The Golden Age Comedia

Vern
Williamsen

The Golden Age Comedia

Text,

Theory,

and

Performance

edited by
Charles Ganelin and
Howard Mancing

Purdue University Press
West Lafayette, Indiana

98   97   96   95   94   5   4   3   2   1

The paper used in this book meets the minimum requirements of American National Standard for Information Sciences—Permanence of Paper for Printed Library Materials, ANSI Z39.48-1984.∞

Printed in the United States of America
Design by Anita Noble

Library of Congress Cataloging-in-Publication Data
The Golden Age comedia : text, theory, and performance / edited by Charles Ganelin and Howard Mancing.
      p. cm.
      Includes bibliographical references and index.
      ISBN 1-55753-042-4 (alk. paper)
      1. Spanish drama—Classical period, 1500–1700—History and criticism. 2. Spanish drama—Classical period, 1500–1700—Criticism, Textual. 3. Theater—Spain—History—16th century. 4. Theater—Spain—History—17th century. I. Ganelin, Charles. II. Mancing, Howard, 1941– .
PQ 6105.G65 1994
862'.309—dc20   93-1959   CIP

Contents

Acknowledgments

The compilation of a volume of this nature is never an easy task, but what labor of love ever is? The purpose of this collection of essays—to honor a scholar who has contributed immeasurably to the development of *comedia* studies in the past few decades—makes the travail well worth the effort. This thing of beauty owes its existence as well as excellence to those who did the real work. The contributors who have joyfully shared their intellectual endeavors have shown saintly patience with the long gestation the volume has undergone. Their willingness to withstand, and their understanding of, the many day-to-day interruptions incumbent upon the editors in their academic positions are truly appreciated.

The clerical staff of the Department of Foreign Languages and Literatures at Purdue University is made up of people who define the word *support.* Two individuals must be pointed out for recognition: Diane Lasic, head of the clerical staff of the department, often stayed in the office late to handle our mass mailings and to make up for the occasional blunder committed by the well-intentioned editors; her good nature and even temperament have been exemplary; and Deborah Starewich, to whom go the spoils of victory. She undertook myriad tasks involving word processing, program translations, and other technical matters—many of them thankless—and often completed her work long before the editors had the opportunity to move to the next step. Her efficiency and patience are truly outstanding. Thanks also to Yolanda Gamboa for her generous and expert assistance in the translation of some of the manuscripts from Spanish to English.

We extend both sincere appreciation and awe to Margaret Hunt, editor for Purdue University Press. Her keen eye for style and and her knowledge of the intricacies of documentation have saved the editors from many embarrassing errors. We are also grateful to graphic designer Anita Noble, whose skill and artistic talent make our efforts a pleasure to read. They, and the entire staff at Purdue University Press, have helped us immeasurably with the difficult crossing of this literary Rubicon.

Finally, thanks to Vern for being the kind of person for whom the editors enthusiastically produce this homage. The size of *The Golden Age* Comedia attests to the widespread esteem he enjoys within the profession and to the many friendships he has nurtured over the years. We know that these essays mark not the end of a career but a transition to a "retired" active life still dedicated to the Spanish *comedia.*

We happily dedicate to Vern our *Varia Editio Rerum Novarum.*

Introduction

Spanish *comedia* studies enjoy today what might be considered a Golden Age. Important journals and a growing quantity of books present an exciting array of critical studies by a varied body of scholars dedicated to the classical theater of Spain. In this poststructuralist and postmodern final decade of the twentieth century, a multitude of approaches yields new readings of old plays that prove Northrop Frye's claim in *The Anatomy of Criticism* that "the two essential facts about a work of art, that it is contemporary with its own time and that it is contemporary with ours, are not opposed but complementary facts" (51):

- *comedia* textual criticism has incorporated the theory and practice that its scholars were often accused of ignoring;
- groundbreaking essays in genre studies, reception theory, Lacanian, Bahktinian, and feminist analyses are prominent;
- *comedia* texts are frequently discussed as performed texts (pre-texts and pretexts to performance), thus opening the way to performance studies that have much to offer Shakespearean specialists;
- and new quality translations, and the theory of translation, have become a major concern.

It is our privilege to bring together the work of a group of outstanding and innovative scholars whose writings exemplify the above trends and to dedicate the essays in this volume to a colleague who in many ways anticipated and helped initiate the current Golden Age: Professor Vern Williamsen. For over twenty years Vern Williamsen has devoted himself to the study and teaching of the Golden Age *comedia.* He has been instrumental in training a generation of scholars, many of whom have become prominent in their own right. When one person has had an impact not only on intellectual pursuits but also on the professional and personal formation of so many colleagues and students, the most fitting tribute could come only from those who have worked with him and have benefited in myriad ways.

In many ways, Williamsen's career mirrors closely the evolution of the profession in the 1970s and 1980s. His earliest published scholarship consisted of excellent editions of *comedia* texts, including Mira de Amescua's *No hay dicha ni desdicha hasta la muerte* (1971), Mira's *La casa del tahur* (1973), and Ruiz de

Alarcón's *Don Domingo de Don Blas* (1975); all are models of textual scholarship, all are standards in the field.

But Williamsen's concentration on textual criticism was only the first phase of his career. Later his interests turned primarily to theory, especially as expressed in his compact volume on dramatic structure, *The Minor Dramatists of Seventeenth-Century Spain* (1982), and in a series of articles, of which we might draw particular attention to his essays on Sor Juana's "simetría bilateral" first published in the *Actas del XVIIº congreso internacional de literatura iberoamericana* (1975) and on Calderón's dramatic structure in *Comparative Literature Symposium* (1981).

Later, Williamsen's interest turned to performance. His most recent works have dealt with the aesthetics of reception and the role of the audience. Subtle, original pieces on the aural cues that Golden Age audiences recognized and responded to, published in *Neophilologus* (1984) and the *Actas del IXº congreso internacional de hispanistas* (1986), exemplify this phase of his scholarship; also noteworthy is his article on the use of polymetry and its importance in the editing of *comedia* texts (*Editing the "Comedia" I*, 1985).

Finally, his prominence in the development of the prestigious annual *comedia* festival of El Chamizal and his performed translations of Lope de Vega's *La discreta enamorada* (*In Love but Discreet*) and Mira de Amescua's *La casa del tahur* (*The Gambler's House*) are, in many ways, the capstones of this most recent phase of his scholarly work. He has also reflected on the theory and aesthetics of literary translation in his essay "The Critic As Translator," published in *Translating the Theatrical Experience* (1987).

From textual criticism to theory to performance: this has been, in the broadest sense, the evolutionary path that *comedia* studies have taken in recent decades. Characteristically, Vern Williamsen has always been at the forefront of his profession.

The collection presented within these pages represents, we believe, an excellent compendium of the state of the art in *comedia* studies and may take its place beside one classic and two more recent anthologies: the 1971 homage to William L. Fichter (Madrid: Castalia, 1971) and the volumes honoring John E. Varey and Bruce Wardropper. The first of these consists of more than fifty essays from scholars worldwide and covers *comedia* as well as other Golden Age topics. The

Varey and Wardropper collections, published respectively by Dovehouse Books (Ottawa, 1989) and Juan de la Cuesta (Newark, Del., 1989) each consists of nearly thirty studies by renowned scholars, a number of whom are contributors to this book; the Varey volume, because of the honoree's groundbreaking work in staging, contains a number of articles related to that area of endeavor. It is of no small importance that John Varey is represented here as well, an affirmation of Vern Williamsen's activities in, and contributions to, the performance aspects of the *comedia.*

The scholars selected to contribute to *The Golden Age* Comedia have excelled either within seventeenth-century studies on the whole or in specific aspects of the *comedia.* Their work represents, too, a variety of critical approaches that in itself summarizes the most recent theoretical applications to Spain's Golden Age theater. This book, then, has been divided into two sections, dedicated to textual analyses and to theoretical and performance studies. Any division, of course, is always open to question. Our purpose in organizing these essays under such broad rubrics is in part to reflect the status of *comedia* studies as well as to suggest further directions. We hope that none of these essays is "definitive" because of the implication that discussion is at an end. Some will undoubtedly lead to revisions of accepted wisdom; others may be more polemical.

The section on textual studies opens with Dian Fox's investigation of both the historical context of Lope's *El caballero de Olmedo* and the celestial imagery used to characterize Don Alvaro de Luna, a key to understanding the tragic nature of Don Alonso. Susan Niehoff McCrary develops the notion of a king's spiritual maturation or consciousness, which allows him theatrical redemption, thus restoring the ruler's credibility as national hero and facilitating the reintegration of the body mystical and the body natural (or *geminata persona*). Matthew D. Stroud applies Girard's *Violence and the Sacred* to Lope's *El castigo sin venganza* to illuminate rivalry, imitation, violence, sacrifice, and the sacrificial victim. Constance Rose offers a concise and brilliant analysis of fifteen verses of Tisbea's "yo, de cuantas el mar" soliloquy from *El burlador de Sevilla,* revealing how Tisbea has deceived herself before Don Juan's seduction. Frederick A. de Armas furthers the rehabilitation of Andrés de Claramonte by showing how his *El secreto de la mujer* is constructed around the contradictory meanings of *pharmakon,* elucidated by Plato and Derrida, whereby writing is transformed from poison to remedy. William R. Blue outlines the "economy" of exchange, the orderly distribution of elements in a system, in Rojas Zorrilla's *Entre bobos anda el juego*. Margaret Rich Greer discusses *La dama duende* in relation to economic issues and the legal status of widows and concludes that the real "ghost" of the play is the phantasm of control. Daniel L. Heiple argues that Calderón's *autos sacramentales* of 1671, celebrating the canonization of Saint Ferdinand, are adapted from an unknown hagiographic *comedia*. Susana Hernández Araico continues the rich vein of recent studies on the *palacio* of the Buen Retiro to propose a new reading of Calderón's mythological play *El mayor encanto amor;* she highlights how the playwright transfigures Cosme Lotti's stage design for the play to mould the visual signs to his own concept of representation as a critical expression of the Count-Duke Olivares's adulatory manipulation of scenery and theatricality. Thomas Austin O'Connor clarifies the Calderonian notion of *fineza* as applied both to *villanos* and nobles alike: *finezas de noble* urge the noble individual to treat the other as a self, and *finezas de amor* affirm unity in place of opposition. Teresa S. Soufas examines the feminine response to established *comedia* conventions in her study of María de Zayas's *La traición en la amistad*. Michael McGaha studies textual and historical evidence deduced from a number of manuscripts of Francisco de Villegas to determine that Villegas was but one more pseudonym of the New Christian playwright Antonio Enríquez Gómez. Nancy L. D'Antuono's original work detailing the relationships between the Golden Age *comedia* and the Italian theater focuses on yet another Italian adaptation, this time of Lope's *El bastardo Mudarra*.

Part 2, "Theory and Performance Studies," begins with Catherine Larson, who traces the history of metatheater to suggest a model of its future potential for explicating *comedia* texts; she reveals how Lionel Abel's influential 1963 book *Metatheater* offers possibilities for textual analysis. Henry W. Sullivan reopens the question of the double plot in the *comedia* with his application of Lacanian poetics to the *comedia,* focusing particularly on the notions of law and desire. James A. Parr maintains the dialogue between theory and practice in his treatment of canons and related cultural questions. Dawn L. Smith reveals how Cervantes's *El retablo de las maravillas* offers a penetrating study of the relationship in theater between performers and spectators given that the *entremés* appears to be an ironic anticipation of the modern concept of metatheater. Catherine Connor (Swietlicki) proposes a revision of the propaganda-oriented theories of theater prominent in the last two decades of *comedia* criticism by focusing on the power

of popular culture. Her approaches take into consideration the dialogic process of ideology, changing notions of popular culture, and the carnivalesque in everyday life. Emilie L. Bergmann discusses the metaliterary representation of reading and writing in *La Estrella de Sevilla* and Lope's *La dama boba.* The integration of the oral mode both of the honor code and of *Estrella* with writing and reading determines the fate of Estrella; literacy for Lope's *boba* integrates her into the symbolic and empowers her in courtship and marriage. Carol Bingham Kirby, in an examination of the *refundición* within the seventeenth century, proposes a statistical method to analyze poetic, dramatic, and structural differences among versions of *El rey don Pedro en Madrid,* thus improving our understanding of the *comedia* and its transmission. Amy R. Williamsen continues the long-overdue revival of Mira de Amescua's theater by focusing on its past and present reception. Sharon Dahlgren Voros extends Greimas's semiotic model of adjuvancy in connection with Thomas Pavel's plot dynamics to an analysis of the feminine supporting roles of Calderón's *El príncipe constante* and *Los tres mayores prodigios.* J. E. Varey and Charles Davis continue to provide fundamental and necessary details about the physical arrangement of theaters; in the present article, they bring to light previously unavailable material about the seating accommodation in the two commercial theaters of Madrid in the seventeenth century, particularly the *bancos* and the *taburetes,* the prices charged for the various localities, and the social background of those who took up extended leases. Teresa J. Kirschner outlines and describes four types of montages to further clarify the staging of the national/historical plays of Lope de Vega. Louise Fothergill-Payne analyzes a performance of Alarcón's *El examen de maridos* in which the genre and style of a *comedia* shift into farce and ridicule. By pinpointing specific differences in plot, character, mood, language, and message, she concludes that farcical adaptations of *comedias* risk losing the best of both farce and drama. Victor Dixon, developing Vern Williamsen's indications that verse forms afford an important key to the interpretation of *comedias,* examines significant features of the versification of six well-known Lope plays, thus reaffirming and extending Williamsen's conclusions.

Trends in recent critical practice thus find ample representation in the essays we have included. To those who would maintain that *comedia* studies traditionally lag behind other scholarly endeavors, these examples will prove them wrong; those who would deny the worth of outgrowths of the time-honored New Criticism will find that a text-oriented analysis can probe depths of meaning and can work hand in hand with Lacanian psychoanalysis or deconstruction. And to those who would argue that *comedia* scholars rely too much on the text without realizing the value of performance, the essays in this volume demonstrate an acute awareness of its centrality in *comedia* studies.

Finally, a few words about the composition of this volume are in order. The collection in your hands is not a stepchild, nor scattered verses, but the "gala y flor" of a labor of love. We as editors have endeavored to select outstanding essays to be read by many and to impart a coherent overall design to the whole. Most, if not all, readers will choose essays according to their interests; the volume may thus be a valuable reference work as well as a compilation of critical excellence. We hope that the sum of the parts—as in Vern Williamsen's own work—is greater than the whole.

Part One

extual Studies

Dian Fox

History, Tragedy, and the Ballad Tradition in
El caballero de Olmedo

ope de Vega's *El caballero de Olmedo* has taxed the ingenuity of
Hispanists, who sense that it should be classified as tragedy and who
cite Lope's own designation of the work as a trágica historia"[1] and
yet are divided concerning what the hero's flaw might be, or whether
he even has one. A. A. Parker blames the sad conclusion on the im-
prudence of the two lovers, Alonso and Inés, "que se dejan absorber tan
completamente por su mutua pasión que se ciegan a la razón y la conciencia y
procuran obtener un objetivo bueno y honrado por medios deshonrosos" (329).
That is, they employ a go-between and deceive Inés's good-natured father, Don
Pedro. David H. Darst believes that Don Alonso is destroyed by an "intellectual
tragic flaw," pride; he ignores signs and warnings of trouble and insists on proceeding home to Olmedo despite the danger (14). Thomas Austin O'Connor contends that, like that of Oedipus, Alonso's tragedy results "not from moral weakness but from moral strength"; and he "foolishly" fails to heed warnings (391,
392). I propose that attention to *El caballero de Olmedo*'s historical context, in
conjunction with some crucial imagery shared by the play and the ballad tradition, will help clarify Lope's conception of tragedy, at least as it applies here. Not
incidentally, the discussion will bring to light a ballad that may well be a previously unidentified source of the play.

Golden Age playwrights often associate a work's protagonist with the historical character and fate of the king who oversees the denouement; this is recognized, for example, to be the case in Calderón's *El médico de su honra* and *A
secreto agravio, secreta venganza*. I argue elsewhere that the same principle holds
true in Lope's *El mejor alcalde, el rey* and *Peribáñez* (Fox, 76–91, 101–40). *El
caballero de Olmedo* has a historical setting during the reign of King Don Juan II

of Castile (1406–54). Yet in this case, Lope links his hero not with the presiding monarch but with an intimate subordinate to the King.

For many years the Condestable Don Alvaro de Luna (1390?–1453) was the closest advisor of Don Juan II. Eventually the *privado's* influence was eclipsed; he lost favor and, at the king's own instruction, was executed. Most commentaries and chronicles—for example, Fernán Pérez de Guzmán's *Generaciones y semblanzas,* Galíndez de Carvajal's *Crónica del Rey Don Juan II,* and Juan de Mariana's *Historia general de España*—represent the Condestable as a ruthless and presumptuous man well deserving his fate. However, poets preferred the more romantic, sympathetic version of the character described in the *Crónica de Don Alvaro de Luna,* which was probably composed by one of the Condestable's partisans.[2] This work portrays Don Alvaro as an innocent victim of others' envy and wickedness. His last moments are related in a chapter entitled "De la muerte del mejor caballero que en todas las Españas ovo en su tienpo, e mayor señor sin corona, el buen Maestre de Santiago":

> Cavalgó pues el bueno e bienaventurado Maestre en su mula, con aquel gesto e con aquel senblante e con aquel sosiego que solía cavalgar los pasados tienpos de su leda e risueña fortuna. La mula cubierta de luto, e él con una capa larga negra. E como de los mártyres se cuenta que iban con el alegre cara a rescibir martyrio e muerte por la Fe de Jesu-Christo, semejantemente iba el bienaventurado Maestre, sin turbación alguna que en su gesto pareciesse, a gustar e tragar el gusto e trago de la muerte, conosciendo de sí mismo que siendo inocente, e sin cargo nin culpa alguna contra el Rey su señor e por aver usado todos tienpos de bondad e de virtud e de lealtad acerca dél, le daban la muerte que yba a rescibir. (432)

Poetic imaginations spurned the generally unfavorable historical tradition. Raymond R. MacCurdy points out that it was rather the hagiographic version of the character engendered in the eponymous chronicle that flourished in the *romancero* (46). During the seventeenth century only the Cid was the subject of more historical ballads than was Don Alvaro de Luna (Pérez Gómez, 12).[3]

Poets also enthusiastically availed themselves of the various connotations of the name "Luna," which lend it an air of beauty and mystery (MacCurdy, 82). While, according to Juan-Eduardo Cirlot, the sun is masculine and represents controlling reason and the active life, the moon is traditionally feminine and emotional, a heavenly body symbolizing the imagination and the irrational (283–85; 416–18; see also de Vries, 326b). Because the moon influences liquids, it can upset the balance in the bodily humors, resulting, traditional psychology holds, in lunacy. The moon's phases may connote changes in fortune, as "nueva," "creciente," "llena," "menguante," or "eclipsada." In the Bible, a bloodied moon is a sign of Armageddon. The prophecy in Joel 2:31 reads, "The sun shall be turned into darkness, and the moon into blood, before the great and the terrible day of the Lord come." In St. John's vision of the Apocalypse (Revelation 6:12–13), "Lo, there was a great earthquake; and the sun became black as sackcloth of hair, and the moon became as blood; And the stars of heaven fell unto the earth."

"Luna" in Spanish can also refer to the glass in a mirror as a passive and reflective object. Appropriately, in some *romances* Don Alvaro de Luna is a mirror in which King Don Juan sees himself. Many of the poems refer to the phases of the moon; finally Don Alvaro finds his fortunes, like the moon, waning and then eclipsed. Since the Condestable of these verses (as of the chronicle) is always a man of superlative character who is ruined by the malice of others, since the moon's cyclical nature suggests rebirth, and since his *Crónica* emphasizes Christological motifs, Don Alvaro often becomes a Christ figure in the *romances*.[4] He is made to carry "un Christo Crucificado a su muerte" (XL); his last supper consists of bread and wine (XVI); and the iron weapon that cuts his throat is associated with the spear that pierced Christ's side (XXXVI). In XXI, the earth quakes when he dies; in XX he is called "Fénix," evoking the Resurrection.

The moon also suggests the political relationship between a counsellor and his king, the sun—a subject that was dear to the hearts of Golden Age playwrights and their public (Heninger, 345). Early in the seventeenth century, royal ministers had acquired considerable power due to the weakness or ineptitude of kings Philip III (1598–1621) and Philip IV (1621–60). Many thoughtful Spaniards were alarmed. Not only political treatises but also fiction, including drama, alluded to what was felt to be the excessive influence on the reigning monarchs of the Duque de Lerma and, afterwards, the Conde Duque de Olivares (Elliott, 319–45). The *comedia de privanza,* meant to show the influential favorite how he ought to behave, or the consequences of his failure to live up to his commission rightly, is a result of this political situation. MacCurdy points out that the *comedia de privanza* received a significant impetus from the trials and fate of Don Rodrigo Calderón, who had come to power with Lerma under Philip III (42). After his mentor's eclipse, Calderón was incarcerated in 1619 and finally executed in 1621. "It is conjectured," MacCurdy states, that some playwrights and other authors of fiction "composed works dramatizing the tragic end of Don Alvaro de Luna as a means of urging the king to extend clemency to Calderón" (45). Logically, these theatrical pieces, following the lead of the ballads and the *Crónica* of Don Alvaro, and consistent with the defense of Don Rodrigo Calderón, would stress the good character of King Juan's counsellor.

I propose that such a mitigating intent also pervades *El caballero de Olmedo,* which S. Griswold Morley and Courtney Bruerton date at 1620–25 (178; see also Socrate, 99–105). Here the King appears on three occasions, always accompanied by the Condestable, Don Alvaro de Luna. Although their dialogue is peripheral to the main action of the drama, the relationship between king and counsellor is of utmost importance for understanding the moral character of the play's protagonist. An examination of the analogies between the *privado* and Don Alonso should contribute to an understanding of the hero's debated tragic status.

Beyond considerations of character, recognition of thematic affinities between the historical/romanticized Don Alvaro de Luna and the fictional Don Alonso Manrique will shed further light on possible poetic sources for *El caballero de Olmedo.* Over recent years Francisco Rico has elaborated on Lope's debt to popular verse in the composition of the play (Vega 1981; see also Rico 1967, 38–56). According to Rico, a ballad, now lost but derived from the events surrounding the death of Don Juan de Vivero in 1521, was the basis for a dance about *El caballero de Olmedo* that Lope incorporated into his drama. However, although the lyrics from the *romance* and the dance evidently inspired Lope's plot line, Willard F. King observes that we have found no external explanation for the supernatural element and ominous tone infusing the play's third act: none of Lope's known sources "introduces the omens, forebodings, and mysterious apparitions—or the elaboration of the original four-line song ('Shades have warned him / not to set out,' etc.)—which loom so large in Lope's dramatization" (Vega 1972, xvii).

King Don Juan II and the Condestable Don Alvaro de Luna appear for the first time near the center of the work, from lines 1554 to 1609. The ruler is anxious to leave for a meeting with "el Infante"—who, Jack Sage has explained (90–

104), is the Infante Don Enrique of Aragón—who awaits Don Juan in Toledo. There the two will discuss a crucial peace treaty. The King brusquely orders Don Alvaro not to bother him now with business, to which the Condestable replies that the papers "contienen sólo firmar; / no has de ocuparte en oír" (1556–57). Is Don Alvaro attempting to take advantage of his king's haste in order to effect some dishonesty? The monarch's good judgment prevails; he decides to take the time to hear this business. As it turns out, it consists of innocent confirmation of the King's own initiatives, which Don Alvaro has scrupulously committed to paper. First, the King's decree with respect to the habits of the Order of Alcántara:

Cond:	Su Santidad concedió
	lo que pidió Vuestra Alteza
	por Alcántara, señor.
Rey:	Que mudase le pedí
	el hábito, porque ansí
	pienso que estará mejor.
Cond:	Era aquel traje muy feo.
Rey:	Cruz verde pueden traer. (1560–67)

Clearly, the King acted independently of the Condestable on this matter. Next, they discuss the ruler's legislation concerning, in Don Alvaro's words, the "diferencia que pones / entre los moros y hebreos / que en Castilla han de vivir" (1577–79). The monarch responds devoutly and in terms that can leave no doubt about his personal involvement in the issue:

Rey:	Quiero con esto cumplir,
	Condestable, los deseos
	de fray Vicente Ferrer,
	que lo ha deseado tanto.
Cond:	Es un hombre docto y santo.
Rey:	Resolví con él ayer
	que en cualquiera reino mío
	donde mezclados están,
	a manera de gabán
	traiga un tabarde el judío

> con una señal en él,
> y un verde capuz el moro.
> Tenga el cristiano el decoro
> que es justo: apártese dél;
> que con esto tendrán miedo
> los que su nobleza infaman. (1580–95)

Don Alvaro de Luna's only remarks support whatever his superior sees fit to undertake. Finally, let us examine the King's determination regarding the chivalric habit of the hero, Don Alonso Manrique:

> Cond: A Don Alonso, que llaman
>   "el caballero de Olmedo,"
>   hace Vuestra Alteza aquí
>   merced de un hábito.
> Rey: Es hombre
>   de notable fama y nombre.
>   En esta villa le vi
>   cuando se casó mi hermana.
> Cond: Pues pienso que determina,
>   por servirte, ir a Medina
>   a las fiestas de mañana.
> Rey: Decidle que fama emprenda
>   en el arte militar,
>   porque yo le pienso honrar
>   con la primera encomienda. (1596–1609)

It has been argued that the above scene reveals the manipulative character of Don Alvaro and the weakness of the King. William C. McCrary writes, "The image of John and Alvaro on stage could not fail to remind the spectator of the strange and unnatural domination which the Condestable reputedly exerted over the mind of the monarch" (112). According to Alison Turner, the conversation shows the monarch "unable to recognize the real danger to his kingdom, his evil advisor to whom he is speaking, the Condestable Don Alvaro de Luna" (182). However, these critics do not take into account the fact that the popular version of the character—the one prevailing in the oral and dramatic traditions, which would have reached this play's public—is almost unfailingly positive, to the point of apotheosis. A contemporary audience, immersed in that reverential oral tradition, would be predisposed to view Don Alvaro in a complimentary light. This central scene, in fact, ratifies the upright character of the Condestable by clearly establishing his utter subservience to his sovereign. And Lope makes it plain that if the King has hesitated to deal with business as usual, it is because the Infante Don Enrique—and with him the nation's peace—await the monarch in Toledo (Sage, 100). Even so, despite his very understandable impatience to leave, Don Juan still insists on examining the documents before signing them. The Condestable, for his own part, has discerned the monarch's apprehension and merely tries to expedite his departure.

Furthermore, Lope makes it apparent that each of the three matters addressed involves solely the King's own initiative. The pope concedes *Don Juan's* request for the attire of the Order of Alcántara; *Don Juan* enforces different dress for Moors and Jews; *Don Juan,* personally impressed with Alonso Manrique's valor, means to confer on him the "merced de un hábito." If the Condestable were so jealous of influence, no doubt he would have opposed the elevation of a potential rival for the King's favor. Quite to the contrary, however, not the slightest hint of impropriety on Don Alvaro's part—or weakness on the King's—characterizes this discourse: in proposing that Don Juan just sign the papers, it is obvious that the Condestable's motives are unimpeachable.

In the second dialogue between king and counsellor (2078–2105), Don Alvaro expresses nothing but admiration for the protagonist Don Alonso. Throughout the play, the *privado* scrupulously maintains the decorum of his office and respect for the King. In short, Lope dramatically endorses the idealization of Don Alvaro de Luna in the *romancero,* thus exonerating him of the misconduct charged in the majority of the chronicles.

C. Alan Soons has noted a further significant aspect of the second *jornada's* central scene, which will lead in the third act to a climactic figurative doubling of the exemplary Don Alvaro and of the tragic Don Alonso (161–64). Each of the three issues discussed by king and counsellor involves a change of clothing in the interest of propriety; dress is emphasized as the fitting emblem for the person who wears it. The King confirms that Don Alonso Manrique, as a knight of a military and religious order, will wear a cross on his breast. And, in fact, all major characters throughout the play seem particularly interested in apparel, continually changing or exchanging articles of clothing. Doña Inés disguises herself as a peasant maiden for the *feria* of Medina; next she becomes a lady but gradually surrenders her señorial wear—the green ribbon from her slipper and her neckband—as signs of her love. She pretends to anticipate dressing in the "galas celestiales" (1406) of a nun; finally the *burlas* become *veras,* for she will enter the convent as the bride of Christ.

Fabia, the *celestina,* muses over the vestments of her own bawdy youth, when she arrayed herself in silk (329); afterwards she dons the "hábito monjil" in order to invade the house of Inés's father. Fabia imagines her charade so distinctly that she complains about the discomfort of wearing her sackcloth (1443–44). Inés's and Fabia's changes in clothing indicate spiritual ascent, whether or not they are meant to be taken seriously.

Raiment also preoccupies the clown, Tello, who lays claim to the night cloak that the villain, Don Rodrigo, has lost. It is this cape that allows Don Rodrigo to identify his rival (1345–53), the hero, whom he will later murder. Tello receives a suit from his own master, Don Alonso, in gratitude for his service (1741–42); later, as Fabia's accomplice, the *bufón* disguises himself "de gorrón," as a Latin teacher, to "instruct" Inés. All of Tello's acquisitions of clothing—garments of a knight and of a scholar—likewise rehearse metaphorical ascent. Tom Drury has noted that at one point Tello refers to himself as "Martín Peláez" (1486; Drury, 49a n. 1), the name of a character associated with the legends of the Cid. In that tradition, Peláez, at first a coward and a fool, becomes a hero out of shame. His namesake in *El caballero de Olmedo* undergoes a similar amelioration: the dignity of his acquired attire turns from fraudulent to mournfully real in the third act, when Tello discovers his master on the road to Olmedo, dying. In the drama's culmination, Tello makes his way into the company of the King to disclose the death of the protagonist and to demand justice. The feigned master of Latin at the end becomes *advocatus* of Don Alonso.[5]

Attending Tello's climactic discourse are all the principal characters of the play, including the Condestable, Don Alvaro de Luna. Tello narrates the catastrophe in *romance* verse. The nuncio begins, "Invictísimo Don Juan / que del castellano reino, / a pesar de tanta envidia / gozas el dichoso imperio" (2629–32). Tello proceeds to describe the scene and the characters of the tragedy in the apocalyptic language of the bloody moon:

> . . . *La luna,* que salió tarde,
> *menguado el rostro sangriento,*
> me dio a conocer a [Don Rodrigo y Don Fernando];
> que tal vez alumbra el cielo
> con las hachas de sus luces
> el más escuro silencio,
> para que vean los hombres
> de las maldades los dueños,
> porque a los ojos divinos
> no hubiese humanos secretos.
> Paso adelante, ¡ay de mí!
> y *envuelto en su sangre veo*
> *a Don Alonso espirando.* (2675–87; emphasis mine)

Tello's striking speech bathes in blood both *la luna* and the victim of treachery, metaphorically staining the future of his listener, Don Alvaro *de Luna,* with the fate of the dying Alonso.

The apocalyptic vision continues in the *romance* narrative that follows. Tello carries his failing lord home to Olmedo, where Don Alonso receives his parents' benediction. Then,

> [C]ubrió de luto su casa
> y su patria, cuyo entierro
> será el del fénix, Señor,
> después de muerto viviendo
> en las lenguas de la fama,
> a quien conocen respeto
> la mudanza de los hombres
> y los olvidos del tiempo. (2701–8)

Such precise poetic language—in *romance* verse, playing on *la luna* and Christological motifs such as the resurrection of the hero—vividly recalls the supremely popular ballads relating the legend of Don Alvaro de Luna. I would now like to submit a source not identified by Rico for that lugubrious and portentous third act of *El caballero de Olmedo.* A ballad, published in 1622,[6] describes, with a striking correspondence to the third act of Lope's *tragicomedia,* Don Alvaro de Luna's dance of death. In this dark, dreamlike poem, which begins on the eve of Don Alvaro de Luna's execution, the anonymous narrator comes face-to-face with Death. The apparition, after predicting Don Alvaro's fate, is transfigured into the exemplary Condestable himself as he heroically meets his executioner. I quote the ballad in full:

Apriessa llega la noche
embuelta en su manto negro,
con que a penas se diuisan
formas, y plantas del suelo.
Escassa su luz mostrauan
las bellas lumbres del cielo
pronosticando desdichas
con infelices portentos.
Escondiose el claro dia
passose a Occidente Febo,
dexando de sus reliquias
el calor mustio, y enfermo.
Era más de media noche
quando en profundo silencio
dan descanso los mortales
a los fatigados cuerpos.
Quando el cansancio diurno
se restaura con el sueño,
y todo vela y reposa,
solo gime, y ladra el perro.
Que con mortales aullidos
dauan espanto sus ecos,
como que anuncian ruina
del venidero sucesso.
A tal hora vide vn bulto
formado de secos huessos
con vna Luna puesta al cuello.
Yo soy la muerte, me dixo,
culpa del padre primero

de inobediencia nacida
para pena y daño vuestro.
Soy del diuino juyzio
embiada contra vn reo
que en esta Luna subido
tuuo su felice assiento.
Condenale la malicia
siendo la embidia del pueblo
el Fiscal del acusado,
yo el cordel y el instrumento.
Mañana a las diez del dia
conocereys mis efetos,
y el rigor de mi cuchillo
sobre el ombro mas enhiesto.
Daré en tierra con la cumbre
del edificio mas bello
que leuantó el Rey Don Iuan
y que han visto nuestros tiempos.
Bolui a mirarle los ojos,
y vile cercado y preso
a cauallo en vna mula
cubierto de luto negro.
Aduerti el vulgo afligido,
sordo, lloroso, y suspenso,
contemplando esta cayda
como en el cristalino espejo.
De dos en dos diuididos
le siguen de trecho en trecho
los ojos enternecidos,
aunque algunos van contentos.
Miré bien, y conoci,
al Condestable del Reyno
Maestre de Santiago
de la vida humana exemplo.
En las manos del verdugo
inclinaua el graue cuello,

> cuya sentencia publica
> en voz alta el pregonero.
> Cumplase la justicia
> que manda el Rey, y quiere la malicia,
> sobre este desdichado
> del cuerno de su Luna derribado.

Clearly, this elegy in *romance* form suggests some key elements of *El caballero*'s haunting final act when, on his way home to Olmedo at night, Don Alonso meets first the Sombra, then the enigmatic peasant, and ultimately his death at the hands of an envidious few. The date of publication of the song, together with the play's favorable rendition of the Condestable and with Tello's *romance* relation of the death of the Christlike protagonist, would support a conjecture that Lope knew and was influenced by this and perhaps other ballads about Don Alvaro de Luna as he composed his "trágica historia."

Furthermore, *El caballero de Olmedo* could, like so many other plays of the period, be an argument in defense of the former favorite, Don Rodrigo Calderón, or, if written after 1621, be in part a requiem. And at this point in Lope's life, his own fortunes were on the wane, with the disappointments of age and the illness of Marta de Nevares. It has been suggested elsewhere (Socrate, 99–100, 109, 114; Sage, 12–13) that the playwright himself, "Fénix de los ingenios," a heroic if not entirely innocent victim of fortune, would identify with the calamity of the "poeta de Olmedo" (1111).

Finally, I would propose recognizing *El caballero de Olmedo* as a sort of dramatized *romance,* a tragic ballad of the kind that Edward M. Wilson described, not in Aristotelian or Christian, but in popular terms (231). Simply, the hero's enviable prosperity ends in sorrow.[7]

Notes

1.   The words are actually spoken by King Juan II in the closing lines (2731–32) of the play. Here and hereafter, references to *El caballero de Olmedo* are to Vega 1981, with line numbers specified.

2.   Attributed to Gonzalo Chacón and first published in 1546; see Chacón.

3.   All references to the ballads will be to Pérez Gómez.

4.   "Muy peculiar de [la *Crónica de don Alvaro de Luna*]," writes María Rosa Lida de Malkiel,

en contraste con toda la historiografía castellana, y quizá otra prueba de contagio poético—es la hipérbole sacroprofana, cultivada por los poetas coetáneos y por el propio don Alvaro. Constante es el cotejo entre la caída del Condestable y la Pasión, implícita en la comparación de los traidores al Condestable con Judas . . . ; cuando, después de largo discurso, don Alvaro promete allanarse a la voluntad del Rey con las palabras *fiat voluntas tua* . . . , a pesar de que se da expresamente como fuente el Padrenuestro, la situación sugiere mucho más la oración de Jesús en el Huerto (San Mateo, XXVI, 42) donde también se hallan. Unas páginas más adelante . . . la comparación con Jesús es franca, y al comenzar a narrar la muerte . . . , el Cronista rodea a su idolatrado héroe de una aureola de martirio . . . , y emplea como epíteto constante ya no "ínclito" sino "bienaventurado." (249n. 96)

5.   It is likely that Lope knew the 1606 *comedia* entitled *El caballero de Olmedo,* probably written by Cristóbal de Morales. In this play, the *gracioso,* Galapagar, also undergoes a marked transformation. After the death in the second act of the hero, Don Alonso Girón, Galapagar spends much of the third act wreaking vengeance on the servants of the villain (the wicked English Conde). The work ends with Galapagar's decision to journey to Montserrat "y en San Antón ser santero" (ed. Eduardo Juliá Martínez [Madrid: CSIC, 1944], 165). My thanks go to Erik Urdang for suggesting to me Tello's final vocation.

6.   Number 34, according to Pérez Gómez (50), first published in *Sylva de varios romances.*

7.   This essay is based on "Identificaciones trágicas en *El caballero de Olmedo,*" a paper presented at the Octavo Congreso Internacional de Hispanistas, Providence, R.I., August 1983. After that, Kenneth Stackhouse's article "Don Alvaro de Luna and the Unity of Lope de Vega's *Caballero de Olmedo*" (1989) was published. Stackhouse arrives at very different conclusions from my own regarding the dramatic significance of the figure of the Condestable for *El caballero de Olmedo* and maintains that the negative portrayal of the Condestable in the historiographical tradition would move a seventeenth-century Spanish audience to conclude that in the play, the sinister Don Alvaro de Luna must be behind the murder of the protagonist.

Works Consulted

Chacón, Gonzalo. 1940. *Crónica de don Alvaro de Luna.* Edited by Juan de Mata Carriazo. Madrid: Espasa-Calpe.

Cirlot, Juan-Eduardo. 1979. *Diccionario de símbolos.* 3d ed. Barcelona: Labor.

Darst, David H. 1984. "Lope's Strategy for Tragedy in *El caballero de Olmedo.*" *Cuadernos hispanoamericanos* 6:11–17.

Drury, Tom. 1981. "'Martín Peláez, aquel tímido asturiano.'" *Hispania* 64:41–52.

Elliott, J. H. 1963. *Imperial Spain 1469–1716.* New York, Mentor.

Fox, Dian. 1991. *Refiguring the Hero: From Peasant to Noble in Lope de Vega and Calderón.* University Park: The Pennsylvania State University Press.

Heninger, S. K., Jr. 1974. *Touches of Sweet Harmony: Pythagorean Cosmology and Renaissance Poetics.* San Marino, Calif.: Huntington Library.

Lida de Malkiel, María Rosa. 1952. *La idea de la fama en la Edad Media castellana.* Mexico: Fondo de Cultura Económica.

McCrary, William C. 1968. *The Goldfinch and the Hawk: A Study of Lope de Vega's Tragedy* El caballero de Olmedo. Chapel Hill: University of North Carolina Press.

MacCurdy, Raymond R. 1978. *The Tragic Fall: Don Alvaro de Luna and Other Favorites in Spanish Golden Age Drama.* Chapel Hill: University of North Carolina Press.

Morales, Cristóbal. 1944. *El caballero de Olmedo.* Edited by Eduardo Juliá Martínez. Madrid: Consejo Superior de Investigaciones Científicas.

Morley, S. Griswold, and Courtney Bruerton. [1940] 1966. *The Chronology of Lope de Vega's Comedias.* New York: Kraus Reprint Corporation.

O'Connor, Thomas Austin. 1980. "The Knight of Olmedo and Oedipus: Perspectives on a Spanish Tragedy." *Hispanic Review* 48:391–413.

Parker, A. A. 1976. "Aproximación al drama español del Siglo de Oro." In *Calderón y la crítica: Historia y antología,* edited by Manuel Durán and Roberto González Echevarría, 1:329–57. Originally published in English as *Approach to the Spanish Drama of the Golden Age.* Diamante, vol. 6. London: The Hispanic and Luso-Brazilian Council, 1957.

Pérez Gómez, Antonio. 1953. "Introducción." *Romancero de don Alvaro de Luna (1540–1800).* Valencia: n. p.

Rico, Francisco. 1967. "*El caballero de Olmedo:* Amor, muerte, ironía." *Papeles de Son Armadans* 139:38–56. Rpt. rev. in *II jornadas de teatro clásico español, Almagro, 1979,* 169–85. Madrid: Ayuntamiento de Almagro, 1980.

Sage, Jack. 1974. *Critical Guides to Spanish Texts. Lope de Vega*: El caballero de Olmedo. London: Grant & Cutler.

Socrate, Mario. 1965 [1967]. "*El caballero de Olmedo* nella seconda epoca di Lope." In *Studi di letteratura spagnola: Ricerche realizzate col contributo del C. N. R.,* 95–173. Rome: Società Filologica Romana.

Soons, C. Alan. 1961. "Towards an Interpretation of *El caballero de Olmedo.*" *Romanische Forschungen* 73:160–68.

Stackhouse, Kenneth. 1989. "Don Alvaro de Luna and the Unity of Lope de Vega's *Caballero de Olmedo.*" In *Texto y espectáculo: Selected Proceedings of the Sym-*

posium on Spanish Golden Age Theater, edited by Barbara Mujica, 55–63. Lanham, Md.: University Press of America.

Sylva de varios romances. 1622. Barcelona.

Turner, Alison. 1966. "The Dramatic Function of Imagery and Symbolism in *Peribáñez* and *El caballero de Olmedo.*" *Symposium* 20:174–86.

Vega, Lope de. 1972. *The Knight of Olmedo.* Translated by Willard F. King. Lincoln: University of Nebraska Press.

———. 1981. *El caballero de Olmedo.* Edited by Francisco Rico. 3d ed. Madrid: Cátedra.

Vries, Ad de. 1974. *Dictionary of Symbols and Imagery.* Amsterdam: North Holland Publishing Company.

Wilson, Edward M. [1958] 1980. *Tragic Themes in Spanish Ballads.* Diamante, vol. 8. London: The Hispanic and Luso-Brazilian Council. Reprint in *Spanish and English Literature of the 16th and 17th Centuries: Studies in Discretion, Illusion and Mutability,* edited by Donald William Cruickshank, 220–33. Cambridge: Cambridge University Press.

Susan Niehoff McCrary

Theatrical Consciousness and Redemption

he criticism that exists to date on Lope's *Las paces de los reyes* has run the gamut from hostile to sympathetic. Earlier critics, such as Marcelino Menéndez y Pelayo, Federico C. Sainz de Robles, James Castañeda, and C. A. Soons, have focused on the rupture between the first act and the second two and believe that the lack of historical continuity prevents the piece from ever being considered among the major works of Lope de Vega. The later scholars David H. Darst, William C. McCrary, and Frederick de Armas have suggested that there is, indeed, a unity in the drama, one that transcends the historical time lapse and draws the acts together thematically rather than temporally. Following this latter group of "advocates of unity," I would like to add some further comments. All three of these critics have focused on internal unifying elements that surpass the seeming rupture of time in the drama, yet each has perceived the harmony of the work in a different light. It is my contention that perhaps there is an even broader unity that encompasses all three approaches; that is, the drama and, therefore, the unity in the work center on the theatricalization of consciousness responding to the knowledge of limitation and vulnerability.

Darst was the first to perceive that Lope's treatment of the life of Alfonso VIII closely imitates the construct of the universal hero in all of its stages: "the hero's royal birth, exile and education away from his people, return and recognition, initiation into manhood, heroic feats, fall, death, and spiritual rebirth" (225–26). McCrary, expanding on the premises of Darst, adds that the hero pattern exists in the chronicle material which inspired the dramatist, and he argues that the unity of *Las paces,* this *crónica dramática,* lay in its *poesis:* the proposition that "plot imitates action" (1973, 3). Through the art of homologous retrospection, then, McCrary concludes, "what emerges is a sacramental representation that assimilates the present to the past and thus transports the past to the present. Properly speaking, with *Las paces,* rather than look at the spectacle, one looks into and through it, back to the ancient stories of judgment and reconciliation or damnation which preceded it, and which in turn repeat even more archaic rituals" (16).

De Armas, though a proponent of unity, disagrees with one of the major premises of Darst and McCrary: that the investiture of the child Alfonso contravenes the last will and testament of Sancho el Deseado and is, thereby, the cause of all of the evils that follow, namely, the siege of Zurita and the murder of Lope de Arenas. De Armas argues that the coronation is a just and lawful act, and that together with the subsequent scenes serves "to portray a child who represents the ideal of Kingship and fights injustice and treason aided by the patron of Spain" (68). De Armas envisions a different kind of unity than that proposed by Darst and McCrary, one that becomes apparent in the recapitulation of the themes of passion, treason, and blindness throughout the action of the play. He concludes that "*Las paces de los reyes* is a panoramic presentation of a monarch's life, commencing with an idealized figure of kingship in childhood, passing through the *mocedades* where war is displaced by lust thus endangering the kingdom, and ending with a restoration of the Christian order previously threatened by Raquel" (73). The rupture between the first act and the second two, then, represents to de Armas the break between the ideal monarch and the man who abandons himself to blind passion, thus neglecting his royal duties.

Both appraisals of this play clearly offer valid interpretations which demonstrate that *Las paces* is definitely worthy of having been penned by the *Fénix* and that the subtle harmony of its design attests to its being a work of high caliber. I agree that there is a unity within the play that substantiates the favorable attention that it has received in recent years. Darst, McCrary, and de Armas have looked beyond the obvious, as we all must do with the *comedia,* and have discerned what Lope perceived when he set out to dramatize the somewhat turbulent life and reign of Alfonso VIII. In examining the seemingly discordant interpretations of these critics, a harmony emerges among them that seems to indicate that they are not mutually exclusive. If we approach the work as a theatricalization of the genesis of consciousness in Alfonso, then we can confirm both the poetic and thematic unity previously suggested. As such, the three acts become dramatizations of the development from aconsciousness to moral-spiritual diminution to consciousness.

In Christian thought, the myth of the Fall addresses the painful awareness of the finiteness of consciousness and the constraints of nature laid upon Adam after his disobedience. The apparent moral and mental awakening effected by his transgression is recorded in the phrase from Genesis: "Then the eyes of both were opened" (Gen. 3:7). Rather than referring to a heightened perception, which would appear to be the inference here, the phrase actually implies a diminution of consciousness. Upon eating the fruit from the forbidden tree, Adam's eyes were opened to the presence or substance of good and evil, or life and knowledge, but not to the consequences of disobedience. It would appear from the biblical account that Adam takes a great leap forward in consciousness, his "eyes now opened," as if prior to this time he was in a deep stupor or asleep. Adam's fall into sin, however, has the effect of dulling or limiting his consciousness because it alienated him from God and required that his intelligence and consciousness cope with guilt and shame. In other words, new spiritual-psychic complexes were introduced that drew Adam's spiritual strength away from consciousness. Far from experiencing an expansion of his spirit, Adam underwent a diminution of it, thus concentrating his powers on himself and away from God. He and all of mankind fell into a kind of sleep or lack of consciousness, which was the metaphor of sin's consequences (McCrary 1987, 93–101).

If we examine the first act of *Las paces* in light of this Genesis account, what we witness is a child who is too young and inexperienced to understand the consequences of his sudden assumption of power. Even though the terms of Sancho's will are violated, as William McCrary so strongly argues, it appears that the heavens have actually sanctioned this act as necessary to the continuity of Christendom in the realm, as witnessed by the seemingly miraculous entrance of Alfonso into Toledo, a city whose doors are guarded "con tanta vigilancia" (504a) and which should be "imposible entrar" (504a), along with the spatial disposition of the young heir in the tower, which draws the attention of the spectator upward, toward the heavens. The providential confirmation comes when Alfonso is *armado* by the statue of Santiago, the protector sent by the heavens to watch over and guide this youth who is suddenly transformed into king. The appearance of Santiago serves a dual function here: first, it demonstrates the charity of a loving and forgiving God who, at the very least, understands the reasons for Alfonso's naive contravention of his father's will, although He may not agree with the deceptive manner in which it was carried out; and second, it is this statue of the apostle that actually anoints the young monarch, empowers him with the ability necessary to function in his role as king, and serves as political and spiritual mentor as the youth assumes his grave royal responsibilities. It is thus solely through the power invested in the *niño-rey* by Santiago that the young monarch is able to perform the duties accorded him in this ceremony.

The initial emphasis of, and therefore the disparity among, critics has focused on whether or not Alfonso is the rightful heir to the throne at this time in his life. What these arguments do not address is that Alfonso, who is but an innocent child, cannot yet understand the impact of history or the consequences of the contravention of his father's will. He is not responsible for his coronation because he is not yet old enough to grasp the significance of right and wrong. Alfonso is like humanity after the Fall in that he represents the innocent child who has come into the world stained with original sin and is, therefore, aconscious. The operative word here is "innocent." He has not consciously transgressed—committed a grave mortal sin—because he is too young and inexperienced in the ways of the world to make a choice of such magnitude. It is not within his purview to enter into the world of kingship—an adult world—without the spiritual guidance of Santiago and the political encouragement and support of the count and the other *castellanos*. He has been led like an innocent lamb to the throne and beseeches the apostle: "Sed mi padre en defenderme / de mi tío, que es león, / y quiere en esta ocasión / como a cordero ofenderme" (507a). The loyal Castilians have acted out of a sense of duty to the kingdom in offering the crown to Alfonso before the time indicated by Sancho rather than place the realm in jeopardy under the ruthless Fernando. It is thus the faithful *hidalgos* who are responsible for the premature investiture of the child.

The *castellanos* readily accept and acknowledge the young heir to the throne, as witnessed by the comments of Conde Don Manrique: "¡Toledo por Alfonso, rey legítimo / de Castilla! ¡Toledo por Alfonso, / hijo del rey don Sancho el Deseado, / y del emperador de España nieto!" (503a) and of Don Esteban Illán: "¡Toledo por Alfonso, castellanos, / no por Fernando de León, su tío! / ¡Alfonso es vuestro rey, Alfonso viva!" (503a). Only Lope de Arenas remains staunch in adhering to the letter of the law. Unmoved by the fervor of the crowd and its wholehearted decision to embrace Alfonso as the rightful ruler, Lope de Arenas holds fast to the "testamento del rey" (504b) and believes that "guardalle es más justa ley" (504b). He voices his fears when he rhetorically asks: "¿Qué sé yo cuál de vosotros, / si con las fuerzas se ve, / querrá ser rey?" (505a).

It is clear that Lope de Arenas is incapable of understanding the world in which he lives. He staunchly fights to support the past, unable to see the dangers of the present. He is blinded by his sense of loyalty to Sancho and the kingship and therefore believes that the last will and testament should be upheld at all costs. His fear that there may be those who intend to manipulate Alfonso in order to gain power causes him to stand firm in his conviction that by denying Alfonso entrance into Zurita, he is, in fact, protecting the youth. Sancho el Deseado could not have known that Fernando would mistreat the loyal Castilian subjects and abuse the power entrusted to him, or surely the monarch would not have left the kingdom at the mercy of his brother's hands until Alfonso would reach the age of fifteen. Lope de Arenas cannot comprehend that the immediate threat to the kingdom is Fernando, not the infidels. By denying Zurita to Alfonso, Lope is actually responsible for his own destruction. He is analogous to Alfonso in his inability to grasp the ramifications of his tunnel vision. Each understands only part of the whole picture: Lope sees only the present, the small world in which he lives, and is blind to the gravity of the problems caused by both Fernando and the Moors; whereas Alfonso looks beyond the present to the greater picture, ignoring the consequences that his present actions will have on the loyal subjects of his kingdom.

Alfonso certainly does not represent the ideal of kingship in most of the first act, but we must keep in mind that the young monarch simply fulfills the duties of his office through the power invested in him by Santiago rather than through his own conscious knowledge of kingship. He does not yet understand that his authority was bequeathed by his father, who came into it by divine decree. He is unaware that kingship represents the continuity of tradition, law, order, convention, and the social infrastructure of cohesion on which tribal continuity rests. He wisely places himself in the hands of Santiago, however, knowing that the apostle will guide him in his efforts to vanquish the treachery and abuses of both his uncle and the Moorish infidels. It is through his bond with, and trust in, this *santo patrón* rather than through his own God-given talents that Alfonso is able to mirror the "ideal kingly qualities and virtues" stressed by de Armas (66). Like Adam and all of humanity after the Fall, Alfonso the child is aconscious, that is, his entire reign as *niño-rey* is carried out in a dreamlike state as he relives the fate of his prototype in suffering the consequences of original sin.

The episode at Zurita demonstrates well this mental "swoon" of the young monarch, which paralyzes his ability to reason. Wide-eyed and innocent like the child he is, he enters into the battle with no sense of fear but rather with a desire to prove that the sword entrusted to him by Santiago will, indeed, uphold justice. It does not seem to occur to Alfonso that justice could be served in other ways. Here again, his intentions are valid, but his manner of achieving them leaves something to be desired. His control of the fortress is obviously essential if the Castilians are to rebel against the unjust rule of Fernando. Alfonso's concern is to restore law and order to the Christian lands, and thus he undertakes this campaign in good faith with the ultimate goal of ridding the kingdom of Fernando's injustice and treason. Protected and guided by Santiago, then, the *niño-rey* does what he thinks is best for Castile. He is, however, unaware of the full impact of his actions. Thus, as he exercises his royal power, his first victim is neither the usurping Leonese nor the marauding Moor but rather the loyal Christian Lope de Arenas. In commissioning Dominguillo, he has unconsciously transgressed the laws of God and the holy faith, further violated his father's decree by being responsible for the death of one who sought only to uphold it, and, finally, deprived Costanza of her husband. What is important here is that thus far the monarch still has not consciously transgressed because he remains an innocent child. Given his youth, he cannot be held completely responsible for his actions. He comes away from act 1 still innocent, still unaware of his purely temporal-temporary status.

Alfonso's character shifts dramatically as the innocent child of act 1 becomes the "hombre ya" (515b) of act 2. What were minor offenses committed out of ignorance or inexperience now become deliberate transgressions as the monarch willfully and knowingly oversteps his authority as king. We witness his first major infraction with the bathing scene in act 2, in which he espies the Jewess Raquel. What begins as a simple survey of his lands and the damage done by the swollen Tajo ends with Alfonso's chance encounter with the Jewish bathers. The vision of the exquisite nude "ninfa del Tajo" (518a) entrances the king—"¿Cuál escultor jamás hizo figura / de pario mármol tan perfecta y bella, / ni la imaginación de nieve pura? / No sé qué pueda comparar con ella?" (518a)—and causes him to lose himself. It is only after he has been completely captivated by her beauty that he sees her clothed and realizes "que es hebrea" (518b). Alfonso has already made his decision to pursue this forbidden woman, and no amount of rationalization or warning from Garcerán—"guárdate de emprender cosa tan fea" (518b)—will deter him from his goal: "Garcerán, el servir tiene dos caras, / verdad, y gusto del señor. Agora / ponte en la de mi gusto" (518b).

Blinded by passion and an overwhelming desire to possess something that lies beyond his authority, Alfonso struggles within himself before yielding to the temptation. He refuses to listen as he is cautioned by both Garcerán and the *villano,* Belardo, that the object of his passion is forbidden fruit. The *villano* admonishes him: "Y a vos, señor, os defienda / de dar en tan gran error; / porque si cristiana fuera, / ya tuviérades disculpa; / mas, en su ley, es bajeza" (520b). The innocence of youth can no longer be blamed for his waywardness. The monarch is obviously aware that his actions cannot be sanctioned by either moral or divine law when he responds: "Parece que el Cielo enseña / hasta los rudos villanos. / ¡Oh amor, terrible es tu fuerza!" (520b). The king is—or at least should be—bound by the holy bonds of matrimony when he first glimpses Raquel, thus his estrangement from his wife and his kingdom in order to pursue the delights of the flesh constitutes an infraction against both the *nomos,* the laws of man, and the *hodos,* the divine law.

In his state of virtual oblivion, the monarch cannot see beyond the satisfaction of his cupidity. Like his prototype, Adam, Alfonso is experiencing a moral-spiritual diminution of consciousness and is unable to perceive the effect that his actions will have on the kingdom. The king appears to be possessed and confused by the force of his attraction for the lovely Jewess. He neglects his royal duties and withdraws from both the realm and his family in order to satisfy his own personal needs and desires. Despite Garcerán's final efforts to convince the monarch to "vencerse a sí mismo" (520b), the temptation is too strong, and Alfonso's will too weak.

What we witness in act 2, then, is Alfonso's fall and the serious personal and political consequences of his transgression. This *jornada* theatricalizes the monarch's spiritual state after the temptation and violation. Like Adam in the Genesis material, Alfonso now becomes conscious of good and evil but not of the consequences of his disobedience. His fall into sin has dulled or limited his consciousness as he focuses inwardly to cope with his guilt and shame. His spiritual capacities are impaired so much that he is unable to perceive the truths of the world. His compromised consciousness takes two modes in act 2: a moral one, in which he refuses to acknowledge his responsibility to his wife; and a political-military one involving his refusal to participate in the impending war.

After Adam ate the fruit, he felt immediate guilt and shame and became conscious of his nakedness or vulnerability, and thus of his alienation from God.

Alfonso's reaction imitates that of Adam when the monarch returns after his initial encounter with Raquel only to find his wife inconsolable at his short absence. The scene depicts his guilt and shame as the king struggles within himself to understand the confusion that consumes him. He has lost control of his emotions and has ceased to function in a rational manner. He struggles with his conscience, unaware of the depths and source of his guilt: "No la engaña el pensamiento; / que el basilisco que vi / me tiene fuera de mí / desde hoy. ¡Qué extraño tormento!" (522a). He cannot yet "see" that the wages of sin are vulnerability, nakedness, and death. He has been stripped of his protective royal demeanor and stands naked in his shame, exposed, like all of humanity, unable to hide from the wrath of God and his own conscience:

> And they heard the sound of the Lord God walking in the garden in the cool of the day, and the man and wife hid themselves from the presence of the Lord God among the trees of the garden. But the Lord God called to the man, and said to him, "Where are you?" And he said, "I heard the sound of thee in the garden, and I was afraid, because I was naked; and I hid myself." He said, "Who told you that you were naked? Have you eaten of the tree of which I commanded you not to eat?" (Gen. 3:8–11)

Alfonso appears to be just as "naked" militarily as he is personally. With his energies turned inward to cope with his guilt, he is incapable of preparing the troops for the impending battle against the Moors. When Don Illán enters for military instructions, Alfonso sends him away saying, "que de un nuevo accidente / tengo el alma ofendida. / Di que cuelgue la espada" (523a). His confusion and diminished perception have placed the kingdom in jeopardy. It is clear that the king's responsibility to his people is no longer his major concern. He is so consumed with his own dilemma that he has neglected to protect the realm from the threat of enemy invasions. The body personal has prevailed over the body mystical, causing the office to be subordinated to the whims and urges of the individual. Alfonso has knowingly abused his royal power, yet does not seem to realize that his wrongdoings will occasion potentially devastating consequences for himself and for his people.

Alfonso's indecisiveness becomes evident once again in the second *jornada* as he struggles with his conscience. The heavens blatantly forewarn him of the dangers should he enter the garden house where Raquel has been taken. The violent storm, an omen from Santiago (524b), rages only over the garden: "Y están los cielos serenos / sobre la misma ciudad. / Sólo en la huerta parece / que el Cielo muestra su furia: / debe de ser que mi injuria / siente, riñe y aborrece" (524b). The effect of the tempest is compounded by the sound of Voz, the monarch's own conscience, which attempts, to no avail, to reason with Alfonso: "desde que fuiste niño, / te ha sacado libre el Cielo / entre tantos enemigos. / No des lugar desta suerte, / cuando hombre, a tus apetitos. / Advierte que por la Cava / a España perdió Rodrigo" (525a). Neither Voz nor the appearance of Sombra deters the startled king from fulfilling his destiny. The extent of his vulnerability and limitations becomes evident as we witness his obvious fear, an emotion hitherto unknown to Alfonso. He acknowledges a consciousness of his moral-spiritual diminution, but he lacks the power to alter his role in history, as he confides to Garcerán: "que amor me quita el juicio; / y perdida la razón, / conozco el daño, y le sigo, / porque, donde está sujeto, / ¿de qué sirven los sentidos?" (526a–b).

While act 2 theatricalizes Alfonso's sense of diminished perception, it is in the third *jornada* that the monarch finally becomes fully conscious not only of his actions but, more importantly, of their consequences. As the last act opens, it is clear that the monarch has completely abandoned his kingdom for his passions. His political and military neglect will allow the realm to fall into Moorish hands if immediate action is not taken. In the absence—both physical and mental—of the king, the queen resolves to act as head of state in an effort to preserve Christianity and maintain law and order in the kingdom. With her son, Enrique, "de luto los dos" (526b), she convenes a secret meeting of the noblemen and vows that justice will be done. She argues that Raquel has endangered the realm because "a vuestro rey tiene preso, / sin darle tan sola un hora / de libertad en siete años" (527a). Her concern for the kingdom and for the rights and privileges of her son force her to deliver an ultimatum: "éste es Enrique, mi hijo: / o matadme esa traidora, / o él y yo, pues no tenéis / manos, fuerzas, sangre ni honra, / a Inglaterra nos vamos" (527b).

As the queen prepares to intercede on behalf of the kingdom and her son, Alfonso remains oblivious to the dangers incurred by his continued absence. Lope has very carefully organized the scenes so that the first, in which the queen and the nobles determine to restore justice in the realm, is juxtaposed to the second, in which the monarch and the Jewess set out placidly on a fishing expedition. The audience's perception is that of simultaneous occurrences in which the tension in the first scene tends to heighten the peacefulness of the second, and vice versa. The fishing scene, which both reflects the past and foreshadows the future, serves as an initial awakening for Alfonso, who is still experiencing a "sueño de los sentidos." The *caña,* which symbolizes for Sebastián de Covarrubias y Horozco human fragility and inconstancy (1943, 291), symbolizes Alfonso's state of mind and the weakness of human nature. The skull and the olive branch pulled from the river indeed "inform the remainder of the drama" as William McCrary suggests (7). He continues: "Death, as depicted by the skull, represents the end of living, while the olive branch speaks of peace and hope, and therefore, the beginning of a new life. . . . This is no ordinary skull, but rather an infantile one. The child to whom it was once attached has passed on, presumably to meet its maker—an idea beautifully suggested by the retrieval of the olive branch in the same waters which have entombed the skull" (7). De Armas perceives the skull as "possibly a symbol of frustrated love, a confluence of Cupid and a hoped-for offspring" (73). In light of the monarch's passage in the play from aconsciousness to consciousness as presented here, the skull can further be seen as an omen of the death of the child-man, Alfonso, who must learn that the wages of sin are death. As such, the skull and the olive branch symbolize the king's past life and at the same time foreshadow his imminent return from the body personal to the body mystical: the impending death of his former life of transgression and his rebirth into a future life as God's anointed representative on earth. When the river water is understood with the *calavera* and the olive branch that it engulfs, it would be difficult not to experience an infiguration of baptism. The implication of a baptism for the king prefigures the restoration of peace and harmony through atonement and redemption.

Historically and theatrically, the etiological legend of Raquel effectively divides the life of Alfonso into two phases: a period of providential preparation, unrecognized as such by the young sovereign; and a second period during which the Castilian monarch is fully conscious of his mission and denomination as one of the chosen vessels. The point of demarcation between these two intervals in the drama is provided by God's angel, who appears to the grief-stricken and enraged king after the execution of his beloved *Fermosa,* Raquel. It is here that Alfonso finally undergoes a direct experience with the divine will, is painfully obliged to acknowledge his former cupidity as an offense to God, and repents his transgressions. His desire to avenge the murder of Raquel blatantly contradicts the moral-ethical code and would, therefore, be yet another grave infraction against both the *nomos* and the *hodos*. By taking the law into his own hands, he would fall further into the depths of the evil that has ensnared him. He must awaken from his "sleep" and accept responsibility for his actions. He directs his anger, a visible symbol of his limitations, toward the heavens. He has not yet fully realized that he is destined to suffer the consequences of his own actions before he can atone and be forgiven. In other words, he is obliged to accept Raquel's murder as part of the greater providential plan in order to rise above his own self-centered existence and submit himself to divine providence.

Alfonso's encounter with the angel brings him face-to-face with the reality of his own life and his role in the world theater. He must come to understand that the answers do not lie in the Old Testament justice of "an eye for an eye" but rather in submission to a higher authority. The carefully chosen phrase: "vuelve en ti" (534b) with which the angel implores the sovereign implies that the latter has obviously not been acting within the proscribed limitations of his role. The king's infractions have turned his energies inward, causing him to lose himself in the confusion and guilt that he has experienced. The angel serves as a mirror which reflects a reality that Alfonso can no longer ignore or deny. It is as if he is finally awakening from a long slumber and must gradually rise to consciousness. Awareness dawns slowly as he is struck by the words of God's messenger: "Alfonso, muy ofendido / está Dios de tus palabras, / de las blasfemias de que dices / y de que tomes venganza. / Vuelve en ti; que si no enmiendas / lo que has dicho y lo que tratas, / grande castigo te espera" (534b). The monarch, at last fully conscious of the ramifications of his actions, heeds the warning and responds accordingly: "Pequé, Señor, ofendí / vuestra majestad; perdón" (534b). He will go forth now with a greater understanding of what it means to be king and what the duties and privileges thereunto are.

Like Adam's descendants, Alfonso has struggled to come to terms with the limitations and vulnerability imposed by the Fall. He fulfills his role in history as he becomes cognizant of the nature of sin and its consequences and is finally allowed to experience a higher level of consciousness. The figural baptism of the fishing scene has opened the heart and mind of the monarch and prepared him for the rebirth that he now undergoes. Humanity is destined to experience the knowledge of creatureliness, dependency, and humility appropriate to created beings, yet faith and baptism will allow one to recognize one's limitations and rise above them through complete submission to God. The unity of *Las paces,* then, can be seen not only in the repetition of the themes of passion, treason, and blindness, or in the art of the hero construct, or even in the homologous retrospection, but also in the movement of Alfonso from the aconscious innocent child of act 1 to the conscious anointed king of act 3. As Alfonso comes to understand the necessity of acknowledging divine authority, he achieves a hitherto unexperienced level of consciousness and thus reintegrates the fragments of the kingship shattered by his former transgressions. The monarch who emerges from this encounter is finally conscious of his role in history and is a transformed man, as indicated in the *Crónica general de España:* "y de allí adelante temió siempre a Dios e fizo siempre buenas obras, e emendó mucho en su vida e fizo mucho su façienda" (Ocampo, 87). The restoration of harmony, not only in the kingdom but also between creator and creation, allows Alfonso to begin his reign anew, a reign that, sanctioned now by divine providence, will withstand the threat of enemy invasion at the Battle of Las Navas.

Works Consulted

Castañeda, James A. 1962. *A Critical Edition of Lope de Vega's "Las paces de los reyes y judía de Toledo."* Chapel Hill: University of North Carolina Press.

Covarrubias y Horozco, Sebastián de. [1611; 1674] 1943. *Tesoro de la lengua castellana o española.* Edited by Martín de Riquer. Reprint. Barcelona: S. A. Horta de Impresiones y Ediciones.

Darst, David H. 1971. "The Unity of *Las paces de los reyes y judía de Toledo.*" *Symposium* 25:225–35.

De Armas, Frederick. 1978. "Passion, Treason and Blindness in Lope's *Las paces de los reyes.*" In *Studies in the Spanish Golden Age: Cervantes and Lope de Vega,* edited by Dana B. Drake and José A. Madrigal, 65–75. Miami, Fla.: Ediciones Universal.

McCrary, Susan Niehoff. 1987. El último godo *and the Dynamics of* Urdrama. Potomac, Md.: Scripta Humanistica.

McCrary, William C. 1973. "Plot, Action, and Imitation: The Art of Lope's *Las paces de los reyes.*" *Hispanófila* 48:1–17.

Menéndez y Pelayo, Marcelino. 1949. *Estudios sobre el teatro de Lope de Vega.* Vol. 4. Santander: Consejo Superior de Investigaciones Científicas.

Ocampo, Florián de. 1853. *La crónica general de España.* Continued by Esteban de Garibay in *Las glorias nacionales,* edited by Manuel Ortiz de la Vega. Vol. 2. Madrid: Librería José Cuesta.

Soons, C. A. 1966. *Ficción y comedia en el siglo de oro.* Madrid: Castalia.

Vega, Lope de. 1958. *Obras escogidas de Lope Félix de Vega Carpio.* Edited by Federico C. Sainz de Robles. Vol. 1. Madrid: Aguilar.

Matthew D. Stroud

Rivalry and Violence in Lope's

El castigo sin venganza

esáreo Bandera published *Mimesis conflictiva* in 1975, at least a decade ahead of its time in terms of its reception by the *comediantes.* Using the ideas of René Girard, Bandera focuses primarily on *Don Quixote,* but a significant section of the monograph is devoted to a discussion of *La vida es sueño.* His discussion is wide ranging, dealing with the relationship between subject and object; the nature of, and processes surrounding, the sacrificial victim; the necessary relationship between truth, violence, civilization, reason, and illusion; the role of desire and (in)differentiation in rivalry; and the all-pervasive influence of the other in human relations. Unfortunately, Bandera's book and his approach to the *comedia* have been largely ignored or vitiated as unable to account for every detail in the play. Ciriaco Morón-Arroyo accuses Bandera (along with Freud and Derrida) of trying "to find a radical principle or a radical reality out of which the rest of things would become meaningful" (85), dismissing most of Bandera's arguments with the statement that literature "cannot be approached only from this point of view" (79). Not only is this assertion unfair to Bandera's work, which in no way excludes the possibility of multiple approaches to the *comedia* or any other literary texts, but it also neglects the interesting perspective that Girard and Bandera have to offer. The purpose of this present study is to continue the discussion of Girard's *Violence and the Sacred,* not with respect to *La vida es sueño* but rather to Lope's *El castigo sin venganza.* Considering the nature of Girard's ideas regarding the relationship among sex, violence, the sacred, rivalry, and the double bind, his study would seem to have a natural association not just to this *comedia* but to the wife-murder plays in general.

Let us begin with Girard's observation that "sexuality is a permanent source of disorder even within the most harmonious communities" (35). The entire plot of Lope's masterpiece revolves around the relationship between sex and violence. So that political violence will not erupt when he dies, the Duke of Ferrara weds Casandra to produce legitimate heirs (676–81).[1] After only one night with Casandra in an entire month, the Duke, a notorious womanizer, abandons her (1034–43). To get even, Casandra resorts to the violence at her disposal. First, she promises that she will bear no heirs for the Duke (1109), then she decides to seduce the Duke's illegitimate son, Federico (1811–25). The two have a sexual relationship while the Duke is away in the service of the pope (during which he is said to have had a religious conversion [2351–63]). When he returns, he discovers the adultery. To punish the lovers, he has Federico kill Casandra as an enemy of the state (2927–53), then he orders his soldiers to kill Federico for murdering Casandra (2981–87). The Duke's sexual habits provoke the revenge of Casandra's sexual liaison with Federico, which results in the final violence.

As with any love triangle, this plot involves rivalry. Girard's thoughts provide an interesting description of the situation of these characters: "Rivalry does not arise because of the fortuitous convergence of two desires on a single object; rather *the subject desires the object because the rival desires it.*"[2] The Duke of Ferrara demonstrates his lack of interest in Casandra by abandoning her and returning to his nightly debauchery. When he learns, however, that Federico and Casandra are having an affair, he responds quickly and violently. He once again asserts his role as husband, and, even though he did not care much for her before, he cannot allow the illicit relationship to continue. The Duke's desire is quite different from that of Federico and is, in fact, much more political than erotic— he asserts his domination over Casandra in order to forestall the threat she has become to the duchy.

Girard continues, "Two desires converging on the same object are bound to clash. Thus, mimesis coupled with desire leads automatically to conflict" (145–46). In other words, rivalry leads to violence because violence is a direct consequence of a loss of difference, that is, a loss of distinctions in identification necessary to the proper functioning of social institutions and taboos.[3] In the case of adultery, for example, the husband loses his distinction as the wife's sex partner when the other man assumes that role. Additionally, *El castigo sin venganza* presents another, more socially unacceptable loss of difference, that between parent and child; the sin of adultery is compounded by the sin of incest.[4] Not only is the difference erased between insider (the Duke, the husband) and outsider

(Federico, the other man) but also the difference between father and son (both identifications based upon sex roles).

One of the ironies of the father-son rivalry is that, in large part, Federico is merely following in his father's footsteps. Cintia, remarking on the inappropriateness of the Duke's womanizing, clearly compares the actions of the father and his son: "si en Federico fuera / libertad, ¿qué fuera en él?" (119–20). Even more to the point, Casandra tells the Duke that Federico was "un retrato vuestro" (2656) during the Duke's absence, ironically referring to the illicit sexual habits of both father and son. A clear indication of the loss of difference occasioned by the illicit love affair is the statement by the Duke: "De que la llame madre / se corre, y dice bien, pues es su amiga / la mujer de su padre, / y no es justo que ya madre se diga" (2624–27).

Even the *gracioso* comments on Federico's loss of identification when he refers to him as a hermaphrodite, suspended as he is between life and death (1216–22), a description that we may easily extend to Federico's dilemma between acting on impulse (as his father has done) and restraining the sexual urge that threatens himself, his father, his stepmother, the state, and the institution of marriage. Finally, Federico's statement, "Yo me olvido de ser hombre" (2215), is significantly ambiguous. It could mean that he has lost his human reason, he has been made cowardly by the return of the Duke, or he has forgotten his role as illegitimate son.

Federico's dilemma between lust and duty, between being a good son and following his father's example, is symptomatic of Girard's concept of the double bind: "Man cannot respond to that universal human injunction, 'Imitate me!' without almost immediately encountering an inexplicable counterorder: 'Don't imitate me!' (which really means, 'Do not appropriate *my* object!')" (147). On many occasions, he has wanted to be like his father, as when he wanted to go to battle with the Duke (1695–99). Also, whether he admits it or not, he wants to assume his father's role with the father's wife. In neither case is it permissible. The double bind produces in Federico a great melancholy of frustration and confusion (958–64, 1197–1215), which is typical of Federico's lackluster character.

The Duke, as the aggrieved husband, is placed in his own double bind—he can allow the treason to go unpunished to the detriment of the state, or he can kill the two people he loves the most. More than for Casandra, it is for Federico that he grieves as he prepares the deaths of the lovers: "dar la muerte a un hijo, / ¿qué corazón no desmaya? / Sólo de pensarlo ¡ay triste! / tiembla el cuerpo, expira el alma, / lloran los ojos, la sangre / muere en las venas heladas" (2868–73). Of course, he chooses action over inaction, violence over passivity, but it is at the great cost of destroying his own image, his own "retrato."

Thus, violence is the result of the rivalry in the play, but the Duke seems aware, at least at some level, of the nature of violence and its ability to go beyond the bounds of its original purpose. Again according to Girard, violence can be good or bad (115). Good violence is generative and fulfills a necessary function in the maintenance of the society; bad violence is reciprocal. Objectively, there is no difference between good and bad violence, from which we derive a basic irony inherent in all the ambiguous wife-murder plays: a sacrifice is both a sacred obligation and a criminal act at the same time (Girard, 1, 40); it is precisely the controlled execution of violence that allows society to avoid a crisis. So beneficial is good violence that it can even be considered an act of piety or devotion (Girard, 298, citing Gernet, 326–27). In order to avoid reciprocal violence, the Duke must carry out his punishment according to the precepts of the sacred, and he attempts to convince us that his actions are good violence (justice: for the sake of the state) rather than bad (revenge: for personal reasons).[5]

The sacred is a dehumanized and external force that alone is capable of changing bad violence into good violence, and it functions with the approval of society (Girard, 30–31). In other words, the sacred is simply socially acceptable violence. Indeed, without nominal unanimity, sacrificial violence deteriorates into reciprocity. The sacrificial rite is a sacred obligation; the wishes of the individual are clearly inferior to the demands of the society. Because of its inherent violence (both good and bad), the sacred is desirable and fearful at the same time (Girard, 267). As a consequence of the nature of the sacred (eliciting both devotion and terror), societies that revere the sacred are extremely conservative (Girard, 134, 282). The sacred in *El castigo sin venganza,* as invoked by the Duke, is the combination of honor, the authority of the state, and divine sanction. Of great dramatic interest is the fact that all three come to be embodied in the personage of the Duke.

Honor represents a system of codified actions that clearly favors the society over the individual: honor is more important than life itself, regardless of the particular life in question.[6] Honor is an all-pervasive force in the play, rarely mentioned before act 2 but, due to the nature of sex and its accompanying violence, always close at hand. Honor alone, however, is not impersonal enough to avoid reciprocity, and revenge is the term most often associated with violence in the name of honor, as we can see in the titles of plays such as *A secreto agravio, secreta venganza, La venganza honrosa,* and *La mayor venganza de honor.*

For the Duke, honor is judge, sentence, and executioner (1746–47). Typical of those who administer sacred violence, the Duke both accepts his duty and condemns the necessity, calling honor a fierce enemy (2811). In the soliloquy in which the Duke laments this turn of events and tries to discover why and how he has been put in this position, his arguments clearly revolve around the ideas of good and bad violence, but he calls them "punishment" and "revenge" (2545). He separates his roles as father (with its attendant political authority to punish) and aggrieved husband (with its imperative to avenge the dishonor). Because he is the embodiment of law and order, there is no external legal system to which he can refer the matter; he alone must decide. His decision is to act as a punishing father rather than to take a husband's revenge, which would be a sin against heaven:

> No es venganza de mi agravio;
> que yo no quiero tomarla
> en vuestra ofensa, y de un hijo
> ya fuera bárbara hazaña.
> Este ha de ser un castigo
> vuestro no más, porque valga
> para que perdone el cielo
> el rigor por la templanza.
> Seré padre y no marido,
> dando la justicia santa
> a un pecado sin vergüenza
> un castigo sin venganza. (2838–49)[7]

Thus the Duke adds to his arguments his claim to be acting as an instrument of heaven, making the deaths of the lovers satisfy, in one action, the demands of divine justice, parental authority, and honorable revenge (he will still make some of his motives for violence secret, just to be sure [2850–57]). Whether the actions reflect *castigo* or *venganza,* of course, the violence is the same; only the reasons for it change.

The effect of having the cause of the violence exterior to people themselves is that the violence can be seen as unanimous rather than the idiosyncratic deed of an individual. The Duke is, as he sees it, only upholding the prohibitions of the sacred; and in discharging the sentence, he enlists his soldiers, anonymous men whose task it is to carry out orders without question or personal involvement. The Duke as father is the authority figure; to disobey would be treason and could threaten the very foundations of the society. In addition, upholding the law is a positive reinforcement of the social *status quo;* as an instrument of impersonal justice (even though he himself is the incarnation of that justice), the Duke can renounce personal blame for his actions and include himself in the unanimous, restored society that will exist after the executions have taken place.[8]

Another function of the sacred is that it hides the true workings of violence from the members of society. The Duke, who takes on the role of honor's instrument, confesses that he does not understand the nature of the blood expiation:

> ¡Ay, honor, fiero enemigo!
> ¿Quién fue el primero que dio
> tu ley al mundo? ¡Y que fuese
> mujer quien en sí tuviese
> tu valor, y el hombre no!
> Pues sin culpa el más honrado
> te puede perder, honor,
> bárbaro legislador
> fue tu inventor, no letrado. (2811–19)

The perpetrators of revenge frequently decide to keep their violence secret or lie about its true nature, and the Duke is no exception. Ostensibly, such secrecy keeps the original dishonor from public notice, thus saving the reputation of the husband. As a side effect, the secrecy also keeps the violence from becoming reciprocal (Hesse, 203–10). The concealment of true motives also allows the Duke to perpetrate a falsehood regarding the deaths of the two lovers. A leitmotiv throughout the play is that Federico's unhappiness stems from his loss of inheritance rather than from the love triangle. No one wants to investigate other possible causes of his melancholy. It is easier for society to ascribe his dilemma to a nonsexual—and therefore nontaboo—reason, financial and political interests. This pretense is carried through to its conclusion, even when the Duke has found out the truth. The public reason for the death of Casandra is that she was a traitor to the state; for Federico, that he killed his mother because of his inheritance (2927–45, 2981–86).

It is in large part the nature of the sacrificial victim that determines whether the violence perpetrated will be considered good or bad. The sacrificial victim, the *pharmakos,* has a dual nature. On the one hand, he is the object of scorn, insult, and violence, and he is weighed down with guilt; on the other hand, he is surrounded with a quasi-religious aura of veneration—he has become a sort of cult object. Moreover, to insure that the ritual violence will not escalate into reciprocal violence, the ritual victim tends to be chosen from groups marginal to society (Girard, 12–13, 271). Such is the status of women in the society depicted in this play; they are both hated and idolized. Throughout the play, women are referred to as untrustworthy (1171–72, 2932) and traitorous (1726, 1845) and are compared to ferocious lions (296–303), sirens (2016), and enchantresses (38–39). Women are also compared to the sun (1442–44, 1628), angels (36, 2597), flowers (625–43), and objects of idolatry (1731–32) and are described as celestial (1861). Women are by no means trivial, since they are both the guardians of reproduction of the human race in their role as mother and are repositories of men's honor in their roles as wife, daughter, and sister. However, they are not central to male society outside of those two roles. It is of interest that the Duke grieves the death of Federico; he hardly even mentions Casandra's. As a wife, she is her husband's property and therefore suitably marginal to the society, so that her death, carried out according to the precepts of the sacred, will not cause social collapse.

Because people do not understand the true nature of violent unanimity, they naturally examine the victims to determine whether they are somehow responsible for their own violent deaths (Girard, 85). As the Duke says of Federico: "pagó la maldad que hizo / por heredarme" (3016–17). The *pharmakos,* the threatening force, has been driven out, and the stage society achieves catharsis, a concept that Girard defines as the "mysterious benefits that accrue to the community upon the death of a human *katharma* or *pharmakos*" (287). From the deaths of Casandra and Federico comes a strengthening of social institutions. Aurora and the Marqués will marry, thus completing the tragedy-comedy cycle of death and regeneration and achieving Arnold Reichenberger's "order restored" (307).

Batín tells us in the final speech that we are to take what we have seen as an example. Tragedy, according to Girard, is in itself an intermediary "between the ritual performance and the spontaneous model that the ritual attempts to reproduce" (132). As with the sacred, violence in tragedy is impersonal and operates without regard to other concepts of good and bad (Girard, 47, 204). It is to be hoped that, just as in the primitive rite, "the spectators will be purged of their passions and provoke a new katharsis, both individual and collective. . . . Every true work of art might be said to partake of the initiatory process in that it forces itself upon the motions, offers intimations of violence, and instills a respect for the power of violence; that is, it promotes prudence and discourages hubris" (Girard, 290, 291–92). In other words, it is Batín's "ejemplo."

There is one principal obstacle to the direct application of Girard's theories of tragedy to Lope's play: *El castigo sin venganza* is not a tragedy in an Aristotelian sense. Girard notes that in tragedy, the responsibility for what happens is evenly distributed among all (77). What Lope's play lacks is the concentration in a single individual of the traits of both protagonist and victim. In other words, there is no tragic hero here in the sense that Oedipus is one. Because of the status of Federico and Casandra as (illegitimate) son and wife, there is disagreement concerning their appropriateness as sacrificial victims and concerning the benefits that accrue to society by their deaths. In Aristotelian tragedy, the spectator tends to divide the tragedy and characters into categories of good and bad, focusing on the extremes rather than the nature of the conflict itself (Girard, 149). Here, where there is much less unanimity regarding the validity of the sacrifice, spectators and critics alike vary greatly in their interpretations depending upon individual differences of opinion about the roles of Casandra and Federico in the society.

The debate over the meaning of the play (e.g., is this a moral example or a shocking illustration of violence and perversity?) hinges in large part on whether one agrees that the Duke's violence has indeed been purified and made socially good. Is the Duke really acting only as an impartial judge? Are the deaths of Casandra and Federico likely to reunite the society? What happens after the curtain falls? Those who are outraged, such as Morris, Pring-Mill, and May, see the Duke's actions as less than pure: he may indeed be the Duke, but he is also a jealous husband whose own actions cast suspicions on his legitimacy as an authority. Others, including Alonso, Kossoff, and Nichols, assert that the Duke has a legitimate responsibility to the state and believe that he has truly replaced jealous revenge with pious justice. There is in both arguments a separation of characters into good and bad. It is the nature of Golden Age drama, however, to present characters who share responsibility for the actions.[9] As Edward M. Wilson stated, they are all bad (292). Bandera notes that with regard to the plays of Calderón, although we may have a desire to establish fixed boundaries, Calderón fully recognizes the danger inherent in such oversimplification and prefers twilight (259). In a sense, the lack of a clear dichotomy between good and bad is what makes this play a masterpiece worthy of study again and again. There is no single, correct interpretation; each spectator and critic is called upon to judge the validity of the sacrifice on an individual basis.

Notes

1.   All references are to line numbers in Kossoff's edition of *El castigo sin venganza* (Vega Carpio 1970).

2.   Girard, 146. A psychoanalytic basis for Girard's assertion can be found in the writings of Jacques Lacan (1–29), especially in "The Mirror Stage" and "Aggressivity in Psychoanalysis." For Lacan, rivalry is the manifestation of the desire for the object of the other's desire, thus implicating the triangle of others, the ego, and the object (19). It is in the mirror stage, through which all must pass between six and eighteen months of age, that the subject's ego is constituted through its relation to the Other and to others. One of its effects, according to Anika Lemaire, is "the constitutional aggressivity of the human being who must always win his place at the expense of the other, and either impose himself on the other or be annihilated himself" (179). By way of example, Lacan cites St. Augustine: "Vidi ego et expertus sum zelantem parvulum: nondum loquebatur et intuebatur pallidus amaro aspectu conlactaneum suum" (20) ["I have seen with my own eyes and known very well an infant in the grip of jealousy: he could not yet speak, and already he observed his foster-brother, pale and with an envenomed stare" (Sheridan trans.)].

3.   Girard, 57–58, 146–47, 169, 180, 281.

4.   At that time, sex between a son and a stepmother was considered incest. See Wilson, 278.

5.   Anthony Wilden notes that violence always accompanies civilization (481). It occurs in the name of education, of rationality, of science, of culture, or of order, and we justify it as a defense against aggressivity coming from those we control. For Juliet Flower MacCannell, the civilization that is promised as the solution for primal violence is itself the source of aggression; it is "uncivilized" (73).

6.   Cf. Lope's *Porfiar hasta morir* (719a): "Creo / si ya he vengado mi honor, / que estimo la muerte menos." For general overviews and bibliographies regarding honor in the *comedia,* see Castro, 1–50, 357–86; and Artiles, 235–41.

7.   The meaning of lines 2844–45 is open to debate; see Dixon and Parker, 157–66. That revenge was a sin was well known in the Golden Age and caused an ongoing conflict in the drama between what was honorable (revenge) and what was moral (mercy or punishment). See Dunn, 24–60.

8.   Parker believes that the Duke ultimately suffers a punishment of frustration for his actions. He may be part of the surviving society, according to Parker, but he pays dearly for it (1970, 698).

9.   The idea of shared responsibility for tragedy was discussed in relation to the plays of Calderón by Parker (1962, 222–37).

Works Consulted

Alonso, Amado. [1952] 1962. "Lope de Vega y sus fuentes." *Thesaurus* 8:1–24. Reprint in *El teatro de Lope de Vega: Artículos y estudios,* edited by José Gatti, 193–218. Buenos Aires: EUDEBA.

Artiles, Jenaro. 1969. "Bibliografía sobre el problema del honor y la honra en el drama español." In *Filología y crítica hispánica: Homenaje al Prof. Federico Sánchez Escribano,* edited by Alberto Porqueras-Mayo and Carlos Rojas, 235–41. Madrid: Alcalá; Atlanta: Emory University Press.

Bandera, Cesáreo. 1975. *Mimesis conflictiva: Ficción literaria y violencia en Cervantes y Calderón.* Madrid: Gredos.

Castro, Américo. 1916. "Algunas observaciones acerca del concepto del honor en los siglos XVI y XVII." *Revista de filología española* 3:1–50; 357–86.

Dixon, Victor, and Alexander A. Parker. 1970. *"El castigo sin venganza:* Two Lines, Two Interpretations." *Modern Language Notes* 85:157–66.

Dunn, Peter N. 1965. "Honour and the Christian Background in Calderón." In *Critical Essays on the Theatre of Calderón,* edited by Bruce W. Wardropper, 24–60. New York: New York University Press.

Gernet, Louis. 1968. *Anthropologie de la Grèce antique.* Paris: F. Maspero.

Girard, René. 1977. *Violence and the Sacred.* Translated by Patrick Gregory. Baltimore, Md.: Johns Hopkins University Press.

Hesse, Everett W. 1976. "The Art of Concealment in Lope's *El castigo sin venganza."* In *Oelschläger Festschrift,* edited by David Darst et al., 203–10. Estudios de *Hispanófila,* vol. 36. Madrid: Castalia.

Lacan, Jacques. 1977. *Ecrits: A Selection.* Translated by Alan Sheridan. New York: Norton.

Lemaire, Anika. 1979. *Jacques Lacan.* Translated by David Macey. London and New York: Routledge and Kegan Paul.

MacCannell, Juliet Flower. 1986. *Figuring Lacan: Criticism and the Cultural Unconscious.* London: Croom Helm.

May, T. E. 1960. "Lope de Vega's *El castigo sin venganza:* The Idolatry of the Duke of Ferrara." *Bulletin of Hispanic Studies* 37:154–82.

Morón-Arroyo, Ciriaco. 1978. "Cooperative Mimesis: Don Quixote and Sancho Panza." *Diacritics* 8:75–86.

Morris, C. B. 1963. "Lope de Vega's *El castigo sin venganza* and Poetic Tradition." *Bulletin of Hispanic Studies* 40:69–78.

Nichols, Geraldine Cleary. 1977. "The Rehabilitation of the Duke of Ferrara." *Journal of Hispanic Philology* 1:209–30.

Parker, Alexander A. 1962. "Towards a Definition of Calderonian Tragedy." *Bulletin of Hispanic Studies* 39:222–37.

———. 1970. "The Spanish Drama of the Golden Age: A Method of Analysis and Interpretation." In *The Great Playwrights,* edited by Eric Bentley, 1:679–707. New York: Doubleday.

Pring-Mill, R. D. F. 1961. "Introduction." Lope de Vega, *Five Plays,* edited by Jill Booty, i–xxxvi. New York: Hill and Wang.

Reichenberger, Arnold G. 1959. "The Uniqueness of the *Comedia.*" *Hispanic Review* 27:303–16.

Vega Carpio, Lope de. 1964. *Porfiar hasta morir.* In *Obras escogidas de Lope Félix de Vega Carpio,* edited by Federico C. Sainz de Robles, 1:689–719. 4th ed. Madrid: Aguilar.

———. 1970. *El perro del hortelano. El castigo sin venganza.* Edited by A. David Kossoff. Madrid: Castalia.

Wilden, Anthony. 1980. *System and Structure: Essays in Communication and Exchange.* 2d ed. London: Tavistock.

Wilson, Edward M. 1963. "Cuando Lope quiere, quiere." *Cuadernos hispanoamericanos* 161–62:265–98.

Constance Rose

Reconstructing Tisbea

isbea's role in *El burlador de Sevilla* has always aroused comment. Critics muse on whether or not she deserves her fate, and the consensus is yes; some see her as Eve, the original cause of original sin; others as the eternal temptress, the perennial tease, a vampire woman out to destroy men. Many believe that she suffers from hubris.[1] This may be claiming too much for Tisbea, who has no imperial ambitions and who is, after all, only a poor fisherwoman, despite her absurdly affected manner of speaking. *Presumida,* yes, but hubris seems too strong a term to apply to Tisbea. Nevertheless, the spectacle of this fisherwoman speaking in such convoluted Gongoristic terms is somewhat disconcerting; such a speech act is obviously a breach of decorum and defies any semblance of verisimilitude. Since the playwright[2] had to be well aware of this, what, then, was his intention with the creation of this character? What exactly did he hope to accomplish?

In Tisbea, it would appear, the author has created a character for whom he has nothing but contempt.[3] He sets Tisbea's character in her long introductory soliloquy, and the process of deconstructing Tisbea begins with this very speech, which could be called an ironic variation on the *beatus ille* theme.[4] He is well aware of the impact of her words and her manner of speaking upon the audience/reader. And it is his intention to undercut everything she says; he does so, in fact, by turning her very words against her. He simply negates everything she says so that the disparity between what is and what Tisbea thinks becomes apparent. In this way, he exposes the contradictory tendencies in her nature and demonstrates that she is not the person she thinks she is. Instead, his Tisbea is a serious study in self-deception.

The playwright, then, must unmask Tisbea without intervening in the action; he must conspire with the audience to evaluate and judge what Tisbea says, thinks, feels, and imagines through a variety of means. No simple job. As Edward Friedman has pointed out, "the playwright faces the complex task of governing discourse without the benefit of a narrative persona. Each of the characters speaks in a voice which appears to be unmediated but which bears the marker of authorial intervention" (77). The task that the author of *El burlador de Sevilla* has set for himself is seemingly made all the more difficult by the fact that in her initial appearance Tisbea delivers a lengthy monologue.[5] She has not been previously described—she has, in fact, never been mentioned; unknown and unannounced, she simply appears alone on the stage. No one is playing off her, no one is conversing with her, no one is listening to her or even overhearing thoughts spoken out loud. No one, that is, except the audience.

The piscatory incident in which Tisbea is involved is, in reality, another type of pastoral; while not present in classical literature, piscatory pastoral makes an appearance in the Renaissance with such masters as Sannazaro and Góngora.[6] This seaside episode in *El burlador de Sevilla,* as a reflection of rural life, is used to balance the later, more traditional land-bound pastoral incident in which Aminta appears; Tisbea, the fisherwoman, and Aminta, the shepherdess, are two examples of peasant women swayed by the charms of the noble Don Juan.[7]

The scene in which Tisbea first appears contrasts with what has occurred before. *El burlador de Sevilla* is a play characterized by the rush of time (Aubrun). There is little time for reflection—and appropriately, the work contains no sonnet. The play is action oriented, and Don Juan, as the protagonist, is always on the move. Tisbea, on the other hand, is presented on stage for the first time alone, still, absorbed in her own thoughts: a thinking peasant woman. But what she is thinking about is how different she is from the rest, how she, alone of all others, is free from the chains of love. In a play where sexual encounters abound, she imagines that she alone is exempt from passion's power. Unlike Segismundo, whose observance of the natural world in *La vida es sueño* leads him to protest (in *décimas*) that all creatures of nature have more freedom than he, Tisbea congratulates herself (in *romancillo*) that she has more liberty than all others. How little she knows herself.

In order to understand the total meaning of the passage and to observe how the author reveals her true nature, let us first look at the first sixteen lines of her speech:

1.	Yo, de cuantas el mar,	375
2.	—pies de jazmín y rosa—	
3.	en sus riberas besa	
4.	con fugitivas olas,	
5.	sola de amor esenta,	
6.	como en ventura sola,	380
7.	tirana me reservo	
8.	de sus prisiones locas.	
9.	Aquí donde el sol pisa	
10.	soñolientas las ondas,	
11.	alegrando zafiros	385
12.	el que espantaba sombras,	
13.	por la menuda arena,	
14.	—unas veces aljófar,	
15.	y átomos otras veces	
16.	del sol que así la dora—[8]	390

Tisbea is standing by the sea alone. Whether one is part of an audience present at a performance or whether one is reading the play, Tisbea is the center of attention. Both the external and the internal lines of space coalesce to focus on her.[9] She is framed by the stage as in a full-length portrait, holding "una caña de pescar," the sign of her office. She alone occupies the stage, and the first word she utters is "yo," thus doubling the effect of her solitary presence and bringing herself all the more clearly into focus. And it is she who further directs the audience/reader's gaze more intensely upon herself by focusing on herself. All eyes are literally upon her as the theatre audience is transformed, for the moment, into voyeurs and eavesdroppers.

The first eight lines of the soliloquy are entirely devoted to Tisbea's self-description; only later is any attempt made to describe the setting. The very first line establishes the "yo," the subject of the sentence, as the dominant word in the entire passage. The rest of line one contains a subordinate clause whose verb does not appear until the end of line three, interrupted as it is by line two, a parenthetical phrase in praise of her beauty, which refers back to the word "yo." The subordinate clause in lines one and three is adjectival and modifies the word "yo," which it locates in space—in a maritime community. Lines five and six are in apposition to the "yo" of the subject but are self-contained, introduced and ending with the same word, "sola," thus emphasizing her separateness from the rest of the community. Finally, the main verb appears in line seven, where it is introduced by the word "tirana," a noun in apposition with the subject pronoun "yo." I shall discuss line eight later, but suffice it to say that line eight is a prepositional phrase and appears, at first glance, to have nothing to do with explaining the "yo" with which these closely connected lines begin.

One might diagram the first eight lines of Tisbea's soliloquy thus:

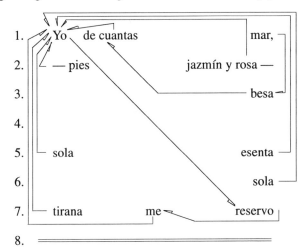

1. Yo de cuantas mar,
2. — pies jazmín y rosa —
3. besa
4.
5. sola esenta
6. sola
7. tirana me reservo
8.

This passage reveals more about Tisbea than she realizes. Its language emphasizes her immobility—it surrounds and entraps her. Because of the syntactical constructions she employs, it becomes evident that what she says is in contradiction to the overall meaning of the passage—in brief, syntax is used here to contradict sense. "Yo" does not find a verb until the seventh line, and when it does, with "me reservo," it is blocked by the verb, which throws the action back upon "me," the pronoun object reflective of the subject, "yo." Line eight, rather than modifying Tisbea ("yo"), physically blocks her exit. Thus, while she may think that she has escaped the force of love and its "prisiones locas," she herself is a prisoner of her own words, of her own verbal creation.

Tisbea is beautiful and proud of it, but her thinking is faulty. Poetic portraits should begin at the top, not the bottom, but we never see her face because she directs our gaze immediately to her feet, her beautiful bare feet. It was so important for her to do so that she interrupted the flow of her thought, shifting her eyes from the sea to her own feet—which, we soon discover, are kissed by the waves. Perhaps no other feet in Spanish literature are so famous except for those of Dorotea in *Don Quijote,* who is first observed washing her bare feet, feet as white and precious as alabaster, in a stream (Johnson, 118–28). Though their situations may differ, both of these sensuous women have their feet in the water; metaphorically and physically they are both in danger, sexual danger, and while Dorotea is at least vigilant, Tisbea is not.

Upon closer observation, all of Tisbea's words take on new significance, as the author continuously manages to negate what she is saying. Her statement, "pies de jazmín y de rosas," not only reveals the beauty of her skin—and by synecdoche reflects the beauty of her entire being—but also echoes the poetic phrase "entre rosas y azucenas."[10] Tisbea is a flower among flowers. Thus transformed, she then ceases to be human; she is nothing more than a beautiful flower, there for the plucking.

The next eight lines are devoted to describing the setting, the shore on which Tisbea stands. An ice maiden, as unyielding as diamonds, as she begins to observe her surroundings, she soon becomes part of the whole bejeweled immobile landscape, while the sun plays upon the sapphire waves—"el sol pisa / soñolientas las ondas / alegrando zafiros." The very shape of the verses she utters creates a many-faceted prismatic pattern, like the waves that they refer to, like the precious stones that they conjure up. Tisbea is the crowning jewel in this splendid setting. She is a jewel among jewels, among the pearls and sapphires set in gold. She is a golden maiden—"unas veces aljófar / y átomos, otras veces, / del sol que así la dora,"[11] washed by the same sun that casts a golden light upon the beach. But, in truth, the pattern of the phrases she utters, as they crisscross back and forth, seems to seal her in—indeed, she seems to seal herself in with her words, like a fly enclosed in amber, forever entrapped.

Tisbea passes through another series of metamorphoses. She is first a Venus born on the waves, reminding one of Botticelli's painting, a true goddess of love, lovely herself with her pink and white complexion. But then her self-absorption transforms her into a female Narcissus,[12] adoringly transfixed by her own image and the image she projects, or would project. As Tisbea stares down at her own reflection in the sea, she does not really see herself clearly. Water makes an imperfect mirror, especially when its surface is disturbed by rippling waves, and the image it casts is never so clear as the original—and indeed can be quite distorted. Tisbea would also have us believe that she is a follower of Diana, that chaste and virginal goddess, but her glance at her comely feet, kissed by the sea, belies the intent of her words—that she is exempt from the force of love. Quite the contrary. Tisbea, in truth, is far from free; she is a passionate creature, a prisoner of her own nature.

In her own mind, Tisbea has already shown herself capable of being transported into mythic situations, and another is at hand with the shipwreck of Don Juan. In classical literature, shipwrecked men rarely augured well for the women who found them. The play's many references to Troy (a war started by Venus, after all) tell us to look in that direction.[13] First, Odysseus comes to mind. His washing up on the shores of the island of Drepane and finding himself in the company of the princess Nausicaa would appear to be one of the archetypical situations against which the Spanish dramatist is playing. While Odysseus personally caused no harm to Nausicaa herself, the aid that her parents gave to him resulted in great damage to their own subjects, for the gods intervened to make sure that kindness was not paid in kind. Aeneas also comes to mind, and, indeed, Tisbea refers to Don Juan as an Aeneas when he rescues Catalinón from the sea (502–3).[14] The association becomes even more explicit when Don Juan boasts that he will treat Tisbea as Aeneas treated Dido—namely, he plans to seduce and abandon her (899–900). For while Aeneas may have thought he had a mission to fulfill and had a right to leave Dido, she—and posterity—felt otherwise (Lida).

While Tisbea is unaware of Don Juan's imminent arrival, the audience is well aware of his impending presence, not only because we already know of his existence and his travel plans but also because we are constantly reminded of him during Tisbea's soliloquy. Her speech is delivered in *romancillo,* with assonantal rhyme in *o-a,* which echoes the name Don Juan; endlessly repeating this rhyme, Tisbea has, unknowingly, been anticipating and announcing the arrival of Don Juan, who will be swept into her arms.

So absorbed is Tisbea in contemplating her beauty and in declaring her independence that she hardly notices the shipwreck and dramatic events which are occurring before her eyes. She would have if she had been looking out, not in.

"Dichosa yo mil veces" (1.415), she announces to herself in this feminine variation on the *beatus ille*—she has substituted "blessed is she who lives separate
from love" for the Horatian "blessed is he who lives far from the trouble and
intrigue of the court." Far indeed from the intrigue of the court—the court has just
washed up at her feet and invaded her rural sanctuary, this seaside *lugar ameno*.
Tisbea views this occurrence as providential, as an opportunity; but we know that
her thinking is faulty and her perceptions topsy-turvy, as that gaze upon her feet
revealed. She is neither a female goddess nor a queen nor even a princess. She
may try to speak like one, but she aims too high; she is, after all, only a humble
fisherwoman—she may have cast her net and caught a big fish,[15] but she is no
match for the aristocratic Don Juan. She has no need to beg him, "Plugiere que
no me mintáis." As the playwright has shown, Tisbea has already deceived herself.

Notes

1.   For a discussion of Tisbea's character in general, see Rogers, 49–52; for Tisbea
as Eve, see Maurel, 558–75; and for the culpability of all the women in the play, see
Lundelius. For additional studies on *El burlador de Sevilla,* consult Williamsen and Poesse.

2.   I use the words "playwright" or "author" in this study as a way of remaining
neutral in the attribution controversy that Rodríguez López-Vázquez has raised. One thing
remains clear, however; the play is quite didactic, leading me to believe that the work
does indeed portray "una concepción frailuna y misógina de la vida" (Feal Deibe, 312).

3.   Although Singer remarks that "the *Burlador* certainly shows Tirso scornful of
women's worth" (68), he later qualifies this statement by adding that "this play . . . shows
a great love of women—in their subordinate, pleasure-giving place" (70).

4.   Since Horace's ode is already satirical, it would seem most unpromising to
satirize a satire, but the author of *El burlador de Sevilla,* like most Golden Age writers,
many of whom omitted the irony of the ending—cf. Fray Luis de León's "Vida retirada"—
takes the work at face value.

5.   Gitlitz would call this type of soliloquy an "intermedio lírico" (126–63); Tisbea's
speech, nevertheless, is more than just a lyrical interlude, as it contains valuable information for judging her. For more on soliloquies and monologues in Golden Age plays, see
Marín, 11 and passim, and Morley and Bruerton, 5 and passim.

6.   Jacobo Sannazaro is credited with composing the first piscatory pastoral by
transporting the constants of Arcadia and its shepherds to the Neapolitan shore in his
Piscatoriae (1526); see Kennedy, 158–68. For the piscatory pastoral in Spain, see

Beverley's introduction in Góngora 1980. Examining more modern examples of this subgenre, Marx casts *Moby Dick* as a pastoral (277–319)—even though putting a whale in the garden would seem a bit of an exaggeration.

7.   In addition, it should be pointed out that through this doubling—two peasant women, two noblewomen—the author suggests that the number of women who fall victim to Don Juan—or whom he exposes—is infinite.

8.   All quotations refer to the edition of Fernández; the first sixteen lines of Tisbea's soliloquy occur on pages 89–90.

9.   For a discussion of view lines in literature, see Uspensky (passim).

10.   Mauricio Molho discussed the implications of this and similar phrases in lectures held in Paris and Santander. See also Molho 1977.

11.   Editors disagree about the reading of this line; many, Rodríguez López-Vázquez among them, give the line as "del sol, que así le adora." I have accepted Fernández's rendering of the line as more consistent with the bejeweled and golden surface that the author has created.

12.   Parain remarks that "la jeune émule de Narcisse devient une image féminine de Don Juan" (129).

13.   McGaha lists all the references to the Trojan War in both *El burlador de Sevilla* and *Tan largo me lo fiáis* (83b–84a).

14.   The ambiguous nature of the passage that treats the shipwreck and the rescue of the drowning man suggests a possible ironic interpretation. Line 503 in particular is troublesome; most editors render it as "Anquises le hace Eneas," though in one widely used edition (Martel and Alpern), the editors, perhaps trying to make sense of the line, overcorrect to "Anquises se hace Eneas." Just who is Aeneas and who is Anchises in this equation? Is there role switching going on? In his bilingual edition, Edwards, who, like most scholars, holds to the first reading, does not clarify the matter with his translation of the line: "The one Aeneas to the other's Anchises." Now while Aeneas rescued his aged father from burning Troy, it is not totally clear if Don Juan saved his servant (an ancient retainer?) from drowning—or if the reverse is true. Perhaps the line is deliberately ambiguous; at times, it seems, the playwright holds Don Juan in almost as much contempt as he does Tisbea.

15.   Clearly the playwright has stacked the deck against Tisbea. When he identifies her as a fisherwoman, by indicating in the stage directions that she is holding a "caña de pescar," he is also identifying her as a sinner. The Golden Age word play that allows the association of *pescar/pecar* condemns Tisbea before the fact, even before she begins her soliloquy, and undermines whatever she may say: a woman who fishes is a woman who

sins, and the sin that she commits is that of the flesh. Her avowal that she is free from the chains of love is rendered ridiculous because, according to the sign of her office, her "caña," she is actively "fishing" for a man for sexual pleasure.

Works Cited

Aubrun, Charles V. 1957. "Le Don Juan de Tirso de Molina: Un essai d'interpretation." *Bulletin hispanique* 59:26–61.

Claramonte, Andrés de. 1987. *El burlador de Sevilla.* Edited by Alfredo Rodríguez López-Vázquez. Kassel: Reichenberger.

Feal Deibe, Carlos. 1975. "El *Burlador* de Tirso y la mujer." *Symposium* 29:300–313.

Friedman, Edward H. 1987. "'Girl Gets Boy': A Note on the Value of Exchange in the *Comedia.*" *Bulletin of the Comediantes* 39:75–84.

Gitlitz, David M. 1980. *La estructura lírica de la comedia de Lope de Vega.* Valencia: Albatrós Hispanófila.

Góngora, Luis de. 1980. *Soledades.* Edited by John Beverley. Madrid: Cátedra.

Johnson, Carroll B. 1983. *Madness and Lust: A Psychoanalytical Approach to* Don Quijote. Berkeley and Los Angeles: University of California Press.

Kennedy, William. 1983. *Jacobo Sannazaro and the Uses of Pastoral.* Hanover, N.H.: University Press of New England.

Lida de Malkiel, María Rosa. 1942. "Dido y su defensa en la literatura española." *Revista de filología hispánica* 4:209–52, 313–82.

Lundelius, Ruth. 1975. "Tirso's View of Women in *El burlador de Sevilla.*" *Bulletin of the Comediantes* 21:5–13.

McGaha, Michael. 1977. "In Defense of *Tan largo me lo fiáis* . . ." *Bulletin of the Comediantes* 29:75–86.

Marín, Diego. 1962. *Uso y función de la versificación dramática en Lope de Vega.* Valencia: Castalia.

Marx, Leo. 1964. *The Machine in the Garden: Technology and the Pastoral Ideal in America.* New York: Oxford University Press.

Maurel, Serge. 1971. *L'univers dramatique de Tirso de Molina.* Poitiers: Université de Poitiers.

Molho, Maurice. 1977. *Semántica y poética: Góngora y Quevedo.* Barcelona: Crítica.

Morley, S. Griswold, and Courtney Bruerton. 1940. *Chronology of Lope de Vega's "Comedias."* New York: Modern Language Association.

Parain, Georges. 1980. "La pastorale dans le *Don Juan* de Tirso." In *Le genre pastoral en Europe du XVe au XVIIe siècle,* edited by Claude Longeon, 127–49. Saint-Etienne: Université de Saint-Etienne.

Rogers, Daniel. 1977. *Tirso de Molina: El burlador de Sevilla.* London: Grant and Cutler.

Singer, Armand E. 1981. "Don Juan's Women in *El burlador de Sevilla.*" *Bulletin of the Comediantes* 33:67–71.

Tirso de Molina. 1968. *El burlador de Sevilla.* In *Diez comedias del siglo de oro,* 2d ed., edited by José Martel and Hymen Alpern; revised by Leonard Mades, 235–321. New York: Harper and Row.

———. 1982. *El burlador de Sevilla.* Edited by Xavier A. Fernández. Madrid: Alhambra.

———. 1986. *The Trickster of Seville and the Stone Guest.* Edited and translated by Gwynne Edwards. Warminster: Aris and Phillips.

Uspensky, Boris. 1973. *A Poetics of Composition: The Structure of the Poetic Text and Typology of a Compositional Form.* Translated by Valentina Zavarin and Susan Wittig. Berkeley and Los Angeles: University of California Press.

Williamsen, Vern G., and Walter Poesse. 1979. *An Annotated, Analytical Bibliography of Tirso de Molina Studies, 1627–1977.* Columbia: University of Missouri Press.

Frederick A. de Armas

Balthasar's Doom:

Letters That Heal/Kill in Claramonte's

El secreto en la mujer

At a time when canon formations and exclusions are undergoing close scrutiny, little attention is being paid to the so-called minor drama tists of the Spanish Golden Age. Vern Williamsen has made us aware of this oversight in his book-length survey on the topic, stating that "the approximately 1,750 extant texts left by nearly 100 minor authors are rarely read and even more infrequently investigated" (ii). Williamsen focuses on eleven playwrights and shows how these writers utilized, incorporated, and further developed the dramatic structures and techniques they inherited from Lope de Vega. One of the three early dramatists of Lope's school included in his book is Andrés de Claramonte, a producer-director of *comedias* who also authored quite a few plays, of which at least thirteen are extant. He is perhaps the most maligned dramatist of the period. Even his contemporaries used the name Claramonte as a synonym for literary thievery: Alonso de Salas Barbadillo, for example, calls Ruiz de Alarcón a "segundo Claramonte" (Hernández Valcárcel, 29) to emphasize his borrowings. Modern critics have followed suit. Luis Fernández Guerra y Orbe, Emilio Cotarelo y Mori, and Marcelino Menéndez Pelayo are largely responsible for this continuing view of Claramonte as an author who "se dedicó a la piratería literaria" (Menéndez Pelayo, 78). Blanca de los Ríos also speaks against his "piraterías" (3:90) and calls him an "usurpador y profanador" (2:533) of Tirso's plays. Vern Williamsen, however, is more balanced in his presentation, stressing that "his works as a whole exhibit a remarkable ability to stage plays (he was, after all, primarily a manager of a stage company) in such a way as to increase their popular appeal" (41). But Williamsen echoes the charges of *piratería* when he adds: "In many instances, the plays seem to be built from bits and pieces lifted from the works of others" (41).

Mirroring the present concern over canon formation, Alfredo Rodríguez López-Vázquez reacts to such attacks on Claramonte by attributing to this maligned playwright some of the masterpieces of Golden Age drama, including *El burlador de Sevilla, La Estrella de Sevilla,* and *El condenado por desconfiado.* He claims that since Claramonte died without having prepared a will, his plays became part of the public domain and were immediately attributed to better-known authors (31). López-Vázquez's claims have elicited strong reactions. James Parr exclaims: "Now we have a *cause célèbre,* however, a full-fledged frontal assault on one of the articles of faith—Tirso's paternity of *El burlador de Sevilla y convidado de piedra.* The Mercedarians will be merciless in their counterattack" (288). And yet, this view of Claramonte as a writer of masterpieces is not totally original; more than sixty years ago, Sturgis Leavitt argued for his authorship of one of the most admired plays of the period, *La Estrella de Sevilla.*

It may be that such contradictory opinions of Claramonte as author of masterpieces and as plagiarist or epigone will be difficult to resolve in the near future. Rather than dealing with such thorny questions of authorship and priority, I would suggest that we look at the thirteen *comedias* of rather certain authorship[1] in order to determine if there are elements here worthy of interest and investigation. If actions and characters evince a depth and complexity that are incompatible with random borrowing; if they are structured and developed in such a way as to elicit interest and suspense; and if the images and concepts inscribed in the action are such that they open the texture of the work so that the revealed palimpsest can be said to mirror our critical concerns, then perhaps it would be possible to look at the *cause célèbre* with a clearer perception of the centrality of these marginal texts.

The first steps in this direction have already been taken by a few critics. To the previously mentioned studies by Vern Williamsen and Alfredo Rodríguez López-Vázquez should be added the work of María del Carmen Hernández Valcárcel and Charles Ganelin. These five critics are engaged in editing and examining Claramonte's works, many of which are only available in manuscript.

My own perusal of these *comedias* has led me to single out the opposition of poison/remedy as central to Claramonte's dramaturgy. Indeed, in at least ten of his thirteen plays, this conceptual pair serves as a key image that reveals and elucidates a central conflict. This opposition has occupied an important position in the history of thought, for the term *pharmakon,* meaning both venom and anti-dote, appears in works of Western philosophy separated by more than two millennia, that is, in the works of Plato and Jacques Derrida. Indeed, this fascinating term was well known to seventeenth-century thinkers in Spain, as is evinced by the entry *veneno* in the *Tesoro de la lengua castellana o española.* As Sebastián de Covarrubias explains: "Es nombre genérico y tómase en buena y en mala parte, pues algunas vezes significa medicina. . . . Y el nombre *pharmacon* comprehende en sí ambas significaciones" (999).

The vehicle for the *pharmakon* in Claramonte's theater can vary significantly from play to play. In *El valiente negro en Flandes,* for example, he utilizes the Senecan image of the poison found in golden cups; in other *comedias,* such as *Deste agua no beberé* and *La Estrella de Sevilla,* it is Hercules' poisoned tunic that threatens madness but can also bring enlightenment; while in yet others a woman's beauty is both venom and antidote. In *De lo vivo a lo pintado,* the source of contagion is a lady's portrait, thus reminding us that *pharmakon* also serves to designate pictorial color (Derrida, 129). Painting, particularly the portrait, is linked to writing in Plato's *Phaedrus,* where both arts are criticized (Derrida, 136). And indeed, the most important vehicle for the *pharmakon* in Claramonte is perhaps writing or, more clearly stated, the letter, by which I mean both *letras* and *cartas.* Through them the playwright reveals the power of the written word to both save and destroy. From pacts with the devil that can be erased, as in the *Auto del rosario,* to letters that will actually poison the addressee, as in *La católica princesa,* Claramonte's texts are replete with writing as *pharmakon.* The written word is often imbued with magical or supernatural qualities. In *La infelice Dorotea,* for example, a Moor makes magical characters appear on a wall that predict the lady's tragic demise. In two other plays, divine writing also serves to prophesy death. This essay will focus on one of these two *comedias* in order to investigate how the *pharmakon* as Balthasar's doom serves to highlight the central conflict and add new visions and dimensions to Claramonte's dramaturgy.

The two *comedias* in question are very different in nature and use divine writing in opposite manners. *El secreto en la mujer* has been defined by Hernández Valcárcel as a *comedia novelesca* (59). It begins in the manner of a *comedia de capa y espada* but soon becomes a serious and even tragic meditation on love, jealousy, and parental disobedience. *Púsoseme el sol, salióme la luna,* on the other hand, is a *comedia hagiográfica* on the life of Santa Teodora, taken from one of the numerous sixteenth-century accounts based on Jacobo Vorágine. Like *El secreto en la mujer,* it deals with the potential for tragedy found in love and jealousy. It also includes the notion of parental disobedience from a heavenly perspective. A reference to Balthasar's doom appears at the beginning of *El secreto en la mujer* and at the conclusion of *Púsoseme el sol.* This essay will focus on the first of these two *comedias,* since it contains the most explicit formulation of the *pharmakon* and its relationship to writing.

Clavela in *El secreto en la mujer* is immersed in the secrets, *mudanzas,* and deceptions common in the woman in love found in the comedies of the period. She claims to love Antonio, who often visits her ("por él muero / que es de mi estrella influsión" [50–51]),[2] but on hearing that she is to marry him, she reveals to her servant that she actually prefers Ursino and would like to elope with him that very night. A third suitor, the one who appears to have the least chance of marrying the lady, is perhaps the most interesting. She despises him because he is poor: "ya es feo y villano el pobre. / No hay pobre galán aunque él / sea noble y caballero" (55–57).

Not only is Lelio a nobleman and a gentleman; he is also a poet, an occupation that fits him perfectly, according to Clavela: she believes that poverty engenders poetry, since the lack of food inflames the imagination. Indeed, Clavela can testify as to Lelio's poetic productivity, having collected "mil fábulas secretas" in spite of her indifference toward him. As the play opens, Tisbeo, Clavela's servant, manages to read to her yet another poetic missive from this impoverished suitor and is able to obtain yet one more reply. Since Tisbeo had asked her for only "dos letras" (116), she gives him precisely that. It is through Lelio's hermeneutic efforts to interpret the two *letras* found in Clavela's *carta* that the text foregrounds its concern with writing.

Lelio's first reaction to the letter is one of joy. He calls the *letras* comets, since they are "de fuego amoroso y fiel" (307). From the start, his attitude evinces a certain inconsistency, since comets in the literature of the period never stand for constant love. Rather, they often symbolize a fiery passion that is of short duration.[3] The notion of burning letters on the page reminds Lelio's servant, Pánfilo, of those "que vió escritas Baltasar / en el templo" (313–14). In order to temper his master's joy, the servant is pointing to the tragic consequences of Balthasar's letters in the Bible. But in so doing, Pánfilo has unwittingly introduced the notion of the divinity of Clavela, since she is the author of the letter(s).

The biblical tale of Balthasar's doom was the subject of an *auto sacramental* by Cristobal Suárez performed in Sevilla in 1613 (Sánchez Arjona, 283; Parker, 160). It may well have been a model for *La cena del rey Baltasar* (1634), which, according to Parker, constitutes "a splendid example of Calderón's special and valuable qualities as a dramatic poet. These qualities find a more elaborate expression in his later *autos*. In many of them the analysis is carried much further and many more factors are introduced in the scheme. But the unity of idea, form, and purpose which he achieved in this early work is only repeated in them, not surpassed" (193). Calderón's *auto* depicts the struggle between Balthasar and Daniel. At its most basic level, Parker refers to it as "a conflict between a vain, idolatrous King and the Prophet of God's chosen people whom he has enslaved" (194), but this critic reminds us that, in reality, most characters are aspects of Balthasar's mind. The King's desire for power and irresponsible freedom is countered by Daniel's "moral sanity" (Parker, 167), which is the aspect of Balthasar that is sacrificed in the end. The King's rejection of *juicio* leads to divine punishment. At the final banquet, Death appears in disguise and presents him with one of the golden cups that Balthasar's father had stolen from the temple in Jerusalem:

> Este vaso del altar
> la vida contiene, es cierto,
> cuando a la vida le sirve
> de bebida y de alimento:
> mas la muerte encierra, como
> la vida; que es argumento
> de la muerte y de la vida
> y está su licor compuesto
> de néctar y de cicuta
> de triaca y de veneno. (101)

Death offers Balthasar the drink of life, explaining to him how opposites may inhabit the same object. In the golden cup of life can be found both nectar and hemlock, antidote and poison. In this sense, life itself can be seen as a *pharmakon,* hiding within itself its very opposite. Once Balthasar drinks from the cup, a disembodied hand descends from above and writes three words. Daniel must interpret "aquellas letras" (104), since they are written in Hebrew. They represent God's judgment and Balthasar's doom.

In *El secreto en la mujer,* Pánfilo's biblical allusion does not dampen Lelio's enthusiasm and joy, since it opens the way for the suitor's contemplation of Clavela's letters as divine. He will attempt to interpret the two *letras* in terms of the "alfabeto hebreo" (352), thus following closely the biblical tale, where God communicates and operates through the Hebrew alphabet. Clavela, Lelio's divinity, has written the letters *b* and *t.* Of the first one, Lelio states: "La Be en alfabeto hebreo / siempre el bien significaba, / y era el blasón y el trofeo / que en su estandarte pintaba / el pueblo de Dios" (352–56).

Such an interpretation of Hebrew letters immediately recalls the Cabala. Abraham Abulafia, a thirteenth-century Spanish exponent of the Cabala known to engage in the "white magic" of "self directed mystical operations" (Swietlicki, 3), clearly states: "The letters are in essence signs and hints in the image of characters and parables, and were created because they are instruments by which man is taught the way of understanding" (quoted in Idel, 54). Indeed, the whole notion of flaming letters found in the tale of Balthasar and foregrounded by Lelio in his comparison of Clavela's letters to comets is also typical of Jewish mysticism, since it was believed that the Torah was handed to Moses in the form of white fire engraved with black fire. The Cabala attained great popularity in its Christianized form during the Renaissance and into the seventeenth century. Pico della Mirandola, for example, combined his interest in the hermetic tradition with this other type of ancient wisdom, since they both foregrounded the notion of creation by the word. Frances Yates explains Pico's interest in the Cabala: "In Genesis, God spoke to form the created world, and, since He spoke in Hebrew, this is why for the Cabalist the words and letters of the Hebrew tongue are subjects for endless mystical meditations, and why, for the practical Cabalist, they contain magical power" (85). Johannes Reuchlin (1455–1522), another major representative of the Christianized Cabala, includes his own interpretation of these letters: "Each letter has a symbolical meaning, representing an angel, a heavenly body, or an element" (quoted in Blau, 59). Even non-Cabalists accepted the importance of Hebrew letters. Damasio de Frías in his *Diálogo de las lenguas* (1579), for example, considers as factual the notion that prior to the Tower of Babel mankind spoke one language, which was probably Hebrew. He thus speculates on the magical powers of such a language (Cozad, 215–16). Perhaps one of the functions of the lengthy speech on the Tower of Babel in Calderón's *La cena del rey Baltasar* (which some critics view as a mere interpolation) is to contrast the confusion and powerlessness of modern speech with the Hebrew letters that appear at the fateful banquet and have the power to kill the King.

Lelio's exercise is typical of the cabalist, whose contemplation of the sound, form, and meaning of the Hebrew letters is essential to the apprehension of divinity. Lelio, of course, is utilizing this mystical principle in a profane manner, since he has replaced God with Clavela. Whatever the actual source of his interpretation of the letter *b,* it was certainly consonant with the beliefs of the period. The pseudo-Lullian treatise *De auditu kabbalistico,* actually written in a fifteenth-century hand, includes as its first section a discussion of nine letters of the Latin alphabet, beginning with *b.* This letter stands for goodness, or *bonitas* (Blau, 16; Yates 1966, 177–79), which is precisely the meaning given to it by Lelio: "el bien."

The second letter written by Clavela is the *t,*[4] and it recalls the second term that God uses in his judgment of Balthasar. *Tecel* is judgment itself: "y que en el peso / no cabe una culpa más" (Calderón, 105–6). Lelio's interpretation also refers to judgment, but it stretches to the limit the leniency of the censor of Claramonte's play, since it enters into questions of predestination and apocalypse: "es la Te letra sagrada, / y tiene tanto balor / que en su Apacalipsis Juan / de esta letra señalados / vió los que en el Libro están / del Señor predestinados" (370–75). Having thus completed his cabalistic interpretation of Clavela's divine letters, Lelio concludes: "y así aquí juntas dirán / que me ofrecen bien, y que / me predestina y señala / por su esposo la Be y la Te" (376–79).

Harold Bloom reminds us that the Cabala, with its ten names of God or *Sefirot,* is like astrology or the tarot. They "fascinate because they suggest an immutable knowledge of a final reality that stands behind our world of appearances" (28). However, this immutable reality must be read or interpreted by humans. Even if the Hebrew language were to capture the essence of things, human beings may not have the understanding or degree of consciousness necessary for unveiling the mysteries. In Lelio's case, his Bloomian misreading stems from a consciousness clouded by amorous passion. He is not even aware that such an interpretation is easily deconstructed through allusions to the evanescent comet and to Balthasar's tragic fate.

Lelio's misreading does not detract from the mystery and allure of the immutable letters, just as a wrong astrological prediction did not detract from the interest in this occult science during the period. Lelio's servant actually accentuates the mystery by relating the letters to hieroglyphs: "Que los egipcios han hecho / para hablar y responder / jeroglíficos y letras" (335–37). This increases the impact of the mysterious letters, since, as Catherine Swietlicki has noted, "Renaissance humanists saw hieroglyphs as cryptic sources of syncretic wisdom handed down by ancient Cabalists along with Egyptian Hermeticists" (28). We have already seen how Pico tied together the Cabala and the works of Hermes Trismegistus. In the dialogue between Lelio and Pánfilo, hermeticism is brought into the discussion of the Cabala, not only through the servant's reference to the Egyptian mysteries but also through the *gracioso*'s surprising knowledge of ancient texts.

When Lelio provides his interpretation of the two letters, the servant predictably laughs at this hermeneutic practice by associating the letters to drinking red wine, since *b* and *t* are found in "beber" and "tinto" (399, 400). He then relates the *b* to "borrico," claiming: "que al amante / así Apuleyo le llama" (402–3). Pánfilo is here referring to Apuleius's *Golden Ass,* a work where the hero-lover is transformed into an ass, or *borrico.* Significantly, this work was considered as a hermetic text during the Renaissance because it contains a description of the mysteries of the goddess Isis, who transforms the ass back to human form and makes him her priest once he acquires the secret wisdom she imparts to her priests.[5] While Lelio wanders aimlessly through the mysteries of the Cabala, his servant, amidst his many witticisms, imparts knowledge to his master. First he suggests to him the power of the written word but warns him of Balthasar's doom, and then he reminds him how the foolish Lucius was transformed into an ass.

But Lelio is intent in his analysis and will not listen to warnings. He does, however, partake of his servant's occult interests, not only through his use of the Cabala but also through his interest in the Platonic-hermetic tradition. Apuleius was erroneously thought to be the translator of the *Asclepius,* the basic hermetic text. Its author, Hermes Trismegistus, was the founder of what Ficino, Pico, and others called the ancient theology, or *prisca theologia.* He was followed by Orpheus, Pythagoras, and many other sages, "culminating in the Divine Plato" (Yates 1964, 14). While Pánfilo delves into the Egyptian mysteries, Lelio introduces Plato, the master of the *prisca theologia,* through a reference to Athenian philosophy. Speaking of Clavela's letters, Lelio states: "que estas letras están llenas / de cuanta sabiduría / pudo cifrar[se] en Atenas. / Todas son filosofía" (323–25).

This philosophy of love ("que Amor / filosofía es del alma" [327–28]) originating in Athens is most probably the philosophy of Plato's *Symposium.* In this manner, Lelio counters Pánfilo's image of Balthasar's banquet of doom with a Platonic banquet of love. His allusion is particularly apt, since the Platonic text includes the myth of Porus and Penia, Resource and Poverty, considered to be the parents of Love (81). Clavela's rejection of Lelio is based on his poverty— the mother of Love—but this god also has Resource for his father. It is precisely Lelio's resourcefulness that leads him to write poems which the lady collects in spite of her apparent disdain for him. Indeed, poetry is a central analogy for love used by Plato in the discussion of the Porus and Penia myth (83–84).

And yet, the very text that Lelio utilizes to defend his love can serve to undercut his arguments. Immediately following the discussion about the parents of love and how they shape the god's attributes, the dialogue turns to the other qualities of Eros, one of them being sophistry. In his commentary on the *Symposium,* Marsilio Ficino explains: "A *sophist* Plato defines . . . as an ambitious and crafty debater who, by the subtleties of sophistries, shows us the false for the true. . . . This lovers as well as beloveds endure at some time or other. For lovers, blinded by the clouds of love, often accept false things for true, while they think that their beloveds are more beautiful, more intelligent, or better than they are. They contradict themselves on account of the vehemence of love, for reason considers one thing, and concupiscence pursues another" (126). Lelio's misreadings of Clavela's letters are thus based on this particular quality of love. But the servant once more proves superior to his master in argumentation through allusion, although he ought not be called a sophist, since he does not "show us the false for the true." Pánfilo at this point may have recalled that after being labeled a sophist, Eros is called a magician (Ficino, 127) or *pharmakeus,* a noun that Derrida includes in the constellation of words that are related to *pharmakon,* the terminological nucleus of his discussion about the patterns of language in Plato's *Phaedrus.* It is not surprising, then, that the unusually learned and atypically philosophical *gracioso* evokes the language of this crucial dialogue in his arguments. Again, it is the letter *b* that helps Pánfilo to undercut Lelio: "También yo en cierta botica /

la vi escrita, y harto bien, / en un bote que decía / 'basilicón,' y era bueno / porque de él más bien vendía / el boticario" (360–65).

Following his master's explanation of *b* as "bien" (another Platonic allusion to which we will soon turn), Pánfilo cleverly introduces the term "bien" twice in his own description of *b,* using, in addition, several words beginning with *b.* Pánfilo claims to have seen this ubiquitous letter in a "bote," or jar (a word beginning with *b*) in a "botica," or pharmacy (another word beginning with *b*), where the pharmacist, or "boticario" (again the *b*) sold the "basilicón," or unguent. Clavela's *b* refers to "el bien" in that the *basilicón* is a good potion (*bueno*). Moreover, this drug has a label on which the letter *b* is well written (*bien*), and it sells well (*bien vendía*). This extensive and clever use of *b* serves to turn the discussion away from the magic of love found in the *Symposium* and to turn attention toward the *Phaedrus,* a dialogue where the Greek philosopher discusses writing in terms of a potion or drug. Indeed, the introduction of "pharmacy" (*botica*) and "pharmacist" (*boticario*) recalls the many permutations of the term *pharmakon* in the *Phaedrus,* beginning with the introduction of a character named Pharmacia (Derrida, 70), something that has been thoroughly documented by Derrida in his appropriately titled study, "Plato's Pharmacy."[6]

In the *Phaedrus,* Theuth, a god who was the inventor of many arts, brought them to the god-king of Egypt, Thamus, "desiring that the other Egyptians might be allowed to have the benefit of them" (Plato, 184). Writing, he claimed, "will make the Egyptians wiser and give them better memories" (184). Theuth thus refers to writing as a *pharmakon,* or remedy. Thamus replies with the classic condemnation of writing: "And so the specific [remedy or *pharmakon*] which you have discovered is an aid not to memory but to reminiscence. As for wisdom, it is the reputation, not the reality that you have to offer to those who learn from you; they will have heard many things and yet received no teaching . . . having acquired not wisdom, but the show of wisdom" (184). The remedy proposed by Theuth turns out to be a drug that can only cure the symptom. Furthermore, it is "a debilitating poison for memory" (Derrida, 110). In Plato's pharmacy, the *pharmakon* is a dangerous supplement to speech; it is a term without a stable essence, having among its meanings both poison and cure.

The letter *b,* Pánfilo makes clear, is part of Plato's pharmacy. It is found on one of those dangerous "botes" that give the "boticarios" their name (Covarrubias,

232). Writing (the letter *b*) appears to be beneficial, since the container is filled with "basilicón," an unguent often made by "boticarios" (Covarrubias, 198) and much prized for its curative qualities. Even though the name, according to Covarrubias, is derived from the Greek and means "regio" (198), it is dangerously close to the *basilisco,* the mythical snake with its dangerous poison. Furthermore, whatever the curative properties of the potion might be, it can be poison or antidote depending on the dosage: "y assí los boticarios por esta razón se llaman venenarios, y si por nuestra desdicha exceden en la composición de la cantidad o dosis, son sus porciones mortíferas" (Covarrubias, 999).

Thus, utilizing the *Phaedrus,* Pánfilo points to the dangers of Clavela's writing. But, through allusions to this dialogue, the *gracioso* is also bringing into question his master's occupation, poetry or writing. Indeed, he is even questioning the type of textual interpretation in which his master is engaging. The instability of writing (as opposed to the certainty inherent in sacred letters when used by or for divine purposes) derives from its lack of presence. We do not have to turn to Derrida to discover this. The question is made clear by Plato and was much debated in Spain during the seventeenth century. For example, Mateo Alemán, in his *Ortografía castellana* (1609), includes what Mark D. Johnston calls "a veritable catalog of logocentric themes" (762). Here, "Mauricio compares the relation of speech to writing as that of the living to the dead." Written texts are both dead and silent. In the *Phaedrus,* Socrates explains: "I cannot help feeling, Phaedrus, that writing has one grave fault in common with painting; for the creations of the painter have the attitude of life, and yet if you ask them a question they preserve a solemn silence. And the same can be said of books" (Plato, 185). Lelio's questioning of Clavela's writings is simply an empty exercise. He can misread, he can be a sophist, since her letters cannot correct him. Socrates adds: "If they are maltreated or abused, they have no parent to protect them" (Plato, 184). Derrida explains that for Plato, *logos* is the true son, the speech uttered by the father, while writing is an orphan (77). He further explains: "The figure of the father, of course, is also that of the good (*agathon*)" (81). Lelio had equated the good ("el bien") with Clavela through her use of the letter *b*. Pánfilo, however, has shown him that the good cannot be contained in writing, for it is an unstable and even poisonous form, a supplement to speech that lacks presence. Where, then, can the good be found? Certainly not in poetry, but in philosophy, which is a verbal art, as defined in the *Phaedrus*. While Lelio insists on poetry, writing, and love making, the *gracioso* attempts to teach him philosophy through dialogue, thus following the Socratic method.

Furthermore, Pánfilo teaches Lelio that even though writing lacks presence, one can aspire to understanding it through contextualization.[7] He asks his master to read the poem-letter he sent to Clavela. In it, Lelio threatens to depart from Milan if the lady fails to reciprocate. In this sense, the mysterious letters make sense. Pánfilo explains: "Pues junta la Be y la Te / y verás qué dice" (435–36). Clavela's response is thus "bete," the familiar command to leave. Rather than becoming a catalyst for a move from poetry to philosophy, these words elicit from Lelio yet another poem, one in which words beginning with the letters *b* and *t* serve to represent his torment and fear (*temor*). Lelio's love places him under the protection of Eros, whose parents, as noted, are Porus and Penia. Having been rejected by Clavela because of his poverty, he is able to win her through resource. As she prepares to elope with Ursino, a rival, Antonio, fights with him, leaving the street empty. As Lelio passes by his beloved's house one more time before his exile, he hears Clavela calling from the window: "¡Ah, esposo, ah, Ursino! / . . . / Tu Clavela soy, espera!" (666, 668). In the darkness of the night, Lelio pretends to be Ursino and escapes with Clavela.

When Lelio was readying to leave Milan in response to his lady's demands, he had visited his father and had lied to him concerning his reasons for departure. The father had responded by giving his son advice in the form of three commandments:

> Y tanbién te encargo Lelio
> tres cosas, de ellas te guarda:
> La primera es que no fíes,
> en grande o pequeña causa,
> tu secreto de mujer,
> animal que no le guarda.
> Lo segundo es que no dotes
> ni prohijes en tu casa
> jamás, hijo que no sea
> nacido de tus entrañas.

La tercera es que no vivas
aunque más mercedes te haga,
en lugar, ciudad o villa
de señor. Esto te manda
tu padre, y a la partida
te lo ruego envuelto en agua,
que si estas tres cosas no haces
te verás en mil desgracias
y te acordarás de mí. (546–64)

Having obtained Clavela's favors through resourcefulness, Lelio chooses to ignore his father's advice, and the rest of the play will show how he "sins" against these three commandments. He will pursue the "bien," or goodness, he finds in love and writing, ignoring that in a logocentric culture, the father is goodness ("el bien"), and his oral commands serve to actualize this quality in his children's world. Lelio's concerns with poetry (writing) and love for a woman, both marginal to logocentrism, lead him to the immediate breaking of two of the father's commands, thus turning against patriarchal presence and the oral tradition of philosophy. Significantly, these two interdictions have to do with paternity and progeny. The last command is the one he disregards first. His father had warned him not to accept the authority of another lord, much less live under him. Lelio and Clavela take up residence in Florence, where the Duke shows Lelio such favor that he soon becomes a rich and powerful subject. The Duke in many ways replaces Lelio's true father, in the same way as writing seeks to replace the living word, the speech of the father. In Derrida's analysis of the *Phaedrus,* we discover that "the father is always father to a speaking/living being" (80), in other words, the father's true son is speech. The desire of writing, Derrida claims, is "denounced as a desire for orphanhood and patricidal subversion" (77). The middle commandment has to do precisely with orphanhood. Having accepted an adopted father, Lelio now accepts an adopted child, an orphan. Conceptually he had done this long before, when he chose poetry over philosophy, the orphan over the true child. When Aurelio is adopted as a son, when the counterfeit is accepted as true, it is time for the labyrinth of deceit and unknowing to be generated. The child Aurelio is really Aurelia, a woman whom Lelio had spurned long before. She has allied herself with Ursino to avenge Lelio's amorous misdeeds.

It is time for Lelio's third transgression. Clavela feels abandoned now that her husband has the Duke's favor and the two are always at the hunt. She also feels jealous of the Duchess, who, she claims, sees her husband more than she does. In order to show Clavela his love, Lelio decides to steal the Duke's favorite falcon and have Pánfilo serve it for dinner. This anecdote, probably taken from either Lope de Vega's *El halcón de Federico* or its Boccaccian model,[8] serves to exemplify the breaking of the third commandment. Lelio tells Clavela what he has done and urges her to keep this secret, since the Duke has decreed that the thief will be executed. Once more, Lelio values that which in a logocentric culture is devalued: woman, like writing, is a dangerous supplement. After all, in the biblical story, woman was created as an afterthought.

Having broken all three commandments, the lover must be punished. Clavela reads a letter that she mistakenly believes is addressed by the Duchess to Lelio. In her jealousy, she denounces her husband, who stands condemned to die. Astounded at Clavela's cruelty, the Duchess tells her: "eres áspid que convierte / su flor en ponzoña infiel" (2724–25). Having rejected true goodness, Lelio's "bien" is revealed as a creature that, unlike the bee, transforms the flower's nectar into poison. Writing (a false letter), Aurelio (an "orphan," which recalls the status of writing), and a woman (Clavela) have emerged as dangerous. They are the poison, or *pharmakon,* that leads Lelio to destruction. Having espoused the false letter *b* (Clavela), he must accept the consequences of the false *t*—an apocalyptic conclusion and a *temor,* or fear, that can exist in those who do not embrace philosophy.

But Lelio's aloneness in the last moments is relieved by the arrival of the father. His presence leads Lelio to understand his failings:

> ¡Ay padre de mis entrañas!
> por no tomar tus consejos
> y por ser desobediente
> en este punto me veo
> . . . .
> y estoy sobre el gran teatro
> donde represento al tiempo
> la figura del engaño
> y al fin la del escarmiento. (2772–75; 2782–85)

In the midst of life, Lelio has found death, since life is nothing other than the *pharmakon* that hides within itself its very opposite. This leads Lelio to understand his errancy and to arrive at *desengaño*. Since he has accepted his true father,[9] it is now time for philosophy to appear and dispel his fear, evincing once again the power of transmutation found in the *pharmakon*. In the *Phaedrus,* this drug "is presented to Socrates as a poison; yet it is transformed, through the effects of the Socratic *logos* and of the philosophical demonstration in the *Phaedrus,* into a means of deliverance, a way toward salvation, a cathartic power. The hemlock has an *ontological* effect: it initiates one into the contemplation of the *eidos* and the immortality of the soul" (Derrida, 127). Since Lelio has now glimpsed the power of this drug and seeks its positive effects rather than pursuing woman and poetry, the philosopher of the play, the *gracioso,* can now save him. Pánfilo brings the Duke his falcon. This apparent act of magic does not make the *gracioso* a *pharmakeus,* or magician. Rather than killing the bird for his master's dinner, Pánfilo, aware of the danger, had roasted a different bird. The philosopher is not alien to the deceits of the world. Rather, he uses them to teach and to save. If the banquet of love has turned out to be poisonous, at least Balthasar's doom has not been actualized. In this misogynist and logocentric drama, the main concerns of the dramatic genre (love and poetry) are seen as poisonous and dangerous. And yet, the work can also be regarded as a response to the Platonic exile of the poet from the republic,[10] for the dialogic nature of this *comedia* aspires to the philosophical realm where the *pharmakon* of writing can be transformed from venom into remedy.

Notes

1.   The thirteen *comedias* that most critics agree are the work of Claramonte are *El ataúd para el vivo, La católica princesa, De Alcalá a Madrid, De los méritos del amor, De lo vivo a lo pintado, Deste agua no beberé, El gran rey de los desiertos, El infante de Aragón, La infelice Dorotea, El nuevo rey Gallinato, Púsoseme el sol, salióme la luna, El secreto en la mujer,* and *El valiente negro en Flandes.* In addition, many believe that *La Estrella de Sevilla, El mayor rey de los reyes,* and *El tao de San Antón* are also by this producer-director. Claramonte also wrote several *autos sacramentales,* including the *Auto del rosario* and *El horno de Constantinopla.*

2.   I would like to express my appreciation to Charles Ganelin for having provided me with his transcription of the manuscript as well as with copies of other manuscripts by

Claramonte. Since that time, Alfredo Rodríguez López-Vázquez has published an edition of the play (1991). All verse references in the text are to this edition.

3.   The comets of fiery passion are common in the theater of Lope de Vega. Claramonte was an actor and producer of a number of Lope's plays and must have been well aware of this commonplace. See de Armas 1987.

4.   According to Derrida, "The ninth letter of the Hebrew alphabet, corresponding to our 't' is linked to the comet" (349). Lelio has already alluded to this celestial configuration in an amorous context. But comets were more often signs of disaster and judgment.

5.   This text was well known in the Spanish Golden Age. For its hermetic connotations, see de Armas 1983.

6.   I am using Derrida's essay to lay bare some of the inherent assumptions and oppositions found in the Platonic texts. It is not my purpose here to follow his study into its deconstructive phase.

7.   This notion, of course, goes counter to Derrida's statement that "meaning is context-bound but context is boundless" (Culler, 128).

8.   For a discussion of this play and its model (*Decameron,* 5:9), see D'Antuono (21, 79–90). For the relationship between Lope de Vega's play and Claramonte's *comedia,* see Rodríguez López-Vázquez (35–39).

9.   Lelio has relied up to this point on Resource, one of the parents of Eros, as depicted in the *Symposium.* Now he must run to his true father. In Derrida's reading of the *Phaedrus,* Resource has a very different genealogy: "The good (father, sun, capital) is thus the hidden illuminating, blinding source of logos. . . . Logos is thus a resource" (82, 84). In this sense, Lelio is turning to speech and philosophy.

10.   It is interesting to note that at the end of *El secreto en la mujer* the supposed orphan is exiled, while Clavela is sent to a convent, which can also be seen as an exile from the realm. The conclusion of the *comedia* thus parallels Plato's exile of the poet from the republic and points to the marginality of the orphan (writing) and of the woman. Although the play echoes Plato's logocentric concerns, it also fashions a place for itself by denying its poetic heritage and foregrounding its philosophic qualities. According to B. W. Ife, picaresque novels during the Golden Age can also be seen as subtle replies to the Platonic critique of writing. The Platonic notion that "the poet, like the orator is a *psychagogos,* a man who tries to influence the psyche and uses language as a bewitching tool of illusion" (Plato, 61) is often mirrored in moralistic texts of the Golden Age through the image of literature as poison, as in the works of Juan Luis Vives (Ife, 13–14), Juan de la Cerda (15), Luisa María de Padilla Manrique, Benito Remigio Noydens, Juan Sánchez Valdés de la Plata, and Alejo Venegas (34). Their notion of sweet poison parallels the image of Clavela as an asp who turns sweetness (the flower) into poison.

Works Consulted

Alemán, Mateo. 1950. *Ortografía castellana.* Edited by José Rojas Garcidueñas. Mexico: Colegio de México.

Barceló Jiménez, Juan. 1980. *Historia del teatro en Murcia.* Murcia: Academia Alfonso X el Sabio.

Blau, Joseph Leon. 1964. *The Christian Interpretation of the Cabala in the Renaissance.* Port Washington, N.Y.: Kennikat Press.

Bloom, Harold. 1984. *Kabbalah and Criticism.* New York: Continuum Publishing Co.

Calderón de la Barca, Pedro. 1926. *Autos sacramentales.* Edited by Angel Valbuena Prat. Madrid: Ediciones de "La lectura."

Claramonte, Andrés de. *El secreto en la mujer.* Biblioteca Nacional (Madrid) MS. R-169.

———. 1983. *Andrés de Claramonte. Comedias.* Edited by María del Carmen Hernández Valcárcel. Murcia: Academia Alfonso X el Sabio.

———. 1985. *Púsoseme el sol, salióme la luna.* Edited by Alfredo Rodríguez López-Vázquez. Kassel: Reichenberger.

———. 1987. *La infelice Dorotea.* Edited by Charles Ganelin. London: Tamesis Books.

———. 1991. *El secreto en la mujer.* Edited by Alfredo Rodríguez López-Vázquez. London: Tamesis Books.

Cotarelo y Mori, Emilio. 1893. *Tirso de Molina: Investigaciones biobibliográficas.* Madrid: Imprenta de Enrique Rubiños.

Covarrubias, Sebastián de. [1611; 1674] 1987. *Tesoro de la lengua castellana o española.* Edited by Martín de Riquer. Barcelona: S. A. Horta.

Cozad, Mary. 1983. "A Platonic-Aristotelian Linguistic Controversy of the Spanish Golden Age: Damasio de Frías's *Diálogo de las lenguas* (1579)." In *Florilegium Hispanicum: Medieval and Golden Age Studies Presented to Dorothy Clotelle Clarke,* edited by John S. Geary et al., 203–27. Madison, Wis.: Hispanic Seminary of Medieval Studies.

Culler, Jonathan. 1982. *On Deconstruction.* Ithaca, N.Y.: Cornell University Press.

D'Antuono, Nancy. 1983. *Boccaccio's "Novelle" in the Theater of Lope de Vega.* Madrid: Porrúa Turanzas.

De Armas, Frederick A. 1983. "Lope de Vega and the Hermetic Tradition: The Case of Dardanio in *La Arcadia.*" *Revista canadiense de estudios hispánicos* 7:345–62.

———. 1987. "The Threat of Long-Haired Stars: Comets in Lope de Vega's *El maestro de danzar.*" *Bulletin of the Comediantes* 39:21–36.

———. 1988. "Diomedes' Horses: Mythical Foregrounding and Reversal in Claramonte's *Deste agua no beberé.*" *Gestos* 6:47–63

Derrida, Jacques. 1981. *Dissemination.* Translated by Barbara Johnson. Chicago, Ill.: University of Chicago Press.

Ebersole, Alva. 1978. "Simbolismo en *Deste agua no beberé* de Andrés de Claramonte." *Perspectivas de la comedia,* edited by Alva Ebersole, 119–32. Colección Siglo de Oro, vol. 6. Valencia: Albatros-Hispanófila.

Fernández Guerra y Orbe, Luis. 1871. *D. Juan Ruiz de Alarcón y Mendoza.* Madrid: Rivadeneyra.

Ficino, Marsilio. 1985. *Commentary on Plato's Symposium.* Translated and edited by Sears Jayne. Dallas, Tex.: Spring Publications.

Idel, Mashe. 1988. *The Mystical Experience in Abraham Abulafia.* Albany: State University of New York Press.

Ife, B. W. 1985. *Reading and Fiction in Golden-Age Spain.* Cambridge: Cambridge University Press.

Johnston, Mark D. 1988. "Mateo Alemán's Problem with Spelling." *PMLA* 103:759–69.

Leavitt, Sturgis. 1931. *The "Estrella de Sevilla" and Claramonte.* Cambridge, Mass.: Harvard University Press.

Menéndez Pelayo, Marcelino. 1941. *Estudios y discursos de crítica histórica y literaria.* Vol. 3. Madrid: Consejo Superior de Investigaciones Científicas.

Mesonero Romanos, Ramón, ed. 1924. *Dramáticos contemporáneos a Lope de Vega.* Biblioteca de Autores Españoles, vol. 43. Madrid: Sucesores de Hernando.

Parker, Alexander A. 1968. *The Allegorical Drama of Calderón.* Oxford: Dolphin Book Co.

Parr, James A. 1988. Review of Andrés de Claramonte, *El burlador de Sevilla atribuído tradicionalmente a Tirso de Molina,* edited by Alfredo Rodríguez López-Vásquez. *Hispania* 71:288–89.

Plato. 1953. *The Dialogues of Plato.* Vol. 3. Translated by B. Jowett. Oxford: Clarendon Press.

Sánchez Arjona, J. 1887. *El teatro en Sevilla en los siglos XVI y XVII.* Madrid: A. Alonso.

Swietlicki, Catherine. 1986. *Spanish Christian Cabala.* Columbia: University of Missouri Press.

Tirso de Molina. 1952. *Obras dramáticas completas.* 3 vols. Edited by Blanca de los Ríos. Madrid: Aguilar.

Yates, Frances A. 1964. *Giordano Bruno and the Hermetic Tradition.* Chicago, Ill.: University of Chicago Press.

———. 1966. *The Art of Memory.* Chicago, Ill.: University of Chicago Press.

Williamsen, Vern G. 1982. *The Minor Dramatists of Seventeenth-Century Spain.* Boston, Mass.: Twayne.

William R. Blue

The Diverse Economy of
Entre bobos anda el juego

$\mathcal{S}$panish Golden Age comedies that deal with odd, exaggerated, and eccentric characters, the *comedias de figurón,* caricature and censure nonconformists. In plays from this subgenre, a bizarre character momentarily takes control of, and provokes chaos in, the otherwise smooth running of a homogeneous society bent on repeating its fixed patterns of behavior. The experienced audience present for such plays has the archetype firmly in mind and waits, expectantly, to see the preposterous blocking force overthrown and removed.[1] *Entre bobos anda el juego* seems to present just such a case when the crass, miserly Lucas stands in the way of marriage between the lovely Isabel and the equally handsome Pedro, Lucas's cousin. Antonio, Isabel's greedy father, arranges a marriage between his daughter and the rich Lucas, but before the marriage was arranged, Pedro had saved Isabel's life. The two fell in love, each ignorant of the other's name and lineage. Further complicating matters, Pedro has been promised in marriage to Lucas's weak-kneed sister, Alfonsa. Lucas sends Pedro to fetch his bride, the two young people meet, and their smoldering, but apparently blighted, love bursts into flame. They must now overcome Lucas, Antonio, Alfonsa, and Isabel's pesky suitor, Luis. Almost all of the play takes place on the road between Madrid and Toledo, Lucas's hometown. Though the play ends with Pedro marrying Isabel, just as the audience might have hoped, Lucas—not the *graciosos* or the young couple—controls the outcome. He forces the young couple to marry as revenge for deceiving him. Why and how their marriage is revenge, why the traditional happy end may be seen as potentially devastating "poetic justice" depends on a series of economies established in the play. I use the word "economy" in a general sense as an orderly distribution of elements in a system. The play establishes economies of wealth, language, desire, and social and familial relationships.

Antonio has but one child, Isabel, yet he arranges her marriage without once consulting her about what she wants or how she feels. Even after discovering how crass, stingy, and obnoxious Lucas is, after listening to his daughter's complaints about, and desires to avoid, the marriage, Antonio persists because of Lucas's wealth: "Sea lo que fuere, en efecto, / yo os he de casar con él / . . . / Cásoos con un caballero / que tiene seis mil ducados / de renta, ¿y hacéis pucheros?" (362–63, 368–70).[2] Isabel wants to marry for love, not money, a feeling she shares with Pedro, who finds himself in a situation perfectly parallel to hers.

Lucas, oldest son in his family, has inherited all its wealth, an annual amount he knows down to the last penny ("Yo tengo seis mil cuarenta y dos ducados de renta de mayorazgo," he says in a letter), and must care for his sister and cousin. To kill two birds with one stone, he plans to marry them to each other and give them an income. Pedro has nothing; he depends totally on Lucas for his subsistence. The assumed economy of family, then, projects Antonio and Lucas as heads of their respective families, watching out for their charges, helping them along, doing things for their benefit. Consequently, Isabel, Alfonsa, and Pedro ought to respect the wishes of their "father figures," just as the father figures ought to try to respect the wishes of their charges. Obviously, Lucas and Antonio have arranged marriages that Pedro and Isabel detest. The two young people then revolt against what they perceive as oppressive control, citing love as supreme over all other matters. The audience would, no doubt, find the lovers' decision appealing because of Lucas's character and because, though Antonio tries to deny it, Isabel is like a commodity to be bought and sold. Antonio, noble but poor, wants to assure both Isabel's and his futures by marrying her to money; Isabel becomes a means to an end.

Lucas wants to assure that his inheritance will pass intact to his own offspring because "me hereda mi primo si no tengo hijos." He views Isabel as a baby-producing machine. In his first contact with her, in a letter, he baldly states his condition and his proposition: "Hermana: yo tengo seis mil cuarenta y dos ducados de renta de mayorazgo, y me hereda mi primo si no tengo hijos; hanme dicho que vos y yo podremos tener los que quisiéramos; veníos esta noche a tratar del uno, que tiempo nos queda para los otros." At the same time, he sends Antonio the following note: "Recibí de don Antonio Salazar una mujer, para que lo sea mía, con sus tachas buenas o malas." Antonio, no matter how carefully he avoids saying so, barters his daughter; Lucas, who says so in no uncertain terms, buys the merchandise provided it is not used; and Pedro, whom Lucas sends to collect Isabel, acts as a partially trusted receiving clerk.

For Antonio, Isabel's marriage means financial security, his and hers, thus desire or love matters little. For Lucas, marriage means the future integrity of his inheritance; love is immaterial. Although Antonio and Lucas do not factor love into the account, Isabel certainly does, for she believes in true love. She would most likely be the audience's sentimental and pragmatic touchstone in the economy of desire. Love at first sight, for example, she declares a fantasy; true love comes from getting to know someone well: "No entre amor tan de repente / por la vista; amor se engendra / del trato, y no he de creer / que amor que entra con violencia / deje de ser como el rayo: / luz luego, y después pavesa" (851–56). Marriage, she says, depends on mutual respect, and the true lover's actions count much more than mere words, "menos habla quien más siente, / más quiere quien calla más" (63–64). But she gives lie to her own self-righteous assertions when, in the first scene, she says that she saw Pedro only once before the play began and now, she confesses to her maid, "Andrea amiga, sabrás / que tengo amor ¡ay de mí! / a un hombre que una vez vi" (145–47). In that, Pedro is her soul mate because, for him, love sprang full-blown upon seeing Isabel one day bathing in the Manzanares (981–1110).

The audience, therefore, must listen attentively to what the characters say, as well as to how they express themselves. Language and style, a topic the characters comment on throughout the play, form an economy of expression. On one extreme stands Luis, Isabel's ardent pursuer. His affected speech is barely understood by his frustrated servant:

Carranza:	Di, ¿qué tienes señor?
Luis:	Desvalimiento.
Carranza:	Deja hablar afeitado
	y dime, ¿qué vienes a buscar?
Luis:	Busco mi objeto.
Carranza:	¿Qué objeto? Habladme claro, señor mío.
Luis:	Solicito mi llama a mi albedrío. (552–58)

Pedro, declared the best-spoken of the noblemen, has his pretentious moments, too, especially in descriptive passages: "Era del claro julio ardiente día, /

Manzanares al soto presidía, / y en clase que la arena ha fabricado, / lecciones de cristal dictaba al prado" (981–84). But when he declares his love to Isabel, he achieves heights in lyrical clarity, as in his "Amor alas tiene, vuela" speech (790–836). So well spoken is he that Lucas, who knows that he is not eloquent, makes Pedro his John Alden, "Oyes, llega / y di por la boca verbos, / o lo que a ti te parezca; / háblala del mismo modo / como si yo mismo fuera; / dila aquello que tú sabes / de luceros y de estrellas" (762–68). The bottom level in the nobles' linguistic economy belongs to Lucas.

However, below him on the social scale exist other speakers: the servants, whose patterns range from the long-suffering Carranza, who spends most of his time trying to get Luis to speak more clearly, to the wittily nasty Cabellera, Pedro's man. He describes Lucas, in an adjectival tour de force, to the progressively more horrified Isabel:

> es un caballero flaco,
> desvaído, macilento,
> muy cortísimo de talle,
> y larguísimo de cuerpo.
> . . . .
> zambo un poco, calvo un poco,
> dos pocos verdimoreno,
> tres pocos desaliñado
> y cuarenta muchos puerco.
> . . . .
> que es tan mísero y estrecho,
> que no dará lo que ya
> me entenderán los atentos,
> que come tan poco el tal
> don Lucas, que yo sospecho
> que ni aun esto podrá dar,
> porque no tiene excrementos. (209–12; 217–20; 260–66)

Three factors, however, complicate this rather straightforward economy of speech patterns: deceit, word choice, and what I call "alien presence." At the point where Isabel and Pedro declare their love to each other, they have yet to discover a way out of their respective arranged marriages; however, they wish to continue to speak to each other, something they can accomplish by secret meetings, or by a kind of double-talk when they are together publicly. In those moments, Pedro pretends to speak for Lucas (790–887). Their words, purportedly, go from Isabel to Lucas and from Lucas to Isabel, with Pedro as a neutral translator: "la voz de Lucas habla / en mi voz; yo soy quien, ciego, / a ser intérprete vine / de aquel amor estranjero" (443–46), but *traduttore traditore*. Pedro speaks his own feelings; the words exceed their boundaries, unhinging relationships of truth and falsehood, of family, of trust, of duty.

In another context, Terry Eagleton has noted that language, desire, and money are systems that "involve exchange and equivalence" and as such may be considered stabilizing factors in a given society (57). But "they are necessarily indifferent as systems to particular objects or uses, they tend to breed an anarchic state of affairs in which everything blurs. . . . There is, in other words, something in the very structures of stability themselves which offers to subvert them." Subversion, doubt, recrimination, and near chaos result when words come unhinged in *Entre bobos*. Lucas is not so stupid that he does not wonder if something is going on between Pedro and Isabel. Pedro, in turn, gets into trouble with Isabel when she hears him declare—though dissembling and in an attempt to throw Lucas off the trail—his love for Alfonsa. Likewise Pedro doubts Isabel's fidelity when he hears Luis say that she promised to marry him. If language can get out of control, the characters seem to show and believe, then so, too, can desire. Since desire can be motivated by so many reasons—a handsome face, money, security, chance, opportunity—its object may change, too, according to the circumstance. In addition, if the self can be counterfeited—Pedro "loves" Alfonsa, Pedro "obeys" his cousin, Isabel "agrees" to her father's plan as dutiful daughter—then whom can one trust? Fiction's inherence in reality is more than a simple truism; "being yourself," Eagleton says, "always involves a degree of play-acting" (13); expressed in a more economic way, "the self is a commodity which lives only in the act of barter, love operating as the 'universal commodity'" (24). If that is true, then perhaps what makes this play seem different is its naked honesty.

Underlying the speech of all the play's characters runs a subterranean economic vocabulary. Lucas is obviously and openly mercantilist, but even in the conversations between the two young lovers, barter and exchange enter, though perhaps unconsciously. On the conscious level, however, Isabel, like her father, openly acknowledges a desire for money and what it can bring. One reason she rejects Lucas is that he is miserly, "yo no quiero / sin el gusto la riqueza" (324–25). Pedro becomes her love, her "dueño," a commonplace though still meaningful metaphor used continually by the pair. Pedro, though poor, is a verbal spendthrift, for if he had money, he would shower Isabel with gifts, so highly does he value her: "vos sois *más* que aquello, *más* / que cupo en toda mi idea, / y aun *más* que aquello que miro, / si hay *más* en vos que *más* sea" (819–22, emphasis mine). In their lengthy exchange about love, the word *trato* becomes central to their discussion, "amor se engendra del *trato* . . . El *trato* engendra el amor . . . es de esencia / que haya *trato,* luego el *trato* / es el que el amor engendra . . . Con *trato,* amor, yo confieso / que es perfeto . . . en fin, amor se acendra / en el *trato*" (852–73, emphasis mine). *Trato* does mean "tener conocimiento," as Covarrubias says, but its first meaning is "negociar comprando y vendiendo mercadurías." In addition, their love alternates from *ganado* to *perdido,* depending on the changing circumstances. A vocabulary of buying and selling, of negotiation, of loss and gain characterizes the expressions of their most inner, most profound feelings.

But there are yet other voices to be heard in *Entre bobos,* and I use the word "voices" advisedly. These are the "alien presences": voices that are heard but that have no physical presence on stage, for each time they speak, the passages are marked "dentro." The voices belong to those who inhabit the roads where the action of the play takes place. The innkeepers, coachmen, wagon drivers, mule skinners, and itinerants of all sorts speak a rough, scathingly funny, jargon-filled language of disrespect, principally to Lucas. In their presence, Lucas's power vanishes. The voices are not simply the voices of subversion speaking irreverently to the voice of dominance, for no such simple polarity obtains; rather, these voices broker power in their context as Lucas does in his. Lucas correctly perceives the taunting threats in the voices.

The threats come in doublespeak. *Carnero* is both mutton and cuckold. Alfonsa becomes "ese fiambre" and "la ninfa," who, "si va a Madrid . . . a estar de asiento, / en la calle del Lobo hay aposento" (631–32). They call her Doña Melindre and Dulcinea, as Lucas, for them, is Don Quijote and Don Langosta. Deceit and trickery are operative in their life and language. The innkeeper sells "un gato que parezca liebre," and he is both *liebre* (coward) and *gato* (clever thief). In this world of quicksilver language, the tongue-tied Lucas has no chance, no matter how much he huffs and puffs, draws his sword and threatens. In the final act, language turns coarse when the wedding party's coach breaks down on the road.

Suddenly surrounded by muleteers and itinerants, they must listen to curses, "puto, beata, aquel hijo de aquélla," and sexually oriented jokes:

Caballera:	¿Adónde va el patán en el matado?
Caminante (dentro):	A buscar voy a tu mujer, menguado.
Caballera:	Dígame, si va a vella,
	¿cómo va tan espacio?
Caminante:	Tal es ella. (2007–10)

Immediately following that dialogue, wandering musicians pass by, offering a snippet of a song—*dentro,* of course: "Mozuelas de la corte, todo es caminar, / unas van a Güete y otras a Alcalá" (2013–14). That little verse may well be, in the end, a very scary line.

The voices of the invisible people constantly remind the characters, and the audience, too, of what lies just below the surface of the "noble" world in which the principal characters move. And move they do, spatially from Madrid to Toledo, temporally toward the future, but they move personally, socially, and economically as well. The topos of life as a voyage comes alive in the play. The itinerant musicians sing of movement, of the young women of the court, some who go to Guete (Huete), others to Alcalá. In those two towns were located women's correctional institutions.

In the final scenes, Lucas steps forward like a judge to decide everyone's fate. He has found out about Pedro's and Isabel's deceptions and swears that "he de tomar tal venganza, /. . . / que dure toda la vida" (2621–23). To take their lives for the affronts he has suffered would be "venganza venial." A life sentence is what he has in mind. Calling all the characters together, he makes Isabel and Pedro confess their love and their deceit. He then reminds them how poor they are and how he was to have been their financial lifeline. He commands them to "dar la mano," adding:

> ella pobre, vos muy pobre,
> no tenéis hora de paz;
> el amar se acaba luego,
> nunca la necesidad;
> hoy con el pan de la boda,

> no buscaréis otro pan;
> de mí os vengáis esta noche,
> y mañana, a más tardar,
> cuando almuercen un requiebro,
> y en la mesa, en vez de pan,
> pongan una "fe" al comer
> y una "constancia" al cenar,
> y, en vez de galas, se ponga
> un buen amor de Milán,
> una tela de "mi vida,"
> aforrada en "¿me querrás?,"
> echarán de ver los dos
> cuál se ha vengado de cuál. (2735–52)

He also proposes a marriage between Alfonsa and Luis.

The latter two will live well, financially speaking, though they will have to put up with Lucas. Isabel and Pedro, on the other hand, will have to eat their words, wear their promises, since words and promises are all they have (MacCurdy 1968, 133). All of their linguistic cleverness, all of their lyrical flights will likely provide meager nourishment. As Luis, Alfonsa, and Lucas continue on the road to Toledo, Pedro, Isabel, and Antonio head off down another path, perhaps toward Huete or Alcalá. Their road turns downward, downward toward those heard but unseen voices who surrounded them on the journey. Love without money will be slow starvation; noble birth without money is a crumbling facade. While not necessarily bringing grace, beauty, respect, or a silver tongue, money is power, raw, brutal power.

In the late 1630s, when *Entre bobos* was written, as Domínguez Ortiz has shown on numerous occasions, monetary questions were uppermost in the minds of nobles, including those in the highest reaches of the nobility.[3] It was a problem for the king, for the upper classes, and it was a frightening reality for those on the edge of the financial precipice, a reality Lucas brings home in the most direct way. With luck, one could rise in this society, but one could more easily fall. The play presents the characters with opportunity and choice, but the choices are not easy. Is it literally worth it to marry a crass and slovenly man or a hypochondriacal, overprotected woman to assure one's financial future? Or is love worth more than money and status? It is not an easy choice, and, in the end, they are not even allowed to choose. The audience may feel that the right man wound up with the right woman, but at the same time, their hearts must go out to the young couple, for the road they are now forced to walk will be a rough one.

It will be a rough one, that is, if they persist in the values that Isabel's father seeks. Antonio must reinforce the facade crumbling before his face. Nobility is a status that, in order to be maintained, requires money, for which he has attempted to barter his daughter. For him, the descent will likely be unbearable. But for the young couple, the "descent" into the plebeian community may be seen in another light. The social and material life "of the common people in early modern Europe may be described in terms of cooperation, engagement with material life, and a resourcefulness that enables them to conserve valuable institutions and to create new ones. By virtue of this capacity, 'the people' are able to retain authority and initiative, thus to act purposefully and reciprocally on the dominant culture" (Bristol, 23). In *Entre bobos,* that community engages with and opposes the "official" culture represented by Lucas, Alfonsa, and Luis. The lovers, then, by refusing the safe though distasteful path of facade and financial security, by opposing the official culture, may be welcomed into the other life. By means of their inversion of traditional economies of language, family, and social relations, Isabel and Pedro may already be prepared to find a new and enjoyable home among the common people. There, their love may flourish, their opposition be seconded, their rebellion against the "de jure relations of dependency, expropriation, and social discipline" (Bristol, 22) find harmonious echo if they integrate themselves into the communal economies. Their attitude toward their future and toward themselves will determine all.

The audience, made up as it was from all sectors of society, may view the end of the play from differing perspectives as well. There may be some wealthy nobles who, while not perhaps liking Lucas's portrayal, may see his actions at the end of the play as poetic justice or as terrible but righteous vengeance exercised by a powerful man upon those who try to fool him. Some members of the less privileged classes may hear and applaud the alien voices' ability to make Lucas squirm. In that ability, they would see their own powers, in their context, reconfirmed. Those people might welcome Isabel and Pedro with understanding and open arms should they, in turn, neither fear nor abhor the less fortunate. Those same people might see in Lucas's slovenly, gross, and mercenary character and in Alfonsa's weak-kneed and spiteful portrait a confirmation of their suspicions about the wealthy, while in the fallen Pedro and Isabel, they might find a fanciful self-image to hold dear. On the other hand, any "Lazarillos" among them might see Pedro and Isabel as fools because men and women are indeed commodities and the two young lovers have just made a losing deal. The economy of responses may be as varied as the other economies presented in the play.

The play, then, offers not only a number of possibilities for the characters but for the audience as well. It presents a series of "traditional" economies—of wealth, of family, of language, of expectations, and of responses—but brings each into question. Whether characters have succeeded or failed, fallen or risen, whether the end of the play presents a rough or smooth road ahead for the characters, whether the audience will respond positively or negatively to what they have seen or to what they project as the implicit future of the characters—all depends largely on the contexts and parameters that the member of the audience brings to bear on the play. This suggestive play is an open-air market in which all its customers can find something they can afford to take home.

Notes

1.   See Bruce Wardropper's introduction to his edition of *El lindo don Diego* in his *Teatro español del Siglo de Oro* (New York: Charles Scribner's Sons, 1970), 885; Frank Casa and Berislav Primorac's introduction to their edition of the play (Madrid: Ediciones Cátedra, 1977), especially 22–27; and my *Comedia: Art and History,* University of Kansas Humanistic Studies, vol. 55 (New York: Peter Lang, 1989).

2.   All quotes are from Raymond R. MacCurdy's edition in his *Spanish Drama of the Golden Age* (New York: Appleton, Century, Crofts, 1971).

3.   See, for example, *Política y hacienda de Felipe IV* (Madrid: Ediciones Pegaso, 1983), 35–59 and also Manuel Garzón Pareja's *Historia de la hacienda de España* (Madrid: Instituto de Estudios Fiscales, 1984).

Works Consulted

Bristol, Michael D. 1985. *Carnival and Theater: Plebeian Culture and the Structure of Authority in Renaissance England.* London: Methuen.

Covarrubias, Sebastián de. [1611; 1674] 1943. *Tesoro de la lengua castellana o española.* Edited by Martín de Riquer. Barcelona: S. A. Horta.

Eagleton, Terry. 1986. *William Shakespeare.* Oxford: Basil Blackwell.

MacCurdy, Raymond R. 1968. *Francisco de Rojas Zorrilla.* New York: Twayne Publishers.

————. 1971. *Spanish Drama of the Golden Age.* New York: Appleton, Century, Crofts.

Margaret Rich Greer

The (Self)Representation of Control in
La dama duende

lose to the center of Calderón's comedy *La dama duende,* we find a pair of sonnets spoken as a witty exchange between two secondary characters, Don Juan and Doña Beatriz. At first reading, the sonnets seem to be mere rhetorical decoration voiced by characters who serve primarily to facilitate the development of the plot and to underline the hypocrisy of male concern for the virtue of women. However, on closer reading, puzzling or apparently frivolous passages in a well-worked Calderonian play often prove crucial to a complete understanding of the drama. I believe that this pair of sonnets is close to the thematic as well as the textual center of this play, and that an explanation of them can help to integrate a variety of elements in the plot that have not been sufficiently explained. What follows does not pretend to constitute a radically new interpretation of *La dama duende;* my reading of the play is related both to Anthony Cascardi's understanding of the power of illusion (24–36), and to A. A. Parker's emphasis on the "tyrannical concept of authority" that it illustrates (143–47). Rather, my intent is to enrich our appreciation of the play by calling attention to certain neglected aspects of the text and to its relationship to the sociohistorical setting in which it was written and performed.

La dama duende is a very funny play whose humor derives from the exploitation of a variety of theatrical resources: lively comic dialogue; a successful use of visual effect,[1] and an elaborate plot that "intrigues" the spectator/reader to the end. We have evidence of Calderón's care in structuring this play in the survival of two versions of it, published nearly simultaneously in 1636. The now-standard version was first published in the Madrid *Primera parte* of Calderón's works, and another version with a very different third act appeared in separate editions in Valencia and Zaragoza.[2] Audiences ever since have shown their abiding enthusiasm for Calderón's achievement. *La dama duende* was, as Henry W. Sullivan points out, the first play of Calderón to appear on a foreign stage, in a French version of the 1640s (56–60), and can still today arouse diverse reactions among German spectators, including outbursts that evince an involvement similar to that of Don Quixote before Maese Pedro's *retablo* (383–87).

Although one modern German critic who reviewed a production of Hugo von Hofmannsthal's version of the play in 1957 found the two love sonnets of Don Juan and Doña Beatriz the high point of the performance (Sullivan, 385), they have been little noted by Spanish and Anglo-American critics. Angel Valbuena Briones describes them as "dos buenos sonetos de tema amoroso y profano, cuya factura recuerda la del famoso soneto *A Cristo crucificado,* de inspiración mística" (121). The link with that anonymous mystical poem would seem to be tenuous at best, and the amorous and secular nature of the sonnets is obvious to the hastiest reader. John Varey does offer an accurate, if brief, characterization of the interchange of sonnets between Don Juan and Doña Beatriz, "en que se descubren su amor recíproco basado en el libre albedrío" (330).

In this witty poetic debate, Don Juan and Doña Beatriz debate the relative value of determinative stellar influences and free will in the course of true love.

Don Juan:	Bella Beatriz, mi fe es tan verdadera,
	mi amor tan firme, mi afición tan rara,
	que aunque yo no quererte deseara,
	contra mi mismo afecto te quisiera.
	Estímate mi vida de manera,
	que, a poder olvidarte, te olvidara,
	porque después por elección te amara;
	fuera gusto mi amor y no ley fuera.
	Quien quiere a una mujer, porque no puede
	olvidalla, no obliga con querella,
	pues nada el albedrío la concede.
	Yo no puedo olvidarte, Beatriz bella,
	y siento el ver que tan ufana quede,
	con la victoria de tu amor mi estrella.
Doña Beatriz:	Si la elección se debe al albedrío,
	y la fuerza al impulso de una estrella,

> voluntad más segura será aquella
> que no viva sujeta a un desvarío;
>   y así de tus finezas desconfío,
> pues mi fe, que imposibles atropella,
> si viera a mi albedrío andar sin ella,
> negara, vive el cielo, que era mío;
>   pues aquel breve instante que gastara
> en olvidar, para volver a amarte,
> sintiera que mi afecto me faltara;
>   y huélgome de ver que no soy parte
> para olvidarte, pues que no te amara
> el rato que tratara de olvidarte. (1889–1916)[3]

Don Juan attributes to the stars all control over his love for Beatriz; they will not let him cease loving her even if he would. Denying the possibility of exercising free will in the matter, he pretends to lament that he cannot forget her, at least briefly, in order to renew his commitment to her and prove the greater value of a love based on free choice. Doña Beatriz rejects this argument as a suspect "fineza." Her sonnet contains more potential ambiguity than his, for her relative valuation of stellar predetermination and free will depends on whether one relates the possibility of a "desvarío" to heavenly bodies or to human will. If we assume that the latter is more probable, Beatriz declares she is content that she has no personal election to forget Don Juan, that "no soy parte," because her commitment to loving him is such that if she saw her free will stray from him, she would swear by the heavens that that will was not hers. In sum, each denies having free will in the determination of love, and Don Juan laments this as a defect, while Beatriz values it as an assurance of constancy.

We should then ask how truthfully this stylized debate reflects their actual postures in the dramatic world that Calderón has crafted. Critics such as Stephen Greenblatt and Louis Marin have pointed out the complex relationship in the sixteenth and seventeenth centuries between the possession of power and its representation. In question in this drama is, I believe, the relationship between the *possession* of control over one's destiny, the *representation* of that control to others, and the consciousness or *self-representation* of control. Aside from providing the dramatic framework and advancing the encounters of Don Manuel and

Doña Angela, the most obvious thematic value of the Don Juan–Doña Beatriz subplot is that of underlining the hypocrisy of the male obsession with scrupulous maintenance of both the appearance and the reality of female virtue. In welcoming Doña Beatriz's presence in their house in order to court her away from the restrictions of her father's surveillance, Don Juan and Don Luis are condoning precisely the sort of freedom that they deny their sister. In general terms, then, Don Juan's sincerity is inherently suspect.

As a noble male head of household in a patriarchal society, Don Juan is in a position of power—over his own life and over that of his younger brother, Luis, and sister Angela as well. He not only acts this role with assurance (in arranging living quarters, dictating his sister's confinement, and inviting a guest over Luis's objections) but also voices his awareness of their resentment of his power. Commenting on Doña Angela's feigned and Don Luis's real displeasure at Don Manuel's presence, Don Juan says: "tú y don Luis mostráis disgusto, / por ser cosa en que yo he tenido gusto" (1869–70). In general terms, he represents himself both as possessing authority and consciousness of his own authority. In the course of love, he adopts the conventional pose of powerlessness; yet in his actions, he belies this enslavement, for as Golden Age suitors go, he seems less than dedicated. His pattern of courtship involves brief appearances, either opened or closed with a complaint by Doña Beatriz over his absence, which he answers with a polished declaration of dedication, only to depart again, claiming the press of other obligations.

Beatriz, as a single woman in this society, is theoretically as powerless to choose her lover as she claims to be, for the selection belongs to her father. One might even say that her pose in the sonnet represents an internalization of the socially dictated powerlessness of women. She is consistent, at least in her rhetoric, for she uses the same excuse of stellar determination in rejecting the attentions of Don Luis: "no puedo pagarlas; / que eso han de hacer las estrellas / y no hay de lo que no hacen / quien las tome residencia" (283–86). In fact, however, she is exercising a choice by admitting Don Juan's courtship, talking to him at the *reja* to her father's displeasure, and then taking advantage of her father's ignorance of the identity of her *galán* to live in her suitor's house. Both Don Juan and Beatriz, in their practice of choice, contradict their rhetorical representation of control in this interchange of sonnets. This discrepancy between possession, consciousness, and representation of control extends to the remaining characters of the play as well.

The character who comes closest to an accurate representation of his condition is Cosme, who is acutely and vocally aware that he occupies a very low rung on the socioeconomic hierarchy. He displays independence of action, albeit only in brief flashes: in the opening scene, it is Cosme who comes up with the idea of protecting the fleeing Doña Angela by asking Don Luis to read the address on a letter, and when Don Manuel orders him to unpack his bags, he mutters his resentment: "Mas porque él lo mandó, ¿se ha de hacer presto? / Por haberlo él mandado / antes no lo he de hacer, que soy criado" (774–76). Taking comic counsel with himself, he decides to perform his devotions at a tavern because "antes son nuestros gustos que los amos" (780). In the Valencia version of *La dama duende,* Cosme recounts a funny scene in which he is literally on the bottom, squashed by his master in the chair they take to meet the phantom lady. They both get in the chair in the cemetery, Cosme tells us: "Los dos en efecto allí / juntamente nos sentamos / en la silla yo, y tú en mí / que por entonces jugamos / a arráncate nabo" (Pacheco-Berthelot, 60). "Arráncate nabo" is described by Sebastián de Covarrubias as a children's game in which "uno está en el suelo y otro prueva a levantarle, y dízele: Arráncate nabo; responde: No puedo de harto. Arráncate cepa; responde: No puedo de seca" (quoted by Pacheco-Berthelot, 60).

With comic symbolism, Cosme represents himself as virgin in relation to the two fundamental sources of power—physical force and economic strength. Rodrigo, servant to Don Luis, challenges him to take out his sword, but Cosme refuses, saying: "Es doncella / y sin cédula o palabra / no puedo sacarla" (178–80). He gloats that his pocketbook has lost its virginity, as he fattened it at Don Manuel's expense during their journey: "buena está y rebuena, / pues aquesta jornada / subió doncella y se apeó preñada" (764–76). That happy state soon ends in miscarriage, however, as Isabel changes his coins for charcoal.

Cosme is subject not only to all those natural beings above him in the socioeconomic hierarchy but also to the whole range of demons who populate his imagination. Much has already been said about the contrast between his fearful, superstitious approach to life and Don Manuel's insistence on rational explanation and response to events. As many readers have observed, the verbal and visual play on his fears provide a major source of the humor of the play. What has been overlooked is that Cosme seems to squirm out of the grasp of the conventional structures of social and literary control at the very end of the play. Don Manuel would round off the play with the standard weddings, marrying his servant to Isabel as he gives his hand to Doña Angela. Cosme, often accused of drunkenness, refuses, saying that he really would be drunk if he agreed to marry, and that, furthermore, he does not have time to waste on such things.

With this closing, Cosme brings the play back full circle to his apparently extraneous speech on time in the opening scene. In the first instance, his lamentation for having just missed the festivities for Prince Baltasar Carlos is a topical reference guaranteed to please the audience, which might have included the king and queen themselves. Yet Calderón, through Cosme, turns the allusion into a comic discourse on the ultimate power over all human existence—time, whose passage determines whether we reach the arms of love or death. After proceeding through a litany of classical tragedies, Calderón lightens the topic and turns to Spain with Cosme's reference to Abindarráez. That story has a triple relevance to the plot about to unfold: first, in the play of power relationships and chivalry between Abindarráez and Rodrigo de Narváez; secondly, in the the evasion of patriarchal authority by a pair of lovers; and finally, in its comic resolution.

While Cosme verbalizes his powerlessness in humorous terms that endear him to the audience, Don Luis expresses his complaints in a very different mode. Valbuena Briones cites a José Luis Alonso production of the play in which Don Luis was portrayed as a comic figure (101), which could easily be accomplished by exaggerating his alternation between bellicose poses and tirades of whining self-pity. The dramatic text itself, however, does not suggest such a characterization, and most readers perceive him as a dark and unappealing figure. Edwin Honig sees in him a latent incestuous attraction to his sister. Barbara Mujica concurs and calls him a "study in frustration," a potentially tragic figure who is "partially responsible for his own unhappy situation of frustrated lover and domineering brother because he accepts honor as an absolute" (305, 317). Don Luis himself refers to the darkness of his character as he asks: "¿Soy yo la noche?" and wails: "tan infeliz nací / que huye esta beldad de mí / como de la noche el velo / de la hermosa luz del día / a cuyos rayos me quemo" (1460–65). In his paranoic self-image, "No hay acción que me suceda / bien" (294–95); "Cada día / mis hermanos a porfía / se conjuran contra mí" (1392–94). Therefore, he considers his only option to be a spoiler: "el estorbar es último remedio / de un celoso" (1824–25). Sword play also serves to represent Don Luis's lack of control. In the first act, he offers his own sword to Don Manuel in an elaborate display of apology for having attacked his brother's friend. And in the last act, Don Manuel breaks Don Luis's sword in two.

We need not attribute Don Luis's attitude to a dark and deep-seated personality defect, however, for it is an understandable response to his position in society. He is a younger brother in a patriarchal structure and as such must accept his brother's decisions, however grudgingly. Doña Angela counsels him: "Pues deja los sentimientos; / que al fin sufrirle es mejor; / que es nuestro hermano mayor, / y comemos de alimentos" (533–36).

A key factor in the preservation of the aristocratic order in Spain was the *mayorazgo,* which dictated that the great bulk of an estate should pass to the eldest son rather than being divided equally among heirs, and that the property could neither be sold nor mortgaged. This system was a mixed blessing for the nobility: on the one hand, it protected them against potential ruination by spendthrift sons, and by preserving their wealth in land, it enabled the aristocracy to survive the crisis years of the late sixteenth and early seventeenth centuries; on the other hand, it was a system designed for a localized, agrarian economy, not a commercial and monetary one (Jago 1973, 220). As Jago puts it, "Entails embodied a deep commitment to the family over the individual, and as such they ensured the long-term survival of aristocratic estates by placing the interests of multi-generational families ahead of those of individual nobles" (1979, 90).

The system clearly works against younger sons, such as Don Luis, and his paranoia about a family conspiracy against him would not be altogether unjustified. At best, a small inheritance that would provide a modest living would have been set aside for him in his father's will. However, Doña Angela's comment would suggest that Don Luis does not possess even that degree of financial security but rather is totally dependent on the support of his older brother. Furthermore, the return of a young, attractive widowed sister *is* a threat to him, if not in terms of honor, then for economic considerations related to her dowry, as we will see below. And finally, although Doña Beatriz never mentions "filthy lucre" in her choice of Don Juan and rejection of Don Luis, she would have been less than human not to consider their relative financial prospects. A younger son was generally considered an inferior marriage prospect; María de Zayas structures two stories, "Al fin se paga todo" and "El imposible vencido," around the disastrous consequences of the loves of younger sons.

Calderón plays on the economic dependency of younger brothers and their resulting disadvantage in courtship in the *auto La que va del hombre a Dios.* In that work, Vida and Amor Propio are courting Muerte and Culpa, respectively.

Whereas Muerte asks that Vida pay for a "manto de gloria," Culpa says to Amor Propio that she will accept only "un hábito" because "sois menor hermano / de la Vida—claro está, / sin más caudal que el que os da / de alimentos" (283–86).

Yet despite his inferior economic position and his acute consciousness that he is weak, it is Don Luis who works the "happy ending." After a second loss of his sword to Don Manuel, he returns ready to surrender his sword yet a third time (3067–69). Nevertheless, when he finds his sister rather than Doña Beatriz implicated with Don Manuel, it is Don Luis who demonstrates the strength and resourcefulness to command that Don Manuel marry his sister; and it is Don Manuel who prostrates himself at Don Luis's feet in gratitude for his "prudencia y constancia" (3084).

The character who complains most resentfully of oppression is, of course, Angela:

> ¡Válgame el cielo! Que yo
> entre dos paredes muera,
> donde apenas el sol sabe
> quién soy, pues la pena mía
> en el término del día
> ni se contiene ni cabe;
> donde inconstante la luna,
> que aprende influjos de mí,
> no puede decir: "Ya vi
> que lloraba su fortuna";
> donde en efeto encerrada
> sin libertad he vivido,
> porque enviudé de un marido,
> con dos hermanos casada;
> ¡y luego delito sea,
> sin que toque en liviandad,
> depuesta la autoridad,
> ir donde tapada vea
> un teatro en quien la fama,
> para su aplauso inmortal,
> con acentos de metal
> a voces de bronce llama! (379–400)

The severe restriction of women in this patriarchal society has been much discussed in relation to Doña Angela and other young women in Golden Age drama. What has not been sufficiently addressed is the question of why Calderón makes this heroine a widow. On first reflection, our answer might be that a handsome young widow, having known a measure of independence and sexual experience through marriage, would be less likely than an inexperienced girl to accept passively paternal or fraternal control. However, Isabel justifies that fraternal surveillance, saying: "este estado [widowhood] es el más ocasionado / a delitos amorosos" (406–8) and goes on to describe the antics of lighthearted widows in Madrid.

Widowhood does more than provide psychological plausibility for this "mujer-duende-torbellino," however; it also gives her claim to independence a legal grounding and makes her an economic problem for her family. Widows were the only women in seventeenth-century Spain who had legal independence. They had the right to administer family affairs and to arrange the marriages of sons and daughters, and they were the only women entitled to go to court in their own names (McKendrick, 17; Kagan, 86). In practice, however, their independence was contested, particularly during the first year after a husband's death. According to the old *Fuero juzgo,* a woman who remarried or committed adultery within a year of her husband's death forfeited half her dowry to her children by that marriage or, if there were none, to her dead husband's relatives: "Si la mugier despues de muerte de su marido se casa con otro ante que cumpla el anno, ó fiziere adulterio, la meetad de todas sus cosas reciban los fiios della é del primero marido. E si non a fiios, los parientes mas propinquos del marido muerto ayan la meytad" (2.2.1). This one-year stricture descended from Visigothic law, which expressed concern about the paternity of children born to a recent widow (Dillard, 44–45). It is thus rooted in the fundamental reason for the obsession with female chastity in a paternalistic society, the need to control women's reproductive capacity to ensure that the man's property passed only to his legitimate heirs. The *Nueva recopilación* of 1569 reaffirmed the penalty against adultery but granted widows the right to remarry whenever they wished without suffering loss of the dowry (McKendrick, 16).

Legally, the financial assets of a married couple were of three kinds, hers, his, and theirs: the bride's dowry; the goods that the bridegroom brought to the marriage; and acquisitions after marriage, which belonged equally to both (Dillard,

69). The dowry legally reverted to the woman on her husband's death; further-more, she could not be held responsible for her husband's debts (McKendrick, 17). Legal texts are one matter, however, and social practice another, and in prac-tice it seems that widows often had to fight to defend their legal rights.[4] Kagan cites the case of a widow from Ventas named Catalina Morales who in 1580 filed a suit against the creditors of her recently deceased spouse in order to protect her dowry (82–83). She seems thereby to have forced them to an out-of-court settle-ment. Records of local lawsuits from the sixteenth and seventeenth centuries are scarce, apparently because they were discarded after the *residencia* or judicial review performed at the end of the term of office of the royal *corregidores*. How-ever, in one surviving exception, the *fiel de juzgado* of Toledo, at least one fifth of the cases were brought by widows.

> Typically, a widow went to the *fiel* seeking to protect her dowry from her dead husband's creditors. Luisa de Aguilera, for example, did this after her husband, Bernal Hernández, died in 1582 leaving debts amounting to over 11,000 mrs. At the request of his creditors, Hernández's property had been seized by the alcalde of Ventas, but Luisa protested and asked the *fiel* to separate the goods belonging to her dowry from her husband's property. The *fiel* so ordered, and in similar cases involving widows he generally did the same. Ostensibly, the *fiel* appeared as a champion of widows' rights, but he was only acting in accordance with laws stipulating that, in the event of the death of the husband, dowries were to be returned to the widow intact. (Kagan, 86)

Calderón thus had a very good reason for making Doña Angela a widow. As such, she had a legal right to independence, but this right, at least in the economic sphere, was not easily conceded. A contemporary audience would certainly have recognized this situation when Rodrigo explained her presence in the house:

> Ya sé que su esposo era
> administrador en puertos
> de mar de unas reales rentas
> y quedó debiendo al rey
> grande cantidad de hacienda,

> y ella a la corte se vino
> de secreto, donde intenta,
> escondida y retirada,
> componer mejor sus deudas;
> y esto disculpa a tu hermano;
> pues, si mejor consideras
> que su estado no le da
> ni permisión ni licencia
> de que nadie la visite . . . (330–43)

Doña Angela has come home to straighten out her financial situation, that is, presumably to protect her right to her dowry from her husband's creditors.[5] The comment that her condition precludes all visitors has to do with proper conduct for a recent widow but also with the fact that due observation of the prescribed rites of mourning was considered proof that the widow was also honoring her dead husband by remaining chaste. Failure to carry them out aroused suspicions of a new amorous involvement (Dillard, 106). This explains the scandalized reaction of Don Juan and Don Luis at seeing Doña Angela out of widow's weeds. Aside from his concern for the family honor, Don Luis has good cause, in economic terms, to insist that Don Manuel not take Doña Angela out of the house except by marrying her, for if she commits adultery, her dowry is surely lost.

The question of the dowry was yet more complex, however, in the crisis years of the early seventeenth century. Lisa Jardine suggests that in *The Duchess of Malfi* Webster presents a woman in the one way she threatened the patriarchal structure in seventeenth-century England—through the obligation of providing her with a dowry upon marriage, which strained the resources of a landed aristocracy under pressure in a changing economic world. The Spanish nobility suffered similar financial difficulties. Their base in land insured long-term survival but left them in a "liquidity crisis" in the early decades of the century. Most of their holdings were entailed and thus could not be sold or mortgaged to raise cash. Prices had quadrupled during the course of the sixteenth century, and inflation continued apace in the seventeenth except when curtailed by severe currency devaluations, which had other painful consequences. Most of the nobility also felt obliged to live in Madrid, a very expensive city where social prestige was directly linked to an elaborate display of wealth in clothes, servants, carriages, and the like, which had to be paid for in cash.

In 1627–28, just before the presumed 1629 composition date of *La dama duende,* there had been a sudden deterioration of the Castilian economy. Due to a variety of factors, including large-scale minting of the copper *vellón,* the country was suffering from a severe rise in prices in that currency. After price-fixing and then withdrawing *vellón* coins in circulation, the crown in August 1628 devalued the *vellón* by 50 percent, bringing instant relief to the royal treasury but heavy losses to private individuals (Elliott, 329–30). It was not only Cosme who suddenly found his vile *cuartazos* turned to charcoal. In the wake of such a devaluation, Isabel's comments on the worthlessness of the *cuartazo* in the hierarchy of money (863–68) would presumably have had special resonances for the audience of 1629.

In this economic climate, providing a dowry could severely strain a noble family's resources and even liquidate a fortune. For example, Henry Kamen cites the duque de Infantado, who spent more than 370,000 *ducados* in a generation on dowries for his many daughters (390). The one way a noble could manage to raise cash by a mortgage on his entailed lands was through securing a license for a *censo,* granted by the crown on a restricted, case-by-case demonstration of sufficient cause. Approximately 20 percent of such licenses were granted for necessary family expenditures, especially for dowries (Jago 1973, 223–25). María de Zayas tells two stories in which women are brought to grief by covetous relatives who resist the financial drain of providing them a dowry. In one tale, the half sisters Magdalena and Florentina suffer from the covetousness of an uncle, in whose care they have been left on the death of their parents. The uncle endlessly postpones finding suitable marriages for them because he would then lose the benefits of administering their estate. Magdalena finally determines to marry anyway,

> sin la voluntad de su tío, conociendo en él la poca que mostraba en darle estado, temeroso de perder la comodidad con que con nuestra buena y lucida hacienda pasaba. Y así, gustara más que fuéramos religiosas, y aun nos lo proponía muchas veces; mas viendo la poca inclinación que teníamos a este estado, o por desvanecidas con la belleza, o porque habíamos de ser desdichadas, no apretaba en ello, más dilataba el casarnos; que todo esto pueden los intereses de pasar con descanso. (486)

In the other story, a father refuses to provide a dowry for his daughter, Doña Mencía, in order to preserve the estate intact for his son, Don Alonso:

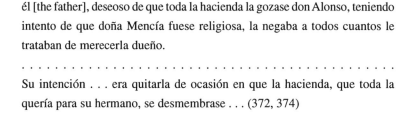

él [the father], deseoso de que toda la hacienda la gozase don Alonso, teniendo intento de que doña Mencía fuese religiosa, la negaba a todos cuantos le trataban de merecerla dueño.

. . . .

Su intención . . . era quitarla de ocasión en que la hacienda, que toda la quería para su hermano, se desmembrase . . . (372, 374)

To ward off potential suitors for the beautiful Doña Mencía, her father and brother keep her hidden, just as Don Juan and Don Luis attempt to hide Doña Angela.[6] Audiences familiar with this economic problem would be likely to recognize, therefore, that brothers of a beautiful young widow such as Doña Angela had a concrete economic reason for guarding the "honor" of a sister. In the first instance, they needed to insure that she not lose the dowry from her first marriage to her dead husband's relatives by forming an illicit attachment in the first year of widowhood. Secondly, they might be inclined to discourage a second marriage and a renewed dowry outlay that would weaken their own financial position.

Aside from Doña Angela's reminder to Don Luis of their financial dependence on Don Juan, direct references to financial concerns are restricted to lower-class characters. Rodrigo brings up the issue of Doña Angela's husband's debts; Isabel talks of the hierarchy of coinage; Cosme gloats over pilfering a few coins from Don Manuel and goes into agonies over their "transformation." He also pledges his silence in financial terms: "No hablaré más que un pariente / pobre en la casa del rico" (2508–9) and makes a pun on the double meaning of *sustentar,* "to uphold a cause in a chivalric tournament," and "to feed" (45–50).

Don Manuel, nevertheless, does make an oblique reference to certain "deudas" that Don Juan owes him, which can be read both as a discrete indication of financial obligation and a reminder that the noble code of good taste does not permit discussion of such matters. Don Manuel explains to Cosme his friendship with Don Juan—they studied together and were comrades in arms. When Don Manuel was made a captain, he chose Don Juan as his *alférez* and even saved Don Juan's life by nursing him back to health after a bad wound. After such a litany, Don Manuel certainly needs add no further justification of Don Juan's friendship for him. Yet he goes on to say:

> La vida, después de Dios,
> me debe; dejo las deudas
> de menores intereses,
> que entre nobles es bajeza
> referirlas; pues por eso
> pintó la docta Academia
> al galardón, una dama
> rica, y las espaldas vueltas;
> dando a entender, que, en haciendo
> el beneficio, es discreta
> acción olvidarse de él. (69–79)

Why would Calderón have Don Manuel add such a mysterious yet graphic passage except to say the unsayable, that Don Juan was also financially indebted to him? Presumably Don Manuel is in a stronger financial position than Don Juan, for he was the one made captain, and he has arrived in Madrid to collect a promised royal reward for his services.

In foregrounding these economic issues, I do not suggest that Calderón meant to make them central to the drama.[7] My purpose, rather, is to illuminate the power relations between the characters based on a legal and economic subtext that was well known to audiences of the day but is not familiar to twentieth-century readers or viewers.

Within the world of the play, then, the three empowered males are Doña Beatriz's father, Don Juan, and Don Manuel. The first, believing himself in control of his daughter, sends her packing to her cousin Doña Angela to prevent her from talking to an unknown suitor by night. In fact, he is playing into her hands, sending her to the very house of her *galán*. Don Juan is the visible wielder of authority in the play. He redesigns his house to cloister his beautiful, ebullient sister, yet she escapes his control at every turn. When he finds her out of widow's weeds in a splendid dress, he leaves with the dictatorial parting shot, "Quédate con Dios, y advierte / que ya no es tuyo ese traje" (2466–67). This is not just a reminder that her dress is inappropriate to mourning but also a dictum that the dress, presumably part of her dowry and therefore hers while she was married, is back under his control now. Doña Angela recognizes the pronouncement as such and, in the manner of subordinates everywhere, mutters her resentment behind his back, saying after he departs, "Vaya Dios contigo, y vete" (2468). Our delight in the drama derives from watching her escape his control time and time again. Don Juan finally catches her alone before Doña Beatriz's house at night and is reduced momentarily to silent impotence equal to that of his sister, as Doña Angela recounts:

> Quiso [Don Juan] hablarme y no pudo;
> que siempre ha sido el sentimiento mudo.
> En fin, en tristes voces,
> que mal formadas anegó veloces
> desde la lengua al labio,
> la causa solicita de su agravio.
> Yo responderle intento
> —ya he dicho como es mudo el sentimiento—
> y aunque quise, no pude,
> que mal al miedo la razón acude. (2967–76)

Finding his voice again, he curses his "hermana fiera," labels her the first stain on their ancient honor, and again endeavors to control her by locking her up, only to shut her in with Don Manuel, the very man she desires.[8]

Because Don Juan and Doña Beatriz's father both attempt to exercise authoritarian control over others, the audience takes pleasure in seeing their rule overturned. With regard to the third empowered figure, Don Manuel, the situation is different. Despite his insistence on the possibility of rational explanation and control of events, he does not attempt to dominate anyone but Cosme and, briefly, the beautiful "duende" who has invaded his room. The reader/viewer is satisfied with the resolution of the drama in his marriage to Doña Angela because both are presented sympathetically. Yet at the same time, we are left with a shadow over our pleasure, the suspicion that this is not what Don Manuel would have elected had he had free choice. Although he enjoys the epistolary flirtation with the "dama duende," marvels at Doña Angela's beauty when he sees her, and expresses a desire to enjoy her, nowhere in the play does he declare his love for her. Furthermore, he carries with him another woman's portrait, which throughout Golden Age drama is the conventional symbol for a commitment of love. Calderón at no time dissolves the shadow of competition cast by that portrait. Rather, he juxtaposes the scene in which Doña Angela plans to steal the threatening portrait— "porque no ha de tener, contra mi fama, / quien me escribe, retrato de otra dama"

(1883–84)—with the exchange of sonnets in which Don Juan and Doña Beatriz debate the value of free will and celestial predetermination in love.

Critics such as Cascardi and Mujica have posited a development, a personal maturation of Don Manuel and/or Doña Angela during the course of the play. Such a reading seems questionable, however, given the circular structure of the plot, which, like the mysterious voyage to meet the phantom lady, begins and ends in the same place. As Parker points out, Don Manuel acts as an automaton of the code of chivalry at the end of the play as in its beginning (146–47). When Cosme asks him in the first scene what he will do about Doña Angela's request for protection, he answers: "¿Eso me preguntas? / ¿Cómo puede mi nobleza / excusarse de excusar / una dicha, una afrenta?" (115–18). And in the last scene, he finds himself a "humano laberinto de mí mismo" (3008), torn by conflicting obligations posed by the code of chivalric behavior. After debating this quandary for which he finds no reasonable solution, he resorts again to reflex action dictated by noble chivalry: "Pues de cualquier manera / mal puesto he de quedar, matando muera. / No receles, señora; / noble soy; y conmigo estás ahora" (3031–34). Despite his favored position in the socioeconomic hierarchy, he is more controlled by its codes of conduct than other, much less powerful figures, such as Don Luis and Doña Angela. Even Cosme seems to squirm out of his control at the end, rejecting the marriage that Don Manuel orders for him.

To view Doña Angela's final speech as proof of maturity through submission to male authority is, I believe, to accept the legitimacy of the authoritarian structures that the drama mocks. Furthermore, her conduct is as circular as is that of Don Manuel. Her first words in the play are a plea for protection: "Si, como lo muestra / el traje, sois caballero / de obligaciones y prendas, / *amparad* a una mujer / que a valerse de vos llega" (100–104; emphasis mine). Moreover, her very last word in the final scene echoes that same plea: "que me valgas, me ayudes y me *ampares*" (3004; emphasis mine). The experience she has just undergone and which she recounts to Don Manuel is a humiliating experience that most contemporary female readers would not wish on this vibrant woman:

> mi casa dejo, y a la oscura calma
> de la tiniebla fría,
> pálida imagen de la dicha mía,
> a caminar empiezo:

> aquí yerro, aquí caigo, aquí tropiezo;
> y torpes mis sentidos,
> prisión hallan de seda mis vestidos.
> Sola, triste y turbada,
> llego de mi discurso mal guïada
> al umbral de una esfera,
> que fue mi cárcel, cuando ser debiera
> mi puerto o mi sagrado. (2926–37)

We see through her words the pathetic sight of Doña Angela stumbling alone through the dark streets, panic-stricken and imprisoned by her own dress, fleeing from her own home to another house that should have offered her a safe haven. Instead, she fled from one prison to another.

At the same time, it would be a distortion to make of Calderón a defender of women's rights *avant la lettre.* Women are consistently portrayed herein as *duendes, diablos, livianas,* and this negative evaluation, characteristic of patriarchal societies, is expressed by the female characters as well as by the male. When Doña Angela protests her brothers' domination, Isabel justifies it as necessary to control the disruptive sensuality of widows. Doña Angela says, "para hacer sola una / travesura dos mujeres, / basta haberla imaginado" (797–99); she describes her curiosity about Don Manuel as "necio" (624, 820); and says that Don Manuel's bundles of documents cannot be women's love letters because "si fueran de mujeres / ellos fueran más livianos" (828–29). Rather, Calderón seems to be using women as a vehicle to make fun of all those who presume to have the right and the capacity to control their own lives and those of others.

The real "ghost" of the play is the phantasm of control; those who believe they hold that *duende* find themselves holding a basket of underwear, while some of those who complain of powerlessness actually shape events. No one, however, achieves the blessed state of combining the possession of power with the consciousness of that possession. The play thus reflects its historical moment in ways more profound than the reference to the festivities for the baptism of the crown prince.[9] *La dama duende* undoubtedly is, as Varey says, an artificial and self-consciously literary play (321); yet it is also a product of the climate of the early decades of the seventeenth century, a time of social change, economic crisis, and a generalized consciousness of national decline, both political and moral. Doña

Beatriz's and Don Juan's witty denials of the force of free will in love offered the audience more than the aesthetic pleasure of a courtly debate. In such a time, few could share Don Manuel's assurance that reason and the codes of chivalry and honor could answer all questions and put all to right. Beneath the laughter, many might see more psychological truth in Cosme's view of a world controlled by forces beyond one's grasp that attack relentlessly and turn hard-earned cash to charcoal. The best hope might then be to squirm out of the grasp of the structures of authority at the end, like Cosme; and the best entertainment, to laugh at those who presumed to live in a world within their own control.

Notes

1.   For a careful study of its probable staging, see Varey, 319–35. Ruano offers a different explanation of key ingredients of the set, including the placement of the *alacena.*

2.   Pacheco-Berthelot, who published the variant third act, does not yet come to any conclusions about the authority of the two versions or about the priority of one over the other. My own guess is that both are authorial and that the Madrid version is a reworking of the Valencia text, but this would need to be tested by a careful comparison of the three editions along with the manuscript states of the text in the Biblioteca Nacional.

3.   All citations are from the Valbuena Briones edition unless otherwise indicated.

4.   In the *auto La que va del hombre a Dios,* Calderón incorporates into his allegory not only the disadvantaged status of younger brothers but also the legal strictures regarding women's dowries. When Hombre accuses his wife of causing his downfall, the Christ figure says that no woman can be imprisoned for debts but that penalties for her guilt can be exacted against her dowry: "podéis hacer en su dote / excursión de bienes; cumpla / la deuda hasta lo que alcance, / pues se obligó en la escritura, / donde la escritura dijo / que eras dos en carne una" (285–90).

5.   Young widows, such as Doña Angela, often had to return home even when the dowry was not contested because it was not sufficiently large for them to live independently.

6.   Don Alonso and Doña Mencía's father also refuse to "sully the family blood" by allowing her to marry a wealthy man of lower social standing who is willing to marry her without a dowry; Don Alonso kills his sister to prevent such a union.

7.   Tirso de Molina does foreground economic issues and their centrality in marriage negotiations in *En Madrid y en una casa,* a *comedia* that is closely related to *La dama duende* and that repeatedly cites the Calderonian comedy, either directly or indirectly. Tirso, however, inverts the names and the economic power of the central charac-

ters—rather than Don Manuel and Doña Angela, they are Doña Manuela, a rich young widow, and Don Gabriel, an impoverished noble playboy.

8.   In the Valencia version, which I take to be anterior to the Madrid one we know, Don Juan is a more sympathetic figure who appears less dictatorial because he reports directly his own indecision and suffering. If the Madrid version is a rewrite, then it would appear that Calderón deliberately exaggerated the authoritarian picture of Don Juan in order to increase the pleasure of seeing him fooled.

9.   The one "character" hovering in the wings of the play whose authority is never challenged is that of the king. To see his celebration of a son, Doña Angela puts aside, "deposes" her brother's authority (395); her former husband's debt is to the king; Don Manuel comes to Madrid to seek advancement through the king's favor. The crown did, in fact, have increasing control over this aristocracy, not only through direct grants of land, titles, offices, and other favors, but also through the granting of licenses for the *censos* that the nobles needed to raise cash (Jago 1973, 219). However, Calderón in no way questions the nature of royal authority in this play, although he would soon do so in the court play *El mayor encanto amor.* See Margaret Greer.

Works Consulted

Calderón de la Barca, Pedro. 1984. *La dama duende.* Edited by Angel Valbuena Briones. Madrid: Cátedra.

Cascardi, Anthony J. 1984. *The Limits of Illusion: A Critical Study of Calderón.* Cambridge: Cambridge University Press.

Dillard, Heath. 1984. *Daughters of the Reconquest: Women in Castilian Town Society, 1100–1300.* Cambridge: Cambridge University Press.

Elliott, J. H. [1963] 1966. *Imperial Spain, 1469–1716.* Reprint. New York: Mentor Books.

Fuero juzgo, o libro de los jueces. 1968. [Edited by Jaime Uya.] Barcelona: Ediciones Zeus.

Greenblatt, Stephen. 1980. *Renaissance Self-Fashioning: From More to Shakespeare.* Chicago, Ill.: University of Chicago Press.

Greer, Margaret. 1989. "Art and Power in the Court Spectacle Plays of Calderón." *PMLA* 104:329–39.

Honig, Edwin. 1972. *Calderón and the Seizures of Honor.* Cambridge, Mass.: Harvard University Press.

Jago, Charles. 1973. "The Influence of Debt on the Relations between Crown and Aristocracy in Seventeenth-Century Castile." *The Economic History Review.* 2d ser., 26:218–36.

———. 1979. "The 'Crisis of the Aristocracy' in Seventeenth-Century Castile." *Past and Present* 84:60–90.

Jardine, Lisa. 1987. "A Case Study in the Literary Representation of Women." In *John Webster's* The Duchess of Malfi, edited by Harold Bloom, 115–27. New York: Chelsea House Publishers.

Kagan, Richard L. 1981. *Lawsuits and Litigants in Castile, 1500–1700.* Chapel Hill: University of North Carolina Press.

Kamen, Henry. 1983. *Una sociedad conflictiva: España, 1469–1714.* Madrid: Alianza Editorial.

McKendrick, Melveena. 1974. *Women and Society in the Spanish Drama of the Golden Age: A Study of the "mujer varonil."* Cambridge: Cambridge University Press.

Marin, Louis. 1988. *Portrait of the King.* Translated by Martha M. Houle. Minneapolis: University of Minnesota Press.

Mujica, Barbara. 1980. *Calderón's Characters: An Existential Point of View.* Barcelona: Puvill.

Pacheco-Berthelot, Ascensión. 1983. "La tercera jornada de *La dama duende* de Pedro Calderón de la Barca." *Criticón* 21:49–91.

Parker, A. A. 1988. *The Mind and Art of Calderón: Essays on the* Comedias. Edited by Deborah Kong. Cambridge: Cambridge University Press.

Ruano de la Haza, J. M. 1987. "The Staging of Calderón's *La vida es sueño* and *La dama duende.*" *Bulletin of Hispanic Studies* 64:51–63.

Sullivan, Henry W. 1983. *Calderón in the German Lands and the Low Countries: His Reception and Influence, 1654–1980.* Cambridge: Cambridge University Press.

Varey, John. 1988. *Cosmovisión y escenografía: El teatro español en el Siglo de Oro.* Madrid: Editorial Castalia.

Zayas y Sotomayor, María de. 1983. *Parte segunda del sarao y entretenimiento honesto [Desengaños amorosos].* Edited by Alicia Ylleras. Madrid: Cátedra.

Daniel L. Heiple

Transcending Genre:

Calderón's *El santo rey don Fernando*

For Vern, evidence of another *comedia*

n 4 February 1671, Pope Clement X announced that the medieval Spanish king Fernando III (1199–1252), who had long had the cognomen "el Santo," was officially canonized (*Acta,* 379b). This news was the occasion for great celebrations in Seville (in whose cathedral the king is buried) and Toledo. The saint's day is 30 May, and the news did not reach Seville until 3 March (*Acta,* 380a); this late announcement left little time for preparations. Elaborate paintings and decorations were prepared, and the lavish celebrations began on Sunday, 24 May, and lasted through the saint's holy day (Torre Farfán, 272–335). Madrid appears not to have been the center of celebrations, but since Corpus Christi that year fell on 28 May, just two days before the new saint's day, both of Calderón's *autos sacramentales* performed for Corpus Christi in Madrid that year celebrated the piety of Spain's newest saint. These two *autos, El santo rey don Fernando, primera parte* and *El santo rey don Fernando, segunda parte,* are quite different from the rest of Calderón's *auto* production. Not only is it the sole occasion when two *autos* are on the same topic, but, in addition, the plays themselves, especially the second one, are markedly different from other *autos* in their treatment of allegory. Angel Valbuena Prat says that in the first part the characters were "admirablemente delineados," a clear reference to the realistic aspects of the play; he summarized his views of this *auto:* "Es un auto donde hay escenas valientes, trozos realistas, grandeza, devoción y fanatismo" (1263a). Valbuena's emphasis on the realism of this play is made clear by his introduction to the second part: "Continuación del auto anterior es éste, aun más *historial,* si cabe, que aquél" (1289a). Realism does abound in the second part, which has twelve historical characters and only four allegorical characters—who are in fact more supernatural than allegorical.

A. A. Parker (1968) takes into account the unique character of these plays by contrasting them with the *comedia de santos*. He maintains that two separate generic solutions existed for hagiographical and biblical material: either the *auto* in the tradition of the morality play or the *comedia de santos*. While most saint's lives were adapted to the representational action of the *comedia,* Calderón preferred the genre of the morality play. He "effected this assimilation by using such material as an allegory from which to extract a meaning that could be presented in more general and universal terms than would be possible were it dramatized representationally" (Parker 1968, 161). This explanation highlights the great diversity of form within Calderón's *autos* while at the same time establishing clear categories and tendencies. Even so, the two San Fernando plays, which are the most realistic and representational of Calderón's *autos,* seem to fit uncomfortably into any classification of allegorical drama.

In this study, I will carry Parker's distinction a step further and will argue that the San Fernando plays must have existed first as a *comedia de santos* that Calderón transformed into the two *autos sacramentales* for the year the saint was canonized. This generic transformation not only produced two *autos* that are definitely unique in their structure; it also left intact sufficient and substantial amounts of the original *comedia* to allow its reconstruction. As a chronological hypothesis on which to fit my arguments, I would suggest that Calderón was commissioned to write a *comedia de santos* for the celebration of the canonization, and then, either because the celebration was cancelled or because the play had been performed in another city, he could count on sufficient audience unfamiliarity with the *comedia* to be able to adapt it into the two *autos* for the annual Corpus Christi celebration.

The adaptation of *comedias* to the *auto sacramental* was not new. Both Lope and Valdivielso used the plots of their secular *comedias* as the basis for *autos sacramentales*, most often the honor plays (Wardropper 1951). Calderón continued the tradition by adapting his honor play *El pintor de su deshonra* into an *auto.* He also adapted other successful *comedias,* such as *La vida es sueño* and *Ni Amor se libra de amor.* These transformations seem to indicate the popularity of the original plays and the attraction their titles and plots held for the audiences who attended the subsequent *autos sacramentales.*

The adaptation of an unknown play on Fernando el Santo into the two *autos* for Corpus Christi in 1671 follows a different procedure. First, the original play, as far as we know, had not been presented in Madrid, and the title and plot would not have served to pique audience expectation. Even more important, the play is not really allegorized in the way the previous *comedias* had been. By and large, Calderón presented the play in all its historicity, inserted several allegorical characters in the first *auto,* and added a number of statements claiming that history and allegory are essentially of the same nature. The second *auto* may not have been changed at all. The alterations are so minimal that one can still recognize the structure of the *comedia* within the text of the *autos,* making them substantially different not only from other *autos* that were transformed from *comedias* but also from all other *autos.*

The method of transformation was different in each of the two *autos.* I would suggest that the first act of the *comedia* was transformed, by making it much longer, into the first of the San Fernando plays (1,836 lines). This was achieved by changing four individual characters into allegorical characters and by adding several other allegorical characters and scenes. The second *auto* (2,237 lines) was formed from the last two acts of the *comedia,* and it has little allegorical action and few allegorical characters. The text of the *comedia* must be nearly intact in this unusual *auto.*

The first *auto* deals exclusively with San Fernando's faith as a Catholic ruler, while the second play concentrates on his virtues as a crusader against the Moors. The first *auto* has four principal moments: the finding of a mysterious tablet, the conversion of the Jews, the execution of Apostasía, and the preparations for war against the Moors. On this representational action is superimposed a very unimposing allegory. The *loa* tells us that the action will represent a competition among Faith, Hope, and Charity to see in which of the cardinal virtues San Fernando excelled most. Rather than announce, as he does in other historical *autos,* that the allegory will arise from the history, in this play Calderón says the allegory is "contained" in the history itself: "A cuyo efecto en mi idea, / había imaginado hacer / a dos luces atenta, / un Auto, que en lo historial / lo alegórico contenga" (1268a).

In the *auto,* Hebraísmo, Alcorán, and Apostasía form a pact opposing the cardinal virtues: Hebraísmo against Caridad, Alcorán against Esperanza, and Apostasía against Fe. Apostasía argues that since they all have allegorical names, they should live up to their roles. The phrasing almost suggests that the figures at one time existed as nonallegorical characters: "Que ya que nuestros sucesos / (el día que a ti te aclaman / Hebraísmo, a ti Alcorán, / y a mí Apostasía) se pasan / desde Historia a Alegoría, / procuremos apurarla" (1276b). Hebraísmo takes up his role, proclaiming an ideal of a mixture of history and allegory: "y la licencia / usando, de que no haya / de ser siempre Alegoría, / ni siempre Historia" (1276b). The roles of Fe, Esperanza, and Caridad are simply superimposed on the action. The other characters never address them, and only at the end do they address another character. Throughout most of the play, they speak directly to the audience, commenting on the action. These allegorical characters are not integrated into the plot but are simply additions to it.

I would claim that four of the characters in the first *auto* were individual characters in the original *comedia*. These four characters, Alcorán, Hebraísmo, Apostasía, and La Religión de Santo Domingo, have allegorical names, but they are more individualized than Calderón's typical allegorical characters, and their actions are not allegorical but particular. Valbuena Prat notes that it is the only case of a Jew who converts in Calderón's *autos*. The reason for the absence of such an incident in the other *autos* is that it is allegorically incorrect for a character named El Hebraísmo to convert to Catholicism. El Hebraísmo represents the Jewish people and the Hebraic traditions, and historically they did not convert to Catholicism during the reign of Fernando III. The conversion in this play is a historical event, the action of one Jew, whose conversion serves to exalt the noble piety of Fernando el Santo. It is not an allegorical event but rather a pseudo-historical event typical of the *comedia de santos*.

The character of La Religión de Santo Domingo is even more inconsistent in its representational and allegorical roles. The King explains the generic duality of the character:

> Volveré en busca de aquella
> joven Religión Sagrada,
> que a dos luces se interpreta,
> Domínica; una, fundada
> en ser el Domingo Día
> de Dios, pues en él descansa;
> y otra, en que fuese Domingo
> de Guzmán su Patriarca;
> con que debajo del nombre

de Religión, se retratan
Historia y Alegoría. (1274a)

The weakness of the allegory of "el Domingo Día de Dios" is typical of Calderón's use of etymology, but it never serves as a principle of allegory, as it must here. A more typical type of allegory occurs later at the point when the King has invoked Religión and is about to go in search of her:

Rey: Divina Religión Santa,
                            ya sé la letra, a saber
                            tu sentido iré.
                Sale Domingo, de estudiante.
Religión: No vayas,
                            que la Religión no espera
                            que la busque quien la llama. (1275b)

This allegorical nicety, so typical of Calderón's style, is absent in most of the play. Even though the assignment of the speaking part calls him "Religión," the stage directions always label him as "Domingo," and the King later addresses the character as Domingo.

Valbuena Prat mentions fanaticism as a characteristic of the first *auto,* and he recognizes that this type of play did little to help Calderón's reputation as a humanist: "todo eso, en contraste valiente de piedad y barbarie, y humanismo y sequedad hace de esta obra una de las más típicas del Calderón discutido y apasionadamente juzgado, de un lado, como el excelso dramaturgo cristiano, y de otro, como el poeta de la Inquisición" (1263a). The action in this play presents a mythical founding of the Inquisition in the reign of San Fernando. At the beginning of the play, Apostasía is heard arriving offstage as he falls from his horse, a symbolic opening familiar from other Calderón *comedias.* The religious figure of Santo Domingo, in his pursuit of Apostasía, becomes the founder of the Inquisition, a poetic truth not far from the real truth, since the Dominicans were always closely associated with the workings of the Inquisition.

The oppressive nature of the Inquisitional methods are developed fully. After meeting Apostasía, La Religión de Santo Domingo says: "Este hombre importa seguir / y saber su nombre y Patria, / su oficio, vida y costumbres" (1277a).

Apostasía tries to murder Hebraísmo when he betrays the pact against the cardinal virtues, and Hebraísmo reveals that Apostasía is an Albigensian. When Apostasía fails to abjure his false beliefs, San Fernando decides to execute him. The execution is for matters of faith and has nothing to do with Apostasía's attempt to murder Hebraísmo: "advirtiendo en su castigo, / que del Cuerpo de la Iglesia / éste es nervio cancerado; / y así, es forzoso que sea / su cura el Fuego, que el cáncer / sólo el Fuego le remedia" (1283b).

San Fernando proclaims to Religión that this will be the first *auto de fe,* and his only sign of reluctance seems to be that they have spent so much time talking about it:

> El primer Auto de Fe,
> que público el Mundo vea,
> este ha de ser: Tú el primero
> inquisidor, que le ejerza;
> y yo el primero ministro
> que le asista; pues. . . . Mas estas
> resoluciones no son
> para dichas, antes que hechas.
> Y así, basta que te diga,
> que yo encenderé la hoguera. (1283b)

The crowd becomes inflamed, singing "Viva la Fe, y el Albigense muera," and Apostasía is burned, with San Fernando the first to light the fire. With the conversion of Hebraísmo and the execution of Apostasía, San Fernando has fulfilled his works of charity and faith, and his final work, of hope, will be the wars against the Moors. A Viejo Venerable appears to announce that Amanzor has ravaged the city of Santiago and destroyed the temple of the patron saint of Spain. San Fernando swears to avenge this anachronistic deed, which occurred two centuries before the action of this play. Saints Isidore and Leander appear to urge him on to restore Seville to Catholic dominance. These wars, which occupy the major part of the action of the second *auto,* will be the work of hope.

In the final moments of the first *auto,* the three cardinal virtues appear with symbols that they combine to form the seal of the Inquisition. Thus, the allegorical competition among the three virtues has led to a holy apotheosis and the formation of the institution that will preserve the purity of the faith, an act deemed worthy of the sainthood of the new saint. The first San Fernando *auto* is certainly not for modern tastes.

The second *auto* is quite different in structure but is, nevertheless, unified as a work. The action is essentially representational, not allegorical. The only really allegorical figure is Sultana, Secta de Mahoma, who presides over the action, urging her troops on to victory, only to lose to the Christians. She, like the other three characters—the two angels and a girl dressed as a statue of the Virgin with only seventeen speaking lines—is more supernatural than allegorical. The figure of Sultana had appeared in both earlier Calderonian *autos* that deal with medieval history, *El cubo de la Almudena* (1651) and *La devoción de la misa* (1658).

The second San Fernando *auto* lacks an allegorical superstructure. The action is purely representational, concerning the battle of Seville, the arrival of two angels who sculpt a statue of the Virgin according to San Fernando's dream, and the death of San Fernando. The 2,237 lines of the second *auto* could easily form two acts of a *comedia,* both in length and in structure. The break between the second and third *jornadas* must have occurred at the bottom of the first column on page 1306 (after line 1023), after Sultana has recommended war. At this point, the stage directions indicate the entrance on stage of San Fernando and the Christian nobles. Although no stage directions have indicated that Abenyuceph and Sultana have exited, they in fact seem to be offstage during the next scene, and when Sultana next appears, the stage directions indicate that she enters: "Sale cayendo a sus pies Sultana" (1308b). The break between the two acts divides the matter almost in half (1,023 lines in act 2; 1,214 lines in act 3) and occurs after the Christian troops have broken the supply line to the city and the Moors have decided on an all-out battle. The action of the second *auto* on San Fernando clearly comes from a *comedia de santos.*

The allegorical figure of Sultana serves to narrate the previous Moorish battles with San Fernando and to spur Abenyuceph, king of Seville, on to battle. She gives a certain structural unity to the play by appearing at the beginning, in the middle, and at the end in defeat. She also narrates the battle scene to the audience and gives battle plans to the Moors. She announces early in the play that history and allegory are not intertwined in this work: "y la licencia / usando, que ya asentada / quedó de que Alegoría, / e Historia no se embarazan, / mirando a dos luces" (1298a). Only once more is allegory mentioned in the play, when San

Fernando interrupts a comparison: "no es bien que porque caiga / otro en una Alegoría, / caiga yo en una jactancia" (1300b). The only moment of allegorical explanation occurs when Sultana falls from her horse at the end of the battle, and San Fernando explains that her captivity has allegorical meaning: "Sin hablar de la cautiva, / que es reservada materia / que no toca a lo historial, / pues sólo toca a la idea / de explicar que la africana / Ley quedó en España presa" (1309b). This apologetic explanation of the only allegorical moment in the *auto* suggests that the whole of the second part is simply a *comedia* transcribed with the title of an *auto sacramental.*

Even though Calderón conceived of the historical *auto* as a genre distinct from the allegorical *auto,* the allegory in the San Fernando *autos* is quite distinct from that of other historical *autos*. The table of contents of the 1677 edition of the first volume of Calderón's *autos,* prepared by Calderón himself for publication, distinguished between two types of *auto sacramental,* "Auto Sacramental Alegórico" and "Auto Historial Alegórico." Exactly what this distinction was to indicate is lost, since the other volumes prepared by Calderón did not reach the press, and when the *autos* were edited by Pando y Mier in 1717, he did not retain the generic distinctions in the table of contents. The 1677 volume contained four *autos* labeled as *historial alegórico.* They are the two parts of *El santo rey don Fernando, ¿Quién hallará mujer fuerte?* and *No ay instante sin milagro.* The San Fernando plays are indeed historical, and *¿Quién hallará mujer fuerte?* is based on biblical history, but the label for *No ay instante sin milagro* must be a mistake, since the play is a composed allegory. The same phrase, "Auto Historial Alegórico," is used in the *loa* to introduce the second San Fernando *auto.*

The relation of history and allegory in the San Fernando *autos* differs greatly from that of the earlier *autos* treating medieval history. Both *El cubo de la Almudena* (1651) and *La devoción de la misa* (1658) make clear Calderón's usual method of constructing allegory out of history. Like the San Fernando plays, these *autos* deal with the medieval struggle against the Moors. *El cubo de la Almudena* treats the battle of Madrid against the Moors and the discovery of the statue of the Virgin of Almudena. In this play, the historical action is completely allegorized. There is only one real historical character with a nonallegorical name; the rest are all allegorical figures. Calderón argues that both senses are necessary to his play: "Permitid que aquí / del alegórico estilo / al histórico me pase, / pues de entrambos necesito" (568b).

Calderón makes clear that there are two separate actions in the play: one treating the struggle of the Christians against the Moors and the other the importance of the host for the Christian believer:

> . . . con que a un tiempo
> viniendo los dos sentidos
> de Historia y de Alegoría,
> hará de entrambos un mixto,
> pues tocarán a la Historia
> los asaltos y peligros,
> y a la Alegoría la falta
> de aquel Misterioso Trigo.
> Dirá la historia el suceso
> de nuestro rencor antiguo;
> y la Alegoría dirá,
> cuando llegan los Auxilios
> del Pan. (569a)

The two senses of history and allegory are clearly intertwined in this play. At one point, this combination is called "lo mixto" (571a), and the whole action is conceived of as telling two stories at the same time: "y así, a ambas luces el campo / marcha" (569a).

In *La devoción de la misa,* there are more historical characters, and the action is less allegorical; but even so, the action is given an allegorical sense. This play also deals with the war against the Moors, the forces of Count Garci-Fernández in battle against the troops of Almanzor. The history allegorized in the play is the medieval legend of a soldier who was so devout that while at mass he forgot to go to battle, but his reputation was saved by an angel who stood in for him and carried the day against the Moors. The major action of the *auto* consists of the battle between the Christians and Moors. The battle is preluded and presided over by the custodial angel of Spain and La Secta de Mahoma. In their beginning debate, the angel explains the workings of providence, by which the Moors were allowed to take Spain as a punishment for Rodrigo's sins. The hero of the *auto,* Pascual Vivas, had killed a man and atones for his sin by attending mass so that his faith will save his soul. He gives a very long description of the mass before the action begins.

Unlike the second part of the San Fernando *auto,* the historical action in this play is allegorized. The angel argues that allegory is made out of history: "pues a segundas causas / se remite la experiencia, / haciendo de lo historial / alegórica materia, / atiende y atiendan todos / para que nada se pierda" (249b). The character Secta insists that the hero of the *auto* must have an allegorical function, an element that is completely missing in the San Fernando plays, where none of the historical characters have true allegorical functions:

> Pues que ya tan misterioso
> lo historial quieres que sea
> alegórico, ¿qué hombre
> de cuantos la historia cuenta,
> sin que le añada el ingenio
> circunstancia que no tenga,
> representará en común
> el que a dos luces intentas
> introducir? (249b)

She claims that the hero must be a real person, and that the allegory must not add an element that would distort the true facts of the historical figure.

The allegory comes from two aspects of the play. Calderón introduces Demonio and an assistant, Lelio, who are trying to win Pascual's soul. Just as the Moors are trying to win Spain, so is the devil trying to condemn Pascual. Demonio says that even though he has lost Pascual's soul, he will send the Arab troops to reconquer Spain (268a), but the angel explains that the Moors will finally be expelled from Spain by the great Philip III. The second-story doors on one of the carts open and reveal "retratado a Felipe III a caballo y a sus pies la Secta" (268b). The triumph of Pascual Vivas over sin is compared to the triumph of the Christians over the Moors, not only in the battle in the play but in the whole course of history.

The battle is compared to the mass. Just as Pascual conquers evil in the church, so do the Christian soldiers conquer the Moors in battle. Also, Pascual has two forms, just as Christ assumes two forms in the host of the mass. Calderón is careful to explain that there is a difference, since in the mass, the host is the real presence of Christ, whereas Pascual in the battle is an image of his real self. The angel sings and is answered by the chorus:

Angel:	¿Cómo puede en dos partes
	estar un cuerpo?
Músicos:	Solo Dios en la Hostia
	del Sacramento.
Angel:	Pues ¿cómo hoy en dos partes
	Pascual se ha visto?
Músicos:	Como uno era su imagen,
	que no era él mismo. (268a)

The final allegorical correlation occurs when Pascual confesses to his great shame that he was in the church and not in the battle. He denies with great vehemence that he was in the battle, and this confession becomes both his salvation and the denouement of the drama:

Pascual:	Todo aqueso es afrentarme
	cuando yo, señor, confieso
	mi culpa a voces.
Demonio:	Porque
	aun no falte este pequeño
	rasgo de la alegoría
	con la confesión que ha hecho
	y propósito a la enmienda,
	bien con la Gracia se ha puesto,
	pues ella le da los brazos. (267a)

The allegorical elements in this play are obviously different from those in the San Fernando *autos*. In *La devoción de la misa,* the characters and the action are seen "a dos luces," that is, the story is retold as an allegorical action. Even though Calderón makes similar arguments in the first San Fernando *auto* about the relation of history and allegory, the action in both plays is historical and not allegorical, and it cannot be interpreted "a dos luces." The treatment of history and allegory in these two *autos* makes clear that the San Fernando *autos* were not conceived of as *autos sacramentales* but rather as a historical *comedia de santos* that was then hurriedly converted into the *autos* performed on Corpus Christi two days before the celebration of the new cult of Saint Ferdinand in 1671.

An archaeological dig into the two San Fernando *autos* produces almost intact the remains of a previous *comedia de santos*. By eliminating the explanations of allegorical character names, the allegorical characters, and the allegorical action from the 1,837 lines of the first *auto,* it is possible to reduce it in structure and extension to the norms of the act of a *comedia.* The second *auto* can stand as it is as the second and third acts of the *comedia.* The resulting play takes the form of a celebratory play of the type typical not only of the *comedia de santos* but also of Shakespeare's *Henry V* and Guillén de Castro's *Las mocedades del Cid.* Clearly the generic differences between the *auto* and the *comedia* had always been fluid (Bataillon, 197), and some of the *autos* in the early 1670s often contained more nonallegorical representational material than the earlier *autos.* The example of the San Fernando *autos* is unique in the elimination of generic boundaries and the absorption of one genre into the other.

Works Consulted

Acta Sanctorum. 1866. Vol. 20. Rome: Victor Palmé.

Bataillon, Marcel. 1964. "Ensayo de explicación del 'auto sacramental.'" In *Varia lección de clásicos españoles,* 183–205. Madrid: Gredos.

Calderón de la Barca, Pedro. 1677. *Autos sacramentales, alegóricos y historiales.* Vol. 1. Madrid: Joseph Fernández de Buendía.

———. 1717. *Autos sacramentales, alegóricos y historiales.* Edited by Pedro de Pando y Mier. 6 vols. Madrid: Manuel Ruiz de Murga.

———. 1959. *Autos sacramentales.* Vol. 3 of *Obras completas.* Edited by Angel Valbuena Prat. Madrid: Aguilar.

Parker, Alexander A. 1968. *The Allegorical Drama of Calderón.* Oxford: Dolphin Book Co.

———. 1969. "The Chronology of Calderón's *Autos Sacramentales* from 1647." *Hispanic Review* 37:164–88.

Pérez Pastor, Cristóbal. 1905. *Documentos para la biografía de D. Pedro Calderón de la Barca.* Madrid: Real Academia de la Historia.

Torre Farfán, Fernando de la. 1671. *Fiestas de la S. iglesia metropolitana y patriarcal de Sevilla al nuevo culto del señor rey S. Fernando el Tercero de Castilla y León.* Seville: Viuda de Nicolás Rodríguez.

Wardropper, Bruce W. 1951. "Honor in the Sacramental Plays of Valdivielso and Lope de Vega." *Modern Language Notes* 66:81–88.

———. 1967. *Introducción al teatro religioso del Siglo de Oro.* Salamanca: Ediciones Anaya.

Susana Hernández Araico

Official Genesis and Political Subversion of

El mayor encanto amor

n their impressive book on the Retiro palace, Jonathan Brown and John Elliott initiate their analysis of that architectural complex of sumptuous symbols of power with the following quotation from Calderón (7): "¿Qué fábrica ésta ha sido? / ¿para quién? ¿para quién se ha prevenido / esta Casa, este Templo, / última maravilla sin ejemplo?" (Calderón 1717, 394). Brown and Elliott use this question, posed by the allegorical figure of Judaism in the *auto El nuevo palacio del Retiro* (1634), as a point of departure for evaluating the construction, decoration, and sporadic use of the palace conceived by the Conde Duque de Olivares for Philip IV. By touching on the relation between the royal favorite and Portuguese Jewish investors, and the charges of Hebraiophilia lodged against him, Brown and Elliott underscore the ambivalent status accorded the allegorical figure of Judaism in Calderón's *auto* (100, 230).[1] Nevertheless, they consider this Corpus Christi play to be another example of the artistic adulation fostered by Olivares in his quest for public support. According to Brown and Elliott, the poetry and theater commissioned by Olivares to entertain the king and his court simultaneously praise the grandiose construction of the Retiro and fulfill the aim of adulation, as does the rest of the art commissioned for the new palace. Barbara Von Barghahn concurs in her remarkable study of Philip IV and his "Golden House," the Buen Retiro (1986, 76, 90).[2] Such "official" theatrical homage aims, however, to defuse strong criticism of the new palace in letters, lampoons, and popular satires (Brown and Elliott, 232–35). Authorities on Spanish art and history thus consistently ignore Calderón's posture and that of other dramatists with regard to the architectural monument that, as a new space for staging *comedias,* was to modify the emission and reception of their dramatic art.

Such carelessness is evident in readings of *El mayor encanto amor,* the first of Calderón's mythological *comedias,* conceived with spectacular stage machinery for the Retiro's great central pond on midsummer night 1635 but not actually staged until July 29.[3] Both Brown and Elliott (230) and Von Barghahn (89) make the mistake of interpreting this play solely on the basis of set designer Cosme Lotti's draft (Hartzenbusch 1851, 386–90), probably due to Emilio Cotarelo y Mori's assertion (1924, 165) that it is an early version of Calderón's, prior to the one published in the *Segunda parte* of his *comedias* in 1637.[4] In 1889, Leo Rouanet demonstrated clearly that the document in question is actually Lotti's staging draft, to which Calderón objected in a letter of 30 April 1635. N. D. Shergold (1958) reiterates Rouanet's views, and Brown and Elliott cite this article (276n. 20), but they have not read Rouanet, Shergold, or Calderón. Unfortunately, such carelessness reinforces for readers with limited knowledge of Golden Age theater the impression that dramatic productions in the Retiro were merely spectacles to praise the very power that sponsored them. Calderón's revision of Lotti's scenographic plan in the dramatic text of *El mayor encanto amor* belies this fallacy.

Lotti, a superb hydraulic engineer and gifted designer of stage machinery, was dedicated to the entertainment of the king and the celebration of his power (Shergold 1973). His interests thus depended completely on Olivares's politics and found their highest expression in the Retiro. His adulation is hardly surprising, then, in the *Circe y Ulises* fête, which was written "a petición de la Excelentísima Señora de Olivares" (Calderón 1851, 386), that is, commissioned in detail by the Conde Duque de Olivares.[5] Lotti's draft personifies the new palace as a giant hermit—thus calling attention to the Buen Retiro's size and importance—far from Circe's pleasures. With another allegorical character named Virtue, the favorite—more so than the queen—is represented as the beneficial promoter of this retreat.[6] The spectacle, as propagandistic support for the king's isolation, the source of Olivares's power, was conceived to appease public resentment toward Olivares for the enormous expenses on the new palace as well as on the king's idleness—which it encouraged—especially during time of war.

Lotti no doubt pursued his own interests in producing a play about Circe in praise of the new palace and its gardens of stunning aquatic engineering that he himself had conceived (Shergold 1973, 589). The theme of Circe constitutes the motif for an aquatic festival, or *naumaquia,* with elaborate fireworks, in keeping with courtly spectacles in vogue in Italy and France (Egido, 24n.29). Circe and her magic were already a standard pretext for impressive stage transformations to highlight nature's mutability through its four elements. Logically, the scenographic art of mutations and optical illusion centers the action on the pond, i.e., water, the symbol of fluidity and the fleetingness of experience (Rousset, 142–43); hence the prominent role of water in Lotti's scenographic draft. It is also understandable that, of all of Lotti's instructions, Calderón accepted first of all that "el teatro ha de ser en el estanque" (Rouanet, 198), the ideal location for the deceptive meta- morphoses that his text would feature. But, in principle, the dramatist refused to write the *comedia* following the "memoria . . . que Cosme Lotti hizo del teatro y apariencias que ofrece hacer a su majestad . . . [porque] no es posible guardar el orden que en ella se me da" (Rouanet, 197–98). His refusal to write his first mytho- logical *comedia* according to Lotti's spectacular staging project, as well as his documented presence at the rehearsals of his later *autos* and courts fêtes (Pérez Pastor, 250, 279; Cotarelo y Mori 1924, 297, 300), proves that Calderón did not permit his works to be used as mere fillers for stage designs planned as sensa- tional entertainment in the palace. In response to Lotti's proposal, Calderón wrote that "aunque está trazada con mucho ingenio . . . no es Representable por mirar más a la invención de las tramoyas que al gusto de la Representación" (Rouanet, 197–98). Calderón, keenly aware of, and always concerned with, the reception of his dramatic texts, knew of the deeply felt public dissatisfaction with Olivares's enormous public expenditures for the monarch's sensual amusement. Neverthe- less, the playwright had to accept the challenging task of injecting dramatic sense into a spectacle designed to astonish visually and to justify Olivares's position. "Haciendo elección de algunas de sus apariencias, las que yo habré menester . . . para lo que tengo pensado," he stated (Rouanet, 197), and proposed to adapt the stage designer's visual signs to his own theatrical concept.

Lotti intended to reflect the magnificence and power of a monarchy capable of transforming everything into theater.[7] Hence the gigantic hermit, *disforme* and *muy viejo* (Calderón 1851, 390), that personifies the Buen Retiro palace. Evi- dently, Lotti wanted to stress the transformation of the ancient site—a hermit's retreat—into the new gardens he himself designed as enormous and "venerable" (Calderón 1851, 390).[8] Calderón retained a giant in his dramatic text probably because Prince Baltasar found such colossal characters entertaining (Shergold and Varey 1961, 29). But by transforming the character into a carnavalesque figure, as seen in *autos* or in the midsummer night celebrations,[9] Calderón undercut its importance vis-à-vis Ulysses. In fact, in his own scenographic instructions list that he selected from Lotti's original list, the giant appears last (Rouanet, 198). Its comic effect is complemented by a dwarf and a *dueña*—both familiar figures in the palace whose function as spies Calderón ridiculed in *El mayor encanto amor.* The dwarf was also very much to the taste of the prince, the favorite, and the nobility in general (Gallego, 16–23; Moreno Villa, 18–21). The laughter that the *dueña* would cause—at the expense of the Condesa de Olivares and her retinue—is a prelude to, or perhaps has its echo in, the *entremés* entitled *Las dueñas* that Benavente wrote for the same occasion (Bergman, 175, 289–92).[10] Thus Lotti's venerable allegorical giant becomes a carnivalesque monster in Calderón's text, where, moreover, ridiculous characters displace Virtue to introduce him onto the stage.

In Lotti's draft, Virtue appears disguised as a magician; she separates Ulysses from Circe, directs the passive hero to recognize his moral weakness in the reflection of a fountain, and introduces him to the giant hermit, "Buen Retiro." For Calderón, however, it is impossible to reach the truth through an aquatic reflection that can only produce an optical illusion. He changes the imagery from water to a mirror yet maintains an emblem of self-deceit in the humorous metamorphosis of the *gracioso* into a monkey (Covarrubias 1973, 98a).[11]

As a powerful politician, Olivares becomes for the opposition an object of accusations of witchcraft (Marañón, 190–211).[12] By personifying him in the figure of Virtue, who only pretends to be a magician, Lotti contradicts the rumors that the favorite bewitched the king with celebrations and sensual pleasures.[13] With that allegorical figure, Lotti uses the marvelous fountains in the palace gardens and the entire Retiro to represent as a moral force the mesmerizing effect that Olivares exercised on the monarch. But Calderón did not allow Virtue—or genuine valor—to be debased by the disguise of a magician feigning friendship with Circe and carrying out enchantments similar to those of the classic seductress.[14] Calderón's text therefore replaces the Virtue of Lotti's draft with Achilles, the valiant warrior whom Philip IV should emulate in taking to the battlefield and leaving behind Olivares's magic.

Evidently, the playwright himself devises the stage effect of Achilles's ghost in order to spur the king's desire—frustrated by the politics of the favorite—to follow the Cardinal Infante's example of military heroism. It is precisely in this use of the spectre in the *comedia* that Calderón demonstrates the power of his verbal artistry over stagecraft, as his text determined the machinery that the appearance of Achilles's spirit may have required. Thus, verbal and aural elements dominate in the stage production over the visual and its illusions. In the first place, Ulysses's rejection of sloth takes place through the powerful impact of Achilles's voice instead of through the visual magic that Lotti had intended for Virtue. Nor is Achilles's "grabado arnés ilustre"—a visual object with which Ulysses's comrades hope to spur him to leave Circe—able to arouse him from his erotic lethargy until he is moved to valor by a voice. Then "abre para quejarse una boca y de ella escape pardas nubes de humo y fuego" (Calderón 1973, 24d–25a), which expels the spirit of Achilles. It is not coincidental that the voice introduces the impressive apparition, which emerges from a "mouth." It is worth noting that this effect, whose sonorous prelude lifts the protagonist from his sensual abjection, is a horrifying vision, the spectre of death, the disillusionment of all appearances.

The changes in stage effects through which Calderón eliminates Lotti's excessively laudatory elements in turn reveal to the monarch the deception around him, especially in the person of his favorite. With the allegorical character of Virtue replaced by Achilles, the symbolic association of the former with Olivares is automatically transferred to Circe; her "suntuoso palacio" and "jardín delicioso" in Lotti's outline (Calderón 1851, 387) coincide with the construction of the Retiro much more logically than the ridiculous giant hermit does. Besides, Lotti's outline itself had already postulated in visual terms a political correlative with the traditional connotation of Circe as a fearsome seductress.

Lotti has Circe appearing in the midst of flowers and "compuesta con un bizarro y rico vestido a la persiana" (Calderón 1851, 387)—that is, in a rich floral pattern (*Diccionario de autoridades,* 2:234). Circe appears as Flora, who not only typifies the elegant courtesan (see Antonio de Guevara's *Epístolas familiares* [Gallego, 36]) but also personifies the fundamental deceitfulness of institutionalized politics and its official poetry (according to the 1494 Spanish translation of Boccaccio's *De las ilustres mujeres* [fol. 68]).[15] Lotti's Circe, therefore, visually conceived as Flora, already connotes the abuse of political power, from which the favorite, represented as Virtue, was supposedly to save the king, personified in Ulysses. Calderón uses this original political projection but subverts it, astutely intensifying it.

Since Achilles replaces the allegorical figures of Virtue and the giant hermit (which represent Olivares and the Retiro respectively), the meaning of Lotti's

flattering signifiers is transferred in Calderón's dramatic text to the visual-philosophic sign of the classical bewitcher Circe. The moral connotation of the latter then confirms in the spectators' minds the censure against the favorite, particularly due to his role in the construction of the palace.[16] The popular attribution of witchcraft to Olivares and the opposition to his extravagance in the Retiro thus merge with the political projection of the visual sign of Circe-Flora, originally conceived by Lotti, and to which Calderón expressed no objection in his letter (Rouanet, 196–200).

Calderón's process of linguistic-representative subversion is seen in the Gongoristic metaphors that initially describe Circe and her gardens and palace when Antistes, having escaped from those dangers, urges Ulysses to escape before seeing them:

> Discurrimos ese monte;
> hasta que hallándonos dentro,
> vimos un rico palacio,
> tan vanamente soberbio,
> que embarazando los aires
> y los montes afligiendo,
> era para aquéllos nube
> y peñasco para éstos,
> porque se daba la mano
> con uno y otro extremo;
> pero aunque viciosos eran,
> *la virtud no estaba en medio.*
>
> (4b; emphasis added)

Describing Circe's deceptive demeanor when she orders drinks that would transform Ulysses's companions into beasts, Antistes continues: "cautelosamente humana / . . . / . . . haciendo / con urbanas ceremonias / político al cumplimiento" (4b–c). Thus Calderón's metaphoric language ironically alludes to the referents of the visual signs. Suppressing the character Virtue and developing instead a symbolic link between the *Conde Duque* and Circe, Calderón decodifies the classic witch, endowing her with dignity and *admiratio*.

As a chaste, spirited woman of profound passion, Circe appears respectable and worthy of compassion in her emotional complexity. The rupture of the code of the classic witch-seductress demonstrates Calderón's intention to preclude any burlesque interpretation in the dramatic representation of Olivares. While, on the one hand, he eliminates the political sycophancy in Lotti's *memorial,* on the other, he avoids the ideological simplification and deceptive exaggeration of satire in the symbolic representation of the favorite and thus intensifies the mordant impact of his criticism. Just as Lotti's draft proposes, Calderón also produces an allegory of an undeniably philosophical tradition, in keeping with the customary reading of the Ulysses-Circe episode. But by imposing his verbal control over its visual signs and dramatizing it with conflicting characters, he manages to introduce a notable twist in Lotti's static, adulatory stage plan.

Calderón's efforts to energize the weak plot in Lotti's outline are demonstrated by Albert Sloman (128–58) and John Richard Le Van (1981, 124–86), who compare *El mayor encanto amor* to earlier works, especially *Polifemo y Circe* (1630), whose third act only was written by Calderón.[17] Nevertheless, these and other critics continue to place value primarily on the universal symbolism of *El mayor encanto amor* as an antecedent to the *auto Los encantos de la culpa.* Except for Shergold's monumental history (1967), which does not, however, address problems of intended emission and/or reception, critics have concentrated on a purely philosophical reading of *El mayor encanto amor* and have shown limited interest in the Calderonian text's audiovisual signs or the great care with which the dramatist chooses them.[18] Calderón is so concerned that his text would be adapted to the initial project by the Italian stage designer—notorious as an untrustworthy braggart[19]—that he binds the latter legally to carry out without any alteration the scenes "que están dispuestas por Don Pedro Calderón y que firmado de su mano sea [se ha?] entregado al dicho Cosme Lotti" (Caturla, 44). For an innocuous fable of universal symbolism, it would not be worth such an effort to protect the integrity of his dramatic text. Calderón foresees that his adaptation of Lotti's initial draft would not please those preparing the royal celebration—ultimately, Olivares. While mutilations of his *comedias* in public theaters and pirated editions of his works were frequent, for an official court occasion, Calderón wished to ensure that his text be staged exactly as he had conceived it. The ambivalent effect would be a genuinely dramatic spectacle that would please its chief patron and the royal audience far more than Lotti's static plan but, at the same time, a subtle expression of solidarity with public opposition against the costly Retiro palace and the favorite's politics.

Already the previous year, Calderón's *auto El nuevo palacio del Retiro* presented a clear expression of criticism against "el pomposo gallinero" (Caturla, 17) converted into a garden of delights for the five senses. While Calderón praised there the new palace as an image of the Triumphant Jerusalem of the Apocalypse (1717, 396), at the same time he compared it through the very different image of Judaism to the earthly paradise (with its rivers, fountains, fish, birds, and beasts), where man, the God-king's favorite, "del bien, y del mal llegó en poco tiempo a saber" (1717, 395). The following rhetorical question posed by Judaism on the one hand affirms the political referent of "man-favorite" and, on the other, reduces the importance of potential criticism: "pero qual Privado, qual / no supo del mal, y el bien?" (1717, 395a). The pause of the comma emphasizes "mal," so that "el bien" is almost conciliatory.

Calderón uses the comparison of the Retiro to the earthly paradise as an ambiguous warning to Olivares by means of the figure of the queen:

> Y assi, pues, el hombre fue
> Alcaide de aquel primero
> Jardin, mas feliz espero,
> que oy el cargo se le dè
> deste mas feliz, porque
> si alli padeciò mudança,
> en su privança hoy alcança
> el hombre tanto favor,
> que yà sin aquel temor
> ha de gozar tu privança.
> (1717, 400)

By appearing to praise the increase in power that the Retiro means for the favorite, Calderón ironically draws attention to its fragility.[20] The merry expression of assurance from the queen ultimately suggests the new garden is a threat to its "alcalde." The irony arises from the well-known opposition between queen and favorite, especially over the new palace that separates her even more from her husband (Hume, 173).[21]

Furthermore, in *El nuevo palacio del Retiro,* Calderón already presents the sense of sight, which begins to defy dramatists precisely with the arrival of Lotti at court (Whitaker, 46), as the most presumptuous, the most deceitful and least reliable, of the five senses (Calderón 1717, 400). On the other hand, hearing, the vaguest and most ethereal sense, the one most defiant of human comprehension, is ultimately the least deceptive due to the very distrust that it elicits (401). By affirming the superiority of hearing, Calderón suggests that rumors about the new palace and the "quejas que abaten al valido" (402) are more trustworthy than the pleasurable impressions of the other four senses. Thus the *auto* of 1634 preludes Calderón's refusal (by means of language or "una voz" [401b]) to subjugate his art to the visual deceits proposed by Lotti the following year for the Circe spectacle.

The *auto El nuevo palacio* also anticipates the volcanic destruction of the mythological palace in *El mayor encanto* in June 1635. In the *auto,* the comparison of the new palace to the triumphant church (396b, 403a, 405a) remains doubtful in the favorite's own ironic reference to the Old Testament, such as "Si el Señor no edificare la Casa, en vano presume trabajar quien la edifica" (402b). On the other hand, the apocalyptic image of the "victoriosa . . . gran Jerusalén" gives rise to a kind of *Dies irae* (403–4) whose violent incendiary images point to the vanity of the new royal house, undercutting the festive occasion.[22] In this sense, the *auto* anticipates the final fire in *El mayor encanto amor* when Circe, out of vengeance and indignation against Ulysses, destroys her palace with a volcano eruption.

Calderón accepts Lotti's stage design for this effect of "quedar todo destruido[,] correr fuego las fuentes y abrasarse todo" (Rouanet, 198), since midsummer night is a celebration of the victory of light over darkness on the summer solstice. Moreover, it highlights the triumph of Philip IV's role as a sun god personified by Ulysses (de Armas, 141–42, 149). But, identified spatially and linguistically with Olivares's Retiro (Hernández Araico 1987b, 277–78), the incineration of Circe's palace in Calderón's text would give expression above all to public resentment against the favorite and the Retiro.[23] The visual symbolism of a festive renewing fire includes, then, the destruction of this vain edifice of pleasure, while the image of a sun deity responds to Achilles's call to military valor.

It is not surprising that *El mayor encanto amor* was staged only once, although its great cost would justify more performances. This single production suggests an official displeasure with Calderón's text, despite its great success as a spectacle. A contemporary commentary suggests that it was not repeated due to the fire that the staging produced.[24]

Did the flames come from the machinery for the volcano or from that of the mouth where Achilles emerged? What a strange coincidence if a malfunction in Lotti's machinery had made the symbolic fire of the new royal palace in Calderón's text a reality! Or was the fire alarm perhaps the result of Lotti's intent to silence Calderón's critical drama without compromising the legal agreement between the two? It is clear that, from its scenographic conception in praise of Olivares and the Retiro up to its staging with Calderón's veiled criticism of the *Conde Duque, El mayor encanto amor* is produced on the basis of a dialectic between set designer and dramatist, between the deceit of optical illusion and the irony of a dramatic text. A careful reading of Lotti's *memorial,* Calderón's response, his dramatic text, contemporary reactions to the production, and the text of the *auto* from the previous year contradict Brown and Elliott's interpretation, as well as Von Barghahn's, regarding the young Calderón's political posture vis-à-vis the *Conde Duque*'s grandiose architectural project. While the construction of the Retiro and Lotti's marvelous engineering irrevocably modify the concept of his theater, in no way does Calderón sacrifice the originality of his dramatic art, nor does he succumb to political exigency and produce mere poetic fillers for spectacles praising the very power that commissions them.

Notes

This paper, originally intended for publication in Spanish, was read at the 1987 MLA in San Francisco. Hence the lack of references to important works on Calderón's mythological plays published since.

1.   For a more detailed analysis of the role of Judaism in *El nuevo palacio del Retiro,* see Alice Pollin 1973.

2.   In *Elogios al palacio real del Buen Retiro* (Covarrubias y Leyva 1635), several poems contain veiled criticism or expressions of resentment against the sumptuous palace, which Brown and Elliott fail to take into account. It seems strange that Calderón is absent from a volume including Felipe Godínez, Rosete Niño, Pérez de Montalbán, Valdivieso, and Vélez de Guevara. An exceptional call to military action for the king, similar to that of *El mayor encanto amor,* is found in a sonnet by a pseudonymous Arminda:

> En tanto (o Gran Filipo) que en las lides
> Donde estragos seràn las amenazas,
> El hasta [sic] empuñas, y el escudo embraças,
> Y en un trueno Andaluz los vientos mides;

>Campo de Marte, y fábrica de Alcides
>Sea el amfiteatro, en que hoy abrazas
>Imperios que en perfiles de oro enlazas,
>Y en quarteles sus términos divides.
>
>Marcial Palestra sea, y del Tebano
>Alcaçar, sino templo sin segundo,
>A los trofeos del orgullo Hispano:
>
>Bien que será y (en tu valor lo fundo)
>A los que espero de tu Heroica mano
>Bobeda estrecha el ambito del mundo. (n. p.)

As late as 1641, the palace of the Buen Retiro is an object of satire and a symbol for Spain's growing lack of military bravery, as epitomized by the king:

>Si cariños del Retiro,
>Señor, tan apriesa os tornan:
>rey que a retirarse llega
>mucho sus armas desdora;
>No se castiguen soldados,
>aunque se vuelvan a tropas,
>que buen ejemplo les da
>el mismo rey en persona.
>(Egido López, 131)

3.   The production was delayed because of the war with France, the death of the Cardinal Infante in the battle of Tirlemont (*Cartas de algunos pp. . . . ,* 200; 208–24), and Philip IV's displeasure with his favorite for not allowing him to leave the court for the battlefield. Elliott observes that Olivares drafted a document indicating his disposition to support the king's sally to fight in Cataluña (494). He does not clarify whether this political tactic was merely a strategy to dissipate the opposition's strong criticism of his deceitful manipulation of the king, as Hume suggests (293–98). The date for the staging of *El mayor encanto amor* has been the object of a long controversy (Calderón 1851, 385–86; Cotarelo y Mori 1924, 157–66; Shergold 1958). For a definitive conclusion, see my forthcoming "Más sobre el primer y único montaje de *El mayor encanto amor* de Calderón: Confusión jesuítica."

4.   In the first volume of his edition of Calderón's *Comedias,* Hartzenbusch considers this "curioso papel . . . muy a propósito para que se aprecie el trabajo que hizo Calderón sobre la traza del maquinista" (Calderón 1851, 385). Since it is his intention to demonstrate that "el drama de espectáculo" was not staged for midsummer night in 1640,

it is incumbent on him to point out that a mistake was made by "el que puso *al plan de Lotti* el encabezamiento con que está publicado" (my emphasis), basing this opinion perhaps on the *Anales de Madrid* by León Pinelo. There is no doubt that for Hartzenbusch the *memorial* is "la traza del maquinista" and not a Calderonian outline, although he is mistaken about the year of the production.

5.   For the careful attention of both the Conde Duque and the Condesa de Olivares in planning court celebrations for the king and queen, see Hume's commentary on the open-air fêtes that they prepared in June 1631 (230–36).

6.   Without reference specifically to *El mayor encanto amor,* Von Barghahn (89–90) observes that in imitation of the Platonic symbolism of Italian *intermezzi,* English masks personified the queen as "belleza virtuosa ejemplar." By the same token, Isabel de Borbón ruled as a Neoplatonic goddess of love in Lotti's spectacles, according to Von Barghahn.

7.   Brown and Elliott, conscious of the fact that the Retiro palace provided an architectural form for dramatizing the power of the monarchy, entitle their chapters in theatrical terms: "The King on Stage," "The Theater of the Court," "Grooming the Actor," "Behind the Scenes," and—clearly inspired by Calderón—"The Theater of the World."

8.   Brown and Elliott (230) consider this gigantic hermit, which they attribute to Calderón, an obvious reference to the hermitages of the Retiro. The venerable old age of the giant represents the "fundación antigua" of that land as a place of retreat for the Spanish monarchs since Henry IV founded a monastery there between 1460 and 1468 (Caturla, 17–18). In fact, the room next to the old monastery of San Jerónimo, where ever since Philip II the kings retired for mourning (Brown and Elliott, 8–9), was called the "cuarto viejo."

9.   For discussions on the use of gigantic figures, see *Cartas de algunos pp. . . ,* 63; Cotarelo y Mori 1924, 251; Shergold and Varey 1961, xxiv–xxv; Caro Baroja 1949, 198.

10.   Yet another jab at *dueñas* is found in the *Academia burlesca en buen retiro a la Magestad de Philippo Quarto el Grande,* in which *dueñas* and dwarfs were included with political satire, as noted in the following title of a "fantasía política" written, according to Mercedes Etreros, in imitation of Quevedo in the second half of the century: "A vos los serenísimos bufones mis Primos, Mondongas [frecuente apodo para dueñas] Moças de servicio, Damas y Duendes. Guardadamas, Parientes, Dueñas locas de palacio, Jergones asquerosos. Y los de mi consejo, cocineros, Acroyes, Ujieres y otros sabandijos [frequent derogatory term for midgets]. A los hombres malos, Condes, Duques y Marqueses de la putrefacción de España" (1983, 201).

11.   In Covarrubias there are two emblems, apparently an error, in *centuria* 1 with the number 98; the reference is to the first of these, the emblem of a monkey; Covarrubias's

explanation begins: "Siendo la mona abominable, y fea, / Si a caso ve su rostro, en un espejo / Queda de sí pagada, y no desea / Otra gracia, beldad, gala o despejo."

Sloman observes that Calderón establishes a parallel between the monkey and the Ulysses—who also contemplates his image in the water—of *Polifemo y Circe* (written in collaboration with Mira de Amescua and Pérez de Montalbán) (145–47). Closer would be the parallel with the Ulysses of Lotti's *memorial*, who also sees his reflection in the water. Furthermore, the monkey fits in with the carnivalesque element of giants in the *autos*, documented on at least one earlier occasion as a technique used by Lotti (Cotarelo y Mori 1924, 258n. 1; Shergold and Varey 1955, 265). Curiously, after the fall of the *Conde Duque*, the Condesa de Olivares is insulted as a "mona," according to a story that Marañón considers of doubtful authenticity (267). As another example of the association of this insult with the erotic witchcraft analyzed by Caro Baroja (1974, 67), note the following outburst about the *Condesa*'s sister in the second act of Lope's *El galán castrucho:* "Abre la puerta, vejona, / cara de mona. / Abre, hechicera, bruja, / la que estruja / cuantos niños hay de teta: / por alcahueta / once veces azotada / y emplumada."

12.   Pennethorne Hughes observes that political opposition often provided a motive for an accusation of witchcraft (39, 170–71, 176–77). Caro Baroja points out that "al enemigo del poder constituido se la acusa del crimen de magia. . . . La acusación hacia el hombre de personalidad poderosa también puede basarse en que subyuga o domina mediante la magia" (1974, 232).

13.   For the popular criticism about the distracting of the king with the pleasures that Olivares provided for him, see particularly "La cueva de Meliso" (Egido López, 137–72), "sátira menipea, apócrifa, . . . la más copiada . . . de cuantas se escribieron contra Olivares y se atribuyen a Quevedo" (Egido López, 342). Consult also the *pasquín* cited by a Jesuit (*Cartas de algunos pp. . .* , 191): "El rey de Francia está en campaña y en el Retiro el de España" (a letter dated 18 June 1635).

14.   For the typology of Circe as a classic whore and witch, consider Alciato's emblem no. 76 (in a Spanish translation of 1549), which concludes as follows: "Circe es una ramera de gran fama; / Y pierde la razón cualquiera que la ama" (Daly and Callahan, vol. 2, n. p.).

15.   Curiously, in *Elogios al palacio real del Buen Retiro,* there is an engraving of Flora at the end of the first poem and another one following the last poem. Perhaps they are an allusion to the "juegos florales" that, according to Boccaccio, make up the official symbol of the immoral courtesan Flora (68).

16.   For the correspondence of Calderón's linguistic signs and Lotti's visual signs to the palace and the gardens of the Buen Retiro, see my essay "Revisión semiótica del drama mitológico calderoniano" (1987b, 277–78).

17.   Unfortunately there is no documentation about the *mise-en-scène* of this work.

18.   For Jack Sage, Calderón's first mythological drama is no more than "una farsa con algunos momentos musicales de inspiración humanista" (1973, 223). In his note to the English translation of this study, Sage explains that beginning with Lope de Vega dramatists handled the Neoplatonic tradition with "nice irony" (1973, 217); but this does not modify in any way his interpretation of the musical devices in *El mayor encanto amor.* I would like to elaborate somewhat on my earlier brief interpretation of them (1987, 275). That Calderón was particularly interested in the musical aspect of the representation is clear from his own selection of eleven *apariencias* from Lotti's *memorial:* "El carro plateado que ha de venir sobre el agua y la senda para que anden junto a él los que le han de venir acompañando con música" (Rousset, 198) is one of the first scenic details that Calderón mentions.

19.   The Tuscan ambassador in Madrid, Avelardo Medici, describes Lotti in a letter to Andrea Cioli dated 15 April 1627: "Io gia lo havevo squadrato per huomo che nelle sue cose particolari si governava et mutava per via di ragion di stato, *preziandosene molto et dandose ad intendere d'haver habilita di guadagnarsi la grazia d'ognuno, ridendo in bocca e dicendo a lor modo; et poi facendo al suo*" (Whitaker, 62)

20.   Calderón offers other ironic warnings to Olivares through the figure of Pleasure: "En passadas Monarquias / fue de los tiempos costumbre / aver mudanças, ya vimos" (1717, 402a). Calderón's irony can also be perceived in the figure of the man-favorite: "No es posible, que del Rey / Sagradas palabras tuve / de que ha de vivir eterna / esta fabrica, que oy sube / al Sol, porque aunque à la vista / de otras privanças se funde, / no la amenaza el peligro" (402a–b). In *La hija del aire,* there is an echo of this theme with the same words (*privanza-mudanza*) in Nino's affirmation to Menón in the first act: "El sol testigo / será de una privanza / a quien nunca se siga la mudanza."

21.   Hume cites Sir Arthur Hopton with respect to the queen's displeasure with the love affairs that the favorite arranged for the king: "The Queen hath had her little saying to him also, for some opinion she had of some secret pleasures there brought to the King" (283–84). Marañón cites the observation of a Valencian ambassador that "la Reina poco contenta de ver al Rey tan dado a los placeres y de tenerla a ella casi abandonada" (242). But he does not consider these circumstances a cause of the resentment against Olivares (346–48); rather the countess is "la tutela puritana de su camarera mayor" (265–66, 346–48). Brown and Elliott affirm that "Philip's delight in his new palace was apparently not shared by his queen, partly perhaps because of its association with Olivares, whom she did not like" (197). Elliott barely alludes to the friction between the queen and the favorite (112, 264).

22.   Perhaps the apocalyptic poetic images coincided with fireworks or other light and sound effects appropriate to the celebration of Corpus Christi, especially since it was in June, almost Saint John's day or the summer solstice (Shergold and Varey 1955, 286).

23.   In *Elogios al palacio real del Buen Retiro,* there are two curious references to the fire in the Temple of Diana, one in the sonnet of Guillén de Castillo and the following from the final "Panegírico": "Allà en Efeso enmudezca / El Templo, cuyo cadaver / Sacrilego incendio pudo / Arderle en hoguera infame" (n. p.).

According to Caro Baroja, the celebrations of midsummer night in Spain and throughout Europe include the following rituals of fire or destruction: bonfires; the burning of effigies, procession and burning of a hide; and procession and destruction of a figurine (1949, 196–99). Covarrubias explains under "fuego" or "foguera" that "se prenden por regocijo, para purificar el aire como en tiempos de peste, y para execución en autos de fe" (1943, 610–11). "Fuegos" are also lighted "en las atalayas de la costa, para advertir si hay enemigos," adds the *Diccionario de autoridades* (2:805). The destructive sense of fire against the enemy is also observed by Covarrubias in the phrase "a fuego y a sangre . . . la cruel y bárbara determinación del vencedor . . . aunque suelen los príncipes invertir esta clásula en sus mandatos, pocas veces la ejecutan con todo rigor" (1943, 611). A notable antecedent of a symbolic burning of Olivares took place in France a few weeks before the staging of *El mayor encanto:* "Por el suceso que tuvieron los franceses contra el príncipe Tomás [de Saboya en Flandes donde cayeron muchos españoles e italianos] se hicieron en París luminarias en nombre de los seis mil que dicen degollados, y últimamente pintaron en un lienzo grande un español con bigotones muy crecidos y le tiraron con todas las inmundicias de las de acá, y al cabo le quemaron . . ." (*Cartas de algunos pp. . . ,* 210).

24.   Monanni's report dated August 4 (I am grateful to Shirley Whitaker for a copy) compares the "desgracia" of this fire with that of "otra tragicomedia" at Aranjuez, *La gloria de Niquea* by Villamediana, "donde por un incendio corrieron peligros las mismas personas reales." For another fire associated with a political plot, see *El hijo del sol, Faetón* (1662) (Shergold 1967, 325–26; Hernández Araico 1987a, 79).

Works Cited

Academia burlesca en buen retiro a la Magestad de Philippo Quarto el Grande (MS. Madrid 1637). 1952. Edited by A. Pérez Gómez. Valencia: Tipografía Moderna.

Barrera y Leirado, Cayetano Alberto de la. 1860. *Catálogo bibliográfico y biográfico del teatro antiguo español, desde sus orígenes hasta mediados del siglo XVIII.* Madrid: Rivadeneyra.

Benavente, Luis Quiñones de. [1635] 1911. *Las dueñas.* In *Colección de entremeses, loas, bailes, jácaras, mojigangas desde fines del siglo XVI a mediados del XVIII,* edited by Emilio Cotarelo y Mori, vol. 2:566–67. Nueva Biblioteca de Autores Españoles, vol. 18. Madrid: Bailly/Baillière.

Bergman, Hannah E. 1965. *Luis Quiñones de Benavente y sus entremeses.* Madrid: Castalia.

Boccaccio, G. [1494] 1951. *De las ilustres mujeres en romance por Juan Boccaccio.* Zaragoza. Reprint. Madrid: Real Academia Española.

Brown, Jonathan, and John H. Elliott. 1980. *A Palace for a King.* New Haven, Conn.: Yale University Press.

Calderón de la Barca, Pedro. 1717. *El nuevo palacio del Retiro.* In *Autos sacramentales, alegóricos y historiales,* edited by P. de Pando y Mier, 2:386–415. Madrid: M. Ruiz de Murga.

———. 1851. *El mayor encanto amor.* In *Comedias,* edited by Juan Eugenio Hartzenbusch, 1:390–410. Biblioteca de Autores Españoles, vol. 7. Madrid: Rivadeneyra.

———. [1637] 1973. *El mayor encanto amor.* In *Segunda parte de comedias,* edited by D. W. Cruickshank and J. E. Varey, fols. 1–27a. Vol. 5 of *Comedias de Pedro Calderón de la Barca.* London: Gregg International and Tamesis.

Caro Baroja, Julio. 1949. *Análisis de la cultura.* Barcelona: CSIC.

———. 1974. "Arquetipos y modelos en relación con la historia de la brujería." In *Ritos y mitos equívocos,* 215–58. Madrid: Ediciones Istmo.

———. [1944] 1984. "La magia en Castilla durante los siglos XVI y XVII." In *Algunos mitos españoles,* 11–132. Madrid. Reprint in *Del viejo folklore castellano.* Valladolid: Ambito.

Cartas de algunos pp. de la Compañía de Jesús sobre los sucesos de la monarquía entre los años de 1634 y 1638. 1861. Memorial Histórico Español, vol. 13. Madrid: Real Academia de la Historia.

Caturla, María Luisa. 1947. *Pinturas, frondas y fuentes del Buen Retiro.* Madrid: Revista de Occidente.

Cotarelo y Mori, Emilio. 1911. *Don Francisco Rojas Zorrilla: Noticias biográficas y bibliográficas.* Madrid: Revista de Archivos, Bibliotecas y Museos.

———. 1924. *Ensayo sobre la vida y obras de D. Pedro Calderón de la Barca.* Madrid: Revista de Archivos, Bibliotecas y Museos.

Covarrubias Horozco, Sebastián. [1610] 1973. *Emblemas morales.* Edited by Duncan Moir. Menston, England: Scolar Press.

———. [1611; 1674] 1943. *Tesoro de la lengua castellana o española.* Edited by Martín de Riquer. Barcelona: S.A. Horta.

Daly, P. M., and V. W. Callahan, eds. 1985. *Andreas Alciatus.* Emblems in Translation, vol. 2. Toronto: University of Toronto Press.

De Armas, Frederick. 1986. *The Return of Astraea: An Astral-Imperial Myth.* Lexington: University of Kentucky Press.

Egido, Aurora. 1982. *La fábrica de una auto sacramental: "Los encantos de la culpa."* Salamanca: Universidad de Salamanca.

Egido López, Teófanes, comp. 1973. *Sátiras políticas de la España moderna.* Madrid: Alianza.

Elliott, J. H. 1986. *The Count-Duke of Olivares: The Statesman in an Age of Decline.* New Haven, Conn.: Yale University Press.

Elogios al palacio real del Buen Retiro escritos por algunos ingenios de España. [1635] 1949. Edited by A. Pérez Gómez. Valencia: Tipografía Moderna.

Etreros, Mercedes. 1983. *La sátira política en el siglo XVII.* Madrid: FUE.

Gallego, Julián. 1986. *Monstruos, enanos, y bufones en la Corte de los Austrias (A propósito del "Retrato del enano" de Juan Van der Hamen).* Madrid: Amigos Museo del Prado.

Garasa, Delfín Leocadio. 1964. "Circe en la literatura española." *Boletín de la Academia Argentina de letras* 29:227–71.

Hernández Araico, Susana. 1987a. "Mitos, simbolismo y estructura en *Apolo y Climene* y *El hijo del sol, Faetón,*" *Bulletin of Hispanic Studies* 64:77–85.

———. 1987b. "Revisión semiótica del drama mitológico calderoniano," *Bulletin of the Comediantes* 39:273–280.

———. Forthcoming. "Más sobre el primer y único montaje de *El mayor encanto amor* de Calderón: Confusión jesuítica." *Bulletin of Hispanic Studies.*

Hughes, Pennethorne. [1952] 1967. *Witchcraft.* Baltimore, Md.: Penguin Books.

Hume, Martin. 1907. *The Court of Philip IV: Spain in Decadence.* New York: Putnam.

Le Van, John Richard. 1981. "From Tradition to Masterpiece: Circe and Calderón." Ph.D. diss., University of Texas at Austin.

MacCurdy, Raymond R. 1958. *Rojas Zorrilla and the Tragedy.* Albuquerque: University of New Mexico Press.

Marañón, Gregorio. 1945. *El conde-duque de Olivares: La pasión de mandar.* Madrid: Espasa-Calpe.

Moreno Villa, J. 1939. *Locos, enanos, negros y niños palaciegos.* Mexico: Presencia.

Pérez Pastor, Cristóbal. 1905. *Documentos para la biografía de D. Pedro Calderón de la Barca.* Madrid: Fortanet.

Pollin, Alice M. 1973. "El Judaísmo: Figura dramática del auto *El nuevo palacio del Retiro,* de Calderón." *Cuadernos hispanoamericos* 276:579–88.

Rouanet, L. 1899. "Un autographe inédit de Calderón." *Revue hispanique* 6:196–200.

Rousset, Jean. 1954. *La littérature de l'Age Baroque en France: Circe et le Paon.* Paris: José Corti.

Sage, Jack. 1956. "Calderón y la música teatral." *Bulletin hispanique* 58:275–300.

———. 1973. "The Function of Music in the Theatre of Calderón." In *Studies of Calderón's Comedias*, edited by J. E. Varey, 209–230. Vol. 19 of *Comedias de Pedro Calderón de la Barca*. London: Gregg International and Tamesis.

Shergold, N. D. 1958. "The First Performance of Calderón's *El mayor encanto amor.*" *Bulletin of Hispanic Studies* 35:24–27.

———. 1967. *A History of the Spanish Stage*. Oxford: Clarendon Press.

———. 1973. "Documentos sobre Cosme Lotti, escenógrafo de Felipe IV." In *Studia Iberica: Festschrift für Hans Flasche,* edited by K. H. Körner and K. Rühl, 589–602. Bern/Munich: Franz Steiner Verlag.

Shergold, N. D., and J. E. Varey. 1955. "Documentos sobre los autos sacramentales en Madrid hasta 1636." *Revista de la Biblioteca, Archivo y Museo* 24:203–311.

Shergold, N. D., and J. E. Varey, eds. 1961. *Los autos sacramentales en Madrid en la época de Calderón, 1637–1681.* Madrid: Ediciones de Historia, Geografía y Arte.

Sloman, Albert. 1958. *The Dramatic Craftsmanship of Calderón.* Oxford: Dolphin Book Company.

Von Barghahn, Barbara. 1986. *Philip IV and the "Golden House" of the Buen Retiro: In the Tradition of Caesar.* New York: Garland Press.

Whitaker, Shirley B. 1984. "Florentine Opera Comes to Spain: Lope de Vega's *La selva sin amor.*" *Journal of Hispanic Philology* 9:43–66.

Thomas Austin O'Connor

The "Grammar" of Calderonian Honor:
The *Fineza*s of *Fineza contra fineza*

I t has been observed that Calderón's dramatic worlds consist of masculine preoccupations grounded on an understanding and praxis of honor and its demands (Casa). The hierarchical world of the *comedia,* with its representation of the chain of being—descending from God to king, to nobility, and finally to the people—establishes relationships of mutuality that define each person's place and role in the cosmos. In one regard, *La vida es sueño,* as a play set at court, depicts the chaos and violence that threaten Polish society; the obvious cause of this disharmony must be sought at the center of Polish political life, at the court of King Basilio. This ruler shuns political responsibility in favor of private study. If the King is to serve as a model for his people, if the nobility's role and function as a social and political elite are to model proper conduct, then the Polish people are being ill served by their ruling classes. To understand the deep structure of honor in this play and to anticipate a similar but better-defined structure in a less well-known play set at court, *Fineza contra fineza,* we must closely examine how this noble virtue defines both one's place in society and the behavior one is expected to exhibit. In other words, honor is an ideal that seeks to guide and to form personality and character according to its understanding of humankind's place in the hierarchical structure of the universe.

The world of honor recognizes duality in human life and the apparently contradictory demands placed on its inhabitants. Concretely, *Vida* foregrounds vengeance as a noble obligation while its immature or not fully developed understanding of the obligations of *fineza* constrains and limits honor's presence and force. The word *fineza* appears several times in the play, but it is associated in large measure with love intrigues. There are, however, two principal manifestations of *fineza* that may be summarized under the rubric "finezas . . . cortesanas" (497) and "finczas amorosas" (2753).[1] The former define the general conduct expected of the noble person, focusing on the proper regard for others, both men and women. The latter proceed from the dynamics of love for the other sex, and they entail a higher order of action and value that will be explained later.

The Calderonian corpus presents magnificent examples of the duality *honor-fineza*. Let us begin with the honor tragedies and with *El médico de su honra* as a paradigm for them. This play dramatizes the intersection of the private worlds of Gutierre, Leonor, and Mencía with the public world of the palace, typified by King Pedro and Prince Enrique. Although honor in this case is not a positively energizing principle of conduct, as it should be, the reason for its negative value rests with Gutierre's exaggerated practice of, and dedication to, what may be labeled degenerate honor, with Prince Enrique's refusal properly to honor his subjects, and with King Pedro's failure to rule with efficacy the social order under him. The obligations of *fineza,* though acknowledged in the play,[2] have been bracketed in this bleak dramatic world. In other works, such as *Fineza contra fineza,* Calderón draws a dramatic picture of life-giving honor that demonstrates how the public world of the palace may positively influence the private world of the characters when all are attuned to the obligations of *fineza.* Ciriaco Morón Arroyo correctly notes that honor is a secular ethic (69), and Calderón presents it as such. But, by and large, critics of his plays have not recognized the vital and complex nature of his understanding and depiction of honor because they have overlooked the countervailing force found in the practice of *finezas,* a practice that even opposes the call for vengeance.

The code of honor seeks to establish the ideal as norm for human conduct. There are two principal modes or manifestations of the codification of masculine and feminine behavior. The first, an immature and egotistical variety, looks inward, preoccupied with the "yo" and how one is regarded by others. In its most exaggerated form, it views "the other" as a threat to one's social identity, and therefore its recourse to vengeance as curative for real or perceived injury is immediate. The second mode is what I would call "mature" honor in that it is outward looking. This form of honor acknowledges *fineza*'s demand to be of service to the other, for it views the other as a manifestation of the self, as an opportunity to affirm oneself and one's nobility. These two codifications of honor recognize adherence to obligation as the defining essence of the noble soul. The phrase "yo soy quien soy" is its formulaic acknowledgment. Nevertheless, as I have suggested above, how one views the other determines the quality of one's response to the call of duty or obligation. In Calderonian theater, the most positive recognition of the fulfillment of honor's obligations proceeds from the application to one's actions of the term *hidalguía,* defined in the *Autoridades* as follows: "Metaphoricamente vale generosidad, magnanimidád y nobleza de ánimo." Ismenia, a character in *Fineza contra fineza,* denominates her enemy's self-sacrifice for her sake as "¡Qué generosa hidalguía!" (2133b).[3] Honor is not a monolithic structure of defined conduct but rather a complex set of expectations that seeks to harmonize social utility with personal preeminence.

La vida es sueño contains an implicit though undeveloped recognition of the dual nature of *fineza* as a motivational force of human conduct. In the myth play *El mayor encanto amor* (1635), Calderón has Ulises emphasize the distinct sources from which the two classes of *fineza* spring. He states: "que una cosa / es cortesana fineza, / y otra fineza amorosa" (1523a). While Robert ter Horst has addressed the importance of the concept of *fineza* in the later plays, he has not satisfactorily clarified the issue. He opines that *finezas* are principally a moral refinement and adds that

> [s]uch acts of civilized self-sacrifice in connection with the competitions of love at court or in a courtly atmosphere Calderón terms *fineza.* A quite late play, *Fineza contra fineza,* is constructed on an increasing scale of clear though muted sexual sacrifice. *Fineza,* a concept which I despair of rendering into English with even several words, springs from sexual rivalry and transmutes the crassness particularly of the struggle between two men for a woman's body into an elevating, ennobling process powered by the apparent renunciation by one of the competitors. (180)

The dynamics of *fineza* are much broader than ter Horst suggests, for its essence resides in two complementary concepts that the *Academia* and *Autoridades* summarize under *amor* and *benevolencia.* The play *Fineza contra fineza,* like *Encanto* and *Vida,* indicates that the wellspring of *fineza*'s deliberate acceptance of self-sacrifice comes "de nobleza" and "de amor," two different though complementary virtues. Ter Horst has accurately identified the essence of *fineza*'s virtue as the assumption of risk, for, "*obligaciones,* being a commitment to people, involve a very high degree of risk" (158).

To clarify the distinction between "fineza cortesana" and "fineza amorosa," let us examine how and why Calderón considers that *finezas* that proceed from love are of a higher order than those that come from nobility. The acceptance of risk in both cases demonstrates and confirms one's regard for the other. But exposing oneself to love involves greater risk, hence greater pain and suffering, than that incurred from commitment to others in a more altruistic though less personal manner. *Finezas de amor* involve one's soul and one's very being, whereas *finezas de nobleza* are more intellectual and social in character, reflecting a more detached attitude toward life. Joseph Campbell has observed that there are three categories of love, represented by Eros, Agape, and Amor: biological desire, spiritual or altruistic love, and personal love, "the highest spiritual experience" (186). While Eros reflects the body's needs, Agape identifies "other" with "self," thus purifying the love instinct. It is only in Amor, however, that the "personal ideal" (Campbell, 187) takes significant form in the other, which demands a higher axiological commitment than Agape's love of neighbor. Amor establishes harmony, reducing duality (the condition of human existence) to unity, the primordial state of human experience. *Finezas de amor* are greater acts than kindness, the practice of doing good, for they demand that one expose oneself to risk and rejection, open oneself to experience, and accept whatever may result.

In the myth plays of Calderón's late period, such as *Fineza contra fineza,* there is a clear agenda that he proposes for the renovation of Spanish national life. I summarize this agenda as a movement from a politics of privilege, rape, and abuse of others to one of obligation, love, and service to others. Calderón points toward a social structure in which the other is an end in himself or herself, another self, rather than toward one that views the other as a means to self-aggrandizement. Only through a voluntary assumption of honor's ideals as manifested in the two forms of *fineza* can the Spanish nobility justify itself and fulfill its primarily social responsibility in the existing hierarchical order. In this agenda, self-sacrifice, the recognition and acceptance of risk as an opportunity for service, becomes the hallmark of nobility. In this manner, the elite must lead the way to a better society by modeling the conduct that will realize this goal. Adherence to the demands of *fineza* transforms both male and female personality and, in so doing, heals a society rent by social, political, and personal strife. Forgiveness of injury is not a sign of weakness but rather the proof of one's true nobility of soul.

Marriage is not principally an economic, dynastic, or social transaction; it is a personal fulfillment that preserves society.

One way of approaching Calderón's duality of vision demands that we integrate the separate manifestations of honor and *fineza* into his broader social agenda. His depiction of degenerate honor, as seen in *El médico de su honra,* rests upon a preoccupation with *gusto* as the motivating principle of personal and social existence. *Gusto* is grounded on a politics of privilege, rape, and dehumanization of the other. It is egotistical and socially destructive. The dialectic in operation in his theater opposes the ideals of honor, the obligations of *fineza,* to the egotistical and degenerate praxis of honor as a private concern. The acceptance of risk for the other's sake focuses on and finally unmasks the deadly character of *gusto.* Although this view of the nature and significance of human experience informs in some manner all of Calderonian drama, it evolved over the dramatist's lifetime. Its most pristine manifestations are found in two myth plays, *Amado y aborrecido* and *Fineza contra fineza.* We shall now turn our attention to this latter work, in which the nature and value of *fineza* become both dramatic theme and ideological statement.

Fineza contra fineza celebrates pardon and forgiveness over vengeance and retribution, an apparent denial of one of honor's fundamental tenets. The harmony of the other and the "yo" is symbolized in the concluding marriages, whose wholeness transcends duality through the exaltation of oneness in body and soul. Calderón is not an old man yearning for some resolution of human conflict but a serious dramatist who attempts to make palpable his insight into the nature and meaning of human experience. Although *Fineza contra fineza* is an optimistic play, it does not ignore that suffering is the characteristic that defines our being-in-the-world, and only through a willing embrace of that suffering do we humans transcend finitude.

The plot of *Fineza contra fineza* is relatively straightforward, but it needs to be recounted here because few scholars are familiar with it. Anfión, the king of Chipre and son of Acteón, has invaded and conquered Tesalia, a land dedicated to Diana. To avenge his father's death at Diana's hands, he plans on laying waste to the country, but, having been importuned by Diana's nymphs to show mercy, he relents on condition that they and their temple be rededicated to Venus.

Ismenia appears to lead this reorientation of life from disdain to love, while Doris, who loves Tesalia's defeated general, Celauro, is incorrectly judged to be a recidivist nymph continuing to champion Diana's cause. After much intrigue involving love, mistaken identity, and the call to vengeance, the action focuses on a statue of Venus that has disappeared from Diana's erstwhile temple. Although Celauro discovers that Ismenia removed the effigy, as a true nobleman—a quality demonstrated repeatedly throughout the play—he promises to guard her secret and to protect her. When lots are drawn and Doris is selected by chance to die for Ismenia's crime, Celauro is placed in a most difficult situation that tests the quality of his nobility. How can he permit that his beloved Doris die for Ismenia's crime? How can he denounce Ismenia, whom he has sworn to protect? This ingenuous and admirable character declares himself guilty of the crime. This occasions a series of self-denunciations, which accounts for the play's title. Doris, imitating her lover's noble renunciation, declares to Anfión that she removed the statue to avenge Diana's injury. With two "guilty" parties before him, Anfión declares that the one to hand over the statue will die and save the other. When neither can do this, he condemns both to die. At this point, Ismenia confesses her crime and is sentenced to death. Cupido then appears from the trapdoor and, insisting on the axiological differences between *fineza de amor* and *fineza de noble,* condemns Ismenia in Venus's name. At the conclusion, Anfión, declaring his motivation to be a *fineza de amor,* pardons Ismenia, who willingly accepts him as her husband. The victorious general and the vengeance-driven nymph recognize the superior nobility of Celauro and Doris, and their desire to emulate the other couple's self-sacrifices leads to the play's final marriages, symbolically curative of personal disharmony and prophylactic of societal destruction.

I have written elsewhere at length about a fundamental structure of Calderonian dramaturgy that I label "the offense-vengeance mechanism." To be human is to be fallible, and the legacy of that fallibility is the inevitable suffering that characterizes human existence and experience. That an injury demands retribution forms an integral part of the codification of honor's obligations and manifests itself throughout *Fineza.* Anfión's avowed purpose in the invasion of Tesalia was to avenge his father's death by the not so innocent and chaste Diana. Her love affair with Endimión suggests to Anfión that enmity toward Chipre was the motive of her vengeance and not a just retribution for error. This political leader accepts vengeance as a proper and necessary course of action. Ismenia, too, is ruled by a desire to avenge her brother's death at Celauro's hands. Both Anfión and Ismenia accept honor's demands at face value, and thus their lives are stalked by, and dedicated to, death. Celauro and Doris, however, represent a higher order of life and a more profound understanding of honor's role in guiding human conduct. They include or allow room for compassion, "which is the healing principle that makes life possible" (Campbell, 112). Many Calderonian plays depict the cycle of violence and death that vengeance exacts, but there are many others, such as *Ni Amor se libra de amor, La estatua de Prometeo,* and *Fineza contra fineza,* which dramatize that only compassion and forgiveness can control this pernicious human legacy.

Fineza contra fineza links forgiveness to the obligations of honor as understood through *fineza.* As Celauro ponders the implications of Anfión's possible pardon of Doris, he says: "es fuerza también que haga / mérito de la fineza / que ha de hacer en perdonarla" (2127b). One reason he fears this act of clemency is that the performance of a *fineza* has markedly social and personal ramifications. When Celauro acknowledges Anfión as "rey piadoso" and "invicto dueño," the latter replies: "A darme por entendido / de esas dos deudas me atrevo, / en fe de que las finezas / logren su agradecimiento" (2109a). The performance of *finezas* leads to their recognition by others and to the incurrence on their part of a debt of gratitude. In our play, Calderón lays bare through dramatization the dynamics of *finezas* and their social efficacy and power. While acknowledgment of noble acts is a passive response, a higher and more perfect response is the emulation of that noble conduct. Once Celauro denounces himself, Ismenia *recognizes* his *fineza:* "¡Qué generosa hidalguía!" (2133b). But Doris, with her more perfect response, sacrifices herself, declaring: "haya pues en mi nobleza / *fineza contra fineza*" (2134a).

Once Doris and Celauro denounce themselves, Ismenia realizes that her interior sense of nobility is being challenged by their *finezas.* Her passive recognition of them is no longer adequate, for she now finds herself "en tan noble competencia" (2135a). She responds according to her inherent noble self-image, her *amor propio:* "Pues vea / el mundo que entre Celauro / y Doris, también Ismenia / tiene valor para hacer / fineza contra fineza" (2135a). It is precisely the virtue of valor that encourages her to dare great deeds regardless of the danger involved, and valor is a characteristic of true nobility. What these *finezas contra finezas* reveal is more than their social power, for they also contain properties that transform personality and character. Joseph Campbell places great emphasis on compassion, for it "is the awakening of the heart from bestial self-interest to humanity" (160). Celauro and Doris were already awakened to their full humanity because they had discovered it in their love for one another. Ismenia, on the other hand, only responds out of social motivation to equal these characters' greatness of soul and nobility of spirit. Nevertheless, the power of *fineza* to transform and to perfect a fallible mortal is just now beginning to take effect in her heart and soul.

Cupido arrives to the accompaniment of music and song that declare: "Finezas contra finezas, / mas la madre de Amor, / que las castiga, las premia" (2136b). He subsequently acknowledges Celauro's and Doris's "tan amante competencia" (2136b) and, granting them life, condemns Ismenia to death for her sacrilege. His reasons are clear: "con que Ismenia, / pues su fineza no fue / de amor, sino de nobleza, / sea la víctima que ellos / habían de ser" (2136b). Although Cupido affirms love's superiority over nobility, he continues to be motivated by the latter's exigency of vengeance and punishment rather than by the former's call to forgiveness and life. At this point, Anfión intervenes and declares Ismenia absolved of guilt due to his *fineza de amor,* in other words, his pardon of her sacrilegious act of having removed Venus's effigy. Anfión's *fineza* of pardon translates an intellectual acknowledgment of love's superiority into a life-conferring reality for him and Ismenia. Love is of a higher order than honor, and therefore its fruits are of a higher value than those of honor. As a conqueror seeking to establish Venus's cult of love in Diana's realm of disdain, he himself was not fully aware of the scope and reach of love's powers. His *fineza* makes palpable the superiority of Venus's cult over that of Diana and justifies the substitution.

Anfión utilizes a significant formulaic expression in Calderonian theater to affirm the motivation for his pardon of Ismenia: "Ya es triunfo de amor vencerme / yo a mí mismo" (2137a). *Vencerse a sí mismo* signals the domination of self-interest, of *gusto,* in favor of a higher value, the acceptance of risk, the acceptance of full humanity as symbolized in his love for Ismenia. Both Ismenia and Anfión have to progress from their immature, yet noble, understanding of honor as an obligation that may at times require vengeance to that held by Celauro and Doris. Curiously, even Cupido needs to mature in his understanding of the very values he professes to uphold and to disseminate. Ultimately all the characters acknowledge love's superiority over honor in informing and guiding human affairs.

At this point, we can speak about the "grammar" of Calderonian honor. Each noble person is obligated to affirm his or her nobility through acts that are socially oriented. The first rule recognizes that the self, the "yo," lives in an imperfect world where fallible people may impugn or tarnish one's self-image and the opinion others have of it. The maxim is "protect yourself." This understanding of honor is mechanical, for it states categorically that any offensive act, any injury to the person, must be quickly avenged. But there are rules governing the application of vengeance to concrete and particular circumstances. For instance, even the gods are restrained by rules of conduct for the taking of vengeance. In *Celos, aun del aire, matan,* Diana reveals her baseness when she seeks to pursue vengeance beyond the death of the offending party and when she excessively gloats over vengeance executed. In other words, the rule of vengeance, the shedding of blood (the symbol of life's force), is truly mechanical in that it is a prescribed response to some offending behavior on the part of another. This code, however, seeks to limit the damage and to prevent it from infecting the entire body politic. The second rule recognizes the other as forming society and living in a relational mode to the "yo." The other is, moreover, not a potential threat to nobility but rather an opportunity to demonstrate it. The other is part of oneself, part of the body politic. The maxim is: "serve others,"[4] be of service to the community, demonstrate through external acts the quality of one's soul, the foundation of all honor. This form of honor is transformational in that it seeks to make the person into its image. That is why the voluntary acceptance of risk is the hallmark of all nobility, for it exposes the interior person and his or her self-image to exterior testing and confirmation. It is in fact the most demanding requirement of being noble. These exteriorizations may be classified into *finezas de noble,* a consciousness of class obligation, and *finezas de amor,* a consciousness of personal obligation. *Finezas cortesanas* or *de noble* energize social consciousness and responsibility by placing the power to do good in the hands of those living in that society. *Fineza* here is *social* power. *Finezas amorosas* or *de amor* energize personal awareness and responsibility by relating the power to do good to a particular individual, which allows one to mediate the "I-Thou" relationship. This becomes *personal* power in the true sense of pertaining to the person. What it permits us to see is that what one does to and for others one does to and for oneself. In loving another, one's capacity to love multiplies beyond measure. Celauro demonstrates this truth not only in his love of Doris but more clearly in his voluntary self-sacrifice for Ismenia. *Personal* power humanizes the social being.

Calderón's dramatic worlds reveal these deep structures of noble conduct and the consequences of adhering to a particular understanding and practice of honor's obligations. The elementary conception of honor maintains the duality of "yo-el otro" and thus affirms the imperfection of life divided into a progressive series of oppositions such as good-evil, male-female, night-day, light-dark, etc. Honor itself participates in this characteristic opposition of human existence and experience, but its term is not only *villanía* but, on a higher plane, *fineza*. *Fineza* assures the noble person that he or she and the other are bound together in a social or relational manner that intimates unity. The *finezas de noble* urge the noble person to accept risk for the other's sake, to treat the other as a self, as oneself. But *finezas de amor,* because they demand the ultimate risk of exposure not only of one's noble self-image but of one's very being to rejection and suffering, do not intimate unity in place of duality and opposition but rather affirm personal wholeness and integrity.

Although the notions of *fineza* appear early in Calderonian drama, in *Vida, Médico, Los tres mayores prodigios,* and *Encanto,* for example, it is not until the 1650s and afterwards that they begin to play a significant role in his understanding of human life and experience and his dramatization of them. There is a definite evolution and development of *fineza*'s importance in humanizing individuals subject to the codifications of human perception, understanding, and action, especially through honor. What Calderón left to us as a dramatic and vital legacy was the realization not just that living in time and space signals humankind's condemnation to imperfection, duality, and opposition, but also that it offers us the opportunity to transcend these limitations of human experience. His greatness as an artist rests securely on the profundity of his vision and understanding of human life and of its ability to move us to action.

Notes

1.   See also 512, 1750, 1761, and 1929 for other examples of *finezas amorosas* and 852 and 2832 for those of *finezas cortesanas.*

2.   See 2:161–70; 662–64.

3.   All references to the Valbuena Briones edition of the *Obras completas* are by page and column, and when other plays are cited in this manner, they proceed from this edition.

4.   For a Christian perspective on this issue, see Mark 10:42–45.

Works Consulted

Calderón de la Barca, Pedro. 1965. *El médico de su honra.* In *Dramas de honor.* Edited by Angel Valbuena Briones, 2:11–118. Madrid: Espasa-Calpe.

————. 1969. *Fineza contra fineza.* In *Obras completas.* Edited by Angel Valbuena Briones, 1:2099–2137. Madrid: Aguilar.

————. 1985. *La vida es sueño.* In *Diez comedias del Siglo de Oro.* Edited by José Martel and Hymen Alpen; revised by Leonard Mades, 607–99. Prospect Heights, Ill.: Waveland Press.

Campbell, Joseph, with Bill Moyers. 1988. *The Power of Myth.* Edited by Betty Sue Flowers. New York: Doubleday.

Casa, Frank P. 1977. "Honor and the Wife-Killers of Calderón." *Bulletin of the Comediantes* 29:6–23.

Diccionario de autoridades. [1726–39] 1969. Madrid: Gredos.

Morón Arroyo, Ciriaco. 1982. *Calderón: Pensamiento y teatro.* Santander: Sociedad Menéndez Pelayo.

O'Connor, Thomas Austin. 1988. *Myth and Mythology in the Theater of Pedro Calderón de la Barca.* San Antonio, Tex.: Trinity University Press.

Ter Horst, Robert. 1982. *Calderón: The Secular Plays.* Lexington: University Press of Kentucky.

Teresa S. Soufas

María de Zayas's (Un)Conventional Play,

La traición en la amistad

... the plots of women's literature are not about "life" and solutions in any therapeutic sense, nor should they be. They are about the plots of literature itself, about the constraints the maxim places on rendering a female life in fiction.—Nancy K. Miller

... pues ni comedia se representa, ni libros se imprime que no sea todo en ofensa de las mujeres, sin que se reserve ninguna.—María de Zayas y Sotomayor

In her only play, *La traición en la amistad,* María de Zayas offers dialectical responses to established theatrical conventions of seventeenth-century Spain.[1] Examining and challenging some of the dramatic models developed and popularized by the predominantly male writers and viewers of Golden Age plays, Zayas offers her critique of these categories through a focus on the courtship conventions of the noble class, a favorite subject for theatrical depiction in Golden Age Spain. In so doing, she scrutinizes both the *comedia* as an art form and the values of the society represented and addressed by the performers on stage. The present study of Zayas's play proceeds from a point of view shared by such feminist critics as Jean Kennard and Lillian Robinson, who are concerned with the way literary conventions are imposed by the ideology and beliefs of the contemporary society that celebrates them. This reading of *La traición en la amistad* is premised upon a feminist emphasis "on the fact of literature as a social institution, embedded not only within its own literary traditions but also within the particular physical and mental artifacts of the society from which it comes" (Kolodny 1985, 147).

My focus is upon the ways in which Zayas depicts the disorder of the community that the *comedia* reflects and upon her insistence on the inaccessibility of transcendence for the *comedia*'s female characters as they are regularly portrayed. Zayas thus begins by challenging the stereotypical gendering of the *dramatis personae*. Her characterization of Fenisa, who has been described as a female Don Juan,[2] is at the center of this undermining of conventions. Through Fenisa, Zayas presents to her public an example of the social, political, and literary intolerance for a woman or her fictional representation who does not fulfill the conventions or "maxims" of the dominant cultural ideology. Some of Nancy Miller's observations about *La Princesse de Clèves* are applicable to Zayas's dramatic development of Fenisa: "To build a narrative around a character whose behavior is deliberately idiopathic . . . is not merely to create a puzzling fiction but to fly in the face of a certain ideology (of the text and its context); to violate a grammar of motives that describes while prescribing."[3]

In addition, by incorporating into her drama standard models of *comedia* women, Zayas dramatizes the rejection of her idiopathic character by the proponents of the prevailing cultural, social, and literary codes, who are as limited by them as Fenisa is at the end of the play. None of the depicted women is shown triumphant within the system of maxims and literary conventions that Zayas critiques—the majority because they conform to the literary expectations, and Fenisa because the standards of the textual world she inhabits will not accept her or provide her with satisfactory alternatives. By grounding her play squarely within the conventional system, Zayas thus suggests the impossibility of being or becoming an admirable character of either sex, given the demands for conformity to an inadmirable model. She communicates a cynical regard for the literary stereotypes that make the process of falling in love and devoting oneself to a beloved simply part of a predictable, cyclical game of insincerity and trickery whose end is the standard pairings of often mismatched couples in the last act.

Zayas's literary reputation among twentieth-century scholars is as the author of collections of short prose pieces, but evidence afforded by her contemporary Juan Pérez de Montalbán indicates that her seventeenth-century audience recognized her more limited theatrical contribution: "Décima musa de nuestro siglo, ha escrito á los certámenes con grande acierto; tiene acabada una comedia de excelentes coplas, y un libro para dar á la estampa, en prosa y verso, de ocho novelas ejemplares."[4] In this century, Agustín G. de Amezúa discusses the play in his "Prólogo" to the *Novelas amorosas y ejemplares de doña María de Zayas y Sotomayor*, saying:

> *La traición en la amistad* . . . es una de tantas piezas de enredo como entonces se llevaban a la escena; solamente que esta vez, y contra los impulsos defensivos femeninos de doña María, los enredos no parten del hombre, sino de una mujer, que, por ambiciosa en amores, se queda a la postre compuesta y sin novio. . . . Lo mejor de ella es la versificación, suelta y graciosa; . . . La

comedia, a creer lo que nos refiere Montalbán, estuvo precedida de cierta fama, aunque no sepamos si, al representarse, alcanzó o no el buen éxito que de ella se esperaba.[5]

Amezúa's critical lens permits him elsewhere only a view of Zayas in relation to her male contemporaries: "Toda la comedia tiene el corte de las de Lope, a quien doña María imita francamente: tanto era entonces el señorío drámatico del Fénix" (xl).[6] Such a bias is also upheld by Irma Vasileski, who opines: "Dentro del panorama general del teatro del Siglo de Oro, no nos parece posible incluir a María de Zayas en un lugar eminente por la razón mencionada de que no conocemos muchos de sus dramas, y sobre todo si consideramos las grandes figuras de dramaturgos contemporáneos suyos con quienes tendríamos que compararla" (33).[7]

By approaching *La traición en la amistad,* however, as a work that reveals its author's questioning of the social and literary conventions upheld by the male-dominated culture and dramatic circles in which she had to write and publish, one can appreciate this play's uniqueness in Zayas's production. This very uniqueness is indicative of her pessimism over the constraints of convention as well as of the admittedly limited access for women to the theatrical world, whether as playwright, spectator, or disparaged performer. This play can, moreover, be considered as a complement to Zayas's *novelas,* whose content challenges literary and social stereotypes and whose structure is developed through a frame tale about young nobles begun in the first published collection and continued in the second work (now known, respectively, as *Novelas amorosas y ejemplares* and *Parte segunda del sarao y entretenimiento honesto [Desengaños amorosos]*). Costumed decoratively, these characters take turns telling stories to an audience of friends in a decidedly theatrical manner.

The plot of *La traición en la amistad* involves a mixture of the components in the love intrigues so often dramatized in *capa y espada* works. The initial dilemmas faced by each of the principal characters result from their having fallen in love with someone who does not, at least as the play begins, return that affection.[8] Marcia, for instance, has continually rejected Gerardo, her suitor of seven years, and is currently attracted by Liseo. This man is unfaithful to Laura, who nevertheless hopes to force him to honor an earlier promise of marriage. Marcia's cousin Belisa loves Juan, but he, like Liseo, Lauro, and other unnamed noblemen referred to in passing, openly woos Fenisa. The plot is thus replete with elements typical of numerous *comedias*—the court setting, an honor dilemma, a persistent though rejected courtly lover, secret liaisons, deceits, role-playing, seductions, jealousy—all part of the complicated courting practices of the noble classes that threaten or effect unhappiness or even disaster for many women (and some men as well) in numerous Golden Age plays.

Though it is obvious that Fenisa is a target for censure by the characters in the play because of her flirtations with many suitors and her competition with her female friends for this attention, she merely perpetuates the amorous games that the other characters play on a temporary basis, as befits convention. Their court-ships also involve numerous betrayals, and rather than serving as the primary vehicle for Zayas's denouncement of a woman's untrustworthy behavior and atti-tude concerning her women friends, Fenisa serves as the central component in the playwright's condemnation of the whole system of courtship as regularly depicted in the *comedia.*[9]

In a short soliloquy in act 1, Fenisa laments her competition with Marcia: "¿dónde, voluntad, caminas / contra Marcia, tras Liseo?";[10] later she reiterates: "¿no miras que vas perdida? / el amor y la amistad / furiosos golpes se tiran" before affirming: "cayó el amistad en tierra / y amor victoria apellida" (591). Such declarations seem to contrast with Marcia's reaction when she learns that Laura has been betrayed and abandoned by Liseo: "mas, Laura hermosa, sa-biendo / que te tiene obligación / desde aquí de amarle dejo" (600). Marcia's response here is more appropriately understood as motivated by Laura's honor predicament rather than specifically by feelings of friendship and loyalty to this woman. She does not necessarily best the questionable ethics of Fenisa, since she is called upon to respond to different information. The first evidence that Fenisa knows of Liseo's relationship with Laura, in fact, comes in act 2, when he men-tions to her that—as he has been given to understand—Laura will enter a convent ("del mundo engañoso escapa" [604]). Fenisa thus would seem to consider her-self in competition only with Marcia, who, like herself, is an eligible candidate for premarital courtship.

Although some of the criticism heaped upon Fenisa results from what is said to be *her* betrayal of friends, we must ask what *their* attitude and behavior toward her are. The only woman who attempts to counsel Fenisa or urge her to take another course of action is her maid Julia. The other noblewomen merely talk about her, but none speaks to her directly. Marcia, Belisa, and Laura enact the

stereotypes of Golden Age love intrigues without ever breaking with literary convention. All three move in reaction to what is done to them and move progressively
closer to the standard wedding in the final scene instead of envisioning another
possibility for action or interaction. The new model provided by Fenisa is, however, unacceptable for two reasons: at the moral level because of her selfish attitudes and demeanor; and theatrically because, as a female character (who is
supposed to be seen publicly with only one suitor and to welcome his attention
alone), she does not supersede the conventional realm in which she is ultimately
portrayed as trapped. From the fixed categorical system, Fenisa thus chooses a
well-known masculine model whose tenets allow for greater freedom to indulge
in multiple amorous relationships merely as diversions and with relative impu-
nity: "Hombres, así vuestros engaños vengo; / guardémonos de necias que no
saben, / aunque más su firmeza menoscaben, / entretenerse como me entre-
tengo" (605).[11]

The use of the word *amistad* in the title and throughout the play suggests an
additional level of Zayas's examination of the conventions. The definition of this
term in the *Diccionario de autoridades* is significant, for along with the primary
meaning ("amór, benevoléncia y confianza recíproca"), there is also listed the
following: "Vale tambien lo mismo que Amancebamiento" (270). *Amigarse* is
also described as "Lo mismo que Amancebarse," and *amigo* as "[s]ignifica tambien
el que vive amancebádo" (269). Likewise, *amigado* is "Lo própio que amancebádo: y assi esta voz amigado ordinariamente se toma en mala parte, y se entiende
por el que está enlazado en alguna torpe amistád" (269). Such an emphasis cannot be overlooked in Zayas's play. In Fenisa's conversation with Liseo in act 2,
for example, the two discuss his involvement with Marcia and the supposedly
cloistered Laura, after which Fenisa asks "¿Somos amigos?" His answer suggests
the ambiguous quality of the term that they bandy about: "¿Pues no?" (605). In a
subsequent scene, Fenisa speaks with Gerardo, who seeks her help in his hereto-
fore unsuccessful suit with Marcia. Requesting that she serve as his intermediary
and appealing to her as a friend of Marcia—"pues su amiga eres" (606)—he thus
hints at the two meanings of the word. Fenisa answers his petition with a seductive speech that reinforces the disjuncture of the two definitions of *amistad:* "yo
te quiero, señor mío; / ¿por qué, mi bien, no pretendes / olvidarla?" (606). Gerardo's
rejection of her proposition includes the charge that she represents "amiga destos
tiempos" (606). As the scene ends, Fenisa summarizes the whole dramatized situ-

ation when she declares to her maid: "¡Ay, Lucía, / enredo notable es éste! / ¡Traición en tanta amistad!" (606).

Both Laura's predicament and Marcia's decision to sacrifice her feelings for Liseo are typical of the emotional turmoil that women characters experience as consequences of the courtship practices in which they all participate. Belisa and Laura commiserate over their similar circumstances: about Laura's honor dilemma Belisa asserts, "pierdo / el juicio, imaginando / tal traición"; and, upon learning of Juan's inconstancy, Laura exclaims to her new friend, "¡Ay cielo! / ¿también tú estás agraviada?" (601). Laura also informs Marcia of Fenisa's and Liseo's relationship: "que este cruel lisonjero / si a mi me desprecia, á ti / te engaña, pues sé por cierto / que ama á Fenisa tu amiga / que á ti te engaña cumpliendo / con traiciones" (600).

The distress the three women articulate in this scene is thus provoked not only by Fenisa's behavior but also by the deceptions perpetrated by the male suitors. Their own adherence to misogynistic stereotypes, however, leads them to blame Fenisa more heavily than Liseo for their unhappiness. Marcia assures Laura that "que ya he pensado el remedio / tal que he de dar á Fenisa / lo que merece su intento" (600); Belisa likewise blames Fenisa for Juan's fickleness: "y que si puedo / le he de quitar á don Juan, / mi antiguo y querido dueño, / que también le persuadió / á que no me viese" (601).[12]

The above conversation ends with Laura's statement: "La traición en la amistad / puede llamarse este cuento" (601), which brings the title within the play's text and symbolizes further the dissolution of the division between the internally represented microcosm and the external macrocosmic realm beyond the enacted text, to which the *comedia* normally looks for its transcendent message. The figures that Zayas depicts in *La traición en la amistad* are, in effect, caught in the circular space of the court and in the customs and consequences of courtship in which they engage. The female characters in this play, moreover, do not escape from this ambiance as do the noble women of the frame narrative of her *novelas*. These latter characters renounce the courtly secular realm and choose to enter the female community of the convent, where they are free from the calumny and abuse of men and the constraints upon their own educational and personal development that social codes impose.[13]

Though the courtships that Zayas portrays in *La traición en la amistad* do progress toward marriage for three of the noble couples, just as in some other

Golden Age plays (Ruiz de Alarcón's *La verdad sospechosa* and Calderón's *No hay cosa como callar* are examples), this so-called remedy of disorder does not bring together two completely happy individuals in any of the pairings. Marcia, for instance, sacrifices any possible relationship with Liseo for Laura's sake, and she finally accepts Gerardo as her fiancé after having rejected him for seven years. Hers is an intellectual decision to promise herself to him, and although she does profess her affection for him in later passages, she explains to Belisa her reasons for changing her mind: "Porque viendo, Belisa, los engaños / de los hombres de ahora . . . / aposento a Gerardo" (607). The low esteem in which Marcia holds not only Liseo but "los hombres de ahora" collectively is the catalyst for her present reversal of attitude toward Gerardo. In the process, however, she pronounces what Zayas elsewhere presents as a mistaken attitude—that is, directing the sort of stereotypical calumny usually reserved for women to men.[14] Marcia thus reiterates her own dependence on the fixed quality of the categories that she helps to represent in the dramatized society.

Gerardo, of course, gains the partner of his choice, but his union with Marcia stands for the suspected reality—sensual and emotional—behind the courtly love tradition; that is, the faithful and long-suffering male's success in winning the desired but disdainful woman leaves questions unanswered about the woman's fulfillment. Like Cervantes's Marcela, Marcia voices the woman's response to the complaints aimed at her because she does not reciprocate a devotion she never sought to inspire.[15] The romantic love she has felt for Liseo is apparently not what she feels for Gerardo; she has simply chosen a safe relationship with a man whom she believes she can trust. This seems to be the most hopeful choice that Zayas offers any of her stereotypical female characters in *La traición en la amistad,* thanks to the rampant misconduct and skewed ethical system in which they interact.[16]

Liseo represents a particularly abusive practitioner of the courtship values and their double standard. In one conversation between him and his servant, León, the faithless nobleman articulates sentiments reminiscent of other despicable males of Golden Age drama (Tirso's Don Juan in *El burlador de Sevilla,* Calderón's Don Juan in *No hay cosa como callar,* and Lope's Comendador de Calatrava in *Fuenteovejuna,* for example). Recounting his treatment and feelings for the women with whom he is involved, he says: "Es Marcia de mi amor prenda querida / y Fenisa adorada en tal manera, / que está mi voluntad loca y perdida. / Laura ya no es mujer, es una fiera; / Marcia es un ángel; mi Fenisa diosa; / éstas vivan, León, y Laura muera" (603). Rejecting Laura in these cruel terms, he goes on to explain in greater detail his intentions regarding Marcia and Fenisa. Of the latter, he says: "León, si yo á Fenisa galanteo, / es con engaños, burlas y mentiras, / no más de por cumplir con mi deseo" (803). With regard to Marcia, however, he claims: "á sola Marcia mi nobleza aspira; / ella ha de ser mi esposa, que Fenisa / es burla" (603). The audience, nevertheless, is provided further information about the basis of Liseo's process of choosing his favorite from among these women. In the list of Marcia's attributes, he cites: "hermosura y perfecciones raras: / su hacienda, su nobleza, su hermosura, / su raro entendimiento" (603). Physical beauty and financial worth are the first recalled, and given his consistently self-serving attitude, his speech further suggests his practical rather than emotional attachment to this woman.

Fenisa's repeated statements about her many suitors are also revealing in their callous and/or frivolous sentiments. At one point, for example, she says to her maid Lucía: "diez amantes me adoran, y yo á todos / los adoro, los quiero, los estimo, / y todos juntos en mi alma caben, / aunque Liseo como rey preside" (605). Through such statements, Fenisa and Liseo expose the faulty nature of the aristocracy's concept of love. The dichotomous relationship between *amor* and *amistad* that Fenisa ponders in her early soliloquy, then, not only articulates the problems for friends who are simultaneously attracted to the same romantic partner; it also makes clear the questionable nature of declared romantic devotion in the intrigues and love affairs (the *amistad*) as regularly depicted on the seventeenth-century stage. Indeed, the sincerity of Fenisa and Liseo is certainly suspect, but it cannot be forgotten that all the other characters continuously interact with them in game playing and inconstancy. Juan is the first *galán* to appear on stage with Fenisa and does so in a scene in which he tries to calm her professed jealousy, wooing her just as Liseo and Lauro do later. Gerardo does not surrender to Fenisa's amorous advances, but his efforts to engage her services as a Celestinesque go-between cannot help but imply the potential disaster in such a proposition, based as it is on the obvious literary antecedents in Rojas's famous novel or Lope's *El caballero de Olmedo*. Liseo's charming deceptions likewise attract three of the four female principals.

The arrangement of conversations that Zayas organizes in the play also supports her disapproving depictions of the theatrical courtships at court. The discussion between Juan and Fenisa, in which she admits in an aside, "Aunque á don Juan digo amores / el alma en Liseo está," is based on his protestations of jealousy. Sensing her coolness toward him ("tú pagas mal / mi amor"), he merely responds to her role-playing technique. She hopes to keep him unbalanced and to gain needed information about Liseo ("[Aparte] 'Desta manera le engaño'" [592]). This same sort of language is soon imitated in Juan's conversation with the jealous Belisa, who labels as traitorous both Juan and his treatment of her (601). At this point, Juan continues to evince his propensity to emotional treason through a statement about Fenisa: "accidente fué el querer / á esa mujer" (602). This whole reversal of stated devotion is presumably a parallel of his disregard for Belisa during his courtship of Fenisa. Very soon he promises renewed devotion to Belisa with the telling request, "dame de amiga la mano" (602).

In addition, immediately after Juan's conversation with Fenisa in act 1, Zayas arranges a scene in which Liseo speaks with his servant, León. The latter offers his own crude remarks about relations with the opposite sex—the size and measurements of the most desirable women, for instance, and, in particular, the availability of "fregoncillas cortesanas" and his preference for "las fregoncillas que estos años / en la Corte se usan" (593). León's insistence upon the futility of chastity, his admiration of the unchaste woman ("que si fuera / mujer, que había de ser tan agradable / que no había de llamarme naide, esquiva"), and the anecdotes he uses to convince his master about the validity of his observations heighten the irony of the comparison of his lower-class attitudes with those of the noble class he serves (593).[17] León's stories and remarks further strengthen the negativity of Zayas's depiction of the entire society and its social and literary common-places. Later, when Fenisa and Liseo engage in mutually jealous and seductive banter—reminiscent of their respective conversations with the other principals—León constantly interjects his own comic complaints about the loss of his remaining two teeth due to a slap from Liseo. The ridiculous quality of the *gracioso*'s statements, coming as they do between those of the courting nobles, reduces the seriousness of what these two say (604). The scene ends with Fenisa's and Liseo's arrangement of a tryst in the "prado" in, significantly, the courtly setting of "la huerta del Duque," where she also plans to meet other suitors that same night (605).

As is the case in many *comedias,* dishonesty has caused the problems, but it is also the means employed by the characters to effect the conventional resolution. In the process, trickery is further institutionalized. With the help of Marcia and Belisa, Laura engages in a standard theatrical ruse—role-playing in the dark to deceive a lover. Pretending to be Marcia, she obtains Liseo's signature on a written marriage contract and in the final scene produces it, to his embarrassment and chagrin. His acquiescence in the marriage does not portend a happy future for the couple.[18] Having arrived at Marcia's house precisely to claim her as his bride, he even declares to Fenisa, "De Marcia soy, no pretendas / estorbar mi casamiento" (619). Now married to the woman upon whom he earlier wished death, Liseo participates in the final scene without ever having given any evidence of moral development. He has not behaved honorably to any woman, including Marcia, whom he has often claimed to want to marry—a claim he made about Laura in the play's prehistory. Though he is indeed the man whom Laura loves, the courtship system that has led to his unkind treatment of her has also allowed her reciprocal deception to trap him into marriage. They have fulfilled the conventions of the court's games of love and honor and the *comedia*'s demand for marriage, but they merely reassemble in the relationship that led to the dramatized dilemma. A line delivered by Belisa midway through act 2 is thus significant as a summary of the cyclical and inescapable nature of the literary conventions examined by Zayas: "porque al fin todas las cosas / vuelven á lo que solían" (603).

Zayas's approach to her subject matter in this play belongs to the female writer's strategy described by Miller in the quotation at the beginning of this study. Zayas does not put forth suggestions for change. Through Fenisa she envisions an alternative within the fixed conventional characterizations of women in the *comedia*. Developing this alternative in a way that demonstrates its untenability in the conventional literary structure in which it must struggle for recognition, Zayas also exposes its inescapable conversion to convention in that system, which will not accommodate anything but the codified theatrical categories that audiences popularize. Fenisa's unconventionality partakes of the characteristics of both the male and female stereotypes. Like many of the *damas* of Golden Age theater, she is flirtatious and marriageable, but she insists on prolonging indefinitely the games she plays with a multitude of suitors instead of deciding to love only one. Like her sisters, she is also ill-treated by the most unscrupulous of her male admirers, for, as Liseo admits, he intends to deceive her with attention and promises until he marries Marcia. Fenisa nevertheless overtly models her attitude toward, and behavior with, her suitors on their male pattern of comportment.

Liseo and Juan, however, are reconciled into the acceptable pattern of relation-ships, even without any moral development on their own part. Indeed, faithless male characters usually end up by honoring their original commitments to women whom they have abandoned, but only after being tricked into doing so; this is the case with Liseo and Laura.

Zayas does not, on the other hand, portray the reabsorption of Fenisa into society. Never renouncing her dedication to perpetual courtship, this character continues to reject the conventional resolution enacted at the end of most *comedias,* while at the same time she is rejected by the formulaic characters who obey this tradition. In the last scene, Fenisa is rebuffed by Juan and Liseo, who are now reunited with Belisa and Laura respectively; even León hastily contracts mar-riage with Lucía in order to avoid any possibility that he will have to marry the ostracized Fenisa. Joining Gerardo and Marcia, these couples form or reform the pairings that the dramatic conventions demand, returning the relationships to their original and/or initially potential status, just as Belisa has anticipated. In this undertaking, they reject Fenisa not only as a renegade from the social system they validate and preserve but also as a symbol of the activities of courtship they must renounce in order to marry and fulfill the literary precepts. Fenisa is therefore a representative of what must always be overcome in the dramas of love intrigues: a character's inability or unwillingness to love only one partner. She becomes, therefore, a conventional element herself even in her unconventionality because of the pessimistic view that Zayas suggests about change in *comedia* practice. Rejecting the rules that the other characters follow and affirm, Fenisa becomes a permanent fixture herself precisely because of the open-ended quality of Zayas's play and the implied ongoing nature of the conventional system. Fenisa does not revolutionize the stereotypes that will continue to be portrayed as demanded by theatrical audiences. In order to celebrate a *boda* at the end, the world of court-ship will have to be sacrificed, just as Fenisa is renounced by the other characters in *La traición en la amistad.*

Courtship should be the means to an honorable matrimonial end. Fenisa makes of courtship an end in itself and, in so doing, violates the sense of propriety that the conventions are supposed to promote. She also exposes, however, the hypoc-risy of *comedia* theory, since the formulaic repetition of *enredos de amor* seems to be the goal of playwright and playgoer alike at the expense of the characters' moral progress. The very fact that the characters in *La traición en la amistad* are reunited in the pairings of the play's prehistory implies a possible repetition of the disruption of those unions that has just been dramatized. León's invitation to the audience ("Señores míos") to come and claim the unclaimed Fenisa ("qual ven, sin amantes queda; / si alguno la quiere, avise / para que su casa sepa" [620]) is thus doubly significant. Like his master, Liseo, who affirms that the play is "historia tan verdadera / que no ha un año que en la corte / sucedió como se cuenta" (620), León ends the play by insisting on the specular quality of the stage world and on the audience's responsibility for the repetition of the dramatized conventions. Though spectators' demands are shaped by traditions that they learn to expect, it is they who popularize the conventions perpetuated by the playwrights, who must then satisfy their viewers. Zayas's play questions this whole process. It does not close but rather points toward the sure repetition of the fixed dramatic categories that she has examined and challenged but has not replaced.

Finally, it is significant that Zayas embodies the deviation from conventions in a female character who eventually proves to be their prisoner. The gender differences upheld by the social and literary double standard are consistently affirmed in *La traición en la amistad*. Neither Juan nor Liseo is ever considered by the abandoned lovers or by any other member of the dramatized society to be unworthy of reassimilation into the resolved pattern at the end of the drama. Such a privilege is typical of depictions of numerous male suitors in countless Golden Age dramas, whereas just as many female characters left abandoned by these very men are considered temporarily or permanently dishonored, dishonorable, and unmarriageable. Fenisa embodies this dichotomy, as she is criticized throughout the drama by the other figures for doing what Liseo also does without loss of social status. It is she who is left alone and isolated, whereas all three of the other women work together to bring Liseo back into the circle of resolution. And yet Fenisa is also free to continue her preferred process of courtship at the play's end. As the character who has disrupted the romances of at least two of the couples during their courtships, she might later be the disruptive figure in an imagined adulterous affair in a subsequent drama about conjugal honor. Zayas and her audience, of course, are not accustomed to honor dilemmas proposed by adulterous husbands. Thus what is suggested by the unmarried status of Fenisa is therefore more subject matter for an unconventional plot that would reaffirm the conventions of injustice for female characters as developed by the dramatic formulas.

Notes

I wish to thank Joan Bennett, Valerie Greenberg, Babette Spaeth, Susan Tucker, Maryann Valiulis, and Beth Willinger, members of the Feminist Research Group at Tulane University, who read and critiqued an early draft of this essay. Their suggestions were helpful as I revised the final version.

1.   The importance of the Golden Age plays and/or playwrights currently relegated by institutional consensus to noncanonical status is an issue appropriate for consideration by Hispanists. Vern Williamsen has challenged his colleagues to reconsider the importance to *comedia* development of less well known seventeenth-century authors (all but one of those he studies are male) whose contributions to the theatrical production of that period need to be recognized. Feminist scholars, of course, regularly reexamine the ideology that underlies both the literature of any given age and the discourse of subsequent interpretive scholarship. In the introductory remarks to their edition of essays on topics pertaining to social and cultural patterns of representation of women in the Renaissance, Ferguson, Quilligan, and Vickers reiterate that "feminists mount a challenge to the very notion of a canonical tradition; they further challenge that notion by reading canonical texts, generally by men, in heretical ways" (xxi).

2.   Stroud asserts, for example: "[Fenisa] is, in short, a kind of Doña Juana" (543).

3.   Miller, 340. Elsewhere Miller notes: "For sensibility, sensitivity, 'extravagance'—so many code words for feminine in our culture that the attack is in fact tautological—are taken to be not merely inferior modalities of production but deviations from some obvious truth. The blind spot here is both political (or philosophical) and literary. It does not see, nor does it want to, that the fictions of desire behind the desiderata of fiction are masculine and not universal constructs. It does not see that the maxims that pass for the truth of human experience, and the encoding of that experience in literature, are organizations, when they are not fantasies, of the dominant culture" (357).

4.   Juan Pérez de Montalbán, fol. 359r. Zayas eventually published twenty *novelas*.

5.   Agustín G. de Amezúa, xl–xli. Serrano y Sanz likewise describes *La traición en la amistad* as "[m]anuscrito de mediados del siglo XVII" (590). See Place, 53–55.

6.   This statement is not necessarily supported by any evidence from Zayas. At the beginning of her "El traidor contra su sangre," for instance, her narrator does praise Lope's poetic skill: "En tanto que duró la música que todos escucharon con gran gusto, oyendo en este romance trovados los últimos versos de uno que hizo aquel príncipe del Parnaso, Lope de Vega Carpio, cuya memoria no morirá mientras el mundo no tuviere fin" (1983, 369). Her play, however, actually offers a challenge to the sort of dramatic portrayal that Lope helped to popularize in the seventeenth century. Amezúa nevertheless persists in his

traditional critical orientation and ends his discussion of *La traición en la amistad* with this final supposition: "el hecho es que doña María no volvió a las tablas dramáticas, creyendo, acaso, impropio de una mujer andar por ellas" (xli).

7.   See also Yllera's introduction to the *Desengaños amorosos* (21–22). Beyond the scant critical treatment already mentioned, *La traición en la amistad* has suffered the general neglect of scholars of the Spanish classical drama until the publication in this decade of the studies by Alessandra Melloni and Matthew Stroud. Examining the play from a formal standpoint, Melloni compares Zayas's dramatic technique with her narrative strategies and argues that the ending devised for the play is a "happy" one. Stroud claims that the play's ending is weak and is justifiable only: (1) if it is understood to show the risk run by a woman who betrays the female community, to which she should remain true regardless of her sexual appetite or interest in marriage; (2) if a character such as Fenisa is understood as a victim of the societal double standard that allows more freedom to men than to women in the courting practices; or (3) if Zayas's treatment is considered part of the more limiting dramatic system that provides playwrights fewer opportunities for direct communication with the audience for expressing personal views about the events presented within the inflexible plot development. My reading produces different conclusions, however, by means of its emphasis on Zayas's critique of the rigid literary codes that promote so much social and moral disorder, including gender inequities (Serrano y Sanz 1975, 545–46).

8.   This situation repeats certain elements in the frame tale of Zayas's prose works, in which a young noblewoman named Lisis is betrothed to Don Diego, even though she loves Don Juan. Juan, in turn, loves Lisarda.

9.   For a different interpretation, see Stroud, 543–45.

10.   Zayas (1975, 591). All quotations from the play are taken from this edition and will be identified henceforth in the text by page number.

11.   Even the notion of vengeance against the men who deceive women seems to lose its primacy for Fenisa as she adheres more and more closely to the flawed male model she has chosen.

12.   Later, in a conversation with the *gracioso* León, Belisa reiterates these conventional sentiments. Answering León's complaints about "las mujeres destos tiempos," who, according to him, take advantage of lovers and their cuckolded husbands, she says, "no son mujeres; / sucias harpias son" (616). She soon points out, though, that "también los hombres tienen cien mujeres / sin querer á ninguna" (616), a statement that does not elicit a parallel diatribe against these faithless males. León enhances this stereotypical misogyny by claiming that in the case of such men, "si engañan, los hombres aprendieran / de los engaños que hay en las mujeres" (616).

13.   Not only do the majority of the young noblewomen of the frame tale of Zayas's prose collections make this decision; her protagonists in the following *novelas* do as well: *La fuerza del amor; El desengaño andando y premio de la virtud; La esclava de su amante; La más infame venganza; La inocencia castigada; Mal presagio casar lejos; La perseguida triunfante;* and *Engaños que causa el vicio.* For further information about the benefits of the cloister for women in seventeenth-century Spain, see Arenal and Arenal and Schlau.

14.   Near the end of the final *novela* in *Desengaños amorosos,* "Estragos que causa el vicio," Zayas's authorial voice is raised on various topics, among them the following: "Bien ventilada me parece que queda, nobles y discretos caballeros y hermosísmas damas . . . la defensa de las mujeres, por lo que me dispuse a hacer esta segunda parte de mi entretenido y honesto sarao; pues, si bien confieso que hay muchas mujeres que, con sus vicios y yerros, han dado motivo a los hombres para la mucha desestimación que hoy hacen de ellas, no es razón que, hablando en común, las midan a todas con una misma medida. Que lo cierto es que en una máquina tal dilatada y extendida como lo del mundo, ha de haber buenas y malas, como asimismo hay hombres de la misma manera" (1983, 503).

15.   In the first scene, Marcia responds to Fenisa's advice to favor Gerardo as follows: "No digas, / que á nadie estoy obligada / sino á mi gusto" (591). For a feminist reading of the Marcela-Grisóstomo episode in *Don Quijote,* see Munich, 244–50.

16.   Stroud, moreover, questions even Gerardo's values, since he alone of the three principal males has not enjoyed the physical relationship he ultimately seeks with the woman he professes to love (540). If Liseo and Juan are representative of the male participants in the court's double standard, what could be expected of Gerardo were he to gain Marcia's assent to sexual relations? Marcia's initial confidence in Gerardo's integrity is thus perhaps as misplaced as Laura's and Belisa's has been with regard to Liseo and Juan.

17.   See also 595–96. Fenisa's maid Lucía offers similar sorts of anecdotal information at the same time that she warns the noblewoman of the social risk she runs due to her unorthodox behavior. See, for example, 605–6. León's carnivalesque suggestion of gender reversal is also indicative of the disorder of the society and is reiterated during the scene when Laura visits Marcia and Belisa for the first time. Impressed by the beauty of their visitor, the two cousins use language that suggests an erotic attraction to Laura. Belisa ends the exchange with the following lines: "No hay más bien / que ver cuando viendo estoy / tal belleza; el cielo os dé / la ventura cual la cara, / si hombre fuera, yo empleara / en vuestra afición mi fe" (599). These three women thus frame their conversation about female solidarity and their plot to trick Liseo with this tone of underlying inversion of the conventional order. As with the chaos of carnival reversals, however, the disorder cedes to the traditional cultural configurations. Marcia, Belisa, and Laura do not return to

this sort of communication during the rest of the play but instead dedicate themselves to fulfilling the traditional plot development, which leads to what should be recognized as a questionable fulfillment for them.

    18.   See Stroud, 544 on this same point.

Works Consulted

Arenal, Electa. 1983. "The Convent As Catalyst for Autonomy: Two Hispanic Nuns of the Seventeenth Century." In *Women in Hispanic Literature: Icons and Fallen Idols,* edited by Beth Miller, 147–83. Berkeley and Los Angeles: University of California Press.

Arenal, Electa, and Stacey Schlau, eds. 1989. *Untold Sisters: Hispanic Nuns in Their Own Works.* Albuquerque: University of New Mexico Press.

Diccionario de autoridades. [1726–39] 1979. Madrid: Gredos.

Ferguson, Margaret W., Maureen Quilligan, and Nancy J. Vickers, eds. 1986. *Rewriting the Renaissance: The Discourses of Sexual Difference in Early Modern Europe.* Chicago, Ill.: University of Chicago Press.

Kennard, Jean E. 1978. *Victims of Convention.* Hamden, Conn.: Archon Books.

Kolodny, Annette. 1985. "Dancing through the Minefield: Some Observations on the Theory, Practice, and Politics of a Feminist Literary Criticism." In *The New Feminist Criticism: Essays on Women, Literature, and Theory,* edited by Elaine Showalter, 144–67. New York: Pantheon.

Melloni, Alessandra. 1981. "María de Zayas fra *comedia* e *novela.*" In *Actas del coloquio Teoría y realidad en el teatro español del siglo XVII: La influencia italiana,* 485–505. Rome: Instituto Español de Cultura y de Literatura de Roma, 1981.

Miller, Nancy K. 1985. "Emphasis Added: Plots and Plausibilities in Women's Fiction." In *The New Feminist Criticism: Essays on Women, Literature and Theory,* edited by Elaine Showalter, 339–60. New York: Pantheon.

Munich, Adrienne. 1985. "Notorious Signs, Feminist Criticism and Literary Tradition." In *Making a Difference: Feminist Literary Criticism,* edited by Gayle Greene and Coppélia Kahn, 238–59. London: Methuen.

Pérez de Montalbán, Juan. 1632. *Para todos.* Madrid.

Place, Edwin B. 1923. *María de Zayas, an Outstanding Short-Story Writer of Seventeenth Century Spain.* Boulder: University of Colorado Press.

Robinson, Lillian S. 1978. *Sex, Class, and Culture.* Bloomington: Indiana University Press.

Stroud, Matthew D. 1985. "Love, Friendship, and Deceit in *La traición en la amistad,* by María de Zayas." *Neophilologus* 69:539–47.

Vasileski, Irma. 1973. *María de Zayas: Su época y su obra.* Madrid: Playor.

Williamsen, Vern G. 1982. *The Minor Dramatists of Seventeenth-Century Spain.* Boston, Mass.: Twayne.

Zayas y Sotomayor, María de. 1948. *Novelas amorosas y ejemplares de doña María de Zayas y Sotomayor.* Edited by Agustín G. de Amezúa. Madrid: Real Academia Española.

———. 1975. *La traición en la amistad.* In *Apuntes para una biblioteca de escritoras españolas,* 2:590–620. Edited by Manuel Serrano y Sanz. Madrid: Rivadeneyra.

———. 1983. *Desengaños amorosos.* Edited by Alicia Yllera. Madrid: Cátedra.

Michael McGaha

Who Was Francisco de Villegas?

he playwright known as Francisco de Villegas is one of the most enigmatic, original, and interesting dramatists of Spain's Golden Age. Cayetano de La Barrera described him as an "ingenioso escritor dramático
de la segunda mitad del siglo XVII" (494) and observed that he used
the honorific "Don" in the signature of most of his plays but not in a
sonnet published in a collection of *Saynetes y entremeses* in 1674. La Barrera
listed six plays written entirely by Villegas—*Dios hace justicia a todos, Lo que
puede la crianza, El rey don Sebastián, Cuerdos hacen escarmientos, La culpa
más provechosa,* and *El más piadoso troyano*—as well as three written in collaboration with Jusepe Rojo: *La esclavitud más dichosa y Virgen de los Remedios,
Las niñeces de Roldán,* and *El esclavo de María.* Two other plays, *El nacimiento
de San Francisco* and *El Eneas de la Virgen,* were collaborations with Román
Montero de Espinosa and Pedro Lanini Sagredo, respectively. Eight of these plays
were published in the collection of *Comedias nuevas escogidas* in Madrid between 1663 and 1673. The Biblioteca Nacional, Madrid, possesses seventeenth-
century manuscripts of two others: *Dios hace justicia a todos* and *El Eneas de la
Virgen;* the earliest published versions I have been able to locate of those two
plays are *sueltas* printed by Orga in Valencia in the mid-eighteenth century. *El
esclavo de María* seems to have disappeared without a trace, or it may just have
been an alternate title of *La esclavitud más dichosa.*

Contemporary references to Villegas are few and tantalizing. In 1660–61 the
company of Sebastián García de Prado toured France. The tour led to a well-
known lawsuit because Prado failed to perform in the Madrid *corrales,* as he had
contracted to do, during that season, causing grave financial reverses to the
arrendadores of the *corrales.* The first witness called to testify at the trial, on 27
August 1661, was a Francisco de Villegas, "que así se dixo llamar y ser vecino

desta uilla que come de su hacienda y posa en la Calle de Cantarranas en casas de Ana de Villegas, su hermana." After stating that he was forty years old, Villegas "dixo que desde que tiene vso de raçon asiste a los corrales de las comedias desta Corte y a tenido mucho conocimiento, trato y comunicazion con todas las compañias que an representado en todo este tiempo en los dichos corrales desta Corte" (Varey and Shergold 1973, 179). There is, however, no indication that this Francisco de Villegas was a playwright. The anonymous two-volume manuscript *Genealogía, origen y noticias de los comediantes de España* edited by Varey and Shergold contains a reference to a Juan de Villegas, "hermano de Francisco de Villegas, el poeta, y conocido por las comedias que escriuio. Después de auer continuado Juan en representar tomó el auito de relixioso franciscano. Sus hermanas Maria de Villegas y Ana de Villegas y amuas fueron representantas, y Ana fue despues beata" (1985, 215). Since the passage distinguishes between the poet Francisco and his brother, who was known for his plays, this Francisco was surely not our playwright. The passage adds that the compiler of the *Genealogía* thought that this Juan de Villegas was the same one who gave alms while a member of the company of Malaguilla in 1638. The reference is almost certainly to the actor-playwright Juan Bautista de Villegas, who is known to have been writing plays by 1621 (La Barrera, 495). If so, in spite of the coincidence that both men had sisters named Ana, it is unlikely that Juan's poet brother was the same Francisco who at age forty testified at the trial in 1661.

Varey and Shergold have unearthed two additional references to Villegas. A document dated 16 July 1657 states that Pedro de Rosa contracts to perform "seis comedias nueuas, nunca bistas ni representadas," including one by Francisco de Villegas (1973, 122). Another document states that Juan de la Calle and Sebastián de Prado did not perform in the *corrales* on 8, 9, and 10 February 1660, although they had rehearsed a new play by Agustín Moreto and another by Francisco de Villegas (Varey and Shergold 1973, 233).

Francisco de Villegas has often been confused with Juan Bautista de Villegas, the actor-playwright of an earlier generation whom I have already mentioned, and the confusion is compounded by the fact that there may have been still another playwright named simply Juan de Villegas. Medel del Castillo in his 1735 *Indice general alfabético de todos los títulos de comedias que se han escrito por varios autores, antiguos y modernos* lists the plays *Cuerdos hazen Escarmiento, Culpa mas Provechosa, Dios haze Justicia á Todos, Lo que puede la Crianza,*

Mas Piadoso Troyano, and *Rey Don Sebastian,* as well as sixteen others, as by Juan de Villegas, attributing only *Verdades Venturosas* to Juan Bautista de Villegas and failing to mention Francisco de Villegas at all.[1] In his catalogue of dramatic manuscripts in the Biblioteca Nacional, Antonio Paz y Meliá (1934) states that both *El más piadoso troyano* and *El rey don Sebastián* are actually by Juan Bautista de Villegas. Of the latter play, he writes: "Es de Juan Bautista de Villegas, y no de Francisco, como dicen los Indices, e idéntica a la que imprimió como anónima con ambos títulos Gibert y Tutó en Barcelona" (479).

I have not had an opportunity to examine either of the manuscripts of *El rey don Sebastián.* I have seen the manuscript of *El más piadoso troyano,* however.[2] It is true that the title page lists the author as "Don Juan de Villegas," but it is also clear that the manuscript is merely a copy of the version printed in part 32 (1669) of the *Comedias nuevas* series. The title page states in the same handwriting as the rest of the manuscript—which, according to Paz y Meliá, is that of Cañizares— "esta ympresa en la Parte 32 de Varias" (MS. 18.074). Since the printed version attributes the play to Francisco de Villegas, that evidence would seem to be more reliable. The scant documentary evidence indicates that Francisco de Villegas's dramatic career spanned approximately the eighteen years from 1657 to 1674. The Francisco de Villegas who testified at the trial in 1661 was probably not the playwright. If he had been, he would surely have said so, because that would have given greater credibility to his claim to intimate familiarity with the theater companies of Madrid.

A manuscript copy of one of the Villegas plays, *La culpa más provechosa,* dated 15 June 1710, attributes the play to Don Fernando de Zárate (MS. 16.869). As is now well known, Fernando de Zárate was a pseudonym used by Antonio Enríquez Gómez after his clandestine return to Spain from a fifteen-year exile in France. When I first read *La culpa más provechosa,* my subjective hunch, based on familiarity with Enríquez's other works, was that he was indeed the author. The play, based on medieval legends about the early life of Pontius Pilate, is a *refundición* of *El dichoso desdichado, Poncio Pilato* by an obscure author called Don Juan de Espinosa Malagón y Valenzuela.[3] Although *La culpa más provechosa* is vastly superior to the earlier play in almost every way, the most striking difference is that the *refundición* goes to extreme lengths to eliminate all the unfavorable characteristics attributed to Pilate in *El dichoso desdichado.* Pilate is presented as a truly tragic figure, caught in the grip of cosmic forces beyond his control or comprehension, whereas his principal antagonist in the play, St. Veronica, is portrayed as a nagging, vindictive shrew.

There is some rather significant circumstantial evidence to support attribution of the play to Enríquez. The play's *gracioso* is called Caimán, a name used by Enríquez for the *gracioso* of his play *La soberbia de Nembrot.* The generally pessimistic—indeed fatalistic—tone of the play is consistent with Enríquez's other work, as is the political preoccupation with the conflict between *razón de estado* and ethical behavior. Both the title of the play and its concern with original sin and predestination recall Enríquez's *La culpa del primer peregrino* (Rouen, 1644). One of the most notable characteristics of Enríquez's theater is his creation of strong, independent female characters (Dille 1980), and the Veronica of *La culpa* is certainly one of the best developed and most aggressive female characters in all of Golden Age drama. The image of the hydra, used to describe turbulent Rome after the death of Augustus (Enríquez Gómez 1669, 4), was a favorite of Enríquez's and occurs almost constantly in his work. The references to David, Solomon, and Samson are also characteristic of Enríquez (1669, 21). His epic poem *Sansón Nazareno*—the same epithet, "Sansón, el valiente nazareno" occurs in the play— treats Samson's exploits. In Enríquez's play *La conversión de la Magdalena,* Jesus appears to Mary Magdalen in a dream. Her description of him closely parallels Pilate's description of Veronica's portrait of Jesus in *La culpa.* The passage is too long to quote in full, but among other things Mary describes Jesus' hair as "de rayos de sol formada / la ondeada cabellera" (act 2, fol. 4r), while Pilate says: "El cabello . . . desafiaba a los rayos del sol, en ondas partido" (Enríquez Gómez 1669, 66), going on to observe that Jesus' fiery locks, unlike the sun, "no queman y alumbran."[4] In *La conversión,* Mary tells one of her would-be lovers: "Vos decís que soy un sol: / alumbro, pero no quemo" (act 1, fol. 4r).

The parallels between *La culpa más provechosa* and Enríquez's *Las misas de San Vicente Ferrer*[5] are even more striking. Pilate is remarkably similar to the Muley of *Las misas,* another sympathetic but flawed character who is portrayed as tragically doomed and unable to resist his fate. The many elements that Muley's account of his life in act 1 of *Las misas* have in common with Pilate's *relación* in act 1 of *La culpa* seem to betray the hand of a single author. Muley and Pilate were each the sole survivor of a shipwreck. Each man made it to shore, where he encountered a poor but learned old man who befriended him, took him into his home, and educated him. Muley's teacher baptized him, changing his name to Juan. Poncio adopted his teacher's surname Pilato. Later in his *relación,* Muley tells how he was captured by Turks and became a pirate. Pilate explains how he became a bandit. Pilate is ultimately slain because of Veronica's vindictiveness. The equally vindictive Francisca Ferrer—St. Vincent's sister—murders Muley.

Jesús Antonio Cid, one of the few scholars who has thoroughly studied Enríquez/Zárate's works, also believes that *La culpa más provechosa* is by Enríquez. He has described the play as "obra insólita en todo el teatro clásico en cuanto que presenta un conflicto entre acción y 'destino' que la ortodoxia del momento consideraba escandaloso aun imaginarlo" (294). However, proving that Enríquez was the author obviously required a careful stylistic comparison with both Enríquez's other plays and the other nine Villegas plays. When I undertook this analysis, I hoped that the Villegas plays would prove sufficiently different from *La culpa* to rule out Villegas's possible authorship.

My task was made easier by the fact that Carlos Romero Muñoz had recently carried out the first extensive analyses of the plays of Enríquez/Zárate in an attempt to prove that the play *La conquista de México* was not his work but was almost certainly written by Lope de Vega. Romero Muñoz analyzed thirteen plays attributed to Enríquez with relative certainty. Enríquez claims twelve of the thirteen as his own in the prologue to his *Sansón Nazareno;* the remaining one, *No hay contra el honor poder,* was published under his name in part 2 of the *Escogidas* collection in 1652. It was probably written after the prologue, which we know was finished by 1649, though not published until 1656. The twenty-five plays attributed to Zárate that Muñoz analyzes are somewhat more problematic because the attribution of these plays is far less certain. It is especially unfortunate for my purposes that Muñoz included the disputed *La culpa más provechosa* among the plays analyzed. At least one other play he included, *Los hermanos amantes,* is probably not the work of Zárate.[6] Nevertheless, the sampling is sufficiently large not to be drastically skewed by the inclusion of these two plays. I applied Muñoz's procedure—compiling statistics on the length of plays, percentages of *redondillas, quintillas, romance,* and *octavas,* metric forms in which each act begins and ends, number of "passages" (i.e., sections of the play written continuously in a single verse form), maximum and minimum length of passages in the various verse forms, and percentage of Spanish verse forms—to the nine remaining Villegas plays and was startled to find that they turned out to be re-markably consistent with the Enríquez/Zárate plays. Space does not permit me to give the detailed statistics I have mentioned, but the summary is as follows:

	length	redondillas	quintillas	romance	octavas	no. of passages	Spanish verse
average of 13 Enríquez plays	2,623	18%	5%	67.2%	3.3%	25	91.3%
average of 25 Zárate plays	2,878	22.7%	3.6%	64.9%	2.8%	36	94.2%
average of 9 Villegas plays	2,791	25.8%	6%	64.4%	4.7%	23	93.3%

These figures led me to the hypothesis that not just *La culpa más provechosa* but all ten "Villegas" plays are really the work of Enríquez, that is, that Don Francisco de Villegas, like Don Fernando de Zárate, was just another pseudonym adopted by Enríquez during the years (c. 1650–61) when he was living in Seville as a fugitive from the Inquisition. In choosing the name Francisco de Villegas, Enríquez may have playfully hoped that the public would mistakenly consider these subversive plays the work of his archrival, the bigoted ultraconservative Francisco Gómez de Quevedo y Villegas. I think it is very likely that the Villegas plays were the "legajos de comedias" ("Copia," fol. 1r) that the Inquisitors found on Enríquez's desk when they arrested him in September 1661, and that the Inquisition arranged for publication of the plays after Enríquez's death in 1663, since they were the only items of value in his estate, which the Inquisition had confiscated. But what about the collaborators on some of those plays—José Rojo, Román Montero de Espinosa, and Pedro Lanini y Sagredo? Lanini is known to have been employed by the Inquisition as a *censor de comedias;* in fact, he censored Enríquez's *Las misas de San Vicente Ferrer* in 1688 and *La conversión de la Magdalena* in 1699, approving both for performance after making certain emendations and deletions. It is quite plausible that his collaboration on *La Eneas de la Virgen* was of exactly the same nature. Much less is known about the other two collaborators. José Rojo, an actor who played *barbas,* was employed in the company of Juan Pérez in 1655 (Varey and Shergold 1985, 2:91) and in 1662 was working as a copyist for the company of Simón Aguado (Varey and Shergold 1973, 240). Aside from his collaboration on *La esclavitud más dichosa* and *Las niñeces de Roldán,* the only dramatic work he is known to have written is a *loa* for the company of Vallejo published in the *Flor de entremeses, bailes y loas* in 1676 (La Barrera, 344).

Montero de Espinosa published a volume of *Diálogos militares y políticos discurridos por Eráclito y Demócrito* in Brussels in 1654. It is worth noting that the contrasting philosophies of Heraclitus and Democritus was one of Enríquez's favorite themes, figuring especially prominently in his *Academias morales de las musas* (1642) and providing the subject matter for the play *Los dos filósofos de Grecia.* Montero also produced some poetic glosses on St. Teresa's seven meditations on the Lord's Prayer and a Spanish verse translation of the penitential psalms (La Barrera, 270). I have been unable to find any proof that either Rojo or Montero worked for the Inquisition; unfortunately, the Archivo Histórico Nacional, where most of the remaining Inquisitional files are housed, does not have an index of censors. However, Rojo's background in theater and training as a copyist and Montero's religious writings make it at least credible that they might have been hired by the Inquisition to "clean up" the "Villegas" plays for publication.

A brief examination of the other nine Villegas plays provides further indications of their ideological, thematic, and stylistic consistency with Enríquez's works. Although the play *El rey don Sebastián* is subtitled *y portugués más heroico,* the play frequently and forcefully makes the point that Sebastian is really foolhardy rather than heroic. The play's most sympathetic character is the Moor Maluco. Sebastian, who sees himself as the champion of Christianity, is presented as the antithesis of everything a king should be—reckless, more interested in personal fame and territorial conquest than in his duty to preserve his kingdom, and heedless of the fate of his subjects. The play is a powerful argument against unnecessary warfare, even when its ostensible aim is the propagation of the Christian faith. Enríquez had a more than usual interest in Portuguese history. He had been employed by the Portuguese government as a propagandist in France during the 1640s but had fallen out with the Portuguese ambassador over the publication of his controversial *Política angélica* in 1647. The *Política angélica* also condemns religious wars, and Sebastian is the very opposite of the ideal Christian ruler described in that work and dramatized in Enríquez's play *El rey más perfeto.*

Lo que puede la crianza is the story of a girl named Juana and her brother, Félix. For reasons too complicated to explain here, Juana was brought up as a boy, and Félix as a girl. On the threshold of adulthood, brother and sister must teach each other the behavior proper to their respective sexes. Finally, both end up being paired with appropriate partners, but neither is entirely reconciled to the rigid sex roles imposed by their society. Juana will continue to be independent and demand that she be treated with respect, and Félix will never embrace mindless violence.

It would take many pages to summarize the outrageously complicated and improbable plot of *La esclavitud más dichosa y Virgen de los Remedios.* The play revolves around the stories of two friends, Don Juan de Peralta[7] and Don Luis de Silva. The impoverished Juan wastes his time and little remaining money gambling while his wife and daughter pray to the Virgin for a miracle. Luis falls in love with a woman named Clara de Cabrera, who turns out to be a Morisca. Luis and the Peralta family are shipwrecked and taken prisoners by the Moors but are finally freed through the intervention of the Virgin. Don Juan and his wife, Beatriz, who have declared themselves "slaves of the Virgin," are ridiculous figures. The Morisca Clara is the most admirable character in the play. The Moors are presented as kind and civilized, in contrast with the cruelty, ignorance, and racist bigotry of the Spaniards. The play's plot recalls that of Enríquez's *El valiente Campuzano,* in which the ignorant and violent but staunchly *cristiano viejo* thug Pedro de Campuzano destroyed his sister Leonor's life by preventing her from marrying the kind, gentle, wealthy Morisco Don Pedro (Dille 1983).

Cuerdos hacen escarmientos is a comedy based on the love between two characters whose personalities are diametrically opposite. Carlos is an extrovert. He wears his heart on his sleeve, trusts everyone, and his greatest pleasure in life is bestowing lavish gifts on all those around him. Laura is pathologically reserved, incapable of expressing her love, and too haughty to accept gifts. These qualities almost lead to disaster for both of them, but they learn their lesson in time— *hacen el escarmiento*—and end up happily married.

El más piadoso troyano, the story of Dido and Aeneas, closely parallels *La culpa más provechosa,* also raising troubling questions about divine justice. Aeneas survives the burning of Troy only to suffer the greater misfortune of being commanded by the gods to abandon his beloved Dido. The gods, envious of men's happiness, reward piety and merit with the most terrible suffering. Aeneas's ultimate "piety" is made to seem cruel, irrational, and unjust.

Las niñeces de Roldán is based on medieval legends concerning the early life of Roland. Roland grows up as a peasant, unaware of his noble origins, but soon demonstrates uncommon bravery, intelligence, leadership, and recklessness. Although he ultimately proves to be of royal blood, while still unaware of his true rank, Roland defiantly refused to accept the inferior status imposed by his apparently low birth, insisting that all men are equal, and that individual merit is more important than inherited privilege.

El nacimiento de San Francisco deals with the career of the power-mad emperor Frederick Barbarossa, whose long struggle with Pope Alexander III plunged Italy into the needless and devastating warfare between Guelphs and Ghibellines—also the theme of the second part of Enríquez's *El gran cardenal de España.* The play culminates in the birth of St. Francis, presaging a new period of peace and fruitful cooperation between church and state. St. Francis plays a similar messianic role in Enríquez's *El rey más perfeto.* The play's message is that each of the three estates—church, nobles, and commoners—has its own rights and privileges, and harmonious government—what Enríquez termed *la política angélica*—requires that none of them try to exceed its proper sphere of influence.

La Eneas de la Virgen, a thoroughly silly play that relies heavily on the use of stage machinery, is the least admirable of the Villegas plays. The main character, Ana de Lara, is another woman warrior. Though Dimén, Moorish king of Aragon, is madly in love with her and offers her everything he has if she will marry him, she spurns his advances. She and her brother Pedro are taken captive by Dimén, and Dimén, maddened by thwarted love, hangs Pedro when Ana refuses to marry him. The Christian forces later conquer Dimén. Ana cruelly wants to kill him, but Pedro intervenes. It turns out that he has not died at all; though hanged, he has been held in the air by the Virgin for three days. This miracle causes Dimén to convert to Christianity. The play's title refers to Ana's rescue of a statue of the Virgin from the Moors, reminiscent of Aeneas's rescue of his father, Anchises, from the flames of Troy. No intelligent reader can miss the point that if Ana had simply married Dimén, much unnecessary violence and death could have been avoided.

The last of the Villegas plays, *Dios hace justicia a todos,* is also one of the most interesting. The play is loosely based on the life of the great Hungarian statesman János Hunyadi, though most of the events portrayed in it are fictitious. The Grand Turk Amurates invades Hungary but is persuaded by Hunyadi's son Rodulfo to extend very generous peace terms after Hungary's surrender. However, King Casimir breaks the peace treaty and plans a surprise attack on Amurates, arguing that he is not obliged to keep his word to an infidel. Both Rodulfo and his father are horrified and shamed by Casimir's dishonorable behavior. Amurates at first appears to be losing the battle, but he begs for divine assistance: "¿Cómo, Dios de los cristianos, / esta sinrazón consientes? / ¿Tú amparas al que te rompe / la paz que te promete?" (1763, 34).[8] God intervenes, and the tide of the battle turns. Dying, Casimir recognizes that God is punishing him for his sins. The play forcefully implies that Moslems and Christians are equal in the sight of God, and that God's justice extends to all.

Taken together, these plays, like the other writings of Antonio Enríquez Gómez, constitute a severe indictment of the mainstream values of seventeenth-century Spanish society. They are an impassioned plea for justice, arguing that merit should be rewarded above noble birth and wealth, and that all human beings have equal rights, regardless of their sex, race, or religion. Though superficially they appear innocuous and orthodox—their titles are especially misleading—lurking just below that surface one finds a repugnance for the mindless violence and prejudice that often passed for heroism, and even nagging doubts about divine justice in a world where evil so often triumphed and virtue was oppressed.

Some of the "Villegas" plays—I would single out particularly *La culpa más provechosa, El rey don Sebastián, Lo que puede la crianza,* and *Dios hace justicia a todos*—are extraordinary dramatic achievements and compare favorably with the best-known Golden Age plays. Their well-developed, highly individualized characters are forced to come to grips with crises that have faced men and women in all civilized societies throughout history. Conventional wisdom does not offer satisfactory solutions to their complex problems. There is a stubborn rejection of closure in these plays; the restoration of order that occurs at their conclusion is always relative and leaves the audience pondering the unresolved dilemmas posed by its ambivalence. All of this casts very serious doubt on the generalization so often voiced in studies of Golden Age theater that "the foundation stones of the Spanish Theater of the Golden Age, honor and faith, are dogmatic and exclusive of any other thought conflicting with these two tenets. The rigidity of the ideology is the reason for the relative remoteness of this national theater from modern Western thought" (Reichenberger 1959, 314). Perhaps the reason why such statements have been so widely accepted and so rarely questioned is that our knowledge of Golden Age theater is severely limited. What we know as Golden Age theater is really but a handful (out of the many thousands of plays written in Spain between about 1580 and 1680) of "masterpieces" that a small group of conservative, neo-Catholic nineteenth-century German and Spanish critics found most appealing. Examination of the "Villegas" plays supports Américo Castro's view of seventeenth-century Spain as an *edad conflictiva,* an age much more similar to our own in its inner doubts and anguish than Reichenberger was prepared to admit. I am convinced that further study of the theater of Enríquez Gómez and of the many other less known Golden Age playwrights, as well as study of the less known works of the more famous ones, can revitalize *comedia* scholarship and will ultimately result in a drastic alteration of our view of that theater.

Notes

1.   The author index was prepared by John M. Hill from Medel's alphabetical listing by titles.

2.   I would like to express my gratitude to Enrique Rodríguez-Cepeda for obtaining copies of this and other Villegas manuscripts for me from the Biblioteca Nacional.

3.   I am grateful to Bruce Wardropper for calling this play to my attention.

4.   Thus in the manuscript; the printed version has "queman, y no alumbran."

5.   The manuscript of *El admirable maior prodgio* [sic] *de las misas de S. Biçente Ferer* in the Biblioteca Municipal, Madrid, dated Seville, 10 March 1661, is one of only two known autograph manuscripts of "Fernando de Zárate."

6.   This is the opinion of John B. Wooldridge, who is presently at work on a detailed stylistic comparison of the Enríquez/Zárate plays in an attempt to weed out the works falsely attributed to Zárate (personal letter to the author, 18 May 1987). Muñoz's own analysis demonstrates that *Los hermanos amantes* is an anomaly: it is the longest of the Zárate plays, the one with the highest percentage of *quintillas* and the lowest percentage of *romance,* and also contains the only long passage in *quintillas* (405 verses) of the Zárate plays.

7.   In Enríquez's *La presumida y la hermosa,* Don Diego de Peralta is impersonated by his friend Don Juan; Peralta, a town in Navarre, is the setting for the Villegas play *La Eneas de la Virgen,* which portrays the legend concerning the origin of the town's name.

8.   The same passage occurs on fol. 41v of MS. 16.662 in the Biblioteca Nacional. I am grateful to Frank Casa for obtaining a copy of this manuscript for me.

Works Consulted

Cid, Jesús Antonio. 1978. "Judaizantes y carreteros para un hombre de letras: A. Enríquez Gómez (1600–1663)." In *Homenaje a Julio Caro Baroja,* edited by Antonio Carreira, Jesús Antonio Cid, and Rogelio Rubio. Madrid: Centro de Investigaciones Sociológicas.

"Copia del Secuestro de los V[ien]es de Ant[oni]o EnRiquez Gomez Veçino de Seu[ill]a Alias Don fernando de zarate." Archivo Histórico Nacional. Inquisición, Leg. 2067, N° 25.

Dille, Glen F. 1980. "Notes on Aggressive Women in the *Comedia* of Enríquez Gómez." *Romance Notes* 21:215–21.

———. 1983. "The Tragedy of Don Pedro: Old and New Christian Conflict in *El valiente Campuzano.*" *Bulletin of the Comediantes* 35:97–109.

Enríquez Gómez, Antonio. 1669. *Parte treinta y dos de comedias nvevas, nvnca impressas, escogidas de los mejores ingenios de España.* Madrid: Andrés García de la Iglesia for Francisco Serrano de Figueroa.

———. *La conversión de la Magdalena.* Biblioteca Nacional, MS. 16.732.

Hill, John M. 1929. "Indice general alfabético de todos los títulos de comedias que se han escrito por varios autores, antiguos y modernos." *Revue hispanique* 75:144–369.

La Barrera, Cayetano de. 1968. *Catálogo bibliográfico y biográfico del teatro antiguo español.* London: Tamesis Books.

Paz y Meliá, Antonio. 1934. *Catálogo de las piezas de teatro que se conservan en el Departamento de Manuscritos de la Biblioteca Nacional.* Vol. 1. Madrid: Blass.

Reichenberger, Arnold G. 1959. "The Uniqueness of the *Comedia.*" *Hispanic Review* 27:303–16.

Romero Muñoz, Carlos. 1983. "Lope de Vega y 'Fernando de Zárate': *El Nuevo Mundo* (y *Arauco domado*) en *La conquista de México.*" *Studi di letteratura ispano-americana* 15–16:243–64.

———. 1984. "*La conquista de Cortés,* comedia perdida (¿y hallada?) de Lope de Vega." In *Studi di letteratura ibero-americana offerti a Giuseppe Bellini,* 105–24. Rome: Bulzoni.

Varey, J. E., and N. D. Shergold, eds. 1973. *Fuentes para la historia del teatro en España.* Vol. 4, *Teatros y comedias en Madrid: 1651–1665.* London: Tamesis Books.

———. 1985. *Fuentes para la historia del teatro en España.* Vol. 2, *Genealogía, origen y noticias de los comediantes de Espana.* London: Tamesis Books.

Villegas, Francisco de. 1763. *Dios hace justicia a todos.* Valencia: Viuda de Joseph de Orga.

————. *Dios hace justicia a todos*. Biblioteca Nacional. MS. 16.662.

————. *El más piadoso troyano*. Biblioteca Nacional. MS. 18.074.

————. *La culpa más provechosa*. Biblioteca Nacional, MS. 16.869.

Wooldridge, John B. 1987. Personal letter, 18 May.

Zárate, Fernando de. 1661. *El admirable maior prodgio* [sic] *de las misas de S. Biçente Ferer.* Biblioteca Municipal, Madrid, dated Seville, 10 March.

Nancy L. D'Antuono

Lope's *Bastardo Mudarra* as
Scenario and Opera Tragicomica

he impact of the *comedia* on the evolution of the Italian theater of the seventeenth century has attracted sustained attention over the last century. Histories of Italian literature on the whole, however, tend to view negatively the corpus of Italian seventeenth-century plays that draw on Spanish sources. At most, one or two plays are singled out for their shortcomings as misguided dramatic experimentation rather than for the distinctiveness of their artistic vision and execution. The fact that the two dramatic manifestations, though generically united, speak to two distinct audiences at differing points in the development of each nation's theater and that they were performed under widely varying circumstances seems to have had little effect on the judgments handed down. While it is true that many of the Italian translations or adaptations were inspired solely for personal profit, others were motivated by admiration and respect for the works of Spain's master playwrights—Lope and Calderón in particular—and by the desire to arrive at a comparable Italian art form. In light of this, a comprehensive, more balanced study of the Italian recastings is long overdue. While the international symposium convened in 1981 to celebrate the tercentenary of Calderón's death brought renewed interest in the diffusion of his theater abroad, the influence of Lope's theater on Italian dramaturgy of the seventeenth century remains largely untouched.[1] My preliminary examination and evaluation of several Italian pieces—*commedia dell'arte* scenarios as well as *commedie letterarie* deriving from Lope's theater—indicate that the subject does indeed warrant further attention.[2]

The texts I have chosen to analyze in this essay are *Sette infanti del' Ara* [*sic*], a scenario belonging to the latter half of the seventeenth century, and *Il Tradimento della moglie impudica o sia L'Ingiusta morte de i sette Infanti dell'Ara* (1667); both are modeled on Lope's *Bastardo Mudarra* (1612).[3] The scenario is unique in that it marks a departure from the humor typically associated with the *commedia dell'arte,* despite the insertion of masks such as Tartaglia and Pulcinella. *Il Tradimento della moglie impudica* speaks to those elements in Golden Age drama that most impressed the Italians: the sense of national pride, the chivalric dignity of its protagonists, and the power of the honor code. Unfortunately, these forceful and dynamic elements are often undercut by expansions intended to insure audience appeal.

Several factors, extraliterary as well as literary, account for the warm reception accorded Spanish Golden Age plays in Italy. Spain's domination of southern Italy, which had begun with the Aragonese presence in Sicily as early as 1282, was a *fait accompli* by the first decade of the sixteenth century. In those areas not directly under Spanish rule (i.e., everything north of the Papal States), the crown had secured the support of powerful nobles through concessions of land and privileges or through dynastic marriages. Paralleling the high regard among Italians for Spanish discoveries and conquests in the New World was their esteem for Spain's literary genius and especially for the *comedia,* which exemplified Spanish religious, social, and monarchical values. Spaniards were seen as the embodiment of Christian chivalric values, the new crusaders to be admired and emulated. Such was their impact that Italians soon began to imitate them in manner, dress, and speech. Italian clerics took to imitating the preaching style of their Spanish fellow priests.[4] All was not rosy for long, however, in this political marriage of cultures. By the end of the sixteenth century, many Italians had begun to resent not only the Spanish presence on home soil but also what they perceived to be the arrogance and pretensions of their political masters.

The ambivalent attitude toward Spanish domination notwithstanding, the impact of Spanish Golden Age drama on Italian dramaturgy of the seventeenth century was unmistakable and long-lived. It was also perfectly natural. Spanish comedy was, by the time it reached Italy's shores, already Italianate in form, the direct result of the contact between the *commedia dell'arte* players performing in Madrid, Seville, and Valencia and Spain's budding dramatists, among them Lope de Vega.[5] Lope codified for Spain's national theater elements that were at the heart of the *commedia dell'arte:* a three-act structure, balance and duplication in plot and characters, and a fast-paced story line centering on the tribulations of young lovers who must overcome the inevitable obstacles to their union. The *comici* also offered Lope, in the person of Zanni, the model for his *gracioso.*[6]

Lastly, they made possible the appearance of women as actresses on the Spanish stage, thus allowing for the inclusion in Golden Age comedy of one of the Italian players' favorite devices, the woman disguised as a man.

This was the shape and form of the *comedia* that Spanish acting troupes brought to viceregal Naples and from there to ambassadorial courts in Rome, Florence, Mantua, Milan, and Venice. Their arrival was most propitious for Italian dramaturgy. The early decades of the seventeenth century found Italy's theater, both erudite and popular, in serious need of revitalization. The Renaissance comedies of Ariosto, Machiavelli, and Bibbiena had produced no successors. The court-oriented theater, tied to the norms of that society and its perception of drama, had degenerated into a rigid, bloodless art form governed more by Aristotelian principles than by theatrical instinct. Moreover, no single playwright had emerged who could bring together successfully the classical tradition and a more flexible art form, as Lope de Vega had done for Spain.

The arrival of Spanish theatrical companies in Italy proved advantageous for the *comici dell'arte* as well. Reigning masters of the Italian stage since the mid-sixteenth century, the *comici* were now hampered by a repertory near exhaustion from repetition. In their unrivaled capacity for survival, the *comici* turned to the Spanish *comedia* for new plots. The acquisition of Spanish texts in printed form, as *sueltas* or as performance texts, was facilitated by the many friendships and mutual respect shared by the Italian players and their fellow actors from Spain ever since the latter group's arrival in Naples in 1620 (Croce 1966, 55–80). Of the approximately 700 extant scenarios, almost all of which remain unedited, 104 have their roots in Spanish materials (these include scenarios that are recastings of earlier versions). There are 27 scenarios deriving from plays by Lope de Vega, 4 of which were uncovered by this writer.[7]

The adjustment of Spanish materials to the exigencies of *commedia dell'arte* performances and to the masks was a relatively simple matter. The tripartite structure common to both art forms facilitated the transposition of content, broadly speaking. This did not preclude adjustments stemming from a particular actor-director's dramatic vision or from the need to accommodate the masks of a particular troupe. Here, too, however, the rearrangement was easily accomplished. The *galán* and *dama* of the Spanish original became the *primo innamorato* and *prima donna* of the Italian company. Similarly, the roles of the second pair of lovers (if the plot or subplot so demanded) could be passed on to the second lover and second lady. The blocking figure might now be Pantalone, the Venetian patriarch and senior elder, occasionally assisted by Dottor Gratiano, the Bolognese pedant and second elder, or the role might be assigned to a third male acting as the leading lady's brother. If the Spanish plot contained an unsuccessful second suitor, the role usually went to the *Capitano,* who was always mercilessly ridiculed by the *prima donna.* The *dama's* female servant found her standard counterpart in the *servetta,* or *soubrette,* of the Italian troupe. The *gracioso* reverted easily back to his progenitor, Zanni. By the beginning of the seventeenth century, the single comic servant had evolved into two: one *servo astuto* to assist the lovers in their schemes and the other, a dim-witted fellow, to act as foil for the requisite *lazzi* (comic stage business) that were the mainstay of *commedia dell'arte* performances. Such was the drawing power of the *comici dell'arte* that dramatists for the regular theater found it expedient to incorporate some of the masks, roles, or slapstick humor into their plays if they expected to capture their share of the theater-going public. We shall see precisely this type of borrowing in the discussion of *Il Tradimento della moglie impudica.*

Before approaching Lope's play and the Italian imitations to which it gave rise, a brief résumé of the legend of the *Siete infantes de Lara* is in order. The legend, as found in the *Primera Crónica General,*[8] recounts the slaughter and beheading of the seven sons of Gonzalo Gustios at the hands of the Moors. The *infantes* are led into ambush by their uncle, Ruy Velázquez. Their deaths are subsequently avenged by Mudarra González, bastard half-brother of the *infantes.* Ruy Velázquez's act of betrayal is the result of a series of three altercations between Gonzalo González, youngest of the *infantes,* and a member of Ruy's family, Ruy himself, and a vassal of Ruy Velázquez's wife, Doña Lambra.

On the day of Ruy Velázquez's wedding to Doña Lambra, Gonzalo González kills Alvar Sánchez, a cousin of his hosts, in a dispute over who had dealt a better blow to the *tablado.* Ruy Velázquez, hearing his wife's screams, strikes Gonzalo twice, whereupon Gonzalo retaliates by thrusting his goshawk into Ruy's face. Further violence is avoided when Gonzalo Gustios, the *infante's* father, steps in to make peace.

As Doña Lambra and the wedding party travel to Barbadillo, they stop at a meadow to rest and to dine. There, angered by the sight of Gonzalo González stripped to his underclothes to bathe his goshawk, Doña Lambra sends one of her men to throw a melon filled with blood in Gonzalo's face. The *infantes,* recognizing the deed as a deliberate insult, kill the man even as he clings to Doña Lambra for protection. The brothers then depart for Salas, their village.

When Ruy Velázquez returns, he readily accedes to his wife's demand for vengeance and devises a plan to rid himself of all the *infantes* and their father as well. On the pretext of needing financial assistance to defray the costs of the wedding, he asks Gonzalo Gustios to deliver a formal letter to Almanzor requesting help. The sealed letter, written by a Moor whom Ruy Velázquez later kills, asks Almanzor to decapitate the bearer and to then proceed to Almenar, where, by a ruse, Ruy will bring the *infantes*. Almanzor shows the letter to Gustios but does not kill him. He imprisons Gustios temporarily and sends a Moorish noblewoman to care for him. Shortly thereafter the lady becomes pregnant with Gustios's child.

Ruy Velázquez now asks the *infantes* to join him in battle in the Campo de Almenar. Their tutor, Nuño Salido, troubled by what he believes to be evil omens, tries to dissuade the *infantes* from participating in the sortie. The *infantes* do not heed him. Nuño leaves but returns just in time to be insulted for his premonitions by Ruy Velázquez. When Nuño calls Ruy Velázquez a liar, one of the latter's vassals steps forward to attack Nuño, only to be killed by the young Gonzalo. Ruy Velázquez commands his men to kill the *infantes*. When the *infantes* offer to pay five hundred *sueldos* for the man's death, Ruy feigns acceptance, not wishing to prejudice his plan.

As the *infantes* march toward Almenar, Ruy Velázquez steals away to meet with two Moorish kings, Viara and Galve, to insure that they will kill the *infantes*. Nuño Salido overhears the plot and rushes back to warn the *infantes,* but is too late. They are surrounded by fifteen companies of Moors. To bolster their courage, Nuño tells them that the omens were good, and to prove it he joins them in the first sally, in which he is killed.

Impressed by the *infantes'* prowess, the Moors back off, but not before Fernán, one of the brothers, is killed. Diego González, another brother, who is as yet unaware of the treachery, goes to Ruy Velázquez for help. Ruy refuses, saying that he has not forgotten their insults in the past. As Diego leaves, several hundred sympathetic soldiers steal away to help the *infantes*. In the ensuing battle, all the Christians are killed save the six *infantes*. The Moorish kings take pity on the *infantes* and bring them to their tents to be fed and washed. Ruy Velázquez, enraged by news of the gesture, threatens to denounce Viara and Galve to Almanzor and to demand that their lives be taken. Viara and Galve return the *infantes* to the battleground, and the fighting resumes. All are killed and beheaded. Viara and Galve carry the heads of the *infantes* and that of their tutor to Almanzor.

Almanzor has the heads washed and placed on a white sheet in the order in which they were born, with Nuño's head at the end. He then sends for Gonzalo Gustios (who believes he is being freed) and asks him to identify the heads of some people from Salas. At the sight of the heads, Gustios begins to cry, taking them in his hands one by one and reviewing the deeds of each. In a fury, Gustios then takes up a sword, kills seven Moors and asks Almanzor to kill him. Instead, Almanzor once more asks the Moorish noblewoman to comfort Gustios. She makes up a story about once having had twelve sons who were slain in a single battle. Almanzor frees Gustios and gives him the heads to take back. Before he leaves, the lady tells Gustios that she is pregnant and asks his instructions. Gustios orders that if the child is a boy, he is to be sent to Gustios upon reaching the proper age. Gustios then gives her half of a ring, which will serve to identify the boy as his son. Shortly after his departure, she gives birth to a son, whom she names Mudarra González.

At the age of ten, Mudarra is knighted by Almanzor. Later, when he learns of the fate of his half brothers, Mudarra sets out with a company of men to see his father in Salas. When Gustios sees the ring, he is pleased, especially when Mudarra announces that he wishes to avenge the death of his seven brothers. Mudarra goes to Count Garci Fernández and in his presence challenges Ruy Velázquez. Mudarra is about to wound Ruy Velázquez when the count declares a three-day truce. Mudarra kills Ruy Velázquez later that night, however, when Ruy tries to steal away. Not wanting to take vengeance on Doña Lambra while the count is alive (she is a relative), Mudarra waits until Garci Fernández has died before destroying Doña Lambra by fire.

Although the legend was repeatedly dramatized during the Golden Age, Lope's *Bastardo Mudarra* remains the most faithful rendition of the legend. Juan de la Cueva's *Tragedia de los siete infantes de Lara* (1579) begins with the events after the death of the *infantes,* as does the anonymous 1583 version, *Los famosos hechos de Mudarra* (cited by Menéndez y Pelayo, 3:315). In his 1615 recasting of the legend as *Gran tragedia de los siete infantes de Lara,* Alfonso Hurtado de Velarde takes several liberties with the chronicle materials, perhaps in an effort to differentiate his work from Lope's, although the debt to his predecessor is apparent. Two plays by Alvaro Cubillo de Aragón, *El rey de Andalucía* and *El genízaro de España,* both published in 1654 (cited by Menéndez y Pelayo, 317), barely hold to the legend and contain many invented episodes centering on Mudarra. Juan de Matos Fragoso's *El traydor contra su sangre y siete infantes de Lara* (n.d.),[9] written before 1650, eliminates the episode of the *tablado* as well as that of the melon filled with blood and begins with the altercation between Gonzalillo and Ruy Velázquez. Doña Sancha is already dead as the play begins, and Doña Lambra has no role in the work. Just as the Carolingian epics degenerated into mock epics, so did the legend of the *siete infantes.* In 1650, Jerónimo de Cáncer y Velasco and Juan Vélez de Guevara presented their two-act *comedia burlesca, Los siete infantes de Lara,* to Philip IV in the Retiro.

Lope's *Bastardo Mudarra* incorporates almost in its entirety the legend as found in the *Primera Crónica General,* chapters 736–42 and chapter 751, as well as some elements from the second version intercalated into the recasting of 1344. Lope alters the name of Gonzalo Gustios to Gonzalo Bustos. The Moorish noblewoman who attends him is now called Arlaja (Lope is the first dramatist to use this name). Act 1 of Lope's play takes up, with minor shifts, the essential data from chapters 736 through 738, up to the point where Ruy Velázquez kills the Moor who writes the letter of betrayal for him. Lope eliminates the episode in which Gonzalillo bathes his goshawk. The *infantes* are merely relaxing when Doña Lambra's servant hurls the blood-filled melon in Gonzalillo's face. This allows for immediate retaliation on the part of the *infantes.* Also eliminated is Ruy Velázquez's lie to his sister, Doña Sancha, regarding the reason for her husband's departure. Lope underscores Ruy's villainy by having the nobleman envision himself as "otro conde Don Julián," who, as vengeance for an affront to his daughter, allowed the Moors to enter Spain. By contrast, Lope's Gonzalo Bustos is respected not only by his peers but by his enemies as well—so much so that Almanzor cannot bring himself to kill him.

Act 2 begins with Almanzor's reception of Gonzalo Bustos and takes us through the death of the *infantes* and Gonzalo's eulogy, the emotional climax of the legend. Once more, Lope, while holding to the essence of the tale, adjusts the material to the demands of dramatization. Ruy Velázquez, at variance with the *Primera Crónica General* and the recasting of 1344, plays on the *infantes'* sense of chivalric honor to lure them into ambush. Ruy announces that as a knight he cannot stand idle while the Moors lurk on Castile's borders, for a sheathed sword "no da honor, sino afrenta" (676a), and asks the *infantes* to stay behind to protect his home and their own. Ruy knows full well what their reaction will be, and the trap is sprung. For the sake of the play's swift forward movement, once the fighting has begun, Lope discards the episode in which Diego goes to Ruy for help and is rebuffed. Also eliminated is the pause in the battle when the knights are granted food and rest by their enemies, Viara and Galve. Rather, we learn of it as Galve recounts to Arlaja the details of the battle as well as Ruy Velázquez's threat to have them killed for their compassion toward the *infantes*. The narration is strategically placed immediately before the scene in which Almanzor asks Bustos to identify the eight heads. Gonzalo's lament is somewhat compressed. While the *infantes* are named individually, there is no lingering over each to memorialize their noble exploits. Rather, we have a general lament for their youthful destruction and Gonzalo Bustos's oath of vengeance. Amplifications to the original material include the novelistic embellishment of Gonzalo González's love for Doña Constanza, the fruit of which is Doña Clara, who inspires the love of Mudarra in act 3.

Lope's penchant for autobiographical reflections in his own works is evident in the character of Lope, a squire who refers to himself as "Honrado montañés soy, / nací en el solar de Vega" (194a). He chastises Nuño Salido (the *infantes'* tutor) for referring to the power of omens as the *infantes* march into battle, insisting that omens are "reprehendidos por la iglesia / contrarios a nuestra fe / y a toda intención discreta" (194a). The comment may well have been added to satisfy the censors. In similar obeisance, Gonzalo Bustos not only instructs Arlaja to send his son to him when he is of age, but also to have him baptized by one of the many priests held captive in Córdoba.

The third act moves quickly from a chess game during which Almanzor calls Mudarra a bastard to the latter's discovery of his true identity from Arlaja and his subsequent departure for Salas and the reunion with his father. From the second *cantar* (1344), Lope picks up the tribulations of Gonzalo Bustos over the years (recounted by Clara to Mudarra). The dramatist underscores further the perversity of Doña Lambra through the episode of the seven stones that she hurls every morning at Gonzalo Bustos's window to remind him of his loss and his powerlessness to avenge himself. Also from the second *cantar* is Bustos's instantaneous regaining of his eyesight when he embraces Mudarra for the first time.

As the play moves toward its climax, Lope expands upon his sources to offer us a sleepless, tormented Ruy Velázquez who cannot lay the death of his nephews to rest. The *infantes* haunt his imagination with accusations of treason. When Lope's Mudarra comes upon the psychologically weakened Ruy, he does not kill him outright but spells out who he is and why he challenges Ruy. Ruy is allowed to defend himself but is no match for the younger man. Having decapitated Ruy, Mudarra goes on to kill Doña Lambra, saying, "Tú has de morir abrasada / con la gente que te sigue" (220a).

The play ends quickly thereafter. Bustos places Clara under the protection of Count Garci Fernández. News of Mudarra's vengeance is coupled with Bustos's explanation of Ruy Velázquez's treachery, in turn confirmed by Lope, eyewitness to the slaughter. Mudarra, returning with the severed head of Ruy Velázquez, offers to serve the count in fighting the Moors, to become a Christian, and to marry Clara. His gestures meet with warm acceptance.

Sette Infanti del'Ara [*sic*] is one of ninety scenarios in the first Naples miscellany (Biblioteca Nazionale, Codex XI. AA. 40).[10] Although the collection was compiled in 1700, the *Sette Infanti del'Ara* may have been staged as early as 1634. In a letter of February of that year, Leonora Castiglione, an actress, refers to "I 7 *infanti dell'Ara*" with the machines needed for an allegorical prologue and epilogue" (Rasi, 1:606–7). Whether Castiglione refers to the staging of this particular scenario or yet another version cannot be confirmed, since the Naples piece is the only one that has survived. We can be sure, however, that the legend, through Lope, was on the boards at that time and that it was still popular up through the end of the seventeenth century.

Although *El bastardo Mudarra* had its first performance in 1612, it was not published until 1641. It is most likely that unpublished copies reached viceregal Naples in the hands of Spanish actors. I would speculate further that the preparer of the scenario had probably heard Lope's work performed by Spaniards under its original title, *Los siete infantes de Lara*. Impressed by the drama, the scriptwriter set about casting his own version. Several misspellings in the Naples scenario argue for the primacy of an oral source. The title reads *Sette Infanti "del'Ara"* rather than *"de Lara";* "Gonzalo Bustos" is written as one word, "Gonzalbusto"; and "Doña Lambra" is now "D[onna]. Alambra." These shifts are most likely the result of a nonnative speaker's transcription of the Spanish he heard. I cannot, however, discard the possibility that the discrepancies may be charged to the copyist or to an earlier Italian version now lost to us.

The Naples scenario follows Lope's plot fairly closely, though not mechanically. The title page alerts us to a number of shifts. Caught between fidelity to his source and accommodation to the acting troupe on hand, the scriptwriter makes the following adjustments. The role of Doña Sancha is eliminated. This may have been because the average troupe had only two leading ladies, who would be needed to take up the roles of D. Alambra and Arlacca; or because Doña Sancha has no role beyond the opening scenes of Lope's play. The suppression of her part results in a second adjustment: Ruis Velasco (Ruy Velázquez) and Gonzalbusto (Gonzalo Bustos) are now brothers rather than brothers-in-law. The new arrangement is dramatically effective, since it serves to underscore Ruis Velasco's perversity, now directed against his own brother.

The role of Nuño Salido, tutor to the *infantes,* is taken up by the Dottore, first elder of this scenario, while Tartaglia, often second elder, assumes the role of Mendo, servant to Ruis Velasco. Lope, servant to the *infantes,* who lives to tell of the treachery, is replaced by Pollicinella. The latter, contrary to custom, does not engage in any comic nonsense. The scriptwriter eliminates the part of Count Garci Fernández. There is only brief mention of a count of Barcelona, in whose name Gonzalbusto goes to Almanzorre. The cast of characters lists "7 Infanti," but Gonsadiglio, whose name does not appear listed separately, is the only one with a speaking role. I am at a loss to explain why Alvar Sánchez is renamed Lisardo, or why the Moor Alí is now Braim, since neither Lisardo nor Braim are masks. The remaining characters' names are Italianized: Arlacca (Arlaja), Almanzorre (Almanzor), and Modarra (Mudarra).

The extensive list of props, which includes trumpets and drums for the battle scene in which the seven *infantes* are to appear along with "turchi, e soldati mori," points to concern for detail and, by extension, to an elaborate production. The letter of Leonora Castiglione noted above would appear to support this supposition. There are, however, two stage properties that suggest either the possibility of a source other than Lope or the scriptwriter's imaginative amplification. The first is a scarf that Ruis Velasco wears wrapped around his arm at Almanzorre's request so that he may be recognized and escape injury when the Moors attack. The second prop is a handkerchief stained with Ruis Velasco's blood, which, when passed over Gonzalbusto's blind eyes, restores his sight. Both elements, the scarf and the blood-soaked handkerchief, reappear in *Il Tradimento della moglie impudica.* Since the scenario is not dated separately from the collection in which it appears (1700), there is no way to determine the direction of the borrowing or whether, in fact, both recastings took these elements from an earlier Italian version that is no longer extant.

As for the narrative content of the scenario, act 1 includes all of the action of the Lopean source up to Gonzalbusto's announcement that he must go to Cordova. There are, however, several details in act 1 at variance with Lope's plot. Lope's Ruy Velázquez sends Gonzalo Bustos to Almanzor on the pretext of retrieving the tribute promised him. In the scenario, Ruis sends Gonzalbusto as an ambassador to conclude the peace between the kingdoms. The Italian plot calls for D. Alambra's servant to be instructed to not only throw a blood-filled melon in Gonzadiglio's face but also to kill him should he take umbrage, whereas Lope's Estébañez had been told only to insult Gonzalillo with the gesture. Ruis Velasco's letter of betrayal asks Almanzorre only to imprison Gonzalbusto, not to behead him, as in the Lopean original. Indeed, it appears that the scriptwriter, as he constructed the plot, chose details for the plan as they occurred in the original play contrary to Ruy's designs.

One major revision is the absence in the scenario of Lope's own expansion of the legend: Gonzalillo's love for Doña Constanza. It was probably discarded because it was unmanageable within the time limits of the average evening's entertainment. Also eliminated is Ruy's allusion to himself as a second "Don Julián," which would have had little meaning for an Italian audience.

The changes in act 2 reflect considerable originality, especially as concerns the relationship between Gonzalbusto and Arlacca. According to the scenario, they had met and loved earlier and already have a son named Modarra, who is in Africa learning to fight like his father. This departure from Lope and the facts of the legend may have been intended to shorten the time lapse between Ruy's betrayal and Modarra's revenge. Once again, the scenario coincides with *Il Tradimento della moglie impudica.* It should be noted, however, that Lope's Arlaja is drawn to Gonzalo Bustos because she has long admired him by reputation (188a), which might just as easily have suggested the emendation found in the scenario.

Another innovation is the manner in which Ruis Velasco prepares for his nephews to be ambushed. Whereas Lope's Ruy Velázquez had made this clear in his letter, the Ruis Velasco of the scenario makes a separate trip to Almanzorre to work out the details. In order to lure the *infantes* to their death, Lope's Ruy Velázquez plays on their pride as Christian knights. In the scenario, Ruis Velasco exhorts his nephews to vengeance by focusing on their father's imprisonment by Almanzorre. Once the battle begins, the action moves swiftly and without interruption. There is no mention in the scenario of the auguries or of any awareness on the part of the *infantes* that their uncle has betrayed them.

As act 2 comes to an end, the scenario moves closer to the Lopean source. Gonzalbusto is ostensibly invited to dinner only to find a table on which are the heads of his seven sons and their tutor. The actor is cued simply: "lui suo lamento" (he makes his lament). The fleshing out of the lament is left to the actor's own talents. I suspect that the lament, following Lope's cues, was somewhat abbreviated in the interest of maintaining the flow of the play.

Act 3 begins, as in Lope's version, with the chess game between Almanzorre and Modarra, in which the former, in a moment of anger over the game, calls Modarra a bastard and leaves. Modarra ascertains from Arlacca the facts of his birth and learns of the betrayal of his father and brothers. Modarra sets out to avenge the affront, carrying the half-ring that will serve to identify him.

The scriptwriter retains, with some variation, the first seven lines of Lope's recasting of the *romance* "Convidárame a comer."[11] Each line of verse in the scenario is punctuated by the throwing of a stone ("ad ogni verso si butta un sassolino" [fol. 8]). The episode, with Donna Alambra's accusation that Gonzalbusto's men had killed one of her doves and Gonzalbusto's response that one against seven is hardly fair, is fused with one that appears later in Lope.

As we come to the end of the play, the preparer of the scenario strikes off again on his own. He eliminates Mudarra's encounter with Doña Clara and moves quickly toward the finale. Having killed Ruis Velasco, Modarra returns with Ruis Velasco's head wrapped in a handkerchief dipped in the latter's own blood. Upon passing it over his eyes, Gonzalbusto's blindness is cured (in Lope's version, it is cured when Mudarra and Gonzalo Bustos embrace). It bears repeating that this scenario is unusual in that while masks such as Tartaglia (usually played with a stutter) and Pollicinella are included in the cast, there are no cues whatsoever for the traditional *lazzi* (comic business). The *comici* sensed the power of the material before them and held to its original tenor.

I believe it is safe to assume that the legend of the *infantes* was offered this way on more than one occasion. Unfortunately, no performance data has come down to us other than Leonora Castiglione's letter. That it still held enormous appeal at the end of the seventeenth century is verified by the fact the count of Casamarciano would wish it included in the scenarios he ordered copied.

There are two editions of *Il Tradimento della moglie impudica o sia L'Ingiusta morte de i sette Infanti dell'Ara* (1667 and 1683) in the Biblioteca Casanatense in Rome. The texts of the plays are identical. Variations between the editions are confined to the matter of publisher (Giacomo Monti, 1667; Gioseffo Longhi, 1683—both in Bologna), the lack of a dedication in the 1683 edition, and a slight modification in the spelling of one of the minor character's names (Arsere, in the 1667 edition, becomes Arsette in the later piece).

The dedication of the 1667 edition, addressed to Girolamo Alamandi, offers information as to the matter of performance: "it was then with regal pomp, and noble mastery, represented in the theater erected in the great hall of the most illustrious counts of Bentivogli" (3; my translation). The comment suggests that the work may have been commissioned for a specific occasion or celebration and not necessarily intended for public consumption thereafter. To date, no information regarding subsequent performances has surfaced, although this does not preclude its having been taken up by regular acting troupes once it appeared in print. The fact that it was reissued in Bologna sixteen years later points to continued interest in the material. As of this writing, I am unable to verify the existence of any other editions of the work.

The designation of the work as an *Opera tragicomica riordinata e vestita dal Sig. Angelo Vandani* raises several questions. What exactly did Vandani "reorder" and "dress up"? Was there an earlier version? Does it refer to the plot expansions and the radical name changes that he introduced into the Spanish legend as dramatized by Lope? I am inclined toward the latter interpretation because of the substantial amplification the work undergoes while still remaining faithful to the essentials of the legend. The description of the play as an "opera tragicomica" suggests musical accompaniment and a substantial enlargement of the comic aspect, especially since the cast includes a servant named Piccariglio, clearly intended to strike a familiar chord in the mind of the audience.

That the playwright appears determined to create a tragicomedy centering on the honor theme rather than to reproduce the medieval legend may be gleaned from the total rejection of the traditional names for the cast. Vandani's list of characters reads like that of any seventeenth-century Spanish honor play. For purposes of clarity, I reproduce the cast of Lope's play, rearranged to correspond to the Italian personages as listed.

Bastardo Mudarra	*Il Tradimento*
Garci Fernández (Conde)	Rè di Castiglia
Doña Constanza	D. Clara, sua nipote
Gonzalo Bustos	D. Federico, favorito del Rè
Gonzalo González (Gonzalillo)	D. Carlo, con sei fratelli, figli di D. Federico
Nuño Salido	D. Garzia, aio dei sette fratelli
Lope	Piccariglio, loro servo
Alvar Sánchez	D. Duarte, Cavaliere principale di Castiglia
Ruy Velázquez	D. Ferrante, Generale del Rè
Doña Lambra	D. Eleanora, sua moglie, e cugina di D. Duarte
Almanzor	Rè di Granata
Arlaja	D. Elvira, sua sorella
Mudarra	D. Pietro, figlio naturale di D. Federico e D. Elvira
Viara, Galve	Seriffe, consigliero del Rè di Granata
Alí, moro	Alí Moro Granatino, servo dello stesso D. Ferrante

Vandani's major amplification to the Lopean source material is visible immediately in the play's first title, *Il Tradimento della moglie impudica* (*The Treachery of the Wanton Wife*). It is the scorned D. Eleanora who is the motivating force behind *L'Ingiusta morte de i sette Infanti dell'Ara* (*The Unjust Death of the Seven Infantes of Lara*), the play's secondary title. The adjustment to the original plot suggests that the dramatist did not view the altercations between the young knight and members of Doña Lambra's family as being sufficient reason for the bloodbath that ensues. The shift in focus may have been inspired by Doña Lambra's charge in Lope's play regarding "mi honor, muerto ya" (179b), although there is no reference to improper advances. It may also have its roots in a French version of the legend embedded in Honoré D'Urfé's *Savoysiade* (1606), a panegyric to the Italian house of Savoy. D'Urfé's Doña Lambra is madly in love with one of the *infantes*. When her advances are rejected, her love turns to implacable hatred.[12]

Whatever the source, Vandani was clearly determined to recreate an Italian version of a Spanish Golden Age honor play. D. Ferrante's choice of words after D. Eleanora tells him of D. Carlo's improper advances make this abundantly clear. Having sent his wife to rest, D. Ferrante mulls over the question of revenge and decides that killing Carlo is not enough; the entire memory of that family must be wiped out, for "macchia d'honore solo con sangue si lava" (a stain on one's honor can only be washed away with blood, 43). The words are a literal translation of one of the basic tenets of the honor code, "mancha de honor solo con sangre se lava," as repeated with variations in many a Golden Age play.

D. Federico's prior diplomatic contacts with the Moorish king allow for significant plot changes in act 2 concerning the birth of D. Pietro (Mudarra). When D. Federico is about to be killed by the king of Granada, his life is spared only on the insistence of D. Elvira (Arlaja). It is at this point that we learn that the two had been lovers at an earlier time and that their son, D. Pietro, is locked in a tower. Elvira hopes that D. Federico's presence will bring about his release.

Act 2 also contains several seriocomic episodes. I can find no justification for their inclusion, other than as a concession to popular tastes. These scenes involve D. Duarte, who, unlike his Lopean counterpart, Alvar Sánchez, is not killed by the youngest *infante* but escapes. Pretending to be a mute Moor, he comes to serve D. Carlo, waiting for an opportunity to kill him but never quite succeeding. That we are not expected to take the attempts seriously may be gleaned from the cue in the text: "fa lazi [*sic*] da voler uccidere D. Carlo" (he does the routine of wanting to kill D. Carlo) repeated three times in act 2, scene 5, as D. Carlo writes a letter of farewell to D. Clara. The use of the word *lazi*, a variation of *lazzi*, a term used by the *comici dell'arte* to signify improvised comic action, points to the author's intent to amuse. Act 2, scene 11 finds the Moor headed for D. Carlo's room once more, with a stiletto in hand, only to be seen by Piccariglio, who shoves him into the empty room and locks the door from the outside. The scene stands in sharp contrast to the episodes that follow: D. Ferrante's arrival at Granada and his meeting with the king to solidify his plans for the ambush and the Moor's entry into Castile.

Act 2, scene 14 is once again a seriocomic circumstance. The Moor succeeds in convincing D. Carlo that he wishes to defend him, not to kill him, and D. Carlo helps the Moor escape Piccariglio's wrath. The counterpoint is so jarring as to seriously undermine the legendary material. Vandani was probably trying to re-create comic relief as he had read, or seen performed on stage, in Spanish Golden Age drama. Unfortunately, he was not quite up to the skill of his models.

As Vandani approaches the battle episodes, he inserts one more scene, which functions effectively to remind us of who is to blame for the tragedy about to unfold. It is a double monologue with D. Clara at one end of the stage expressing her love for the absent D. Carlo and D. Eleanora at the opposite side giving vent to her bloodthirsty hatred and desire for revenge.

The battle scenes (2.17–23) follow the Lopean source sequentially, with only one variant, namely, the death of D. Duarte at D. Carlo's side and the former's confession in the presence of Piccariglio. The servant, like his Spanish counter-part, is a witness to the slaughter and returns to testify to the betrayal at the appropriate moment in act 3.

The remainder of act 2, as in Lope, is taken up with D. Federico's release by the king of Granada, but not before he is presented with the heads of the seven *infantes* and that of their tutor, D. Garzia. Vandani builds up to the power of that moment most effectively. As the king leaves the room under the pretext of being called to a secret council, the stage directions call for the coloring of the walls to suddenly change to black ("si muta l'adobbo colorito della stanza in nero," 105), thereby creating a barren, funereal ambience for the uncovering of the table. D. Federico's reaction is intense but brief. Only D. Carlo and D. Garzia are named individually. D. Federico realizes it has been a plot, longs to die, and loses consciousness.

Lope's act 3 moves at a lively pace once Mudarra learns his true identity. Vandani, on the other hand, while essentially holding to the same basic episodes, feels obliged to underscore one more time the perfidy of D. Ferrante and D. Eleanora before each meets the fate he/she deserves. D. Ferrante, angered by D. Federico's survival and determined to see him dead, tries to discredit D. Federico with the king, suggesting that D. Federico is in collusion with the Moorish king. He points to the arrival of a young Moor with a secret letter for D. Federico as evidence of his betrayal. Don Ferrante's plan backfires when D. Federico shows the letter to the king. His charges of treason against D. Ferrante are supported by Piccariglio, who witnessed the ambush, and a servant who acknowledges being bribed by D. Ferrante.

Vandani's expansion of the duel between D. Pietro and D. Ferrante is well executed dramatically. Whereas Lope has the audience learn through Ruy Velázquez's musings that he has been haunted by the memory of his nephews, Vandani brings those recollections to life. The ghosts of the seven brothers appear with swords in hand to defend D. Pietro. The latter insists, however, that to do so would cloud his name and render the revenge ineffective. When D. Ferrante is dead, D. Pietro dips his handkerchief in his blood and returns with it to D. Federico. D. Federico touches the handkerchief to his eyes and instantly regains his sight. As stated above, in Lope's version Bustos regains his sight when he and his son embrace.

As for D. Eleanora, her hatred now focuses on D. Clara, whom she plans to poison at the ball that evening. Her scheme goes awry, however, when D. Clara, suspicious of the drink Eleanora tries to force upon her, orders Eleanora to drink it. D. Eleanora cannot refuse an order from the king's niece. As she lies dying, D. Eleanora confesses all—her rejection by D. Carlo out of love for D. Clara and the false accusation passed on to her husband. Her admission of guilt is strategically placed near the close of the play, since, in the dramatist's eyes, she is the prime mover of the tragedy. D. Ferrante was merely a tool to execute her desire for vengeance. The last verses of the drama, uttered by Piccariglio, serve to underline the lady's evil deed. Piccariglio says that he has no desire to return to Granada, where he nearly lost his skin "servendo à i sette bravi, trucidati così miseramente per *Tradimento della moglie impudica*" (serving seven brave men, slain by the treachery of a wanton wife, 155).

The popularity in Italy of the legend of the seven *infantes* as dramatized by Lope de Vega spans more than half a century. Although *El bastardo Mudarra* was not published until 1641, there exists an autograph manuscript dated 27 April 1612. We may assume that a copy of the original or perhaps a performance text was circulating among Spanish actors and that it was accessible to Italian playwrights and actors. Leonora Castiglione's letter confirms its existence in the repertory of the *comici dell'arte* as early as 1634. I would, however, posit that the scenario *Sette Infanti del'Ara* is a later version because of the points of contact with Vandani's *Tradimento della moglie impudica,* which is known to date from 1667. In both, the *infantes'* father and the Moorish lady had been lovers years earlier and already have a son; the nobleman who betrays the *infantes* wears a scarf around his arm so that he may be spared in battle; and the father's sight is restored when a handkerchief stained with the blood of the traitor touches his eyes. It is entirely possible that Vandani, familiar with the scenario, decided to pick up the details noted above and incorporate them into his recasting. The reverse of the borrowing is not likely, since the scenario does not reproduce Vandani's cast, nor does it aim to be an honor tragedy. Both works, however, clearly have their roots in Lope. Those details not found in Lope may be credited to the creative imagination of the scriptwriter and/or the dramatist or, perhaps, to a secondary Spanish source. Two elements point to a familiarity with Hurtado de Velarde's refurbishing: the traitor's use of a red scarf wrapped around his arm as a signal that he is to be spared and the appearance of the ghosts of the seven brothers as D. Pietro (Mudarra) prepares to kill D. Ferrante. Not to be discounted is the likelihood of an intermediate Italian source that Vandani "reordered" and dressed up" and that, unfortunately, has not yet surfaced if, indeed, it still exists.

Notes

This essay, with slight variations, was presented as a paper at the Midwest Modern Language Association meeting in Chicago, 11–14 November 1991. I wish to express my deepest gratitude to those institutions whose generosity made possible the consultation of works in Italian libraries pertinent to this study: the National Endowment for the Humanities (Travel to Collections Grant,1990), Saint Mary's College (Summer Research Grant, 1990), The American Council of Learned Societies (1991), and The American Philosophical Society (1991).

1.   The most recent studies are those of Profeti (1985; 1987; 1991).

2.   See D'Antuono (1981; 1982; 1983;1984; 1992; 1993; in press).

3.   Vega Carpio, 165–222. All references to *El bastardo Mudarra* are taken from this edition and given in parentheses. The autograph manuscript in the Biblioteca de la Real Academia de la Lengua bears the title *Los siete infantes de Lara*. *Los siete infantes de Lara* is also the title listed in Lope de Vega's *Peregrino en su patria* [1618], edited by Myron A. Peyton (Chapel Hill: University of North Carolina Press, 1971).

4.   Croce (1899) as cited by Farinelli (1929, 2:215 n. 7).

5.   For data corroborating the performance of the *comici dell'arte* in Spain, see Pellicer, Sánchez Arjona, Pérez Pastor, Díaz de Escovar, and Falconieri.

6.   For a discussion of the evolution of the *gracioso* from Zanni and specifically from Harlequin, see Place.

7.   The four scenarios are *La dama scaltra* (Lope's *La discreta enamorada*), no. 22 of Adriani; *Il castico della disonesta moglie* (Lope's *El castigo del discreto*), in *Cinquant'un scenari; Il cavaliere perseguitato* (from Lope's *El perseguido*); and *Nerone imperatore* (Lope's *Roma abrasada*), in Bartoli. Bartoli reproduces the scenarios of Codex II.1.90. of the Biblioteca Magliabecchiana, Florence. For an alphabetical listing of all extant scenarios, see Lea (2:506–54). See Pandolfi (vol. 5) for plot summaries of all extant scenarios.

8.   Alfonso X (2:431–42; 446–48). See also Menéndez Pidal. The 1971 edition reproduces Menéndez Pidal's original study of 1896 along with additions made during the periods 1929–30, 1934, 1950–51, and 1968. For a discussion of the differences in the facts of the legend between the *Primera Crónica General* and the intercalation of the legend in the recasting of 1344, see also Lathrop.

9.   The volume is a collection of *sueltas,* of which *El traydor . . .* is the fourth play. See Microfilm Edition of the *Comedia* Collection, University of Pennsylvania Libraries, Reel 37.

10.   Spellanzon, 271–83. Spellanzon hypothesizes that the Italian actors playing in Madrid may have seen Juan de la Cueva's version or that of Hurtado de Velarde on the Spanish stage. She confuses, however, Hurtado's play with the anonymous version of 1586 and draws no conclusions. Spellanzon offers a plot summary of the scenario, noting the main points of variance with Lope's play. A transcription of the scenario follows. I am indebted to Spellanzon's article for stimulating my interest in *El bastardo Mudarra* and its Italian recastings.

11.   On the *romance* "Convidárame a comer" in both Lope's and Hurtado de Velarde's plays, see Menéndez Pidal, 98.

12.   Benedetto, 253–70. Benedetto reproduces, with a substantial introduction, *Le quatriesme livre de la "Savoysiade,"* which treats the legend of the seven *infantes* by focusing on their avenger, their half brother, Mudarra. The poem from which this is excerpted celebrates the deeds of Beroldo, legendary head of the house of Savoy. Beroldo's feats include a sojourn in Spain at the time of Almanzor and direct contact with Mudarra. As for D'Urfé's familiarity with Lope's *Bastardo Mudarra,* Benedetto notes that in D'Urfé's 1615 revision of the *Savoysiade,* the name of Mudarra's mother, Zelinda in the 1606 version, is changed to Halhage (sometimes spelled Halhaje or Halhaja), clearly related to Lope's Arlaja.

Works Consulted

Adriani, D. Placido. 1734. *Selva overo Zibaldone di concerti comici.* Codex A. 20. Biblioteca Comunale di Perugia.

Alfonso X. 1977. *Primera Crónica General de España.* Edited by Ramón Menéndez Pidal and Diego Catalán. 3d ed. Madrid: Gredos.

Allacci, Leone. 1666. *Drammaturgia.* Rome: Mascardi.

———. 1755. *Drammaturgia . . . accresciuta e continuata fino all'anno MDCCLV.* Venice: Giambattista Pasquale.

Ancona, Alessandro d'. 1891. *Origini del teatro italiano.* 2 vols. Turin: Loescher.

Arróniz, Othón. 1969. *La influencia italiana en el nacimiento de la comedia española.* Madrid: Gredos.

Bartoli, Adolfo. [1880] 1969. *Scenari inediti della commedia dell'arte.* Bologna: Forni.

Belloni, Antonio. 1904. "Per la storia del teatro italo-spagnolo nel secolo XVII." *Biblioteca delle scuole italiane* 10:1–3.

———. 1929. *Il Seicento.* In *Storia letteraria d'Italia.* Milan: Vallardi.

Benedetto, Luigi Foscolo. 1912–13. "Una redazione inedita della legenda degli infanti di Lara." *Studi medievali* 4:231–70.

Bertini, G. M. 1951. "Drammatica comparata ispano-italiana." *Letterature moderne* 2:418–37.

Cairo, Laura, and Piccarda Quilici. 1981. *Biblioteca teatrale dal '500 al '700: La raccolta della Biblioteca Casanatense.* Rome: Bulzoni.

Cáncer, Jerónimo de, and Juan Vélez de Guevara. 1653. *Los siete infantes de Lara, comedia burlesca.* In *El meior de los meiores libros que han salido de comedias nuevas,* 439–56. Madrid: María de Quiñones por Manuel López.

Cinquant'un scenari composti per il teatro San Cassiano. MS. Correr 1040. Museo Correr, Venice.

Correa, Gustavo. 1958. "El doble aspecto de la honra en el teatro del siglo XVII." *Hispanic Review* 26:99–107.

Croce, Benedetto. [1891] 1966. *I teatri di Napoli.* Naples: Pierro; Bari: Laterza.

———. [1899] 1948. "I predicatori italiani del Seicento." In *Saggi della letteratura del Seicento.* Vol. 1 of *Scritti di storia letteraria e politica,* edited by Benedetto Croce, 155–81. Bari: Laterza.

Cubillo de Aragón, Alvaro. 1654. *El rayo de Andalucía. El genízaro de España.* Madrid.

Cueva, Juan de la. [1579] 1965. *Los siete infantes de Lara.* Madrid: Espasa-Calpe.

D'Antuono, Nancy L. 1981. "Lope de Vega y la commedia dell'arte: Temas y figuras." *Cuadernos de filología* (Universidad de Valencia) 3:261–78.

———. 1982. "The Spanish *comedia* in Italy: Lope's *La discreta enamorada* and Its *commedia dell'arte* Counterpart." In *La Chispa '81: Selected Proceedings,* edited by Gilbert Paolini, 69–81. New Orleans, La.: Tulane University Press.

———. 1983. "Theatrical Innovation: The Role of the *Commedia dell'Arte.*" Chap. 5 of *Boccaccio's Novelle in the Theater of Lope de Vega.* Madrid: Porrúa Turanzas.

————. 1984. "Bandello, Lope de Vega and an Unedited *Commedia dell'Arte* Scenario: *Il castico della disonesta moglie.*" In *La Chispa: Selected Proceedings,* edited by Gilbert Paolini, 79–87. New Orleans, La.: Tulane University Press.

————. 1989. "Pantalone Hispanicized: The Comic Father Figure in Lope de Vega's *La francesilla.*" In *Italo-Hispanic Literary Relations,* edited by J. Helí Hernández, 41–55. Potomac, Md.: Scripta Humanistica.

————. 1992. "The Evolution of *Il cavaliere perseguitato:* Literary Interdependence in Bandello, Lope de Vega and the *Commedia dell'Arte.*" *Bulletin of the Comediantes* 44:103–12.

————. 1993. "La comedia española en la Italia del siglo XVII: La *commedia dell'arte.*" In Press. *Cuadernos de teatro clásico.*

Díaz de Escovar, N. 1910–11. "Anales del teatro español correspondientes a los años 1581–1599." *La ciudad de Dios* 82:432–40; 789–96; 83:146–56; 209–24.

Falconieri, John V. 1956–57. "Historia de la *commedia dell'arte* en España." *Revista de literatura* 11:3–37; 12:69–90.

Farinelli, Arturo. 1902. *España y su literatura en el extranjero.* Madrid: Tello.

————. 1929. *Italia e Spagna.* Turin: Bocca.

Fucilla, Joseph G. 1945. *Relaciones hispanoitalianas. [Revista de filología española, Anejo LIX].* Madrid: Consejo Superior de Investigaciones Científicas.

Hurtado de Velarde, Alfonso. 1616. *Gran tragedia de los siete infantes de Lara.* In *Flor de las comedias de España de diferentes autores.* Barcelona: Cormellas.

Lathrop, Thomas A. 1971. *The Legend of the Siete Infantes de Lara.* Chapel Hill: University of North Carolina Press.

Lea, Katherine M. [1934] 1962. *Italian Popular Comedy.* New York: Russell and Russell.

Levi, Ezio. 1935. *Lope de Vega e l'Italia.* Florence: Sansoni.

Lisoni, Alberto. 1895. *Gli imitatori del teatro spagnuolo in Italia.* Parma: Pellegrini.

————. 1898. *La drammatica italiana.* Parma: Pellegrini.

Listerman, Randall W. 1976. "Some Material Contributions of the *Commedia dell'Arte* to the Spanish Theatre." *Romance Notes* 17:194–98.

Madden, David. 1975. *Harlequin's Stick. Charlie's Cane: A Comparative Study of* Comedia dell'Arte *and Silent Slapstick Comedy.* Bowling Green, Ohio: Bowling Green State University Popular Press.

Matos Fragoso, Juan de. [n.d]. *El traydor contra su sangre y siete infantes de Lara.* n.p. In *Comedias* [binder's title] [a collection of *sueltas*]. Microfilm Edition of the *Comedia* Collection, University of Pennsylvania Libraries, Reel 37.

Menéndez Pidal, Ramón, ed. 1971. *La leyenda de los siete infantes de Lara.* 3d ed. Madrid: Espasa-Calpe.

Menéndez y Pelayo, Marcelino. 1949. *Estudios sobre el teatro de Lope de Vega.* Vol. 3. Madrid: Consejo Superior de Investigaciones Científicas.

Meregalli, Franco. 1974. *Presenza della letteratura spagnola in Italia.* Florence: Sansoni.

Molinari, Cesare. 1985. *La commedia dell'arte.* Milan: Mondadori.

Navarra, Teresa. 1919. *Un oscuro imitatore di Lope de Vega: Carlo Celano.* Bari: Società Tipografica Pugliese.

Nicoll, Allardyce. 1931. *Masks, Mines and Miracles.* New York: Harcourt.

Pandolfi, Vito. 1957–60. *La commedia dell'arte: Storia e testo.* 6 vols. Florence: Sannsoni.

Pérez Pastor, Cristóbal. 1901. *Nuevos datos acerca del histrionismo español en los siglos XVI y XVII.* Madrid: Imprenta de la Revista Española.

Pellicer, Casiano.1804. *Tratado histórico sobre el origen y progresos de la comedia y del histrionismo en España.* Madrid: Real Arbitrio de Beneficencia.

Petraccone, Enzo. 1927. *La commedia dell'arte.* Naples: Ricciardi.

Place, Edwin. 1934. "Does Lope de Vega's *gracioso* Stem in Part from Harlequin?" *Hispania* 17:257–70.

Profeti, Maria Grazia. 1985. "Lope a Roma: Le traduzioni di Teodoro Ameyden." *Quaderni di lingue e letterature* 10:89–105.

———. 1987. "Jacopo Cicognini e Lope de Vega: 'Attinenze strettissime'?" *Quaderni di lingue e letterature* 12:221–29.

———. 1989. "'Armi' ed 'amori': La fortuna italiana di *Los empeños de un acaso.*" *Estudios sobre Calderón y el teatro de la Edad de Oro: Homenaje a Kurt y Roswitha Reichenberger,* edited by Francisco Mundi Pedret, 299–322. Barcelona: PPU.

———. 1991. "L'amistà pagata opera scenica del Signor Lopez di Vega Carpio, tradotta dal Signor Mario Calamari." In *Homenaje a Alonso Zamora Vicente,* 3:93–103. Madrid: Castalia.

Rasi, Luigi. 1897. *I comici italiani: Biografia, bibliografia, iconografia.* Florence: Bocca.

Sánchez Arjona, J. 1887. *El teatro en Sevilla en los siglos XVI y XVII.* Madrid: A. Alonso.

Sanesi, Ireneo. 1938. "Note sulla commedia dell'arte." *Giornale storica della letteratura italiana* 3:5–76.

———. 1954. *La commedia.* Storia dei generi letterari, vol. 1. Milan: Vallardi.

Sette Infanti del' Ara [sic]. 1700. In *Gibaldone comico di vari suggetti di comedie ed opere bellissime copiate da me Antonio Passanti detto Orazio il Calabrese. Per comando del Ecc.mo Sig.r Conte di Casamarciano.* Codex XI.AA.40. Biblioteca Nazionale, Naples.

Shergold, N. D. 1956. "Ganassa and the *Commedia dell'Arte* in Sixteenth-Century Spain." *Modern Language Review* 51:359–68.

Siracusa, Joseph, and Joseph L. Laurenti. 1972. *Relaciones literarias entre España e Italia.* Boston: G. K. Hall.

———. 1983. "Literary Relations between Spain and Italy: A Bibliographic Survey of Comparative Literature. Third Supplement (1901–1980)." *Bulletin of Bibliography* 40:12–39.

Smith, Winifred. [1912] 1964. The *Commedia dell'Arte.* New York: Benjamin Blom.

Spellanzon, Giannina. 1925. "Uno scenario italiano ed una commedia di Lope de Vega." *Revista de filología española* 12:271–83.

1667. *Tradimento della moglie impudica o sia L'Ingiusta morte de i sette Infanti dell'Ara, Il, opera tragicomica riordinata, e vestita dal Sig. Angelo Vandani e consecrata all'illustriss. Sig. Girolamo Alamandi.* In Bologna, per Giacomo Monti. Biblioteca Casanatense, Comm. 268/4.

1683. *Tradimento della moglie impudica o sia L'Ingiusta morte de' sette Infanti dell'Ara, opera tragicomica riordinata, e vestita dal Sig. Angelo Vandani.* In Bologna per Gioseffo Longhi. Biblioteca Casanatense, Comm. 588/3.

Vega Carpio, Lope Félix de. [1910–1913] 1966. *El bastardo Mudarra.* In *Obras de Lope de Vega,* volume 7. Madrid: Real Academia Española. Biblioteca de Autores Españoles, vol. 196, 165–222. Madrid: Atlas.

———. [1618] 1971. *Peregrino en su patria.* Edited by Myron A. Peyton. Chapel Hill: University of North Carolina Press.

Part Two

Theory and Performance Studies

Catherine Larson

Metatheater and the *Comedia:*
Past, Present, and Future

S
ince the appearance of Lionel Abel's seminal *Metatheatre: A New
View of Dramatic Form* (1963), critics have attempted to define metatheater and to explore its manifestations in a number of dramatic texts.
The concept has proven particularly relevant to *comedia* scholarship
due to the large number of metadramatic techniques that abound in
Golden Age drama. This essay proposes a reexamination of the topic in which a
number of key issues will be addressed, including the development of a working
definition of metadrama, an analysis of how it has responded to the critical inquiry of the past twenty-five years, and an exploration of its future role in *comedia* studies.

Although *self-referential* theater has existed for centuries, the general hy-
potheses posited by Abel have formed the basis of much contemporary interest in
the phenomenon. Studies of *self-conscious* theater are abundant in the criticism
of Shakespeare and modern drama, and more recent attempts to expand upon
Abel's analysis represent an increasingly sophisticated and detailed approach to
the study of *self-reflexive* theater. In recent years, theater critics have tried to refine the terminology and to categorize different types of metadramatic techniques.
Comedia critics have also appropriated Abel's ideas—as they pertain to the definition of metatheater itself and as they might apply to *comedia* texts.

The first, most obvious, and, at the same time, most difficult issue at hand is
the definition of metadrama. At first glance, this might seem easy—we understand
the etymology of the prefix "meta" and have read about the concept in other contexts: metapoetry, metafiction, and even metahistory. We know that on a most
basic level, metadrama is drama about drama (Hornby, 31), and we tend to unite
under that umbrella term such all-inclusive notions as dramatic self-consciousness,

self-referentiality, the play-within-the-play device, and multilayered role-play-ing. When we teach the concept to our students, we often cite the two stock phrases that form the heart of Abel's definition: "All the world's a stage" and "Life is a dream." Beyond these basic intuitions, however, certain larger issues remain un-resolved: we have been unable to agree on our approaches to the terminology and to the nature and varieties of metadrama; we are even less able to articulate what to make of a play once we have determined that it *is* a metadrama. As schol-ars, we often muse self-consciously about the uncanny nature of this phenome-non, which played such a vital role in the plays of writers from Shakespeare and Calderón to Pirandello, Beckett, and Genet.[1]

Abel self-consciously analyzed his own role in "discovering" a new view of dramatic form: "I have asked myself: can I be the first one to think of designating a form which has been in existence for so long a time, about three hundred years? It is a strange and not undramatic fact of life that something seemingly individual will continue to be seen darkly until it has been given a name" (77). Indeed, Abel emerged as a kind of *post facto* founding father of the concept, defining a set of techniques and attitudes that had never before been given their full measure of legitimacy precisely because they lacked a name.

I see Abel's study as an important and necessary first step, but one that left a great deal for subsequent theater critics to debate, refine, and augment. Metadrama is a phenomenon that has been interpreted in numerous—often conflicting—ways, particularly, as we will see, by *comedia* scholars. Subsequent attempts to affix a working definition to the concept necessarily had to be general enough to pertain to a large number of cases, yet specific enough to respond to some of the issues that Abel did not undertake.

In order to analyze how other scholars have been able to build on Abel's work in the field, it is useful to begin by defining metadrama in terms of his often-cited thesis. According to Abel, metaplays

are theatrical pieces about life seen as already theatricalized. By this I mean that the persons appearing on the stage in these plays are there not simply because they were caught by the playwright in dramatic postures as a cam-era might catch them, but because they themselves knew they were dra-matic long before the playwright took note of them. What dramatized them originally? Myth, legend, past literature, they themselves. They represent to the playwright the effect of dramatic imagination before he has begun to exercise his own. (60)

Abel's definition did, indeed, capture the very essence of metatheater. Yet, my quarrel with Abel's *Metatheatre,* as with many other early excursions into uncharted critical and theoretical waters, is that its definitions are at once too broad and too narrow. Abel's interest lay in describing a dramatic form that was neither tragedy, comedy, nor tragicomedy, not in delineating the multiplicity of ways that metatheater could manifest itself in a dramatic text or in its staging. Moreover, he was little concerned with the effects that the phenomenon produced in and on the reader/spectator. Although he notes the frequent use of the play-within-the-play device in Shakespeare's comedies and history plays, he excludes these plays as not being fully representative of the form; his criticisms of such dramatists as Molière and Marlowe rest on the argument that both writers created characters who were not contained by the generic bounds of their own plays, at least in part because the dramatists' dramatic horizons did not mesh with the inherent theatricality of their characters (61–63).

I would suggest that Abel's adherence to the idea of the metaplay's generic purity is an unnecessary complication of the issue. We might, then, focus less on what metatheater *is* than on what it *does,* stressing the process as well as the product, or at least the results produced by that product. In that light, articles debating whether or not a specific play is a "true" metadrama—in Abel's strict definition of the term—tend to leave us wanting more.

I will therefore briefly present a few of the principles that have guided my own understanding of metadrama in the hope that this working definition will enable us to move on to a discussion of the effects of post-Abelian scholarship on *comedia* criticism. The first point I would like to stress is that metatheater is not really a critical methodology per se, or even a theory (except in the most abstract of senses), although it could certainly be argued that an understanding of the phenomenon is a useful interpretive tool. Consequently, as a term, "metadrama" is more descriptive than prescriptive.

In metadramatic texts, playwrights use certain self-referential devices that may be tied to the play's theme, plot, characterization, or structure in order to achieve specific effects. Such techniques by definition foreground the tension that exists between art and reality. Richard Hornby's *Drama, Metadrama, and Perception* catalogues these devices by type:

1. The play within the play
2. The ceremony within the play
3. Role-playing within the role
4. Literary and real-life reference
5. Self-reference (32)

Hornby's study has one clear advantage over many earlier treatises on the topic of metatheater: rather than taking Abel's general formulations as a given, Hornby's five categories offer a substantive set of descriptive tools to use in discussing theatrical self-consciousness. The critic can then isolate the number and nature of the metadramatic devices that the dramatist employed, analyze the patterns that emerge, and study the effects produced.

Moreover, different plays contain varying amounts of metadramatic techniques and produce different reactions in the reader or spectator. In that sense, we might see metadrama as a continuum on which plays may be placed at different points, depending on the degree of their self-reflexivity. In addition, it is obvious that reader or audience reactions to a metaplay will vary—at least to a certain extent—due to the same kinds of reader-response factors that govern any type of reaction to literature: as Jauss reminds us, readers respond to a given text based on their own horizons of experience and expectations, that is, on their own past experiences with other literary texts and with life itself.[2]

With that caveat in mind, the effects of these metadramatic techniques on the reader or audience are crucial to our understanding of the phenomenon. Hornby maintains that metadrama causes the audience to "see double," to recognize on some type of conscious level that he or she is witnessing theater about theater (32). In a similar vein, Herbert Weisinger describes the blurring of illusion and reality that occurs in the *theatrum mundi* metaphor:

> The strain between what we know ought to be there and what we actually see breaks down our hold on our instinctive acceptance of our three-dimensional, perspectived, space-time, cause and effect universe. The results of our ordinary processes of perception and logic are deliberately and systematically reversed, misdirected, and even repudiated, and we are thus startled

into a fresh perception of experience but often at the cost of our confidence in that as well. The metaphor and like devices must by their nature carry with them the overtones of suspicion and anxiety: one can never be sure any more, either in the displaced or the new vision, for, having been tricked once, we feel sure we will be tricked twice. Once the actor has stepped out of his role, can we be sure that he really has returned to it; does the dream really end; if objects cast no shadow, are they really real; and if last year is either a dream of the past or a projection of the future, is there really no present? (67–68)

These descriptions of the experiential effects of metadrama underline the conflict between illusion and reality that is produced by a self-conscious play. By causing the reader/spectator to contemplate the links between art and life, the dramatist raises any number of questions about the nature of the theater, about the metaphysical problems of the age, and about society in general.[3]

Like other literary trends, metadramas tend to rise and fall in popularity in different ages. Hornby notes that "whenever the play within the play is used, it is both reflective and expressive of its society's deep cynicism about life. When the prevalent view is that the world is in some way illusory or false, then the play within the play becomes a metaphor for life itself" (45). One of those ages whose society Hornby describes is the Baroque. Frank Warnke views the distinction between the Renaissance and the Baroque in terms of a theatrical metaphor, maintaining that while the Renaissance saw the world as being *like* the theater, in the Baroque, the world *was* the theater (69–70). Manfred Schmeling echoes this distinction: "Le théâtre dans le théâtre répondait particulièrement bien à l'esprit baroque, fasciné par l'apparence, l'idée de la *vanitas* et du *theatrum mundi*" (18). The twentieth century has engaged in yet another revival of self-reflexive literature, since contemporary society has made self-reflexive art "a correlative for the complex intellectual and philosophical temperament of our age" (Schlueter, 4).

Due to the proliferation of self-conscious literature in the twentieth century, as well as the attendant interest provoked by Abel's *Metatheatre* and numerous other scholarly treatments of metafiction in general, the topic became a critical commonplace in the 1960s and 1970s. In theater criticism, dozens of books and articles described the metadramatic techniques found in Shakespeare and in countless modern plays. Hispanic critics joined that trend. Alan Trueblood's 1964 article, "Rôle-playing and the Sense of Illusion in Lope de Vega," which wrestled with the relationship between the dramatic imagination and the play spirit in role-playing, stressed the importance of the world-stage metaphor in *Lo fingido verdadero*. In 1970, Bruce Wardropper also dealt with the role of the imagination in his analysis of Calderonian theater, particularly the honor plays. Although both critics treated the topics of role-playing and the imagination, Trueblood used Huizinga's *Homo Ludens* as the theoretical model for his article, while Wardropper based many of his observations on Abel's *Metatheatre*.[4] In addition, Susan L. Fischer's dissertation, which examined the psychological and aesthetic implications of role-change in Calderonian drama, anticipated much of the interest in metadrama and the *comedia* that would follow.

In the mid-1970s, a major debate was waged vis-à-vis the application of Abel's ideas to the *comedia*. Thomas A. O'Connor's "Is the Spanish *Comedia* a Metatheater?" (1975) initiated this debate, modifying Abel's focus on the character's theatricalized self-image in order to describe the dramatist's worldview (276). He maintained that metatheater must be adapted to seventeenth-century Spain's theocentric and moral view of the world, which held that acting and role-playing essentially signaled inauthenticity and self-deception: "To be an actor is to be false, a mime or mimic of what really is. The Christian cannot be thus and be sure of salvation. While *metatheater* gives many insights into the structure and form of the serious Spanish *comedia,* it fails to explain the Christian response to pretense and theatricality" (287). O'Connor concluded that metatheater as described by Abel was more applicable to Shakespeare than to Spanish dramatists of the Golden Age. In a subsequent article on *La vida es sueño* (1978), O'Connor again stressed that although Abel's term "may provide some new insights into the nature of the *comedia*," we should nonetheless "be circumspect in applying it indiscriminately."[5]

Arnold Reichenberger (1975) had previously supported just such a position: his own claims regarding the uniqueness of the *comedia* bolstered O'Connor's arguments. In addition, Robert Sloane's complementary analysis of *El príncipe constante* (1979), while centering on the problem of role-playing, likewise concludes with the observation that Calderón's drama is not a true metaplay, since God is the controlling "dramatist"; this would seem to underscore O'Connor's theocentric approach to the *comedia*. Thus, O'Connor's view of the applicability of metatheater to the *comedia* garnered support from a number of scholars who believed that Abel's ideas needed to be modified to take into account the unique nature of seventeenth-century Spanish values.

A number of critics, however, represented the opposite position in this debate, finding O'Connor's thesis problematic. Frank P. Casa (1976) objected both to O'Connor's general analysis of role-playing and his specific examples of the phenomenon. Casa maintained that the *comedia* does not exhibit true role reversal or character betrayal but rather the self-realization of inherent characteristics (28–29); moreover, he observed that role-playing per se is not necessarily as negative as O'Connor had described it. Casa noted the influence of social factors other than religion on the *comedia* and Golden Age Spain. As a result, he found it difficult to reconcile O'Connor's theocentric view with the multitude of realities that surrounded seventeenth-century society and that served as sources for Golden Age dramatists.

Stephen Lipmann (1976) also objected to O'Connor's theocentric approach, claiming that he "overlooks Abel's point on the primacy of the dramatic imagination. And he misrepresents Abel's point on 'theatricalized life'" (232). Although Lipmann conceded that much of this polemic might derive from Abel's own lack of thoroughness and digressions in *Metatheatre,* he nonetheless rejected O'Connor's thesis, affirming that Abel's use of the term "metatheater" is "entirely appropriate to the *comedia*" (231).

Finally, in the early pages of her article on *Los cabellos de Absalón* (1976), Susan L. Fischer adds her criticism of O'Connor's "excessive faith in a particular critical creed" and his narrow definition of the *comedia* as "a form of instruction without due consideration of it as a form of experience" (104). She then discusses the dual nature of role-playing in metatheater, distinguishing theatrical role-playing from the psychic or mental mode of role-play.

These three studies, all of which explore some of the debatable aspects of O'Connor's view of the *comedia,* helped to clarify the complexity of the issues surrounding metadrama's possible application to Golden Age theater. In that sense, O'Connor's article served a purpose similar to that of Abel's book: it led to the type of scholarly debate that ultimately helped to refine the original concept and to reexamine its usefulness as a tool for explicating seventeenth-century dramatic texts.

In the late 1970s and early 1980s, a number of critics used the concept of meta-theater to study the theme and structure of several serious Golden Age dramas. José Antonio Madrigal discussed role-playing in his analysis of Lope's *Fuente-ovejuna* (1979), uniting Abel's ideas on metatheater with Joseph Moreno's theories on the topic of psychodrama. Particularly interesting in Madrigal's article is his validation of Abel. Madrigal contended that Abel's metadramatic theories are beneficial in that they offer the critic a focus or dramatic perspective, serving as a vehicle to promote a better understanding of a play's theme (21–22). In that context, Madrigal observed, it is appropriate to apply the nucleus of Abel's ideas, since they were never intended to function as a rule-governed method or system of interpretation (17, 22).

Many other *comedia* scholars used just such an approach to the topic, distilling the essence of Abel's theories and combining them with the ideas of Wardropper and others. William C. McCrary (1978) and Susan L. Fischer (1981) analyzed Lope's *El castigo sin venganza* as a metadrama; both articles emphasized how the characters' role-playing functions on multiple levels, especially in the case of the duke. Fischer summarized the role of metatheater in Lope's play in this way: "By endowing his play with a metatheatrical structure, Lope has used the raw materials of the playwright's craft to show that the human imagination is simultaneously a productive and destructive faculty. On the one hand, it is the source of man's creativity, and on the other, it is the origin of his self-deception" (32).

Carol B. Kirby's article on Calderón's *El médico de su honra* (1981a) paralleled William C. McCrary's 1979 analysis of the interplay between theater and history in *El rey don Pedro en Madrid*. McCrary, who saw Pedro as the protagonist of a great national drama, reiterated his debt to Abel's two central metaphors (the world-theater topos and the life-dream metaphor), which he fused with the "Ciceronian teleology of the dramatic art which predicated that a play was an *imago veritatis*" (149). Kirby's approach to Calderón shared many of McCrary's views; she concluded that Calderón was less interested in the dramatization of a particular king's reign than in the "process by which art imitates itself through the remembrance and repetition of previous models and scripts" (134).

In addition to these studies, a number of other *comedia* texts have also been analyzed as metadramas. *La vida es sueño* and *El gran teatro del mundo* have continued to attract attention for their use of self-referential theatrical techniques.[6]

In *The Limits of Illusion: A Critical Study of Calderón* (1984), Anthony Cascardi observed that "in some of Calderón's most interesting works, there are overt recognitions of the contiguities between theatrical form and the thematics of illusion" (xi). Roger Moore's analysis of *El mágico prodigioso* (1981) further discussed the play-within-the-play technique; Moore stated that *El mágico prodigioso* is not "a simple play with a demonstrable unity of theme and action, but rather a series of plays composed at different times by different authors" (130). The list of critical studies describing metadramatic aspects of the *comedia* has continued to grow, although the approaches themselves have varied significantly in their response to Abel's postulations.

As is readily apparent from this survey, critics have explored the self-conscious nature of the *comedia* in many forms and styles during the last twenty-five years. The topic that Abel initiated has sparked such a degree of critical interest that it could certainly be labeled one of the dominant trends of contemporary *comedia* criticism. Yet, even though the theatrical metaphor has come to be recognized as a major aspect of Golden Age drama, it is far from exhausted as a subject for textual explication. As Hornby's study suggests, metadrama remains an important issue in theater criticism; as new theories modify existing concepts, we see the analytical tools that we once took for granted in a new light, allowing our understanding of the *comedia* to build upon established ideas in an ever-expanding, metonymic chain of interpretation.

A relatively unexplored aspect of metatheater's role in Golden Age drama is its relationship to comedy. As part of our reexamination of the concept, we should note that many questions relating to the appearance of metadrama in comedy remain unanswered. Perhaps part of this general critical neglect derives from an overly strict adherence to one of Abel's principal goals in *Metatheatre,* the definition of a new form that differs in certain key respects from traditional definitions of tragedy, comedy, and tragicomedy. It is certainly clear that critical treatments of metatheater in Hispanic texts have tended to focus on serious dramas. As I have noted earlier in this essay, however, Abel's insistence on separating metatheater from other theatrical genres unnecessarily complicates the issue. This is particularly true when the discussion involves the *comedia,* which already deviated greatly from classical generic definitions of comedy or tragedy. Moreover, the most recent studies of metadrama tend to concern themselves less with questions of generic purity and more with issues of contemporary interest: what metadramas do and how they are perceived by their audiences.[7]

In order to examine these issues, we need to survey the ways that self-consciousness manifests itself in all types of *comedias*. I would argue that self-conscious devices appear as frequently in Golden Age comedy as in other types of theater, classic examples being Cervantes's *El retablo de las maravillas* and Calderón's *La dama duende*. Role-playing is often made explicit in the disguises and theatrical manipulations inherent in the *capa y espada* plays, the *comedias de enredo,* and the *comedias de figurón*. Characters may become self-dramatizing or function as intratextual dramatists or directors, writing new scripts or directing the actions of other characters in a patently self-referential attitude. In that context, the lighter *comedias* often help to highlight the differences between the sexes, since women often must resort to using role-playing and other theatrical devices in order to achieve some measure of power or authority. Explorations of identity, which involve questions of reality versus role-playing or being versus seeming, are the stuff of which many nonserious *comedias* are made.

In a number of these less serious plays, the self-conscious nature of role-playing leads the reader/audience to experience the "seeing double" that Hornby has described as a recognition of the theatrical metaphor in action (32). In other comedies, the play-within-the-play device serves to achieve that effect: the interior play's relationship to the exterior play parallels the relationship that exists between the outer play and reality (Nelson, 10). In each case, the metaplay produces a double-layered perspective for the spectator, just as it does in more serious dramas. Patricia Waugh's comments on metanarratives are directly applicable to our discussion of the effects of metatheater in Golden Age comic works: these texts not only provide readers with a better understanding of the fundamental structures of the theater; they also offer "extremely accurate models for understanding the experience of the world as a construction, an artifice, a web of interdependent semiotic systems" (9).

As I have tried to underscore, these effects of metatheater do not belong exclusively to the serious dramas of the Golden Age. Consequently, I would suggest that Abel's observation that many metaplays "instill a grave silence—a speculative sadness—at their close" (59) is relevant only to the extent that by raising questions about the relationship between the theater and human identity, metadramas may provoke more than superficial musing about the connections between art and life, between the world of the theater and the world outside the theater. That kind of ontological questioning can certainly result from plays that are less serious than those that Abel initially discussed. Thus, as critical discussions of metatheater continue to expand the limits of Abel's theories, we may well find any number of texts that lend themselves to the insights that the approach offers.

Yet another area of interest to contemporary literary theorists is that of the relationship existing between and among texts. The notion of intertextuality, discussed by Roland Barthes, Julia Kristeva, Gustavo Pérez-Firmat, and numerous others, refers not just to the appearance of one text inside another but also to a chain of references and allusions that form part of the place a text occupies in history. Hornby relates the concept of intertextuality to metadrama by including literary references ("direct, conscious allusions to specific works" [90]) within his five categories of metadramatic types. While I would quarrel with some aspects of Hornby's discussion of the topic,[8] I do agree with his conclusion that

> the degree of metadramatic estrangement generated is proportional to the degree to which the audience recognizes the literary allusion as such.
>
> When they do recognize it, the result is like an inset play within the play in miniature: the imaginary world of the main play is disrupted by the reminder of its relation, as a literary construct, to another literary work or works. (88)

It is clear that literary citation, a concept directly linked to contemporary discussions of intertextuality, offers the critic a wealth of material for investigation. The intrusion of antecedent literary texts in a later one can lead to an interrogation of the authority of literature itself. In addition, the use of literary references as a distancing device within a text raises questions of audience appreciation, especially since the audiences of the *corrales* displayed a vast range in education and knowledge of other texts.[9] It might be useful to study from a sociological perspective how these variables in an audience's literary sophistication would relate to its ability to recognize such estranging devices in a metaplay. Discussions of metatheater can thus go far beyond the mere acknowledgment that a text is self-conscious.

In a similar vein, a number of valuable insights might be gleaned from examining other variables inherent in an audience's recognition and appreciation of metatheater. If an acquaintance with literary allusions affects an audience's ability to "see double," it must surely be true that similar cases could be made for other

types of metadramatic devices. This issue clearly relates to the motivations behind a dramatist's use of self-conscious structures. Whether he was challenging
traditional forms of the theater, striving to question the social order of his day, or
designing an artifice of excess, the self-conscious playwright of the Golden
Age made decisions that affected his intended audience in specific ways. An
audience's response was therefore directly tied to its ability to break through what
Robert Alter called "real-seeming artifice" (x) in order to move to new levels of
interpretation.

Yet another area that invites critical engagement is that of the staging of self-
conscious *comedias*. This could include an analysis of the conflict between theatrical conventions and their subversion in many Golden Age metadramas, or it
could extend to a discussion of the *comedia*'s endings, specifically the appeal for
applause made directly to the audience at the conclusion of a play. In addition, the
ways that metadramatic devices actually functioned onstage—as well as the props
that facilitated their staging, the self-conscious use of costume (e.g., in the cases
of the *mujer vestida de hombre* and the *hombre vestido de mujer*), and the use of
the aside—represent related issues that merit further attention. Once again, the
field offers a great deal to the *comedia* scholar.

Finally, recent discussions of metalanguage and metadiscourse are obvious
examples of issues related to self-conscious theater. The tenuous relationship existing between signs and referents is as applicable to the level of discourse as to
the other semiotic systems that function in the theater. In that sense, Keir Elam
notes:

> In the drama, the metalinguistic function often has the effect of foregrounding
> language as object or event by bringing it explicitly to the audience's atten-
> tion in its pragmatic, structural, stylistic or philosophical aspects. At an ex-
> treme of linguistic self-consciousness, such commentary serves to "frame"
> the very process of character-to-character or actor-to-audience verbal com-
> munication, and so becomes part of a broader metadramatic or metatheatrical
> superstructure. (1980, 156)

As Elam's comments suggest, studies of the links between self-conscious language and self-conscious theater proffer real interpretive possibilities for *comedia*
scholars. Dramatic discourse, yet another fruitful avenue for exploration, could

serve as an appropriate vehicle for explaining the relationship between a drama's rhetorical strategies and its structural self-reflexivity.

In this essay, I have tried to suggest both the richness of more recent discussions of metatheater and the possibilities available to the critic who wonders if the topic has exhausted theoretical examination. As part of this effort, I have included a relatively lengthy bibliography at the end of this study in the hope that it will be useful to scholars interested in the subject. We need to evaluate what remains to be done from the perspective and context of what has been written before, distinguishing what works from what does not. I would submit that the relationship between metatheater and the *comedia* still offers the critic much material for textual analysis. *Comedia* scholars have accomplished a great deal, but the field nonetheless remains open for future exploration and study.

Notes

1.   Ernst Robert Curtius, for example, offers a clear explanation of the theatrical metaphor and its development from Plato through John of Salisbury to Hofmannsthal (see especially pages 138–44).

2.   See Hans Robert Jauss (1982a and b) for a discussion of the relationship between literary history, literary theory, and reader reception and response.

3.   John W. Kronik's analysis of *El gesticulador* makes just such a point; Kronik observes that Usigli's drama "is one of those plays which all the while that it makes the theatrical medium into a vehicle of socio-political commentary also turns onto itself to unmask and probe the medium that it is" (5). In the *comedia,* this kind of dialogue between the theater and sociopolitical issues is manifest: Golden Age metadramas deal with the honor code, the role of women in society, the social power structure, and questions of religion, to cite just a few of the many issues that are raised.

4.   Bruce Wardropper's 1970a essay is closely allied with Abel's study; see also 1970b and 1973 for further discussion of self-consciousness in Golden Age drama.

5.   O'Connor 1978, 13. He concludes that "Abel's underlying principles for metatheater must be altered and modified when applied to Calderón and other Spanish dramatists. If not, one will miss the point and fail to understand the basic moral attitude implicit in the *comedias* of the seventeenth century. Metatheater can be a useful term which helps us to comprehend the serious dramas of the period, and therefore an altered understanding of it . . . is imperative for its application to *La vida es sueño*" (24).

6.   Michele F. Sciacca, Peter W. Evans, Jackson I. Cope, Federica de Ritter, Domingo Ynduráin, and Eugenio Suárez-Galbán figure among the many scholars who have examined the theatrical metaphor in *La vida es sueño* and *El gran teatro del mundo.*

7.   In particular, note such contemporary treatments of metadrama as those of Sidney Homan, Robert Egan, James Calderwood (1979), Keir Elam (1984), Robert Nelson, June Schlueter, and Richard Hornby.

8.   Hornby claims that these allusions must be "recent and popular" (90), a caveat that seems entirely unnecessary. I would submit that as long as the reader/spectator recognizes that the allusion is to another text, the dramatist will have produced the kind of self-conscious reflection that breaks the mimetic reality created in the play up to that moment.

9.   The audience's appreciation of literary self-reflexivity parallels, of course, its ability to "see double" in related areas, such as Golden Age art. Indeed, the links between self-conscious theater and the plastic arts offer yet another avenue for interpretation.

Works Consulted

Abel, Lionel. 1963. *Metatheatre: A New View of Dramatic Form.* New York: Hill and
        Wang.

Alter, Robert. 1975. *Partial Magic: The Novel as a Self-Conscious Genre.* Berkeley and
        Los Angeles: University of California Press.

Archer, Robert. 1988. "Role-Playing, Honor, and Justice in *El alcalde de Zalamea." Jour-
        nal of Hispanic Philology* 13:49–66.

Barthes, Roland. 1975. *The Pleasure of the Text.* Translated by Richard Miller. New York:
        Hill and Wang.

Berry, Francis. 1965. *The Shakespeare Inset: Word and Picture.* London: Routledge and
        Kegan Paul.

Calderwood, James L. 1971. *Shakespearean Metadrama.* Minneapolis: University of Min-
        nesota Press.

———. 1979. *Metadrama in Shakespeare's Henriad:* Richard II *to* Henry V. Berkeley
        and Los Angeles: University of California Press.

———. 1983. *To Be and Not to Be: Negation and Metadrama in* Hamlet. New York:
        Columbia University Press.

Casa, Frank. 1976. "Some Remarks on Professor O'Connor's Article 'Is the Spanish
        Comedia a Metatheater?'" *Bulletin of the Comediantes* 28:27–31.

Cascardi, Anthony J. 1984. *The Limits of Illusion: A Critical Study of Calderón.* Cam-
        bridge: Cambridge University Press.

Case, Thomas E. 1990. "Metatheater and World View in Lope's *El divino africano." Bul-
        letin of the Comediantes* 42:129–42.

Cope, Jackson I. 1973. *The Theater and the Dream: From Metaphor to Form in Renais-
        sance Drama.* Baltimore, Md.: Johns Hopkins University Press.

Culler, Jonathan. 1981. *The Pursuit of Signs.* Ithaca, N.Y.: Cornell University Press.

Curtius, Ernst Robert. 1953. *European Literature and the Latin Middle Ages.* Translated by Willard Trask. New York: Harper and Row.

Darbord, Michel. 1983. "Cervantes et le théâtre." In *Vérité et illusion dans le théâtre au temps de la Renaissance,* edited by Marie-Thérèse Jones-Davies, 21–25. Paris: Touzot.

Egan, Robert. 1975. *Drama within Drama: Shakespeare's Sense of His Art.* New York: Columbia University Press.

Elam, Keir. 1980. *The Semiotics of Theatre and Drama.* London: Methuen.

———. 1984. *Shakespeare's Universe of Discourse: Language-Games in the Comedies.* Cambridge: Cambridge University Press.

Evans, Peter W. 1984. "Calderón's Portrait of a Lady in *La vida es sueño.*" In *What's Past Is Prologue: A Collection of Essays in Honour of L. J. Woodward,* edited by Salvador Bacarisse et al., 46–56. Edinburgh: Scottish Academic Press.

Fischer, Susan L. 1974. "Psychological and Esthetic Implications of Role-Change in Selected Plays of Calderón." Ph.D. diss., Duke University.

———. 1975. "The Art of Role-Change in Calderonian Drama." *Bulletin of the Comediantes* 27:73–79.

———. 1976. "Calderón's *Los cabellos de Absalón:* A Metatheater of Unbridled Passion." *Bulletin of the Comediantes* 28:103–13.

———. 1981. "Lope's *El castigo sin venganza* and the Imagination." *Kentucky Romance Quarterly* 28:23–36.

Fly, Richard. 1986. "The Evolution of Shakespearean Metadrama: Abel, Burckhardt, and Calderwood." *Comparative Drama* 20:124–39.

Friedman, Edward H. 1982. *The Unifying Concept: Approaches to the Structure of Cervantes' Comedias.* York, S.C.: Spanish Literature Publications.

Gass, William H. 1970. *Fiction and the Figures of Life.* New York: Knopf.

Hernández-Araico, Susana. 1983. "Texto y espectáculo en 'La hija del aire': Escenificación de un metadrama trágico." *Segismundo* 37–38:27–36.

Hesse, Everett W. 1980. "Tirso and the Drama of Sexuality and Imagination." *Iberoromania* 12:54–64.

Holt, Marion Peter. 1988. "The Metatheatrical Impulse in Post–Civil War Spanish Comedy." In *The Contemporary Spanish Theater: A Collection of Critical Essays,* edited by Martha T. Halsey and Phyllis Zatlin, 79–91. Lanham, Md.: University Press of America.

Homan, Sidney. 1981. *When the Theater Turns to Itself: The Aesthetic Metaphor in Shakespeare.* Lewisburg, Pa.: Bucknell University Press.

Hornby, Richard. 1986. *Drama, Metadrama, and Perception.* Lewisburg, Pa.: Bucknell University Press.

Hubert, Judd D. 1991. *Metatheater: The Example of Shakespeare.* Lincoln: University of Nebraska Press.

Huizinga, Johan. 1950. *Homo Ludens: A Study of the Play-Element in Culture.* Boston, Mass.: Beacon.

Hutcheon, Linda. 1980. *Narcissistic Narrative: The Metafictional Paradox.* New York: Methuen.

Jacquot, Jean. 1957. "'Le théâtre du monde' de Shakespeare à Calderón." *Revue de littérature comparée* 21:341–72.

Jauss, Hans Robert. 1982a. *Aesthetic Experience and Literary Hermeneutics.* Translated by Michael Shaw. Introduction by Wlad Godzich. Minneapolis: University of Minnesota Press.

———. 1982b. *Towards an Aesthetic of Reception.* Translated by Timothy Bahti. Introduction by Paul de Man. Minneapolis: University of Minnesota Press.

Kirby, Carol Bingham. 1981a. "Theater and History in Calderón's *El médico de su honra.*" *Journal of Hispanic Philology* 5:123–35.

———. 1981b."Theater and the Quest for Anointment in *El rey don Pedro en Madrid.*" *Bulletin of the Comediantes* 33:149–59.

Kristeva, Julia. 1973. *Séméiotiké: Recherches pour une sémanalyse.* Paris: Seuil.

———. 1986. *The Kristeva Reader.* Edited by Toril Moi. New York: Columbia University Press.

Kronik, John W. 1977. "Usigli's *El gesticulador* and the Fiction of Truth." *Latin American Theatre Review* 11:5–16.

Larson, Catherine. 1991. "Lope de Vega and Elena Garro: The Doubling of *La dama boba.*" *Hispania* 74:15–25.

Lipmann, Stephen. 1976. "'Metatheater' and the Criticism of the *Comedia.*" *Modern Language Notes* 91:231–46.

McCrary, William. 1978. "The Duke and the *Comedia:* Drama and Imitation in Lope de Vega's *El castigo sin venganza.*" *Journal of Hispanic Philology* 2:203–22.

———. 1979. "Theater and History: *El rey don Pedro en Madrid.*" *Crítica hispánica* 1:145–67.

Madrigal, José Antonio. 1979. "*Fuenteovejuna* y los conceptos de metateatro y psicodrama: Un ensayo sobre la formación de la conciencia en el protagonista." *Bulletin of the Comediantes* 31:15–24.

Moore, Roger. 1981. "Metatheater and Magic in *El mágico prodigioso.*" *Bulletin of the Comediantes* 33:129–37.

Moreno, Joseph. 1972. *Psychodrama.* New York: Beacon House.

Muller-Bochat, Eberhard. 1984. "Las ideas de Cervantes sobre el teatro y su síntesis en *Pedro de Urdemalas.*" *Arbor* 119:81–92.

Nelson, Robert. 1958. *Play within a Play; The Dramatist's Conception of His Art: Shakespeare to Anouilh.* New Haven, Conn.: Yale University Press.

Nolting-Hauff, Ilse. "Lope de Vega: *Lo fingido verdadero.*" In *Das spanische Theater: Vom Mittelalter bis zur Gegenwart,* edited by Volker Roloff, 70–89. Dusseldorf: Schwann-Bagel.

O'Connor, Thomas A. 1975. "Is the Spanish *Comedia* a Metatheater?" *Hispanic Review* 43:275–89.

———. 1978. "*La vida es sueño:* A View from Metatheater." *Kentucky Romance Quarterly* 25:13–25.

Paredes L., Alejandro. 1983. "Nuevamente la cuestión del metateatro: *La cisma de Inglaterra.*" In *Calderón: Actas del congreso internacional sobre Calderón y el teatro español del Siglo de Oro,* edited by Luciano García Lorenzo, 1:541–48. Madrid: Consejo Superior de Investigaciones Científicas.

Pennington, Eric. 1990. "Metatheatrical Techniques in Alfonso Sastre's *Jenofa Juncal.*" *Gestos: Teoría y práctica del teatro hispánico* 5:77–89.

Pérez-Firmat, Gustavo. 1978. "Apuntes para un modelo de la intertextualidad en literatura." *Romanic Review* 69:1–14.

Persin, Margaret H., Andrew P. Debicki, Nancy Mandlove, and Robert Spires. 1983. "Metaliterature and Recent Spanish Literature." *Revista canadiense de estudios hispánicos* 7:297–309.

Reichenberger, Arnold G. 1975. "A Postscript to Professor Thomas Austin O'Connor's Article on the *Comedia.*" *Hispanic Review* 43:289–91.

Righter, Anne. 1962. *Shakespeare and the Idea of the Play.* London: Chatto and Windus.

Ritter, Federica de. [1952] 1953. "El gran teatro del mundo: La historia de una metáfora." *Revista nacional de cultura* 14:133–53. Reprint. *Panorama* 2:81–98.

Schlueter, June. 1979. *Metafictional Characters in Modern Drama.* New York: Columbia University Press.

Schmeling, Manfred. 1982. *Métathéâtre et intertexte: Aspects du théâtre dans le théâtre.* Paris: Lettres Modernes.

Scholes, Robert. 1970. "Metafiction." *Iowa Review* 1:100–115.

———. 1979. *Fabulation and Metafiction.* Urbana: University of Illinois Press.

Sciacca, Michele F. 1950. "Verdad y sueño en 'La vida es sueño' de Calderón de la Barca." *Clavileño* 1:1–9.

Sito Alba, Manuel. 1983. "Metateatro en Calderón: *El gran teatro del mundo.*" In *Calderón: Actas del congreso internacional sobre Calderón y el teatro español del Siglo de Oro,* edited by Luciano García Lorenzo, 2:789–802. Madrid: Consejo Superior de Investigaciones Científicas.

Skrine, Peter N. 1978. *The Baroque: Literature and Culture in Seventeenth-Century Europe.* New York: Holmes and Meier.

Sloane, Robert. 1979. "Action and Role in *El príncipe constante.*" *Modern Language Notes* 85:167–83.

Stoll, Anita K. 1992. "Teaching Golden Age Drama: Metatheater as Organizing Principle." *Hispania* 75: 1343–47.

Suárez-Galbán, Eugenio. 1966. "Calderón y Pirandello." *Boletín de la Academia de artes y ciencias de Puerto Rico* 2:907–18.

Trueblood, Alan S. 1964. "Rôle-playing and the Sense of Illusion in Lope de Vega." *Hispanic Review* 32:305–18.

Wardropper, Bruce W. 1958. "Poetry and Drama in Calderón's *El médico de su honra.*" *Romanic Review* 49:3–11.

———. 1970a. "La imaginación en el metateatro calderoniano." In *Actas del Tercer congreso internacional de hispanistas,* edited by Carlos Magis, 923–30. Mexico: El Colegio de México.

———. 1970b. "Introduction." *Teatro español del Siglo de Oro.* New York: Scribner's.

———. 1973. "The Implicit Craft of the Spanish *Comedia.*" In *Studies in Spanish Literature of the Golden Age Presented to Edmund M. Wilson,* edited by R. O. Jones, 339–56. London: Tamesis Books.

Warnke, Frank J. 1972. *Versions of Baroque: European Literature in the Seventeenth Century.* New Haven, Conn.: Yale University Press.

Waugh, Patricia. 1984. *Metafiction: The Theory and Practice of Self-conscious Fiction.* London: Methuen.

Weisinger, Herbert. 1964. "*Theatrum Mundi:* Illusion as Reality." Chap. 4 of *The Agony and the Triumph: Papers in the Use and Abuse of Myth.* East Lansing: Michigan State University Press.

White, Hayden. 1973. *Metahistory: The Historical Imagination in Nineteenth Century Europe.* Baltimore, Md.: Johns Hopkins University Press.

Ynduráin, Domingo. 1974. "El *Gran teatro* de Calderón y el mundo del XVII." *Segismundo* 10:17–71.

Ziomek, Henryk. 1986. "A New View in Renaissance and Baroque Drama." *Kwartalnik Neofilologiczny* 33:137–47.

Henry W. Sullivan

Law, Desire, and the Double Plot:
Toward a Psychoanalytic Poetics of the *Comedia*

y purpose in this essay is to reengage with two old—and stub-born—issues stemming from our aesthetic appreciation of the Golden Age Spanish theater: the question of multiplicity of plot versus the simple unity of action advocated by Aristotle and the question of the place of humor and the clown (*gracioso*) in serious plays. The methodology I am using brings together the critical dyad, or odd couple, that I term "psychoanalytic poetics." Strictly speaking, the two problems under discussion are formal in nature and have traditionally been discussed since Aristotle—in treatises on poetics, "arts of poetry," and the like—in formalist terms.

Following Terry Eagleton, psychoanalytic literary criticism can be broadly divided into four kinds, depending on what it takes as its object of attention. It can attend to the *author* of the work, to the work's *contents,* to its *formal construction,* or to the *reader* (Eagleton, 179). Now, we can find analogies among the "formal construction" of works of literature and dreams in Freud's description of "dream-work" and the elaboration of "latent content" into a coherent narrative by the process known as "secondary revision." But I am here proposing something rather different by a "psychoanalytic poetics" of the *comedia.*

In a series of essays written over the last decade, I have endeavored to show that literary drama is a genre which derives its power of reference from the Oedipal experience, which lies at the basis of human psychic formation. In various writings on Tirso de Molina, in particular, I have preferred the Lacanian account of the Oedipal experience to that of Freud (Sullivan 1985, 1986, 1988, 1989a). Lacan once said that the Oedipus complex was Freud's own neurotic dream (Ragland-Sullivan, 267). By this he did not mean that the supposed desire of a five-year-old boy to murder his father and sleep with his mother was a psychically and literally true paradigm. But the Oedipus complex was, Lacan argued, true in its structure. The position of the infant in the family triangle and in its parents' discourse is precisely what gives rise to his or her subjectivity and specificity as an ethical being. In another place, Lacan talked of the Oedipal experience as "the passage through the defile of the signifier" (Lacan 1977, 58), by which he meant the unique structuring of consciousness—and unconscious signifying chains—in the formation of the subject, a structuring that results from the impact of all signifiers preexisting in the language and culture that are imposed on the speechless human animal. Viewed from this language-and-culture perspective, the Oedipus complex is not just a mythical story or an offshoot of abnormal psychology; it is a description of how everyone comes to be human.

Fundamental to the structure of the ethical human subject is the dialectic of law and desire. For a detailed account of the genesis of the speaking subject, I refer to my previous essays on the topic (1986,1989a). Suffice it to say here, on the issue of a psychoanalytic poetics of the Spanish *comedia,* that the universal dialectic of law and desire as a structuring phenomenon gives the clue to the unusual structure of the Spanish *comedia*'s "double plot." Law and desire arise in the human subject as the inverse expression of each other in consequence of the process that Lacan termed "castration." Castration, or the "eclipse of the subject by the signifier," is to be understood here as the advent of language in the neonate and its injunction both to prohibition as such as well as to an obedience of social laws. The loss and lack implicit in this division of the subject, now a speaking subject (*je*) as well as the earlier subject of ontology (*moi*), establish desire as the lacking condition of a person. Individual desire is the source of drive and motivation, and this explains why the constraints of law push to inhibit and tame desire socially, while law must always contend with the pressure of desire to subvert its own claims.

Now, while it is true that Hegel, for example, was very taken with tragedies such as Sophocles' *Antigone* as works displaying a dialectic of law, or conflicts of rights and claims (and he was one of the first philosophers to take desire seriously), to my knowledge, no aesthetic system has argued for the dialectic of desire and law as the basis of a dramatic procedure. And yet a prolonged scrutiny of the Spanish *comedia* reveals that precisely this dialectic is at work in the apparent splitting of the dramatic action into two plots. Because neo-Aristotelian critics in the Enlightenment found the idea of multiple plots offensive to reason and their conception of order, writers of the stripe of a Voltaire systematically denounced this feature of the Spanish drama. While Romantic critics, especially in Germany, found a lot of good to say of Calderón and the *comedia,* they were generally content to praise the multiplicity of action they found but not to attempt any explanation for it (Sullivan 1983b, 169–209). In the last hundred years, readers of the *comedia* have assumed an apologetic or defensive posture toward these multiple plots, or—as in the case of Alexander Parker—attempted a neo-Aristotelian path out of the dilemma (see, for example, his *Approach to the Spanish Drama of the Golden Age*).

The novelty of the approach that I am suggesting resides in the following principles: the main actions of Golden Age Spanish dramas concern law, expressed as issues of *power* politics, and the secondary actions concern *desire,* expressed as issues of love and passion. Typically, the main action will put forward a political dilemma in the shape of a looming crisis of succession. In Calderón's *La vida es sueño,* the apparent unsuitability of Segismundo to succeed his father is an obvious example. In Lope's *El castigo sin venganza,* the need to provide a legitimate heir for the duke of Ferrara is another example. In Guillén de Castro's *Las mocedades del Cid,* King Fernando I of Castile is concerned that his son and heir, the intemperate and indomitable Prince Sancho, will prove incompetent as ruler unless drilled in the art of prudent government by a tutor. Fernando's unwise appointment of the senile Diego Laínez (the Cid's father) to this post is what sets the political action of the play in motion. Other main plots with law as their center concern dynastic battles (Tirso's *La prudencia en la mujer*), civil wars with a crown at stake (Lope's *Fuenteovejuna* or Calderón's *Lances de amor y fortuna*), the restitution of a fallen favorite to royal favor (Tirso's *El vergonzoso en palacio* or *Privar contra su gusto*), or the rise and fall of a favorite (such as Mira de Amescua's *Próspera y adversa fortuna de don Alvaro de Luna* in two parts), and many more.

The secondary action of the *comedia,* revolving around desire, sets forth relationships based on love and sexual attraction between one, two, or three *galán-dama* couples, with the attendant complications of rivalries and jealousy, prior seduction before the play begins, promises of marriage, or clandestine marriages, and so on. There is no Golden Age Spanish drama of any category that does not have such abundant love interest, or focus on desire, at its affective center. Any *comedia* one can think of, therefore, provides an example of what I am saying, and I shall not spend time dealing with particular cases.

While the law issues at stake in the main action and the desire complications at stake in the secondary action separately provide dramatic interest and conflict, it is a key feature of Golden Age dramaturgy that the playwright always sets the two actions on a collision course. This produces a direct confrontation of law and desire in the imaginative realm that counterfeits the dialectic of law and desire in life itself. The law plot places difficulties and hindrances in the way of the desire plot, while the desire plot exercises a subversive effect on the will and proscriptions of law. While the two actions are clearly separate in their exposition during the opening scenes of any *comedia*'s act 1, they come increasingly to intermingle and influence each other as the play progresses. Thus the inherent dramatic interest of the main and secondary actions gains a much heightened impact by virtue of the inevitable collision between them.

At this point, I should like to introduce a note of reservation. I do not wish to suggest that the two Lacanian principles of law and desire surface in the *comedia* in some sort of clean split or Manichaean dualism: pure law versus pure desire, or the reverse. On the contrary, law is simply the codified desire of the individual or group that holds power in the symbolic order. This law also wills or "desires" someone to act in some fashion. But its characteristic feature as law lies in the *negativity* of its prohibitions. Actually, the law wills you *not* to do this or that. It is rare to find, generally speaking, laws that set out a complex code of permissions or dispensations. Thus, even in the law plot, desire is also in play.

By the same token, it should not be thought that desire, love, and sex in the secondary plot are simply anarchic forces of subversion. Sexual desire is also structured around very clear norms in the Spanish *comedia*. These concern the licit or taboo objects of sexual attraction, for example; or the Spanish code of wooing and seduction; and even the poetic and neo-Petrarchan language in which the experience of desirous love is expressed in the text. Tirso de Molina, in particular, by introducing strong elements of illicit sexuality and—through the stage trick of cross-dressing in male disguise plots—by suggesting lesbian and homosexual implications or necrosadistic and coprophiliac elements, etc., could be said to have dramatized the anarchy of desire. But he does so against a clear set of codes of normalcy and convention, licitness, decorum, and taboo. In other words, Tirso—like his contemporaries—portrays desire also as structured by law.

Thus the contrast of desire and law in the main and secondary actions of the *comedia* comes down to a matter of degree. But precisely in this question of degree lies, in my view, the answer to the vexing question of the tragic-comic distinction, which has hitherto eluded devotees of the *comedia*. It has always been understood, even in contemporary writings such as Lope's *Arte nuevo de hacer comedias* (1609), that the Spanish *comedia* was a hybrid genre. That is, it contained tragic and comic elements side by side. This was another aesthetic feature of the genre that rendered it anathema to the neoclassical critics of the Age of Reason. Elsewhere I have argued that tragedy depicts the fate of the victims of law's arbitrariness (Sullivan 1989a; Ragland-Sullivan & Sullivan). Comedy, on the other hand, depicts the successful subversion of law by desire.

According to this interpretation of tragic praxis, the noble or outstanding hero is typically flawed in some way, as Aristotle stated centuries ago, but in death is punished far beyond his or her actual measure of wrongdoing. The punishment does not fit the crime. There is, therefore, an excess of punishment over wrongdoing exacted for the hero's flaw. But, on the basis of the reasons set out in the preamble to this essay, each of us suffers an inner sacrifice of our desire to the demands of societal law as the price of living in our human community in sanity. When personal desire is sacrificed, according to Lacan, it gives rise to feelings of guilt, even though we have not committed any particular crime. These guilt feelings may be said to accumulate as an excess of guilt over wrongdoing present in the spectator. What the process known as tragic catharsis does is overcome the spectator's excessive (and strictly unwarranted) guilt feelings by means of the excessive punishment of the hero. The collective mass of audience guilt is drained off as through a poetic "black hole" in the crisis and denouement of the tragedy, and so purgation and ritual cleansing—as Aristotle claimed—is what catharsis or tragic effect is really about. The two excesses on each side of the balance sheet of psychic economy between drama and spectator cancel each other out.

In comedy, on the other hand, desire depicts law as trivialized and triumphs over it. Moreover, in line with the truth of the arbitrariness of human culture as a fictitious construct superimposed on nature, law itself is shown to be lacking and empty. The law is an ass. The figure of authority in the Spanish comedy, in the strict sense of the term, is a father, a jealous brother, or other guardian, perhaps a duke or grandee (as in Calderón's *El galán fantasma*), who performs a blocking function. The hero in the comedy is usually a young suitor who seeks to gain access to the daughter, sister, or ward of the blocking figure, in a fairly obvious displacement of the Oedipal triangle. Thus, the father lays claims of law to "possession" of the female character in his care (the place of the "mother") and prohibits the "son's" access to this taboo woman. The cunning young suitor (or "son") discovers the means to dupe the father and circumvent his prohibition, thus generating the comic intrigue that constitutes the play's action.

The theory I am outlining here eliminates the need to think of the *comedia* as a bungled genre or a monstrous hybrid. The greatest single difficulty posed to critics of the *comedia,* on formal grounds, was to understand how an exactly similar aesthetic procedure in the art of playwriting could lead, apparently indifferently, to a tragic feeling and outcome in one case and a comic feeling and outcome in another. I think that the division of the main action and secondary action into law plots and desire plots, respectively, provides the answer to this riddle. However, such a theory would be incomplete if it did not address the question of the comic elements as such. As observed at the outset, *all comedias*— whatever their ethos and final resolution—contain humorous or farcical touches, most often embodied in the indispensable role of the clown (*gracioso*).

Perhaps the best model to invoke for an understanding of the aesthetic structure that I envision here would be the praxis of baroque music. Not surprisingly, the baroque drama and baroque music display numerous analogies, which I have outlined elsewhere in an essay on Calderón, J. S. Bach, and the art of fugue (1989b). Specifically, I am referring here to the normal baroque practice of arranging the musical voices, or counterpoint, on four lines of interweaving musical argument corresponding to the soprano, alto, tenor, and bass parts. The most important and audible part is the soprano, or top voice, which may be compared to the *comedia*'s main action. The alto line, by extension, may be compared to the secondary action. But what of the other two?

In my view, the comic elements in the Spanish drama should be accorded a subsidiary but still important status as a third, comic action. This would, then, correspond to the tenor line of the baroque fugue. Comicality, or the ludic element, in the Spanish *comedia* does not intrude in block scenes, set off sharply from the tragic or serious action, as is sometimes the case in Shakespeare (the drunken porter's scene in *Macbeth,* for example). On the contrary, the *gracioso*— usually the hero's valet or lackey—keeps a running comic commentary going on events in the two plots, often providing a parodic inversion of them. He is sometimes abetted or augmented by a female comic part—the *graciosa* or leading lady's maidservant—while there may also be jokes, puns, anecdotes, or humorous play in the mouths of other characters than him. Thus wit, or *agudeza,* on some plane of intensity and frequency, may pervade the whole play. This dimension of comic continuum, therefore, deserves to be recognized as a third action, subliminally but distinctively interwoven among the other two.

The question now arises: What is the purpose of the third or comic action in the psychic economy of a dramatic tradition pitched around the dialectic of law and desire? The answer to this question, in my view, lies in the unconscious effect produced in the audience by the spectacle of law and desire in collision. Since these components structure every human subject in a proportion or mix decided by that subject's unconscious positioning toward the phallic signifier, the dramatist's deliberate teasing and provocation around those components must prove troublesome to the spectator. According to Lacan, the conflict aroused by law and desire locked in an unsettling relationship opens up the human subject to anxiety. By shaking up these cultural constructs and putting them in question, the dramatist exposes the spectator to the order that Lacan defined as the source of anxiety. The real is the unsayable realm—beyond unconscious imagining or conscious symbolization—that always hollows out a void, referred to as a hole in the Other, at the center of the subject's reframed inner world. Art, indeed, may be defined in part as a process that brings this real into view.

Now, it is an observable truth that a standard human response to anxiety is laughter. It may be nervous laughter or explosive mirth, a titter or a snicker, but all of these may be subsumed under the broader concept of a "comic catharsis." In other words, the unsettling of the ethical structure of the subject—just as, *mutatis mutandis,* is the case with a tragic catharsis—is discharged through comedy. This, then, provides the clue to the place of the third, comic action in the Spanish *comedia:* it provides a continual, sporadic discharge or catharsis to the upset created by the ineffable presence of the real in the law/desire conflict. It is not an incidental feature or a concession to audience demands but an integral part of the drama's widening ripples of affective impact.

But we have not yet said anything about the fourth voice or line in the contrapuntal mix: the dramatic action that would correspond to the bass. This, the most subliminal and intangible of all four dramatic continua, is what I would term the "poetic action." One of the glories of the Spanish *comedia* is its poetry. But while the poetic language of the seventeenth-century drama owed great debts to the Castilian lyric tradition and the Italianate innovations of the sixteenth century, its function was never merely decorative. It was *dramatic* poetry in the truest sense of the word. It had to work for a living. It placed extraordinary resources at the dramatist's disposition, especially in the realm of poetic imagery.

In an essay on Vélez de Guevara's memorable drama, *Reinar después de morir,* I advanced a theory of model classical tragedy in Spain that saw the continuum of poetic imagery as an essential reinforcement of the play's overall effect (Sullivan 1983a). I argued that careful analysis of the repeated images in a given drama would reveal an authorial intentionality that was clearly not random. The series of repeated images were threaded like three long strings of metaphor throughout the play. The three basic metaphors were derived from the dramatic situation itself, distilled so to speak from the very stuff of the double plot. In *Reinar después de morir,* the three base images revealed themselves as the "forest creature at bay" (the doomed Inés de Castro's sequestration at Pedro's country villa); "grief and mourning" (Pedro's sorrow over his dead queen); and "the sun in heaven" (the solar authority of Pedro's father and the reason of state). These images can be clearly shown combining and crossing in the play's text to furnish a rich interweave of subliminal import and commentary on the evolving tragic situation.

An important factor in this process is the degree to which the events in the playwright's story line are foreknown. To the new student of the *comedia,* it is sometimes surprising to learn that not only the dramatist but even the audience— above all in plays with a historical or legendary basis—already knew the outline of the story and how the play would end. How, asks the newcomer to the genre, can there be any real suspense or dramatic tension if all concerned know the outcome from the start? The answer lies, however, not in what will actually happen but how the events will be treated. An important and useful distinction here is the division, suggested by the Russian Formalist critics, between the tale (or the sequence of events represented) and the plot (the way the author gives these events a particular relationship); or, to quote Emile Benveniste, the difference between the *énoncé* and the *énonciation* (quoted by Todorov, 130–32).

Having decided on the outline of the dramatic tale or fable, the Spanish dramatist could exploit the poetic action for its proleptic or anticipatory effects. That is to say, the text could be infused with imagistic suggestions *prior to* the particular dramatic situation from which the base image is derived. So, for example, in *Reinar después de morir,* the death and posthumous coronation of Inés de Castro provides the climax and denouement of the whole. It occurs at the end of act 3, when the drama is virtually over. One might, therefore, expect that images of grief and mourning would not appear till late in the play. But this is not the case. Such images occur from the start and create a mood or ethos of gloom that permeates the drama and primes the audience in subliminal fashion for what is to come. By the same token, imagery can be used retroactively to recall events that have already occurred. Such anticipatory and retroactive use of the base images in the poetic action therefore belong to the *énonciation,* or plot, and contradicts the strict time sequence of the tale itself. The poetic action, then, is one of the most important ways in which the playwright tells his tale in his own unique fashion.

To round out and illustrate my theoretical discussion, I propose to analyze a particular text—not a tragedy this time, but a comedy: Moreto's *El desdén con el desdén.* If the theory of the four concurrent actions that I outlined above—main action, secondary action, comic action, and poetic action—is to hold true, then it must apply equally to tragic praxis *and* comic praxis. The aesthetic procedures of such a psychoanalytic poetics must be valid for all full-length, three-act dramas of seventeenth-century Spain. The universal validity of the theory would finally lay to rest the problem of why Spanish tragicomic dramas could employ a single methodological technique with such widely differing outcomes. The test is successful, I believe, in the case of Moreto's celebrated comedy of reference.

As in so many *comedias,* the primary concern of the main or law plot is the question of succession. The story is set in Barcelona, and the ruler of the realm, the Count of Barcelona, worries about the continuation of his bloodline and securing an appropriate heir. His only child, Princess Diana, has become cold and aloof toward all men and rejects the various suitors who court her. Should she stick to her chaste resolve and to her books of philosophy, never marrying, then the house of Barcelona would be without issue after her death. Such a situation would almost inevitably bring on civil dissension, warring factions and parties, perhaps foreign intervention, and maybe even civil war. It is this contingency that the count wishes at all costs to avoid.

This overriding concern is what lends a special urgency to the events in the secondary or desire plot. Diana has three suitors: Carlos, Count of Urgel; the Prince of Bearne; and Count Gaston de Foix. They are all in love with her, but she spurns them equally. Eventually Carlos, following his servant Polilla's shrewd advice to treat her with the same or even greater disdain than she treats him, arouses her pique and then her desire for him, thus finally winning her hand. In this sense, and in keeping with our definitions at the outset, the main plot is at odds with the secondary plot: there is a dialectic of law and desire in play. The law of the realm expects that the heir apparent, Princess Diana, will take her dynastic and genealogical responsibilities seriously. But instead, her desire—or rather her perverse refusal to desire—stands in the way of law's expectations. This refusal is characterized by Carlos as "unas iras / contra el orden natural / del Amor" (Moreto, 783), where one should read the expression "natural order" rather as "cultural order" or law. The crux of the play, therefore, depends on this conflict between the two actions as per our definition.

But the elements of desire, love, and sexuality in this secondary action really occupy center stage. Inasmuch as they provide the main business of the comedy, they are not "secondary" in a qualitative sense, but only in their structural relationship to the main, legal action. And this is an important hallmark of a Spanish *comedia* that is truly a comedy: the preponderance of the love interest in the secondary action over the power political issues at stake in the main action. Another hallmark of the truly comic *comedia* is the enlarged or prominent status of the third, comic action in the whole.

In *El desdén con el desdén,* the prominent comic action is carried forward by the person of Polilla. Apart from being an unusually well-drawn and witty *gracioso,* Polilla intervenes in the intrigue almost with the capacity of a prompter or master of ceremonies. He invents his noble lord's stratagem and coaches him continually in what to say and when to say it. At times, when Carlos's facade of cold aloofness almost breaks down under the pressure of his true desire, Polilla provides him with the determination and single-mindedness to tough it out and win his bride. Polilla further takes the initiative when he introduces himself into Diana's presence and wins her confidence by his wit and his imposture as the Latin-spouting doctor Caniquí.

The change of name here—Polilla to Caniquí—provides a good example of how witty poetic imagery may be employed in the generation of comic situations. Though it is not one of the three base images of the play, *polilla* in Spanish means a moth, a caterpillar, or ravager. The usual object of a moth's ravages is fabric or cloth. Polilla plans to worm his way into Diana's confidence by getting into her clothes and irritating her in a sexual manner: "me sabré introducir en sus camisas / . . . / yo sabré apolillarle las entrañas" (792). When he adopts the pseudonym of Caniquí, this name extends the image of fabric, since the word refers to a kind of fine linen that might be used to make undergarments. At the end of the scene, Laura says he has taken her fancy and she would like to use him as a linen handkerchief (*lienzo*) to dab her nostrils. In the garden interlude of act 2, scene 8, possibly the most erotic scene in the play, this image of cloth and clothing is presented visually, since Diana and her ladies-in-waiting are shown in casual, domestic attire, wearing long underskirts or *guardapieses* with tight waists.

If we study the poetic imagery of the play carefully, the materials of the poetic action—the three base images—suggest themselves easily enough. These are, in textual sequence of introduction, "the chaste goddess," "festive celebration," and "the fruit and vegetable orchard." Diana, of course, is the chaste goddess of Greek and Roman mythology, hostile to men and devoted to reading and hunting. There are many echoes of this appropriate association throughout the text. But Moreto has extended the base image in numerous ways. In the first place, the Spanish Diana, like her mythical counterpart, is surrounded by virgin nymphs or attendants, called Cintia and Laura. Now, Cynthia was the Greek name of the triple deity Cynthia-Artemis-Hecate, who occupied heaven as the moon goddess, earth as the goddess of the hunt, and Hades as an infernal sorceress. Thus Cynthia reduplicates the associations of chaste virgin. Similarly, Laura evokes the Spanish *lauro* and *laurel,* the bush or leaves of the laurel or bay tree. According to a well-known myth, the god Apollo attempted to ravish chaste Daphne, who was converted into a laurel tree by divine intervention in order to save her from his grasp. This story is recalled early in the play during the description of the scenes with which Diana has decorated her apartments: "a Dafne huyendo de Apolo" (784).

Moreto develops an interesting example of image crossing out of his base metaphor of virgin/laurel in the climax of the third act, where it is combined with the image of festive celebration or celebratory triumph. The laurel or crown of bay leaves was, of course, the reward of the victor in the Olympic Games or in a military triumph. Bearne says: "que yo el laurel consigo / de ser vuestro"; Cintia says: "en él gano / un logro para el deseo, / para mi nobleza un lauro"; Diana says: "El ser querida una dama / de quien desea, no es lauro, / sino dicha de su estrella"; and Cintia again: "yo me aparto / de mi esperanza por ella / y por vos, si es vuestro el lauro" (849, 851, 853, 855).

The second base image—that of festive celebration—comes straight out of the secondary action. The three lovers have outdone themselves in throwing lavish festivities, jousts, and tourneys to beguile the reluctant princess. Words such as *fiestas, festejos, festejar, galanterías, Carnestolendas, sarao,* and so on abound in the text. Moreto, indeed, has chosen to set his story at Carnival time in Barcelona, thus imparting the carnivalesque element of which Bakhtin wrote. Not only does Diana's behavior seem to set normalcy on its head and make the world of the play a dizzy place; Moreto develops the image of celebration into a whole scene by dramatizing a *sarao,* or masked soirée, in act 2, scene 3. The metaphor or image is, once more, visualized on the stage in the game of partners, colors, favors, and dancing.

The third base image—that of the fruit and vegetable orchard—is introduced by the flippant Polilla early on. He compares the efforts of the suitors to topple Diana's resistance to those of small boys tossing stones at a fig tree in order to knock down the *breva,* or early fruit of the season (789). There are many references to different fruits and vegetables and to the orchard in the inevitable proverb "el perro del hortelano," which arises from the context of Diana's jealousy of Cintia; Carlos feigns love for Cintia as a ruse to provoke the princess. Diana does not want Carlos, she thinks, but will not let another have him.

The most elaborate development of this image is again a whole scene brought onto the stage: the garden interlude of act 2, scene 8. Here, Diana and her maids are singing in this idyllic setting, a kind of paradise to tempt the male. Carlos, however, threatened at knife point by Polilla, takes no notice but simply examines and admires the plants in the garden: the ivy, the laurels once more, the hyacinths, cherry trees, and so on. Another crossing of base images is implicit here: the combination of the orchard and the chaste goddess. Carlos is, so to say, an intruder in the garden, with its fountain and flowers; he has penetrated Diana's abode and seen her *en déshabillé:* "¿Como, atrevido, / habéis entrado aquí dentro, / sabiendo que en mi retiro / estaba yo con mis damas?" (831). This recalls the story of Actaeon, who, while out hunting with his hounds, came upon Diana with her nymphs bathing naked in a pool or fountain. The outraged Diana then changed Actaeon into a stag, which was promptly torn to pieces by his own hunting dogs. The inversion in the *comedia* is Carlos's studied averting of his eyes instead of an illicit gaze; it is also a clever crossing of two of the base images.

Thus Moreto's *El desdén con el desdén* fulfills in all respects the desiderata and conditions for the definition of the *comedia* that I am proposing here. This is a definition based on an aesthetic procedure derived from what I am terming a psychoanalytic poetics. Although psychoanalytic criticism and various kinds of formalist aesthetics (New Criticism, structuralism, etc.) may seem to be incompatible forms of discourse, they appear to join felicitously here. The forms of the *comedia* appear to arise out of the ethical structuring of the human psyche, itself a result of the Oedipal genesis of the subject, which is the essence of the human condition. Any play of baroque Spain contains four actions: main, secondary, comic, and poetic. The first is pitched around law, the second around desire. The collision of the two produces anxiety, which is periodically relieved by the third action in a comic catharsis. The double storyline provides the material of the fourth, poetic action in the shape of three base images that are ingeniously extended, developed, and crossed at the subliminal level of the textual metaphors.

This is certainly not classical Greek procedure, but it produced classics of a different kind. Far from being bungled in its tragicomic form, the *comedia* reflects immense psychological refinement and sophistication in its structure. Above all, the role of laughter should not be seen as aesthetically problematic but rather as an integral part of the varied cultural catharsis that the Spanish *comedia* provided for its audiences in its Golden Age.

Works Consulted

Bakhtin, Mikhail. 1968. *Rabelais and His World.* Translated by Helene Iswolsky. Cambridge, Mass.: MIT Press.

Eagleton, Terry. 1983. *Literary Theory: An Introduction.* Minneapolis: University of Minnesota Press.

Lacan, Jacques. 1966. *Ecrits.* Paris: Seuil.

———. 1977. *The Four Fundamental Concepts of Psychoanalysis.* Translated by Alan Sheridan. New York: Norton.

Moreto y Cabaña, Agustín. 1939. *El desdén con el desdén.* In *Diez comedias del Siglo de Oro,* edited by José Martel and Hymen Alpern. New York & London: Harper.

Parker, Alexander A. 1957. *The Approach to the Spanish Drama of the Golden Age.* Diamante, vol. 6. London: The Hispanic and Luso-Brazilian Council.

Ragland-Sullivan, Ellie. 1986. *Jacques Lacan and the Philosophy of Psychoanalysis.* Urbana & Chicago: University of Illinois Press.

Ragland-Sullivan, Ellie, and Henry W. Sullivan. 1989. "A Lacanian Theory of 'Christian' Catharsis." Unpublished MS.

Sullivan, Henry W. 1983a. "Vélez de Guevara's *Reinar después de morir* as a Model of Classical Spanish Tragedy." In *Antigüedad y actualidad de Luis Vélez de Guevara: Estudios críticos en el IV centenario de su nacimiento,* edited by C. George Peale, 144–64. Purdue University Monographs in Romance Languages. Amsterdam and Philadelphia, Pa.: Benjamins.

———. 1983b. *Calderón in the German Lands and the Low Countries: His Reception and Influence, 1654–1980.* Cambridge: Cambridge University Press.

———. 1985. "Love, Matrimony and Desire in the Theater of Tirso de Molina." *Bulletin of the Comediantes* 37:83–99.

———. 1986. "Sibling Symmetry and the Incest Taboo in Tirso's *Habladme en entrando.*" *Revista canadiense de estudios hispánicos* 10:261–78.

———. 1988. "Towards a Definition of Tirsian Tragedy." In *Proceedings of the VII Annual GASDS* (El Paso), edited by Barbara Mujica, 67–76. Landham, Md.: University Press of America.

———. 1989a. "The Incest Motif in Tirsian Drama: A Lacanian View." In *Parallel Lives: Spanish and English National Drama, 1580–1680,* edited by Louise Fothergill-Payne, 180–92. Lewisburg, Pa.: Bucknell University Press.

———. 1989b. "The Art of Fugue: Inevitability and Surprise in the Works of Calderón and J. S. Bach." In *Estudios sobre Calderón y el teatro de la Edad de Oro: Homenaje a Kurt y Roswitha Reichenberger,* edited by Francisco Mundi Pedret, 121–28. Barcelona: PPU.

Todorov, Tzvetan. 1972. "Literature and Language." In *The Structuralist Controversy,* edited by Richard Macksey and Eugenio Donato, 125–33. Baltimore, Md.: Johns Hopkins University Press.

James A. Parr

Partial Perspectives on Kinds, Canons, and the Culture Question

Kinds

Although the term *comedia* is itself limiting vis-à-vis the much more comprehensive "Golden Age drama" (which would include *pasos, entremeses,* and *autos*), there is obviously more than one kind of *comedia.* Problems arise when we begin the difficult work of subdivision into tragedy, comedy, tragicomedy, and whatever other forms there may be. Since tragedy is historically the originary form, we might look at it first. Three decades ago, Lionel Abel advanced the notion that there is little prospect of any early modern, modern, or postmodern tragedy; what arises instead, under the aegis of Calderón and Shakespeare, is something he calls metatheater, or "pieces about life seen as already theatricalized" (60). Now, this is a clever conception, but what it means in the final analysis is that drama, in the early to mid-seventeenth century, became self-conscious as it came to focus more on its ingenious devices than on implacable destiny. As any number of exercises over the past twenty-five years have demonstrated, and as Abel himself recognized, metatheater manifests itself in the *comedia* well before Calderón.

Metatheater is primarily a device, a technique, a strategy for describing an early modern substitute for classical tragedy in which philosophical questions (e.g., "To be or not to be?" [Abel, 55]) are foregrounded, thus contributing to self-consciousness on the part of certain characters; and this is seen, in turn, to mirror the self-awareness of authors. I have difficulty considering a dramatic device— one that involves the baring of devices, no less (for that would seem to be in the nature of self-consciousness)—to be a true dramatic form or genre. Indeed, there may be reasonable doubt whether metatheater exists in and of itself, beyond the formulation given it by Abel and the exercises prompted by his perspective. If metatheater is primarily a formal feature—an aspect, not an essence—it is hardly sufficient to constitute a genre. At best, it seems an anemic substitute for classical tragedy. This is not to deny that self-conscious drama exists; certainly it does, and these metadramatic aspects have received further elaboration by Richard Hornby. What I question is the idea that this particular "dominant"—in the terms of the Russian Formalists—is adequate to the demanding task of constituting a philosophical alternative to classical tragedy.

What alternatives to classical tragedy might there be, then? There is surely more than one, and while I can do little more than suggest possibilities here, the first would seem to be Christian tragedy per se (exemplified in *El príncipe constante*); the second would be a more secularized—sometimes paganized—dramatic universe set in the days of an earlier dispensation (*El dueño de las estrellas* or *La hija del aire*); while a third would be a similarly secularized world of more recent vintage in which destiny remains a paramount consideration, although it is made clear that the protagonist determines his or her destiny (*La adversa fortuna de don Alvaro de Luna* or *La serrana de la Vera*).

It does not seem to me that the nominally Christian environment shared by poet and audience in seventeenth-century Spain precludes the appreciation of tragedy. I doubt very much that any spectator would have been moved to reassure another, after viewing *El caballero de Olmedo,* that "It's all right; only the flesh has perished; as Christians, we know there is life after death." This would assume a level of naivete equal to Alonso Quijano's—a failure to distinguish between reality and an artful simulacrum of reality, in other words. I am willing to grant audiences of the time the ability to discriminate between the two and to "suspend belief." It has always puzzled me that otherwise serious and sensitive commentators should disallow Christian tragedy, as though suffering and death *as such* had somehow lost their sting since the New Dispensation and, more important, lost their capacity to move an audience.

Even Northrop Frye, whose insights are generally cogent and compelling, has it that "Christianity . . . sees tragedy as an episode in the divine comedy, the larger scheme of redemption and resurrection. The sense of tragedy as a prelude to comedy seems almost inseparable from anything explicitly Christian" (215). In theory this may perhaps be the case, but I am quite confident that theology has no more bearing on the average theater-goer's experience of drama than it has on other aspects of daily life. Roger L. Cox is perceptive in remarking that the "tragedy as a prelude to comedy" approach "defines tragedy right out of existence, because it asserts that without transcendence these events remain below the level of tragedy and with transcendence they stand above the tragic level" (563).

Three of the more ill-conceived and ill-considered notions that continue to prejudice our understanding of tragedy are these: (1) all tragedy must be like classical tragedy, that is, of a sort that offers instances of ultimate, irremediable disaster tantamount to damnation for eternity, as was supposedly the case for those who lived and died on the stages of antiquity. This is a transparently narrow and reductive view, but, sadly, many moderns continue to endorse it. There is possible, I trust, a more ample and generous perspective that is satisfied with suffering in, and frequently loss of, this life. This alternative view would eschew the pursuit of fictional characters beyond their fictional graves—and if we pause to consider the silliness of that scenario, it may speak for itself; (2) the second ill-conceived notion is complementary to the first in that it maintains the impossibility of Christian—which is to say, modern or early modern—tragedy for reasons that correlate with those just adduced; (3) the third is also a hand-me-down from classical tragedy—or, rather, from a misreading of classical tragedy—and has to do with the moralist's insatiable search for "tragic flaws," or *hamartía,* and the corresponding need to see transgressors punished through "poetic justice."

Eric Bentley urges a thoughtful realignment of sensibility that might help set us on a better path. Rather than the moralizing of the late, great thematizing school, or the focus on poor-man's philosophy advocated by Lionel Abel with his claim that metatheater is a "comparably philosophic form of drama" (vii) (comparable to ancient tragedy, that is), Bentley would stress aesthetic and psychological dimensions. He maintains, quite rightly I think, that the experience of tragedy ought to be aesthetic and psychological rather than moral and philosophical. Richard Levin offers a complementary perspective in some comments on "the paradox of thematism":

> In attempting to elevate . . . plays by making them seem more profound [the thematic approach] has actually debased them, for when the drama, even the greatest drama, is treated as a species of intellectual discourse, it becomes a decidedly inferior species. If the meaning and purpose of the plays really can be found in this kind of general proposition, if *that* is what they add up to, then it is hard to see why any adult would be interested in them. (59)

It is not a difficult matter to reach in one's thumb and pull out the plum of a theme or a moral contained in a given *comedia.* What I am suggesting, buttressed by Bentley and Levin, is that there may be a better approach that would focus instead on the aesthetic and psychological realms. Let me illustrate briefly.

There are any number of plays in which the aesthetic and the psychological coalesce in the denouement. A prime example would be *El médico de su honra.* The play is not a tragedy, despite A. A. Parker's otherwise persuasive ruminations, but rather a dark tragicomedy. The tragic tone is dissipated at the end by comic integration through marriage, as Eros supersedes Thanatos. Lope's *gracioso* remarks with ironic detachment in *El médico de su honra:* "Aquí hay una boda / con un entierro, señores; / esto es abreviar parolas" (972). Thus we have generic artifice amusingly laid bare.

Calderón's reworking of *El médico de su honra* offers the same ending, but without the overt commentary. The effect of baring the device is nevertheless identical. Both dramatists have juxtaposed tragic and comic endings, and the audience response that can reasonably be assumed is a psychological anagnorisis centering on recognition of the artifice coupled with an aesthetic sense of wonder (*admiratio*) at this novel invasion of the tragic by the comic. Thus we find combined in the denouement of *El médico de su honra* the aesthetic and psychological dimensions that Bentley considers pertinent in the appreciation of tragedy. But it is not a tragedy, strictly speaking. Rather, Lope and Calderón were able to achieve through tragicomedy effects that are sometimes associated with the more venerable form called tragedy.

The symbiosis of the aesthetic and the psychological—bearing always on audience response—is by no means isolated to the play just touched upon. It occurs also in *El caballero de Olmedo* and *El burlador de Sevilla,* to mention only two. In the former, there is again ironic juxtaposition, this time of a potentially comic ending with a very real tragic ending. Just after the scene of Alonso's ambush and murder comes the one where Inés and her father discuss, belatedly, what a fine match Alonso would make for her. The current notion of the "intentional fallacy fallacy" confirms that Lope was indeed aware of what he was about, both here and in *El médico.* In *El burlador,* a potentially comic ending of integration into society through marriage to Isabela is proffered as a possibility, but Don Juan chooses to fulfill another social obligation first, and it turns out to be his last. In both instances, the reality of comic integration through marriage that we find in *El médico de su honra* is replaced with the insinuation of that prospect. In neither instance can the insinuation be considered innocent, however, juxtaposed as it is, in both cases, to the typically tragic real ending. In *El caballero* and *El burlador,* audience response can be conjectured to involve both a psychological dimension—anagnorisis—and an aesthetic dimension—*admiratio*—although it seems likely that intellect will also come into play here to facilitate the process of anagnorisis or generic awareness, for these two plays are more subtle in the baring of their artifice than was the case in *El médico de su honra.* Beyond that consideration, however, lies the fact that it is difficult to separate the psychological and the aesthetic, for they are really two facets of what can be thought of as a single, unified response. For that reason I referred earlier to their fusion, indicating that they coalesce.

The peculiar performance context of the *corrales* must have mitigated against the writing and staging of tragedy, for how could the playwright hope to maintain a tragic tone through three acts when, between those acts, there would be farcical interludes? Lope probably had these constraints in mind when he composed *El caballero de Olmedo.* Knowing that any tragic mood established during the first two acts would be undermined by the intervening farces, he set aside the more lugubrious aspects until act 3, where they might receive concentrated attention unavailable until then. We may do Lope and his art a disservice when we apply our ingenuity to treating his performance texts as well-wrought urns, imposing unity at all costs while disregarding the realities of their staging. It may be proper to think of *El caballero de Olmedo* as a funeral urn for the preservation of the hero's memory, but it is less justifiable to treat it as a "well-wrought urn" in terms of the old New Criticism.

In the class of plays that concerns us, the domain of tragedy is largely a masculine enclave, while the world of comedy tends to be manipulated by feminine wiles and wit, as Bruce Wardropper (1978) has explained. In tragicomedies such as *El caballero de Olmedo,* that distinction continues to be maintained. Don Alonso's tragic qualities—his *areté,* valiant deeds, deprivation, and death—contrast markedly with the scheming and prevaricating of the female figures, especially Fabia and Inés. The contrast is most apparent in the peculiar devotion to his parents that obliges Alonso to return home to reassure them, whereas his true love's deception of her parent is representative of feminine guile and comic convention generally. The astute females provide the comic dimension, while the noble knight plays the role befitting a tragic hero. The masculine, tragic world is brought into contact with the feminine, comic world, and in the process it becomes apparent that the latter is an inverted image of the former. That inversion centers on values, attitudes, actions, and, not least of all, the sex of the central characters.

Not all comic characters are female, of course. One has only to think of *el mentiroso,* Don García, who can readily be perceived as the antithesis of medieval paragons such as Don Alvaro de Luna or the Knight of Olmedo. Don García displays a mental imbalance that makes him obsessive-compulsive and a moral imbalance that leads him to equate fame with infamy. Whether these misprisions are owing to a humoral imbalance, to the trauma of being reared a *segundón,* or simply to the need to excel at being different lends itself to conjecture. The traditional values of chivalry found in the medieval models mentioned above have been modernized and urbanized, however, and thus perverted (Paterson, 366). García is a pathetic, gesticulating automaton, despite his ingenuity and apparent congeniality. We are amused at the complications he creates and dazzled by his discourse, but he lacks substance, and we are ultimately distanced from him due to his topsy-turvy values, compulsiveness, and mechanistic responses.

Although I have not offered enough examples to make a proper case, an inference that begins to take shape is that comedy in the *comedia* can be thought of as an inversion of tragedy, which is, in a sense, "always already" there, whether as an ingredient of the plot (*El caballero de Olmedo*) or as an implicit world against which to measure the amusing travesties of its norms and values (*La verdad sospechosa*). Comedy is a distorting, sometimes esperpentic mirror held up to tragedy.

The protagonist of works whose dominant mode is tragedy is ordinarily a man, whereas the lead characters of comedy tend to be women (*Marta la piadosa, La dama duende, La dama boba, El perro del hortelano,* etc.); or, if they happen to be men, like Don García, they display stereotypical feminine strategies for coping with an oppressive patriarchal society, such as mendacity. Conversely, if the protagonist of a tragedy is a woman, she will ordinarily display *virtus,* the better qualities of manliness, possibly by usurping a stereotypically masculine role. Two somewhat disparate examples would be Semíramis of *La hija del aire* and Gila of *La serrana de la Vera.* My point is that the societal conventions of the time considered *virtus*—moral fortitude, valor, worth—to be inseparable from its root word, *vir,* and the plays therefore illustrate that it requires the *vir* or the *vira*go (virtuous or not) for its exemplification. Conversely, the lack of *virtus* associated with the feminine finds its expression through a form traditionally thought to be similarly deficient and inferior, comedy.

The frequent attempts to dignify comedy by bringing out its serious side are well intentioned but largely misguided. Richard Levin offers pertinent, if provocative, commentary:

> Anyone familiar with the recent thematic scene will not be surprised to learn that some of the most solemn and portentous—not to say pretentious—statements are attributed to comedies, for that has become a well-established trend, and one more indication of how far this approach has taken us from our dramatic experience. In order to make comedies seem more profound, it has, in effect, decomicalized them. (59–60)

Marriages in comedy frequently respond to the ancient convention of what may strike moderns as arbitrary pairing off rather than to the imperatives of romantic love or poetic justice. A good example is Segismundo's loveless arrangement with Estrella at the end of *La vida es sueño,* complementing the necessary union of Astolfo and Rosaura. Don García's disappointment at the end of *La verdad sospechosa* need not be taken to illustrate poetic justice (by frustration), but can be viewed in nonmoralistic terms as again illustrating hallowed comic convention. Walter Kerr draws upon Francis Cornford's classic study in some remarks that help to clarify the matter:

> Any wedding will do so long as there is a wedding, that marriage which Cornford takes to be "the survival of one moment in a ritual action older than any form of comic literature." And it is the revel in celebration of this marriage—so often a forced marriage—that has apparently given us our word for comedy: *Komoidia.* "If tragedy and comedy are based on the same ritual outlines," Cornford concludes, "the Satyr-play at the end of the tetralogy must stand for the sacred marriage and its *Komos,* which form the finale of Comedy." But the point here, as it is very much Cornford's, is that the finale of comedy bears no organic relationship to the body of comedy. Historically regarded, it is an extraordinarily convenient device for cutting short an action that might have been improvised indefinitely and swiftly imposing upon that action—at the very last moment—a boisterously "happy" atmosphere. (66)

I believe that the standard generic categories continue to stand us in good stead in talking about the *comedia*. Metatheater, as a device, can be found in all the forms: tragedy, comedy, and tragicomedy. It may nevertheless be appropriate to stake out a fourth catchall category—a sort of holding area—for problem plays that resist ready classification under one of the three main rubrics. We might call that fourth kind "serious drama," for surely no one would want to be associated with less-than-serious drama.

Canonicity and the Culture Question

One of the paradoxes of Golden Age literature is that the majority of the texts we would today call high canonical began life in much more modest circumstances and with no such aspirations. The plays written by Lope and others for performance in the *corrales* are prime examples of a popular art that, in time, came to occupy a much more exalted niche in the literary hierarchy. This fairly obvious fact shows that the canon is a creature of time and place. It is also, as John Guillory asserts, a product of social contexts and institutions (238–39). What is canonical in one historical moment may not be so in another; or, conversely, texts that were never intended for such high office may come to be prized by succeeding generations. Change is fairly slow, however, and this continues to be the case in our own time in the comparatively conservative field of *comedia* studies.

If Marcelino Menéndez y Pelayo had prevailed, *La vida es sueño* would today be considered a marginal mediocrity. But along came the New Criticism in the guise of the thematic-structural method, and, *voilà,* it can now be seen that Calderón's masterpiece exudes structural integrity from every line. Could it be that certain texts require certain critical approaches to bring out their latent potential? Is Catherine Larson on the mark when she proposes that *Fuenteovejuna* is "a drama that has been waiting for a deconstructive critic" (124)? It is noteworthy in this regard that Frederick de Armas has recently completed a state-of-the-art reading of the plays of Andrés de Claramonte. Possibly his demonstration of how well these texts respond to the critical temper of our time will confer on them new respectability, prompting a bull market in *Claramontiana.* If so, more power to him, and to Claramonte.

There is more to the linkage between criticism and canonicity than meets the eye. If texts fail to respond to the latest innovations in analysis, or, otherwise stated, if they fail to attract able practitioners of the newer criticism, their fate will be the same in either case: they will fade from the scene. At best, they may continue to be read as exemplary of a certain type of play—plays about the lives of saints, for instance. To be at the center of critical attention is tantamount to being at or near the core of the canon. The critical canon and the select canon feed off each other to the increase of both. One cannot exist without the other.

The select canon is that central core of texts thought to be the best of their kinds, or at least the most representative. Criteria for inclusion and exclusion will differ from person to person, but in practice, this select nucleus finds expression in syllabi for undergraduate courses on the *comedia* and in graduate reading lists. At the very heart of that nucleus one would have to situate *El burlador de Sevilla,* partly for its intrinsic merit, but even more so for its historical importance, given the persistence of the Don Juan theme in subsequent literature.

Nowadays the select canon is necessarily much smaller than the critical canon, for the forays into what were once thought to be minor plays or minor dramatists have become legion, as legions of critics seek a place in the sun for themselves and their commitments. Fortunately, there seems to be room for all, due in part to the plethora of professional meetings here and abroad and the corresponding opportunities to organize special sessions on almost any issue. In addition to special sessions at meetings of the Modern Language Association, the division on Golden Age drama now organizes three separate regular sessions, each on a different topic. The year I chaired the division, sometime in the mid-70s—when it was still "Spanish 3"—there was only the one regular session (as had been the case since time immemorial), and there were few if any special sessions. We have come a long way in a relatively short while, both in the quantity of papers being presented and in their relative sophistication. In other words, the critical canon has expanded almost beyond belief.

How has this explosion of commentary affected the select canon? Paradoxically, less than one might imagine. No doubt some of the more esoteric titles and topics have found their way into graduate seminars, but probably not into introductory or survey courses or onto standard reading lists. While this qualifies my earlier point about the complementarity of criticism and canonicity, it does not invalidate it by any means. The fact is that there are practical limitations on the growth of the select canon, as I have defined it. Only so many texts can be assigned in a course on the *comedia,* and only so many can realistically be added to graduate reading lists. So it is apparent that not every work deemed worthy of critical attention can become, *ipso facto,* canonical in the more limited sense. The newer works that are now receiving attention may yet find their way into the select core, however, depending upon the argumentative and critical acumen of their sponsors. This is, after all, the age of *homo rhetoricus,* when truth and value are contingent affairs. Verification and falsification are no longer what they once were. Validity in interpretation is seen to reside increasingly in rhetoric, in the power of persuasion. What is real—or what is canonical—is whatever one's immediate audience can be persuaded of. Maybe life does imitate literature, if we think of the *homo rhetoricus* of *La verdad sospechosa.*

Other considerations affecting our conception of the canon are more political in nature, centering on what has come to be called "identity politics." As Henry Louis Gates puts it in his concise and insightful manner, "The recent move toward politics and history in literary studies has turned the analysis of texts into a marionette theater of the political, to which we bring all the passions of our real-world commitments" (19). Gates's concern is much like my own: to find a middle ground between the sometimes ill-tempered and hurtful rhetoric of both Right and Left. Sadly, it is more and more difficult to hew to the *aurea mediocritas* without giving offense to at least one of those extremes.

It will be a sad day indeed for our specialty if the ethnic and generic fault lines already perceptible are allowed to widen. There is a naive and divisive sentiment about that those brought up in a certain culture are uniquely qualified to deal with the literature of that culture. I am thinking specifically of an unfortunate comment by Bernardo Gicovate to the effect that Adolfo Van Dam failed to capture the full sense of the tragic implicit in the emended title *El castigo sin venganza* because he was from another culture (304). As a matter of fact, we are all products of a rather different culture than that of early seventeenth-century Spain. Carried to its logical extreme, this sort of thinking would maintain that only the English can fully understand Shakespeare, only Spaniards are attuned to the subtleties of Cervantes and Calderón, and so forth. I hope the absurdity of that sort of cultural bias is apparent.

An equally misguided and unconstructive perception is that those born with secondary sexual characteristics typing them as female are, by virtue of that accident of birth, better equipped to comprehend women characters and women writers. We are still at a primitive stage in dealing with such questions, but I am confident that in the not too distant future our awareness of the relationships among sex, sexual orientation, and gender will expand tremendously, and we shall be able to see that some men are as feminine in their generic orientation as some women—and vice versa—and, concomitantly, that some male authors have a very pronounced feminine component to their constitution. Everything depends on how we define masculinity and femininity. If the subversion of cultural norms and the dominant discourse is a defining feminine feature, as the collected studies in Stoll and Smith's *Perception of Women in Spanish Theater of the Golden Age* would lead one to believe, then it is indisputable that Cervantes, Lope, Tirso, Quevedo, and many other male writers give ample evidence of femininity. We should consider the possibility that, while these writers' biologically assigned sex may be male, their psychic affinities may situate them within the feminine in terms of gender. And it should go without saying that comparable considerations apply to male critics.

In practical terms, the impact of identity and gender politics on the select canon is negligible. Where the effect has been most conspicuous is in the expansion of the critical canon, and that, on the whole, is a salutary development. It has fostered the production of scholarly editions, making accessible texts that were difficult to come by, and it has helped to fill many programs, specialized collections, and journals—including the *Bulletin of the Comediantes* —with high-level contributions. The only drawback may be that one is often adrift during presentations at scholarly meetings, because the text under discussion is unfamiliar. It is sometimes possible, at least, to appreciate the theoretical framework.

I should like to end with a word on behalf of that central core called the select canon, as it is evinced, for example, in Martel and Alpern's *Diez comedias* of 1939. My contention is that canonical works such as the ones included there can serve an instrumental function in both intellectual growth and career advancement. Anyone who agrees to match wits with all the others who have written on well-known texts is certain to be challenged intellectually, surely more so than if focusing on marginal authors and titles. To confront the classics, one must compete not only with previous generations of critics but also with one's own by offering new perspectives and fresh insights, often with the aid of cutting-edge theoretical tools, all of which not only keeps us constructively occupied but also is conducive to intellectual growth and, if done particularly well, to career advancement. There can be no denying that the prizes and perquisites of the profession are more likely to accrue to those who dedicate themselves to saying something significant about canonical works. Finally, and not entirely facetiously, a central core of classics gives us a manageable number of texts that confirm our common cultural literacy and allow us to follow oral presentations on them at professional meetings.

Works Consulted

Abel, Lionel. 1963. *Metatheatre: A New View of Dramatic Form.* New York: Hill and Wang.

Bentley, Eric. 1970. *The Life of the Drama.* New York: Athenaeum.

Cornford, Francis M. 1914. *The Origin of Attic Comedy.* London: E. Arnold.

Cox, Roger L. 1968. "Tragedy and the Gospel Narratives." *Yale Review* 58:545–70.

De Armas, Frederick A. "Poison in a Golden Cup: Claramonte's Healing Art." In progress.

Fowler, Alastair. 1982. *Kinds of Literature: An Introduction to the Theory of Genres and Modes.* Cambridge, Mass.: Harvard University Press.

Frye, Northrop. 1957. *Anatomy of Criticism: Four Essays.* Princeton, N.J.: Princeton University Press.

Gates, Henry Louis, Jr. 1992. *Loose Canons: Notes on the Culture Wars.* Oxford: Oxford University Press.

Gicovate, Bernardo. 1978. "Lo trágico en Lope: *El castigo sin venganza.*" *Anuario de letras* 16:301–11.

Guillory, John. 1990. "Canon." In *Critical Terms for Literary Study,* edited by Frank Lentricchia and Thomas McLaughlin, 233–49. Chicago, Ill.: University of Chicago Press.

Hornby, Richard. 1986. *Drama, Metadrama, and Perception.* Lewisburg, Pa.: Bucknell University Press.

Kerr, Walter. 1967. *Tragedy and Comedy.* New York: Simon & Schuster.

Larson, Catherine. 1991. *Language and the Comedia.* Lewisburg, Pa.: Bucknell University Press.

Levin, Richard. 1979. *New Readings vs. Old Plays: Recent Trends in the Reinterpretation of English Renaissance Drama.* Chicago, Ill.: University of Chicago Press.

Martel, José, and Hymen Alpern, eds. [1939] 1968. *Diez comedias del Siglo de Oro.* Revised by Leonard Mades. Prospect Heights, Ill: Waveland Press.

Parker, Alexander A. 1988. "The Tragedy of Honour: *El médico de su honra.*" In *The Mind and Art of Calderón: Essays on the* Comedias, 213–37. Cambridge: Cambridge University Press.

Parr, James A. 1990. "La tragicomedia y otras tendencias genéricas del XVII." In *Confrontaciones calladas: El crítico frente al clásico,* 159–71. Madrid: Orígenes.

————. 1991. "From Tragedy to Comedy: Putting Plot(ting) in Perspective." In *After Its Kind: Approaches to the* Comedia, edited by Matthew D. Stroud, Anne Pasero, and Amy Williamsen, 93–104. Kassel: Reichenberger.

————. "Canons for the *Comedia:* Interrelations, Instrumental Value, Interpretive Communities, Textuality." *Gestos* 14 (1992): 95–104.

Paterson, Alan K. G. 1984. "Reversal and Multiple Role-Playing in Alarcón's *La verdad sospechosa.*" *Bulletin of Hispanic Studies* 61:361–68.

Stoll, Anita K., and Dawn L. Smith, eds. 1991. *The Perception of Women in Spanish Theater of the Golden Age.* Lewisburg, Pa.: Bucknell University Press.

Téllez, Gabriel (pseud. Tirso de Molina). [1630] 1991. *El burlador de Sevilla y convidado de piedra.* Edited by James A. Parr. Valencia: Albatros/Hispanófila.

Vega Carpio, Lope Félix de. 1962. *El médico de su honra.* In *Teatro,* vol. 3 of *Obras escogidas.* Edited by F. C. Sainz de Robles, 944–72. Madrid: Aguilar.

Wardropper, Bruce W. 1966. "Calderón's Comedy and His Serious Sense of Life." In *Hispanic Studies in Honor of Nicholson B. Adams,* edited by John Esten Keller and Karl-Ludwig Selig, 179–93. Chapel Hill: University of North Carolina Press.

————. 1978. "La comedia española del Siglo de Oro." Addendum to *Teoría de la comedia,* by Elder Olson, 183–242. Translated by Salvador Oliva and Manuel Espín. Barcelona: Ariel.

Dawn L. Smith

Cervantes and His Audience:

Aspects of Reception Theory in

El retablo de las maravillas

El retablo de las maravillas has been widely acclaimed for its mordant satire of the aspirations and prejudices of a social class (e.g., by Eugenio Asensio and Nicholas Spadaccini). Critics have also treated it from a psychological point of view (e.g., Teresa Kirschner) or as a cautionary tale based on elements of traditional folklore (e.g., Isaías Lerner and Mauricio Molho). It has been less customary to look at the play as an examination of the nature of theater, except in passing references to the notion of dramatic illusion around which it is constructed (e.g., by Patricia Kenworthy).

Using reception theory as an approach to Cervantes's *entremeses* as a whole, Nicholas Spadaccini speculates that these dramatic interludes represent "an intensification of the dialogic relationship with the *comedia nueva*" (1986, 163). He also suggests that Cervantes turned his failure in the theater in later life into a strategy whereby he "[directed] his writing for the theater away from the public sphere of performance and representation on stage to the private sphere of reading." That is, because he was denied the public reception of a theater audience, he redefined that audience in terms of an ideal reader whose expectations would be shaped by a knowledge of the genre as well as by his previous experiments with demystification in the *Novelas ejemplares* and in the First Part of *Don Quijote*. While this view opens up an interesting critical perspective, it should not be forgotten that although the *entremeses* were published in 1615, they were undoubtedly written much earlier. It is clear that when Cervantes wrote them he expected them to be performed between the acts of his own *comedias*.[1] From this perspective, *El retablo de las maravillas* is a significant statement of Cervantes's view of the relationship between theater and public, expressed in terms that apply to his own experience as well as to the nature of theater in the wider sense.

El retablo de las maravillas offers us the model of a play within a play, which in turn is about a play that turns into an unscripted performance. The proliferation of perspectives involved may be expressed in the form of two circuits, each containing three components:

External Circuit	**Internal Circuit**
1. Cervantes	1. puppeteers
2. audience (17th century—20th century)	2. audience within *entremés*
3. *entremés/comedia+entremés*	3. (nonexistent) puppet show

The components within the internal circuit (corresponding to the play-within-the-play) effectively parallel those of the external circuit.

The process of theatrical communication has been variously defined by recent theorists, particularly in answer to Georges Mounin's provocative assertion that the stimulus-response relationship in theater is unidirectional (Elam, 33–35). Keir Elam proposes a model that involves both the element of intercommunication between members of the audience *and* a process of collective "feedback" to the performers (35–38). A simplified version of this model shows the dramatic "text" directed to an audience through the mediation of auxiliary transmitters that together form the signal emitted in performance.

Sources	**Transmitters**	**Signal**	**Receiver**
dramatic (pre)text director(s)	1. form of performance actors+technicians, etc.	the total performance	audience
	2. movements, sounds, costumes, properties, etc.		

The signal is received by the spectator, who interprets it according to his or her horizon of expectations and reacts with an appropriate response—hostile or approving, puzzled or enthusiastic, etc.[2]

While this model can be applied to most forms of Western theater (including Golden Age *comedia*), in the case of *El retablo de las maravillas* it is obvious that certain modifications are necessary when we examine the internal circuit. Accordingly, the "play-within-the-play" presents the following profile:

Sources	Transmitters
traditions of puppet theater	voice (narrators)
biblical stories, traditions, etc.[3]	(improvised) narrative
Chanfalla & Chirinos as directors/puppeteers	musician's gestures and sounds[4]
	"set"[5]

The signal transmitted to the spectators in this instance is almost entirely acoustic. Nevertheless, the spectators receive the message and interpret it as a *theatrical* text (as opposed to a literary text). They are compelled to do so because they are the victims of a hoax: Chanfalla and Chirinos resort to blackmail (reinforced by the implication of magical intervention) in order to command the acceptance of the audience. Faced with the hoaxers' proviso that only those of pure blood and legitimate birth will be able to see the performance, the townspeople react out of fear and prejudice. This has a direct influence on the reception given to the nonexistent performance. It also explains why the audience is so eager to deny the "absence" of performance and to fill the void with its own "presence." Cervantes thus removes or places in doubt two important features of the theatrical experience: the visual element and the mediating presence of the performers (in this case, puppets). By supposing that the audience (or receiver) is forced to supply both these missing elements, Cervantes questions the very nature of the theatrical transaction.

Elam points out that this transaction does not involve "the Coleridgean notion of the audience's 'suspension of disbelief' in the presented world." Instead, it is based on the spectators' awareness of the fictive nature of what they are witnessing and their active participation in the pretense (108). In *El retablo,* the audience within the playlet is first coerced into accepting the transaction; once they have collectively acquiesced in the hoax (albeit for personal reasons), the "performance" becomes a closed transaction, strictly limited to the participants (i.e., the tricksters and the townspeople). The exclusiveness of the transaction is demonstrated by the reaction of the Quartermaster (*Furrier*), who is unaware of what is going on and is therefore free to react in accordance with his perception that the puppet show is a fraud.

The implications of this short play become complex and ambiguous at the point when the fraudulent puppeteers begin to lose control over their audience.

As the "performance" unfolds, the spectators gradually become immersed in it, so that eventually they take charge of both plot and performance. At one point, Chanfalla and Chirinos find themselves in the awkward position of being threatened by the Mayor—not because their hoax has failed but because it has succeeded too well (234). They are themselves drawn into the performance against their will and are only saved from ultimate failure (and perhaps discovery) because their audience's attention is diverted by the arrival of the Quartermaster. The Quartermaster, too, unwittingly becomes part of the "performance" by representing the intrusion of reality into the illusion. However, before considering how this character represents a means of resolving the dramatic dilemma in both circuits, we shall first examine the question of the fictive audience's involvement in the play-within-the play.

The decision of Chanfalla and Chirinos to deceive the townspeople with a phoney puppet show is a shrewd one, based, it seems, on their understanding of the potential audience and its familiarity with this kind of traveling entertainment. The choice also has a number of practical advantages, since even an authentic puppet show requires no more than two or three people and a minimum of equipment.[6] Although no mention is made of a title for the performance, Chanfalla also sets up his audience's expectations when he makes various references to magic and magicians and gives them to understand that his presence is awaited in Madrid (219). Similarly, when asked to explain the meaning of "el retablo de las maravillas," he replies with a suggestive allusion to "el sabio Tontonelo" (220). The hook is now baited and immediately swallowed when the Governor decides to engage the tricksters to perform that evening in honor of his goddaughter's wedding. The contract is sealed with an advance payment of "media docena de ducados" (222).

When the performance begins, the trick is put to the test. Will the audience call the hoaxers' bluff or go along with the deception? Chanfalla and Chirinos must be careful not to lose the audience's consent and participation, for these elements are essential to the "authorization" of their performance (Wilshire, 3–10). The moment is a delicate one, since, as Elam observes, "If the delegated initiative appears to be abused, the audience is entitled to withdraw from the contract" (96). Once the crucial moment passes, the audience becomes irretrievably involved in the deception. As in the story of the emperor's new clothes, at this point the spectators are too compromised to give the game away. Besides the fact that personal honor is at stake, they have paid good money in the expectation of receiving something in return. Who would want to admit that they have been deceived?

Each one of the townspeople is isolated from the others with the result that, in their anxiety to prove that they see everything that is narrated, they compete with each other in compounding the deception. In a few brief lines of dialogue, Cervantes differentiates among the characters: the Governor and Pedro Capacho (who are better educated than the rest) clearly do not "see" anything, yet neither will admit as much to the others. The Governor, however, confides his dilemma to us, the audience of the external circuit, in several agitated asides. In the end, he also surrenders to the illusion with evident relief that the soldiers provide irrefutable "proof" that he and his friends have not, after all, been the victims of a hoax (234). On the other hand, Juan Castrado, his daughter Juana, and her cousin Teresa enter fully into the pretense: Juan begs Chirinos to bring on less frightening puppets while the two girls react with suitable alarm to the announcement that there are mice running loose (228–29).

The Mayor, Benito Repollo, is more complex in his reactions. Before the puppet show begins, he is shown as pompous, irascible, and unsure of himself.[7] He is also impatient to see the show ("Vamos, Autor, que me saltan los pies por ver esas maravillas" [225]). At the beginning of the "performance," he shows some cynicism, asking truculently when he sees Rabelín: "¿Músico es éste?" (226), and observing that the puppeteers have very little baggage ("Poca balumba trae este autor para tan gran Retablo"). As the figures supposedly appear, however, he reacts vehemently—first begging Samson not to pull down the temple on top of them, then responding in exaggerated fashion to the entry of the bull (228), the mice (229), and the miraculous rain ("Por las espaldas me ha calado el agua hasta la canal maestra" [230]). Finally, he greets the proclaimed appearance of the dancing girl Herodias with undisguised excitement, urging his nephew to dance with her: "Sobrino Repollo, tú que sabes de achaque de castañetas, ayúdala, y será la fiesta de cuatro capas" (232). That he is now caught up in the illusion is evident from his puzzlement at the illogical situation that allows the Jewish dancer to witness the show, which, according to the terms set out by Tontonelo, is invisible to anyone with Jewish blood. At the same time, while he apparently accepts the preposterous illusion proposed in the puppeteers' narration, Repollo is irritated by the *actual* presence of Rabelín. Similarly, when the illusion is interrupted by the arrival of the *real* Quartermaster, his annoyance boils over. He further manages to confuse reality and illusion by attributing the fortuitous arrival of the soldiers to the magical art of Tontonelo. His skepticism is then mistakenly directed against Chanfalla and Chirinos, that is, he threatens them for the *wrong* reasons. Like Don Quijote in the adventure with Maese Pedro's puppet show, Benito Repollo is no longer able to distinguish between reality and fiction or, perhaps, no longer willing to do so.

A similar situation exists with the other townspeople: by the time the Quartermaster makes his entry, it is no longer clear whether they are still reacting out of fear, or whether they have collectively surrendered to the theatrical illusion. Perhaps they have simply become so immersed in the mimetic experience that they have begun to live the text as if it were life (Fischer, 113). What is certain is the solidarity of their reaction: isolated in their individual reception of the phoney puppet show, they are united in their authorization of the total performance. For one reason or another, the audience has "agreed" to play the game, to subscribe to the "lie" that is theater (Ubersfeld, 44).

The intervention of the Quartermaster is therefore a convenient resolution, both for the play-within-the-play and for Cervantes's *entremés*. In the context of the internal circuit, his unexpected arrival solves the townspeople's dilemma, since, by making him the scapegoat, they are able to save face. For the puppeteers, on the other hand, he represents an unforeseen element—the deus ex machina who nevertheless provides them with a timely ending to their performance. In the context of the external circuit, the Quartermaster also provides an ironic twist that directs our attention as audience to the paradoxical fact that the validity of the illusion in this *entremés* is both tested and finally confirmed by the fortuitous intervention of reality. (We have already seen this occur in the Governor's transition from anxious skepticism to relieved authorization.)

Wolfgang Iser suggests that "the virtual position of the [literary] work is between text and reader" (1980a, 106–7). *El retablo* illustrates this theory in the context of drama, providing an example of how a basic text, as proposed by the fraudulent puppeteers, is elaborated and completed by an audience according to its particular horizon of expectations. Iser's proposal that communication is dependent on a series of structured gaps that determine the relationship between text and reader (1980a, 111) allows for a variety of interpretations on the part of the reader/receiver.[8] The fact that the performance is nonexistent implies that the gaps in the relationship between text and receiver are almost limitless. On the other hand, certain expectations are aroused in the spectators by the promise that they are to witness a puppet show. They are thus preconditioned to accept a set of conventions that differ from those of "live" theater: the nature of puppets necessarily limits their movements, which, in turn, are executed within a restricted space constructed for the purpose; the puppets do not speak, change facial expression, etc. However, once an audience consents to these conventions, a puppet show is expected to fulfill a function of theatrical communication similar to that of "live" theater (Varey, passim; Arnott, passim). When the townspeople in *El retablo* agree to be spectators of the proposed puppet show, they not only indicate their willingness to enter into the theatrical contract, they also show that they know what to expect. When these expectations are not fulfilled, they create with their imagination something larger than a puppet show, larger even than what normally transpires within the physical limits of "live" theater (Samson acquires gigantic proportions, the animals inspire terror). Cervantes draws attention to the paradoxical relationship between the restricted physical context of theater and the infinite possibilities of the world that it evokes. Although the relationship between the actor and the dramatic character ("personaje") is a fundamental part of the theatrical transaction, the physical presence of an actor nevertheless limits the options open to the audience to "fill the gap" with its own imagination.[9]

The acceptance of puppets as "believable" performers requires a greater initial effort on the part of the audience, yet at the same time this acceptance permits spectators to exercise their imagination to a greater degree: they "make believe" that the puppets represent *live* performers (i.e., as signs representing signs representing signs). Because the puppets in *El retablo* do not exist, the first sign is rendered ambiguous—thereby further liberating the audience's imagination and casting doubt on the outcome of the performance.

In this way, Cervantes also conveys the sense of risk implicit in theater: the element of uncertainty that always exists in the relationship between what is transmitted and what is received. Anne Ubersfeld suggests that an important part of the spectator's pleasure in theater derives from its negation of reality, its function as exorcism, which permits the safe contemplation of dangerous or forbidden experiences.[10] The nonexistent puppet show is open-ended and threatens to become anarchic until the unexpected arrival of the Quartermaster and the soldiers reasserts a measure of control over the situation, that is, by focusing on an *existing* reality instead of an *imagined* reality. This intervention also allows the *entremés* to be rounded off artistically: for the external audience, the interlude is brought to an end as Chanfalla and Chirinos prepare to move on to the next town. The curtain is lowered for us, literally and metaphorically. It may even occur to us that the puppets have been put away, both in reference to the illusionary performance and to the deceived townspeople, who have allowed themselves to be manipulated. Within the world of the *entremés* itself, however, the incident is not closed, since the Quartermaster and the townspeople have not yet resolved their quarrel, and the soldiers are about to arrive in the town. The hoaxers' little deception has brought about a turmoil far beyond what was intended in their original plans. (It should be noted, incidentally, that *El retablo* breaks with the convention of ending with a dance, providing instead an ambivalent variation on an accepted theme.)

The relationship between the parallel structures that we have called the internal and external circuits is such that what occurs in the internal performance has significant—and even subversive—implications for the external audience. From the perspective of audience reception, it is necessary to define the nature of the audience involved, depending on a number of determinants, such as historical period, national background, etc. The present study is concerned with two categories: a seventeenth-century audience and a twentieth-century audience (in both cases Spanish speaking, with a reasonable awareness of Cervantes and his work). The reaction of each of these respective audiences to the performance of the *entremés* is obviously shaped by very different expectations. In the first case, the play was not performed during Cervantes's lifetime, therefore we can only speculate as to what its reception might have been. However, we may be sure that the reaction of a contemporary audience (like that of a contemporary reader) would have been affected by knowledge of Cervantes's previous work, both as a writer of prose and a dramatist, as well as by familiarity with the type of puppet show parodied in the play (Spadaccini 1986, 172). Undoubtedly a seventeenth-century audience would have responded with amusement to the satirical portrayal of the simple townspeople who make up the audience in *El retablo*. Some spectators might also have been led to reflect on the juxtaposed texts of the *entremés* and the *comedia* that it served as interlude; perhaps they even would have found in it a veiled reference to Lope and to Cervantes's resentment at the intrusion of the *comedia nueva*.[11] Almost certainly, only a few, if any, would have seen in it a reflection of their own weaknesses.[12]

Today's audience has a different perspective on Cervantes, his relationship with Lope de Vega, and the history of the theater in seventeenth-century Spain. We are also in a position to appreciate *El retablo* for itself, as a separate entity, and with an awareness of its special qualities from a variety of perspectives: for example, as a social satire, a psychological study, a synthesis of traditional sources, or a penetrating view of the dynamics of theater.

How, then, does *El retablo de las maravillas* relate to our modern views on audience reception and theatrical communication? We can, I believe, distinguish three important ways in which Cervantes contributes to the debate:

1.   He raises the question of the nature of the transaction between performers and spectators. The hoaxers in *El retablo* resort to blackmail as a means of compelling the compliance of their audience. The stratagem backfires when the audience goes beyond the limit anticipated by the puppeteers, and they lose control of the performance.

2.   By removing the actors as a separate element mediating between the source and the receiver, Cervantes blurs the distinction between the fictional world and the world of the audience. The fiction, which for the audience is safely contained and controlled by the make-believe of theater, appears less distanced and therefore less safe. Our faith in the protective veil of theatrical convention is challenged. What, then, is the meaning of suspension of disbelief or "active participation in the pretense"? At what point does the willed compliance become uncontrolled surrender; or reality merge with illusion so that they mutually confirm and shape each other?

3.   Cervantes illustrates Iser's theory of reader response, adapted to the theatrical context, whereby the spectator completes the process of recreation by "build[ing] his own bridges" between the "gaps" left in the text. The parodic nature of this *entremés* both clarifies the theory and points to the unpredictability of the outcome of the encounter between spectator and theatrical text.[13]

The concept of the ideal reader (and by extension, the ideal spectator) postulated by modern critics is challenged by Cervantes's portrayal of the reluctant spectator (Benito Repollo), who nevertheless eventually surrenders to the pretense (or is overwhelmed by it), and the unwilling (or hostile) spectator (the Quartermaster), who refuses to accept the theatrical text and consequently threatens to subvert it. These are elements of the larger question of authorial control and what happens when the audience either resists or usurps that authority—in this case, transforming the performance and then, in turn, losing control when life itself intervenes and imposes an overriding "script." It would seem that, like Brecht, Cervantes ultimately acknowledged that it is futile to attempt to dominate an audience: the success of the theatrical transaction depends on imaginative collusion between all the parties involved.[14]

It is generally acknowledged that Cervantes's struggles as a dramatic writer profoundly influenced his writing of *Don Quijote.* The book abounds with characters who play roles for the benefit of entertaining or deceiving others: almost everyone is a performer or spectator at some point. Stories are told (or read) to willing audiences; people watch each other—and are themselves watched. The interpretation by spectators or listeners varies, too: Sancho is skeptical about Don Quijote's account of his descent into the Cave of Montesinos; Don Quijote is caught up in the performance of Maese Pedro's puppets; people react in different ways to Don Quijote's apparent madness, yet are reluctant to put an end to his "performance," either because, like the *duques,* they find it entertaining, or because, like Sancho, they enjoy participating in it.

Both *Don Quijote* in its rich complexity and *El retablo de las maravillas* in its pungent brevity point to the conclusion that nothing is certain about audience/ reader response: the nature of reception is infinitely variable. Cervantes himself would have viewed with ironic amusement the changes in critical reception accorded to *Don Quijote* since the seventeenth century (Close 1978). He would also have enjoyed the paradoxical reversal whereby a play neglected in his own time by an audience avid for change is now hailed as a forerunner of modern metatheater.

Notes

A version of this essay has also appeared under the title "Cervantes frente a su público: Aspectos de la recepción en *El retablo de las maravillas,*" in *En torno al teatro del Siglo de Oro: Jornadas I–VI. Almería,* edited by Agustín de la Granja and Antonio Serrano, 3–16 (Almería: Instituto de Estudios Almerienses, 1991).

1.   The title page of the *princeps* refers to "estas ocho comedias y sus entremeses." Cervantes also tells us in the "Prólogo al Lector": "Algunos años ha que volví yo a mi antigua ociosidad, y pensando que aún duraban los siglos donde corrían mis alabanzas, volví a componer algunas comedias; pero no hallé pájaros en los nidos de antaño; quiero

decir que no hallé autor que me las pidiese, *puesto que sabían que las tenía,* y así las arrinconé en un cofre y las consagré y condené al perpetuo silencio"; a few lines later he refers to "algunos entremeses míos que *con ellas estaban arrinconadas*" (Cervantes 1982, 93–94, my emphasis; all subsequent references to *El retablo de las maravillas* are to this edition and appear in the text in parentheses).

2.   See also J. M. Díez Borque's semiotic approach to the *comedia.*

3.   Michel Moner studies the origin and use of religious and profane figures in *El retablo.*

4.   It is not clear from the text that Rabelín actually plays his instrument—indeed, it seems that this effect is illusionary as well! Compare Benito Repollo's remarks (226, 230).

5.   Cervantes implies that the puppet show takes place in a courtyard (or room) in the house of Juan Castrado (220). Benito Repollo comments that the "puppeteers" have brought "poca balumba" (227). The only stage property that seems actually to exist is the blanket used as a curtain (see the final stage direction, 236). Even this is made out to be other than it really is, since Chanfalla calls it a "repostero" (see Cervantes 1982, 226n. 48).

6.   See, for example, the brief description of the preliminaries of Maese Pedro's puppet show in *Don Quijote* 2:25.

7.   However, I cannot agree with Spadaccini's suggestion that Repollo is "effeminate" (1986, 171).

8.   "These gaps give the reader a chance to build his own bridges, relating the different aspects of the object which have thus far been revealed to him" (Iser, "Indeterminacy and the Reader's Response in Prose Fiction," quoted by Fischer, 112. See also Iser 1980a).

9.   Sito Alba insists that it is the presence of the actor *personifying* the character that marks the transition from the literary text to the theatrical text (1987, 107).

10.   It is significant that Brecht considered that the notion of subversion without danger implied in the Aristotelian concept of mimesis was a main source of audience complacency (Ubersfeld, 339).

11.   See Cervantes's ironic allusions to Lope, "el monstruo de naturaleza," in the prologue to the *entremeses* (93).

12.   "Para el público urbano del entremés, los rústicos de *El retablo de las maravillas* se perfilaban como unos atrasados cuya angustia y credulidad alimentaban la hilaridad de los oyentes" (Canavaggio, 1029).

13.   Although the question of parody in relation to *El retablo* goes beyond the scope of the present essay, it adds another interesting dimension. Linda Hutcheon's observation

that parody represents "a method of inscribing continuity while permitting critical distance," and that its use implies an *"informed reader"* (20, 27) are two points in particular that invite further exploration.

14. "The spectator (as Brecht learned, bitterly, when his *Threepenny Opera* succeeded for what to him were the wrong reasons) is the one element the dramatist cannot control, in any form" (Williams, 318).

Works Consulted

Arnott, Peter. 1964. *Plays without People: Puppetry and Serious Drama.* Bloomington: Indiana University Press.

Asensio, Eugenio. 1973. "Entremeses." In *Suma cervantina,* edited by J. B. Avalle-Arce and E. C. Riley, 7–49. London: Tamesis Books.

Canavaggio, Jean. 1981. "Brecht, lector de los *entremeses* cervantinos: La huella de Cervantes en los *Einakter.*" In *Cervantes, su obra y su mundo: Actas del I congreso internacional sobre Cervantes,* edited by Manuel Criado de Val, 1023–30. Madrid: Edi-6.

Cervantes Saavedra, Miguel de. 1982. *Entremeses.* Edited by Nicholas Spadaccini. Madrid: Cátedra.

———. *Teatro completo.* 1987. Edited by Florencio Sevilla Arroyo and Antonio Rey Hazas. Barcelona: Planeta.

Close, Anthony. 1978. *The Romantic Approach to "Don Quijote."* Cambridge: Cambridge University Press.

Díez Borque, José M. 1976. "Aproximación semiológica a la 'escena' del teatro del Siglo de Oro español." In *Semiología del teatro,* edited by J. M. Díez Borque and Luciano García Lorenzo, 49–92. Barcelona: Planeta.

Elam, Keir. 1980. *The Semiotics of Theatre and Drama.* London & New York: Methuen.

Fischer, Susan. 1979. "Reader-Response Criticism and the *Comedia:* Creation of Meaning in Calderón's *La cisma de Ingalaterra.*" *Bulletin of the Comediantes* 31: 109–25.

Hutcheon, Linda. 1985. *A Theory of Parody: The Teachings of Twentieth-Century Art Forms.* New York & London: Methuen.

Iser, Wolfgang. 1980a. "Interaction between Text and Reader." In *The Reader in the Text,* edited by Susan R. Suleiman and Inge Crosman, 106–19. Princeton, N.J.: Princeton University Press.

———. 1980b. "The Reading Process: A Phenomenological Approach." In *Reader-Response Criticism: From Formalism to Post-Structuralism,* edited by Jane P. Tompkins, 50–69. Baltimore, Md.: Johns Hopkins University Press.

Kenworthy, Patricia. 1981. "La ilusión dramática en los *entremeses* de Cervantes." In *Cervantes, su obra y su mundo: Actas del I congreso internacional sobre Cervantes,* edited by Manuel Criado de Val, 235–38. Madrid: Edi-6.

Kirschner, Teresa J. 1981. *"El retablo de las maravillas,* de Cervantes, o la dramatización del miedo." In *Cervantes, su obra y su mundo: Actas del I congreso internacional sobre Cervantes,* edited by Manuel Criado de Val, 819–27. Madrid: Edi-6.

Lerner, Isaías. 1971. "Notas para el entremés del *Retablo de las maravillas:* Fuente y recreación." In *Estudios de literatura española ofrecidos a Marcos A. Morínigo,* 39–55. Madrid: Insula.

Molho, Mauricio. 1976. *Cervantes: Raíces folklóricas.* Madrid: Gredos.

Moner, Michel. 1981. "Las maravillosas figuras de *El retablo de las maravillas.*" In *Cervantes, su obra y su mundo: Actas del I congreso internacional sobre Cervantes,* edited by Manuel Criado de Val, 809–17. Madrid: Edi-6.

Sito Alba, Manuel. 1987. *Análisis de la semiótica teatral.* Madrid: Universidad Nacional de Educación a Distancia.

Spadaccini, Nicholas. 1986. "Writing for Reading: Cervantes's Aesthetics of Reception in the *Entremeses.*" In *Critical Essays on Cervantes,* edited by Ruth El Saffar, 162–75. Boston, Mass.: G. K. Hall.

Ubersfeld, Anne. 1981. *L'école du spectateur.* Vol. 2 of *Lire le théâtre.* Paris: Editions Sociales.

Varey, John. 1957. *Historia de los títeres en España desde sus orígenes hasta mediados del siglo XVIII.* Madrid: Revista de Occidente.

Williams, Raymond. 1973. *Drama from Ibsen to Brecht.* London and New York: Penguin Books.

Wilshire, Bruce. 1982. *Role Playing and Identity: The Limits of Theatre as Metaphor.* Bloomington: Indiana University Press.

Catherine Connor (Swietlicki)

Prolegomena to the "Popular" in
Early Modern Public Theater:
Contesting Power in Lope and Shakespeare

ecent critical studies of the two great national public theaters of the early modern period, Spanish theater in the time of Lope de Vega and the English stage in the Shakespearean era, have tended to focus on related issues of political significance. The term "propaganda" and its political implications have figured rather prominently in Spanish criticism, especially in commentaries of the last two decades written by José Antonio Maravall, José María Díez Borque, and Noël Salomon. However, in current research on English Renaissance theater, the operative word has been "power," even when some type of propagandistic function is assumed. Despite their sometimes differing terminologies, many contemporary critics of English and Spanish public theater are concerned with the same issue: power relationships in society and in dramatic composition. The major difference is that criticism of power operations in the Spanish public theater of the early modern era preceded the current wave of new historicism in English studies, and consequently the Spanish criticism has not until recently been characterized by the same sort of Foucauldian and contemporary Marxist tendencies that underlie the new historicists' project. In the present study, I point out the benefits of studying in tandem such approaches to Spanish and English public theater, and I demonstrate how the political hermeneutics of the current methodologies often overlook issues that are vital to the purported goals of critics. In effect, I want to demonstrate that most contemporary studies of propaganda and power in the public theaters of the period focus primarily on one component of the dramatic code: the play of power in dramatic composition. They are inclined to overlook the opposite end of the process of dramatic communication: the reception of the message and, more importantly, the role of the receptors in the interactive process of theatrical representation. It is on this dynamic and dialogic relationship between producer and receptor, in particular, that I want to refocus attention. My discussion will center on Lope and Shakespeare, two writers whose reputations as the architects of Renaissance public drama and whose roles as kingpins in their respective national literary canons have made them the favorite targets of contemporary revisionist criticism.

The new-historical approach to Renaissance studies can be said to address three interrelated themes: subjectivity, power relationships, and national identity. In Shakespeare studies, the new hermeneutics has deconstructed the previous generations' views of the bard's dramatic works as manifestations of national and universal human values. The new historicism questions, for example, why we have been taught to read a play such as *King Lear* as representative of all "men in all countries and of all times"[1] or why we should value *Othello* for its analysis of the excesses of human passions while disregarding or diminishing the particular historical and sociocultural factors conditioning the Moor's actions.[2] Much of recent Shakespeare criticism presents "alternative Shakespeares," many of which have resulted from uncovering the "essentialist humanism" of nineteenth-century Shakespeare studies and of their twentieth-century formalist heirs.[3] The new hermeneutics calls into question the previous generations' attempts to construct reality through the eyes of a centered human subject whose values were considered to be timeless and whose identity could be incorporated easily into a liberal bourgeois image of the self. As the new historicists see it, Shakespeare's theater was adapted to fit the needs of English studies and English national identity; the bard became emblematic of English artistic excellence as expressed in the creation of transcendent subjects—Hamlet, Othello, Lear, Falstaff, and other characters whose stage lives would enlighten those of spectators and readers.

In the case of Lope de Vega, on the other hand, it is more difficult to criticize scholars for portraying the prolific dramatist as a master analyst of the human psyche. Few would question Lope's ability to depict the human condition in prose or poetry, but—unlike Shakespeare—he is not known as the creator of timeless dramatic characters demonstrating a universal human condition. The case of Lope as dramatist is similar to that of Shakespeare, however, in that he has been canonized as a national dramatic treasure. The author of perhaps as many as eighteen hundred dramatic compositions, Lope has been depicted in mythic terms by a hermeneutics that focuses on the totality of his theater as a panorama of Spanish society and culture. For critics of the late nineteenth and early twentieth centuries in particular, Lope's dramaturgy was loosely associated with the liberal bourgeoisie's visions of itself as heir to the best traditions of Spanish Renaissance humanism and to the glorious Golden Age of Spanish national consolidation and international ascendancy.

In the 1970s social historians of Spain—particularly Díez Borque, Maravall, and Salomon—called attention to the power and propaganda operations in the Spanish national theater as defined and practiced by Lope. To a certain extent, their studies can be seen as a post-Franco response and an outgrowth of Spain's national introspection, the consequences of which we are continuing to witness to this day. Lope de Vega was a natural target of their research because of the emphasis on nationalism in traditional Lope theater criticism. Moreover, his association with the major power brokers of the sixteenth and seventeenth centuries—the aristocracy, the Inquisition, and other church and secular officials—made it easy to question the motives and applications of his theatrical practice. In effect, these critics of Lope's canonical theater did not have to debunk the same type of historical legacy that would confront the new historians of Shakespeare's theater. Critics of English literature have had to challenge such sacred national cows as individualism, democracy, and capitalism—privileged concepts that traditional criticism had associated, at least partially, with the nationalistic *and* essentialist humanistic values in Shakespeare's theater.

Perhaps new historicism's treatment of power operations in the English Renaissance has been articulated best by Stephen Greenblatt. Rather than reading a single, powerful "Elizabethan world view" into Shakespeare's plays (in the manner of E. M. W. Tillyard), Greenblatt writes that the bard's "plays are centrally and repeatedly concerned with the production and containment of subversion and disorder . . . in three modes[:] testing, recording, and explaining" (1985, 29). In other words, Shakespeare did not display monolithic power on stage, but he allowed the forces of subversion to make their presence known before ultimately yielding to the legitimization of, and domination by, the more powerful. Greenblatt (1985, 29) and Jonathan Dollimore (1985b) make this point with regard to *Measure for Measure,* Leonard Tennenhouse concludes similarly in his analysis of *The Taming of the Shrew* (45–52), and so do Paul Brown and Terence Hawkes with regard to *The Tempest.* Similarly revealing studies by Kathleen McLuskie and Catherine Belsey (1985) hold that female subversion was contained in Shakespeare's plays, although other feminist critics, such as Lisa Jardine, Coppélia Kahn, and Juliet Dusinberre, have tried to show that Shakespeare resisted the traditional patriarchal constructions of women that ultimately left them outside the power structures.

Current studies of the power relationships in Lope's plays have not focused on feminist topics. However, there have been several studies dealing with the playwright's treatment of Spanish minorities, such as Jews, Moors, Blacks, and the inhabitants of the New World.[4] Nevertheless, as I mentioned earlier, in these endeavors Hispanists have not made use of the same methodologies as Shakespearean scholars of the new-historical inclination. A notable exception to the trend is the work of Walter Cohen, although his approach is based on a more traditional Marxism than that of other Anglo-American critics of Shakespeare's theater. Cohen has analyzed some of Lope's best-known plays, such as *Fuenteovejuna* and *Peribáñez,* in terms of the power relationships of class struggle.

In general, current approaches to the theatrical works of Lope and of Shakespeare have differed from earlier criticism by focusing on the power operations underlying the transcendent human values present in dramatic texts and by calling attention to social and cultural concerns overlooked by more purely formalist and New Critical methodologies. Stephen Greenblatt may have been one of the first to call this approach new historicism and to see it as "set apart from both the dominant historical scholarship of the past and the Formalist criticism that partially displaced this scholarship in the decades after World War Two" (1982, 7). The continuation of Greenblatt's definition is particularly significant to my topic. He remarks that "earlier historicism tends to be monological; that is, it is concerned with discovering a single political vision, usually identical to that said to be held by the entire literate class or indeed the entire population." A dialogic approach to criticism helps new historicism excavate monologic literary terrain while it simultaneously erodes its own critical grounding or that of other critical methodologies. Nevertheless, complete dialogic opposition to monologic criticism is still lacking, I believe, in new historicism's project for Shakespeare and Lope studies.[5]

As I see it, the real issue is that a truly dialogic reading of the texts of Shakespeare or Lope—two great canonical dramaturges of Western public theater—must recover the *public* element of the power operations within the plays. Most of the studies of power and propaganda in the two dramatists' plays focus on power as a self-reflective and self-imaging force. This approach can be further examined using three theses on power by Michel Foucault. The first is that power is not essentially repressive, since it most frequently incites, induces, or seduces.[6] Secondly, Foucault holds that power is practiced before it is possessed, since it is possessed only in a determinable form, that of class, and a determined form, that of the state. It is the practicing of power that is most studied by the new political hermeneutics of Shakespeare's and Lope's dramatic texts, although many Hispanists have focused just as frequently on power as possessed by determinable forms, the Spanish upper classes, and by determined forms, the monarchy and the Inquisition.

The third Foucauldian thesis on power, the most neglected in the new studies of Shakespeare's and Lope's theaters, is that power passes through the hands of the mastered no less than through the hands of the masters. The new emphasis on power's image of itself as "an infinitely resourceful center of initiative, surveillance, and control" (Bristol, 10) has left little space for commenting on the popular reception of, and reaction to, the power maneuvers of the masters. Moreover, the problem of reception in the context of cultural difference—that is to say of the majority, nonliterate popular culture as compared to the dominant minority of lettered culture—is grossly neglected. Even scholars studying elements of popular culture in Renaissance theater, such as Robert Weimann on Shakespeare or Ricardo del Arco y Garay on Lope, tend to see popular culture as a source of forms, practices, and fragmentary images that come to achieve fuller and more complex realization in the masterpieces of dramatic literature and in the professional theaters where these works were produced.[7] Forgotten in this misfocused view of the popular or plebeian culture's relationship to that of the literate is the fact that critics themselves are products of "Western civilization" and of political and economic conditions. In other words, despite our intellectual or political intentions, we are part of the culture that withdrew from its involvement in traditional society, eventually became victorious and masterful, and continues to focus critical attention on the dominant classes or those that eventually became dominant.

If we are to recover the popular from the dramatic texts of Renaissance public theater and if we are to understand the full meaning of the power and propaganda operations in the reception of those texts, we need critical tools that will help us to overcome our own acculturation. Such tools would situate canonical works in their historical contexts and enable us to see how the would-be masters were still quite intensely involved in the culture of the would-be mastered. This dialogic approach centers on two basic points: first, that the early modern period was one characterized by sociocultural heteroglossia, by colliding discourses and ideologies; and second, that an interdisciplinary and diversified methodology may be instrumental in helping us to recover popular culture and especially its reception of dramatic performance texts in public theaters.

There was no one Renaissance ideology, despite the efforts of scholars who have tried to construct one for us. E. M. W. Tillyard would have us accept "the Elizabethan world picture" as a model for English Renaissance ideology, just as Otis H. Green's vision of "Spain and the Western tradition" would provide an account of Spanish ideology in the period.[8] However, their approach to Renaissance thought disregards the literate classes' very active participation in popular culture, its traditions, customs, and rituals. Moreover, the critics' monologic and orthodox view of the lettered culture ignores several ways in which the very discourse of the dominant classes was itself still bound to the popular culture.

As studies by social historians of the early modern period have shown in recent years, what is commonly called the "popular culture" today did not have the same sociocultural function prior to the Industrial Revolution.[9] Our conceptions of popular culture as that of the nonelite or subordinate classes do not account for rather different connotations that become more apparent when studying early modern social history synchronically as well as diachronically. Succinctly stated, the general culture from roughly 1500 to 1800 *was* the popular culture because it consisted of shared cultural practices of all the people from all social and economic classes. The process by which the lettered and economically favored classes withdrew from genuine participation in the general or popular culture and created an elite culture was an extremely slow and complex one that nevertheless accelerated with the growth of print culture and more highly technical economies.

The interaction of oral and textual cultures is one of the major aspects of the slow withdrawal of the lettered classes from the general culture that has been studied in the last two decades. Studies from anthropology, psychology, and the literatures of the classical, medieval, and early modern periods in Western Europe have shown that literate cultures (particularly in pretechnological societies) remain residually oral long after they have begun to incorporate textual mentalities into their cultural practices.[10] In other words, the languages of literate Western culture—even until the late nineteenth century, but especially during the

Renaissance—were marked by remnants of their ties to popular and largely oral culture, namely, by rhetoric and other structures that betray a sense of being at odds with the supposed Renaissance ideology and psychology of the independent and transcendent human subject. When the interaction of oral and textual modes of thought are considered in tandem with the relationship of all classes to the general or popular culture, all questions on the context of public theater productions in the early modern period become complicated and defy reduction to a simple label such as a "Renaissance world picture."

Another significant dimension to any project that seeks to recover the context of early modern public theater is more specifically sociolinguistic and sociopsychological. Fundamental to this approach are Voloshinov's and Bakhtin's notions of language as inherently dialogic, as a discourse whose meaning can only be grasped in terms of its inevitable orientation toward others. This concept is particularly appropriate for early modern societies demonstrating characteristics of residual orality and simultaneously experiencing the slow process by which lettered culture becomes more clearly distinguished from the popular culture. The dialogic notion holds that the linguistic sign—as a continually modified and transformed component of speech—is always conditioned by social tones, values, and connotations, which are themselves always shifting, just like the heterogeneous speech community itself with all its conflicting social groups and interests. In addition, the concept of speaking as authoring is also significant to understanding the heteroglot nature of early modern society. Not only is anyone who speaks an author, but every act of speaking or authoring always includes the listener/receptor as well as all of the social and cultural factors conditioning their communication.

This concept can help us to think of Shakespeare and Lope not so much as authors in the essentialist-humanist sense of creators of the word passively received, but rather as participants in linguistic acts that are simultaneously social practices. Such an approach can assist us in restructuring theories of performance, closure, and reception in public theaters of early modern England and Spain. Nonliterate spectators in a public audience cannot be considered as merely passive receptors of the power and propaganda messages when they are the ever-present other of the dramatist's acts of authoring. Supporting this view are current studies on the semiotics of stagecraft and historical testimonies on the behavior of audiences in the public theaters. Performance theory has made it clear that the necessarily unpredictable relationships between players and spectators cannot be fore-seen.[11] We have well-documented examples from the early modern public theater in the rowdy antics of the *mosqueteros* and in those of their English counterparts, the groundlings. The relative scarcity of stage settings in the public theaters of the period made the reception of a play more dependent on the purely linguistic as-pects of the performance than was the case in court theater or other more elabo-rately decorated public stages. The spectators in the public theaters were highly attuned to the oral components of the performance not only because the visual aspects were less prominent, but also because they were accustomed by their residually oral culture to interacting among themselves and with the actors during performances. In addition, their participation in the theater event was encouraged by the relative openness of the public stages in England and Spain and by the stages' lack of a comprehensive and authoritative vision. These elements limited the power of the dramatic text to generate a predetermined reception or to con-struct the sort of closure to which we are accustomed as readers from highly literate and technologized societies.

Underlying the sociolinguistic and psycholinguistic aspects of this study on early modern public theater are the attendant sociopolitical implications that arise inevitably from such an interdisciplinary method. A key aspect of this ap-proach is the concept of ideology as a process or system of coding reality and not as a predetermined set of coded messages or beliefs that can be uniformly sent and received *in toto*. This view of ideology as process places it in a linguistic context where the sign becomes an arena for encounters between speakers or, in more political terms, for class struggles.[12] With regard to theatrical signs, a per-formance text becomes the site of a lively and open process of interaction and struggle for meaning among audience, spectators, dramatist, actors, their varied idiosyncrasies, and scores of other factors that can enter into a performance. When receivers are considered a part of the process of production of meaning in such an event, they are not silent recipients of ideological messages coded in dramatic performances.[13] These notions of a theatrical performance as a discursive process and the conception of ideology as a product of a particular signifying practice are appropriate for cultural studies of the early modern period, a time when old and new powers and idea systems collided yet interacted.[14]

This concept of ideology as a process similar to linguistic communication relates to another political aspect of theater reception that might be termed "resistance." Even if it is assumed that the lower classes—who constituted the majority of a public theater audience—were the objects of possible propagandistic intentions on the part of the dramatist or others wielding power in the production of a theatrical performance, the members of that supposedly weak majority exercised resistance to the more powerful in subtle ways that have generally escaped comment in literary discussions. Michel de Certeau's sociohistorical and anthropological approach to culture reveals the multiple "tactics" that the economically and politically weak practice "in everyday life" in order to exercise resistance to the more powerful.[15] These "popular" tactics turn the apparently established order of things to the people's advantage without any illusion that the status quo will change. In early modern times, most participants in such everyday resistance were not literate, and, as a consequence, their resistance was documented only when it occurred on a somewhat larger scale and became manifest as brigandage or rebellion. In the literary realm, these tactics remain visible in the picaresque or in the mischievous actions of manservants, maids, and other *gracioso*-like figures. Indeed, such was the case in many dramatic and narrative works from the early modern period.

Other examples of how popular resistance tactics might become intensified and potentially subversive under specific conditions are to be found in Carnival celebrations and in the carnivalesque activities that proliferated during festivals and related events in the medieval and early modern periods. Certainly Carnival and carnivalesque activities offered ample opportunities for individuals from all levels of society to reverse roles or to turn the established world upside down.[16] Such celebrations have been considered "safety-valve" methods of social control that allow for a release of societal pressures without resulting in permanently successful subversion.[17] Nevertheless, Carnival or carnivalesque activities did result in rebellions, and the overall subversive tendencies of such endeavors can be considered "rehearsals" for the revolutions that eventually took place in Europe.[18] The point is that the misrule of Carnival and other forms of resistance can and should be considered as natural in societies of the early modern period as the supposedly natural conditions of harmony and order.[19] In other words, Carnival and related activities present opportunities for lower-class subversiveness even while they simultaneously affirm the power of traditional customs to create cross-class cohesion. Carnival is the dialogic meeting ground for the celebration of social and cultural diversity as well as of traditional community values cherished by all social classes. The legacy of Carnival and the carnivalesque must not be overlooked by critics studying another performance-oriented activity, the power relationships inherent in the composition and reception of dramatic works written for and performed in public theaters.

The accounts of resistance manifested in Carnival and carnivalesque activities indicate that it may have been just as normal for audiences of Lope's and Shakespeare's time to reject the power represented on stage by the sociopolitical masters as to accept it. Alongside the evidence from Carnival studies, the tactics of resistance used by the mastered classes on a more limited scale in everyday life contribute to our understanding of how audience attitudes work against the propagandistic aspects that may be functioning in the composition and representation of a play. Moreover, other concepts discussed in the present study provide additional grounds for calling into question the supposed manipulation of public theater audiences of the early modern period. The concept of language as dialogic and contextual is highly significant for approaching dramatic texts from the point of view of the would-be masters as well as from that of the would-be mastered. Power may be contested by *both* groups in any signifying practice. Underlying this notion of language is the concept of ideology as a process operating in specific discursive practices and not as a preconceived program of indoctrination. Equally significant for a consideration of dramatic texts from the early modern period are the residually oral condition of the dominant lettered classes and the broad definition of popular culture as the general culture of all the people in that era preceding the total separation of literate groups. Finally, applications of performance theory to dramatic productions from the time of Lope and Shakespeare will provide additionally useful information. As outlined in the present study, an interdisciplinary approach to concepts of European culture in the early modern period can help recover an understanding of the meaning of popular culture in the period and a broader notion of the power relationships operative at that time.

Notes

1.   Samuel Coleridge, 56–57, as cited by Dollimore (1984, 260) in his comments on Coleridge's seminal role in Shakespeare studies and modern literary criticism.

2.   See in particular Karen Newman's article on the critical treatment of racial and sexual difference.

3.   Discovering the effaced contradictions in Shakespeare's plays and the primacy of the transcendental subject in traditional Shakespeare criticism are two aspects of John Drakakis's introduction, and of the essays by contributors, to *Alternative Shakespeares*.

Dollimore outlines the problem particularly well in "Subjectivity and Social Process" (1984, 153–81).

4.   On racial and religious minorities, see Seminario, Gitlitz, and Silverman. My 1988 study takes into account the more dialogic notions of language and society in popular theater.

5.   A case in point is a recent review article by David Harris Sacks on several of the new monographs written in the new-historical manner. He points out that the supposedly new readings of Shakespeare sometimes end by positing a new "univocal" reading (443).

6.   The summary of Foucault's views of power is based on Deleuze, 71.

7.   See Bristol, 47 for comments on Robert Weimann's classic *Shakespeare and the Popular Tradition in the Theater.*

8.   E. M. W. Tillyard's *The Elizabethan World Picture* has been called "the most notorious instance" of monological historical scholarship that claims to describe a single political vision held by the entire literate class and, by extension, the entire population. See Jonathan Dollimore's comments in this regard in his "Introduction: Shakespeare, Cultural Materialism and the New Historicism" (1985a, 5–6).

9.   A major work on the topic is Peter Burke's. His bibliographic references are also highly useful for further study.

10.   For an extensive bibliography and a thorough survey of research on the topic, see Walter J. Ong.

11.   See the studies by Keir Elam, which provide extensive bibliography and detailed descriptions of the complexity of theatrical performance and reception.

12.   Particularly significant to this view of ideology is Voloshinov's study. Also important are the contributions of Barthes and Gramsci, whose views on ideology as applied to media studies are surveyed by Stuart Hall, Tony Bennett, and Janet Woollacott in M. Gurevitch, ed., *Culture, Society and the Media.*

13.   Some of the conclusions by John Fiske and John Hartley on the popular mass audiences of contemporary television may contribute to our understanding of the active role popular audiences play in creating meaning, although historical changes must be taken into consideration.

14.   Catherine Belsey (1985, 1–10; 1980, 86–90) has described this relationship particularly well with reference to Shakespearean theater.

15.   Although de Certeau's essays are primarily concerned with contemporary culture, his text benefits from his extensive knowledge of social history and his frequent references to the past.

16.   See Mikhail Bakhtin's (1984) description of the functions of Carnival in European culture.

17. See Burke, 201–4.

18. This point is demonstrated by Natalie Zemon Davis, whose comments concern European cultures in general, not only that of France.

19. Michael Bristol emphasizes this point with special reference to the public theater in the early modern period (197–200).

Works Consulted

Arco y Garay, Ricardo del. 1941. *La sociedad española en las obras de Lope de Vega.* Madrid: Real Academia Española.

Bakhtin, Mikhail. 1981. *The Dialogic Imagination.* Edited by Michael Holquist. Translated by Michael Holquist and Caryl Emerson. Austin: University of Texas Press.

———. [1968] 1984. *Rabelais and His World.* Translated by Hélène Iswolsky. Bloomington: Indiana University Press.

———. 1986. *Speech Genres and Other Late Essays.* Edited by Caryl Emerson and Michael Holquist. Translated by Vern W. McGee. Austin: University of Texas Press.

Belsey, Catherine. 1980. *Critical Practice.* London: Methuen.

———. 1985. *The Subject of Tragedy.* London: Routledge Chapman & Hall.

Bristol, Michael D. 1985. *Carnival and Theater: Plebeian Culture and the Structure of Authority in Renaissance England.* London: Methuen.

Brown, Paul. 1985. "'This Thing of Darkness I Acknowledge Mine': *The Tempest* and the Discourse of Colonialism." In *Political Shakespeare,* edited by Jonathan Dollimore and Alan Sinfield, 48–71. Ithaca, N.Y.: Cornell University Press.

Burke, Peter. 1978. *Popular Culture in Early Modern Europe.* New York: New York University Press.

Cohen, Walter. 1985. *Drama of a Nation: Public Theater in Renaissance England and Spain.* Ithaca, N.Y.: Cornell University Press.

Coleridge, Samuel. 1907. *Coleridge's Essays and Lectures on Shakespeare.* London: J. M. Dent.

Davis, Natalie Zemon. 1975. *Society and Culture in Early Modern France.* Stanford, Calif.: Stanford University Press.

De Certeau, Michel. 1984. *The Practice of Everyday Life.* Translated by Steven Rendall. Berkeley and Los Angeles: University of California Press.

Deleuze, Gilles. 1986. *Foucault.* Minneapolis: University of Minnesota Press.

Díez Borque, José María. 1976. *Sociología de la comedia española del siglo XVII.* Madrid: Cátedra.

———. 1978. *Sociedad y teatro en la España de Lope de Vega.* Barcelona: A. Bosch.

Dollimore, Jonathan. 1984. *Radical Tragedy.* Chicago, Ill.: University of Chicago Press.

———. 1985a. "Introduction: Shakespeare, Cultural Materialism, and the New Historicism." In *Political Shakespeare,* edited by Jonathan Dollimore and Alan Sinfield, 2–17. Ithaca, N.Y.: Cornell University Press.

———. 1985b. "Transgression and Surveillance in *Measure for Measure.*" In *Political Shakespeare,* edited by Jonathan Dollimore and Alan Sinfield, 72–87. Ithaca, N.Y.: Cornell University Press.

Drakakis, John, ed. 1985. *Alternative Shakespeares.* London and New York: Methuen.

Dusinberre, Juliet. 1975. *Shakespeare and the Nature of Women.* London: Macmillan.

Elam, Keir. 1977. "Language in the Theater." *SubStance* 18–19:139–61.

———. 1980. *The Semiotics of Theatre and Drama.* London and New York: Methuen.

Fiske, John, and John Hartley. 1978. *Reading Television.* London and New York: Methuen.

Gitlitz, David. 1982. "The New Christian Dilemma in Two Plays by Lope de Vega." *Bulletin of the Comediantes* 34:63–81.

Green, Otis H. 1963–66. *Spain and the Western Tradition.* 4 vols. Madison: University of Wisconsin Press.

Greenblatt, Stephen. 1982. "The Forms of Power and the Power of Forms." *Genre* 15: 3–6.

———. 1985. "Invisible Bullets: Renaissance Authority and Its Subversion, *Henry IV* and *Henry V.*" In *Political Shakespeare,* edited by Jonathan Dollimore and Alan Sinfield, 18–47. Ithaca, N.Y.: Cornell University Press.

Gurevitch, M., T. Bennett, J. Curran, and J. Woollacott, eds. 1982. *Culture, Society and the Media.* London: Methuen.

Hawkes, Terence. 1986. *That Shakespeherian Rag: Essays on a Critical Process.* London: Routledge Chapman & Hall.

Jardine, Lisa. 1983. *Still Harping on Daughters: Women and Drama in the Age of Shakespeare.* Sussex: Harvester Press; Totowa, N.J.: Barnes and Noble.

Kahn, Coppélia. 1981. *Man's Estate: Masculine Identity in Shakespeare.* Berkeley and Los Angeles: University of California Press.

McLuskie, Kathleen. 1981–85. "Feminist Deconstruction: The Example of Shakespeare's *Taming of the Shrew.*" *Red Letters* 12:33–40.

———. 1985. "The Patriarchal Bard: Feminist Criticism and Shakespeare: *King Lear* and *Measure for Measure.*" In *Political Shakespeare,* edited by Jonathan Dollimore and Alan Sinfield, 88–108. Ithaca, N.Y.: Cornell University Press.

Maravall, José Antonio. 1972. *Teatro y literatura en la sociedad barroca.* Barcelona: Crítica.

———. 1977. "Relaciones de dependencia e integración social: Criados, graciosos y pícaros." *Ideologies and Literature* 1:3–32.

Newman, Karen. 1987. "'And Wash the Ethiop White': Femininity and the Monstrous in *Othello*." In *Reproducing Shakespeare*, edited by Jean E. Howard and Marion O'Connor, 142–62. New York and London: Methuen.

Ong, Walter J. 1982. *Orality and Literacy*. London: Methuen.

Sacks, David Harris. 1988. "Searching for 'Culture' in the English Renaissance." *Shakespeare Quarterly* 39:465–88.

Salomon, Noël. 1985. *Lo villano en el teatro del Siglo de Oro*. Translated by Beatriz Chenot. Madrid: Castalia.

Seminario, Lee Ann Durham. 1974. "The Black, the Moor and the Jew in the 'Comedia' of Lope de Vega (1609–c.1625)." Ph.D. diss., Florida State University.

Silverman, Joseph H. 1971. "Los hidalgos cansados de Lope de Vega." In *Homenaje al William L. Fichter,* edited by A. D. Kosoff and J. Amor y Vázquez, 691–711. Madrid: Castalia.

Swietlicki, Catherine. 1988. "Lope's Dialogic Imagination: Writing Other Voices of 'Monolithic' Spain." *Bulletin of the Comediantes* 40:205–26.

Tennenhouse, Leonard. 1986. *Power on Display: The Politics of Shakespeare's Genres*. New York: Routledge Chapman & Hall.

Tillyard, E. M. W. 1943. *The Elizabethan World Picture*. London: Chatto and Windus.

Voloshinov, Valentin N. 1986. *Marxism and the Philosophy of Language*. Translated by Ladislav Matejka and I. R. Titunik. Cambridge, Mass.: Harvard University Press.

Weimann, Robert. 1978. *Shakespeare and the Popular Tradition in the Theater.* Baltimore, Md.: Johns Hopkins University Press.

Emilie L. Bergmann

Reading and Writing in the *Comedia*

The *comedia* in performance is primarily a spoken art form, although in the twentieth century, we experience it more often as a written text. In studying the *comedia,* we become accustomed to imagining oral performance, but the presence of actual written texts onstage suggests a dynamic relationship between spoken and written discourse. In *La Estrella de Sevilla* and *La dama boba,* written texts in the form of books, letters, decrees, or contracts are present on stage and are important to the action. Reading and writing are prominent dramatic elements in these two plays, and their role is clearly connected with the inscription of women in systems of exchange in economic and symbolic terms.

Women read in *La dama boba;* a woman is written on—is the object of desire exchanged through written texts—in *La Estrella de Sevilla.* The titles of both plays lead us to expect the *boba* and Estrella to be protagonists; however, their roles differ significantly: the former's success as a reader makes her a coauthor of her marriage, while Estrella is excluded from, and objectified in, the processes of writing and speaking that destroy her solidly contracted marriage. Estrella's single act of writing a letter is ancillary to the marriage arrangements that her brother makes for her: her writing does not make things happen. In act 3, her noble character is exemplified by her long monologues, expressions of renunciation amid the ruins of the marriage that she and Sancho Ortiz had assumed was certain.

These two plays reveal some of the varied aspects of a theme that preoccupied authors in a society in transition from orality to print culture. The interplay of the written and the oral in the *comedia* is varied and complex in its theoretical implications. Speech act theory, semiotics, and feminist literary theory offer productive approaches to the problems arising from the interaction of written and oral language on the dramatic stage.

Elias L. Rivers (115–17; see also Azar) has demonstrated the usefulness of a speech act analysis of *La Estrella de Sevilla* and has shown how the conflict between verbal and written contracts is played out in a moral drama of absolute and misguided power. The possible outcomes of this conflict lead to a question of ideology in the literature of the Golden Age. For the letter to prove more durable than the spoken word, a new order, which Rivers associates with "the shame of writing," must come into being, whereas if the spoken word proves more binding, traditional notions are upheld: the spoken word is imagined to precede the written, the written is seen as nothing more than a debased imitation of the *logos,* and the transcendent value of the spoken word legitimizes the traditional Iberian value of honor. A third possible outcome is that, as happens in *La Estrella de Sevilla* (and other works of the period), neither oral nor written language can be counted on to correspond to reality: the King fails to recognize the binding force of his own word and his signature, and this failure of language reflects moral decadence in a character or in the society depicted. After all, the audience is witnessing an illusion made of words in a period acutely aware of the chasm between sign and referent.

The categories of written and oral together reveal the uncertainty of language itself as exemplified in a young woman's successful and amusing lies in Lope's *La dama boba.* Her apparent initiation into the symbolic order enables her to read, but, once having recognized that letters and words are things—and not the things for which they are made to stand in social interaction—she understands how to manipulate her own use of language to lie. Lope seems to anticipate Lacanian theories of language and the mirror stage: his female character is always outside the law of the father, first from lack of knowledge and later from excess, disrupting and revealing the workings of the symbolic order. The comic plot bypasses questions of honor through a timely betrothal in the presence of witnesses. But underlying this drama, as in *El perro del hortelano* and its improbable assertions of lineage in the interest of marriage, is a transgression of the social order as potentially disruptive in its context as the moral and social irresponsibility of the King's words and deeds in *La Estrella de Sevilla.* In *La dama boba,* humor and the dance of courtship drown out the disturbing undercurrent, while *La Estrella*'s historical setting distances the audience from social and moral disorder in the ruins of language.

By focusing on the role of *papeles* in these two plays, as stage props and objects that influence action on stage, I would like to examine how letters and written promises and commands function amid the oral discourse of the *comedia*. Neither the reader of the dramatic text nor the spectator of a play has access to the writing borne by these objects unless the dialogue includes words to be read by an actor on stage. In addition, there is no reason to suppose that what an actor might read from a stage *papel* is necessarily inscribed on it, since the actor must repeat the same reading with every performance along with the rest of his or her memorized lines. Thus, the problem of the textual object in the dramatic space is a problem of dramatic time: the object is visible but indecipherable until its contents are revealed by an actor who represents the action of reading it—or the contents are not revealed at all in reading but rather revealed indirectly through dialogue or the action it might effect.

This problem of the mysterious object in dramatic time is made evident by the process of reading *La Estrella de Sevilla* and being as uninformed as the fictional characters are (and as the audience would be) of some of its crucial *papeles, cédulas, conciertos,* contracts, and commands; and yet we may expect to have equal access to the representation of written and spoken discourse in the text we are reading. For the audience of a stage performance, the impact of the undeciphered textual object lacks the dimension of discontinuity in written texts, but it has an added semiotic dimension of secrecy.[1] If we recall that a majority of the audience was illiterate and dependent upon a person authorized to read and interpret documents affecting their lives, another dimension is added to the letter's inaccessibility as sign on the stage of a Golden Age *corral*.

That the contents of some *papeles,* particularly the one naming Sancho's victim, remain undisclosed during part of the action is instrumental to the temporal suspense of *La Estrella de Sevilla.* The device is familiar to us from episodes of *Don Quijote,* such as the interruption of the reading of the *Curioso impertinente,* the suspense of waiting to read the translation of the manuscript found in Toledo, and the hinted discovery of a second part. Familiar as it is to the reader of Cervantes's novel, it is nonetheless useful to point out the strangeness of this experience and its possible dramatic functions. The audience can see a piece of paper and knows it bears an inscription, but if it is left unopened or is read silently, only its writer and reader know its contents (unless the actor's facial gestures or verbal response in the process of silent reading give away its contents). In act 2, Sancho

Ortiz reads the good news in Estrella's letter once silently and again aloud for the audience's benefit. Although the technology of the cinema and the higher literacy rate of twentieth-century audiences make it possible for the viewer to read written documents, access to written words remains in the control of the cinematographer, and the stage convention of characters reading aloud continues to be employed for its dramatic potential, although it is often transformed into a voice-over to be understood by the audience as the inner voice of the character.

The playwright's strategy of employing letters and documents on stage places the spectator and the reader in the position of the viewer of Dutch paintings of women absorbed in reading letters: all we know of their contents must be interpreted through the gestures, facial expressions, and surroundings of the readers; the image is an emblem of the interiority of reading. Svetlana Alpers points out in her discussion of Dutch letter paintings that "an essential content remains inaccessible, enclosed in the privacy of the reader's or writer's absorption in the letter. . . . What is suggested is not the content of the letters . . . but rather the letter as an object of visual attention, a surface to be looked at," as well as the letter's "ability to close distances, to make something present, to communicate secretly."[2] To read a document aloud on stage places it in two worlds: the reader's private and personal gaze and privilege of interpretation on the one hand, and, on the other, the represented public world in which the document's words become a verbal rather than a written act. The letter or document as prop constitutes an enigmatic object that is an emblem of deferred meaning: we as readers or spectators can only know what it signifies through the readings carried out by the characters. Moreover, the *papel* in *La Estrella de Sevilla* has a role of its own: it affects the action, and its words have the finality of commands or contracts. It is not only subject to reproduction in oral communication but requires it in order to participate in the drama. In fact, when asked who ordered him to kill Busto, Sancho replies, "un papel" (2935).

La Estrella de Sevilla: Inscription, Gesture, Silence

In the brief penultimate scene of act 1, Don Arias dismisses the other characters on stage: "que quiere el Rey escrebir" (902). Does the King wish to write the past, or is he projecting the future? In fact, he has accomplished nothing worth inscribing in a king's chronicles since his arrival in Seville, and in lines 909–12 it is clear that all he proposes to write is his signature on a *cédula* granting freedom to the slave Natilde, who has promised him access to Estrella in exchange. The statement, however, carries the implication that, as the King's plans have been successful so far, what he wants to write will determine the action of the play, will perhaps be the next two acts of the play. And yet, the King's written word will be invalid: neither he nor Natilde will be able to keep either part of the bargain after Estrella's brother Busto discovers and obstructs the King's entry into Estrella's room and hangs Natilde with the writ of manumission in her hand. The promises and failures of writing are central to the play.

In his speech act analysis of *La Estrella de Sevilla,* Elias Rivers points out the "skirmishes of honor" at the end of act 1 and the beginning of act 2, "in which courtesy can not fully disguise the underlying sexual violence of two men fighting over a woman" (108). I would add that Busto's depiction of himself to the King, "soy de una hermana marido" (406), intensifies the insult to Busto's honor and casts these two men's rivalry in terms of cuckoldry when the King attempts to enter Busto's house. Busto confirms in social terms the parallel images of the Gemini but leaves an unanswered question: if he is committed to having his sister married honorably—so much so that he claims to be wedded to her—how is it that he resists successfully the King's incursions but fails to mention her betrothal at the beginning of the play? Frederick de Armas interprets Busto's conjugal representation of his relationship to his sister as signaling an expected "orderly shift from the care of her brother to the care of Sancho her beloved" (17). Both relationships are represented by Castor and Pollux, but the parallel is subverted and the smooth transition disrupted by the underlying astrological structure of the play revealed by de Armas and James Burke.

Rivers discusses the conflicting obligations in the play, Busto's concealed suspicions, and Sancho's justifiable distrust of written contracts, concluding that "the written contract, as a substitute speech act, destroys the honor system itself, which depends upon the non-reiterable uniqueness of the performative utterance. . . . From a traditional point of view, [a man's] signature is an inadequate substitute for the authentic oral performative utterance" (115). Rivers extends the play's pertinence to "Spain's quixotic attempt to maintain a prehistoric system of social justice" (117), for which Sancho's refusal to accept the King's written immunity is the most dramatic example. The exemplarity of Sancho's behavior is further elaborated when the King fails to fulfill his verbal obligation to protect Busto's murderer, and Sancho, keeping his own promise of secrecy, is forced to remind him of his promise. The King reluctantly makes his confession, professing admiration of "la nobleza sevillana" (2983). His attribution of honor to the population of Seville gives support to Rivers's view of writing, history, and honor in a social and collective context.

Not only verbal and written contracts but also gestures and silence are threatened and invalidated as speech acts in *La Estrella de Sevilla*. It should be noted that Estrella figures as an object of the King's gaze in the dialogue of 1.1 but does not appear on stage as a speaking subject until 1.7. Her communication with the King's cynical advisor, Arias, is atypical: she turns her back on Arias in answer to his indecent proposal in act 1. To free Sancho Ortiz from prison in act 3, she uses the authority of a ring, not a written document, given to her by the King, and she covers her identity with a veil when she speaks to the Alcaide and Sancho Ortiz.

Although it was common enough for the *comedia* to reflect seventeenth-century Spanish women's lack of choice in their marriage arrangements, Estrella's absence and silence with respect to her proposed exchange among the men and her initial anonymity in wielding moral authority are worth noting in the context of the play's enactment of moral disruption on a verbal level and in the context of her often-cited role in moral guidance (Burke, 147–50; de Armas, 11; Sturm and Sturm 1969). Seeing and hearing so little of Estrella herself in the first two acts, however, is an effective dramatic strategy for representing her inviolable virtue: public exposure and discourse could only be detrimental to a woman's honor. Busto unjustly suspects her of dishonoring him; defending herself against Busto's accusations, she asks, "¿En las manos de algún hombre / viste algún papel escrito / de la mía?" (1288–90). The strongest affirmation of her virtue is her absence from writing, and from public discourse, but this absence is nonetheless the mechanism of her victimization.

Silences, omissions, delays in knowledge, and absences are as important to the play's discursive structure as the speech acts and written contracts. When Busto replies to the King's offer of a noble husband for his sister, neither the audience nor the King can know that Busto is concealing his own prior commitment, which invalidates his expression of gratitude—in order to thank the giver, he would have to be in a position to accept the favor. Thus, Busto's omission of crucial information from an exchange initiates the series of faulty speech acts in the play, the broken contracts and promises on the part of other characters that lead from his dishonor to his death by his best friend's hand, the dramatic betrayal of a bond between equals.

The King's offer of a noble and wealthy husband for Busto's sister is clearly made in the context of bribery (419–23), as is Arias's offer, accompanied by flattery (807–8). The vagueness of the King's final "Casarla pienso, y casarla / como merece" (3023–24) culminates the series with a hollow ring of mercantilism. The actions the King plans to carry out amount to defacing a blank page in light of Estrella's absences and emphatic silence in the scenes that involve the King's designs upon her. There is no dialogue of courtship, only a plan to rape a sleeping woman. The title of the play points not to the central figure but to a central absence and to the erasure of inscriptions.

Burke's and de Armas's research reveals astrological structures in *La Estrella*. But a counterdiscourse, the debasing wordplay of coinage, systematically undermines the transcendent inscription of women in astrology. The King establishes the commercial context for the "divinas bellezas" of Seville by asking Arias, "¿Cómo limitas y tasas / sus celajes y arreboles?" The mythological allusion of Phaeton's chariot and the sun is immediately devalued:

> Rey: Sol es, si blanca no fuera,
>
> . . . .
>
> Don Arias: ¿Doña Elvira de Guzmán,
>
> . . . .
>
> qué te pareció?
>
> Rey: Que andaba
> muy prolijo el alemán,
> pues de dos en dos están
> juntas las blancas ansí.
>
> Don Arias: Un maravedí vi allí.
>
> Rey: Aunque amor anda tan franco,
> por maravedí tan blanco
> no diera un maravedí. (75–90)

Estrella's exalted representation as the star of Bethlehem and as the sun in the rest of this scene is thus contaminated by the previous associations of *soles* with coinage. The King's designs on her through bribing her brother Busto inscribe her explicitly in a system of exchange.

In these and later references to coins and in the lines "pagará lo que le has dado; / que al que dan, en bronce escribe" (203–4), an underlying fault in the King's speech acts is revealed. He and his advisor Arias repeat the word "dar" throughout the play, not in the context of gifts but rather with reference to bribing or distracting Busto to gain access to his sister. The King intends to pay for Busto's honor, which by definition cannot be bought. "En bronce escribe" has the resonance of an inscription of eternal validity, but it is only the impression on a coin. The image, by its proximity to the discussion of the women in monetary terms, situates the King and Arias on the relative ground of economics rather than the exalted level of justice.

The image of the gift as an inscription in bronze seems monolithic and eternal, but it has an obverse suggested by the imagery of coins (*soles, blancas, maravedís*) surrounding it. The King's gift has only relative value, as do the women compared on one hand to celestial bodies, inscribing fate indelibly in the heavens, and on the other associated with coinage as objects of exchange. Although she does not specifically address *La Estrella de Sevilla,* Yvonne Yarbro-Bejarano's analysis (624–25) of this aspect of the *comedia* aptly brings together Gayle Rubin's observation that "women are in no position to realize the benefits of their own circulation" (174) with the imagery of coinage cited in English Restoration drama cited by Eve Kosofsky Sedgwick (50–55). The dichotomy between the "actions inscribed on the celestial map" (de Armas, 18) and the debased coinage of the play's speech acts underscores the moral tension generated between expectations of what the King should do and his ill-advised course of action. Sancho's decision not to marry Estrella, although "he has the right to claim her as his recompense for carrying out the King's order" (Sturm and Sturm 1970, 293), is an exposure and rejection of that system of exchange, but the final scenes convey Estrella's and Sancho's loss and estrangement rather than an affirmation of transcendent values.

Moral tension in the play begins with the two neglected *papeles* introduced in 1.4, which remain unread until the King, intending to ignore their contents, hands them to Busto in the next scene. They are *memoriales,* in this case the *curricula vitae,* of Gonzalo de Ulloa and Fernán Pérez de Medina, the two candidates for military command of Archidona, and one is presented as "espejo / del cristal de mi valor," the other as "cristal / que hace mi justicia clara" (271–72, 275–76). Busto refuses the King's unjustifiable offer of this position and instead reads the documents and makes a judgment worthy of a king's councillor. The written documents postpone and displace personal petition before the King, and they make possible a secret process of decision whose dishonesty is subject only to Busto's scrutiny as the beneficiary. Busto treats the *espejo* and the *cristal* as if they were the persons they represent, unlike the King, who equally disregards people and written documents. These apparently insignificant *papeles* establish a connection between writing—representation in the form of documents and contracts—and the questions of justice and honor in the play, and they establish the characters of the King and Busto.

The question of identity suggested in the *espejo* and *cristal* of Gonzalo de Ulloa and Fernán Pérez de Medina is echoed in the variations on "yo soy quien soy" that, over the course of the play, begin to ring false: Busto assures Sancho that the King's authority will protect the signed contract of his marriage to Estrella: "el Rey es Rey" (661); Sancho, rejecting the King's offer of a written immunity, says, "Yo soy quien soy, / . . . / Quien es quien es, haga obrando / como quien es" (2340–45). In both passages, silence, rather than speech or written documents, signifies honor. The broken mirror in 2.17 is a "verdadera cifra" misinterpreted by Estrella and her maid. It serves as an emblem and a foreshadowing of shattered honor and of the disruption of identity in Sancho's mad dialogue with Clarindo in act 3. Sancho seems to have forgotten who he is and lost faith in language as *espejo*. Even honor, in Sancho's satirical view of Hell, has a dual identity: honor that can be bought and true honor that consists in not having it. Sancho is disillusioned with the honor valued by his peers, and true honor is too fragile to keep: "el verdadero honor / consiste en no tenerlo. / . . . / Dinero, amigo, buscad; / que el honor es el dinero" (2482–87). In this "shameful," corrupt social order, honor has exchange value rather than the absolute value that Busto and Sancho had attributed to it. Sancho's identity is defined by renunciation and absence after he is brought back with magical words from Hell to the prison of Seville: he gives up his right to marry Estrella, as was certified in a signed document and as a reward for murdering Busto. In the imagery of the play, coinage and mirrors are only apparently opposing views of identity and value, since the mirror of honor can be broken down into small change. The two sides of the *papel,* the document and the King's role, which commanded and authorized Sancho to kill Busto, are revealed to be equally invalid. The play illustrates the fragility of honor as a social value invested with transcendence, and the fragility of social identity that goes with it, in a world in which written and spoken language has become a medium of exchange in a system of relative values.

Lying, Mirrors, and the Alphabet in *La dama boba*

The word as mirror, understood as representation of the other, is the key to understanding the dramatic function of reading in *La dama boba.* In act 1, the *boba,* Finea, attempts to learn to read while her sister Nise and her cultivated suitors exercise their skills at interpreting and manipulating literary texts. The initial scenes of Finea's futile struggles with the alphabet dramatize her status as outsider; Nise's illuminated volume of Heliodorus and her suitors' elaborately structured sonnets represent their problematic integration into the symbolic order.

Bruce Wardropper has pointed out the importance of mirrors in the play. I would like to discuss their role in Finea's account of her own accelerated, dramatic, and belated psychological and intellectual development. Her understanding of images in mirrors is a necessary step toward her initiation into the symbolic order (Lacan, 93–95). The recurring images of mirrors in *La dama boba* suggest a Lacanian mirror stage, but Finea's narration of this phase of her transformation from *boba* to *discreta* is not only that of her recognition of otherness in symbolic representation but also a dramatization of Neoplatonic concepts of love. She sees the reflection of her lover rather than herself because she believes that in love she has become him. When Finea learns to read, she does not enter the symbolic order so much as invert it through misrepresentation and misnaming parts of her father's house to make room for her own anarchic social arrangement, beginning with a picnic in the attic, which she has renamed "Toledo." Her control, however, is only for the interval left before her father officially gives her to Laurencio. The audience may be assured that her antics are no threat to honor because in act 2 she has given her word in the presence of witnesses to marry Laurencio, but her promise does not fulfill all necessary conditions: she is in love, but she is still a *boba,* with no understanding of marriage or promises. It is more convincing that Laurencio obliges the same witnesses to sign a document. At the same time, it is clear that the *boba,* whatever her dowry may be, is excluded from contractual agreements and other *escrituras* that are vehicles of exchange of women and property.

Like other comic plots, the plot of *La dama boba* derives its kinetic energy from the suitors' shifting objects of desire. The play poses the problem of

education of women in an economy of exchange among men in which male
honor depends upon women's understanding of social rules of shame and honor.
A dialogue between Otavio, father of Finea and Nise, and his friend Miseno establishes the requirements for *discreción:* "virtud y honestidad" (222). *Discreción*
is defined in the first and most comprehensive of three entries in the *Diccionario
de autoridades* as the ability to make distinctions, to separate one thing or quality
from another: "prudéncia, juicio y conocimiento con que se distinguen y reco-
nocen las cosas como son" (2:297). The results of Finea's intellectual lack and
Nise's excess cause Otavio to fear for his honor. Finea threatens his honor not
only because she cannot read or interpret the simplest representation and distinguish it from what it represents but because she cannot distinguish prescribed
from proscribed behavior in the symbolic structures of honor. She is, however,
alarmingly aware of the physical aspects of sexual reproduction: in act 1, she is
fascinated by a new litter of kittens, and she astutely refuses to marry Liseo as he
is represented in a portrait because he is shown only from the waist up: "¿qué
importa que sea pulido / este marido o quién es, / si todo el cuerpo no pasa / de la
pretina?" (872–75). Her father explains to her that the "naipe" to which she thought
she was to be married is "la figura sola, / que estaba en él retratado; / que lo vivo
viene agora" (900–902). By act 3, she has told Otavio that she has been embraced
and "disembraced" by Laurencio far beyond the limits of "virtud," "honestidad,"
and "discreción."

Finea's *bobería* is emblematized in her inability to read. Spoken communication breaks down during a reading lesson in which she cannot perceive the
letters as symbols that form parts of other symbolic structures:

| Rufino: | ¿Qué es ésta? |
| Finea: | ¿Aquesta? ... No sé. |
| .... |
Rufino:	¿Y ésta?
Finea:	¿Cuál? ¿Esta redonda?
	¡Letra! ...
....
Rufino:	Letras son; ¡míralas bien!
Finea:	Ya miro.
Rufino:	*B, e, n: ben.*
Finea:	¿Adónde? (329–43)

Finea likewise "misreads" the ritualized violence of her teacher's punishment. When he says, "¡Vive Dios, que te he de dar / una palmeta!" (349–50), she is shocked to find that the expected "regalo" is painful. Nise, who has learned her place in the symbolic order, supports the teacher's authority and "licencia de castigar," but Finea is still an outsider who calls Rufino "perro" and, acting on an animal level of response to pain, attacks him.

Finea undergoes an intellectual transformation triggered by a recognition not of herself but of the otherness and the *différance* of writing. Desire and absence are her teachers. In the comic plot, she is a "bestia" transformed by love, which first appeals to her through the senses. When she asks her suitor Laurencio what love is, he replies, "¿Amor? Deseo . . . De una cosa hermosa" (769–70). She asks if that is gold or diamonds, and Laurencio replies that it is "la hermosura / de una mujer como vos" (773–74), but we already know that Finea's beauty is equal to Nise's and therefore irrelevant; what Laurencio desires is her wealth. Before introducing Finea to Neoplatonic theories, he teaches a doctrine she understands easily: "Amor con amor se paga" (782). Laurencio's praise of love, a justification to his peers of his decision to court the *boba,* appears to rehearse the traditional praise of its transformative powers, but he simultaneously describes a social economy of desire as motivation for such profitable inventions as language, agriculture, navigation, knowledge, and art:

> es el dotor que ha tenido
> la cátedra de las ciencias;
> porque sólo con amor
> aprende el hombre mejor
> sus divinas diferencias.
> . . . .
> Amor enseñó a escribir
> altos y dulces concetos,
> como de su causa efetos. (1082–1118)

Not surprisingly, an amicable exchange of objects of desire takes the place of a duel between Laurencio and Liseo, the suitor whose parents had promised him to Finea. Liseo has no need for Finea's inheritance and is repelled by her *bobería,* which is initially real and later feigned to ensure his continuing interest in marrying the erudite Nise.

Much has been made of Duardo's Neoplatonic sonnet "La calidad elemental resiste / mi amor, que a la virtud celeste aspira . . ." (525–38) (Wardropper; Holloway), but following close upon the celestial imagery of that sonnet is Laurencio's "Hermoso sois, sin duda, pensamiento . . ." (635–48), which justifies his change of heart from Nise to Finea in purely economic terms (Bergmann, 411–13). Finea, the *boba,* is the inheritor of wealth and is described by her suitor Laurencio as "una casa, / una escritura, un censo y una viña, / y . . . una renta con basquiña" (1634–36), an unequivocal inscription of Finea in a system of exchange. In light of these lines and Laurencio's sonnet, Robert ter Horst sees Lope "as a Spanish Adam Smith professing [an assured materialism] in high-yield verse," "a line of conduct that seeks to re-structure the ideal architecture of love on solid material principles" (357–59). It is not only the "boba," the ignorant woman un-initiated in the symbolic order, who is an object of exchange but also her erudite sister, Nise.

Finea's own narration of the process of her transformation acknowledges the importance of the symbolic order in terms of a process of understanding mirrors and reflections. She explains how the mirror tells truths through the lie of representation. She connects this reflection with her mind's representation of her absent suitor, Laurencio, and her transformation "en otra" to the point of seeing his face instead of her own reflection:

> Finea: Si duermo, sueño con él;
> si como, le estoy pensando,
> y si bebo, estoy mirando
> en agua la imagen de él.
>   ¿No has visto de qué manera
> muestra el espejo a quien mira
> su rostro, que una mentira
> le hace forma verdadera?
>   Pues lo mismo en vidro miro
> que el cristal me representa.
>
> Clara: A tus palabras atenta,
> de tus mudanzas me admiro.
>   Parece que te transformas
> en otra.
>
> Finea: En otro dirás. (1553–66)

Later, she demonstrates her *discreción* in an elaborately *conceptista* explanation
of her love for Laurencio:

> el alma te ve
> por mil vidros y cristales,
> . . . .
> porque en mis ojos estás
> con memorias inmortales.
>   Todo este grande lugar
> tiene colgado de espejos
> mi amor, juntos y parejos
> para poderte mirar. (2410–15)

Laurencio, who effects this transformation, is motivated not by love but by lack
of money. Finea has the money he lacks, and once she learns to read and write,
she reinvents the names of things and controls the outcome of the play.

Finea is attracted first on the simplest physical level, and her progression
from the physical to the intellectual follows in part the Neoplatonic concepts of
Duardo's sonnet, but she attains a level of witty deception rather than the transcendent celestial and spiritual one described by Duardo. To emphasize the role
of desire in the process of reading, Finea's learned sister, Nise, having no love for
Duardo, says she does not understand his sonnet.

La dama boba exposes and parodies the arguments about women's education. In act 1, Otavio laments that too much or too little learning is dangerous, but
so is the basic literacy that enables a young woman to read and respond to her
suitor's messages. Finea tells Laurencio, "Por hablarte supe hablar, / . . . / por
leer en tus papeles, / libros difíciles leo; / para responderte escribo" (2467–71).
When Finea's wit exceeds Laurencio's expectations, he echoes Otavio's views,
first focusing on the impossibility or ineffectuality of women's writing:

> ¿Qué libro esperaba yo
> de tus manos? En qué pleito
> habías jamás de hacerme
> información en derecho?
> Inocente te quería
> . . . .

> no hay mujer necia en el mundo
> porque el no hablar no es defeto.
> Hable la dama en la reja,
> escriba, diga concetos
> en el coche, en el estrado,
> de amor, de engaños, de celos;
> pero la casada sepa
> de su familia el gobierno;
> porque el más discreto hablar
> no es santo como el silencio. (2435–54)

Finea's new *discreción,* in practice more profitable to Laurencio than silence, conceives a new plan: she pretends to be the same *boba* who earlier in the play so disgusted Liseo that he vowed not to marry Finea. In act 2, Finea gave her word to marry Laurencio (who misrepresented her promise as a cure for jealousy, thus giving the promise an equivocal status), and Laurencio had the witnesses sign a document before a notary, but Liseo's parents have an agreement with Otavio, so his renewed interest in the intelligent Finea of act 3 must be diverted by Finea's feigned reversion to an idiocy that exceeds her prior *bobería.*

La dama boba connects the cultural and social phenomena of reading with the interpretation of symbolic forms and with the visual phenomena of mirrors. Central to Finea's transformation is her recognition of the otherness of the reflection she sees in a mirror, and of the ways that representation brings what is absent into her presence. In the comic plot of *La dama boba,* Finea's control of language enables her to marry the man she has chosen. In *La Estrella de Sevilla,* even Sancho's and Estrella's unequivocal gestures of rejection of the King's manipulations and aggressive acts do not suffice to protect their marriage vows from disruptive speech acts and written contracts. Estrella is inscribed as an object in the symbolic systems that determine her fate. She is not completely excluded from writing itself, as her letter to Sancho demonstrates, but her letter's news about her marriage is no longer valid by the time it is received. Sancho reads it between reading the King's written command to Sancho to kill a traitor and his letter identifying the traitor as Busto. As writing and speaking subject, Estrella is excluded from the systems of exchange that move around her. Her lengthy speeches in act 3 create a powerful image of her generosity and dignity, but they are noble acts of renunciation.

In both plays, women are described in mercantile terms, and those terms are connected with the symbolic order through writing. Limited by her role as a virtuous woman to silence, gesture, and anonymity in her response to the authority of speech and writing, Estrella loses her brother and speaks only to free Sancho from prison and from his commitment to their marriage. Finea's control of language is limited but dramatically effective. The fragile *papeles* that move about the stage of *La Estrella de Sevilla* affect the plot as if they were characters but require other characters to give them a voice. Thus Estrella's exclusion is in part shared by the audience, while the audience witnesses Finea's most basic and most elaborate modes of access to reading and writing. Writing in both plays is instrumental to the plot, but it also reflects the ways in which the social order inscribes women in systems of exchange.

Notes

Parts of this essay were read at the Renaissance Society of America Annual Meeting, Harvard University, 30 March 1989; the Eleventh Louisiana Conference on Hispanic Languages and Literatures, Louisiana State University, Baton Rouge, 23 February 1990; and the International Symposium on *La Estrella de Sevilla,* Pennsylvania State University, 2–5 April 1992. I thank Inés Azar for her helpful critical suggestions.

1.   For the reader, however, the expectation is different when the text reproduces rather than refers to another text inscribed on an object that is in turn described in the literary text. A clear example is in lines 241–48 of Garcilaso's *Egloga* III, in which the words carved on a tree are both described and transcribed: "que hablavan ansí por parte della: / 'Elisa soy.'" Garcilaso's reproduction of prosopopeia involves a new set of problems but illustrates the expectation that with the presence of a written text in a fictional world, the substance of it may also be expected to be known to the reader.

2.   Alpers, 192, 196, 200. It must be pointed out that Alpers's study is concerned with distinguishing the Dutch pictorial tradition from the Italian narrative tradition in painting, a tradition to which the function of letters in the *comedia,* and the semiotics of the *comedia* itself, more appropriately belongs.

Works Consulted

Alpers, Svetlana. 1983. *The Art of Describing: Dutch Art in the Seventeenth Century.* Chicago, Ill.: University of Chicago Press.

Azar, Inés. 1986. "Self, Responsibility, Discourse: An Introduction to Speech Act Theory." In *Things Done with Words: Speech Acts in Hispanic Drama,* edited by Elias L. Rivers, 1–15. Newark, Del.: Juan de la Cuesta.

Bergmann, Emilie. 1981. "*La dama boba:* Temática folklórica y neoplatónica." In *Lope de Vega y los orígenes del teatro español: Actas del I congreso internacional sobre Lope de Vega,* edited by Manuel Criado de Val, 409–13. Madrid: Edi-6.

Burke, James F. 1974. "The *Estrella de Sevilla* and the Tradition of Saturnine Melancholy." *Bulletin of Hispanic Studies* 51:137–56.

De Armas, Frederick A. 1980. "The Hunter and the Twins: Astrological Imagery in *La Estrella de Sevilla.*" *Bulletin of the Comediantes* 32:11–20.

Diccionario de autoridades. [1726–39] 1969. Madrid: Gredos.

La Estrella de Sevilla. 1968. In *Diez comedias del Siglo de Oro,* edited by José Martel and Hymen Alpern, 143–233. New York: Harper and Row.

Holloway, James E., Jr. 1972. "Lope's Neoplatonism: *La dama boba.*" *Bulletin of Hispanic Studies* 49:236–55.

Lacan, Jacques. 1966. *Ecrits.* Paris: Seuil.

Larson, Donald R. 1969. "*La dama boba* and the Comic Sense of Life." *Romanische Forschungen* 85:41–62.

Rivers, Elias L. 1980. "The Shame of Writing in *La Estrella de Sevilla.*" *Folio* 12:105–17.

Rubin, Gayle. 1975. "The Traffic in Women: Notes on the 'Political Economy' of Sex." In *Toward an Anthropology of Women,* edited by Rayna R. Reiter, 157–210. New York: Monthly Review Press.

Sedgwick, Eve Kosofsky. 1985. *Between Men: English Literature and Male Homosocial Desire.* New York: Columbia University Press.

Sturm, Harlan, and Sara Sturm. 1969. "The Astronomical Metaphor in *La Estrella de Sevilla.*" *Hispania* 52:193–97.

———. 1970. "The Two Sancho's in *La Estrella de Sevilla.*" *Romanistisches Jahrbuch* 21:285–93.

Ter Horst, Robert. 1976. "Ironies of the Intellect in Lope's *La dama boba.*" *Romanistisches Jahrbuch* 27:347–63.

Vega Carpio, Lope de. 1981. *La dama boba.* Edited by Diego Marín. Madrid: Cátedra.

Wardropper, Bruce W. 1961. "Lope's *La dama boba* and Baroque Comedy." *Bulletin of the Comediantes* 13:1–3.

Yarbro-Bejarano, Yvonne. 1987. "Hacia un análisis feminista del drama de honor de Lope." *La torre, Revista de la Universidad de Puerto Rico* n.s., 1:615–32.

Carol Bingham Kirby

On the Nature of *Refundiciones* of Spain's Classical Theater in the Seventeenth Century

S pain's classical dramatists not only created one of the three great national theaters of Europe; they also inspired a wealth of reworkings in seventeenth-century Spain as well as subsequently, both within and outside their country of origin. The term that traditionally is employed to describe this act of drawing on and remaking an earlier dramatic work is *refundición,* which can be rendered in English as "reworking," "refashioning," or "rehash," although "rehash" carries a more negative connotation. A large number of reworked plays understandably remains unstudied, and more importantly, a systematic critical approach to these plays is lacking. This essay will focus on seventeenth-century *refundiciones* in relation to their sources from the same century and will propose and apply a theoretical methodology to study these reworked plays. *Refundiciones* done in different centuries and in languages other than Spanish will need to be examined using another set of principles. A reworking may be superior or inferior to its source, but whichever the case may be, scholars study refashioned texts because these versions often provide insights into the inner workings of the *comedia,* with its infinite structural, dramatic, and poetic possibilities, which arise from its nature as an open genre.

To analyze the characteristics of *refundiciones,* I propose to use the following six categories as the basis of the comparison of one or more reworked texts with the source text:[1]

1.   one or more verses retained unchanged in the reworking

2.   one or more retained verses, but altered in a minor or major fashion, including modifications in wording, speaker, or location of a verse

3.   a minimum of two or more verses that have been reduced by one or more verses in the reworking

4.   a minimum of one verse in which the source has been amplified into a passage of two or more verses in the reworked version

5.   one or more verses present in the source but deleted in the reworking

6.   one or more new verses added to the reworked text.

Once the degree of retention and modification of the source text—in each act and in the work as a whole—is established on the basis of these categories, this statistical information can be analyzed in conjunction with the poetic and dramatic effect of these relationships.

The textual tradition that I will study to exemplify this methodology is that of *El rey don Pedro en Madrid y el Infanzón de Illescas* (of disputed authorship; henceforth *ERDPM*). This play offers a wealth of material, since the tradition consists of two branches, one of which reworked the other, and also since it produced a second independent reworking. The stemma for the textual tradition of *ERDPM* has the following configuration:[2]

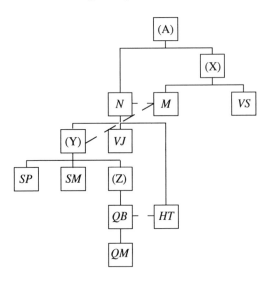

The primary branch of *ERDPM* includes three extant texts: the Biblioteca Nacional manuscript (*N*), which has a *licencia* from 1626; the Biblioteca Municipal manuscript (*M*), which appears to be from the seventeenth century; and the printed text (*VS*) published in the problematic *Parte veinte y siete* (*extravagante*) of Lope ("Barcelona," 1633). *N* has 3,048 verses, while *M* and *VS* represent a shortened version, containing respectively 499 and 505 fewer verses than *N*. Because *N* is the most complete text in the primary tradition, it will serve as the base text of the critical edition that I am preparing for publication.

Two independent reworkings of *ERDPM* were done in the seventeenth century, Moreto's *El valiente justiciero* (*VJ*) and the secondary branch of *ERDPM*. Both versions derive from a text most like *N*, although not necessarily the specific manuscript from the Biblioteca Nacional.[3] *VJ* recasts the work much more substantially than the secondary branch does, although the latter is indeed a substantial *refundición* in its own right. I have analyzed *VJ* as a reworking in another study (see Kirby 1992), in which the same methodology presented in this essay has been applied to Moreto's play.[4]

The *refundición* under study in this essay constitutes the secondary branch of *ERDPM* and is represented by four witnesses from the second half of the seventeenth century: a *suelta* located in the Bayerische Staatsbibliothek in Munich, designated *SM;* a *suelta* located in the Biblioteca del Palacio Real in Madrid, designated *SP;* and the two versions from the apocryphal *Quinta parte* of Calderón, designated *QB* ("Barcelona," 1677) and *QM* (Madrid, 1677). *SP,* with a total of 2,690 verses, will serve as the basis of the statistical comparison between the secondary branch[5] and *N* as the source text,[6] together with a comparative literary analysis of selected passages from the reworking relative to the source.

The statistics for the six categories of analysis in act 1 are as follows:[7]

ACT 1

Category	Total verses in N		% of Act
I (retained)	471 vv. (312/159)	—Total Retained Text 471 vv.	47.38
II (altered)	293 vv. (164/129)		
III (reduced)	101 vv. (—/101)	—Total Modified Text 523 vv.	52.62
IV (amplified)	58 vv. (6/52)		
V (deleted)	71 vv. (14/57)		
		Total Verses Act 1 = 994 vv.	
VI (added)	10 vv. (—/10)		

The statistics reveal that almost half of act 1 is retained, while approximately half of the act is modified. There is also a tendency to retain more verses in the first half of the act and to modify verses, especially in categories 3, 4, and 5, in the second half of the act.

The *refundidor* has recast the figure of Don Pedro by simplifying the enigmatic monarch's hidden motivation.[8] The initial entrance of Don Pedro after he has struggled with his rebellious horse diminishes the immense energy of the stranger:[9]

N, 111-17

Ginesa:	¡Válgate el cielo!
Elvira:	¿Qué es esto?
Ginesa:	Fogoso, espumoso y fiero
	a un bizarro caballero
	un caballo ha descompuesto.
Busto:	En los ijares le ha puesto
	las piernas con tal furor
	que muerto cayó.

SP, 111–17

D. Pedro:	¡Válgame el cielo!
Elvira:	¿Qué es esto?
Busto:	Un monstruo que al rayo imita,
	al llano se precipita
	espumoso y descompuesto.
Ginesa:	Quien lo gobierna le ha puesto
	las piernas con tal valor,
	que muerto cayó.

The text has been reworded (category 2) so that the analogy between rider and horse in the source is shifted to emphasize only the rebelliousness of the animal. In the following passage (category 4), the negative reference to Don Pedro's justice is attenuated, and the passage is expanded to emphasize Tello's abusive behavior:

N, 527–37

Ginesa:	Fueron a buscar justicia
	a Toledo y no la hallaron,
	que dicen que se ha perdido
	después que este rey ganamos.

Antes en ella, después
del tálamo a un mayorazgo
quitó la esposa, con quien
se está por fuerza casando
contra Dios y contra el rey;
y esta sinrazón llorando
estamos de aquesta suerte.

SP, 513–33

Ginesa: Fuimos a buscar justicia
a Toledo y no la hallamos,
porque aun en Toledo están,
de oír su nombre, temblando;
los merinos son su gusto,
los pobres son sus esclavos,
los clérigos sus ministros,
los ricos sus tributarios;
él, de toda esta comarca
es el rey y el dueño, tanto
que a un caballero en Toledo
que se estaba desposando
con una señora hermosa
y rica, se la ha quitado,
y a pesar suyo y del padre,
con ella hoy se casa, dando
ocasión a que en el reino
de Toledo sus vasallos
digan a voces que el rey
es piadoso con los malos,
y con los buenos crüel.

SP deletes (category 5) the entire *Sombra* scene present in *N* (579–96), a scene that is essential to the dramatic structure of the source, since it suggests that Pedro's concern with Tello, which is developed more extensively and to other ends in *N,* is linked to a spiritual *agon* within the monarch himself. The omission of this scene creates an abrupt jump in the plot when the King's courtiers find

Don Pedro in an unexplained turbulent state. *SP,* on the other hand, amplifies (category 4) the following eight verses (*N,* 599–606) to eighteen verses, in which Don Pedro defends María de Padilla as the legitimate queen. The legality of Pedro's marriage to María de Padilla is an issue that Tello alludes to repeatedly in *SP* as justification for his disobedience toward the King. The reworked text has simplified the skillful way in which the source made Tello the imitator of the monarch by shifting the focus of the conflict to more obvious political reasons rather than the more subtle psychological motivation found in *N.*

Act 2 has the following statistics for the six categories of analysis:

ACT 2

Category	Total verses in N		% of Act
I (retained)	406 vv. (226/180) — Total Retained Text 406 vv.		38.52
II (altered)	262 vv. (143/119)		
III (reduced)	171 vv. (26/145)	Total Modified Text 648 vv.	61.48
IV (amplified)	17 vv. (6/11)		
V (deleted)	198 vv. (133/65)		
		Total Verses Act 2 = 1054 vv.	
VI (added)	35 vv. (24/11)		

The figures reveal that *SP* modifies more and also retains less of the source play in act 2 than was the case with act 1. The changes in particular show that more abbreviation (category 3) and less amplification (category 4) occur in act 2 and that considerably more verses are deleted (category 5). More verses are added (category 6) in act 2 than in act 1.

SP eliminates entirely the part of Don Rodrigo as the lesser nobleman, betrothed to Doña Leonor, who challenges Tello in the King's palace as he recovers his lady. The corresponding speeches of Don Rodrigo in *N* are reassigned, at times with some modification, to the peasant Busto. *SP* also expands and strengthens Busto's role; for example, sixteen verses spoken by Busto are added (category 6) in *SP,* following line 1126 in *N.* The structural parallelism established in the source between the three women of different social classes and their respective male counterparts in *SP* is lessened somewhat with the Ginesa-Cordero pair and is eliminated entirely with the Leonor-Rodrigo relationship. Even more significant is the elimination of Rodrigo's role as he relates to the conflict between monarch and nobleman. In *N,* Pedro, as the author of a *comedia palaciega,* has orchestrated an elaborate play to humiliate Tello, whereupon the offended parties, including Don Rodrigo, seek revenge against their offender, but all within the larger framework of preparing for the King's own humiliation of the nobleman in act 3. Don Pedro's equivocal responses to Don Rodrigo in *N* are made less enigmatic in *SP* when said to Busto (category 3):

N, 1115–26

Rodrigo:	¿Qué había de hacer?
Don Pedro:	Hacer
	animoso y prevenido,
	que en toda parte el marido
	es dueño de su mujer.
Rodrigo:	Pues cobraréla.
Don Pedro:	Mi ley
	temed y haced lo que os digo,
	que uno es consejo de amigo,
	y otra advertencia de rey.
Rodrigo:	¿Qué haré?
Don Pedro:	Lo que hiciera yo.
Rodrigo:	Pues atreveréme.
Don Pedro:	Aquí
	don Pedro os dice que sí,
	y el rey don Pedro que no.

SP, 1001–8

Busto:	Pues, ¿qué había de hacer?
Don Pedro:	Hacer animoso y prevenido,
	que en toda parte el marido
	es dueño de la mujer.
Busto:	Pues, ¿atreveréme?
Don Pedro:	Yo
	me atreviera.
Busto:	¿Y yo no?
Don Pedro:	Aquí
	Don Pedro os dice que sí,
	y el rey don Pedro que no.

Later in *N*, Rodrigo's challenge to Tello becomes part of the King's trap of the nobleman, but this segment (*N*, 1363–1400) is deleted (category 5) in *SP*, since the *refundidor* chose not to push the boundaries of social decorum any further than he has in having a peasant seek direct redress against a nobleman.

SP continues to simplify the complexity of the relationship between Pedro and Tello. When the courtiers lead Tello and Cordero from one room to another, one of the King's servants perceptively comments on the interaction between nobleman and monarch (category 2):

<blockquote>

N, 1417–20

Don Juan: Soberbio va el infanzón,

mas él saldrá sin soberbia,

que es, si él arrogante y loco,

temerario el que lo espera.

SP, 1267–70

Fortún: ¡Qué ufano que va! El saldrá,

si ahora tan feroz entra,

tan humilde que aun la sombra

del rey a temor le mueva.

</blockquote>

SP at once removes the suggestion of the similarity and the sense of competition between the two men. It is also significant that *SP* omits (category 5) fifty verses (*N*, 1471–1520), which in part dramatize the further movement of Tello through the rooms of the palace as the embodiment of the King's soul. In these omitted verses, Tello expresses his awareness of the necessity to obey that higher authority invested in the monarch, the body mystical (*N*, 1481–90). Finally, the deletion (category 5) of ten verses in *SP* at the end of Pedro's confrontation with Tello in the palace eliminates a passage that provides important insights into the source of Pedro's drama as it relates to Tello as the King's double (*N*, 1611–20). The end of act 2 (*N*, 1901–2048), in which Pedro's restlessness leads to his challenge to fence with his courtiers, followed by the Shade's appearance, is largely intact. This contrasts with the end of act 1, which is modified considerably.

Act 3 has the following statistics for the six categories of analysis:

ACT 3

Category	Total verses in N		% of Act
I (retained)	543 vv. (267/276) — TOTAL RETAINED TEXT 543 vv.		54.30
II (altered)	262 vv. (105/157)		
III (reduced)	40 vv. (12/28)	— TOTAL MODIFIED TEXT 457 vv.	45.70
IV (amplified)	22 vv. (4/18)		
V (deleted)	133 vv. (99/34)		
		TOTAL VERSES ACT 3 = 1000 vv.	
VI (added)	47 vv. (13/34)		

Among the three acts, act 3 retains the highest percentage of text from the source. Notably there is little abbreviation (category 3), and neither is there a significant amount of amplification (category 4). The *refundidor* has deleted almost twice as many verses as in act 1, but fewer verses than in act 2. Finally, act 3 contains the greatest number of added verses, with a significant number occurring in the second half of the act.

In act 3, *SP* keeps the major plot segments, namely, Pedro's subjugation of Tello and the subsequent appearance of the Shade, as well as the two scenes between Enrique and Mendoza in the countryside. There are several instances in the act in which Pedro makes a speech pointing out the exemplary nature of his justice, either amplifying verses (category 4) present in *N*—seven verses in *N* (2955–61) become thirty-five verses in *SP,* and shortly thereafter two verses in *N* (2971–72) become eight verses in *SP*—or adding new verses (category 6), as in this soliloquy delivered by the King after he has defeated Tello, following line 2616 in *N:*

> *SP,* 2219–26
>
> Don Pedro: Así temblará mi nombre
> éste en su largo destierro,
> y agradecerá la vida
> de que aquí merced le he hecho;
> y los ricoshombres, todos
> se mirarán en su espejo,
> y temblarán mi justicia
> en la piedad que en él muestro.

As was true with act 2, *SP* also reduces in act 3 the role of Cordero by deleting (category 5) part of his speech to Don Pedro in the palace-prison (*N*, 2282–90) and by omitting (category 5) the exchange between Cordero and Ginesa preceding Don Pedro's arrival there (*N*, 2227–58).

Besides the cited changes or additions in *SP* to make Don Pedro, even in his own words, more just, there are other revisions that make the King more stable; for example, when *SP* abbreviates (category 3) a scene in which Pedro is restless about the meaning of the Shade's warning (*N*, 2761–80) and when *SP* deletes ten verses (*N*, 2888–97) revealing the monarch's paranoia about Enrique, apparently because Pedro imagines that his brother has drawn his weapon, when such is not the case. This latter scene is replaced later in *SP* by ten distinct verses (category 6), following line 3038 in *N*. In this passage, Pedro does not imagine a threat but rather interprets an occurrence—the falling of the crown—as a portent of his future tragedy:

	SP, 2671–80
Don Pedro:	Dame esos brazos. Cayóse
	la corona.
Enrique:	Aquí la tienes.
Don Pedro:	La corona y el puñal
	a un tiempo te favorecen;
	no sé, hermano, qué imagine,
	no sé, Enrique, qué sospeche.
Enrique:	Sospecha que en mí un vasallo
	tienes, gran señor, que vuelve
	por tu reino, en la corona,
	y en el puñal, por tus leyes.

The final scene of *N* (2934–3048) and *SP* (2530–2690) varies markedly.[10] *N* has 115 verses, while *SP* has 161 verses. The following figures show statistically that these changes have occurred most notably in categories 4, 5, and 6:

ACT 3 (final scene)

Category	Total verses in N		% of last 115vv. N
I (retained)	51 vv. —— TOTAL RETAINED TEXT 51 vv.		44.35
II (altered)	36 vv.		
III (reduced)	0 vv.	TOTAL MODIFIED TEXT 64 vv.	55.65
IV (amplified)	12 vv.		
V (deleted)	16 vv.		

TOTAL VERSES, FINAL SCENE, ACT 3, N = 115 vv.

VI (added)	18 vv.	

Besides the cited passages relating to the change in emphasis in Pedro's fears of Enrique and the clear attempt to portray the King as *el justiciero,* the plot segments dealing with the resolution of the grievances by the three offended women have been modified. In *SP,* Pedro orders that Tello be executed once he marries one of the offended women, but it is not clear whether the marriage is planned with Leonor or Elvira, since both women respond to the King's order. Elvira then asks the King to pardon Tello and plans to enter the convent to be built by Pedro, while Leonor expresses her desire to serve the queen until she chooses a husband. The King does indeed free Tello. The corresponding text in *N* is briefer. The King initially decides that Tello is to marry Elvira, but subsequently the nobleman is to be executed for having dishonored Leonor. The King changes his decision and frees Tello, who is again to marry Elvira, while the other two couples are constituted by Ginesa-Cordero and, presumably, Leonor-Rodrigo. In both versions, Enrique is witness to the judgments.

This final scene of the play varies not only in *N* and *SP* but also in *M* and *VS*. *M* and *VS* share in common with *SP* eleven identical verses that are lacking in *N* and three other nonconsecutive verses that are closer to *SP* than to *N*.[11] However, *M* and *VS* do not merely alternate text in common with *N* with text shared with *SP*. *M* and *VS* also contain verses that are unique to them only, and the three passages in which *M-VS* agree with *SP* include text not found in *SP* or *N*. Endings clearly are segments that have traditionally been subject to change (see studies by Greer and Ruano). I have decided to reproduce in my critical edition this final scene as it is in *N* for several reasons. *N* is the most complete text, and its ending provides a coherent whole in itself. The evidence provided by the study of the entire textual tradition as represented in the stemma demonstrates that the primary and secondary branches should remain separate. Since *M-VS* show definite contamination with the secondary branch in this final scene, it is unsound to conflate their contaminated readings with *N* in this segment. Furthermore, the way in which *M-VS* have also modified the ending of the play by incorporating other readings, in this case without any demonstrable contamination from the secondary branch, has led me to exclude these readings from the reconstructed text of the primary tradition, although this text from *M-VS* will be recorded in the apparatus for variants in the critical edition.

The phenomenon of Spanish Golden Age plays being reworked by dramatists of the same century, whether by known or unknown author(s), raises several essential questions regarding poetic, dramatic, structural, and textual matters that have not always been approached with the necessary rigor and systematic methodology to illuminate both the source and reworked text. The aim of this essay has been to provide a model for future analyses of other *refundiciones* by presenting and applying such a methodology to the study of two seventeenth-century *comedias*. The statistical data provided by the comparison of one source text with its refashioning according to six categories of analysis have served as the scientific basis on which to analyze the similarities and differences between the two texts. The study has revealed that the secondary branch of *ERDPM* is a reworking that maintains approximately half of the verses of the source and modifies the other half. In most traditional conceptions of *refundiciones,* the secondary branch of *ERDPM* would not constitute a reworking in the sense that Moreto's *El valiente justiciero* does, since only 50 percent of the text is modified and the play's structure has not been substantially changed.[12] Nevertheless, I have shown here that thematically and ideologically the secondary tradition has reworked the source in order to attentuate the psychological conflict present in the source between king and rebellious vassal with the objective of lessening the dramatization of Don Pedro as an unstable monarch.

This study has also revealed textual differences that have great significance for *comedia* editors in general. The extent of the *refundición* represented by the secondary tradition has led me as editor to conclude previously in the preparation of the stemma and again in this essay that these two branches should not be conflated. Certainly no two textual traditions will be identical, but what is gleaned here points out the importance of the larger question for editors as to whether a reworking can or should be used to reconstruct a text that is prepared in a critical edition, since the refashioning almost invariably reveals an altered dramatic conception of the plot and action. The comparison of *N* with *SP*, as well as of *M* and *VS* in the last scene of act 3, reveals how flexible and open the *comedia* was, since the dramatic blocks or segments can be modified in various ways to create new effects, often without bringing attention to the fact that these modifications were made. The role of versification in changing these flexible structural units is a factor that will be studied later as another essential aspect of how texts are reworked. Scholars will also want to consider the importance of different audiences and different historical time periods in the composition and reception of refashioned plays. Ultimately, the critic evaluates the relative artistic value of the *refundición*, but not without gaining new perceptions into the nature of imitation among seventeenth-century dramatists.

Notes

1.   It is not always possible to establish with certainty which text served as the source of the other, as the debate over the priority of *El burlador de Sevilla* and *Tan largo me lo fiáis* demonstrates.

2.   The reader interested in how this stemma was prepared methodologically should consult Kirby 1986 and the revised and expanded translation of the same (1991). This latter version reproduces the same stemma given in this essay. Complete and detailed information about all of the texts of *ERDPM* will be found in the critical edition that I am preparing for publication.

3.   The reader should keep in mind that any of the texts or states included in the stemma could represent numerous actual copies that once circulated but are now lost.

4.   In their comparisons of *VJ* with *ERDPM* as Moreto's source play, Ruth Lee Kennedy and Frank Casa used the defective modern texts of Hartzenbusch (*HT*) and Menéndez y Pelayo respectively. As I have recently demonstrated (1990), all of the modern editions of *ERDPM*, including that of Menéndez y Pelayo, reproduce the *HT* text, which has conflated *N* with *QB*, when in fact the two branches of the tradition should have remained separate. The broken line has been drawn in the stemma between *QB* and *HT* to indicate this contamination. For the bibliographical information on all the modern editions of *ERDPM*, see my article cited in this note.

5.   In the secondary branch, *SP-SM* and *QB-QM* represent two subbranches. Despite the divergences among these versions, they essentially constitute the same text. Because *SP* is the most accurate version, it was chosen for the comparison with *N*. The
reader can consult the secondary text most easily in the facsimile editions of *QB* and *QM*
prepared by Cruickshank and Varey (1973a, 1973b), or in the unpublished edition of *QB*
in Asturias, which mistakenly omits four verses in act 2 (following 1457 in Asturias) and
lacks one verse, found in *SP* alone among the secondary texts (following 1332 in Asturias).

6.   It is worth noting that the primary texts *M* and *VS* in one sense also constitute
reworkings, since they are reduced texts that have been cut for the convenience of performers or printers. The changes made in *M* and *VS,* however, are characterized by two
phenomena that prevent me from considering them *refundiciones,* as I conceive of the
term here. The modifications in *M* and *VS* constantly call attention to the fact that something is missing from what was a larger whole. Furthermore, there is no significant change
in the structure or in the development of the plot or characters in *M* and *VS* that would
demonstrate an overall shift in the direction or a modification in the details of the work.

7.   The figures in parentheses in the charts (for example, 312/159 for category 1,
act 1) indicate the distribution of verses between the first half and the second half of the
act.

8.   The interpretation of the source text presented in this essay remains essentially
the same as that expressed in Kirby 1981.

9.   All quotations from *N* and *SP* have been modernized and regularized. The reader
who consults the reconstructed text of *ERDPM* in my forthcoming edition will need to
add two verses to all verse counts in the present study following v. 620 because the reconstructed text supplies from *M* two verses to complete a defective *décima* in the base text
(*N*) at this point.

10.   In *N,* this final scene corresponds to the last three folios of *N,* which were
copied by a second hand. The last folio includes the *licencia,* dated 1626.

11.   This information provided the main, although not the only, evidence for contamination between *M-VS* and the secondary branch. Because *M* alone shared two readings in common with the secondary branch, the line of contamination was drawn in the
stemma between *M* and (*Y*), the hypothetical intermediate text between the primary and
secondary branches.

12.   The analyses of Casa, Kennedy, and Sloman exemplify traditional conceptions
of seventeenth-century *refundiciones;* namely, that there is extensive, wholesale rewriting in the reworking, as in Moreto's *VJ;* and secondly, that the reworking constitutes a
superior work (see Sloman for Calderón) or one that is original in its refashioning (see
Kennedy and Casa for Moreto).

Works Consulted

Asturias, Sister Rosario Maria. 1963. "A Critical Edition and Study of the Play *El rey don Pedro en Madrid y el Infanzón de Illescas.*" Ph.D. diss., University of Southern California.

Casa, Frank P. 1966. *The Dramatic Craftsmanship of Moreto.* Cambridge, Mass.: Harvard University Press.

Cruickshank, D. W., and J. E. Varey, eds. 1973a. *Quinta parte de comedias.* "Barcelona," 1677. (*QB*). Vol. 12 of *The "Comedias" of Calderón.* Westmead, Farnborough, Hants-London: Gregg International-Tamesis Books.

————. 1973b. *Quinta parte de comedias.* Madrid, 1677. (*QM*). Vol. 13 of *The "Comedias" of Calderón.* Westmead, Farnborough, Hants-London: Gregg International-Tamesis Books.

Greer, Margaret Rich. 1984. "Calderón, Copyists, and the Problem of Endings." *Bulletin of the Comediantes* 36:71–81.

Hartzenbusch, J. E., ed. 1848. *El rey don Pedro en Madrid y el infanzón de Illescas.* (*HT*). In *Comedias escogidas de Fray Gabriel Téllez.* Biblioteca de Autores Españoles, vol. 5. Madrid: M. Rivadeneyra.

Kennedy, Ruth Lee. [1932] 1975. *The Dramatic Art of Moreto.* Reprint. Ann Arbor, Mich.: Xerox University Microfilms.

Kirby, Carol Bingham. 1981. "Theater and the Quest for Anointment in *El rey don Pedro en Madrid.*" *Bulletin of the Comediantes* 33:149–59.

————. 1986. "La verdadera edición crítica de un texto dramático del siglo de oro: Teoría, metodología y aplicación." *Incipit* 6:71–98.

————. 1990. "Performance, Text and Standard Edition: Critical Divergences and Questions of Methodology." *Texto y espectáculo: Nuevas dimensiones críticas de la "comedia,"* edited by Arturo Pérez-Pisonero, 93–100. New Brunswick, N.J.: SLUSA Press.

————. 1991. "The Preparation of a Genuine Critical Edition of Golden Age Dramatic Texts: Theory, Methodology and Application." In *Editing the "Comedia" II,* edited by Frank P. Casa and Michael D. McGaha, 1–38. Michigan Romance Studies, vol. 11. Ann Arbor: University of Michigan Department of Romance Languages.

————. 1992. "Hacia una definición precisa del término *refundición* en el teatro clásico español." In *Actas del X congreso de la Asociación internacional de hispanistas,* edited by Antonio Vilanova, 2:1005–11. Barcelona: PPU.

Menéndez y Pelayo, Marcelino, ed. 1899. *El rey don Pedro en Madrid y el infanzón de Illescas.* In *Obras de Lope de Vega,* vol. 9. Madrid: Real Academia Española.

Ruano de la Haza, José M., ed. 1982. *Cada uno para sí* by Pedro Calderón de la Barca. Kassel: Edition Reichenberger.

Sloman, Albert E. 1958. *The Dramatic Craftsmanship of Calderón*. Oxford: Dolphin Book Company.

Amy R. Williamsen

Reception as Deception:
The Fate of Mira de Amescua's Theater

As literary critics, we are all aware that our experiences and expectations influence our interpretations of literary texts. Scientific experiments have proven that even transitory experiences can affect a reader's understanding (Crawford and Chaffin, 11). A significant number of our expectations stem from our contact with other critical studies of the texts in question, with literary history, and with literary theory. This process can affect not only our understanding of individual works but also our evaluation of an author's entire opus. I contend that contemporary criticism of Mira de Amescua's theater relies, to a great extent, on past judgments of his work. Some of these are damaging, unfounded claims that have been accepted without challenge. Thus, past reception of his *comedias* can act as a deception that misleads critics and precludes them from perceiving vital aspects of his dramatic achievement.

E. D. Hirsch, in his study *Validity in Interpretation,* argues that an interpreter's generic conception of a text "is constitutive of everything that he subsequently understands and this remains the case unless and until that generic conception is altered" (74). Yet the concept of genre represents but one source of expectations that we bring to the study of any given work. Other powerful elements that inform our predisposition toward a text include those resulting from a familiarity with existing interpretations regarding the period, the author, and the work itself. The theoretical stance of Hans Robert Jauss and other proponents of reception theory offers many insights into the problematic relationship between interpretation and the heritage of past reception. I will employ the term "reader," as does Jauss, but I would like to emphasize the polysemic nature of the *comedia,* which cannot be reduced to an evaluation of the written script without considering the production codes. Indeed, although Jauss and his colleagues label the receiver of the text a "reader," the theory applies to all forms of artistic endeavor. In *Towards an Aesthetic of Reception,* he states: "The aesthetic implication lies in the fact that the first reception of a work by the reader includes a test of its aesthetic value in comparison with works already read. The obvious historical implication of this is that the understanding of the first reader will be sustained and enriched in a chain of reception" (20). If, following Jauss's paradigm, each reader does sustain the first understanding of the text, the result may not always enrich the interpretation of the work but rather limit it.

As Annette Kolodny argues convincingly, reading is a learned strategy. As scholars, we are trained to read in accordance with the "dominant critical vision" (588). Julian Hirsch, in his study of the genesis of fame (as summarized and quoted by Robert Holub), dramatizes the pervasive nature of such training in the case of a Shakespearean scholar:

> Having been told from childhood that Shakespeare is the greatest English writer and having later read in journals about Shakespeare's genius and mastery of dramatic technique, this student of English literature could hardly be expected to possess anything but admiration for the English bard. . . . "The power of social heredity already weighs so heavily on the future researcher that he can no longer escape it." If a negative appraisal were perchance offered, it would be treated by other experts as foolishness or as a sacrilege. (48–49)

Although both Jauss and Julian Hirsch cite examples of the perpetuation of positive "myths" regarding texts and authors, the opposite can also occur. A work or an artist can receive unduly harsh treatment based upon unchallenged past evaluations.

One must realize that Hayden White's assessment of the fictionality of history applies to literary history as well. Just as historians "emplot" historical facts according to their personal interpretation, so literary historians and critics elect the "masterpieces" of accepted literary canons according to their tastes, as influenced by their own circumstances. This subjective element cannot be eliminated, nor can it be ignored. We must acknowledge the potential bias inherent in every generation of scholars and respond to the undeniable need for continual reexamination of the presuppositions, including the literary canon, that operate in our discipline. In Jauss's terms, each new paradigm for the study of literature defines not only the accepted methodological procedures with which critics approach literature, but also the accepted literary canon. During different periods, different elements will dominate. Thus, Robert Holub concludes that we must "rethink constantly the works in the canon in light of how they have affected and are affected by current conditions and events" (58).

The concept of literary canon applies to the evaluation of Mira de Amescua's theater on two different levels. First, the accepted canon of works attributed to Mira remains unfixed: it fluctuates from critic to critic. Reception theory lends insight into the impact of this fluctuation upon the appreciation of Mira's dramatic art. Jan Mukarovsky has demonstrated that each individual work of art constitutes a structure dependent upon the others in any given series or system, so that any changes with respect to the system, such as the discovery of a lost work by an author, will alter the perception of other, related structures. This fact reveals the crucial role played by the presence or absence of a fixed canon of works by an author. James Castañeda understood this when he declared that conclusive proof of Mira's authorship of *El condenado por desconfiado* would necessitate "a drastic reassessment of Mira's place among Golden Age dramatists" (23). Thus, the interrelationship between the accepted canon of works by Mira and the place granted to Mira in the canon of *comedia* scholarship becomes clear. Though I do not propose a definitive list of all his *comedias,* I hope to provide sufficient theoretical and empirical evidence to warrant the reevaluation of Mira de Amescua's opus and, consequently, his standing among the canonical literary dramatists of the period.

In the remainder of this study, I explore the relationship between past reception of Mira de Amescua's plays and modern criticism of his theater. Since very few studies recording actual audience response during the Golden Age exist, one must select another measure to gauge a play's success. Assuming that positive response to a play would lead to more editions of the text, I employ the number of extant editions as a rough index of reception. Accordingly, I have compiled a list of titles, giving their frequency and dates of editions. This approach provides a more solid basis for comparison than the number of actual performances (or reactions to them), since the accessibility to printing has remained more constant than recourse to actual *comedia* productions in modern times. I have excluded *autos,* collaborative efforts, and plays of doubtful attribution, including *El condenado por desconfiado, El negro del mejor amo,* and *La ventura de la fea.*

The other crucial index of any work's reception is the critical interest it generates. For the purpose of this inquiry, I have catalogued the number of critical studies dedicated to specific *comedias* during the nineteenth and twentieth centuries. I have not included those writings that merely incorporate a brief synopsis and cursory discussion regarding the *comedias,* although more studies have been devoted to Mira's biography and to general overviews of his theatrical production (fourteen and twenty-seven, respectively) than to any particular play. My chart presents this information in a condensed form. I recognize the tentative nature of the bibliographic information, yet careful analysis reveals several anomalies between past reception and modern criticism that require elucidation.

One of the first discernible patterns demonstrates that the two *comedias* most frequently issued before 1800, *El animal profeta* and *El ejemplo mayor de la desdicha,* are titles mistakenly attributed to Lope de Vega. This raises various questions. Were the plays printed more often because of their association with Lope de Vega's name or simply because they were considered good? Did the attribution to Lope encourage favorable reception then, or did their favorable reception encourage the attribution to Lope? While a definitive answer may never be reached, the inclusion of these *comedias* among the canon of the foremost playwright of the period undoubtedly privileged them in some respects. Nonetheless, the intense popularity reflected by the substantial number of early editions did not translate into continued modern interest. One might speculate that the corrected authorship of the works may have dampened critical curiosity on the part of scholars convinced of Mira's status as a second-rate dramatist. In addition, a change in the dominant taste may account for the decreased appeal of both works. The first, a hagiographic play based on the life of Saint Julian, and the second, the dramatized tale of the tragic fall from favor of Captain Belisario, most probably do not provoke the same interest today as they did then. The most satisfactory explanation would incorporate the mutual influence of both these factors.

The *Don Alvaro de Luna* plays present an interesting contrast. Frequently attributed to Tirso, the two were edited slightly more frequently after 1800 than before, for a total of three and four editions, respectively. Although this modest numerical increase would not lead one to expect a great deal of critical work, the plays have been the subject of a combined total of twenty-one studies. Since various scholars address the problem of authorship in conjunction with other concerns, one must wonder if so much critical energy would have been expended had the plays been originally accepted as Mira's. Indeed, Castañeda has noted that a study that "unfailingly assumes Tirsian authorship without question has, unwittingly, added greatly to Mira's stature as a dramatist" (52). This, as in the case of *El animal profeta* and *El ejemplo mayor de la desdicha,* poses the possibility of serendipitous misattribution.

The comparison of the number of editions before and after 1800 discloses another apparent contradiction. The only modern critical edition of *El conde Alarcos,* one of the two plays issued most frequently before 1800 and attributed consistently to Mira, remains unpublished. *Galán, valiente y discreto,* on the other hand, exists in six modern editions. Conversely, five critical studies have dealt with *El conde Alarcos,* and only two have been dedicated to *Galán.* The discrepancy between early and modern reception of *El conde Alarcos* raises several questions related to the process of reception. Although some suggest that the popularity of the theme in Golden Age Spain accounts for the immediate success of the play, Emilio Cotarelo y Mori's observation that Mira's version quickly surpassed both Lope's and Guillén de Castro's dramatization of the same events (68) would indicate that another variable besides the theme must have contributed to its popularity.

Most modern critics tend, however, to value the other *comedias* over Mira's. The situation, in several ways, seems to parallel that described by Jauss when he explores how Flaubert's *Madame Bovary* eventually overshadowed the early success of Feydeau's *Fanny,* both variations on a common theme. He postulates how the reader's horizon of expectations changed so as to privilege Flaubert's revolutionary style. In the case of *El conde Alarcos,* changing sensibilities could have precluded favorable reception of the intensely gory interpretation proffered by Mira, in which a jealous woman forces her rival to wash her hands in her murdered daughter's blood and then eat the child's heart. (The delayed revelation that the infant actually survived does little to mitigate the initial effect.) If the outrageous extremes of some current forms of entertainment serve as any indication, contemporary society might prove more favorably predisposed to such a work than in the recent past. At the very least, the numerous early editions call for a detailed reevaluation of the work. Castañeda, for example, contradicts the dominant critical dismissal, claiming that Mira's version evidences "more polish, logic, and character development than those by Lope and Castro" (204).

El esclavo del demonio represents a different phenomenon. Modern editions outnumber past ones by a two-to-one ratio. The text, with five early editions, was more accessible than others by Mira, yet this fact alone cannot account for its unprecedented reception. The twenty-two studies dedicated to the analysis of this play indicate a critical interest which far exceeds that generated by Mira's other *comedias*. Critical evaluation of the play, however, varies greatly. Angel Valbuena Prat proclaims that Mira "succeeded brilliantly in a single work, *El esclavo del demonio*" (Calderón, xviii), while Ruth Lee Kennedy feels that it represents "a formless chaotic mass" (155). Since a consensus acclaiming this to be Mira's best effort does not exist, other factors must account for the text's popularity. The modern fascination with the Faust theme could contribute to the play's positive reception; yet *El amparo de los hombres,* also a variation of the Faust theme, remains unpublished in a modern edition, perhaps because of its relative inaccessibility.

No matter what the reason, that one *comedia* could engender such critical activity disproportionate to its past reception leads one to question the process of critical practice. Past critical interest appears to establish a text as an accepted object worthy of scholarly scrutiny. In other words, criticism propagates further criticism. Many possibilities may remain unexplored simply because no one has carried out the first significant critical study or increased the accessibility of the work by providing a satisfactory edition. Critical reception of hitherto little-known texts does improve significantly with the publication of solid modern editions, as the statistics for *La casa del tahur, La fénix de Salamanca,* and *No hay dicha ni desdicha* indicate. The necessity for a reexamination of Mira's canon based on the careful study of the works themselves rather than on past reception, or lack thereof, is evident. Moreover, my statistics support the need for a critical edition of Mira's complete works, since inaccessibility represents one major yet rectifiable problem hindering reception of Mira's theater.

A qualitative analysis of past critical reception corroborates the tremendous challenge facing future investigation, which I demonstrated by the preceding examination of the quantitative data. I will discuss only three cases, ranging from the concrete evaluation of one play to the overall estimation of Mira's place in the literary canon of the Golden Age.

A careful study of individual works will dispute many generally accepted yet misleading statements. For example, a noteworthy critic summarily dismisses *El más feliz cautiverio* as "a youthful effort that does little more than recount the story of Joseph" (Castañeda, 113). The scarcity of early editions and the lack of a modern one seem to support his assertion. Here, as in other instances, a work may have been condemned solely on the basis of past evaluations and cannot be easily reexamined because of the inaccessibility of the text. Castañeda's dismissive description obscures important textual strategies. The work's self-reflexivity, surfacing in the beginning of the first act, transforms it from a straightforward retelling of a Bible story into metatheater. The following exchange between Joseph's brothers, who comment upon the absence of other siblings who were present in the biblical version of the event being dramatized, underscores the problematic relationship between artistic representation and reality, or the version of reality that proclaims itself the truth:

Simeon: Pero digo, camaradas,
            los demás hermanos, ¿cómo
            no están aquí?
Ruben: No hacen falta
            con nosotros, pues a todo
            bastamos sin ellos.
Levi: No haya
            quien de la historia eche menos
            tan precisa circunstancia.
Simeon: Nadie ignora, que a esto y cuanto
            hicimos, todos se hallaban;
            mas la cómica licencia
            estas y otras circunstancias
            omite o añade, y siempre
            que a la historia no haga falta.
            Para el adorno es preciso
            que algún episodio haya.
            Mas volviendo a nuestro asunto,
            ¡juro a Dios que el correr cansa! (Mira n.d., 21–38)

This unexpected digression, which alludes to poetic/comic license in the *comedia,* assumes significance, beyond its light humor, because it questions the relationship of art and reality as it plays with the status sometimes accorded the Bible.

By referring to liberties taken within the *comedia* itself, the dialogue suggests the possibility of liberties that might have been taken in the version generally accepted as definitive. Thus, it undermines the authority of both texts, much as the quote from *Don Quijote* "que no puede faltar un átomo a la verdad" subverts textual credibility.

The excerpt cited is not an anomaly in Mira's works. On the contrary, it represents one of many incidences of self-reflexivity. In the current age, when deconstruction and self-questioning texts constitute the vogue of literary criticism, Mira's appeal to contemporary scholars might increase significantly. A systematic analysis may well provide further support to document the debt that Calderón, often considered the quintessential practitioner of metatheater, owes to Mira.

José Bella reaches another misleading conclusion: "El anti-femenismo o la misoginía, rasgo típicamente medieval, es en pocos autores tan rotundo y sincero como en Mira" (Mira, xxvi). As evidence to prove this assertion, he quotes various passages from Mira's works, including the following from *El esclavo*: "La casada / lleva la cruz más pesada, / y la monja menos grave" (53–55). One could interpret this statement as profeminist in that it does not idealize the lot of a married woman, and it implicitly recognizes the limited options offered to women by society. We should also question the direct attribution of isolated quotes by characters to Mira, the historical author, without an examination of their relationship to other views expressed. If one were to adopt the indiscriminate application of this technique, one could argue that Mira is antimale, since women often lament the shortcomings of men, as does Bartola in *El conde Alarcos:* "es / desdicha tener marido / a disgusto. Siempre habré / de experiencia, porque Gil / es una bestia, y ayer / la desdicha me mató / un asno que era el joyel, / y el marido me ha dejado. / Si la muerte ha menester / un pollino grande y bueno, / ¿por qué me dejó, por qué / el marido?" (221–32). Clearly, the accusation of misogyny does not reflect careful consideration of Mira's texts; nor does it consider the contribution of the strong female leads that dominate the stage in several of his *comedias*. Any conclusion pertaining to Mira's stance vis-à-vis women cannot rely on arbitrarily selected excerpts but rather must incorporate an analysis of the women in his works with attention to subversive textual strategies, such as irony, that can undermine the negative force of apparently acerbic criticism.

Even more damaging to the current reception of Mira's artistry than these evaluations of single works or isolated elements throughout his theater are the widespread negative assessments of his opus as a whole. Many times these judgments have never faced the challenge posed by concrete evidence. After a brief discussion of one play (*El esclavo del demonio,* of course), a very distinguished and usually perceptive critic remarks:

> El puesto que la crítica actual ha dado a este dramaturgo dentro del ciclo de Lope de Vega nos aparece más que discutible, pues no bastan las bellezas de su versificación ni el ingenio, ni la riqueza de observación ni el sentido de la comicidad, ni el "oficio" ni el que haya escrito algunas excelentes comedias para ponerlo a la altura de dramaturgos como Tirso o Ruiz de Alarcón, ni siquiera de Guillén de Castro o Vélez de Guevara. Para ello hubiera sido necesario lo que yo no encuentro en su teatro: dramas realmente valiosos como tales dramas, dotados de la virtud de permanencia más allá del contexto socio-teatral en que nacieron. (Ruiz Ramón, 208)

I doubt that at this embryonic stage in the criticism of Mira's drama, we have sufficient knowledge to justify such a pejorative claim. The majority of his plays have not yet benefited from concerted critical study. While Mira may not rank as high as Lope, Calderón, Tirso, or even Guillén de Castro, it seems imperative to investigate first his production thoroughly to provide a sound basis for any categorical evaluation. The inadequate body of existing criticism precludes the formulation of any sweeping conclusions. All too often, opinions fossilized through years of stagnation become transformed into indisputable facts. We cannot naively accept past reception without falling prey to possible deception.

    I believe that this brief metacritical excursion into the contrastive analysis of past and present reception of Mira's works has demonstrated the self-propagating nature of criticism and the essential need for constant reexamination of past evaluations of the established canon. While this study has concentrated on Mira de Amescua, these conclusions may prove equally valid for other authors and works as well. I do not offer any easy answers; rather I leave you with difficult questions that require us to examine the very underpinnings that inform our scholarly endeavor. The challenge of reception theory to our discipline, like the challenge posed by feminist theory, requires us to consider the dominant critical vision thoroughly, examining the process that determines not only the questions to be asked but also the texts to be studied.

Title	EARLY (pre-1800)			MODERN (post-1800)		
	Ms	Printed Collection	Suelta	Printed Collection	Critical Ed.	Critical Ed. Unpublished
Adúltera virtuosa			1			
Amor, ingenio y mujer	1	2	1			1
Amparo de los hombres			1			1
Animal profeta	3	1 (Lope)	13 (Lope)	1	1	1
Arpa de David	2				1	
Caballero sin nombre		1				
Carboneros de Francia	3	2	8			
Casa del tahur	1				2	1
Cautela contra cautela	1	1		3		
Clavo de Jael	2					
Conde Alarcos		1	13			1
Confusión de Hungría		1				1
Cuatro milagros	1		2			
Desgracias del rey		2				
Don Alvaro, I	1	1		2	1	
Don Alvaro, II	2	1		2	2	
Don Bernardo de Cabrera, I	1			1		
Don Bernardo de Cabrera, II	1	2		1		
Ejemplo mayor de la desdicha	2	5	11 (Lope)		1	
Esclavo del demonio		3	2	3	8	
Examinarse de rey	4					
Fénix de Salamanca		1	1	2	1	

Total Early	Total Modern	CRITICISM (post-1800)		
		Published	Unpub.	Total
1				
4	1		1	1
1	1	1	1	2
17	3	1	1	2
2	1	1		1
1				
13				
1	3	4	1	5
2	3	1		1
2				
14	1	4	1	5
1	1		1	1
3				
2				
2	3	11		11
3	4	10		10
1	1			
3	1			
18	1	2		2
5	11	22		22
4				
2	3	4		4

| Title | EARLY (pre-1800) | | | MODERN (post-1800) | | |
	Ms	Printed Collection	Suelta	Printed Collection	Critical Ed.	Critical Ed. Unpublished
Galán, valiente y discreto	2	1	11	4	2	
Hero y Leandro	2					1
Hija de Carlos Quinto	1					1
Hombre de mayor fama		1	2			
Judía de Toledo	1	2	6	1		1
Lises de Francia		1				1
Lo que es no casarse a gusto			1			
Lo que puede el oír misa	1	1	1			1
Lo que puede una sospecha		2	1			
Mártir de Madrid	2					1
Más feliz cautiverio		1	2			
Mesonera del cielo		2	5		1	1
No hay burlas		1	1			1
No hay dicha	3	1	2	1	1	
No hay reinar		1				1
Obligar contra su sangre	1	1		1		1
Palacio confuso		2	3	1	2	
Primer conde	1					
Prodigios	1					
Rico avariento	1	2				1
Rueda de la fortuna		2	3	1		1
Tercera de sí misma	1	1			1	

Total Early	Total Modern	CRITICISM (post-1800)		
		Published	Unpub.	Total
14	6	2		2
2	1	1	1	2
1	1		1	1
3				
9	2	1	2	3
1	1		1	1
1				
3	1		1	1
3				
2	1	3		3
3				
7	2	1	1	2
2	1		1	1
6	2	4		4
1	1			
2	2	2	1	3
5	3	3		3
1				
1				
3	1	1	1	2
5	2	4	1	5
2	1	2		2

We can only hope that such a metacritical awareness will eliminate statements similar to that of a respected scholar who accepts the authority of a past critical evaluation without hesitation when he acquiesces: "A juicio de Menéndez y Pelayo, de cuyo sentido crítico y conocimiento . . . no se puede uno . . . apartarse ni dudar" (Cotarelo y Mori, 167). The sacred status granted to a mortal critic subject to his or her own foibles—as we are to our own—proves antithetical to the inquisitive spirit essential to the academic quest. Our greatest legacy for future *comedia* scholarship lies not with the provision of definitive answers but rather with the creation of a critical milieu that privileges the question.

Works Consulted

Calderón de la Barca, Pedro. 1942. *Autos sacramentales.* Vol. 1. Edited by Angel Valbuena Prat. Clásicos castellanos, vol. 69. Madrid: Espasa-Calpe.

Castañeda, James A. 1977. *Mira de Amescua.* Boston: Twayne.

Cotarelo y Mori, Emilio. 1931. *Mira de Amescua y su teatro.* Madrid: Tipografía de la Revista de Archivos.

Crawford, Mary, and Roger Chaffin. 1986. "The Reader's Construction of Meaning: Cognitive Research on Gender and Comprehension." In *Gender and Reading: Essays on Readers, Texts and Contexts,* edited by Elizabeth Flynn and Patrocinio Schweickart, 3–30. Baltimore, Md.: Johns Hopkins University Press.

Hirsch, E. D. 1967. *Validity in Interpretation.* New Haven, Conn.: Yale University Press.

Hirsch, Julian. 1914. *Die Genesis des Ruhrnes: Ein Beitrag zur Methodenlehre der Geschichte.* Leipzig: Johann Ambrosius Bartt.

Holub, Robert C. 1984. *Reception Theory.* New York: Methuen.

Jauss, Hans Robert. 1982. *Towards an Aesthetic of Reception.* Translated by Timothy Bahti. Minneapolis: University of Minnesota Press.

Kennedy, Ruth Lee. [1932] 1975. *The Dramatic Art of Moreto.* Reprint. Ann Arbor, Mich.: Xerox University Microfilms.

Kolodny, Annette. 1980. "Reply to Commentaries: Women Writers, Literary Historians, and Martian Readers." *New Literary History* 11:587–92.

Mira de Amescua. 1972. *Mira de Amescua: Teatro.* Vol. 3. Edited by José M. Bella. Madrid: Espasa-Calpe.

———. n.d. *El más feliz cautiverio.* Edited by Vern G. Williamsen. Unpublished.

Mukarosky, Jan. 1978. *Structure, Sign and Function.* Translated by John Burbank and Peter Steiner. New Haven, Conn.: Yale University Press.

Ruiz Ramón, Francisco. 1967. *Historia del teatro español.* Madrid: Alianza.

White, Hayden. 1978. "The Historical Text as Literary Artifact." In *Tropics of Discourse,* 81–100. Baltimore, Md.: Johns Hopkins University Press.

Sharon Dahlgren Voros

The Feminine Adjuvant:
Toward a Semiotics of Calderonian Plot Dynamics

he theoretical approach to the *comedia* that I apply in this essay extends A. J. Greimas's notion of adjuvancy (135), in connection with Thomas Pavel's model for plot dynamics, to an analysis of four feminine supporting roles: Fénix in *El príncipe constante* and Medea, Ariadne, and Deyanira in *Los tres mayores prodigios.*[1] These roles do not merely involve actions of selfless helpmates (Rogers); they also influence the male protagonists' decision-making process. Feminine adjuvancy, the defining characteristic of female helpers or enablers, has a secondary function, even in Greimas's model, since it appears related to those plot structures in which masculine heroic pursuits predominate. I will therefore omit *comedias* in which adjuvancy is often a function of egalitarian relationships and the female heroes, the *mujer varonil,* since this character type has already attracted considerable scholarly attention (e.g., by Pearson and Pope; McKendrick). Calderón's female helpers, however, in supporting male exploits often acquire heroic attributes themselves.

Since the feminine adjuvant as actant has been considered a secondary role, her range of actions has frequently been overlooked or simply condemned (Pearson and Pope, 6). For that reason, I prefer the semiotic term "adjuvant" from Greimas's actantial model, since it removes negative values often given feminine supporting roles and focuses on the functions of a character type. One could argue that since these women are Calderón's dramatic creation, their masculine side is what appears on the stage, not the weaknesses of a "damsel in distress." While twentieth-century notions of female independence are not reliable mediating factors in the *comedia,* Calderón allows his adjuvants to display daring, courage, and discipline, to extremes in Deyanira's case with her suicide accompanying Hercules's ironic death (Pasto, 234).

The term "adjuvant" belongs to a six-point semiotic model that attempts to clarify the relationship of the character to the plot dynamics of the work as a determinant of dramatic function. Any character may assume any one of Greimas's six functions, simultaneously or successively, according to the following semiotic system (Ubersfeld, 62):

Addresser (D1)	Addressee (D2)
Subject (S)	
Object (B)	
Adjuvant (A)	Opposant (Op)

Fig. 1: The actantial model

The model reads from left to right as an addresser (D1) initiates action toward a subject (S) with the intention of attaining an object (B). D1 is assisted by an adjuvant (A) and opposed by an opposant (Op). This action is performed for the benefit of an addressee (D2). In discussing the Holy Grail, for example, Greimas assigns the role of D1 to God, S to the Knights of the Round Table, B to the Holy Grail itself, A to the saints and angels, Op to the Devil, and D2 to humanity (Ubersfeld, 63). Thus, the model, a derivation of Vladimir Propp's morphological analysis of folktales, not only presents a hierarchical scheme on its vertical axes but also permits the notion of characterization to include abstractions or allegorical figures (Elam, 126).

Feminine adjuvants in Calderón carry with them recognizable sets of dramatic signs that make them a dramatic type or, in some cases, an archetype, since they go beyond the confines of a single text and extend to both *auto* and *comedia.* One group of feminine adjuvants includes Fénix in *El príncipe constante* and Hermosura in *El gran teatro del mundo.*[2] Both female figures refuse assistance, Fénix consciously and Hermosura unwittingly. A second group involves those feminine adjuvants willing to assist the male hero, such as Medea, Ariadne, and Deyanira in *Los tres mayores prodigios,* with corresponding allegorical versions in *El divino Jasón* and *El laberinto del mundo.* The Hercules/Deyanira tale is not reworked in an *auto.*

I also distinguish between another binary set involving characterization and action: "mediated adjuvancy" and "unmediated adjuvancy" (Lévi-Strauss, 189). The mediating factor involves objects, special powers, or people that permit the female helper to perform her task. These additional mediators are then the adjuvants of adjuvants. Fénix acts without the assistance of special magical powers or symbolic objects. While her mythological name suggests such special powers, her sphere of dramatic action does not include them. Instead, *in absentia* she influences Muley, captured in battle, but pleads *in presentia* for Fernando, enslaved in order to save Ceuta. In the clearly mythological characters, mediation is already inherently connected to feminine adjuvancy: Medea with her magical powers, Ariadne with her golden clew, and Deyanira with the centaur's shirt. All three actions that influence the male protagonist depend on the feminine adjuvant's ability to manipulate these mediating objects.

Pavel's plot dynamics, a synthesis of the game theory of moves projected onto the tree diagrams of transformational grammar, permits an analysis of the feminine adjuvant's contributions to the central action by relating to key choices responsible for dramatic action (Pavel, 17). The purpose of the model is to trace the dynamics of plot advance and the hierarchical system of dependencies (Pavel, 16) already found in natural language sentence structure. The move quite simply focuses on the choice of action, from among a set of alternatives, that establishes a chain of causality as one move embeds itself in another. Thus, the main dramatic problem carries with it a series of problems and solutions. The move, with its binary structure of problem versus solution, has an intermediary stage, an auxiliary (Pavel, 19), to facilitate the transition from one structural component to another. Pavel then restates the move structure as: move = problem + (auxiliary) + solution. Characters faced with a problem make a series of choices to solve it and in doing so formulate the first move, in which the second move is embedded. With this dual approach in analyzing both positive and negative manifestations of the feminine adjuvant, I hope to establish a working hypothesis for further study of this character typology as a function of the plot style of high drama.

The Unmediated Adjuvant: Fénix in *El príncipe constante*

As representatives of help denied, Fénix in *El príncipe constante* and Hermosura in *El gran teatro del mundo* include the polarity adjuvant/opposant. This semiotic shift from one side of Greimas's model to the other reveals also two distinct levels of consciousness and contradiction: physical beauty does not bring spiritual tranquility. It is this concept, rather than the erotic model proposed by Leo Spitzer (154), that the Constant Prince shares with Fénix, the Moorish princess. The recognition of their own mortality unites them dramatically. Fénix, the phoenix of the birth/death cycle, attempts to intercede for the Christian prince (270ab) after the famous garden scene, in which Fernando's flower image of fading beauty is matched poetically by the princess's "flores nocturnas" (267a). Spitzer, in characterizing Fénix as the narcissistic opposite of Fernando—the main reason, he argues, for her role in the play—emphasizes her feminine wiles and her vanity with the mirror. Yet he cannot account for her "indefinable" pain (140) or explain why the princess's fate is linked to the virtuous prince (160). The mirror, however, like the key stage prop for Hermosura in *El gran teatro,* serves two semiotic functions: it reflects feminine beauty *and* it enhances the sense of one's own mortality. Fernando, the only character who accepts his mortality as a means of serving God, combats his own entourage's fear of "imágenes de la muerte" (254b). These evil omens are fearful for Moors, but not for Christians who do God's will (255a). The central problem of the play, spiritual angst in need of salvation, is confirmed by Fénix as "Sólo sé que sé sentir; / lo que sé sentir no sé; / que ilusión del alma fue" (250a). She further rephrases her anguish as her father, in the first move, announces her marriage to Tarudante, which she states in an aside, "Di sentencia de mi muerte" (250b). Thus, Fénix's physical beauty relates to Ceuta, which signifies beauty: "que Ceido, Ceuta, en hebreo / vuelto al árabe idioma, / quiere decir hermosura" (251a).[3] Both Fénix and Ceuta are semantically and dramatically linked as being in need of spiritual redemption as Calderón typically entangles personal grief with political power in the first move, which is Fénix's forced marriage to Tarudante, whom the King needs to conquer Christian Ceuta (250b). This first move initiates the system of plot dynamics that combines and intertwines the personal lives not only of Fernando and Fénix but also of Fénix's true love, the Moorish knight, her cousin Muley.

In projecting the plot design onto Pavel's model, we see that Fénix as feminine adjuvant remains outside the decision-making process responsible for dramatic development, which confirms the semiotic hypothesis of adjuvancy as a secondary system. Fénix characteristically finds herself confronted with a problem, such as her melancholy or the enigma of her prophetic dream, "¡Ay de mí, que yo he de ser / precio vil de un hombre muerto!" (260b). The solution comes from another character, the Portuguese King Alfonso, who exchanges her for Fernando's lifeless body (277b). Fernando, whose imprisonment and death save Ceuta from Muslim control, also redeems Fénix, who is married to her true love, Muley, at the play's conclusion. The move grammar has the following structure, with modified graphics from Pavel's model:

Move 1 [Fénix, King]

PROBLEM 1	PROBLEM 2	SOLUTION 1
Fénix's melancholy	Ceuta's conquest	King plans to marry Fénix to Tarudante

Move 2 [Fénix, Muley, King]

PROBLEM 1	PROBLEM 2	SOLUTION
Fénix accepts Tar.'s portrait	Ceuta in jeopardy	King sends Muley to battle

Move 3 [Fernando]

PROBLEM	AUXILIARY	SOLUTION
Muley Fern.'s prisoner	Fénix (absent)	Fern. frees Muley for love of Fénix

Move 4 [Fernando]

PROBLEM	AUXILIARY 1	AUXILIARY 2	SOLUTION
Fernando now King's prisoner	Muley intercedes with King (failure)	After garden scene, Fénix intercedes with King (failure)	Fernando is slave to save Ceuta

Move 5 [Muley, King]

PROBLEM	SOLUTION 1	SOLUTION 2
Muley conspires with Fernando (known by King), in love with Fénix (unknown by King)	King makes Muley Fern.'s jailer	King makes Muley Fénix's escort to Tarudante

Move 6 [Fernando]

PROBLEM	AUXILIARY 1	AUXILIARY 2	SOLUTION
Fern. dying asks for help	King blames Fern. for his own fate	Fénix turns away in horror (negative)	Fernando dies in prison (negative, but positive spiritually)

Move 7 [Alfonso, Fernando]

PROBLEM 1	PROBLEM 2	AUXILIARY	SOLUTION 1	SOLUTION 2
Fern.'s death vs. Fénix's beauty	King fears Fénix must die because Fern. is dead	Fénix now offers self in exchange for Fern.	Alfonso accepts Fern.'s body in exchange for Fénix	Alfonso marries Muley to Fénix

Fig. 2: Pavel's move-grammar: Fénix

Thus, in seven moves, or key choices, the plot dynamics of *El príncipe constante* advances to its conclusion, the salvation of Ceuta and the marriage of Fénix to Fernando's friend, Muley. While Fénix is responsible for Muley's freedom from his Christian captor, Fernando (move 3), she is not able to effect the same plot change in move 4 or in move 6 before Fernando's death. In move 4, her action is unsolicited, as she goes to her father, whom she fears as her *dueño* (250b), while in move 6, Fernando requests her assistance, fully aware that she can only intervene by influencing the King: "me amparad / con el Rey" (275b). When Fénix turns away, it is not without pity and horror for the prince's fate. She employs similar phrasing in both her plea before her father, "Horror da a cuántos le ven" (270b), and her reaction to Fernando's suffering, "Horror con tu voz me das" (275a). Thus, Fénix, not insensitive to Fernando's pain as she refuses to look at him ("¡Qué gran dolor!" [275a]), still is incapable of assistance, having been denied her own liberation through marriage to an unloved suitor for reasons of state, thus losing her own power to act independently. Had Fénix not already pleaded for clemency in act 3 (270ab), we could agree with Spitzer's narcissistic hypothesis.

Calderón, in including the pathetic scene of the dying Fernando, sets the stage for the explanation of the enigma, "precio de un muerto has de ser," and the conclusion of the play. Beauty/Fénix cannot contemplate her opposite, physical horror and death/Fernando, just as Hermosura in *El gran teatro* must confront the mirror again to see her true nature, the disintegration of worldly beauty (219). The exchange of beauty for the dead man does not cause the death of beauty, however. Fénix accomplishes the "hero's journey" (Pearson and Pope, 3), normally reserved for male heroism, even though her real journey to Fez to marry Tarudante was against her will. Her capture by Alfonso, King of Portugal, ironically becomes her salvation. Fénix's reprimand of her father indicates her growth and change as developed in the course of dramatic action: "¿Qué es esto, señor?

Pues viendo / mi persona en este trance, / mi vida en este peligro, / mi honor en este combate, / ¿dudas qué has de responder?" (277b). The King hesitates to exchange Fénix, since, knowing that Fernando is dead, he fears for her life and his own (move 7). For the first time in the play, the King is confronted with his own mortality and the destruction of his kingdom, and when he says: "Da muerte a Fénix bella" (277b), it is not because of his desire to rid himself of her, as Spitzer contends (158), but because he has resigned himself to his and his daughter's tragic fate. In turn, Fénix's fierce denial of her father could not have come about had she not progressed spiritually and emotionally by taking pity on Fernando's martyrdom. She verbally strips the male power figure of all authority in her first direct confrontation with him, proof of her transcending her role as a political pawn.

Thus, the feminine adjuvant is first helpless and melancholic, subject to fate in her father's garden-prison, later the heroic Fénix, forcing her father to make the exchange for Fernando, unaware that his untimely death could mean her own. Had the play ended with her death, we could conclude, with Spitzer's vanity/ beauty model, that her actions remain self-centered and ineffective dramatically (160). Yet she places her life in jeopardy, defies her father, and gives the Christian king an opportunity to display his magnanimity by rewarding her with marriage to Muley—which is more of a requited love than Spitzer thinks (141), if we believe Muley's words to Fernando: "En este estado viví / algún tiempo, aunque fue breve, / gozando en auras suaves / mil amorosos deleites" (257a). The erotic model appropriately belongs as an explanation of the Fénix/Muley relationship, which is not without the structural difficulties of a lover in the service of a lady of higher station which, therefore, must remain secret.[4] Much of Spitzer's view that Fénix is cool toward Muley derives from her social rank, not her feelings, as her asides make abundantly clear (250b). Spitzer's erotic/narcissistic model can only account for partial actions of the feminine adjuvant, whereas Pavel's move grammar illustrates her range of action and influence on plot structure as problem in move 1 and move 2, as auxiliary in moves 3, 4, 6, and 7, and as secondary solution in move 7. Yet her independent actions are all performed as auxiliaries in an attempt to provide assistance or deny it and to become a final exchange in fulfillment of the prophesy.

Thus, Fénix is not only an adjuvant in the Greimasian sense, as secondary or supporting figure; her range of action can also be plotted on Pavel's move tree diagram in relation to the decision-making processes of the plot design. While the princess does not make use of mediating objects to perform her tasks, she herself becomes a mediator, making possible the conclusion of the drama. Methodologically, then, Pavel and Greimas allow the examination of plot dynamics as a whole in order to comprehend the dramatic function of a particular character type with respect to a system of key choices that advance the plot to its conclusion.

Mediated Adjuvancy in *Los tres mayores prodigios*

In *Los tres mayores prodigios,* alienation as a factor in feminine adjuvancy becomes problematic. Fénix exists within the sphere of a garden-prison, which restricts her range of action. She breaks free of this peculiar *locus amoenus* only with failed attempts to assist the male protagonists, Fernando and Muley. With the mythological versions of feminine adjuvancy, each female helper not only lives alienated from male spheres of action but makes use of mediation to make her own contributions to plot dynamics.[5] Boccaccio includes biographies of Medea and Deyanira in his *De claris mulieribus* as examples of feminine *virtus,* an attribute associated with male exploits. Medea, removed from courtly life, shifts from opposant against her father, the King, and Friso, who give the Golden Fleece to Mars, to adjuvant in assisting Jason in stealing it. Ariadne and Phaedra, imprisoned by their father, Minos, are attacked by a bear when they leave the palace without permission, which allows them to encounter a male adjuvant, Theseus. Deyanira, abducted by the centaur Nessus, is almost killed by her own husband, Hercules, who states: "tú me mataste con celos, / yo te mato con ponzoña" (1581b). The arrow kills Nessus instead, leaving Deyanira with a husband obsessed with his honor. Thus, feminine adjuvants must first overcome their own situations of restricted mobility, imprisonment, or danger before being able to assist male protagonists in their efforts. The action, then, is clearly reciprocal between feminine adjuvant and male hero.

Even Medea needs Jason's help to steal the Golden Fleece, for she gives him the idea, couched in terms of a debate with his rival Friso, as a hypothetical question, or *acaso*. Both male characters, Friso and Jason, are given a courtly test to define which action is superior, giving or receiving. Each *galán* feels he is the favored one, Jason having to give the ribbon to Medea and Friso having received a ribbon from her. Only Jason picks up the challenge to retrieve the Golden Fleece, with Friso promising to defy him if he does. If we examine the plot dynamics in light of Pavel's move grammar, we see that Medea figures prominently in the decision-making process at the beginning of act 1 and then retreats to the role of auxiliary. I will present a move grammar for each of the three acts, since each involves a different myth.[6]

Move 1 [Medea, her father, the King]

PROBLEM	AUXILIARY	SOLUTION
Golden Fleece offered to Mars against Medea's wishes	King, Friso make offerings	Jason arrives; Medea defends land, but falls in love

Move 2 [Medea, Jason, Friso]

PROBLEM	SOLUTION
Medea in love with Jason, asks for his help for Gold. Fleece	The test: Medea tests Friso/Jason —Jason wins, gives Medea the Fleece, as he gave her the *banda*

Move 3 [Medea, Jason]

PROBLEM	AUXILIARY	SOLUTION
Take the Golden Fleece from Mars's altar [Jason]	Medea uses magic to assist Jason in quest	Medea and Jason escape with Fleece

Fig. 3: Pavel's move-grammar: Medea

Medea's defiance of Mars brings about revenge from Venus (1551a), which causes her to fall in love with Jason. Her own brother, Absinto, rejects the spiteful sorceress and calls her "injusta," as she indulges in "estudios locos" (1549b). Her father fears her magic and is relieved at her change of heart upon Jason's arrival: "¡Gracias al cielo que un día / tratable, Medea, te muestras!" (1555b). Medea's self-description rivals Jason's exploits on the Argos: "Aquel pasmo soy del mundo, / aquel horror de las fieras, / escándalo de los hombres, / y de las deidades bellas / asombro, porque yo soy / la sabia y docta Medea" (1554b). Using Greimas's model, we see that Medea's role shifts from one of principal antagonist to adjuvant, with the mediating factor of her love for Jason. According to Pavel's move grammar, Medea is present at each decision-making step. In move 1, only Jason's arrival causes her to redirect her anger to the defense of the land, since he represents a threat, and she is anxious to prove herself more worthy than Mars in protecting her people. Her alienated state of living in the wilderness indicates her semidivine nature as a woman to be feared and revered. Yet she does not reveal her magic arts directly to Jason in move 2 but rather places herself in the secondary role of adjuvant only after his departure to capture the Golden Fleece. She uses the almost formulaic phrase of adjuvancy with *dar:* "daréle ayuda, daréle / favor" (1559b). From backstage we hear: "Medea nos ha vencido" (1560a). Further, after Jason's victory, the play is not over, for the *gracioso* says: "¿Aun no habemos acabado?" (1560b). Medea reveals her magical arts to Jason as "pues de un peligro guardé / tu vida, de otro peligro / guarda la mía" (1560b), and Jason must ask, "¿Qué es esto?" (1560b). The sorceress now confuses the enemy troops, who fight each other, while Jason unwittingly boasts of the Argos as their means of escape: "¿Qué importa si te defiendo / yo, y si te vienes conmigo / volviendo a fiar al mar / ese veloz edificio?" (1560b). Act 1 concludes with the victory of Jason, who liberates not only the Fleece but also the *hermosa* Medea, who remains in the background as a powerful feminine adjuvant who conceals her magical arts or her means of mediation in the plot dynamics. While seventeenth-century audiences were certainly familiar with the tragic consequences of Jason's betrayal of Medea (Edwards, 327), we have here a successful dramatic high point in which the feminine adjuvant is rewarded for her actions by being liberated from her alienated state. She also has a speaking part in the reunion scene with the familiar concluding remarks: "sus faltas / perdonad" (1589b).

In act 2, the feminine adjuvant is also initially alienated and marginalized in semi-imprisonment by her father, Minos, but is not rewarded for her unsolicited assistance. While Jason does not request Medea's help, and she conceals her powers from him, Theseus does demand help from Ariadne and Phaedra, whom he had saved from the bear (1561a). Here Calderón presents two potential feminine adjuvants, although only Ariadne actually performs that role (1567b). Theseus falls in love with Phaedra, who does not assist him, and betrays Ariadne, who does. We have then the following plot grammar:

Move 1 [Theseus, Ariadne, Phaedra]

PROBLEM	SOLUTION
Ariadne & Phaedra attacked by bear	Theseus saves them and they warn him of King Minos

Move 2 [Theseus, Ariadne, Phaedra]

PROBLEM	AUXILIARY	SOLUTION
Theseus captured by Lidoro, Minos's captain, in love with Ariadne	Ariadne & Phaedra refuse to help Theseus	Ariadne plans help with Daedalus

Move 3 [Theseus, Daedalus = sub. for Ariadne]

PROBLEM	AUXILIARY	SOLUTION
Theseus in jail with *gracioso*	Daedalus gives him golden clew, poison, & dagger [from Ariadne, her name not given]	Theseus escapes from Labyrinth

Move 4 [Ariadne, Theseus]

PROBLEM	SOLUTION
Ariadne escapes and is attacked by Lidoro	Theseus saves Ariadne (second time) and slays Lidoro

Move 5 [Theseus, Phaedra, Ariadne]

PROBLEM	AUXILIARY	SOLUTION
Theseus must choose between Phaedra (love) & Ariadne (duty)	Theseus's horse carries only two people	Theseus chooses Phaedra (love) over Ariadne (duty)

Fig. 4: Pavel's move-grammar: Ariadne

While Medea, the adjuvant, must choose between two rivals, Theseus, the addresser (Greimas, fig. 1), chooses between two adjuvants, a choice that necessarily converts Ariadne into an opposant. Her second rescue (move 4) cancels Theseus's moral debt to her, despite her revelation that she facilitated his escape (1573b). As with the Medea contest, nobility is defined as honor, not passion, while Theseus succumbs to the latter: "Todo el pundonor perdone; / que las pasiones de amor / son soberanas pasiones" (1573b), a concept contrary to the ideology of *El príncipe constante:* "Muley, amor y amistad / en grado inferior se ven / con la lealtad y el honor" (269a). According to classical sources, Theseus takes Ariadne to Naxos, where he abandons her in her sleep. The sleep sequence here permits

Calderón to invoke the principle of reciprocity, for Lidoro attacks Ariadne in her sleep as Theseus arrives to save her a second time. While she swears vengeance and even appears at the end of the third act when all three companies are reconvened on the stage (1588a), we still have the same plot dynamics as with Medea: the treacherous daughter who betrays the father and loves the enemy, who then punishes her (Leach, 81). Ariadne then shifts from adjuvancy to opposition, while Medea moves from opposition to adjuvancy, since Calderón excludes her punishment scene.

In act 3, the Hercules/Deyanira/Nessus plot triangle is advanced also through a system of five key choices or moves.[7] Tragedy is brought about by the gift of the feminine adjuvant, who, hoping to restore Hercules's love for her, unwittingly becomes the means of his destruction. Unlike *El príncipe constante* and act 1 of *Los tres mayores prodigios,* acts 2 and 3 begin with the male hero instead of his female helper. In move 1, Hercules captures a group of frightened peasants, witnesses of the abduction of Deyanira by the centaur Nessus. When she reappears, she threatens suicide rather than submit to Nessus's advances. She even manages to change the evil centaur's aggression to fear that she will indeed die at her own hand: "ten que más quiero perderte / viva, que llorarte muerta" (1579b), quite a different stance from his previous statement: "pues ya no puedo / con halagos vencer, vencer con miedo" (1579a). The stage is then set for Hercules's intervention with this model:

Move 1 [Hercules, peasants]

PROBLEM	AUXILIARY	SOLUTION
Hercules jealous after Deyanira's abduction	Peasants have information	Hercules resolves to avenge himself [fire imagery]

Move 2 [Nessus, Deyanira]

PROBLEM	SOLUTION
Nessus tries to force Deyanira	Deyanira uses knife in suicide threat

Move 3 [Hercules, Nessus, Deyanira]

PROBLEM	SOLUTION
Deyanira captive; Hercules's fear of dishonor	Hercules shoots arrow that could kill Deyanira, but kills Nessus

Move 4 [Deyanira, Hercules]

PROBLEM	SOLUTION 1	SOLUTION 2
Hercules proposes Deyanira feign death to save honor	Deyanira rejects his solution	Hercules abandons Deyanira

Move 5 [Deyanira, Hercules, Licas]

PROBLEM	AUXILIARY	SOLUTION 1	SOLUTION 2
Hercules's dishonor and rejection of Deyanira	Licas assists Deyanira with Nessus's shirt	Hercules accepts gift, burned by shirt, suicide on pyre	Deyanira commits suicide on pyre

Fig. 5: Pavel's move-grammar: Deyanira

Deyanira's most significant actions in plot dynamics involve her resolve to commit suicide rather than submit to Nessus (move 1), thus persuading him to shift his attitude so that he would prefer to lose her than see her dead. Such impassioned techniques of persuasion fall on deaf ears with her own dear husband, who, unlike Nessus, prefers to see her death to the shame of her return: "En el poder has estado / de una fiera rigurosa" (1583b). When she rejects the solution of her feigned death, Hercules refuses any further discourse, a decision that leads Deyanira to use the centaur's magic shirt to win him back. Unbeknownst to her, the shirt still contains the poison from Hercules's arrow, with which he had almost killed her. Like Medea and Ariadne, Deyanira conceals her magic, and, in attempting to regain her husband's affections, she destroys him as he faces Jason and Theseus. Deyanira, however, realizing that where she expected life is now death (1588b), follows her husband and reveals to him the source of his downfall: "Y la que en vida te amó / verás si en muerte te ama" (1589b). Honor is restored as husband and wife are consumed in the fire of their own making. Thus, Calderón offers another perspective on the question of feminine adjuvancy in the use of tragic irony in the exploration of characterization and plot dynamics. Comparable to the uxoricide *comedias,* the faithful, devoted wife becomes the unwitting, unwilling instrument of her husband's demise. Mencía's attempts in *El médico de su honra* to remedy her situation only serve to deepen her husband's rage. Similarly, Deyanira's effort to regain her husband's affection causes his death.

Thus, in act 1, with Medea, the feminine adjuvant overtakes the male hero. In the second instance, with Ariadne, the feminine adjuvant's efforts to save Theseus from the Minotaur cause her everlasting sorrow, while in the third instance, with Deyanira, Nessus's shirt given to Hercules brings his death and her suicide. The progression in this play, from positive to negative outcome of the heroic pursuit, shows a closely knit internal organization on the level of the female hero/helper. While the feminine adjuvant is liberated from her alienated state either as semiprisoner of her father (Medea, Ariadne) or victim (Deyanira), each act does not end with this event but concludes with a reciprocating action on her part. Deyanira, the only married adjuvant, is unprepared for her husband's jealousy. The chain of ironies, in which Deyanira hopes to bring life and love back into their marriage and only brings death, is compounded by her actions as the feminine adjuvant.

Conclusion

The four examples of feminine adjuvancy analyzed here, Fénix, Medea, Ariadne, and Deyanira, are not merely stock Calderonian characters designed to offset and enhance male superiority. Calderón allows each female helper a range of action, varying in degree of independence from the male protagonist, with Medea perhaps as the strongest and the most awe-inspiring of the group. The weakest is Fénix, symbol of beauty and vanity, which she nevertheless transcends as she rebels against the father and sympathizes with the enemy, all in support of the Christian cause to liberate Ceuta, a symbol of beauty on the spiritual level. Her liberation and marriage to Muley are analogues for the redemption of the Christian city. While her actions as adjuvant fail, both in the unsolicited and solicited categories, as the following concluding schema indicates, Fénix herself becomes the mediating object of exchange that permits the conclusion of the play, as she transcends her own incompetence to fulfill the divine plan of the Constant Prince. Thus, although the Fénix model of feminine assistance might not be the ideal for women who support male endeavors, Calderón allows his characters a degree of independent action on the stage, with both positive and negative consequences or results. Despite their gender, women are capable of accomplishment, even when serving the male cause.

The following paradigmatic schema shows the two major oppositional sets that characterize feminine adjuvancy and its role in plot dynamics: unsolicited help and solicited help versus unmediated help and mediated help, along with the result, positive (+) or negative (-), of the action for the feminine adjuvant (= f.a.) and male hero (= m.h.):

Unsolicited	Result		Solicited	Result	
UNMEDIATED:					
Fénix	(f.a.)	(-)	Fénix	(f.a.)	(-)
Fern.	(m.h.)	(-)	Fern.	(m.h.)	(-)
Fénix	(f.a.)	(+)			
Muley	(m.h.)	(+)			
MEDIATED:					
1 Medea	(f.a.)	(+)	2 Ariadne/Phaedra	(f.a.)	(-)
Jason	(m.h.)	(+)	Theseus	(m.h.)	(-)
2 Ariadne	(f.a.)	(-)			
Theseus	(m.h.)	(+)			
3 Deyanira	(f.a.)	(-)			
Hercules	(m.h.)	(-)			
OBJECT:					
1 Magic					
2 Clew, poison, dagger					
3 Nessus's shirt					
PERSON:					
2 Daedalus					
3 Licas					

Fig. 6: Summary of feminine adjuvancy

When help is unsolicited and spontaneous, part of the independent action of the adjuvant, it is successful, suggesting the value of free will. In most instances, the feminine adjuvant offers her services without being asked, a Calderonian device for giving the character a certain range of action and credibility in response to a situation. Yet it is precisely the response to a given situational sequence that the Pavelian model is able to track, since it accounts for both positive and negative results of the same functional role. If we look at the feminine adjuvant from the perspective of the narcissistic/erotic model or the treacherous-daughter model, we have only partial accounts of her impact on plot design. When Spitzer limits Fénix to the erotic model, he cannot explain her pain in the opening scene, her unsolicited plea to assist Fernando, or even Calderón's technique used to "complete the male hero's line of development with the help of a female figure" (160), a statement that questions the validity of feminine roles, which Spitzer implies could very well be eliminated. The point is that feminine roles do appear in Calderón and they do influence the male hero and plot dynamics. Even Fénix's failure as an adjuvant is necessary to the fulfillment of the prophesy and divine plan to redeem Ceuta, since Fernando's death is really a victory for spiritual values. Deyanira's role is analogous to Fénix's in that she also decides to employ magic to save her marriage, the consequences of which lead to the tragic conclusion. Like Fénix, she intends no harm but inadvertently causes the male hero's death—Fénix by withholding help, Deyanira by offering it. The structure of *El príncipe constante* is thus an inversion of *Los tres mayores prodigios*. Medea is the only feminine adjuvant rewarded for her deeds, while the play concludes with the death of another female helper, Deyanira. Fénix is unrewarded and manipulated until the end of the play, when she is married to her love, Muley, hence the positive sign in the schema. Had she married Tarudante, she probably would have resigned herself to her fate. Only with her final reprimand of her father and plea for Fernando's release, as well as her own, does her last action as adjuvant reveal her spiritual angst. Thus, her reward concludes the play and restates its message of Christian redemption. The only truly unrewarded adjuvant, Ariadne, leaves an open-ended structure to the play, bringing with it a critique of passion as destructive to the honor code of duty and gratitude. In sum, one thematic or semiotic model is insufficient, even for secondary feminine stage action, to understand Calderón's handling of adjuvancy. Far from condemning his female helpers, Calderón allows them to make mistakes and to move with grace.

Notes

1.   See also Anne Ubersfeld for a clear description of Greimas's actantial model, a six-point semiotic model that attempts to clarify the relationship of characters or actants to the plot dynamics of a literary work.

2.   All quotations from Calderón will refer to the 1969 edition and will be given in the text in parentheses.

3.   Everett W. Hesse discusses the problematics of Fénix (70–82). William W. Whitby includes the etymologies of Fénix as "eternal life" and Ceuta as "beauty." Dian Fox views Fénix negatively as lacking "spiritual vision" (55).

4.   Lisa Jardine points out the problematics for women marrying a social inferior (77), certainly a source of the contradictions apparent in Fénix.

5.   Thomas A. O'Connor analyzes Calderón's handling of myth in *Los tres mayores prodigios* (136–52).

6.   See Frederick A. de Armas for the political implications of the Medea myth in seventeenth-century Spain (149–63).

7.   See Marcia L. Welles on the rape of Deianeira in *El pintor de su deshonra* and Gwynne Edwards's comparison of the two Calderonian plays that treat this myth.

Works Consulted

Boccaccio, Giovanni. 1963. *Concerning Famous Women.* Translated by Guido A. Guarino. New Brunswick, N.J.: Rutgers University Press.

Bulfinch, Thomas. 1970. *Mythology.* New York: Thomas Y. Crowell Company.

Calderón de la Barca, Pedro. 1969. *Dramas.* Vol. 1 of *Obras completas.* 2d edition. Edited by Angel Valbuena Briones. Madrid: Aguilar.

De Armas, Frederick A. 1986. *The Return of Astraea: An Astral-Imperial Myth in Calderón.* Lexington: University Press of Kentucky.

Edwards, Gwynne. 1984. "Calderón's *Los tres mayores prodigios* and *El pintor de su deshonra:* The Modernization of Ancient Myth." *Bulletin of Hispanic Studies* 41:326–34.

Elam, Keir. 1980. *The Semiotics of Theatre and Drama.* London and New York: Methuen.

Fox, Dian. 1986. *Kings in Calderón: A Study in Characterization and Political Theory.* London: Tamesis Books.

Greimas, Algirdas J. 1966. *Sémantique structurale.* Paris: Larousse.

Hesse, Everett W. 1967. *Calderón de la Barca.* New York: Twayne Publishers.

Jardine, Lisa. 1989. *Still Harping on Daughters: Women and Drama in the Age of Shakespeare.* 2d ed. New York: Columbia University Press.

Leach, Edmund. 1974. *Claude Lévi-Strauss.* New York: Viking Press.

Lévi-Strauss, Claude. 1972. "The Structural Study of Myth." In *The Structuralists from Marx to Lévi-Strauss,* edited by Richard and Fernande DeGeorge, 169–94. Garden City, N.Y.: Doubleday.

McKendrick, Melveena. 1974. *Women and Society in the Spanish Drama of the Golden Age: A Study of the "Mujer varonil."* Cambridge: Cambridge University Press.

O'Connor, Thomas Austin. 1988. *Myth and Mythology in the Theater of Pedro Calderón de la Barca.* San Antonio, Tex.: Trinity University Press.

Pasto, David J. 1988. "The Independent Heroines in Ruiz de Alarcón's *Comedias.*" *Bulletin of the Comediantes* 40:227–35.

Pavel, Thomas G. 1985. *The Poetics of Plot: The Case of English Renaissance Drama.* Minneapolis: University of Minnesota Press.

Pearson, Carol, and Katherine Pope. 1981. *The Female Hero in American and British Literature.* New York and London: R. R. Bowker Company.

Rogers, Kathleen M. 1966. *The Troublesome Helpmate: A History of Misogyny through Literature.* Seattle: University of Washington Press.

Spitzer, Leo. 1965. "The Figure of Fénix in Calderón's *El príncipe constante.*" In *Critical Essays on the Theatre of Calderón,* edited by Bruce W. Wardropper, 137–63. New York: New York University Press.

Ubersfeld, Anne. 1981. *L'école du spectateur.* Vol. 2 of *Lire le théâtre.* Paris: Editions sociales.

Welles, Marcia L. 1991. "The Rape of Deianeira." In *The Perception of Women in Spanish Theater of the Golden Age,* edited by Anita Stoll and Dawn Smith, 184–201. Lewisburg, Pa.: Bucknell University Press.

Whitby, William W. 1956. "Calderón's *El príncipe constante:* Fénix's Role in the Ransom of Fernando's Body." *Bulletin of the Comediantes* 8:1–4.

J. E. Varey and Charles Davis

New Evidence on the Leasing of
Seating Accommodation in the Madrid *Corrales,* 1651–55

n 1615 the commercial theaters of Madrid, the Corral de la Cruz and the Corral del Príncipe, were leased to a private businessman. The first lease was for two years, but in 1617 the theaters were leased for four years, and from that date a regular system of four-year leases was initiated (Varey and Shergold 1987, 19–22). The performance of plays was from time to time suspended as a mark of respect on the death of a royal personage or because of some natural disaster, such as plague. Thus the theaters were closed on 7 October 1644 on the death of Queen Isabel de Borbón and re-opened probably on Easter Sunday 1645, after the normal closure during Lent. But in 1646, the theaters were again closed by royal decree during the Lenten period, on this occasion as a result of reforming zeal. They were not to reopen fully until 1651, but from June 1648 a succession of short leases permitted the performance of *autos sacramentales,* puppets and acrobats, and finally plays: "comedias de historias" (Varey and Shergold 1987, 31–36; Varey and Shergold, 1960). An attempt was made in June 1651 by the town council of Madrid to re-open the *corrales* and to renew the lease system; the negotiations did not succeed at once, but renewed pressure resulted in permission to lease the theaters for four years from 1 December 1651 (Varey and Shergold 1987, 35; 137–38). The new lease was granted to Don Bernardo de Villavelarde. Its clauses repeat those of the lease of 1645–49, with an important new clause, a "condizion añadida," which states that if the king were to renew the prohibition of plays during the period of the lease, then the lessee would only be obligated to pay pro rata for the period of time when plays had been permitted (Varey and Shergold 1987, 139–40).

The leases of 1615–49 had all begun on 24 June. The lease of 1651–55 was proclaimed on 4 November, and the final documents were not signed until 30 December. The lease was to run from 1 December 1651 to 30 November 1655, and these dates appear in all subsequent leases up to that of 1703–7 (Varey and Shergold 1973, 55–57; 1987, 194–96). The prohibition and the continuation of the negotiations for the lease up to the date of its commencement account for the fact that the first document printed in our appendix below dates from 22 December 1651, and that documents 2–14 were signed between 11 January and 5 February 1652, although all the individual leases of seating accommodation to which they refer are backdated to 1 December 1651. The new clause added to the main lease is also reflected in documents 2–14, all of which state that if plays are prohibited by royal command, these subsidiary leases will only apply pro rata to the days on which plays are permitted.

As the new lessee, Don Bernardo de Villavelarde formally accepted inventories of the moveable furniture of the two theaters on 11 July 1652, a later date than was to become usual for such documents. The late date can be accounted for by the fact that—no doubt as a result of dilapidations during the long period of prohibition—some of the seating accommodation was renewed in March and April of that year (Shergold 1989, 101–6); the inventory therefore accurately reflects the total number of benches and similar furniture in use on that date. The two documents refer to various types of seating—*bancos* (benches), *banquillos* (short benches), *taburetes* (stools), *tarimones* (platforms), and *escaños* (long benches with backrests)—as well as to awnings and to locks and keys. In this essay, we are concerned with the leasing of *bancos, banquillos,* and *taburetes,* and we therefore extract the relevant information relating to the two commercial theaters:

> *Corral de la Cruz*
> Mas reciui un tablon de 17 asientos que eran taburetes y el respaldar de
>   tablas dellos.
> Mas reciui 26 bancos delanteros.
> Mas reciui 12 bancos segundos.
> Mas reciui dos banquillos de un asiento, todos a cargo de Juan Rodrigues.
> Mas reciui 12 bancos segundos, questan a cargo de Antonio el Frayle.
> Mas reciui 14 bancos bajos que estan en los corredorsillos, a cargo de
>   Manuel Descobar.
> Mas reciui 16 tarimones grandes que se ponen en el patio.
> Mas reciui 19 bancos que se ponen encima del tablado y estan a cargo de
>   Domingo Rodrigues el portugues.

Mas reciui ocho bancos questan en los quatro aposentos delanteros.

Mas reciui sinco escaños que estan en los aposentos que llaman bajos, a

cargo de Domingo Antonio. (Varey and Shergold 1973, 61)

Corral del Príncipe

Mas reciui 22 bancos delanteros biejos y nuebos para el dicho [C]orral.

Mas 15 bancos que son ocho segundos y siete tarimonsillos para detras.

Mas reciui seis banquillos de a una persona.

Mas vn tablon que cauen 17 personas questa en lugar de los tauuretes con

las tablas del respaldar dellos.

Que todo lo dicho esta a cargo de Vicente Diaz, a quien lo tengo entregado.

Mas reciui 16 bancos, ocho segundos y ocho tarimonsillos, que estan a

cargo de Ejenio Gaitan.

Mas reciui 11 bancos que estan en el corredor alto, a cargo de Ernando

Bermudes.

Mas reciui 16 tarimones altos que ponen en el patio.

Mas reciui 19 bancos que se ponen en los corredores de encima del

tablado que son todos, biejos y nuebos, y estan a cargo de Juan

Catalan.

Mas reciui 11 bancos que ay en los aposentos de enfrente del tablado.

Mas reciui seis escaños que ay en los aposentos que llaman bajos, todo a

cargo de Andres Lopez.

(Varey and Shergold 1973, 61–62)

It will be noted that both inventories refer to a long bench that seated seventeen spectators. Behind this extended bench was a separate *respaldar,* or backrest, made of planks. These seats were known as the *taburetes* (Davis and Varey). They are referred to in the repair document of March–April 1652 cited above. The survey of the Corral del Príncipe notes, "En la parte adonde se ponen los taburetes parece sera mejor poner un tablon acepillado con sus dibisiones de los asientos porque no ay taburetes que poner, y reparar el respaldar que oy tienen de tablas" (Shergold 1989, 101). The work subsequently carried out shows that this extended bench rested on seven trestles: "De vn tablon que se a puesto en el sitio adonde solian estar los taburetes y se fijo sobre siete asnillas de madera que tiene 28 pies de largo y tres dedos de grueso. Vale todo 78 reales" (Shergold 1989,

103). John Allen indicates that the length of the bench, 28 feet, corresponds to the width of the stage (Allen, 26). The 1652 survey of the Corral de la Cruz states that it is necessary "en el respaldo de los taburetes y en el aposento de los cultos ade-reçar los atajos de tablas" (Shergold 1989, 102), and the work carried out is similar to that done in the Príncipe: "De 28 pies de tablon y siete asnillas que se an puesto en el asiento donde estauan los taburetes, 63 reales" (Shergold 1989, 105).

Before 1652, the *taburetes* were probably individual seats. The *Diccionario de autoridades* defines *taburete* as "especie de assiento como una silla, con la diferencia de que es raso, y sin brazos, y el respaldar para reclinarse mas estrecho. Guarnecese de baqueta, terciopelo, tafetan, y otras telas, clavadas à la madera." From 1652, the *taburetes* consisted of a long plank with divisions to indicate individual seats, raised from the floor on trestles (providing support for the feet of the spectators) and with a back support consisting of separate planks. The *respaldar* also served to protect those seated on the *taburetes* from the members of the audience who stood behind them in the yard, as is indicated by a further repair document of 1675 relating to work done in the Corral del Príncipe: "Mas se a de poner vn tablon de 27 pies de largo por media vara de ancho que sirue de taburete arrimado al tablado con sus asnillas y aderezar el antepecho de la baya a donde se arriman los mosqueteros, vale 258 reales" (Shergold 1989, 153). Given that these seats were directly adjacent to the stage, and that the stage was, according to Allen's calculations, some six feet above the floor level of the yard (Allen, 29–37), it is clear that they needed to be raised on trestles if the spectators were to have adequate sight lines. At a later date, the *taburetes* were to be divided from the yard, not by a straight plank, as in 1652, but by a curved barrier demarcating an area known as the *luneta*. The *Diccionario de autoridades,* referring to this later period, has the following definition: "TABURETES. En los corrales de Comedias se llama una media luna, que está en el patio cerca del theatro, con sus assientos de tabla, y respaldos de lo mismo. Lat. *Prope proscaenium sedilia in semicirculum disposita.*"

Several of the documents printed in our appendix below refer to seating accommodation on the *taburetes*. On 11 January 1652, Ignacio Noble leased *taburete* 3 in both theaters (doc. 2); on 13 January, Don Alonso de Pareja leased *taburete* 5 in both theaters (doc. 4); and Simón Centón leased *taburete* 2, again in both theaters (doc. 5); on 18 January, *taburete* 4 in both theaters was leased to Don Alonso de Hoyos Montoya (doc. 6); on 18 January Pedro Ortiz leased *taburete* 11 in the Cruz and the Príncipe (doc. 9); and on 26 January *taburete* 12 in both *corrales* went to Don Francisco de Aldana (doc. 13). In every case, therefore, the same seat is leased in both theaters. The documentation demonstrates that these seats, in close proximity to the stage and in what were clearly considered to be prime locations, cost their lessees 10 ducats—or 110 *reales*—per year per seat. References to similar leases of *taburetes* in 1641 are to be found in a copy of the account books.

While the entries do not indicate whether the leases refer to one theater or both, the document indicates that there were in all seventeen *taburetes,* for which the lessees pay 220 *reales* each per year. Some of the names of the lessees listed in 1641 are repeated in the documents published below (Varey and Shergold 1971, 121).

The remaining documents, with the exception of no 15, are leases for seating accommodation on *bancos,* designated as being in the first row ("de la primera orden") or in the second row ("de la segunda orden"). The relative prices of the seats in the two rows is established by document 10, which indicates that a single seat on a *banco* "de primera orden" was leased for 73 *reales* 11 *maravedís* per year, and one in the second row for 50 *reales* per year. Other documents indicating 50 *reales* for seats in the second row are no. 3, for four seats; and no. 7, for three seats. Documents 8, 12, and 14 are for first-row seats costing 73 *reales* and 17 *maravedís*. Document 1 refers to an unspecified number of seats on a first-row bench, the lease of which cost 20 ducats, or 220 *reales,* for each theater. This therefore in all probability refers to a lease of two sets of three seats at 73 *reales* and 11 *maravedís* per seat. Document 11 specifies 150 *reales* but does not indicate how many seats or in what row; it is likely that this lease is for three seats in the second row. The remaining document, no. 15, is for the lease of a *banquillo,* accommodating one person, which costs the same as a seat on a first-row *banco,* 73 *reales* and 17 *maravedís*.

The evidence from 1641 gives a price of 330 *reales* for three seats on a second-row bench in both theaters, at 55 *reales* per seat. There are also payments of 440 *reales,* presumably for a bench seating four in each theater, as in document 3 below, at 55 *reales* per seat, or perhaps for three seats in each theater at 73 *reales* and 11 *maravedís* per seat, as seems to be the case in document 1 below. In 1641, a *banquillo* cost 70 *reales*. The evidence available is not sufficient for an exact equivalence to be struck between the 1641 prices and those for 1652 (Varey and Shergold 1971, 121–22).

The benches in the Príncipe referred to are numbered 3, 10, 16, and 17 in the first row (assuming that the no. 16 referred to is a first-row bench), and 10, 14, and 15 in the second row. Those in the Cruz are numbered 4, 8, 9, 15, and 25 in the first row (assuming that the no. 9 referred to is a first-row bench), and 8, 13, and probably 19 in the second row. This numbering agrees with the inventory, which specifies 22 first-row benches and apparently 16 second-row benches in the Príncipe, and 26 first-row benches and 24 second-row benches in the Cruz (Varey and Shergold 1973, 61–62).

The question of the number of seats per bench is not resolved by the documents printed below. The *banquillo* was evidently for a single person. Allen concludes that "it seems logical to assume that the standard bench accommodated three men" (24). It is clear from document 3 that certain benches (in this case in the second row) seated four, whereas document 1 seems to refer to a bench (this time in the first row) for three persons: the payment, which is for "el arrendamiento del vanco" in each theater, corresponds, as we have said, to three times the standard rate per first-row seat. One cannot be sure, however, whether others also sat on the benches in question. The evidence is not sufficient to come to a clear conclusion, and it is probable that the benches varied in seating capacity more than has hitherto been assumed.

It is also difficult to compare the prices levied per year with those charged for a single performance. These leases are not for all performances but only for those with most appeal. According to the lease itself, the standard price for a bench, as in 1641–45, is 1½ *reales* (of which one *quartillo* went to the attendant), and 20 *maravedís* for a seat on a bench (Varey and Shergold 1987, 118). By 1675, these prices were to rise substantially; the printed list of prices exhibited in that year (itself an indication that the listed prices were on occasion exceeded) gives the charge for "cada lugar en los bancos primeros y segundos en ambos corrales" as 1½ *reales*, "y por vn banco de tres asientos," 4½ (Varey and Shergold 1974, 100–101). These prices treble those stipulated in the lease of 1641–45 and still repeated in the lease for 1675–79 (Varey and Shergold 1987, 148); and they make no distinction between the first and the second rows. At the 1651 standard price of

20 *maravedís* for a seat on a bench, the lessees in these documents are paying for the equivalent of 125 performances (in the case of first-row benches) or 85 (in the case of second-row benches) per year. Since it is unlikely that there could have been so many genuine *comedias nuevas* and *entradas de autores* in a year, they seem to be paying above the daily rate. This indicates that a guaranteed seat in a prime position, especially on what must have been the days of highest demand, is considered worth an extra payment. For the lessee, such leases as here published had the advantage of guaranteeing him an income, which he furthermore received in advance. The documents further underline—were that necessary—the importance given to novelty in the repertoire, stressing the drawing power both of a company of actors recently arrived in the capital and of a new play in the repertoire.

Finally, the documents give us certain indications as to the social rank of those who leased benches and *taburetes* for these special occasions. Several of the lessees were government officials or servants of the crown. Diego Ramírez de Medrano (or Mesa), who leased a bench, was *Pagador de los Reales Consejos* (doc. 1); Don Alonso de Hoyos Montoya, leasing a *taburete,* was *Contador de resultas* (doc. 6); Gabriel Marcos, who joined Pedro de Cartagena on a bench, was also a *Contador* (doc. 7). Don Juan de Miranda, *Escribano de Cámara del Real Consejo de Guerra,* leased a bench in 1652 (doc. 12), as he had done previously in 1641 (Varey and Shergold 1971, 121). Melchor Morán, a *secretario,* had previously occupied the *banquillo* leased by Don Jacinto de Lemus (doc. 15). Don Francisco de Aldana, the lessee of a bench, was a servant of the queen (doc. 13). Two knights of the Order of Santiago also leased seating accommodation: Don Agustín Daza on a bench (docs. 8 and 16), and Don Jacinto de Lemus on a *banquillo* (doc. 15). In 1641, both men are listed as leasing *taburetes* (Varey and Shergold 1971, 121). All these lessees are evidently "gentes de distincion," as the *Diccionario de autoridades,* under the heading *luneta,* describes those theatergoers who took their places on the *taburetes* in the early eighteenth century: "LUNETA. Se llama en los Corrales de Comedias la estancia cerrada que hai delante del tablado, donde se sientan gentes de distincion, que tambien se llaman Taburétes."

The documentation does not give precise information concerning the rank or position of several of the lessees: Don Alonso de Pareja de Rabago (*taburete,* doc. 4); Pedro de Cartagena, who shared a bench with the *contador* Gabriel Marcos and Francisco de Cabredes/Carriedes (doc. 7); Pedro Ortiz (*taburete,* doc. 9); Don Juan Vázquez Garay (*banco,* doc. 10); Miguel de Torronjeras (*banco,* doc. 11); and Don Sebastián Vázquez de Prada (*banco,* doc. 14). We are informed that Don Melchor Alfonso de Valladolid y Canedo, who also leased a bench in the name of Don Francisco de Navarro (doc. 3), did so in accordance with the order of Don Lorenzo Ramírez de Prado, a member of the Council of Castile and *Juez Protector de hospitales y de los teatros.* Two of the lessees of *taburetes,* Ignacio Noble (doc. 2) and Simón Centón (doc. 5), had leased similar accommodation in 1641 (Varey and Shergold 1971, 121).

The lists of witnesses are not without interest. Through documents 9—the lease of a *taburete* by Pedro Ortiz, witnessed by Pedro Pérez, Don Antonio Escudero, and Don Juan Vázquez—and 10—the lease of a seat on a bench by Don Juan Vázquez Garay, witnessed by Pedro Pérez, Don Antonio Escudero, and Pedro Ortiz—we get a glimpse of friends or associates going together to the notary to register leases of seating accommodation in the theaters and testifying to each other's signature. Pérez, Escudero, and Ortiz also witnessed Don Agustín Daza's lease the same day, 18 January 1652 (doc. 8), and Escudero, Pérez, and Felipe Benito were present in December 1653 to witness Daza's second lease, of seats taken over from Vázquez Garay (doc. 16). The same phenomenon can be observed in documents 4 and 5: first Don Alonso de Pareja de Rabago's lease is witnessed by Simón Centón with Diego Osorio and Lorenzo Yáñez, then Centón's own lease is witnessed by Pareja, again with Osorio and Yáñez. Diego Osorio was a well-known *autor de comedias,* and it is therefore possible that the Francisco García who witnessed document 3 was the *autor* of that name known as *el Pupilo* (Shergold and Varey, eds. 1985, 524). The name, however, is common, and another—and possibly stronger—claim can be made for the identification of this witness with the Francisco García who was guarantor of the lease of Villavelarde (Varey and Shergold 1973, 57). Antonio de Rueda, who witnessed document 7, signed documents as guarantor of the lease of the theaters in 1653 and 1654; a well-known actor and *autor de comedias,* he was to become treasurer of the *Cofradía de la Novena,* the actors' guild (Varey 1985, 111). Perhaps the most interesting name among the witnesses is that of Don Pedro de Arce (doc. 6). Arce had leased a bench in 1641 (Varey and Shergold 1971, 121), and his son, Don

Pedro Ignacio de Arce, was to be a guarantor of the lessee of the theaters in 1683–87 (Varey and Shergold 1987, 56). Pedro de Arce, a former secretary of the Council of War and of the Council of the Indies, a member in 1640 of the *Junta de Ejecución* and of one of the three *salas* created by Olivares in 1642, was one of a circle that included Pedro Calderón de la Barca and was also the possessor of a notable collection of paintings, including at one time Velázquez's *Las hilanderas* (Caturla; Elliott 1963, 387n. 3, 454; Cruickshank; Varey 1986; Elliott 1986, 421, 644). The lessee of 1651–55, Don Bernardo de Villavelarde, is a much less well-known figure (Varey and Shergold 1987, 53–54). The notary before whom the documentation was drawn up, Juan García de Albertos, had himself very close association with the theaters. During the period following the total closure of the *corrales de comedias,* he had taken up six short leases of the two theaters between Lent 1649 and 29 May 1652 and had been the guarantor of the lease of Juan Núñez de Prado for Lent 1650 (Varey and Shergold 1987, 34, 126–37, 193). On 29 May 1639, he became the first *escribano de teatros,* or official theater notary (Varey and Shergold 1971, 89–91).

The present essay arises from a preliminary survey of the surviving documents in the Archivo Histórico de Protocolos de Madrid drawn up before Juan García de Albertos. It provides more precise information than was hitherto available about the seating accommodation in the two commercial theaters—particularly the *taburetes,* renewed in 1652—and about the prices charged for the various localities, the social background of those who took up extended leases, and their relationship with other persons associated in various ways with the theater business.

Works Cited

Allen, John J. 1983. *The Reconstruction of a Spanish Golden Age Playhouse: El Corral del Príncipe 1583–1744.* Gainesville: University Presses of Florida.

Caturla, María Luisa de. 1948. "El coleccionista madrileño don Pedro de Arce, que poseyó *Las hilanderas,* de Velázquez." *Archivo español de arte* 21:292–304.

Cruickshank, Don William. 1968. "A Contemporary of Calderón." *Modern Language Review* 63:864–68.

Davis, Charles, and J. E. Varey. 1991. "The *taburetes* and *lunetas* of the Madrid *corrales de comedias:* Origins and Evolution." *Bulletin of Hispanic Studies* 68:125–38.

Diccionario de autoridades. [1726–39] 1984. Madrid: Gredos.

Elliott, J. H. 1963. *The Revolt of the Catalans: A Study in the Decline of Spain (1598–1640).* Cambridge: Cambridge University Press.

———. 1986. *The Count-Duke of Olivares: The Statesman in an Age of Decline.* New Haven, Conn.: Yale University Press.

Shergold, N. D. 1989. *Fuentes para la historia del teatro en España.* Vol. 10, *Los corrales de comedias de Madrid: 1632–1745. Reparaciones y obras nuevas. Estudio y documentos.* London: Tamesis Books.

Shergold, N. D., and J. E. Varey, eds. 1985. *Fuentes para la historia del teatro en España.* Vol. 2, *Genealogía, origen y noticias de los comediantes de España.* London: Tamesis Books.

Varey, J. E. 1985. "Catalina de Acosta and Her Effigy: vv. 1865–68 and the Date of Calderón's *Casa con dos puertas.*" In *Iberia: Literary and Historical Issues. Studies in Honour of Harold V. Livermore,* edited by R. O. W. Goertz, 107–15. Calgary: Calgary University Press.

———. 1986. "An Additional Note on Pedro de Arce." *Iberoromania* 23:204–9.

Varey, J. E., and N. D. Shergold. 1960. "Datos históricos sobre los primeros teatros de Madrid: Prohibiciones de autos y comedias y sus consecuencias (1644–1651)." *Bulletin hispanique* 62:286–325.

———. 1971. *Fuentes para la historia del teatro en España.* Vol. 3, *Teatros y comedias en Madrid: 1600–1650. Estudio y documentos.* London: Tamesis Books.

———. 1973. *Fuentes para la historia del teatro en España.* Vol. 4, *Teatros y comedias en Madrid: 1651–1665. Estudio y documentos.* London: Tamesis Books.

———. 1974. *Fuentes para la historia del teatro en España.* Vol. 5, *Teatros y comedias en Madrid: 1666–1687. Estudio y documentos.* London: Tamesis Books.

———. 1987. *Fuentes para la historia del teatro en España.* Vol. 13, *Los arriendos de los corrales de comedias de Madrid: 1587–1719. Estudio y documentos.* London: Tamesis Books.

Appendix 1

Benches

Benches marked with an asterisk in the following table have been conjecturally assigned to the first or second row, on the basis of the price per seat in the absence of an explicit indication in the documents. The abbreviation *mrs.* stands for *maravedís.*

Bench	Lessee	No. of seats	Price per year (*reales*)	Document
CORRAL DEL PRÍNCIPE: FIRST ROW				
No. 3	Vázquez de Prada	1	73, 17 *mrs.*	Doc. 14
No. 10	Miranda	2	147	Doc. 12
No. 16*	Daza	2	147	Doc. 8
No. 17	Ramírez de Medrano/Mesa		220	Doc. 1
CORRAL DE LA CRUZ: FIRST ROW				
No. 4	Vázquez de Prada	1	73, 17 *mrs.*	Doc. 14
No. 8	Ramírez de Medrano/Mesa		220	Doc. 1
No. 9*	Daza	2	147	Doc. 8
No. 15	Miranda	2	147	Doc. 12
No. 25	Vázquez Garay, luego Daza	1	73, 11 *mrs.*	Docs. 10 & 16
CORRAL DEL PRÍNCIPE: SECOND ROW				
No. 10	Valladolid y Canedo	4	200	Doc. 3
No. 14	Vázquez Garay, luego Daza	1	50	Docs. 10 & 16
No. 15	Cartagena	3	150	Doc. 7
CORRAL DE LA CRUZ: SECOND ROW				
No. 8	Cartagena	2	100	Doc. 7
No. 13	Valladolid y Canedo	4	200	Doc. 3
No. 19*	Torronjeras		150	Doc. 11

Appendix 2

Documents

In the following documents, the norms of transcription employed in the series *Fuentes para la historia del teatro en España* have generally been followed. Capitalization and punctuation have been regularized and the use of single and double consonants modernized. Accents are reproduced (as a modern acute accent) if they occur in the original document and would occur in modern Spanish in the same position. Obsolete accents have been removed; no accents have been added. Cardinal numbers up to and including eleven are reproduced in words (except the numbers of benches and *taburetes*), and those above eleven in figures. Abbreviations in the original documents are expanded. "Su Majestad" has been abbreviated to "S.M.," and "Archivo Histórico de Protocolos de Madrid" to "AHPM."

No. 1. 1651.

22 December. "Sepan quantos esta carta de obligacion vieren como yo, Diego Ramirez de Medrano [?], Pagador de los Reales Consexos de S.M., otorgo por esta carta que me obligo de dar y pagar y que dare y pagare realmente y con efeto a don Bernardo de Villavelarde, a cuyo cargo esta el arrendamiento de los corrales de las comedias, y a quien en su nombre fuere parte, conviene a sauer, 160 ducados castellanos en moneda de vellon vsual y corriente al tienpo de la paga, los quales pagare por el arrendamiento del vanco de la primera orden del Corral del Principe que es el 17 y del vanco 8 de dicha primera orden del Corral de la Cruz, que los e de tener durante los quatro años de su arrendamiento en anbos corrales para ocuparlos en los dias de comedias nueuas no representadas y dias de entradas de autores en la forma y como an estado sienpre en arrendamiento, que los dichos 160 ducados corresponden a 20 ducados de cada vanco por año, que anbos bancos hazen 40 ducados en cada vn año y todos quatro años los dichos 160 ducados, y los dichos quatro años comenzaron a correr desde 1° de dizienbre deste presente año de la fecha desta y se cunpliran fin de nouienbre del año que verna de 1656 [*sic*, for "1655"], y me obligo de los pagar, 20 ducados luego de contado y otros 20 cunplidos seis meses deste arrendamiento, y en esta forma en pagos anticipados e de pagar hasta acauarse el dicho arrendamiento de los corrales, a que me obligo con mi persona y vienes auidos y por auer . . . [legal formulae] . . . ante el presente scriuano publico en la villa de Madrid a 22 dias del mes de dizienbre de 1651 años, siendo testigos don Antonio de Morales, don Juan de Guzman y Seuastian de la Parra, estantes en esta Corte, y el otorgante, a quien doy fee conosco, y lo firmo.—Diego Ramirez de Mesa [?].—Ante mi: Juan Garzia de Albertos."

(AHPM, Juan García de Albertos, 1651, protocolo 5.588, fols. 108r–109r)

No. 2. 1652.

11 January. Lease by Ignacio Noble from don Bernardo de Villavelarde "del taburete terzero de anbos Corrales, Prinzipe y de la Cruz, desta dicha villa, para ver sentado en ellos todas las comedias nueuas, jamas vistas ni representadas, y entradas de autores por precio de 20 ducados cada año anbos taburetes," for four years beginning 1 December 1651, "pero si se quitare la comedia por echo de S.M. no e de pagar mas de hasta el dicho dia y entonzes pagar[e] prorrata y no mas tienpo." Witnessed by don Antonio Escudero, Pedro Pérez, and Jusepe [?] Alvarez.

(AHPM, Juan García de Albertos, 1652, protocolo 5.589, fol. 9r–v)

No. 3. 1652.

13 January. Lease by don Melchor Alfonso de Valladolid y Canedo from don Bernardo de Villavelarde of "los bancos 10 del Principe y 13 del Corral de la Cruz de la segunda orden anbos, de tal forma que pueda ocupar quatro lugares para los dias de comedias nueuas y entradas de autores, que vno de los dichos quatro lugares a de ocupar en anbos vancos don Francisco Nauarro en conformidad de la orden del Sr. don Lorenzo Ramirez de Prado, del Consexo de S.M. y Juez particular de las comedias, autores y conpañias," for four years from 1 December 1651, "por prezio y quantia de 400 reales en cada vn año." Witnessed by Lorenzo Yáñez, Francisco García, and don Bartolomé de Prado.

(AHPM, Juan García de Albertos, 1652, protocolo 5.589, fols. 13r–14v)

No. 4. 1652.

13 January. Lease by don Alonso de Pareja de Rabago from don Bernardo de Villavelarde of "el taburete quinto de anbos Corrales del Principe y de la Cruz para que los ocupe en los dias de comedias nueuas, jamas vistas ni representadas, y entradas de autores," for four years from 1 December 1651, "por precio de 20 ducados en cada vn año a 10 ducados cada taburete." Witnessed by Simón Centón, Diego Osorio, and Lorenzo Yáñez.

(AHPM, Juan García de Albertos, 1652, protocolo 5.589, fol. 15r–v)

No. 5. 1652.

13 January. Lease by Simón Centón from don Bernardo de Villavelarde of "el taburete segundo de anbos Corrales Principe y de la Cruz para que le ocupe en los dias de comedias nueuas, jamas vistas ni representadas, y entradas de autores," for four years from 1 December 1651, "por precio de 20 ducados en cada vn año a 10 ducados cada taburete." Witnessed by don Alonso de Pareja, Diego Osorio, and Lorenzo Yáñez.

(AHPM, Juan García de Albertos, 1652, protocolo 5.589, fol. 16r–v)

No. 6. 1652.

18 January. Lease by don Alonso de Hoyos Montoya, "Contador de resultas de S.M.," from don Bernardo de Villavelarde of "el taburete quarto de anbos Corrales del Principe y del Corral de la Cruz," for four years from 1 December 1651, "por precio de 20 ducados en cada vn año en los taburetes a 10 ducados por año cada vno para que en ellos bea todas las comedias nueuas, nunca vistas ni representadas, y para los dias de entradas de autores." Witnessed by don Pedro de Arce, don Pedro Báez de Guzmán, and don Gregorio Manzano.

(AHPM, Juan García de Albertos, 1652, protocolo 5.589, fol. 20r–v)

No. 7. 1652.

18 January. Lease by Pedro de Cartagena from don Bernardo de Villavelarde of "el banco 15 de segunda orden del Corral del Principe y el 8 de dicha segunda orden del

Corral de la Cruz," for four years from 1 December 1651, "para que los ocupe el del Principe con el Contador Gabriel Marcos y Francisco de Cauredes [or "Carriedes"?] y el 8 de la Cruz con el dicho Cauredes [or "Carriedes"?] que en vn banco y otro son cinco lugares a precio cada lugar de 50 reales en cada vn año que a este respeto montan 250 reales en cada vn año." Witnessed by Antonio de Rueda, don Pedro Báez de Guzmán, and Juan de Osuna.

(AHPM, Juan García de Albertos, 1652, protocolo 5.589, fol. 21r–v)

No. 8. 1652.

18 January. Lease by don Agustín Daza, Knight of the Order of Santiago, from don Bernardo de Villavelarde of "el banco 16 en el Corral del Principe y el 9 en el Corral de la Cruz para que ocupe dos lugares en los dichos vancos que se entiende dos lugares en cada vno dellos, en todos los dias de comedias nueuas, jamas vistas ni representadas, y entradas de autores," for four years from 1 December 1651, "por precio de 294 reales en cada vn año." Witnessed by Pedro Pérez, don Antonio Escudero, and Pedro Ortiz.

(AHPM, Juan García de Albertos, 1652, protocolo 5.589, fol. 22r–v)

No. 9. 1652.

18 January. Lease by Pedro Ortiz from don Bernardo de Villavelarde of "el taburete 11 de anbos Corrales Principe y de la Cruz," for four years from 1 December 1651, "para que le ocupe en todos los dias de comedias nueuas, nunca vistas ni representadas, y entradas de autores, por precio de 20 ducados en cada vn año a 10 ducados cada vno." Witnessed by Pedro Pérez, don Antonio Escudero, and don Juan Vázquez.

(AHPM, Juan García de Albertos, 1652, protocolo 5.589, fol. 23r–v)

No. 10. 1652.

18 January. Lease by don Juan Vázquez Garay from don Bernardo de Villavelarde of "vn lugar en el banco 14 de segunda orden del Corral del Principe y otro lugar en el banco 25 de primera orden del Corral de la Cruz para que dichos lugares los ocupe en los dias de comedias nueuas, jamas vistas ni representadas, y en los dias de entradas de autores," for four years from 1 December 1651, "por prezio y a razon de 50 reales el asiento de vanco segundo en cada vn año y el lugar del banco de primera orden de la Cruz a razon de 73 reales y 11 maravedís cada año." Witnessed by Pedro Pérez, don Antonio Escudero, and Pedro Ortiz.

(AHPM, Juan García de Albertos, 1652, protocolo 5.589, fol. 24r–v)

No. 11. 1652.

19 January. Lease by Miguel de Torronjeras from don Bernardo de Villavelarde of "el banco 19 del Corral de la Cruz" for four years from 1 December 1651, "por precio de 150

reales en cada vn año, para que le ocupe en todos los dias de comedias nueuas, xamas vistas ni representadas, y entradas de autores." Witnessed by don Antonio Escudero, Jerónimo Medina, and Cristóbal de Torres.

(AHPM, Juan García de Albertos, 1652, protocolo 5.589, fol. 25r–v)

No. 12. 1652.

22 January. Lease by don Juan de Miranda, "Escriuano de Camara del Real Consejo de Guerra," from don Bernardo de Villavelarde of "dos lugares en el banco 10 de primera orden del Corral del Principe y otros dos en el 15 de dicha primera orden del Corral de la Cruz, para que los ocupe en todos los dias de comedias nueuas, jamas vistas ni representadas, y entradas de autores," for four years from 1 December 1651, "por precio de 294 reales en cada vn año." Witnessed by Juan Rodríguez, Jacinto de Salazar, and Francisco de Pinón.

(AHPM, Juan García de Albertos, 1652, protocolo 5.589, fol. 26r–v)

No. 13. 1652.

26 January. Lease by don Francisco de Aldana, "criado de la Reyna nuestra Señora," from don Bernardo de Villavelarde of "el taburete 12 de anvos Corrales del Principe y de la Cruz, para que los ocupe en todos los dias de comedias nueuas, nunca vistas ni representadas, y entradas de autores," for four years from 1 December 1651, "por precio de 20 ducados en cada vn año." Witnessed by Pedro Pérez, don Antonio Escudero, and Martín de Arguinao.

(AHPM, Juan García de Albertos, 1652, protocolo 5.589, fol. 27r–v)

No. 14. 1652.

5 February. Lease by don Sebastián Vázquez de Prada from don Bernardo de Villavelarde of "vn lugar en el banco terzero de primera orden en el Corral del Principe y otro lugar en el banco quarto de primera orden en el de la Cruz, para que los ocupe en todos los dias de comedias nueuas, nunca vistas ni representadas, y entradas de autores," for four years from 1 December 1651, "por prezio de 147 reales en cada vn año anbos lugares." Witnessed by Pedro Giraldo, Gabriel Sedeño, and don Antonio Escudero.

(AHPM, Juan García de Albertos, 1652, protocolo 5.589, fol. 32r–v)

No. 15. 1652.

30 April. Lease by don Jacinto de Lemus, Knight of the Order of Santiago, from don Bernardo de Villavelarde of "los banquillos de ambos corrales que son los que tenia el Secretario Melchor Moran que es de vn lugar cada vno, y los a de ocupar en todos los dias de comedias nuebas, jamas bistas ni representadas, y entradas de autores," from 1 May 1652 to 30 November 1655, at 147 *reales de vellón* per year. Witnessed by don Antonio Escudero, Antonio de Almanza, and Pedro de Miranda.

(AHPM, Juan García de Albertos, 1652, protocolo 5.589, fol. 151r–v)

No. 16. 1653. (See also documents 4 and 5.)

4 December. Lease by don Agustín Daza, Knight of the Order of Santiago, from don Bernardo de Villavelarde of the "asiento que estaba repartido a don Juan Bazquez en el banco de la primera orden del Corral del Principe y en el banco de la primera orden del Corral de la Cruz en la misma forma a que estoi obligado para los demas lugares de los dichos bancos y para los dias de comedias nuebas y entradas de autor," until 30 November 1655. Witnessed by don Antonio Escudero, Pedro Pérez, and Felipe Benito.

(AHPM, Juan García de Albertos, 1653, protocolo 5.590, fol. 195r–v)

Teresa J. Kirschner

Typology of Staging in Lope de Vega's Theater

he connection between the staging and the dramatic structure of the plays of the Spanish Golden Age theater is a topic that, until now, has hardly been studied. Within this large framework, my essay will focus on an analysis of the visual signs (set, costumes, movement, gestures, lighting) and the acoustic signs (music, noise, voices, songs) as manifested in Lope de Vega's national-historical-legendary *comedias*. This group of plays,[1] due to its thematic and conceptual variety, is particularly appropriate for the present research project, since many of the *comedias* it incorporates fall within the category of *comedias de cuerpo,* named thus by Suárez de Figueroa in 1617 because their staging often required an elaborate scenic apparatus. These plays supposedly contrast with the *comedias de ingenio,* which need no complicated stage machinery or scenery (74).

However, my idea of staging goes beyond a purely mechanical aspect. It implies the reading of the theatrical sign as the manifestation of a multiplicity of stimuli that, when superimposed, create a new and subtler meaning. By means of a semiotic approach, I will thus examine the extratextual and extraverbal signs of the dramatic production, the "physicity" of the scenic creation, to use José María Díez Borque's terminology (107). I will also study, bearing in mind the subdivisions already established by Alfredo Hermenegildo, the dramatic signs that determine the scenery and the physical aspect of the characters, as well as the signs that indicate both implicitly and explicitly the iconic presence of objects (Hermenegildo, 710).

When delineating the different connections between the spectacular elements and the structure of the plays, I have kept in mind the relationship between what is seen, what is heard, and what is said on stage, as well as the effect created by such a relationship in the spectator. This has led me to identify four categories, which I will define below through the discussion of specific examples and which I have named symbolic staging, articulatory staging, spectacular staging, and totalizing staging, the latter being a metastaging that absorbs the functions of the three preceding categories.

Symbolic Staging

Lope often exteriorizes the mental processes of dreaming or thinking by representing on stage what is dreamed or imagined by his characters (Kirschner 1989). In *Los hechos de Garcilaso de la Vega y el moro Tarfe,* the character of Garcilaso expresses in a monologue his anguish at not having accomplished "outstanding and famous enterprises," ending with the following verses: "Sobre esta verde hierba quiero echarme, / pues agrada a la vista su frescura; / que el trabajo pesado de lo hecho, / hace que el sueño rinda al laso pecho" (fol. 20r). To this implicit stage direction expressing the character's intention to lie down on the grass and go to sleep is added the explicit one, "Echase a dormir" (fol. 20r). Furthermore, in case the public is not yet convinced that Garcilaso indeed has fallen asleep, the first words that Fame addresses to him when she enters the stage are "Dormido joven," which reiterates the idea of his sleeping, followed by "que en el alma velas" (fol. 20r), which introduces the idea of his dreaming.

Fame appears on the top of the wall playing the trumpet (fol. 20r). The sound of the trumpet attracts the spectator's attention to the very entry of the character Fame, but more important still, the sound marks the beginning and end of the dream itself, so that when Fame leaves, Garcilaso awakens, as it is explicitly explained: "Vase la Fama tañendo la trompeta, y levántase Garcilaso al ruido" (fol. 20v).

In this manner, Garcilaso's subconscious wish to become famous is expressed by a dreamt image, embodied in the character Fame. The metaphoric resounding of his renown and glory, which fills everyone with awe (fol. 20r), is duplicated by the blaring sound of the trumpet. Othón Arróniz, when discussing staging techniques between 1580 and 1620, points out the use of the corridor above the dressing area, called "muro" or "muralla" (163–64; 189–90). Thus, one can see the sleeping body at the stage level, while the representation of what he is imagining takes place higher up on the first-floor corridor. This staging establishes the synecdochic spatial connotation of a physical and corporeal floor-leveled "below" with an "above," the high and privileged area where the metaphysical, ethereal, and supernatural operate.

We can associate the relationship—view of the wall/presence of the character Fame/sound of the trumpet—to the psychological context of Garcilaso's inner world, and we can establish in the same manner a parallel correlation with the external world that surrounds him. Within this reified context, the wall refers to the siege of the city of Santa Fe, and the sound of the trumpet alludes to the army's alert. We can thus see why Garcilaso says when he wakes up: "O estoy soñando o en el real cristiano / al arma tocan" (fol. 21v).

Therefore Fame has a denotative function, not only in relation to Garcilaso de la Vega's aspirations but also in the foreshadowing of his heroic deeds. She proclaims the national quest from the dominant power point of view, since the fight between Garcilaso and Tarfe is emblematic of the fight between Moors and Christians. Thus Fame, when appearing high up on the wall, is predicting the eventual triumph of the Christians over the Moors, which has its reverberations toward the future, toward a possible victory over the non-Catholic infidels in Lope's historical times. The following verses, which close the parenthetical scene of the dream, confirm what has been said: "¡Oh! Aguarde el fiero bárbaro inhumano / que Santa Fe, con su española hueste, / puede vencer, y el mundo irá ganando / el poder del Católico Fernando" (fol. 21v).

Garcilaso's dream could have simply been told in a long tirade, as is the case in other *comedias*. Its staging by means of a *"microauto"* inserted in the play is symbolic of the force of the desires hidden within Garcilaso's soul; at the same time, it contributes to the spectator's more active participation in the celebration of a glorious collective future. However, this type of static and abstract staging does not affect the dramatic action at the level of plot except in a focalizing process, similar to description's function in narrative.

In *El último godo,* there is a setting that illustrates another aspect of this same type of staging. La Cava, Count Julian's daughter, after being dishonored, commits suicide on stage by jumping from a tower (act 2, fol. 395). The tower ("la torre") is the corridor above the corridor of the wall previously mentioned. The elevation of this second level in relation to the stage floor is thus equivalent to the elevation of a second story (Ruano de la Haza, 91). The tension of the fatal jump is emphasized by the comments of Julian and the Moor Tarife from the stage floor while looking up at La Cava, who is at the tower, well above them.

"Tente, tente," cries Julian, while Tarife explicitly states the nature of her movement by saying: "¡Echose!" Julian laments his daughter's death when he says: "¡Ay cielo!" Tarife comments more graphically: "Hecha pedazos está con mi esperanza en el suelo" (fol. 396).

But in spite of the fact that Lope the playwright wants to exploit the sensationalist effect of a fall that requires a specific technique (what today we call a special effect), Lope the stagehand wants to protect the actress portraying La Cava and inserts a very funny stage direction: "Echase allá detrás del teatro, porque acá sería lástima, que se haría mucho mal" (fol. 396). The "here" ("acá") refers to the part of the stage visible to the spectator, while the "back there" ("allá detrás") refers to the part behind the curtains that composed the backdrop and also covered the entrance to the dressing room.

La Cava's physical fall (just like Melibea's) externalizes her moral fall, which also evokes Spain's political fall under the Goths. This movement is again a synecdochic movement, from up above at the tower to down below. Both La Cava and Spain are dismembered, dishonored, raped, and invaded, torn to pieces like Tarife's love. Just as in the case of *Los hechos de Garcilaso,* the staging parallels the dramatic action and fixes it in a visual image that reproduces the canonized official interpretation of some supposedly historicopolitical events of the past.

These two different examples of symbolic staging demonstrate Lope's wide use of it. This type of staging mirrors or reproduces an attribute of a character or a thematic-ideologic motif by either a process of abstraction or its reversal, based on a process of externalization and reification.

Articulatory Staging

Articulatory staging is mainly linked to the mechanics of plot exposition and development. This kind of staging usually influences the very rhythm of the development of the dramatic action. In *El casamiento en la muerte,* Bernardo del Carpio (illegitimate son of Count Don Sancho and Doña Jimena, sister of King Alfonse) struggles to free his father from the imprisonment imposed by the King in order to legitimize his own birth with the marriage of his parents. This personal quest, addressed in the title itself, is intertwined with the realm's divisive fights to control the crown. Bernardo, the redoubtable champion of the Leonese military victories, maintains an attitude that is both reticent and honorable toward his king, similar to that of the Cid and characteristic of a good knight toward a bad lord. From the time Bernardo appears on stage with a banner painted with his father's effigy, to whom he refers as an "innocent prisoner" (2, fol. 52v) (surely another incidence of symbolic staging), and with every new victorious undertaking, he asks the King for his father's release. Throughout the *comedia,* the King promises Bernardo time and time again that he will free his father (fol. 52r), but he repeatedly fails to keep his promise.

Lope purposely leaves the plot solution open until the end of the third act, when Bernardo announces to his companions: "El conoció mi razón, / y como Rey obligado, / libre a mi padre me ha dado, / y hoy le saco de prisión" (3, fol. 73r). Upon these words, the warden says: "Tira, Bernardo, esa puerta / y el paño de esa cortina; / verás lo que has deseado" (fol. 73r). Bernardo and the public think that the King has finally granted the Count his freedom. However, this implicit instruction to open the supposed door of the prison, represented here by the curtain, is counterbalanced by the following explicit stage direction: "Descubren una cortina, y ve Bernardo al Conde muerto, sentado en una silla" (fol. 73r). When confronted with the unexpected sight of his dead father, Bernardo, in a series of heartbreaking speeches, expresses his pain as well as his despair at not being able to remedy his bastardy.

The dramatic tension of this scene and the resolution of the play are thus brought about by the power of the delayed action and the surprising qualities of the staging. By keeping the dead father behind the curtain, out of the hero's and the public's sight, Lope has not only increased the expectation of the public, whom he has to keep interested; he has also increased the dramatic tension of the *comedia.* With the anticipation of what seems to be a certain happy ending, he magnifies Bernardo's and the public's disappointment at the duplicity of the King. Moreover, if the false solution rested on a curtain, the real final resolution of the *comedia* depends upon a head's movement. The cryptic title finally becomes clear. Bernardo moves the head of his dead father ("Toma la cabeza con la mano y hácela bajar," says the explicit stage direction), so that he says yes and agrees to the marriage vows with his mother (fol. 74v). The nodding movement of the father's head establishes the married status of Doña Jimena and the legitimation of her son, Bernardo. Thus, the main plot is resolved by means of this articulatory staging based on the surprising effect of drawing the curtain and on the silent gesture of a head. Its retardatory power plays a decisive role in the intensification of the total impact of the dramatic action on the spectator.

Another example of an articulatory staging is in *El asalto de Mastrique por el Príncipe de Parma.* While the staging had a delaying function in the play just discussed, it produces a multiple perspectivism in this one. As we shall see, this is a complex and daring use of an articulatory staging that seems to foreshadow Valle-Inclán's vision of a synchronic time in a limitless space.

The first act of the play opens with the exposition of a twofold point of view: that of the privates, who complain about the hard work required in the war and about the penury and hunger they are experiencing (fol. 53v); and that of the officers, who are aware of the situation but lack the necessary financial means to remedy it (fols. 55r–55v). The latter, to abort a possible mutiny, decide in private council to assault and plunder Maastricht in order to give the soldiers access to booty and so remedy their needs.

Lope presents the arguments of the conflict (the reasons for the unhappiness of the soldiers and the means to remedy the situation by the chiefs) simultaneously by superimposing two settings, which creates a spatial and temporal linking of two realities set apart. Lope thus attempts to reproduce, as concisely and effectively as possible, the multiplicity of actions that take place in the course of some hours in different parts of the camp. These linked situations require action and reaction from each party and follow a logical chronology: while rumors are spreading throughout the camp about the troop's unrest regarding the future success of the military campaign, the prince of Parma meets with his counselors in a tent and makes a decision that will be announced subsequently by different messengers across the camp.

But the order of representation in the theater normally requires seriality, which Lope alters by trying to represent the temporal and spacial contiguousness implied in "while." This way, while the soldier Campuzano on stage describes to his army companions the entrance of each of the commanders into a tent (an action that has already taken place), these army men and the spectators not only are able to see the tent on stage (probably represented by the dressing room covered by a curtain) but are also aware that the meeting itself is taking place inside. Their dialogue shows the different temporal steps through verb tenses that indicate these temporal differences. The past tenses in "Decidme a los que ha llamado" (fol. 54r), "Don Fernando . . . / es el primero que ha entrado" (fol. 54v), and "Cristóbal de Mondragón entró" (fol. 54v) operate in opposition to the present tense in sentences such as "A consejo llama ahora" (fol. 54v), "en la tienda están" (fol. 54v), "Aquí se están de gobierno" (fol. 54v), and "Que ya están todos allí" (fol. 55r).

To the superimposition of past and present and of "here" and "there" must be added the different points of view among the characters and the spectators. After the verses "Quedo; la tienda han abierto; / escuchemos desde aquí" (fol. 55r), Lope inserts the following explicit stage direction: "Córrase una tienda o cortina, y véanse sentados, el Duque de Parma, armado, con bastón y a sus lados . . ." There follows the enumeration of the same gentlemen who had previously been mentioned by Campuzano entering the tent. The stage direction continues with the indication that the soldiers should come closer to the "teatro" (fol. 55v), that is, closer to the back wall. It is, therefore, with the opening of the curtain that the council scene begins, during which the assault is decided.

This is a unique and extraordinary scene because the spectators hear and see what happens inside the tent, but the characters/soldiers that are on stage do not. They cannot hear what happens there because they do not belong to the circle of the empowered. They can only see the tent from the outside and from a distance. The soldiers now only notice the exit of the council members as before they had noticed their entrance. The next explicit stage direction says: "Ciérrese la tienda, y los soldados digan," and then the dialogue of the soldiers, which had been interrupted with the parenthetical council scene, is resumed once again: "Parece que ya se van / de la tienda," says one soldier; "El seso pierdo," says another; while a third replies, "¿Qué habrán hecho en este acuerdo?" (fol. 56r). Later on, Captain Castro will enter and announce to the soldiers what the spectators already know: the decision to attack Maastricht.

With this extremely complex articulatory staging (of which I have only pointed out the most essential traits), Lope manages to accelerate the rhythm of the exposition by grouping in one scenic nucleus elements belonging to different physical and temporal planes, and to different levels of development of the plot. With the representation of the bustle of camp life, of the ups and downs of privates' lives, and of the tensions between the different military echelons, Lope, in an enormous effort of condensation, manages to have the spectators directly participate in the deliberations of different ranks in the army, thus eliciting their admiration toward both the soldiers and the commanders involved in the attack on Maastricht. Therefore, articulatory staging can serve what may seem to be opposite functions: the opening and closing of the curtain in this *comedia* is linked to the acceleration of the action, whereas in *El casamiento en la muerte* it was linked to the delaying of the final resolution. In both works, however, this type of staging deeply affects the play's structure.

Spectacular Staging

The main function of spectacular staging is to explain, describe, or evoke, without influencing either the development of the plot or the personality of the characters. This familiar type of staging exists for the mere pleasure of the senses. With the progressive development of scenography, the use of spectacular staging has been actively maintained to the present day; it is apparent in the type of spectacles that even in Spanish are called "shows." I will examine here two opposite examples: the first one, taken from the *Comedia de Bamba,* will serve as the paradigm of a somewhat clumsy usage due to very poor scenic props; the second one, based on *Carlos V en Francia,* will serve as the perfect model of a grandiose staging requiring considerable apparatus and expense.

In the first *comedia,* a slave warns Ervigio that he is going to poison King Bamba and usurp the Goth's crown. He then predicts the future of the kingdom, from Count Julian's vengeance and the insurrection of Pelayo to the coming of a strong Philip, second of the house of Austria (3, fol. 116v). Not satisfied with such a panegyric, Lope has the legend of La Cava painted on a canvas (fol. 117v). And, more important to this analysis, he has the canvas shown on stage and praised for its painterly qualities (fol. 118r). In a series of questions addressed by Ervigio to the slave, Lope proceeds to identify, figure by figure, what is painted on the canvas: "¿Quién es ésta que está aquí?" "¿Y aquéste . . . ?" "¿Y éste . . . ?" "¿Y esta brava escaramuza?" "¿Y estos . . . ?" (fol. 118r). Lope then has the slave read the written legend aloud, in case the public cannot or does not know how to read it, with encouraging comments such as: "The writing at the bottom can easily be read," "it can be understood with some effort," "what does it say?" "it says as follows . . . " (fol. 118r). As one can appreciate here, and in contrast to the other two types of staging already discussed, the unfolding of the canvas has little relation to the total structure of the play. The function of this spectacular staging is merely decorative and educational; it serves as a "show and tell," as a pictorial remembrance of who is who in the glorified emulation of the canonized past.

However, it is difficult to accept that one single sporadic adornment, no matter how well painted, can fully convey the message of opulence associated with the crown. The *comedia Carlos V en Francia,* on the other hand, exemplifies the ultimate spectacular staging. The whole play paints the splendors of the courtly life. As its editor, Arnold G. Reichenberger, has rightfully observed: "We should not forget that the audience had not only to hear but also to see. As the stage directions indicate, quite a bit of stately pageantry was to unfold before the eyes of the spectators who would find themselves vicariously in the presence of the high and mighty of the past" (Vega 1963, 34).

Indeed, the spectacular scenes found in this *comedia* are just too numerous to be enumerated, let alone discussed. Suffice it to say that in one scene after another the emphasis is placed on showing the ceremonial richness of kings and princes of the church as closely as possible. Thus Pope Paul III and Emperor Charles V, accompanied by their guards, courtiers, and musicians (1, 83), as well as the king of France displaying the Golden Fleece (1, 88), the grandees and the cardinals of Spain (2, 112), the imperial guard dressed in garb as sumptuous as possible ("guarda de alabarderos con librea, si la hubiere") (2, 116), and the French noblemen march from one end of the stage to the other or slowly descend long staircases step by step in prolonged processions and parades in order fully to display their clothes and banners. The play itself culminates in a magnificent final scene that reproduces the pomp of the historic ceremonial welcoming given to Charles V on his arrival in France. Charles, like Caesar, passes through a triumphal arch accompanied by the king and queen of France while their courtiers comment: "¡Brabo triumpho!" "¡Heroyca empresa!" (3, 186–87).

Onto this triumphant courtly procession Lope superimposes a symbolic staging by means of the appearance of the allegoric figures Spain and France in the discovery space. Their embrace symbolizes the political truce between the two countries (3, 187). Lope thus wants to make sure that, beyond the rapture of ceremonial splendor, wealth of costumes, and richness of representation, his audience understands the historical importance of Charles V's trip to France.

Totalizing Staging

Totalizing staging assumes several of the functions of the other three types of scenification previously discussed. It is hardly noticeable because it is deeply embedded in the plot and in the development of the dramatic action. However, its effect is no less important just because it is less apparent. In a sense, totalizing staging is the opposite of spectacular staging, which, as we have already observed, functions so openly on the surface that the spectator is immediately aware of the technical elements used to produce it. Totalizing staging, on the other hand, functions in the underlying text and internalizes the emblematic elements within the dramatic action itself. Since this last kind of staging is interwoven with the structure and extends its effect throughout the play by means of an anaphoric web of associations, and since its explanation requires more elaboration, I will only discuss one example within this category, that of the last scene (*cuadro*) of the first act of *Fuente Ovejuna.*

The dramatic space in which this scene takes place is a solitary field somewhat distant from the brook, in the outskirts of the village of Fuenteovejuna. This natural and peaceful setting, the classic *locus amoenus,* is traditional for love scenes, and it is thus here where the first love words are exchanged between Laurencia and Frondoso. The stereotyped depiction of harmonic love will nevertheless be altered by the Commander's arrival. "Hide in those branches!" (l. 776), Laurencia tells Frondoso when she sees him coming. This implicit stage direction points out the prop needed for this scene to take place. The branches must be painted on a board or, more likely, represented by a real bush. Thus nature protects the couple by hiding Frondoso among its leaves.

Visually, the Commander's black clothing also contrasts with nature's green. It is the color of evil and death and, linked with the red color of the cross, makes Laurencia associate him with the devil (l. 814). The Cross of Calatrava on the Commander's habit is the only detail of costume that is explicitly named. Both Laurencia and Frondoso allude to it (ll. 811, 826) because it seems a discordant and contradictory sign. Its universal message of Christian love, as is pointed out throughout the *comedia* (ll. 988–94, 1628–29), does not fit with the behavior of the person wearing it.

Other than the cross, the other significant element in the characters' attire is the Commander's lack of a sword (ll. 830–31)—the sword being closely linked to his knightly status and to his participation in the war. The fact that he is not armed with a sword is explained by the presence of the crossbow (l. 820), a key accessory in the development of the dramatic action. When the Commander appears on stage, he is hunting, crossbow in hand. This is the way Laurencia interprets his demeanor when she says to Frondoso: "He must be stalking deer" (ll. 776, 810). This is confirmed by the Commander himself when he says that he is stalking "a timid little deer" (ll. 778–79). Hunting is the privileged occupation of noblemen in times of peace, and it is normal that their lord practice it while resting from the recent war. However, hunting alters the pastoral peace.

It is interesting to note that with the gesture of putting the bow on the ground, the Commander abandons the practice of hunting; he has to let the bow go in order to hold the peasant girl, who resists "a la práctica de manos" (l. 816). It is also important to notice that Frondoso leaves his hiding place not when the Commander tries to rape Laurencia but when he sees the crossbow unattended. The explicit stage direction says: "Frondoso enters, and picks up the crossbow" (107). With the crossbow in his power, Frondoso can protect himself and Laurencia. As a consequence, the deep humiliation the Commander feels has more to do with having been unarmed by a peasant boy than with not having been able to enjoy Laurencia. Throughout the play, the Commander will remember "this affront" (l. 855), always alluding to the loss of the crossbow: "And that Frondoso, is he to keep my bow and go unpunished?" (ll. 1031–32; also ll. 1042, 1604).

However, this hunting scene is neither the portrayal of an aristocratic pastime nor the exposition of the attempted rape of a specific character in the play but rather is, above all, the symbolic staging of sexual appetite (Gerli, 55; Weber de Kurlat, 679). The hunter symbolizes the insatiable incontinence of one's desires (Cirlot, 122). The displacement of the big game hunt in favor of the erotic hunt is clearly prepared by the sequence "corzo" / "corcillo temeroso" / "bella gama" / "bella Laurencia" (ll. 776–87). The jump from the animal deer to the person Laurencia is prepared by the diminutive "-illo" and the adjective "temeroso," which, even though grammatically masculine, can be equally associated with deer and with Laurencia, finally to arrive at the grammatically feminine "bella" and "gama," which clearly indicate Laurencia.

Progressively, Lope has been establishing the relationship war/hunt/sex to the point of making it obvious in this scene by visually materializing the sexual assault. The Commander had previously referred to Laurencia as "hermosa fiera" (l. 601) (literally: sightly wild beast), "fiera" being the word that is also used to name a big game animal (Covarrubias, under "caça"). The welcoming song included the verbs "rendir," as in the expression "rendir las tierras" (l. 593). "Rendir," according to Covarrubias, means "sujetar," and thus the "rendido" is the "vencido y sujeto." When Flores forced Laurencia and Pascuala to enter the Commander's house, Laurencia told him: "No nos agarre" (l. 612); and when in this scene the Commander tells Laurencia to give in and surrender (l. 823), he is holding her with both hands. The concupiscence had already been established with the double meaning of "carne" in the welcoming scene and with the following comments, which reveal its sexual connotation: "¡También venís presentadas / con lo demás" (ll. 619–20) and "¿No basta a vueso señor / tanta carne presentada?" (ll. 623–24).

After the staging of the hunt and during the first public confrontation between the peasants and the Commander, the latter renews his complaints by once more using the sexual symbol of the chase to refer to Laurencia: "Quisiera en esta ocasión, / que la hiciéredes pariente, / a una liebre que por pies / por momentos se me va" (ll. 959–62).

Juan-Eduardo Cirlot links the hare to lust and to fertility and thus considers it a symbol with an inseparable feminine character (278), and Raymond Barbera demonstrates that the hare, from medieval times, alluded graphically to the feminine sexual organ (160). Also, as I have shown elsewhere, Lope always uses the image of the hunt to refer to the sexual act (Kirschner 1993, 555).

The persecutory chase of this scene will be reproduced twice in the *comedia*, thus linking it further to the unfolding of the plot. There is a movement progressing from the open attack on the couple and the emblematic sexual assault, to the assaults and attacks on the peasants, and finally to the sung romance of "Al val de Fuenteovejuna," which mythifies the events represented on stage and witnessed by the spectators. Both assaults—the one on Laurencia in the first act and that on Jacinta in the second act—take place, significantly, in the same dramatic space. "Hanme contado que Frondoso, / aquí en el prado, / para librarte, Laurencia, / le puso al pecho una jara" (ll. 1150–53), says Mengo just before his fight with the Commander's servants. The relationship of the first act: Commander/Laurencia/ Frondoso/crossbow is duplicated in the second act with servants/Jacinta/Mengo/ sling. However, the sling is not an effective weapon next to the servants' swords; Mengo will end the quarrel beaten and Jacinta raped.

The song "Al val de Fuenteovejuna," which is sung toward the end of the second act, applies consequently not only to Laurencia but also to Jacinta and to all the women in Fuenteovejuna who have been subjected to the Commander's advances. Therefore, the totalizing staging of the hunt scene, with the adoption of symbolic, descriptive, and articulating functions, permeates and alters the very fiber of the *comedia* in its entirety.

To conclude, beginning with the premise that demands a conceptual differentiation between telling and representing, I hope to have shown the importance of scenic staging in determining dramatic structure. I hope also to have shown that the study of Lope de Vega's theater requires the inclusion of the analysis of extraverbal and extratextual signs because these audiovisual elements are deeply embedded in the complexity of the dramatic form and play a significant role in his dramaturgy.

Notes

A shorter version of this paper was presented in Spanish at the meeting of the Modern Language Association in Chicago, December 1990.

1.   Within these, we will study here the following plays: *El asalto de Mastrique por el Príncipe de Parma, Comedia de Bamba, Los hechos de Garcilaso, El último godo, El casamiento en la muerte, Carlos V en Francia,* and *Fuente Ovejuna.* The English translations of Lope's texts are my own, with the exception of *Fuente Ovejuna,* where I follow Victor Dixon's translation.

Works Consulted

Arróniz, Othón. 1977. *Teatros y escenarios del Siglo de Oro.* Madrid: Gredos.

Barbera, Raymond E. 1968. "An Instance of Medieval Iconography in *Fuenteovejuna.*" *Romance Notes* 10:160–62.

Cirlot, Juan-Eduardo. 1982. *Diccionario de símbolos.* 5th ed. Barcelona: Ed. Labor.

Covarrubias Horozco, Sebastián de. 1611. *Tesoro de la lengua castellana o española.* Madrid: Luis Sánchez.

Díez Borque, José María. 1989. "Teatralidad y denominación genérica en el siglo XVI: Propuestas de investigación." In *El mundo del teatro español en su Siglo de Oro: Ensayos dedicados a John E. Varey,* edited by J. M. Ruano de la Haza, 101–18. Ottawa: Dovehouse Publications.

Gerli, E. Michael. 1979. "The Hunt of Love: The Literalization of a Metaphor in *Fuenteovejuna.*" *Neophilologus* 63:54–58.

Hermenegildo, Alfredo. 1986. "Acercamiento al estudio de las didascalias del teatro castellano primitivo: Lucas Fernández." In *Actas del Octavo congreso de la Asociación internacional de hispanistas,* edited by A. David Kossoff et al., 1:709–27. Madrid: Castalia.

Kirschner, Teresa J. 1989. "El 'velo' del sueño y de la imaginación en el teatro histórico-legendario de Lope de Vega." In *El mundo del teatro español en su Siglo de Oro: Ensayos dedicados a John E. Varey,* edited by J. M. Ruano de Haza, 197–213. Ottawa: Dovehouse Publications.

————. 1993. "El discurso sexual como subversión del amor idealizado en el teatro histórico-nacional de Lope de Vega." In *Estado actual de los estudios sobre el Siglo de Oro (Actas del II congreso internacional de hispanistas del Siglo de Oro),* edited by Manuel García Martín, 2:549–59. Salamanca: Ed. Universidad de Salamanca.

Ruano de la Haza, José. 1988. "Hacia una metodología para la reconstrucción de la puesta en escena de la comedia en los teatros comerciales del siglo XVII." *Criticón* 42:81–102.

Suárez de Figueroa, Cristóbal. 1913. *El pasagero: Advertencia utilísima a la vida humana.* Edited by Francisco Rodríguez Marín. Madrid: Biblioteca Renacimiento.

Vega, Lope de. 1603a. *El casamiento en la muerte.* In *Las comedias del famoso poeta Lope de Vega. Parte 1.* Zaragoza: Angelo Tauanno (Bib. Nac., Madrid, R-13852).

————. 1603b. *Comedia de Bamba.* In *Las comedias del famoso poeta Lope de Vega. Parte 1.* Zaragoza: Angelo Tauanno (Bib. Nac., Madrid, R-13852).

————. 1614. *El asalto de Mastrique por el Príncipe de Parma.* In *Doze comedias de Lope de Vega Carpio. Quarta parte.* Madrid: Miguel de Siles librero (Bib. Nac., Madrid, R-25608).

————. 1647. *El último godo.* In *Parte veinticinco. Comedias.* Zaragoza: Viuda de Pedro Verges (Bib. Nac., Madrid, R-13876).

————. 1963. *Carlos V en Francia.* Edited by Arnold G. Reichenberger. Philadelphia: University of Pennsylvania Press.

————. 1978. *Fuente Ovejuna.* Edited by Maria Grazia Profeti. Madrid: Planeta.

————. 1989. *Fuente Ovejuna.* Translated by Victor Dixon. Warminster, England: Aris and Phillips.

————. n.d. *Los hechos de Garcilaso.* Bib. Nac., Madrid, MS. 16037.

Weber de Kurlat, Frida. 1971. "La expresión de la erótica en el teatro de Lope de Vega: El caso de *Fuenteovejuna.*" In *Homenaje a José Manuel Blecua,* 673–87. Madrid: Gredos.

Louise Fothergill-Payne

Text and Spectacle of Alarcón's *El examen de maridos:* From *Comedia* to Farce

ncreasing numbers of academics now have the opportunity of seeing a dramatic text come to life thanks to the Festival of Spanish Classical Theatre held annually at Chamizal (El Paso, Texas). This experience, invaluable and rare in the world of Hispanic studies, has made many a text-bound scholar review a particular interpretation of a playwright's words but has also made some spectator-critics raise an eyebrow when confronted by the aesthetics of the director's version.

In the last few years, we have witnessed the densely emblematic and controversial interpretation of *Celestina* (1985), the subversive and sexually explicit adaptation of Tirso's *Marta la piadosa* (1986), the world-upside-down of Calderón's *El gran mercado del mundo* in which vices become virtues (1987), and the lighthearted caricature of Alarcón's *El examen de maridos* played by an all-female cast (1987).

Far from questioning a director's freedom to adapt a play for performance (Fothergill-Payne 1985), I simply want to try to pin down what happens when, as in the case of *El examen de maridos,* both the style and the genre of the original play undergo a complete transformation. I will therefore first discuss the text as it speaks from the one-dimensional page to this reader, and then describe how its performance at Chamizal struck this spectator.

The Text

Although it is not Alarcón's best-known *comedia, El examen de maridos* deserves to be taken seriously. As in *La verdad sospechosa* and *Las paredes oyen,* in this, his last play, the plot revolves around the problems of marrying the right partner. The device is a public examination of the prospective husbands declared by the first *dama* (Doña Inés), the dilemma consists of the violation of friendship when the two *galanes* (the Marqués and Conde Carlos) unwittingly at first compete for the same lady's hand, and the complication resides in malicious gossip spread around by the second *dama* (Doña Blanca) to discredit the Marqués. In turn, the denouement revolves around the issue of whether one should marry the suitor with the blameless record or the man one loves "warts and all."

These are the dramatic conflicts and moral issues suggested by the text. But there is more to a play than mere ideas. In *El examen de maridos,* language and concepts go hand in hand; in fact the play is an exuberant celebration of words—both those that are said and those that are left unsaid—of understanding and mis-understanding, of half-truth and wholesale lies, of conspiratorial innuendos, malicious gossip, and paradoxical truths. Within their dramatic conventions, all characters define themselves and each other through language alone. Indeed, dialogue, monologue, and especially asides suffice to make events plausible as each character moves from certainties to doubts and again to newly acquired certainties.

In this play, communication between the dramatis personae is entirely a mat-ter of signals, but these—and here lies the strength of *El examen de maridos*—are confused and confusing. External signals of paternal direction, peer rivalry, so-cial pressure, and especially *malas lenguas* contradict interior signals from the heart, such as loyalty and desire but also anger and revenge. How to make sense out of all these differing messages is a question of judgment, and Alarcón's *inven-tio* resides, perhaps, in the paradoxical truth that the wrong decoding of signals might produce the right message precisely because of all this searching for mean-ing in ambiguity.

The very plot of the play springs from the simple mandate of Doña Inés's father as set out in his will: "Mira lo que haces antes que te cases." Proverbs by definition are ambiguous and applicable to many different situations. Doña Inés's misguided application of her father's last words is to declare an open competition among her suitors. To this end, she compiles a written report of candidates' financial and social assets and habits. The interplay of double meaning, allusions, and veiled criticism starts when each entry is given an official designation: candidates' defects and excellence are recorded as "consultas." "Billetes" are classified as "me-moriales," while "paseos y mensajes" are entered under "recuerdos." The ex-amination, of course, offers much scope for ridiculing a bureaucratic system in which, in the words of one of the *opositores,* "La fingida hipocresía, / la industria, el cuidado, el arte / a la verdad vencerán; / más valdrá quien más engañe" (253–56).[1] Another flaw in the competition, noted by the *gracioso,* is that love does not count and that points are only given to "lo visible," leaving out "las partes interiores, / en que muchas veces vi / disimulados engaños, / que causan mayores daños / al matrimonio" (478–82).

Apart from criticizing a rigid system of promotion and preferment, this examination also serves to ridicule the vanity and self-promotion of the applicants as each presents his *papel.* Doña Inés's cynical asides—"¡Qué retórico marido!" ... "¡Qué amante tan enflautado!" ... "¡Qué meditada oración!" (438–58 passim)— leave no doubt as to her response to their hollow rhetoric and inflated egos.

But cold assessment changes into confusion when *malas lenguas* spread by Doña Blanca concerning the Marqués's running sore, bad breath, and untrustworthiness interfere with Doña Inés's own impressions. "Causóme pena escuchar / los defetos del Marqués, / y de amor sin duda es / claro indicio este pesar" (1221–24). Moreover, appearance contradicts such alleged flaws: "que las señales desmienten / defetos tan desiguales" (1457–58).

As in *La verdad sospechosa* and *Las paredes oyen,* communication in *El examen de maridos* is as much a question of understanding as it is of lending credibility or even importance to information received. And here the voice of Don Beltrán, *viejo escudero,* signals another dimension in the concept of truth. Even if the Marqués's faults were real, he advises Doña Inés, they would not be important: "Porque tener una fuente / es enfermedad, no error; / de la boca el mal olor / es natural accidente; / el mentir es liviandad / de mozo; no es maravilla, / y vendrán a corregilla / la obligación y la edad" (2187–94).

I have argued elsewhere (1983) for similar leniency in judging Don García's *defetos* in *La verdad sospechosa.* In that play, the protagonist's fabrications seem trivial compared to the lies doing the rounds in high society, lies in which the victim's honor and worldly goods are at stake. I also argue for a happy ending of *La verdad sospechosa* in light of Don García's greater suitability to Lucrecia because she, and not Jacinta, the object of his infatuation, is prepared to believe him and love him. Again, judging by what is said and especially by what is not said, Lucrecia seems more compatible with Don García, while Jacinta, so different in character to her, obviously belongs with Don Juan.

The same sort of pairing off takes place in *El examen de maridos*. The characters of Doña Inés and the Marqués, as they speak to us from the text, are similar in their earnest attempt to do the right thing, in their confusion and their mutual feelings. Last but not least, they are equal in rank, and one might even argue that "Doña Inés" and "El Marqués," the names by which they are designated in the text, are words purposely chosen because they rhyme.

Conde Carlos and Doña Blanca are equally similar but are the opposite of the Marqués and Doña Inés as a pair. Both express themselves in angry and vengeful terms when they find they are not the preferred party, and they do not hesitate to tamper with the truth if it suits their purpose. Doña Blanca's ingeniously constructed fabrications again remind us of *La verdad sospechosa* in that all these nontruths in the end land her in the arms of the marriage partner best suited to her, Conde Carlos. Ironically, her fallacious signals concerning an unhappy love affair between herself and Conde Carlos, upon reaching the latter, are immediately decoded as truths. What is more, "la fama / de que a Blanca doy cuidado" (2267–68) is enough to trigger Conde Carlos's amorous response, much to the consternation of Doña Blanca. After an initial frustration of not getting through to each other, they both end up getting the message, which is that each is to the other a means for revenge and, more importantly, that each is the answer to the other's own marriage designs. Lies thus serve the truth, just as the examination, misguided in itself, served to test feelings and identities.

The apotheosis of paradoxical truths in *El examen de maridos* takes place in its denouement when the short list of candidates is reduced to Conde Carlos and the Marqués. As a final test, they each have to prove their worth in a "competencia de ingenios," that is to say, in a debate. The topic set by Doña Inés is "si la mano debo dar / al que tengo inclinación, / aunque defetos padezca, / o si me estará más bien / que el que no los tiene, a quien / no me inclino, me merezca" (2652–57).

The debate is a splendid example of cross purposes as each pleads the other's cause. The Marqués argues in favor of perfections: "amor nace de hermosura, / y es hermoso lo perfeto" (2704–5). Conde Carlos comes out in favor of love: "Quien ama a un defetuoso / ama también sus defetos" (2870–71). The latter argument is so convincing that the jury proclaims Conde Carlos the winner. Doña Inés heroically accepts, but with regret, the outcome of her own ploy, but Conde

Carlos comes up with the ultimate logical paradox: "pues si mi parte ha vencido, / y es la parte que defiendo / la del imperfeto amado, / él [the Marqués] ha de ser vuestro dueño" (2956–59). As a last little lie to clear the way to a happy ending, Conde Carlos now signals to Doña Inés ("baste por señas deciros" [2982]) that the Marqués's faults were mere fabrications spread by a woman "por orden mía" (2986). And so *El examen de maridos* comes to its "dichoso fin," not without a humorous twist when Doña Inés inquires, "Cuando os miro sin defetos / ¿cómo, Marqués, os querré, / si os adoraba con ellos?" (3003–5).

For this reader, *El examen de maridos* is one of Alarcón's finest plays because of its harmonious blend of wit and satire, its message of true love, and the seemingly endless ambiguities of language and communication. In Alarcón's hands, language becomes a confusing and confused sign-system of *señales, señas,* and *indicios.* However, in a *comedia* there is more to language than sense and non-sense producing signals. It is also a musical instrument when different verse forms underscore moods, rhythm sets the pace, and rhyme delights the ear. As Vern Williamsen once said about translating a *comedia,* "One of the most interesting problems for me to deal with has been the polymetric versification of the Spanish originals, an element that . . . *held particular significance for its audience*" (my emphasis).

The Spectacle

El examen de maridos was performed in Chamizal by the Departamento de Producción, Dirección de Teatro y Danza of the Universidad Nacional Autónoma under the inspired direction of Germán Castillo. As is to be expected of this group, the performance was technically perfect and a highly enjoyable event.[2]

Even before the performance, rumors of an all-female cast and an irreverent treatment of the *maridos* had created a mood of joyful anticipation, which was not disappointed when the curtain went up. The otherwise bare stage was dominated by Doña Inés and her servant, both dressed in lavish period costume. Doña Inés seemed rather dolled up however, with her farthingale made to resemble a chocolate box, from which her bodice rose like a fancy knob on its lid. The sound and movement of the two figures was more puzzling, however. Doña Inés's loud wailing was accompanied by exaggerated movements of distress and solicitude on the part of the servant, who, hardly audible above all the noise, explained more to the audience than to her mistress, "Ya que tan sola has quedado / con la muerte del Marqués / tu padre, forzoso es, / señora, tomar estado" (1–4). With Doña Inés's tearful reply that she would obey her father's will in everything, pathos was established as a mood, melodrama as the chosen style of discourse, and exaggeration as the pattern of subsequent movements. When Don Beltrán made his entrance in the second scene, this initial impression was confirmed: both his appearance and movements were exaggerated to the point of ridicule. Doubled over at the waist, he ran around in little circles like a clockwork doll. The exaggeration of the minute figure was then reinforced by the enormous scroll he unwound, which contained no more than the proverb "antes que te cases mira lo que haces." Doña Inés's tearful recitation of his last words, "en lágrimas deshecho el corazón," produced the same peals of laughter in the audience as did her first loud wailing. Obviously, we were in for a great evening of unadulterated fun and ridicule.

But what was it to be: a puppet show? The rigidity of character and mechanical movements might suggest this. A cartoon? Again, the caricature of outline and synchronization of movement pointed in that direction. A *commedia dell'arte?* Possibly, given the stylized acting and acrobatic mime. Or perhaps a burlesque with its mockery of literary form? When the third scene opened with an identical old fogey, Doña Blanca's father, accompanied by young Conde Carlos all decked out in feathers, hat, and *capa y espada,* we began to detect a pattern. What we were about to see was not a *comedia* but a farce, with all its festive gut appeal but also with its hostile and aggressive undertones.

Farce, like laughter and humor, is difficult to analyze; and, being a "lower form" of theater, it has so far enjoyed far less critical attention than tragedy or comedy. The *OED*'s definition of farce as "a dramatic work (usually short) which has for its sole object to incite laughter" still holds true and will serve here as a point of departure, complemented by more recent studies (e.g., by Bentley, Styan, Milner Davis, and Bermel).

Because of the laughter it produces, a farce is used as comic relief within a play or as an *entremés* between the acts. Very seldom do we find sustained farce extended over several acts. The reason for the "usually short" duration of a farce can be found in the nature of a joke and the response it elicits, laughter. As Cuddon's *Dictionary of Literary Terms* so succinctly says, "The object of farce is to provoke mirth of the simplest and most basic kind: roars of laughter rather than smiles" (263). However, an unbroken succession of jokes is an impossible task, according to Eric Bentley: "If one succeeds very well with a first joke, the audience may get into a state of mind where anything seems funny . . . but this state of mind will not last very long unaided. And it may not be wise to try to sustain it indefinitely lest the result be sheer exhaustion" (235).

To judge by the hearty laughter of the audience preserved on the videotape, the spectators were ready to be amused at Doña Inés's first wailing at the curtain's rise. But her last wailing at the end of the last act, when faced with the inevitability of marrying Conde Carlos rather than her beloved Marqués, aroused considerably less merriment. It is possible that the director had overestimated the audience's capacity for laughter, but the reason for the onset of a certain weariness may also lie in the type of plot and characterization in real farce.

Generally, plot and characters are reduced to the simplest of motivations and conflicts in the farce. Jessica Milner Davis identifies three basic plots: "humiliation farces," in which the figure of authority is defied, deceived, and ridiculed (such as Cañizares in Cervantes's *El viejo celoso*); "deception farces," which can best be described as practical jokes practiced by *pícaros* (such as Molière's *Les Fourberies de Scapin*); and "quarrel farces" based on mistaken perceptions (such as Rueda's *El paso de los olivos*). *El examen de maridos,* in the hands of director Germán Castillo, came closest to a "quarrel farce" with its emphasis on the competition between the *opositores* at the expense of all other conflicts and values. The single-mindedness of a farcical plot is usually matched by the monomaniacal mind-set of the characters, who are little more than stock figures or caricatures of well-known types (Milner Davis, 63). But precisely because of their inelasticity, they cannot adapt to changing circumstances or make a change of heart seem plausible. Hence the lack of credibility in the portrayal of the Marqués and Conde Carlos when they become rivals despite their friendship and in the end plead each other's cause. In fact, true to their farcical nature in this production, they are each indistinguishable from the other in appearance and movement. But then, a type's behavior is meant to be repetitive and predictable; indeed, the joke very often resides in this. This tendency toward repetition is related to duplication of characters, as we saw from the similar representations of the two old men. In the farcical representation of the suitors, the same duplication takes place, whether or not they were meant to be ridiculous.

One of the reasons why farcical type characterization is so limited is simply that the short duration of the farce leaves no time to "explore their consciousness" (Milner Davis, 64). Conversely, when a farce does extend over three acts, the rigidity and duplication of character risk becoming tedious. In the staging of *El examen de maridos,* stereotyping was such that facial expression and differentiation were consciously blurred by the plumed hats, moustaches, elaborate headdress, and fans. In actual fact, as in a *commedia dell'arte,* the characters seemed to be hiding behind a mask. According to J. L. Styan, this "masking" "lends impersonality to the experience, frees the spectator from the need to sympathize, frees him to laugh, all without the tiresome restrictions of everyday life" (83). But here, precisely, lies the limitation of farce as against other forms of drama. While in comedy or tragedy one laughs or weeps in empathy with the hero, farce leaves no feeling other than the aggressive delight of witnessing "the deliberate offense to social norms" (Milner Davis, 26).

Among these, love and marriage are, of course, a perennial target, and this is what probably attracted the director to Alarcón's *El examen de maridos.* But while in Alarcón's *comedia,* as in all other Golden Age plays, the audience is confronted with a set of conflicting truths, Germán Castillo's interpretation converted Alarcón's morality into amorality.

All farce is amoral in itself, Styan states, and wonders, "When it reduces all of life, any aspect of man or society to a thing of no dignity, how can we admit that its posture of indifference is valid and valuable in itself?" (83). For Styan, a farce's amorality is a problem. More recent critics, however, celebrate the spirit of farce as it emerged in the twentieth century, thanks to early Hollywood: "Dada, Surrealism, the Absurd and Happenings, although annunciated with flourishes of theory and manifestoes about The Condition of Man, trade in farcical effects and would be unimaginable without them" (Bermel, 14).

In a twentieth-century spirit of lighthearted farce, then, the director of *El examen de maridos* presented us with a tour de force of absurd situations and coincidences. The comic effect of seeing the shape of female outlines and hearing a feminine pitch of voice in male roles accentuated the caricature of the macho ego, obvious butt of the satire. Staccato music and mechanical dance movements brought out the vanity of all the suitors, while Doña Inés's and Doña Blanca's intermittent wailing characterized them as spoiled children whose favorite toy had been taken away. Whether one agrees with this uniform interpretation or not, it was much fun to watch.

Justified by Alarcón's text was the ridiculing of the first three suitors, confirmed moreover by the *gracioso*'s comment, "Gusto es vellos / cuidadosos y afectados, / compuestos y mesurados, / alzar bigotes y cuellos" (411–14). This characterization was then applied to all male protagonists. The confrontation between Conde Carlos and one of the suitors was a successfully stylized duel where movements rhythmically accompanied Conde Carlos's *desafío* "Esta espada sabrá hacer / que sobre decirlo yo / para dejallo" (695–97). Doña Blanca and her servant are first presented as two *majas* in a modern *zarzuela,* but song dissolves into tears as Doña Blanca bursts out, "Desesperada esperanza, / el loco intento mudad, / y de ofendida apelad / del amor a la venganza" (651–54). Conde Carlos's irate reaction to Doña Inés's proclamation of an open competition for her hand, however, risks becoming low comedy as he flings his plumed hat on her chocolate-box farthingale (roars of laughter), choking on the words "cada agravio da más fuego, / cada desdén más amor" (757–58) and throwing in a gratuitous "Ay" (roars of laughter). He invites ridicule with the conventional poetics "¿Podéisme negar acaso / que dos veces cubrió el suelo / tierna flor y duro hielo / después que por vos me abraso?" (769–72) (roars of laughter) and finishes it all off by lifting Doña Inés's chocolate-box skirts with the words "El fiero dolor que paso / por vuestros ricos despojos" (773–74) (roars of laughter). The bravura with which he utters his threat "¡vive Dios que al preferido / ha de hacer mi furia ardiente / teatro de delincuente / del tálamo de marido!" (885–88) thus finishes the tone of the first act, leaving a smile on spectators' faces as they make their way to the foyer.

The second act offers basically the same jokes as the first, presenting us Conde Carlos and the Marqués strutting around with identical brio while Doña Blanca's performance as a spoiled child is duplicated by Doña Inés's bitter disappointment on hearing "los defetos del Marqués" (1222). Both female roles were consciously modeled on the protagonist in Lope's *Los melindres de Belisa,* a play, according to the director, "comparable" in its portrayal of feminine "facetiousness and fraudulent quality" (program notes). In the second act, too, the Marqués's encounter with Doña Inés seems a duplication of that between Conde Carlos and Doña Inés in the first act. Making his presentation, the Marqués solicits bursts of laughter from the audience while he extols his talents: "Si canto . . ." (singing a shrill scale; laughter); "Si danzo . . ." (rigid steps; laughter); "Pues a caballo . . ."

(rides a hobbyhorse; laughter); "En los toros . . ." (veronicas; laughter); etc. The text, of course, justifies the exaggerated portrayal; what is lost in the laughter, however, is Doña Inés's comments "hallo una falta, Marqués. / . . . / Ser vos quien las publicáis" (1353–56). Equally lost is the Marqués's self-defense, "a quien se opone, toca / sus méritos publicar" (1360–61). This important exchange of *indicios* is then crowned by a danced duet with the rhythmic accompaniments of Doña Inés's words "porque inclinada me siento, / si os digo verdad, Marqués, / a vuestra persona" (1392–94). The scene then closes with the Marqués kneeling melodramatically (laughter).

In the last act, the director, aware of the strain of keeping up the merriment, brings out his best bag of tricks. The act opens with an ingenious balancing act on ladders by the two servants as they take turns peeping over an imaginary wall. Amidst shouts of "Vítor" and general applause, the Marqués and Conde Carlos then appear after their match of tilting at the ring, once again moving rigidly as if on stilts. Later on, the pair become cartoon figures as they encounter each other in the darkness of night, each circling the other with Pink Panther music in the background. Very successful, too, is the portrayal of the three unsuccessful suitors in the last scene when they reappear as puppets emerging from the farthingale of one of the *damas*. To be sure, this Punch-and-Judy show in the background illustrates the absurdity of the whole situation, especially when the suitors, gesticulating wildly but helplessly caught in the lap of their *dama,* pronounce the verdict in three consecutive shouts of "¡Vítor!" "¡Vítor!" "¡Venció el Conde!" At this, Doña Inés's loud wailing, accompanied by many gratuitous outbursts of "ayayay," of course, provokes the by-now statutory laughter. In the end, all *galanes* are paired off with the right *damas* in a final *taconeo.*

And so the audience goes home, under the impression that Alarcón is a very funny playwright indeed. But who is the farceur, Alarcón or the director? Eric Bentley rightly says of the farceur that he is the typical teller of jokes in any company, whether in real life or on the stage, whose wish is "to capture and hold captive his audience." The jokester knows his wish is fulfilled only when the audience laughs because laughter is "audible, re-assuring and gratifying" (232–33).

Only in farce is audience reaction so immediately reassuring and easy to ascertain. In comedy or tragedy, the spectators' sympathy and empathy with the dramatic event, be it through smiles or tears, can only be sensed during performance and only gauged by the measure of applause at the end. Could this be why nowadays so many directors opt for the easy success of a farcical adaptation of Spanish classical theater?

The point is, though, that Alarcón's *El examen de maridos* was not meant to be a farce, and by changing the genre and style, one risks losing out on the best of farce and the best of drama. Lacking in this interpretation as a quasi-musical farce was a diversification of character and language, as all expressed themselves visually and audibly in the same sustained rhetorical pathos. Lost, too, was the rich range of conflicts between friendship and desire, reason and inclination, honor, gossip, appearances, and reality—in short, a whole range of paradoxical truths. Missing was any sort of message, be it that one loves not "because" but "in spite of"; or alternatively, the ironical truth that real identities are tested not by competitive examination but by a series of lies; or even simply a feeling of catharsis after all the confusions have been cleared up.

But then, in accordance with the old saw "No conocéis vuestros bienes, sino cuando de ellos carecéis," the performance at Chamizal had an enriching effect, too. There have been many attempts at defining what a *comedia* is. Perhaps, in good scholastic tradition, it might be easier to define the *comedia* in terms of what it is not by contrasting the text and spectacle of *El examen de maridos*.

The *comedia* in general, and Alarcón's play in particular, does not offer a one-track plot but combines many conflicts approached from different angles by different characters in one text. The resulting ambiguity leaves the reader/spectator with many questions as to the "truth" of their solution, thus lending a certain open-endedness to the denouement. The dramatis personae are not simple monomaniacal types, representative of an idée fixe or a well-defined institution, but real characters who fluctuate between certainties and doubts and, in their humanity, invite sympathy and empathy from the reader/spectator.

The language of a *comedia* does not obey a preset pattern of expression but, through the rich variety of versification, adds moods and rhythm as well as musicality to the discourse. Just as characters can offer an ingenious set of paradoxical truths for the audience to resolve, so can the ambiguous sign-system of language and communication *engañar con la verdad*. A *comedia*'s message cannot be reduced to simple ridicule of social norms but offers a set of contradictory perspectives on the human condition, making it a truly committed piece fit to be put before modern audiences without need for adaptation.

Last but not least, let us not forget that the *comedia* is also very funny, but in the right proportion and in the right places. Herein lies, for this reader/spectator at least, the delight of Spanish classical theater.

Notes

1.   All references are by verse number to Ruiz de Alarcón, *El examen de maridos,* edited by Agustín Millares Carlo (Madrid: Espasa-Calpe, 1960).

2.   Thanks to the untiring efforts of Donald Dietz, who has filmed the Chamizal performances live, I was able to refresh my memory and test my own impressions by viewing the recording of the 1987 performance of *El examen de maridos* provided courtesy of the Association for Hispanic Classical Theater, Inc.

Works Consulted

Bentley, Eric. [1964] 1975. *The Life of the Drama.* Reprint. New York: Atheneum.

Bermel, Albert. 1982. *Farce.* New York: Simon and Schuster.

Cuddon, J. A. 1982. *A Dictionary of Literary Terms.* Harmondsworth: Penguin Books.

Fothergill-Payne, Louise. 1983. "La justicia poética de *La verdad sospechosa.*" In *Historia y crítica de la literatura española,* edited by Francisco Rico, 3:884–88. Barcelona: Grijalbo. [Reprinted from *Romanische Forschungen* 83 (1971): 588–95.]

———. 1985. "On Readers, Spectators, and Critics." *Bulletin of the Comediantes* 37:167–69.

Milner Davis, Jessica. 1978. *Farce.* London: Methuen.

Styan, J. L. 1975. *Drama, Stage and Audience.* Cambridge: Cambridge University Press.

Williamsen, Vern. 1991. "The Critic as Translator." In *Prologue to Performance: Spanish Classical Theater Today,* edited by Louise and Peter Fothergill-Payne, 136–52. Lewisburg, Pa.: Bucknell University Press.

Victor Dixon

The Study of Versification as an Aid to Interpreting the *Comedia:* Another Look at Some Well-Known Plays by Lope de Vega

ike the drama of some other great national schools, the *comedia* was written almost entirely in verse. In this of course, as in other respects, its dramatists were following in the footsteps of their sixteenth-century predecessors (with the notable exception of Lope de Rueda).

They can hardly have been unaware that in eschewing prose they were committing, in S. G. Morley's words, "an evident breach of reality in ostensible imitation of reality" (1948, 62). We find their contemporary López Pinciano expressing amazement that the Ancients should have perpetrated "vn disparate tan grande de escriuir las fábulas en metros; y que, proponiendo imitar, deshazen del todo los neruios de la imitación, la qual está fundada en la verisimilitud, y el hablar en metro no tiene alguna semejança de verdad" (1:206–8), pointing out that (as Lope recalls in *La dama boba*) Heliodorus's "*poema*" had been written in prose; so too, he adds, had Italian comedies and Spanish *entremeses*. López Pinciano's interlocutor Fadrique defends verse, however, as productive of greater "deleyte." Later Fadrique argues by contrast that comedies "tan bien parecen en prosa como en metro" and in prose would be more "verisímiles," but goes on to say that "cada vno puede hazer lo que quisiere en este particular sin cometer yerro alguno" (2:221–22). In fact, the dramatists (and their public, presumably) seem to have opted unquestioningly for *deleyte* rather than *verisimilitud*, taking it for granted that the three-act play, however replete with contemporary reference, should be a stylized artifact, that in holding the mirror up to nature it should follow, as Rudolph Schevill stressed, the formula of art and not the formula of life (13).

The *comedia*'s dramatic diction was heir in consequence to a poetic tradition already rich in expressive resources. That heritage offered dramatists in particular a wide variety of verse forms and patterns of rhyme and assonance, both national and Italianate, and their output is distinguished, far more than that of other schools, by polymetry. As Morley put it, "the extraordinary variety of meters employed in the *comedia* surpassed anything known in any other drama of the world" (1937, 283). In exploiting that resource, the dramatists were at one not only with those who preceded them, such as Gil Vicente, Juan de la Cueva, and Cristóbal de Virués, but with all the leading poets of their own age. And above all, their great exemplar, Lope de Vega, delighted in displaying, outside the drama, a phenomenal facility in every existing poetic form. The use of such a diversity of forms was consistent, moreover, with the variety of nature and of human experience, which the *comedia,* refusing to submit to neoclassical restraints on its choice of subject matter and insisting on mingling the lowly and the lofty, the comic and the tragic, demanded the right to depict in all its complexity. On the other hand, verisimilitude could not be entirely disregarded; the concept of *decoro* demanded that dramatic discourse should be adaptable in some degree to situation and character, that style should accord with a constantly changing content. That concern, as J. M. Rozas argued (122; also see Smith, 135), is the "impulso central" of the *Arte nuevo* (printed in 1609), and Lope saw more clearly than anyone that polymetry offered an answer.

His eight famous lines in that poem on the use of different forms can be seen as simply extending to *comedia* versification the classical doctrine of fitness that is the principal burden of the fifty-odd before them. He might in fact be echoing Horace, who, while listing types of meter and the contexts to which they were suited, had advised the dramatic poet: "Let each of these styles be kept for the role properly allotted to it" (82). Lope's first two lines urge similarly: "Acomode los versos con prudencia / a los sujetos de que va tratando" (Rozas, 191, 305–6). The other six, I would note in passing, have often been misinterpreted as if he could have meant them to constitute a complete and coherent catalogue of metrical forms and uses, immune to the experimentation that for another quarter-century was to continue to characterize his huge output. If we regard them rather as illustrations of some of the contexts in which the six forms he lists might be used, we can show that they are in no way inconsistent with his own practice when he wrote them.

Some critics, of course (e.g., Montesinos, 14; and Weiger, 38–40), have doubted whether those who went to hear (as they said then) a play were able to identify during the performance the metrical forms the poet had employed and the changes he had rung upon them. Many perhaps could not; but undoubtedly some could, especially those cultured spectators who were accustomed to hearing verse read, to reading it aloud themselves, or even to composing it. We find indeed in the texts of plays, as I have pointed out elsewhere (1985, 114–15), a host of jocular references that demonstrate such an awareness. I will add here only a brief quotation from the first act of Lope's *¡Ay, verdades, que en amor!* which was written in 1625. Two spectators, Perseo and Albano, comment as follows on the performance of a *comedia* they have just witnessed: "—No he visto cosa más rara / que las décimas que dijo / con tales afectos Arias. / —Laurel mereció Cintor / por el donaire y la gracia / con que dijo aquel soneto" (Vega 1917, 511).

In any case, the poet (who, contemporary writers seem to take for granted, composed his lines aloud) must obviously have been conscious of the different verse forms as he wrote and changed them, and must have felt each to be in some way or other appropriate, even if his choices were sometimes a matter of instinct or routine. And in the theater, those choices must inevitably have affected the impact of the play on its spectators, whether or not they were consciously counting his syllables and registering his rhymes. Rhyme and assonance may well have been a significant factor in that impact. Vern Williamsen has suggested that the dramatists chose their rhyming words with care "as those most likely to stand forth with special vigor as the actor spoke the lines, to emphasize the central theme, action or dramatic intent of the scene in which they fall" (1985, 128). Undoubtedly they did so on occasion, especially perhaps when the speaker was to exit and leave the stage empty. When Lope advised in the *Arte nuevo:* "Remátense las scenas con sentencia, / con donaire, con versos elegantes, / de suerte que, al entrarse el que recita, / no deje con disgusto el auditorio" (Rozas 190, 294–97), he was alluding to a frequent practice of his own (and for that matter, of his English contemporaries). In *Fuente Ovejuna,* for instance, the brief scene in *sueltos* in which the Order of Calatrava is ousted from Ciudad Real, to the disillusionment of its ill-advised young master, concludes with his sententious observation: "¡Ah, pocos años, / sujetos al rigor de sus engaños!" (1470–71).

It may well be that some choices of rhyme and aphoristic coinages were unconsciously suggested by the ideas that were uppermost in the author's mind; but that would hardly render them less illuminating with respect to those ideas. The analysis of rhyming words and the study of *sentencias* that Robert Pring-Mill so ably illustrated in his pioneering article on *Fuente Ovejuna* would throw no less light on an author's preoccupations and on the likely effect of his play if we were to decide that they sometimes reflected concerns he was not deliberately stressing.

My present interest, however, is in what we can learn from a playwright's successive choices of verse forms from among the many at his disposal. Such an interest is hardly new; many scholars have studied the versification of the *comedia,* in attempts to answer in particular questions of attribution and date and to decide what forms were considered most appropriate to different kinds of dramatic discourse and what function those forms were made to serve in the structuring of a play's action. Most serious editors of *comedias,* moreover, provide at least a tabulation of the forms employed by their dramatist (though they would be well advised in addition—as I have proposed elsewhere (Dixon 1985, 121)—to identify each of them in the text as they appear), and many writers of introductions and critical guides make perceptive comments on their use and function. But we have yet to realize the full potential of the study of versification as an aid to interpretation.

Indeed, Vern Williamsen has insisted on that potential (1978, 13). To the five famous principles for the interpretation of Golden Age drama enunciated in the enormously influential studies of Alexander A. Parker, he has suggested that we should add a sixth, which might be formulated as follows: The impact in the theater of the successive episodes of a play is dependent in part on the author's deliberate or instinctive choices in matters of verse technique, and consequently the study of these can assist us to elucidate its "meaning" or impact. What the application of such a principle has to offer can best be determined, I believe, by the careful analysis of individual plays. As a small step in that direction, this essay will therefore consider some of Lope de Vega's most frequently and deeply studied plays and attempt to assess to what extent a study of their versification may be said to confirm or complement the interpretations arrived at by other approaches.

More comprehensive studies are, of course, essential; in the case of Lope, in particular, the work of Morley and Bruerton and of Diego Marín has provided us with a wealth of indispensable data and comment. Their generalizations may at times appear misleading, but above all they offer an overview of the author's habitual practice as it evolved; they thus enable us to identify significant departures from that practice, and—no less important—not to interpret as innovatory what may have been a matter of almost mechanical routine. They confirm that the unit of both poetic and dramatic construction within each of the *comedia*'s three acts was the *cuadro,* or as I prefer to call it, the *salida,* whose conclusion was signaled by the emptying of the stage. It might fill the whole act or be very short; within it, the author might use a single metrical form or many, but at its end he would almost invariably change to a new one for the next (in Lope's case, notoriously, drawing a line across his manuscript between them). What should attract our attention, therefore, is the nature rather than the fact of the change when a new *salida* begins, unless, exceptionally and intriguingly, no such change is made.

Awareness of an author's regular practice, moreover, should warn us to attach less importance to certain forms and certain changes than to others. As Vern Williamsen has said, "early in the development of the *comedia,* the *redondilla* and *quintilla* seem to have been used for the basic action of the plays; by the turn of the century, poets seem to have gone almost exclusively over to the *redondilla* and to have used the *quintilla* only for the sake of variety" (1985, 128). Thus (as he has also put it) the *redondilla* was "the work-horse of the earlier plays." The last of the pieces of advice in the *Arte nuevo* to which I have referred was "y para las de amor las *redondillas,*" and some critics have sought to show that Lope followed that advice himself (Sage, 79–80; Hall, 75–77). That they have had some limited success may perhaps be explained by the fact that love, in a very broad sense, was Lope's constant theme; I am tempted mischievously to suggest that what he should have written (or even did write) was "y para *las demás.*" From about that time, though, he began to rely equally heavily on *romances,* which for later writers such as Calderón were to become the "work-horse"; and it is possible to theorize why in particular contexts Lope may have preferred one to the other.[1] But together these two octosyllabic meters (and the earlier *quintillas*) rarely accounted for less than 70 percent of his lines. These standbys seem likely therefore to prove less interesting for purposes of interpretation than forms that he resorted to more rarely and presumably more deliberately.

Similarly, he chose to open a very high proportion of his acts, throughout his career, in *redondillas;* but to close them—though for many years he also favored *redondillas*—from about 1609 he almost invariably used *romances.* "*Red. - rom.,*" in other words, became his standard, predictable beginnings-and-endings pattern (Morley and Bruerton, 204). Our attention should therefore be aroused, not when that pattern is maintained but when it is broken by the use of another form to begin or end any act.

We should look, I suggest, in an individual play for significant variations from Lope's usual practice at the time it was written, and should speculate, as I shall in the discussions that follow, on his reasons for employing the metrical forms that he relied on less heavily than those I have so far mentioned. In particular, we should study, I believe, the use of the various forms of Italian origin. According to Diego Marín, these were employed by Lope not so much in serious, ceremonial passages as for the elegant expression of lofty sentiments—by either lowly or highly born characters—without implications either for the solemnity of the scene or for the social rank of those concerned (102–3). It seems to me rather that Lope used them invariably as an instrument of emphasis, and that in some cases it is precisely those implications which they appear to emphasize.

In *Peribáñez y el Comendador de Ocaña,* nine *octavas* are used for the ceremonial appearance of Enrique Justiciero and his queen at the beginning of the final *salida.* Otherwise, Italianate lines appear only in three *salidas,* all set in the Comendador's house and dominated by him. The first of these is mainly in *quintillas,* but in the course of the *salida,* the Comendador turns to *liras* to soliloquize about his love for Casilda, in learned language clearly different from that in which Peribáñez, always in octosyllables, speaks of his. Luján, encouraging his master to hope that the peasant's wife can be bribed into adultery, uses a sonnet to suggest—with ironic implications—an analogy with the story of Angelica and the Moor Medoro in *Orlando furioso* (see Dunn, 218–19). The second such *salida* is in *sueltos;* halfway through it, with no change of meter, Peribáñez also appears, but as a suppliant, perhaps as a dupe, and certainly out of his element (786–907). The third, in act 2 (1786–1856), also begins in *sueltos* but concludes with another sonnet, in which Don Fadrique soliloquizes on the peculiar hopelessness of his passion, resorting to classical analogies and topoi and ending, by way of expressing his despair and vindictiveness, with an implied allusion to the suicide of Iphis and the punishment of Anaxarete (see Dunn, 220–21; Dixon 1966, 18–19). The choice of Italianate forms is thus consonant with and underscores the setting, characterization, and language—assists, in short, in evoking the world of the nobleman,[2] which Lope contrasts throughout the play, as many critics since Edward

Wilson have stressed, with the very different world of the peasant, doubtless having taken as his starting point the metonymic opposition inherent in the *copla* that was his principal source: "Más quiero yo a Peribáñez / con su capa la pardilla, / que no a vos, Comendador, / con la vuesa guarnecida" (1925–28).

Another significant feature of the versification of this play consists in the use of traditional lyric forms for the words of its four songs, all of which—as so often in Lope and other dramatists—serve "as functional units and as elements of composition, rather than as mere lyrical parentheses or decorative embellishments" (Umpierre, 2). The first, "Dente parabienes," celebrates the naturalness and sanctity of marriage; the second, "Trébole, ay Dios, como güele," contrasts the fidelity of the wife with the susceptibility of other women; the third, "La mujer de Peribáñez," incorporating as it does the *copla* embedded previously in Casilda's rejection of Don Fadrique's advances, serves both to reassure her husband and to confirm his determination to defend her; the fourth, "Cogióme a tu puerta el toro," recalls the play's most important symbol and its initiating incident, asserting both falsely and truthfully that Peribáñez's wife remained indifferent to the Comendador's fall. All function, consequently, to underline the constancy of the faithful wife, which was surely the original inspiration of the play and remains a central theme. In this respect also, therefore, unusual metrical forms are used to highlight the meaning of the work. A further peculiarity of *Peribáñez,* however, is that at the beginning of several *salidas* Lope fails to change to a different metrical form. In act 2, the second *salida* ends, and the third continues, in *redondillas;* and in act 3, more strikingly, he continues in *redondillas* after the end of a *salida* at no less than five out of six opportunities. We can only conjecture that he meant the climactic events before the scene in which the crown endorses Peribáñez's action to seem more than usually continuous and dynamic; we may decide therefore to perform them accordingly (on stage or in the mind).

In *Fuente Ovejuna,* by contrast with *Peribáñez,* Italianate verse forms appear to be used, except for a brief *salida* in twenty-three *sueltos* for the defeat of the Order of Calatrava at Ciudad Real, to enhance the prominence and dignity of the peasants, which no critic has doubted that Lope meant to stress. *Tercetos*—suitable, according to the *Arte nuevo,* for weighty matters—are used in act 1 for the peasants' attempts at grandiloquent speeches of welcome to Fernán Gómez and again for the deliberations of their assembly at the beginning of act 3—strikingly, for by this time Lope was beginning three quarters of his acts in *redondillas.* Similarly, *octavas* appear for their serious discussions at the beginning of act 2 and reappear in act 3 (perhaps also because they were the favorite vehicle of the cultivated epic) for the *salida* in which they storm Fernán Gómez's mansion and execute their vengeance. The play's only sonnet (and only soliloquy) is especially arresting. We are expecting the climactic torture scene, for which the peasants have rehearsed and which has been delayed already by one in which the Master of Calatrava reacts with anger and threats of violence to news of the rebellion; but it is Laurencia who appears, alone. No longer averse to love and marriage, no longer a virago, she meditates in the octet, in objective terms, on the nature of totally committed love, turning only in the sestet to its exemplification in herself. The sonnet thus states a theme and adds a first variation. Two more are to follow, for that same love will be further exemplified both by Frondoso and by the whole village under torture. As Bruce Wardropper wrote, Lope's insertion of this sonnet "imposes a tone of immense seriousness on the dramatic moment," and creates "a deliberate pause, towards the end of the action, for the purpose of summing up the ideological content of the drama" (1956, 163).

Like *Peribáñez, Fuente Ovejuna* contains four songs, whose words are cast again in traditional metrical (and musical) forms. The first, a *romancillo,* is the peasants' song of welcome, their innocent offer of love, to their victorious overlord: "Sea bien venido / el Comendadore / . . . ¡Viva muchos años, / viva Fernán Gómez!" (529–44). The second, a *coplilla* with an *estribillo,* is a similar outpouring of their goodwill toward Frondoso and Laurencia, expressing their collective hope that the married couple's life may be long, full, and untroubled: "¡Vivan muchos años / los desposados! / ¡Vivan muchos años!" (1472–74). The *romance con estribillo* that follows clearly foreshadows by contrast the violence of the loveless Comendador, which is in fact to interrupt the wedding and so provoke in act 3 the violent but loving response of their rebellion. That violence is expressed not lyrically but in strident slogans taken directly from Lope's historical source. In some of these, nevertheless, we detect excusable perversions of the first song: "¡Mueran tiranos traidores! / . . . ¡Fernán Gómez muera!" (1813, 1887); in others, by contrast, we hear an echo of the second: "¡Los Reyes nuestros señores / vivan! . . . / . . . ¡Vivan Fernando e Isabel!" (1811–12, 1865). Finally, in a third cry they express a new (though not unprecedented) sense of corporate loyalty and mutual love, which anticipates their crucial unanimity under torture: "¡Fuente Ovejuna!" (1874–87). The other slogans, by contrast, will reappear transmuted, together with further echoes of the first and second songs, in the fourth and final one, which is both a celebration of the peasants' own victory and an assertion of loyalty toward the loving couple who rule their nation: "¡Muchos años vivan / Isabel y Fernando, / y mueran los tiranos!" (2028–30). The *coplilla* could clearly be sung to the same tune as that in the wedding scene, and is glossed in very similar *estribillos;* and when we discover that this use of *coplillas* with *estribillos* is unique in Lope's dramatic versification to *Fuente Ovejuna* (Morley and Bruerton, 184), we can have no doubt that the second scene was intended (and should be played) as a mirror image of the first, and that Ferdinand and Isabella are to be viewed as a couple closely analogous to Frondoso and Laurencia.

Again, as in *Peribáñez,* in *Fuente Ovejuna* Lope elects unusually often not to change at the beginning of a new *salida* from *redondillas* to a different form—in this case on five out of thirteen occasions—perhaps to diminish the sense of discontinuity that its sixteen *salidas* might have produced, but perhaps for other reasons. On the first occasion, for instance, Fernán Gómez exits with his henchmen and the Master of Calatrava, having just alluded to the villagers of Fuente Ovejuna; they are replaced on stage by two peasant girls, one of whom prays that Fuente Ovejuna may never see again an at first unidentified "him." The spectators can immediately guess that these are two of Fernán Gómez's vassals, and that they are talking about him in or near the village. The neatness of the montage is undoubtedly enhanced by the choice to continue in *redondillas.* On the last occasion, the torture scene ends with a charming exchange between Frondoso and Laurencia; their place on stage is taken by Ferdinand and Isabella, who address each other in equally loving though courtly terms. The similarity between the two couples, which Lope surely meant to stress yet again, is emphasized by the fact that he continues in *redondillas,* which indeed he persists with until the end— surprisingly, for by this time he invariably concluded his plays in *romances.* The effect, perhaps, is that the turbulent action of this relatively short *comedia* presses urgently forward to a somewhat sudden and open-ended conclusion.

In general we can say that the discrepancies in versification technique between *Peribáñez* and *Fuente Ovejuna* should encourage us to regard them, despite their evident similarities, as fundamentally different plays, especially in their attitudes to class distinctions.

El villano en su rincón has an unusually high proportion of passages in Italianate forms; some 15 out of 33, accounting for 20 percent of its lines. In one passage, in unlinked *tercetos,* the *villano*'s daughter, Lisarda, demonstrates that she is in every way worthy of the King's marshal, Otón, who promises to marry her; the almost central subplot scene thus highlighted may be said to emphasize what has been seen as the essential theme of the play, expressed in one of its lines: "¡Oh amor, gran juntador de desiguales!" (1349). But its other Italianate passages seem mainly to be associated with the rich farmer and the King. The first is the soliloquy "Gracias, inmenso cielo," in which the apparently pious peasant celebrates his self-sufficient prosperity and contentment (350–424). Like Benalcio's "Oh libertad preciosa" in Lope's *Arcadia,* it betrays—no less than by its *beatus ille* content—by its metrical form (that of the strict Petrarchan *canzone*) its indebtedness to Renaissance pastoral, to the second and third *canciones* of Garcilaso, and especially to Salicio's three stanzas in the Second Eclogue: "Cuán bienaventurado / aquel puede llamarse." And two of the ten later passages in *sueltos* and *octavas* are dominated by the peasant, seen as the king of his little corner. Of the other eight, however, two portray his receipt of royal commands, and the remainder appear in scenes in which the King is clearly dominant. The use of Italianate forms seems therefore to underline their roles as rival monarchs, but also the necessary subservience of the lesser to the greater. Of the two sonnet-soliloquies in the final act, Lisarda's "De grado en grado amor me va subiendo" (2706–19) stresses again the leveling power of love, expressing her emotions at her social elevation by fortune; the other, "La vida humana, Isócrates decía" (2306–19), appears to have been inserted by Lope to enhance the status of the king vis-à-vis the peasant as no less of a philosopher but a learned and courtly one. Like his quotation from Philemon, as I have shown elsewhere (1981, 294–96), it is a close paraphrase of two passages by Epictetus that Lope must have looked for and found in John Stobaeus's *Sententiae.* In a sense it is a reply to Juan Labrador's act 1 soliloquy; like Horace's epode, it expresses envy of the peasant's free and innocent tranquillity, but from the townsman's perspective, which in Lope's case is a more comprehensive one.

This play also includes a number of songs and dances, some with lyrics so close to folklore in both language and poetic form that the degree of artistic elaboration is difficult to determine, as Alfredo Rodríguez has pointed out (640). But the song that the peasant has sung to the King, "Cuán bienaventurado / aquel puede llamarse justamente" (1865–76), consists of two six-line *liras* borrowed from a series of seventeen that Lope had said were sung in four-part harmony in his *Los pastores de Belén*. These and three speeches in other Lope plays that begin with the selfsame words were celebrations (like Juan Labrador's *canzone* and Benalcio's) of the rustic's sense of independence and were no less clearly indebted to the *canzone* in the Second Eclogue; thus the form of the song suggests that it is a restatement of Juan Labrador's philosophy. But the song the King has sung near the end to *him* (2880–85, 2918–23), in the same meter and intended surely to be set to the same air, asserts that that philosophy is flawed in two respects. Human life is contingent and communal; no man, as Solon and other classical sages had said, can truly be called happy until his life has ended; no man should feel happy, moreover, to bask with his family in the heat of his own log fire without a harmonious relationship with the larger community, whose sun and center for Lope is the monarch. The metrical (and musical) echo behind the actual words serves to emphasize that, as several critics have argued, the play is not merely a nostalgic gloss on the *beatus ille* topos so dear to the Renaissance but also and more importantly a seventeenth-century ("No man is an island") reaction against that very topos.[3]

La dama boba, like *Peribáñez* and *Fuente Ovejuna*, has only six passages in Italianate meters. Four are in *octavas, sueltos,* or the similar *silva,* type 3; their use coincides exactly with appearances on stage of Octavio, the father of the two heroines (except that in the third case he enters only halfway through the passage). This fact should perhaps incline us to accord his apparently minor role and his sententious pronouncements a certain weight, for instance when he refers to the need for *mesura*, "pues la virtud es bien que el medio siga" (238), and especially when he speaks of the real motivation of marriage: "el buscar un hombre en todo estado / lo que le falta más, con más cuidado" (255–56)—what Robert ter Horst has called the play's "economy of scarcity" (351).

The other two passages are a pair of sonnets, the positioning of which (as well as the self-advertising nature of the form) suggests that Lope meant them both to claim our attention. The play's first act consists of only two *salidas*. The first of these, entirely in *redondillas,* portrays Liseo in Illescas reacting with horror to a report that his intended, Finea, is a fool and proposing therefore to court her sister Nise instead. The scene shifts to Octavio's house in Madrid, and after Octavio's *octavas,* the rest of the act is also in *redondillas,* except that these frame three set pieces. The first is the servant Clara's *Gatomaquia*-style account in *romances,* to the delight of the "linda bestia" Finea, of the *accouchement* of their cat (413–92). The second is a sonnet recited (525–38) and then explained by Duardo to Nise, which expounds the Neoplatonic doctrine that the lover should progress through different stages of love by using the metaphor of three kinds of fire: the earthly element, the sun, and the divine Idea. Lope was undoubtedly proud of this sonnet, for he reprinted it twice later; yet the supposedly clever Nise, even when it is explained, cannot comprehend it. The third set piece is another sonnet, in which her favored suitor, Laurencio, soliloquizes after she has left (635–48). This too deals with love, but with three kinds of *motivation* for it: virtue, beauty, and profit. The impoverished Laurencio calculates in fact that marriage to Nise would gain him the first two ends but not the third; he should therefore court instead her stupid sister—as he will for the rest of the play—since Finea's dowry is much larger. The metrical structure of the *salida* directs our attention to all three set pieces, which surely serve to clarify the characters of Finea, Nise, and Laurencio, as the first *salida* had clarified that of Liseo. Yet most critics have concentrated only on the idealistic sonnet, which James E. Holloway saw indeed as "the most concise statement of the play's meaning" (238).

A few scholars, such as Robert ter Horst (356) and Emilie L. Bergmann (412), have realized the equal importance of its counterpart, the materialistic sonnet, which undermines the former's message with a pragmatism no less apparent throughout the play. Laurencio's courtship of Finea serves to illustrate, to be sure, the Ovidian topos that "love educates," as she herself expounds in the soliloquy in *décimas* that opens act 3; when we realize that Lope started an act in that verse form only once in 133 plays that are certainly datable earlier, we cannot doubt that he meant to give prominence to her speech. But other passages in the play, such as the final scene, imply that this idealistic view of love by no means excludes more down-to-earth feelings, including erotic passion, duplicity, and self-interest. And the two songs with *estribillos,* to which both Finea and Nise dance in this act, underline love's often mercenary motivation: "que más quiere doblones

/ que vidas y almas / . . . que sólo el dar enamora, / porque es cifra de las gracias" (2227–28, 2283–84). Attention to the significant features of the play's poetic structure thus assists us to discern that in *La dama boba,* as in *El villano en su rincón,* Lope's enthusiasm for an idealistic classical topos is balanced and tempered by considerations that afford a broader perspective.

El perro del hortelano contains an unusually high number of passages in Italianate forms, including eleven in *octavas* or *sueltos.* Since the play is preoccupied with questions of rank and social mobility, it is fitting that the Italianate forms are associated above all with the minor characters of lofty status, though this status is belied by their nature and behavior. When one of her nobly born suitors, Marquis Ricardo, is announced in act 1, Countess Diana acknowledges his rank by calling for chairs, and Lope changes to *octavas* until his departure. In act 2, *sueltos* appear for the scene in which she progresses from church and is addressed by both Ricardo and Count Federico; *octavas* are used again for Ricardo's next appearance, though also, briefly, for the earlier moment when Teodoro tells Fabio that their mistress has decided to marry the Marquis. In act 3, Lope turns to *sueltos* for all three scenes in which the *gracioso* Tristán, pretending to be a grandiloquent thug, encounters the Marquis and the Count; however, when Tristán reports to his master both the noblemen's murder-plan and his own scheme to give Teodoro a noble father, the meter is intriguingly *octavas.* And *sueltos* also appear for the scene in which Count Ludovico in fact acknowledges Teodoro as his son.

The nine sonnets spoken by the major characters—one of which, quite exceptionally at this period, is used to end an act—are undoubtedly, however, the most outstanding feature of the play's versification; arresting the action repeatedly for moments of meditation, they suggest that *El perro del hortelano* is an unusually thoughtful play. One critic, seeing it as both a comedy and (with respect to Marcela) a tragedy, has argued that "los sonetos en sí señalan y sostienen como en staccato los puntos básicos de la trama" (González-Cruz, 541), although Jan Bakker has listed the play's ten *romance* passages in an attempt to show that in general "la lectura de los *romances* de una comedia de Lope da su contenido en forma abreviada" (95). As I argued in my edition, the use of these sonnets is nonnaturalistic and undramatic, but deliberately so. They dam momentarily the turbulent flood of activity in which the *comedia* by and large consists and thus let a character stop and think clearly (or fail to) about his emotional situation and determine his response; but at the same time they permit the author, who is speaking to us through the character, to elaborate on the ideas and universal issues that underlie the plot. Thus the sonnets of *El perro,* as I added (Vega 1981, 56–57), both carry forward the action and elucidate the themes; for the subject of all is love—or more specifically, its exacerbation by other emotions, its inhibition by social pressures, and its susceptibility to being "cured."

That love, if genuine, *cannot* be cured—although the three main characters essay in turns several of the *remedia amoris* of Ovid—is indeed, I think, one of the primary themes of the play and is stressed by its only song. Almost at the play's center, in a scene in *redondillas,* the Countess tells Anarda that she is determined to suppress her love for a social inferior. Her statement is symbolically belied by music and specifically by the brief lyric, in *pareados.* Anarda makes the point that "música y amor conciertan / bien" (1642–43) and directs attention both before and after the song to its words: "Oh quién pudiera hacer, oh quién hiciese / que, en no queriendo amar, aborreciese" (Umpierre, 49).

In *El castigo sin venganza,* Lope's versification is "unusual" rather than "irregular," as Morley and Bruerton noted (100); it reveals him in fact at his most self-conscious, and in his old age more experimental than ever. Its metrical diversity—eleven (or arguably thirteen) different metrical forms—he never surpassed.[4] Contrary to his usual practice, moreover, he begins one act (the second) in *décimas;* even more unpredictably, he begins the third in *romances* and ends the second in *quintillas.*

From two thirds of the way through act 1, the action is set entirely in the castle of Ferrara. Act 2, despite eleven changes of form, constitutes a single *salida.* In act 3, the stage is emptied only once, and any sense of discontinuity is diminished by the fact that no change of meter ensues. The overall impression is that Lope's tragedy, despite the passage of some months, preserves a unity of place and time, as well as of action and mood, which only the most inveterate neo-Aristotelian could consider insufficiently classical.

The first of its many passages in Italianate metrical forms (apart from the nine-line *madrigal* recited offstage in the first *salida*), is the *silvas* that Lope uses to start the second and thus to present, as Vern Williamsen has suggested, the "initiating incident" of Federico's encounter with Casandra (1978, 39–41). But most of the other Italianate meters appear to be associated with the Duke as head of state and in his relationship with his son: for his appearance with Federico early in act 2, for his departure to fight for the pope and for his return, as well as for his discovery of the accusation of adultery.

One of the play's most remarkable features is that five of its characters pronounce among them eight more or less formal monologues that are not unlike operatic arias; four are described as *discursos,* three are explicitly introduced, and four are lent prominence by the fact that (though framed by *redondillas* or *romances*) they are cast in less common forms. Most remarkable of all is Federico's climactic confession of love to his stepmother in the highly wrought, self-advertising form of a lengthy gloss on the famous lines " Sin Dios, sin vos y sin mí." As I (1973, 73–76) and many others have argued, the gloss is precisely appropriate, and the fact that the stanza form, *quintillas,* was one that Lope at this time hardly ever employed confirms that his choice of it was made with deliberate calculation.

In addition to these more or less public *discursos,* the three main characters are made to reveal their real feelings to the spectators alone in an unusual number of soliloquies. Federico has only one, in the conspicuous form of a sonnet, in which he appears to have convinced himself that his love is "eternally impossible" (1797–1810). But its static self-containment is given the lie, implicitly, by the "gush of *quintillas*" (Dunn, 217) in the one by Casandra that immediately follows and expresses her determination to seduce him, as much for revenge as out of love. The content of this, on the other hand, though it shows her significantly further advanced on the road to sin, echoes closely her earlier soliloquy in *décimas,* which by its form had recalled in turn both her warm greeting to Federico in act 1 and her bitter complaints against his father at the beginning of act 2.

No less striking, though, are the five soliloquies by the Duke, which emphasize his dominant role in the final act and the play as a whole. The first (2467–2551) is cast in three different forms, as if to stress that this is one of the most intense and ironical moments of the tragedy. The Duke, attempting at last to exercise his proper function as a dispenser of justice—"que deben los que gobiernan / esta atención a su oficio" (2460–61)—begins solemnly in seventeen *sueltos* (mostly *pareados*) to consider the petitions he has been given, but he is intrigued by a mysterious anonymous letter. Reading this—the accusation of adultery—occupies a single *octava;* but at its end the Duke bursts into six realistically incoherent *décimas,* apostrophizing in turn the paper, heaven, his son, and his own absences but above all acknowledging in a moment of tragic anagnorisis that this is a punishment from God, not unlike but worse than King David's, for his own evildoing in the past, which was exemplified at the outset.

His second soliloquy, in which he reacts, still uncertainly, to his interrogation of Federico, is similarly isolated in a new form, four six-line *liras* (2612–35); his third and fourth, by contrast, are metrically undetached from their contexts (2738–59, 2811–23). And by the time he delivers his fifth (2834–2914), in which he seeks to justify but agonizes over the solution on which he has in fact determined, Lope has already set in motion the *romances,* with their ominous *a-a* assonance, with which the spectators can be sure *El castigo sin venganza* will move inexorably to its end.[5]

The artistry displayed throughout the play suggests that the aging Lope may well have hoped that his *tragedia al estilo español* would eclipse the achievement of any rival, ancient or modern; in its mature mastery of polymetric technique it does precisely that.

Notes

1.   For instance, Jan Bakker has argued interestingly (though with no reference to other studies) that in Lope's plays "la parte de la acción escrita en romance, es desenlace de problemas anteriormente expuestos," whereas *redondillas* are used for "la realización concreta de un acto encaminado a evitar una desgracia o a mejorar una situación" (95, 99).

2.   Cf. Ronald E. Surtz: "The changes of scene are indicated not only by the appearance of a different group of characters, but also by the replacement of the more popular national verse forms (the peasants speak in *quintillas, redondillas,* and *romance*) by the more erudite Italianate meters (the villains speak in *liras, sonetos, endecasílabos libres,* and some *quintillas*)" (1979, 191). The final change to *romances,* however (Surtz's note 64 to the contrary), was probably motivated mainly by the fact that the play was ending.

3.   See, for example, studies by Bruce W. Wardropper (1971), Mary Loud, Frances Day Wardlaw, and Victor Dixon (1981).

4.   The play contains *redondillas, quintillas, décimas, romances, tercetos,* a sonnet, two different *silvas* (234–339, 1682–1708), two different *liras* (700–35, 2612–35), a *canción* (*madrigal*), *sueltos* (*pareados*), and an *octava real.*

5.   I tend therefore to disagree with Vern Williamsen's opinion that "the emotional climax is not to be identified with the Duke's reaction to the accusatory letter but rather in

the final moments of truth as he carefully sets up the murder-execution that brings the play to a close" (1978, 39–40n. 12). Intense though those moments are, the play's first spectators must have sensed by then that the die was cast; as Williamsen has also suggested, "whenever they heard a *romance* of this typically closing type, well into the third act, they would expect a prompt conclusion of the play" (1985, 137).

Works Consulted

Bakker, Jan. 1981. "Versificación y estructura de la comedia de Lope." In *Diálogos hispánicos de Amsterdam, No. 2: Las constantes estéticas de la comedia en el Siglo de Oro,* 93–101. Amsterdam: Rodopi.

Bergmann, Emilie L. 1981. "*La dama boba:* Temática folklórica y neoplatónica." In *Lope de Vega y los orígenes del teatro español: Actas del I congreso internacional sobre Lope de Vega,* edited by Manuel Criado de Val, 409–13. Madrid: Edi-6.

Dixon, Victor. 1966. "The Symbolism of *Peribáñez.*" *Bulletin of Hispanic Studies* 43:11–24.

———. 1973. "*El castigo sin venganza:* The Artistry of Lope de Vega." In *Studies in Spanish Literature of the Golden Age Presented to Edward M. Wilson,* edited by R. O. Jones, 63–81. London: Tamesis Books.

———. 1981. "*Beatus... nemo: El villano en su rincón,* las 'polianteas' y la literatura de emblemas." *Cuadernos de filología* 3:279–300.

———. 1985. "The Uses of Polymetry: An Approach to Editing the *Comedia* As Verse Drama." In *Editing the Comedia,* edited by Frank P. Casa and Michael D. McGaha, 104–25. Michigan Romance Studies, vol. 5. Ann Arbor: University of Michigan Department of Romance Languages.

Dunn, Peter N. 1957. "Some Uses of Sonnets in the Plays of Lope de Vega." *Bulletin of Hispanic Studies* 34:212–22.

González-Cruz, Luis F. 1981. "El soneto: Esencia temática de *El perro del hortelano,* de Lope de Vega." In *Lope de Vega y los orígenes del teatro español: Actas del I congreso internacional sobre Lope de Vega,* edited by Manuel Criado de Val, 541–45. Madrid: Edi-6.

Hall, J. B. 1985. *Lope de Vega: Fuente Ovejuna.* London: Grant and Cutler.

Holloway, James E., Jr., 1972. "Lope's Neoplatonism: *La dama boba.*" *Bulletin of Hispanic Studies* 49:236–55.

Horace. 1965. *On the Art of Poetry.* In *Classical Literary Criticism,* 77–95. Translated and with an introduction by T. S. Dorsch. London: Penguin.

López Pinciano, Alonso. 1953. *Philosophía antigua poética.* Edited by Alfredo Carballo

Picazo. 3 vols. Madrid: Consejo Superior de Investigaciones Científicas.

Loud, Mary. 1975. "Pride and Prejudice: Some Thoughts on Lope de Vega's *El villano en su rincón.*" *Hispania* 58:843–50.

Marín, Diego. 1962. *Uso y función de la versificación dramática en Lope de Vega.* Valencia: Castalia.

Montesinos, José F. 1969. "La paradoja del *Arte nuevo.*" In *Estudios sobre Lope de Vega.* Salamanca: Anaya.

Morley, Sylvanus G. 1937. "Objective Criteria for Judging Authorship and Chronology in the *Comedia.*" *Hispanic Review* 5:281–85.

———. 1948. "The Curious Phenomenon of Spanish Verse Drama." *Bulletin hispanique* 50:445–62.

Morley, Sylvanus Griswold, and Courtney Bruerton. 1968. *Cronología de las comedias de Lope de Vega.* Madrid: Gredos.

Pring-Mill, R. D. F. 1962. "Sententiousness in *Fuente Ovejuna.*" *Tulane Drama Review* 7:5–37.

Rodríguez, Alfredo 1971. "Los cantables de *El villano en su rincón.*" In *Homenaje a William L. Fichter: Estudios sobre el teatro antiguo hispánico y otros ensayos,* edited by A. David Kossoff and José Amor y Vázquez, 639–45. Madrid: Castalia.

Rozas, Juan Manuel. 1976. *Significado y doctrina del Arte nuevo de Lope de Vega.* Madrid: Sociedad General Española de Librería.

Sage, J. W. 1974. *Lope de Vega: El caballero de Olmedo.* London: Grant and Cutler.

Schevill, Rudolph. 1918. *The Dramatic Art of Lope de Vega, Together with* La dama boba. Berkeley and Los Angeles: University of California Press.

Smith, Paul Julian. 1988. *Writing in the Margin: Spanish Literature of the Golden Age.* Oxford: Clarendon.

Surtz, Ronald E. 1979. *The Birth of a Theater: Dramatic Convention in the Spanish Theater from Juan del Encina to Lope de Vega.* Princeton, N.J.: Princeton University Press.

Ter Horst, Robert 1976. "The True Mind of Marriage: Ironies of the Intellect in Lope's *La dama boba.*" *Romanistisches Jahrbuch* 27:347–63.

Umpierre, Gustavo. 1975. *Songs in the Plays of Lope de Vega: A Study of Their Dramatic Function.* London: Tamesis Books.

Vega, Lope de. 1917. *Obras de Lope de Vega Carpio.* Nueva edición. Vol. 3, edited by E. Cotarelo y Mori. Madrid: Real Academia Española.

———. 1980. *Peribáñez y el Comendador de Ocaña.* Edited by J. M. Ruano and J. E. Varey. London: Tamesis Books.

———. 1981. *El perro del hortelano.* Edited by Victor Dixon. London: Tamesis Books.

———. 1987. *El castigo sin venganza.* Edited by J. M. Díez Borque. Madrid: Espasa-Calpo.

———. 1987. *La dama boba.* Edited by Diego Marín. Madrid: Cátedra.

———. 1987. *El villano en su rincón.* Edited by Juan María Marín. Madrid: Cátedra.

———. 1989. *Fuente Ovejuna.* Edited and translated by Victor Dixon. Warminster, Wiltshire: Aris and Phillips.

Wardlaw, Frances Day. 1981. "*El villano en su rincón:* Lope's Rejection of the Pastoral Dream." *Bulletin of Hispanic Studies* 58:113–19.

Wardropper, Bruce W. 1956. "*Fuente Ovejuna:* El gusto and lo justo." *Studies in Philology* 53:159–71.

———. 1971. "La venganza de Maquiavelo: *El villano en su rincón.*" In *Homenaje a William L. Fichter: Estudios sobre el teatro antiguo hispánico y otros ensayos,* edited by A. David Kossoff and José Amor y Vázquez, 765–72. Madrid: Castalia.

Weiger, John G. 1978. *Hacia la comedia: De los valencianos a Lope.* Madrid: Cupsa.

Williamsen, Vern G. 1978. "The Structural Function of Polymetry in the Spanish *comedia.*" In *Perspectivas de la comedia,* edited by Alva V. Ebersole, 33–47. Colección Siglo de Oro, vol. 6. Valencia: Albatrós-Hispanófila.

———. 1985. "A Commentary on 'The Uses of Polymetry' and the Editing of the Multistrophic Texts of the Spanish *comedia.*" In *Editing the Comedia,* edited by Frank P. Casa and Michael D. McGaha, 126–45. Michigan Romance Studies, vol. 5. Ann Arbor: University of Michigan Department of Romance Languages.

Wilson, Edward M. 1949. "Images et structures dans *Peribáñez.*" *Bulletin hispanique* 5:125–59.

List of Contributors

Emilie L. Bergmann is an associate professor of Spanish at the University of California, Berkeley. She is the author of *Art Inscribed: Essays on Ekphrasis in Spanish Golden Age Poetry* and coauthor of *Women, Culture, and Politics in Latin America.* Her current research focuses on gender in early modern Hispanic culture.

William R. Blue is a professor of Spanish at the University of Kansas. He is the author of *Development of Imagery in Calderón's* Comedias and of Comedia: *Art and History.* He has written numerous articles on Golden Age theater and poetry and has been the editor of the Renaissance and Baroque Spanish drama section for *The Year's Work in Modern Languages.*

Catherine Connor (Swietlicki) is an associate professor of Spanish at the University of Wisconsin, Madison. She has published *Spanish Christian Cabala: The Works of Luis de León, Santa Teresa de Avila, and San Juan de la Cruz,* as well as numerous articles on Golden Age literature.

Nancy L. D'Antuono is an associate professor of Italian at Saint Mary's College. Her research focuses on Italo-Hispanic literary and cultural relations from the fourteenth to the eighteenth centuries. She is the author of *Boccaccio's Novelle in the Theater of Lope de Vega* and is working on book-length studies of Calderón's and Lope's theater in Italy.

Charles Davis is a lecturer in Hispanic studies at Queen Mary and Westfield College (formerly Westfield College), University of London, and is the founding editor in chief of the *Journal of Hispanic Research.* He is a director of Tamesis Books, Limited, and jointly edits the series *Fuentes para la historia del teatro en España* with J. E. Varey. His recent publications include volume 16 of this series, *Los libros de cuentas de los corrales de comedias de Madrid: 1706–1719: Estudio y documentos.*

Frederick A. de Armas is Distinguished Professor of Spanish and Comparative Literature at The Pennsylvania State University, where he is also a Fellow of the Institute for the Arts and Humanistic Studies. He is the author of a number of books, including *The Invisible Mistress: Aspects of Feminism and Fantasy in the Golden Age* and *The Return of Astraea: An Astral-Imperial Myth in Calderón.* He has coedited several volumes on Calderón and serves as editor of three journals.

Victor Dixon has taught at the universities of St. Andrews and Manchester, and since 1974 has held the chair of Spanish at Trinity College, University of Dublin. He has published three critical editions of plays by Lope de Vega and is the author of thirty articles on Golden Age drama and on Antonio Buero Vallejo. He has directed and acted in some twenty-five productions of plays, in Spanish and in his own translations.

Louise Fothergill-Payne is a professor of Spanish at the University of Victoria, Canada. Her research focuses on the Spanish intellectual history of the late fifteenth, sixteenth, and seventeenth centuries with reference to the *Celestina,* the *auto sacramental,* and the *comedia.* Her books include *La alegoría en los autos y farsas anteriores a Calderón* and *Seneca and Celestina.* With Peter Fothergill-Payne she has edited *Parallel Lives: Spanish and English Drama 1580–1680.*

Dian Fox is a professor of Spanish and comparative literature at Brandeis University, where she has taught since 1987. She is the author of *Kings in Calderón: A Study in Characterization and Political Theory* and *Refiguring the Hero: From Peasant to Noble in Lope de Vega and Calderón.* She has also written numerous articles on Spanish medieval and Golden Age literature, from the *Poema de Mío Cid* to *Don Quijote.*

Margaret Rich Greer is an associate professor of Spanish at Princeton University. Her published work includes *The Play of Power,* a book on Calderón's court dramas, and a critical edition of *La estatua de Prometeo.* Her current research focuses on Calderón's *autos sacramentales* and on the work of María de Zayas.

Daniel L. Heiple is a professor at Tulane University, where he served as chair of the Department of Spanish and Portuguese from 1986 to 1992. His research focuses on the history of medicine and science in Golden Age literature and on seventeenth-century music. He is the author of *Mechanical Imagery in Spanish Golden Age Poetry* and a book on Garcilaso de la Vega and the Italian Renaissance.

Susana Hernández Araico is a professor of Spanish at California State Polytechnic University, Pomona. She is the author of *Ironía y tragedia en Calderón* as well as numerous papers and articles on Spanish Golden Age theater and Latin American women writers. Her edition of Sor Juana Inés de la Cruz's *Los empeños de una casa* is forthcoming in the MLA series on foreign literatures, accompanied by M. D. McGaha's English translation.

Carol Bingham Kirby is an associate professor of Spanish at State University College at Buffalo, New York. Her research has focused on Calderón's conjugal honor plays, Lope's history plays, and King Pedro in the *comedia.* She is completing a critical edition of *El rey don Pedro en Madrid y el infanzón de Illescas.*

Teresa J. Kirschner is a professor in the Department of Spanish and Latin American Studies at Simon Fraser University. She has won the Canadian Association of Hispanists

Prize for her book *El protagonista colectivo en* Fuenteovejuna *de Lope de Vega.* Her research focuses on the relationship between literature and ideology, semiology and intertextuality, and seventeenth-century Spanish drama, especially staging techniques and Lope de Vega.

Catherine Larson is an associate professor of Spanish at Indiana University, Blooming-ton. She is the author of *Language and the* Comedia: *Theory and Practice* and articles on Golden Age Theater and literary theory, the works of Elena Garro, and contemporary stagings of classical theatrical texts. She has served on the Executive Committee for the MLA division on Sixteenth- and Seventeenth-Century Spanish Drama and on the Board of Directors of the Association for Hispanic Classical Theater.

Susan Niehoff McCrary is an administrator of a Title III Strengthening the Institution Grant at Columbia Basin College. She also serves as adjunct faculty in the Department of Languages and Literatures at Washington State University Tri-Cities and is the author of El último godo *and the Dynamics of* Urdrama.

Michael McGaha is a professor of Romance languages at Pomona College. He has served as editor of *Cervantes* and as associate editor of *Hispania* and has published widely on Golden Age theater, *Don Quijote,* and the theater in the Second Republic of Spain.

Thomas A. O'Connor is a professor of Spanish and chair of the Department of Romance Languages and Literatures at Binghamton University, one of the four University Centers in the SUNY system. In 1988 he published *Myth and Mythology in the Theater of Pedro Calderón de la Barca* and currently is preparing an edition of *El encanto es la hermosura / La segunda Celestina* by Salazar y Torres, Vera Tassis, and sor Juana.

James A. Parr is a professor of Spanish at the University of California, Riverside. He has edited the *Bulletin of the Comediantes* since 1973. His publications include *After Its Kind: Approaches to the* Comedia, *Confrontaciones calladas: El crítico frente al clásico,* and Don Quixote: *An Anatomy of Subversive Discourse,* as well as numerous editions and articles.

Constance Rose is a professor of Spanish at Northeastern University. She has written extensively on the Spanish playwright Antonio Enríquez Gómez as well as on other aspects of Golden Age literature.

Dawn Smith is professor of Hispanic studies at Trent University, Canada. She has pub-lished a critical edition of Tirso de Molina's *La mujer que manda en casa,* coedited *The Perception of Women in Spanish Theater of the Golden Age,* and is the author of numerous articles on staging and reception aesthetics. Her current research focuses on the translation of Cervantes's *entremeses* and the performance of Spanish classical theater for modern audiences.

Teresa S. Soufas is an associate professor of Spanish at Tulane University. Among her recent publications is a book entitled *Melancholy and the Secular Mind in Spanish Golden Age Literature.* Currently she is writing a book-length study of the works of seventeenth-century women playwrights in Spain and preparing an anthology of some of their plays.

Matthew D. Stroud is a professor of modern languages at Trinity University. His publications include an edition, translation, and production of Calderón's *Celos aun del aire matan; Fatal Union: A Pluralistic Approach to the Spanish Wife-Murder* Comedias; *The Play in the Mirror: Lacanian Perspectives of Spanish Baroque Theater;* and articles on Golden Age theater.

Henry W. Sullivan is the Middlebush Professor of Romance Languages at the University of Missouri-Columbia. He is the author of numerous books, including *Juan del Encina, Tirso de Molina and the Drama of the Counter Reformation,* and *Calderón in the German Lands and the Low Countries: His Reception and Influence, 1654–1980.* He is the managing editor of the *Newsletter of the Freudian Field,* founded by Ellie Ragland-Sullivan.

J. E. Varey was founding head of the department of Spanish at Westfield College, University of London, and was a professor in that department until his retirement in 1989. He is a Fellow of the British Academy, a Corresponding Member of the Real Academia Epañola, and founder, director, and general editor of Tamesis Books, Limited. His many books include *Historia de los títeres en España (desde sus orígenes hasta mediados del siglo XVIII)* and *Cosmovisión y escenografía: El teatro español en el Siglo de Oro.*

Sharon Dahlgren Voros is a professor of Spanish and chair of the Language Studies Department, United States Naval Academy. Under the name Ghertman, she is the author of *Petrarch and Garcilaso: A Linguistic Approach to Style.* She has published on semiotics, feminism, and gender studies in Golden Age Spanish drama and is treasurer of the Association for Hispanic Classical Theater, Inc., a nonprofit association to promote the performance and translation of classical texts.

Amy R. Williamsen is an associate professor at the University of Arizona, where she specializes in Golden Age literature. She has published various articles on the *comedia* and on women writers of the period. Her book, *Co(s)mic Chaos: Exploring* Los trabajos de Persiles and Sigismunda, has been published by Juan de la Cuesta.

Index

Versification, 384–402

Vicente, Gil, 385

Vickers, Nancy J., 160n. 1

Vida es sueño, La, 37, 49, 108, 137, 139, 146, 209, 211, 216nn. 5, 6, 224, 242, 243

Viejo celoso, El, 378

Villamediana, Juan de Tassis y Peralta, Conde de, 133n. 24

Villavelarde, Bernardo de, 342, 343, 350, 353, 354, 355, 356, 357

Villegas, Ana de, 166

Villegas, Francisco de, 165–76: *Cuerdos hacen escarmientos,* 165, 166, 172; *La culpa más provechosa,* 165, 166, 167, 169, 170, 172, 174; *Dios hace justicia a todos,* 165, 166, 173–74; *El Eneas de la Virgen,* 165, 170, 173, 175n. 7; *La esclavitud más dichosa y Virgen de los Remedios,* 165, 170, 172; *El esclavo de María,* 165; *Lo que puede la crianza,* 165, 166, 171, 174; *El más piadoso troyano,* 165, 167, 172; *El nacimiento de San Francisco,* 165, 173; *Las niñeces de Roldán,* 165, 171, 172–73; *El rey don Sebastián y portugués más heroico,* 165, 167, 171, 174

Villegas, Juan Bautista de, 166; *Verdades venturosas,* 167

Villegas, Juan de, 166, 167

Villegas, María de, 166

Violence, 37–47

Virués, Cristóbal de, 385

Vivero, Juan de, 12

Voloshinov, Valentin N., 268, 272n. 12

Von Barghahn, Barbara, 119, 128

Vorágine, Jacobo, 61

Wardlaw, Frances Day, 399n. 3

Wardropper, Bruce W., 175n. 3, 209, 211, 216n. 4, 240, 285, 288, 391, 399n. 3

Warnke, Frank J., 208

Waugh, Patricia, 213

Weber de Kurlat, Frida, 368

Webster, John, 97

Weiger, John G., 385

Weimann, Robert, 266, 272n. 7

Weisinger, Herbert, 207

Welles, Marcia L., 340n. 7

Whitaker, Shirley B., 127, 133n. 24

Whitby, William W., 340n. 3

White, Hayden, 310

Widow, 95–99, 103; dowry, 95, 104n. 5; dowry and debt, 97; rights of, 95–98

Wilden, Anthony, 45n. 5

Williams, Raymond, 260n. 14

Williamsen, Vern G., 58, 59, 107, 160n. 1, 376, 386, 387, 388, 397, 399n. 5

Wilshire, Bruce, 252

Wilson, Edward M., 20, 45, 390

Women: and *comedia,* 148–64; and reading, 276–95; status of, in society, 43, 54n. 3, 71, 216n. 3, 265, 281, 283, 286, 289, 291, 316; and writing, 276–95

Wooldridge, John B., 175n. 6

Woollacott, Janet, 272n. 12

Writing, 67, 68, 69, 70, 71, 72, 73n. 10, 276–92

Yáñez, Lorenzo, 349, 354

Yarbro-Bejarano, Yvonne, 283

Yates, Frances, 63, 64, 65

Yllera, Alicia, 161n. 7

Ynduráin, Domingo, 216n. 6

Zárate, Fernando de, 167, 169–77

Zarzuela, 380

Zayas y Sotomayor, María de, 93, 98, 148–64; *Novelas amorosas y ejemplares,* 149, 150; *La traición en la amistad,* 148–64